Also by Sam Sykes from Gollancz:

Tome of the Undergates
Black Halo

BLACK HALO

Sam Sykes

www.orionbooks.co.uk

Copyright © Sam Sykes 2011

The right of Sam Sykes to be identified as the author of
this work has been asserted by him in accordance with the
Copyright, Designs and Patents Act 1988.

First published in Great Britain in 2011 by
Gollancz
An imprint of the Orion Publishing Group
Orion House, 5 Upper St Martin's Lane, London WC2H 9EA
An Hachette UK Company

This edition published in 2012 by Gollancz

1 3 5 7 9 10 8 6 4 2

A CIP catalogue record for this book
is available from the British Library

ISBN 978 0 575 09034 7

Typeset by Deltatype Ltd, Birkenhead, Merseyside

Printed in Great Britain by Clays Ltd, St Ives plc

Prologue

The Aeons' Gate
The Sea of Buradan ... somewhere ...
Summer, getting later all the time

*What's truly wrong with the world is that it seems so dauntingly
complex at a glance and so despairingly simple upon close examin-
ation. Forget what elders, kings and politicians say otherwise,
this is the one truth of life. Any endeavour so noble and gracious,
any scheme so cruel and remorseless, can be boiled down like
cheap stew. Good intentions and ambitions rise to the surface in
thick, sloppy chunks and leave behind only the base instincts at
the bottom of the pot.*

*Granted, I'm not sure what philosophical aspect represents the
broth, but this metaphor only came to me just now. That's beside
the point. For the moment, I'm dubbing this 'Lenk's Greater
Imbecile Theory'.*

*I offer up myself as an example. I began by taking orders with-
out question from a priest; a priest of Talanas, the Healer, no less.
If that weren't impressive enough, he, one Miron Evenhands,
also served as Lord Emissary for the church itself. He signed the
services of myself and my companions to help him find a relic, one
Aeons' Gate, to communicate with the very heavens.*

*It seemed simple enough, if a bit mad, right up until the
demons attacked.*

From there, the services became a bit more ... complicated should be the word for it, but it doesn't quite do justice to describe the kind of fish-headed preachers that came aboard the vessel carrying us and stole a book, one Tome of the Undergates. *After our services were required to retrieve this – this collection of scriptures wrought by hellbeasts that were, until a few days ago, stories used to frighten coins into the collection plates – to say that further complications arose seems rather disingenuous.*

Regardless, at the behest of said priest and on behalf of his god, we set out to retrieve this tome and snatch it back from the clutches of the aforementioned hellbeasts.

To those reading who enjoy stories that end with noble goals reached, lofty morals upheld and mankind left a little better for the experience, I would suggest closing this journal now, should you have stumbled upon it long after it separated from my corpse.

It only gets worse from here.

I neglected to mention what it was that drove such glorious endeavours to be accomplished. Gold. One thousand pieces. The meat of the stew, bobbing at the top.

The book is mine now, in my possession, along with a severed head that screams and a very handy sword. When I hand over the book to Miron, he will hand over the money. That is what is left at the bottom of this pot: no great quest to save humanity, no communication with the Gods, no uniting people hand in hand through trials of adversity and noble blood spilled. Only money. Only me.

This is, after all, adventure.

Not that the job has been all head-eating demons and babbling seagulls, mind. I've also been collecting epiphanies, such as the one written above. A man tends to find them bobbing on the very waves when he's sitting cramped in a tiny boat.

With six other people.

Whom he hates.

One of whom farts in her sleep.

I suppose I also neglected to mention that I haven't been alone in this endeavour. No, much of the credit goes to my companions: a monster, a heathen, a thug, a zealot and a savage. I offer these titles with the utmost respect, of course. Rest assured that, while they are undoubtedly handy to have around in a fight, time spent in close quarters with them tends to wear on one's nerves rather swiftly.

All the same … I don't suppose I could have done it without them. 'It' being described below, short as I can make it and ending with a shict's ass pointed at me like a weapon as she slumbers.

The importance of the book is nothing worth noting unless it is also noted who had the book. In this case, after Miron, the new owners were the Abysmyths: giant, emaciated demons with the heads of fish who drown men on dry land. Fittingly enough, their leader, the Deepshriek, was even more horrendous. I suppose if I were a huge man-thing with a fish-head, I would follow a huge fish-thing with three man-heads.

Or woman-heads, in this case, I'm sorry. Apologies again; two woman-heads. The third rests comfortably at my side, blindfolded and gagged. It does have the tendency to scream all on its own.

Still, one can't honestly recount the trouble surrounding this book if one neglects to mention the netherlings. I never saw one alive, but unless they change colour when they die, they appear to be very powerful, very purple women. All muscle and iron, I'm told by my less fortunate companions who fought them, that they fight like demented rams and follow short, effeminate men in dresses.

As bad as things got, however, it's all behind us now. Despite the fact that the Deepshriek escaped with two of its heads, despite the fact that the netherlings' commander, a rather massive woman with sword to match escaped, despite the fact that we are currently becalmed with one day left until the man sent to pick

3

us up from the middle of the sea decides we're dead and leaves and we really die shortly after and our corpses rot in the noonday sun as gulls form polite conversation over whether my eyeballs or my stones are the more tasty part of me ...

One moment, I'm not quite sure where I intended to go with that statement.

I wish I could be at ease, really I do. But it's not quite that easy. The adventurer's constant woe is that the adventure never ends with the corpse and the loot. After the blood is spilled and the deed is done, there's always people coming for revenge, all manner of diseases acquired and the fact that a rich adventurer is only a particularly talented and temporarily wealthy kind of scum.

Still ... that's not what plagues me. Not to the extent of the voice in my head, at least.

I tried to ignore it, at first. I tried to tell myself that it wasn't speaking in my head, that it was only high exhaustion and low morale wearing on my mind. I tried to tell myself that ...

And it told me otherwise.

It's getting worse now. I hear it all the time. It hears me all the time. What I think, it knows. What I know, it casts doubt on. It tells me all sorts of horrible things, tells me to do worse things, commands me to hurt, to kill, to strike back. It gets so loud, so loud lately that I want to ... that I just—

Pardon.

The issue is that I can make the voice stop. I can get a few moments respite from it ... but only by opening the tome.

Miron told me not to. Common sense told me again. But I did it, anyway. The book is more awful than I could imagine. At first, it didn't even seem to say anything: its pages were just filled with nonsensical symbols and pages of people being eviscerated, decapitated, manipulated and masticated at the hands, minds and jaws of various creatures too awful to re-create in my journal.

4

As I read on, however ... it began to make more sense. I could read the words, understand what they were saying, what they were suggesting. And when I flip back to the pages I couldn't read before, I can see them all over again. The images are no less awful, but the voice ... the voice stops. It no longer tells me things. It no longer commands me.

It doesn't just make sense grammatically, but philosophically as well. It doesn't speak of evisceration, horrific sin or demonic incursion like it's supposed to, despite the illustrations. Rather, it speaks of freedom, of self-reliance, of life without a need to kneel. It's really more of a treatise, but I suppose 'Manifesto of the Undergates' just doesn't have the same ring.

I open the book only late at night. I can't do it in front of my companions. During the day, I sit on it to make sure that they can't snatch a glimpse at its words. To my great relief, none of them have tried so far, apparently far more bothered by other matters.

To be honest, it's a bit of a relief to see them all so agitated and uncomfortable. Gariath, especially, since his preferred method of stress release usually involves roaring, gnashing and stomping with me having to get a mop at the end of it. Lately, however, he just sits at the rear of our little boat, holding the rudder, staring out at sea. He's so far unmoved by anything, ignoring us completely.

Not that such a thing stops other people from trying.

Denaos is the only one in good spirits, so far. Considering, it seems odd that he should be alone in this. After all, he points out, we have the tome. We're about to be paid one thousand gold pieces. Split six ways, that still makes a man worth exactly six cases of whisky, three expensive whores, sixty cheap whores or one splendid night with all three in varying degrees, if his maths is to be trusted. He insults, he spits, he snarls, seemingly more offended that we're not more jovial.

Oddly enough, Asper is the only one who can shut him up. Even more odd, she does it without yelling at him. I fear she may have been affected the worst by our encounters. I don't see her wearing her symbol lately. For any priestess, that is odd. For a priestess who has polished, prayed to and occasionally threatened to shove said symbol into her companions' eye sockets, it's worrying.

Between her and Denaos, Dreadaeleon seems to be torn. He alternately wears an expression like a starving puppy for the former, then fixes a burning, hateful stare upon the latter. At any moment, he looks like he's either going to have his way with Asper or incinerate Denaos. As psychotic as it might sound, I actually prefer this to his constant prattling about magic, the Gods and how they're a lie, and whatever else the most annoying combination of a wizard and a boy could think up.

Kataria …

Kataria is an enigma to me yet. Of all the others, she was the first I met, long ago in a forest. Of all the others, she has been the one I've never worried about, I've never thought ill of for very long. She has been the only one I am able to sleep easy next to, the only one I know will share her food, the only one I know who wouldn't abandon me for gold or violence.

Why can't I understand her?

All she does is stare. She doesn't speak much to me, to anyone else, really, but she only stares at me. With hatred? With envy? Does she know what I've done with the book? Does she hate me for it?

She should be happy, shouldn't she? The voice tells me to hurt her worst, hurt her last. All her staring does is make the voice louder. At least by reading the book I can look at her without feeling my head burn.

When she's sleeping, I can stare at her, though. I can see her as she is … and even then, I don't know what to make of her. Stare as I might, I can't …

Sweet Khetashe, this has gotten a tad strange, hasn't it?

The book is ours now. That's what matters. Soon we'll trade it for money, have our whisky and our whores and see who hires us next. That is assuming, of course, we ever make it to our meeting point: the island of Teji. We've got one night left to make it, with winds that haven't shown themselves since I began writing, and a huge, endless sea beneath us.

Hope is ill advised.

ACT ONE
The Stew of Mankind

One

STEALING THE SUNRISE

Dawn had never been so quiet in the country.

Amid the sparse oases in the desert, noise had thrived where all other sound had died. Dawn came with songbirds, beds creaking as people roused themselves for labour, bread and water sloshed down as meagre breakfast. In the country, the sun came with life.

In the city, life ended with the sun.

Anacha stared from her balcony over Cier'Djaal as the sun rose over its rooftops and peeked through its towers to shine on the sand-covered streets below. The city, in response, seemed to draw tighter in on itself, folding its shadows like a blanket as it rolled over and told the sun to let it sleep for a few more moments.

No songbirds came to Anacha's ears; merchants sold such songs in the market for prices she could not afford. No sounds of beds; all clients slept on cushions on the floor, that their late-night visitors might not wake them when leaving. No bread, no water; breakfast would be served when the clients were gone and the girls might rest up from the previous night.

A frown crossed her face as she observed the scaffolding and lazy bricks of a tower being raised right in front of her balcony. It would be done in one year, she had heard the workers say.

One year, she thought, *and then the city steals the sun from me, too.*

Her ears twitched with the sound of a razor on skin. She thought it odd, as she did every morning, that such a harsh, jagged noise should bring a smile to her lips. Just as she thought it odd that this client of hers should choose to linger long enough to shave every time he visited her.

She turned on her sitting cushion, observing the back of his head: round and bronzed, the same colour as the rest of his naked body. His face was calm in the mirror over her washbasin; wrinkles that would become deep, stress-born crevices in the afternoon now lay smooth. Eyes that would later squint against the sunset were wide and brilliantly blue in the glass as he carefully ran the razor along his froth-laden scalp.

'I wager you have beautiful hair,' she said from the balcony. He did not turn, so she cleared her throat and spoke up. 'Long, thick locks of red that would run all the way down to your buttocks if you gave them but two days.'

He paused at that, the referred cheeks squeezing together self-consciously. She giggled, sprawled out on her cushion so that she looked at him upside-down, imagining the river of fire that would descend from his scalp.

'I could swim in it,' she sighed at her own mental image, 'for hours and hours. It wouldn't matter if the sun didn't shine. Even if it reflected the light of just one candle, I could be blinded.'

She thought she caught a hint of a smile in the reflection. If it truly was such, however, he did not confirm it as he ran the razor over his scalp and flicked the lather into her basin.

'My hair is black,' he replied, 'like any man's from Cier'Djaal.'

She muttered something, rolled up onto her belly and propped her chin on her elbows. 'So glad my poetry is not lost on heathen ears.'

'"Heathen," in the common vernacular, is used to refer to a man without faith in gods. Since I do not have such a thing, you are halfway right. Since gods do not exist, you are completely wrong.' This time, he did smile at her in the mirror as he brought the razor to his head once more. 'And I didn't pay for the poetry.'

'My gift to you, then,' Anacha replied, making an elaborate bow as she rose to her feet.

'Gifts are typically given with the expectation that they are to be returned.' He let the statement hang in the air like an executioner's axe as he scraped another patch of skin smooth.

'Recompensed.'

'What?'

'If it was to be returned, you would just give me the same poem back. To recompense the gift means that you would give me one of your own.'

The man stopped, tapped the razor against his chin and hummed thoughtfully. Placing a hand against his mouth, he cleared his throat.

'There once was an urchin from Allssaq—'

'*Stop*,' she interrupted, holding a hand up. 'Sometimes, too, gifts can just be from one person to another without reprisal.'

'Recompense.'

'In this case, I believe my word fits better.' She drew her robe about her body, staring at him in the mirror and frowning. 'The sun is still sleeping, I am sure. You don't have to go yet.'

'That's not your decision,' the man said, 'nor mine.'

'It doesn't strike you as worrisome that your decisions are not your own?'

Anacha immediately regretted the words, knowing that he could just as easily turn the question back upon her. She carefully avoided his stare, turning her gaze toward the door that she would never go beyond, the halls that led to the desert she would never see again.

To his credit, Bralston remained silent.

'You can go in late, can't you?' she pressed, emboldened.

Quietly, she slipped behind him, slinking arms around his waist and pulling him close to her. She breathed deeply of his aroma, smelling the night on him. His scent, she had noticed, lingered a few hours behind him. When he came to her in the evening, he smelled of the markets and sand in the outside world. When he left her in the morning, he smelled of this place, her prison of silk and sunlight.

It was only when the moon rose that she smelled him and herself, their perfumes mingled as their bodies had been the night before. She smelled a concoction on him, a brew of moonlight and whispering sand on a breeze as rare as orchids. This morning, his scent lingered a little longer than usual and she inhaled with breath addicted.

'Or skip it altogether,' she continued, drawing him closer. 'The Venarium can go a day without you.'

'And they frequently do,' he replied, his free hand sliding down to hers.

She felt the electricity dance upon his skin, begging for his lips to utter the words that would release it. It was almost with a whimper that her hand was forced from his waist as he returned to shaving.

'Today was going to be one such day. The fact that it is not means that I cannot miss it.' He shaved off another line of lather. 'Meetings at this hour are not often called in the Venarium.' He shaved off another. 'Meetings of the Librarians at this hour are never called.' He slid the last slick of lather from his scalp and flicked it into the basin. 'If the Librarians are not seen—'

'Magic collapses, laws go unenforced, blood in the streets, hounds with two heads, babies spewing fire.' She sighed dramatically, collapsing onto her cushion and waving a hand above her head. 'And so on.'

Bralston spared her a glance as she sprawled out, robe opening to expose the expanse of naked brown beneath. The incline of his eyebrows did not go unnoticed, though not nearly to the extent of his complete disregard as he walked to his clothes draped over a chair. That, too, did not cause her to stir so much as the sigh that emerged from him as he ran a hand over his trousers.

'Are you aware of my duty, Anacha?'

She blinked, not entirely sure how to answer. Few people were truly aware of what the Venarium's 'duties' consisted. If their activities were any indication, however, the wizardly order's tasks tended to involve the violent arrest of all palm-readers, fortune-tellers, sleight-of-hand tricksters, and the burning, electrocution, freezing or smashing of said charlatans and their gains.

Of the duties of the Librarians, the Venarium's secret within a secret, no one could even begin to guess, least of all her.

'Let me rephrase,' Bralston replied after her silence dragged on for too long. 'Are you aware of my gift?'

He turned to her, crimson light suddenly leaking out of his gaze, and she stiffened. She had long ago learned to tremble before that gaze, as the charlatans and false practitioners did. A wizard's stink eye tended to be worse than anyone else's, if only by virtue of the fact that it was shortly followed by an imminent and messy demise.

'That's all it is: a gift,' he continued, the light flickering like a flame. 'And gifts require recompense. This' – he tapped a thick finger to the corner of his eye – 'is only given to us so long as we respect it and follows its laws. Now, I ask you, Anacha, when was the last time Cier'Djaal was a city of law?'

She made no reply for him; she knew none was needed. And as soon as he knew that she knew, the light faded. The man that looked at her now was no longer the one that had come to her the night before. His brown face was elegantly lined by wrinkles, his pursed lips reserved for words and chants, not poems.

Anacha stared at him as he dressed swiftly and meticulously, tucking tunic into trousers and draping long, red coat over tunic. He did not check in a mirror, the rehearsed garbing as ingrained into him as his gift, as he walked to the door to depart without a sound.

There was no protest as he left the coins on her wardrobe. She had long ago told him there was no need to pay anymore. She had long ago tried to return the coins to him when he left. She had shrieked at him, cursed him, begged him to take the coins and *try* to pretend that they were two lovers who had met under the moonlight and not a client and visitor who knew each other only in the confines of silk and perfume.

He left the coins and slipped out the door.

And she knew she had to be content to watch him go, this time, as all other times. She had to watch the man she knew the night before reduced to his indentation on her bed, his identity nothing more than a faint outline of sweat on sheets and shape on a cushion. The sheets would be washed, the cushion would be smoothed; Bralston the lover would die in a whisper of sheets.

Bralston the Librarian would do his duty, regardless.

'Do you have to do that?' the clerk asked.

Bralston allowed his gaze to linger on the small statuette for a moment. He always spared enough time for the bronze woman: her short-cropped, businesslike hair, her crook in one hand and sword in the other as she stood over a pack of cowering hounds. Just as he always spared the time to touch the corner of his eye in recognition as he passed the statue in the Venarium's halls.

'Do what?' the Librarian replied, knowing full well the answer.

'This is not a place of worship, you know,' the clerk muttered, casting a sidelong scowl at his taller companion. 'This is the Hall of the Venarium.'

'And the Hall of the Venarium is a place of law,' Bralston retorted, 'and the law of Cier'Djaal states that all businesses must bear an icon of the Houndmistress, the Law-Bringer.'

'That doesn't mean you have to worship her as a god.'

'A sign of respect is not worship.'

'It borders dangerously close to idolatry,' the clerk said, attempting to be as threatening as a squat man in ill-fitting robes could be. 'And *that* certainly is.'

Technically, Bralston knew, it wasn't so much against the law as it was simply psychotic in the eyes of the Venarium. What would be the point of worshipping an idol, after all? Idols were the hypocrisy of faith embodied, representing things so much more than mankind and contrarily hewn in the image of mankind. What was the point of it all?

Gods did not exist, in man's image or no. Mankind

existed. Mankind was the ultimate power in the world and the wizards were the ultimate power within mankind. These idols merely reinforced that fact.

Still, the Librarian lamented silently as he surveyed the long hall, *one might credit idolatry with at least being more aesthetically pleasing.*

The bronze statuette was so small as to be lost amidst the dun-coloured stone walls and floors, unadorned by rugs, tapestries or any window greater than a slit the length of a man's hand. It served as the only thing to make one realise they were in a place of learning and law, as opposed to a cell.

Still, he mused, there was a certain appeal to hearing one's footsteps echo through the halls. Perhaps that was the architectural proof to the wizards' denial of gods. Here, within the Venarium itself, in the halls where no prayers could be heard over the reverberating thunder of feet, mankind was proven the ultimate power.

'The Lector has been expecting you,' the clerk muttered as he slid open the door. '*For some time*,' he hastily spat out, dissatisfied with his previous statement. 'Do be quick.'

Bralston offered him the customary nod, then slipped into the office as the door closed soundlessly behind him.

Lector Annis, as much a man of law as any member of the Venarium, respected the need for humble surroundings. Despite being the head of the Librarians, his office was a small square with a chair, a large bookshelf, and a desk behind which the man was seated, his narrow shoulders bathed by the sunlight trickling in from the slits lining his walls.

Bralston could spare only enough attention to offer his superior the customary bow before something drew his attention. The addition of three extra chairs in the office was unusual. The admittance of three people, clearly not wizards themselves, was unheard of.

'Librarian Bralston,' Annis spoke up, his voice deeper than his slender frame would suggest, 'we are thrilled you could attend.'

'My duty is upheld, Lector,' the man replied, stepping farther into the room and eyeing the new company, two men and one visibly shaken woman, curiously. 'Forgive me, but I was told this was to be a meeting of the Librarians.'

'Apologies, my good man.' One of the men rose from his chair quicker than the Lector could speak. 'The deception, purely unintentional, was only wrought by the faulty use of the plural form. For, as you can see, this is indeed a meeting.' His lips split open to reveal half a row of yellow teeth. 'And you are indeed a Librarian.'

Cragsman.

The stench confirmed the man's lineage long before the feigned eloquence and vast expanse of ruddy, tattoo-etched flesh did. Bralston's gaze drifted past the walking ink stain before him to the companion still seated. His stern face and brown skin denoted him as Djaalman, though not nearly to the extent that the detestable scowl he cast toward Bralston did. The reason for the hostility became clear the moment the man began to finger the pendant of Zamanthras, the sea goddess, hanging around his neck.

'Observant,' the Lector replied, narrowing eyes as sharp as his tone upon the Cragsman. 'However, Master Shunnuk, the clerk briefed you on the terms of address. Keep them in mind.'

'Ah, but my enthusiasm bubbles over and stains the carpet of my most gracious host.' The Cragsman placed his hands together and bowed low to the floor. 'I offer a thousand apologies, sirs, as is the custom in your fair desert jewel of a city.'

Bralston frowned; the company of Anacha suddenly seemed a thousand times more pleasurable, the absence of her bed's warmth leaving him chill despite the office's stuffy confines.

'As you can imagine, Librarian Bralston,' Annis spoke up, reading his subordinate's expression, 'it was dire circumstance that drove these ... gentlemen and their feminine companion to our door.'

The woman's shudder was so pronounced that Bralston could feel her skin quake from where he stood. He cast an interested eye over his shoulder and frowned at the sight of something that had been beautiful long ago.

Her cheeks hung slack around her mouth, each one stained with a purple bruise where there should have been a vibrant glow. Her hair hung in limp, greasy strands over her downturned face. He caught only a glimpse of eyes that once were bright with something other than tears before she looked to her torn dress, tracing a finger down a vicious rent in the cloth.

'Of course, of course,' the Cragsman Shunnuk said. 'Naturally, we came here with all the haste the meagre bodies our gods cursed us with could manage. This grand and harrowing tale the lass is about to tell you, I would be remiss if I did not forewarn, is not for the faint of heart. Grand wizards you might be, I have not yet known a man who could—'

'If it is at all possible,' Bralston interrupted, turning a sharp eye upon the Cragsman's companion, 'I would prefer to hear *him* tell it. Master ...'

'Massol,' the Djaalman replied swiftly and without pretence. 'And, if it is acceptable to you, I would prefer

20

that you did not address me with such respect.' His eyes narrowed, hand wrapping about the pendant. 'I have no intention of returning the favour to the faithless.'

Bralston rolled his eyes. He, naturally, could not begrudge an unenlightened man his superstitions. After all, the only reason people called him faithless was the same reason they were stupid enough to believe in invisible sky-beings watching over them. Not being one to scold a dog for licking its own stones, Bralston merely inclined his head to the Djaalman.

'Go on, then,' he said.

'We fished this woman out of the Buradan weeks ago,' the sailor called Massol began without reluctance. 'Found her bobbing in a ship made of blackwood.'

A shipwreck victim, Bralston mused, but quickly discarded that thought. *No sensible man, surely, would seek the Venarium's attention for such a triviality.*

'Blackwood ships do not sail that far south.' Massol's eyes narrowed, as though reading the Librarian's thoughts. 'She claimed to have drifted out from places farther west, near the islands of Teji and Komga.'

'Those islands are uninhabited,' Bralston muttered to himself.

'And her tale only gets more deranged from there,' Massol replied. 'Stories of lizardmen, purple women ...' He waved a hand. 'Madness.'

'Not that the thought of seeking them out didn't cross our minds,' Sunnuk interrupted with a lewd grin. 'Purple women? The reasonable gentleman, being of curious mind and healthy appetite, would be hard-pressed not to wonder if they are purple all over or—'

'I believe it is time to hear from the actual witness.' Lector Annis cut the man off, waving his hand. He shifted his seat, turning a scrutinising gaze upon the woman. 'Repeat your story for the benefit of Librarian Bralston.'

Her sole reply was to bend her neck even lower, turning her face even more toward the floor. She folded over herself, arms sliding together, knees drawing up to her chest, as though she sought to continue collapsing inward until there was nothing left but an empty chair.

Bralston felt his frown grow into a vast trench across his face. He had seen these women who had sought to become nothing, seen them when they were mere girls. There were always new ones coming and going in Anacha's place of employ, young women whose parents found no other way out of the debt they had incurred, girls snatched from the desert and clad in silk that made their skin itch. Often, he saw them being escorted to their new rooms to waiting clients, the lanterns low as to hide the tears on their faces.

Often, he had wondered if Anacha had cried them when she was so young. Always, he wondered if she still did.

And this woman had no tears left. Wherever she had come from bore the stains of her tears, bled out from her body. Violently, he concluded, if the bruises on her face were any indication. He slid down to one knee before her, as he might a puppy, and strained to look into her face, to convey to her that all would be well, that the places of law were havens safe from violence and from barbarism, that she would have all the time she needed to find her tears again.

Lector Annis did not share the same sentiment.

'*Please*,' he uttered, his voice carrying with an echo usually reserved for invocations. He leaned back in his chair, steepling his fingers to suggest that he did not make requests.

'I was ...' she squeaked at first through a voice that crawled timidly from her throat. 'I was a merchant. A spice merchant from Muraska, coming to Cier'Djaal. We were passing through the Buradan two months ago.'

'This is where she begins to get interesting,' the Cragsman said, his grin growing.

'Silence, please,' Bralston snapped.

'We were ... we were attacked,' she continued, her breath growing short. 'Black boats swept over the sea, rowed by purple women clad in black armour. They boarded, drew swords, killed the men, killed everyone but me.' Her stare was distant as her mind drifted back over the sea. 'We were ... I was taken with the cargo.

'There was an island. I don't remember where. There were scaly green men unloading the boats while the purple women whipped them. Those that fell dead and bloodied, they were ... they were fed to ...'

Her face began to twitch, the agony and fear straining to escape through a face that had hardened to them. Bralston saw her hands shake, fingers dig into her ripped skirt as though she sought to dig into herself and vanish from the narrowed gazes locked upon her.

She's terrified, the Librarian thought, *clearly. Do something. Postpone this inquisition. You're sworn to uphold the law, not be a callous and cruel piece of—*

'The important part, please,' Lector Annis muttered, his breath laced with impatient heat.

'I was taken to the back of a cavern,' the woman continued, visibly trying to harden herself to both the memory and the Lector. 'There were two other women there. One was ... tired. I couldn't stop crying, but she never even looked up. We were both taken to a bed where a man came out, tall and purple, wearing a crown of thorns upon his head with red stones affixed to it. He laid me down ... I ... He did ...'

Her eyes began to quiver, the pain finally too much to conceal. Despite the Lector's deliberately loud and exasperated sigh, she chewed her lower lip until blood began to form behind her teeth. Having failed to fold in on herself, having failed to dig into herself, she began to tremble herself to pieces.

Bralston lowered himself, staring into her eyes as much as he could. He raised a hand, but thought better of it, not daring to touch such a fragile creature for fear she might break. Instead, he spoke softly, his voice barely above a whisper.

As he had spoken to Anacha, when she had trembled under his grasp, when she had shed tears into his lap.

'Tell us only what we need,' he said gently. 'Leave the pain behind for now. We don't need it. What we need' – he leaned closer to her, his voice going lower – 'is to stop this man.'

The woman looked up at him and he saw the tears. In other circumstances, he might have offered a smile, an embrace for her. For now, he returned her resolute nod with one of his own.

'When the other woman wouldn't scream anymore,' the female continued, 'when she wouldn't cry, the man burned her.' She winced. 'Alive.' She paused to wipe away tears. 'I'd seen magic before, seen wizards use it. But they always were weak afterward, drained. This man ...'

'Was not,' the Lector finished for her. 'She witnessed several similar instances from this man and three others on the island. None of them so much as broke into a sweat when they used the gift.'

And this couldn't have been sent in a letter? Discussed in private? Bralston felt his ire boil in his throat. *We had to drag this poor thing here to relive this?* He rose and opened his mouth to voice such concerns, but quickly clamped his mouth shut as the Lector turned a sharp, knowing glare upon him.

'Your thoughts, Librarian.'

'I've never heard of anything purple with two legs,' Bralston contented himself with saying. 'If it is a violation of the laws of magic, however, our duty is clear.'

'Agreed,' Annis replied, nodding stiffly. 'Negating the physical cost of magic is a negation of the law, tantamount of the greatest heresy. You are to make your arrangements swiftly and report to our sister school in Port Destiny. You can find there—'

A ragged cough broke the silence. Lector and Librarian craned their gazes toward the grinning Cragsman, their ire etched into their frowns.

'Pardon us for not living up to your expectations of noble and self-sacrificing men of honour, kind sirs,' Shunnuk said, making a hasty attempt at a bow. 'But a man must live by the laws his fellows put down, and we were told that gents of your particular calling offered no inconsequential sum for reports of all deeds blaspheming to your peculiar faith and—'

'You want money,' Bralston interrupted. 'A bounty.'

'I would not take money from faithless hands,' the Djaalman said sternly. 'But I will take it from his.' He gestured to Shunnuk.

Bralston arched a brow, certain there was a deeper insult there. 'A report of this nature carries the weight of ten gold coins, typical for information regarding illegal use of magic.'

'A most generous sum,' the Cragsman said, barely able to keep from hitting the floor with the eager fury of his bow. 'Assuredly, we will spend it well with your honour in mind, the knowledge of our good deed only serving to enhance the lustre of the moment.'

'Very well, then.' The Lector hastily scribbled something out on a piece of parchment and handed it into a pair of twitching hands. 'Present this to the clerk at the front.'

'Most assuredly,' Shunnuk replied as he spun on his heel to follow his companion to the door. 'A pleasure, as always, to deal with the most generous caste of wizards.'

Bralston smiled twice: once for the removal of the stench and twice for the relief he expected to see upon the woman's face when she learned of the justice waiting to be dealt. The fact that she trembled again caused him to frown until he noticed the clenched fists and murderous glare on her face. It was then that he noticed the particular hue of the purple discoloration on her face.

'These bruises,' he said loudly, 'are fresh.'

'Yes, well ...' The Cragsman's voice became much softer suddenly. 'The laws that man has set upon us and such.' Seeing Bralston's unconvinced glare, he simply sighed and opened the door. 'Well, it's not as though we could just *give* her a free ride, could we? After what she'd been through, our company must have been a mercy.'

'Not that such a thing means anything to heathens,' the Djaalman muttered.

Bralston didn't have time to narrow his eyes before the woman cleared her throat loudly.

'Do I get a request, as well?' she asked.

The two sailors' eyes went wide, mouths dropping open.

'You *did* give us the actual report,' the Librarian confirmed.

'You ...' Shunnuk gasped as he took a step backward. 'You can't be serious.'

'What is it you desire?' the Lector requested.

The woman narrowed her eyes, launched her scowl down an accusing finger.

'Kill them.'

'No! It's not like that!' The Cragsmen held up the parchment as though it were a shield. 'Wait! *Wait!*'

'Librarian Bralston ... ' Lector Annis muttered.

'As you wish.'

The next words that leapt from the Librarian's mouth echoed off of the very air as he raised a hand and swiftly jerked it back. The door slammed, trapping the two men inside. The Cragsman barely had time to feel the warm moisture on his trousers before Bralston's hand was up again. The tattooed man flew through the air, screaming as he hurtled towards Bralston. The Librarian uttered another word, bringing up his free palm that glowed a bright orange.

Shunnuk's scream was drowned in the crackling roar of fire as a gout of crimson poured out of Bralston's palm, sweeping over the Cragsman's face and arms as the tattooed man helplessly flailed, trying desperately to put out a fire with no end.

After a moment of smoke-drenched carnage, the roar of fire died, and so did Shunnuk.

'Back away!' Massol shrieked, holding up his holy symbol as Bralston stalked toward him. 'I am a man of honour! I am a man of faith! I didn't touch the woman! Tell them!' He turned a pair of desperate eyes upon the woman. '*Tell them!*'

If the woman said anything, Bralston did not hear it over the word of power he uttered. If she had any objection for the electric blue enveloping the finger that was levelled at the Djaalman, she did not voice it. Her face showed no horror as she watched without pleasure, heard Massol's screams without pity, no tears left for the carnage she watched lit by an azure glow.

When it was done, when Bralston flicked the errant sparks from his finger and left the blackened corpse twitching violently against the door, the Librarian barely spared a nod to the woman. Instead, he looked up to the Lector, who regarded the smouldering bodies on his floor with the same distaste he might a wine stain on his carpet.

'Tomorrow, then?' Bralston asked.

'At the dawn. It's a long way to Port Destiny.' The Lector raised a brow. 'Do bring your hat, Librarian.'

With an incline of his bald head and a sweep of his coat, Bralston vanished out the door. The Lector's eyes lazily drifted from the two corpses to the woman, who sat staring at them with an empty stare, her body as stiff as a board. It wasn't until he noticed the pile of ash still clenched in the charred hand of the Cragsman that he finally sighed.

'Waste of good paper ...'

Two

TO MURDER THE OCEAN

There was no difference between the sky and the sea that Lenk could discern.

They both seemed to stretch for eternity, their horizons long having swallowed the last traces of land to transform the world into a vision of indigo. The moon took a quiet departure early, disappearing behind the curtain of clouds that slid lazily over the sky. With no yellow orb to disperse the monotony, the world was a simple, painful blue that drank all directions.

The young man closed his eyes, drawing in a breath through his nose. He smelled the rain on the breeze, the salt on the waves. Holding up his hands as though in acknowledgement for whatever god had sent him the unchanging azure that emanated around him, he let the breath trickle between his teeth.

And then, Lenk screamed.

His sword leapt to his hand in their mutual eagerness to lean over the edge of their tiny vessel. The steel's song a humming contrast to his maddening howl, he hacked at the ocean, bleeding its endless life in frothy wounds.

'Die, die, die, die, *die!*' he screamed, driving his sword into the salt. 'Enough! No more! I'm sick of it, you hear me?' He cupped a hand over his mouth and shrieked. '*Well, DO YOU?*'

The water quickly settled, foam dissipating, ripples calming, leaving Lenk to glimpse himself in ragged fragments of reflections. His silver hair hung in greasy strands around a haggard face. The purple bags hanging from his eyelids began to rival the icy blue in his gaze. Lenk surveyed the pieces of a lunatic looking back at him from the water and wondered, not for the first time, if the ocean was mocking him.

No, he decided, *it's far too impassive to mock me …*

How could it be anything but? After all, it didn't know what it was requested to stop any more than Lenk did. *Stop being the ocean?* He had dismissed such thoughts as madness on the first day their tiny sail hung limp and impotent on its insultingly thin mast. But as the evening of the second day slid into night, it didn't seem such an unreasonable demand.

The sea, he thought scornfully, *is the one being unreasonable. I wouldn't have to resort to violence if it would just give me some wind.*

'Hasn't worked yet, has it?'

His eyes went wide and he had to resist hurling himself over the ledge in desperation to communicate with the suddenly talkative water. Such delusional hope lasted only a moment, as it always did, before sloughing off in great chunks to leave only twitching resentment in his scowl.

Teeth grating as he did, he turned to the creature sitting next to him with murder flashing in his scowl. She, however, merely regarded him with half-lidded green eyes and a disaffected frown. Her ears, two long and pointed things with three ragged notches running down each length, drooped beneath the feathers laced in her dirty blond hair.

'Keep trying,' Kataria sighed. She turned back to the same task she had been doing for the past three hours, running her fingers along the fletching of the same three arrows. 'I'm sure it will talk back eventually.'

'Zamanthras is as fickle as the waters she wards,' Lenk replied, his voice like rusty door hinges. He looked at his sword thoughtfully before sheathing it on his back. 'Maybe she needs a sacrifice to turn her favour toward us.'

'Don't let me stop you from hurling yourself in,' she replied without looking up.

'At least *I'm* doing something.'

'Attempting to eviscerate the ocean?' She tapped the head of an arrow against her chin thoughtfully. 'That's something *insane*, maybe. You're just going to open your stitches doing that.' Her ears twitched, as though they could hear the sinewy threads stretching in his leg. 'How is your wound, anyway?'

He attempted to hide the wince of pain that shot up through his thigh at the mention of the wicked, sewn-up gash beneath his trousers. The agony of the injury itself was kept numb through occasional libations of what remained of their whisky, but every time he ran his fingers against the stitches, any time his companions inquired after his health, the visions would come flooding back.

Teeth. Darkness. Six golden eyes flashing in the gloom. Laughter echoing off stone, growing quiet under shrieking carnage and icicles hissing through his head. They would fade eventually, but they were always waiting, ready to come back the moment he closed his eyes.

'It's fine,' he muttered.

Her ears twitched again, hearing the lie in his voice. He disregarded it, knowing she had only asked the question to deflect him. He drew in his breath through his teeth, tensing as he might for a battle. She heard this, too, and narrowed her eyes.

'You should rest,' she said.

'I don't want—'

'In silence,' she interrupted. 'Talking doesn't aid the healing process.'

'What would a shict know of healing beyond chewing grass and drilling holes in skulls?' he snapped, his ire giving his voice swiftness. 'If you're so damn smart—'

Her upper lip curled backwards in a sneer, the sudden exposure of her unnervingly prominent canines cutting him short. He cringed at the sight of her teeth that were as much a testament to her savage heritage as the feathers in her hair and the buckskin leathers she wore.

'What I mean is you could be doing something other than counting your precious little arrows,' he offered, attempting to sound remorseful and failing, if the scowl she wore was any indication. 'You could use them to catch us a fish or something.' Movement out over the sea caught his eye and he gestured toward it. 'Or one of those.'

They had been following the vessel for the past day: many-legged insects that slid gracefully across the waters. Dredgespiders, he had heard them called – so named for the nets of wispy silk that trailed from their upraised, bulbous abdomens. Such a net would undoubtedly brim with shrimp and whatever hapless fish wound up under the arachnid's surface-bound path, and the promise of such a bounty was more than enough to make mouths water at the sight of the grey-carapaced things.

They always drifted lazily out of reach, multiple eyes occasionally glancing over to the vessel and glistening with mocking smugness unbefitting a bug.

'Not a chance,' Kataria muttered, having seen that perverse pride in their eyes and having discounted the idea.

'Well, pray for something else, then,' he growled. 'Pray

to whatever savage little god sends your kind food.'

She turned a glower on him, her eyes seeming to glow with a malevolent green. '*Riffid* is a goddess that helps shicts who help themselves. The day She lifts a finger to help a whiny, weeping little round-ear is the day I renounce Her.' She snorted derisively and turned back to her missiles. 'And these are my last three arrows. I'm saving them for something special.'

'What use could they possibly be?'

'This one' – she fingered her first arrow – 'is for if I ever *do* see a fish that *I* would like to eat by *myself*. And this ...' She brushed the second one. 'This one is for me to be buried with if I die.'

He glanced at the third arrow, its fletching ragged and its head jagged.

'What about that one?' Lenk asked.

Kataria eyed the missile, then turned a glance to Lenk. There was nothing behind her eyes that he could see: no hatred or irritation, no bemusement for his question. She merely stared at him with a fleeting, thoughtful glance as she let the feathered end slide between her thumb and forefinger.

'Something special,' she answered simply, then turned away.

Lenk narrowed his eyes through the silence hanging between them.

'And what,' he said softly, 'is that supposed to mean?'

There was something more behind her eyes; there always was. And whatever it was usually came hurtling out of her mouth on sarcasm and spittle when he asked such questions of her.

Usually.

For the moment, she simply turned away, taking no

33

note of his staring at her. He had rested his eyes upon her more frequently, taking in the scope of her slender body, the silvery hue pale skin left exposed by a short leather tunic took on through the moonlight. Each time he did, he expected her ears to twitch as she heard his eyes shifting in their sockets, and it would be his turn to look away as she stared at him curiously.

In the short year they had known each other, much of their rapport had come through staring and the awkward silences that followed. The silence she offered him now, however, was anything but awkward. It had purpose behind it, a solid wall of silence that she had painstakingly erected and that he was not about to tear down.

Not with his eyeballs alone, anyway.

'Look,' he said, sighing. 'I don't know what it is about me that's got you so angry these days, but we're not going to get past it if we keep—'

If her disinterested stare didn't suggest that she wasn't listening, the fact that the shict's long ears suddenly and swiftly folded over themselves like blankets certainly did.

Lenk sighed, rubbing his temples. He could feel his skin begin to tighten around his skull and knew full well that a headache was brewing as surely as the rain in the air. Such pains were coming more frequently now; from the moment he woke they tormented him well into his futile attempts to sleep.

Unsurprisingly, his companions did little to help. *No*, he thought as he looked down the deck to the swaddled bundle underneath the rudder-seat at the boat's rear, *but I know what will help . . .*

'*Pointless.*'

Gooseflesh formed on his bicep.

'*The book only corrupts, but even that is for naught. You can't*

34

be corrupted.' A chill crept down Lenk's spine in harmony with the voice whispering in his head. *'We can't be corrupted.'*

He drew in a deep breath, cautiously exhaling over the side of the ship that none might see the fact that his breath was visible even in the summer warmth. Or perhaps he was imagining that, too.

The voice was hard to ignore, and with it, it was hard for Lenk to convince himself that it was his imagination speaking. The fact that he continued to feel cold despite the fact that his companions all sweated grievously didn't do much to aid him, either.

'A question.'

Don't answer it, Lenk urged himself mentally. *Ignore it.*

'Too late,' the voice responded to his thoughts, *'but this is a good one. Speak, what does it matter what the shict thinks of us? What changes?'*

Ignore it. He shut his eyes. *Ignore it, ignore it, ignore it.*

'That never works, you know. She is fleeting. She lacks purpose. They all do. Our cause is grander than they can even comprehend. We don't need them. We can finish this ourselves, we can … Are you listening?'

Lenk was trying not to. He stared at the bundle beneath the bench, yearning to tear the pages free from their woolly tomb and seek the silence within their confines.

'Don't,' the voice warned.

Lenk felt the chill envelop his muscles, something straining to keep him seated, keep him listening. But he gritted his teeth, pulled himself from the ship's edge.

Before he knew what was happening, he was crawling over Kataria as though she weren't even there, not heeding the glare she shot him. She didn't matter now. No one else did. Now, he only needed to get the book, to silence the voice. He could worry about everything else later. There would be time enough later.

'*Fine*,' the voice muttered in response to his thoughts. '*We speak later, then.*'

Ignore it, he told himself. *You can ignore it now. You don't need it now. All you need is …*

That thought drifted off into the fog of ecstasy that clouded his mind as he reached under the deck, fingers quivering. It wasn't until he felt his shoulder brush against something hard that he noticed the two massive red legs at either side of his head.

Coughing a bit too fervently to appear nonchalant, he rose up, peering over the leather kilt the appendages grew from. A pair of black eyes stared back at him down a red, leathery snout. Ear-frills fanned out in unambiguous displeasure beneath a pair of menacing curving horns. Gariath's lips peeled backwards to expose twin rows of teeth.

'Oh … there you are,' Lenk said sheepishly. 'I was … just …'

'Tell me,' the dragonman grunted. 'Do you suppose there's anything you could say while looking up a *Rhega*'s kilt that would make him *not* shove a spike of timber up your nose?'

Lenk blinked.

'I … uh … suppose not.'

'Glad we agree.'

Gariath's arm, while thick as a timber spike, was not nearly as fatal and only slightly less painful as the back of his clawed hand swung up to catch Lenk at the jaw. The young man collapsed backward, granted reprieve from the voice by the sudden violent ringing in his head. He sprawled out on the deck, looking up through swimming vision into a skinny face that regarded him with momentary concern.

36

'Do I really want to know what might have driven you to go sticking your head between a dragonman's legs?' Dreadaeleon asked, cocking a black eyebrow.

'Are you the sort of gentleman who is open-minded?' Lenk groaned, rubbing his jaw.

'Not to that degree, no,' he replied, burying his boyish face back into a book that looked positively massive against his scrawny, coat-clad form.

From the deck, Lenk's eyes drifted from his companion to the boat's limp sail. He blinked, dispelling the bleariness clinging to his vision.

'It may just be the concussion talking,' he said to his companion, 'but why is it we're still bobbing in the water like chum?'

'The laws of nature are harsh,' Dreadaeleon replied, turning a page. 'If you'd like that translated into some metaphor involving fickle, fictional gods, I'm afraid you'd have to consult someone else.'

'What I mean to say,' Lenk said, pulling himself up, 'is that you can just wind us out of here, can't you?'

The boy looked up from his book, blinked.

'"Wind us out of here."'

'Yeah, you know, use your magic to—'

'I'm aware of your implication, yes. You want me to artificially inflate the sails and send us on our way.'

'Right.'

'And I want you to leave me alone.' He tucked his face back in the pages. 'Looks like we're all unhappy today.'

'You've done it before,' Lenk muttered.

'Magic isn't an inexhaustible resource. All energy needs something to burn, and I'm little more than kindling.' The boy tilted his nose up in a vague pretext of scholarly thought.

37

'Then what the hell did you take that stone for?' Lenk thrust a finger at the chipped red gem hanging from the boy's neck. 'You said the netherlings used it to avoid the physical cost of magic back at Irontide, right?'

'I did. And that's why I'm not using it,' Dreadaeleon said. 'All magic has a cost. If something negates that cost, it's illegal and thus unnatural.'

'But I've seen you use—'

'What you saw,' the boy snapped, 'was me using a brain far more colossal than *yours* to discern the nature of an object that could very well make your *head explode*. Trust me when I say that if I "wind us out" now, I won't be able to do anything later.'

'The only thing we might possibly need you to do later is serve as an impromptu anchor,' Lenk growled. 'Is it so hard to just do what I ask?'

'You're not asking, you're telling,' Dreadaeleon replied. 'If you were asking, you'd have accepted my answer as the decisive end to an argument between a man who is actually versed in the laws of magic enough to know what he's talking about and a bark-necked imbecile who's driven to desperation by his conflicts with a mule-eared savage to attempt to threaten the former man, who also has enough left in him to incinerate the latter man with a few harsh words and a flex of practised fingers, skinny they may be.'

The boy paused, drew in a deep breath.

'So shut your ugly face,' he finished.

Lenk blinked, recoiling from the verbal assault. Sighing, he rubbed his temples and fought the urge to look between Gariath's legs again.

'You have a point, I'm sure,' he said, 'but try to think of people besides yourself and myself. If we don't reach Teji by tomorrow morning, we are officially out of time.'

'So we don't get paid in time,' Dreadaeleon said, shrugging. 'Or don't get paid at all. Gold doesn't buy knowledge.'

'It buys women *with* knowledge,' another voice chirped from the prow.

Both of them turned to regard Denaos, inconsiderately long-legged and slim body wrapped in black leather. He regarded them back, a crooked grin under sweat-matted reddish hair.

'The kind of knowledge that involves saliva, sweat and sometimes a goat, depending on where you go,' he said.

'A lack of attachment to gold is an admirable trait to be nurtured and admired,' Asper said from beside him, '*not* met with advice on whoremongering.'

Denaos' scowl met the priestess's impassively judgemental gaze. She brushed his scorn off like snow from her shoulders as she tucked her brown hair behind a blue bandana. Her arms folded over her blue-robed chest as she glanced from Denaos to Dreadaeleon.

'Don't let it bother you, Dread,' she said, offering a rather modest smile. 'If we don't make it, what does it matter if we go another few weeks without bathing?' She sighed, tugging at the rather confining neck of her robes to expose a bit of sweat-kissed flesh.

The widening of the boy's eyes was impossible to miss, as was the swivel of his gaze to the aghast expression Asper wore. Powerful as the boy might be, he was still a boy, and as large as his brain was, Lenk could hear the lurid fantasies running wild through his skull. Asper's movement had sparked something within the boy that not even years of wizardly training could penetrate.

A smirk that was at once both sly and vile crossed Lenk's face.

'Think of Asper,' he all but whispered.

'Huh? What?' Dreadaeleon blinked as though he were emerging from a trance, colour quickly filling his slender face as he swallowed hard. 'What ... what about her?'

'You can't think she's too comfortable here, can you?'

'None ... none of us are comfortable,' the boy stammered back, intent on hiding more than one thing as he crossed his legs. 'It's just ... just an awkward situation.'

'True, but Asper's possibly the only decent one out of us. After all, she gave up her share of the reward, thinking that the deed we're doing is enough.' Lenk shook his head at her. 'I mean, she deserves better, doesn't she?'

'She ... does,' Dreadaeleon said, loosening the collar of his coat. 'But the laws ... I mean, they're ...'

Lenk looked up, noting the morbid fascination with which Denaos watched the unfurling discomfort in the boy. A smile far more unpleasant than his gaze crept across his face as the two men shared a discreet and wholly wicked nod between them.

'Give me your bandana,' Denaos said, turning towards Asper.

'What?' She furrowed her brow. 'Why?'

'I smudged the map. I need to clean it.' He held out his hand expectantly, batting eyelashes. 'Please?'

The priestess pursed her lips, as though unsure, before sighing in resignation and reaching up. Her robe pressed a little tighter against her chest. Dreadaeleon's eyes went wider, threatening to leap from his skull. Her collar, opened slightly more than modesty would allow at the demands of the heat, slipped open a little to expose skin glistening with sweat. The fantasies thundered through Dreadaeleon's head with enough force to cause his head to rattle.

She undid the bandana, letting brown locks fall down in

a cascade, a single strand lying on her breasts, an imperfection begging for practised, skinny fingers to rectify it.

Lenk watched the reddening of the boy's face with growing alarm. Dreadaeleon hadn't so much as breathed since Denaos made his request, his body so rigid as to suggest that rigour had set in before he could actually die.

'So ... you'll do it, right?' Lenk whispered.

'Yes,' the boy whispered, breathless, 'just ... just give me a few moments.'

Lenk glanced at the particular rigidity with which the wizard laid his book on his lap. 'Take your time.' He discreetly turned away, hiding the overwhelming urge to wash apparent on his face.

When he set his hand down into a moist puddle, the urge swiftly became harsh enough to make the drowning seem a very sensible option. He brought up a glistening hand and stared at it curiously, furrowing his brow. He was not the only one to stare, however.

'Who did it this time?' Denaos growled. 'We have rules for this sort of vulgar need and *all* of them require you to go *over* the side.'

'No,' Lenk muttered, sniffing the salt on his fingers. 'It's a leak.'

'Well, obviously it's a leak,' Denaos said, 'though I've a far less gracious term for it.'

'We're sinking,' Kataria muttered, her ears unfolding. She glanced at the boat's side, the water flowing through a tiny gash like blood through a wound. She turned a scowl up at Lenk. 'I thought you fixed this.'

'Of course, she'll talk to me when she has something to complain about,' the young man muttered through his teeth. He turned around to meet her scowl with one of his own. 'I *did*, back on Ktamgi. Carpentry isn't an exact science, you know. Accidents happen.'

'Let's be calm here, shall we?' Asper held her hands up for peace. 'Shouldn't we be thinking of ways to keep the sea from murdering us first?'

'I can help!' Dreadaeleon appeared to be ready to leap to his feet, but with a mindful cough, thought better of it. 'That is, I can stop the leak. Just ... just give me a bit.'

He flipped through his book diligently, past the rows of arcane, incomprehensible sigils, to a series of blank, bone-white pages. With a wince that suggested it hurt him more than the book to do so, he ripped one of them from the heavy tome. Swiftly shutting it and reattaching it to the chain that hung from his belt, he crawled over to the gash.

All eyes stared with curiosity as the boy knelt over the gash and brought his thumb to his teeth. With a slightly less than heroic yelp, he pressed the bleeding digit against the paper and hastily scrawled out some intricate crimson sign.

'Oh, *now* you'll do something magical?' Lenk threw his hands up.

Dreadaeleon, his brow furrowed and ears shut to whatever else his companion might have said, placed the square of paper against the ship's wound. Muttering words that hurt to listen to, he ran his unbloodied fingers over the page. In response, its stark white hue took on a dull azure glow before shifting to a dark brown. There was the sound of drying, snapping, creaking, and when it was over, a patch of fresh wood lay where the hole had been.

'How come you never did that before?' Kataria asked, scratching her head.

'Possibly because this isn't ordinary paper and I don't

have much of it,' the boy replied, running his hands down the page. 'Possibly because it's needlessly taxing for such a trivial chore. Or, possibly, because I feared the years it took me to understand the properties of it would be reduced to performing menial carpentry chores for nitwits.' He looked up, sneered. 'Pick one.'

'You did that ... with paper?' Asper did not conceal her amazement. 'Incredible.'

'Well, not paper, no.' Dreadaeleon looked up, beaming like a puppy pissing on the grass. 'Merroscrit.'

'What?' Denaos asked, face screwing up.

'Merroscrit. Wizard paper, essentially.'

'Like the paper wizards use?'

'No. Well, yes, we use it. But it's also made *out* of wizards.' His smile got bigger, not noticing Asper's amazement slowly turning to horror. 'See, when a wizard dies, his body is collected by the Venarium, who then slice him up and harvest him. His bones are carefully dried, sliced off bit by bit, and sewn together as merroscrit. The latent Venarie in his corpse allows it to conduct magic, mostly mutative magic, like I just did. It requires a catalyst, though, in this case' – he held up his thumb – 'blood! See, it's really ... um ... it's ...'

Asper's frown had grown large enough to weigh her face down considerably, its size rivalled only by that of her shock-wide eyes. Dreadaeleon's smile vanished, and he looked down bashfully.

'It's ... it's neat,' he finished sheepishly. 'We usually get them after the Decay.'

'The what?'

'The Decay. Magical disease that breaks down the barriers between Venarie and the body. It claims most wizards and leaves their bodies brimming with magic to be made into merroscrit and wraithcloaks and the like. We waste nothing.'

'I see.' Asper twitched, as though suddenly aware of her own expression. 'Well ... do all wizards get this ... posthumous honour? Don't some of them want the Gods honoured at their funeral?'

'Well, not really,' Dreadaeleon replied, scratching the back of his neck. 'I mean, there are no gods.' He paused, stuttered. 'I – I mean, for wizards ... We don't ... we don't believe in them. I mean, they aren't there, anyway, but we don't believe in them, so ... ah ...'

Asper's face went blank at the boy's sheepishness. She seemed to no longer stare at him, but through him, through the wood of the ship and the waves of the sea. Her voice was as distant as her gaze when she whispered.

'I see.'

And she remained that way, taking no notice of Dreadaeleon's stammering attempts to save face, nor of Denaos' curious raise of his brow. The rogue's own stare contrasted hers with a scrutinizing, uncomfortable closeness.

'What's wrong with you?' he asked.

'What?' She turned on him, indignant. 'Nothing!'

'Had I said anything remotely similar to the blasphemies that just dribbled out his craw, you'd have sixty sermons ready to crack my skull open with and forty lectures to offer my leaking brains.'

His gaze grew intense as she turned away from him. In the instant their eyes met as his advanced and hers retreated, something flashed behind both their gazes.

'Asper,' he whispered, 'what happened to you in Irontide?'

She met his eyes, stared at him with the same distance she had stared through the boat.

'Nothing.'

'Liar.'

'You would know, wouldn't you.'

'Well, then.' Lenk interrupted rogue, priestess and wizard in one clearing of his throat. 'If we're spared the threat of drowning, perhaps we can figure out how to move on from here before we're left adrift and empty-handed tomorrow morning.'

'To do that, we'd need to know which direction we were heading.' She turned and stared hard at Denaos, a private, unspoken warning carried in her eyes. 'And it wasn't my job to do that.'

'One might wonder what your job *is* if you've given up preaching,' the rogue muttered. He unfolded the chart and glanced over it with a passing interest. 'Huh … it's easier than I was making it seem. We are currently …' He let his finger wander over the chart, then stabbed at a point. 'Here, in Westsea.'

'So, if we know that Teji is northwest, then we simply go north from Westsea.' He scratched his chin with an air of pondering. 'Yes … it's simple, see. In another hour, we should see Reefshore on our left; then we'll pass close to Silverrock, and cross over the mouth of Ripmaw.' He folded up the map and smiled. 'We'll be there by daylight.'

'What?' Lenk furrowed his brow. 'That can't be right.'

'Who's the navigator here?'

'You're not navigating. Those aren't even real places. You're just throwing two words together.'

'Am not,' Denaos snapped. 'Just take my word for it, if you ever want to see Teji.'

'I'd rather take the map's word for it,' Asper interjected.

Her hand was swifter than her voice, and she snatched

the parchment from the rogue's fingers. Angling herself to hold him off with one hand while she unfurled the other, she ignored his protests and held the map up to her face.

When it came down, she was a twisted knot of red ire.

The map fluttered to the ground, exposing to all curious eyes a crude drawing of what appeared to be a woman clad in robes with breasts and mouth both far bigger than her head. The words spewing from its mouth: *'Blargh, blargh, Talanas, blargh, blargh, Denaos stop having fun,'* left little wonder who it was intended to portray.

Denaos, for his part, merely shrugged.

'This is what you've been doing this whole time?' Asper demanded, giving him a harsh shove. 'Doodling *garbage* while you're supposed to be plotting a course?'

'Who among us actually expected a course to be plotted? Look around you!' The rogue waved his hands. 'Nothing but water as far as the eye can see! How the hell am I supposed to know where anything is without a landmark?'

'You *said*—'

'I *said* I could read *charts*, not plot courses.'

'I suppose we should have known you would do something like this.' She snarled, hands clenching into fists. 'When was the last time you offered to help anyone and not either had some ulterior motive or failed completely at it?'

'This isn't the time or the place,' Kataria said, sighing. 'Figure out your petty little human squabbles on your own time. I want to leave.'

'Disagreements are a natural part of anyone's nature.' Lenk stepped in, eyes narrowed. 'Not just human. You'd know that if you were two steps above an animal instead of one.'

'Slurs. Lovely.' Kataria growled.

'As though you've never slurred humans before? You do it twice before you piss in the morning!'

'It says something that you're concerned about what I do when I piss,' she retorted, 'but I don't even want to think about that.' She turned away from him, running hands down her face. '*This* is why we need to get off this stupid boat.'

They're close to a fight, Gariath thought from the boat's gunwale.

The dragonman observed his companions in silence as he had since they had left the island of Ktamgi two days ago. Three days before that, he would have been eager for them to fight, eager to see them spill each other's blood. It would have been a good excuse to get up and join them, to show them how to fight.

If he was lucky, he might have even accidentally killed one of them.

'Why? Because we're arguing?' Lenk spat back. 'You could always just fold your damn ears up again if you didn't want to listen to me.'

Now, he was content to simply sit, holding the boat's tiny rudder. It was far more pleasant company. The rudder was constant, the rudder was quiet. The rudder was going nowhere.

'Why couldn't you just have *said* you didn't know how to plot courses?' Asper roared at Denaos. 'Why can't you just be honest for once in your life?'

'I'll start when you do,' Denaos replied.

'What's that supposed to mean?'

The humans had their own problems, he supposed: small, insignificant human problems that teemed in numbers as large as their throbbing, populous race. They would be solved by yelling, like all human problems were.

They would yell, forget that problem, remember another one later, then yell more.

The *Rhega* had one problem.

One problem, he thought, *in numbers as small as the one Rhega left*.

'Because we shouldn't *be* arguing,' Kataria retorted. 'I shouldn't *feel* the need to argue with you. I shouldn't feel the need to talk to you! I should *want* to keep being silent, but—'

'But what?' Lenk snapped back.

'But I'm standing here yelling at you, aren't I?'

Things had happened on Ktamgi, he knew. He could smell the changes on them. Fear and suspicion between the tall man and the tall woman. Sweat and tension from the pointy-eared human and Lenk. Desire oozed from the skinny one in such quantities as to threaten to choke him on its stink.

'It's supposed to mean exactly what it does mean,' Denaos spat back. 'What happened on Ktamgi that's got you all silent and keeping your pendant hidden?'

'I've got it right here,' Asper said, holding up the symbol of Talanas' Phoenix in a manner that was less proof and more an attempt to drive the rogue away like an unclean thing.

'Today, you do, and you haven't stopped rubbing it since you woke up.' Denaos' brow rose as the colour faded from her face. 'With,' he whispered, 'your *left* hand.'

'Shut up, Denaos,' she hissed.

'Not just accidentally, either.'

'Shut up!'

'But you're right-handed, which leads me to ask again. What happened in Irontide?'

'She said,' came Dreadaeleon's soft voice accompanied by a flash of crimson in his scowl, 'to shut up.'

Their problems would come and go. His would not. They would yell. They would fight. When they were tired of that, they would find new humans to yell at.

There were no more *Rhega* to yell at. There never would be. Grahta had told him as much on Ktamgi.

You can't come.

Grahta's voice still rang in his head, haunting him between breaths. The image of him lurked behind his blinking eyes. He did not forget them, he did not want to forget them, but he could only hold them in his mind for so long before they vanished.

As Grahta had vanished into a place where Gariath could not follow.

'It's not like this is exactly easy for me, either,' Lenk snapped back.

'How? How is this not easy for you? What do you even do?' Kataria snarled. 'Sit here and occasionally stare at me? Look at me?'

'Oh, it's all well and good for *you* to—'

'*Let. Me. Finish.*' Her teeth were rattling in her skull now, grinding against each other with such ferocity that they might shatter into powder. 'If you stare, if you speak to me, you're still human. You're still what you are. If I stare at *you*, if I speak to *you*, what am I?'

'Same as you always were.'

'No, I'm not. If I feel the need to stare at you, Lenk, if I *want* to talk to you, I'm not a shict anymore. And the more I want to talk to you, the more I want to feel like a shict again. The more I want to feel like *myself*.'

'And you can only do that by ignoring me?'

'No.' Her voice was a thunderous roar now, cutting across the sea. 'I can only do that by *killing you*.'

The wind changed. Gariath could smell the humans change with it. He heard them fall silent at the pointy-eared one's voice, of course, saw their eyes turn to her, wide with horror. Noise and sight were simply two more ways for humans to deceive themselves, though. Scent could never be disguised.

An acrid stench of shock. Sour, befouled fear. And then, a brisk, crisp odour of hatred. From both of them. And then, bursting from all the humans like pus from a boil, that most common scent of confusion.

His interest lasted only as long as it took for him to remember that humans had a way of simplifying such complex emotional perfumes to one monosyllabic grunt of stupidity.

'What?' Lenk asked.

Whatever happened next was beyond Gariath's interest. He quietly turned his attentions to the sea. The scent of salt was a reprieve from the ugly stenches surrounding the humans, but not what he desired to smell again. He closed his eyes, let his nostrils flare, drinking in the air, trying to find the scent that filled his nostrils when he held two wailing pups in his arms, when he had mated for the first time, when he had begged Grahta not to go, begged to follow the pup.

He sought the scent of memory.

And smelled nothing but salt.

He had tried, for days now he had tried. Days had gone by, days would go by forever.

And the *Rhega*'s problem would not change.

You cannot go, he told himself, and the thought crossed his mind more than once. He could not go, could not follow his people, the pups, into the afterlife. But he could not stay here. He could not remain in a world where there was nothing but the stink of ...

His nostrils flickered. Eyes widened slightly. He turned his gaze out to the sea and saw the dredgespider herd scatter suddenly, skimming across the water into deeper, more concealing shadows.

That, he thought, *is not the smell of fear*.

He rose up, his long red tail twitching on the deck, his bat-like wings folding behind his back. On heavy feet, he walked across the deck, through the awkward, hateful silence and stench surrounding the humans, his eyes intent on the side of the tiny vessel. The tall, ugly one in black, made no movement to step aside.

'What's the matter with you, reptile?' he asked with a sneer.

Gariath's answer was the back of his clawed hand against the rogue's jaw and a casual step over his collapsed form. Ignoring the scowl shot at his back, Gariath leaned down over the side of the boat, nostrils twitching, black eyes searching the water.

'What ... is it?' Lenk asked, leaning down beside the dragonman.

Lenk was less stupid than the others by only a fraction, Gariath tolerated the silver-haired human with a healthy disrespect that he carried for all humans, nothing personal. The dragonman glowered over the water. Lenk stepped beside him and followed his gaze.

'It's coming,' he grunted.

'What is?' Kataria asked, ears twitching.

Not an inch of skin was left without gooseflesh when Gariath looked up and smiled, without showing teeth.

'Fate,' he answered.

Before anyone could even think how to interpret his statement, much less respond to it, the boat shuddered. Lenk hurled himself to the other railing, eyes wide and hand shaking.

'Sword,' he said. 'Sword! Sword! Where's my sword?' His hand apparently caught up with his mind as he reached up and tore the blade from the sheath on his back. 'Grab your weapons! Hurry! *Hurry!*'

'What is it?' Kataria asked, her hands already rifling through the bundle that held her bow.

'I … was looking into the water.' Lenk turned to her. 'And … it looked back.'

It took only a few moments for the bundle to lie open and empty as hands snatched up weapons. Lenk's sword was flashing in his hand, Kataria's arrow drawn back, Denaos' knives in his hand and Dreadaeleon standing over Asper, his eyes pouring the crimson magic that flowed through him.

Only Gariath stood unconcerned, his smile still soft and gentle across his face.

The boat rocked slightly, bobbing with the confusion of their own hasty movements. The sea muttered its displeasure at their sudden franticness, hissing angrily as the waves settled. The boat bobbed for an anxiety-filled eternity, ears twitching, steel flashing, eyes darting.

Several moments passed. An errant bubble found its way to the surface and sizzled. Denaos stared at it, blinked.

'What?' he asked. 'That's it?'

And then the sea exploded.

The water split apart with a bestial howl, its frothy life erupting in a great white gout as something tremendous rose to scrape at the night sky. Its wake tossed the boat back, knocking the companions beneath a sea of froth.

Only Gariath remained standing, still smiling, closing his eyes as the water washed over him.

Dripping and half-blind with froth, Lenk pulled his wet hair like curtains from his eyes. His vision was blurred, and through the salty haze he swore he could make out something immense and black with glowing yellow eyes.

The Deepshriek, he thought in a panic, *it's come back. Of course it's come back.*

'*No*,' the voice made itself known inside his head. '*It fears us. This … is …*'

'Something worse,' he finished as he looked up … and up and up.

The great serpent rose over the boat, a column of sinew and sea. Its body, blue and deep, rippled with such vigour as to suggest the sea itself had come alive. Its swaying, trembling pillar came to a crown at a menacing, serpentine head, a long crested fin running from its skull to its back and frill-like whiskers swaying from its jowls.

The sound it emitted could not be described as a growl, but more like a purr that echoed off of nothing and caused the waters to quake. Its yellow eyes, bright and sinister as they might have appeared, did not look particularly malicious. As it loosed another throat-born, reverberating noise, Lenk was half-tempted to regard it as something like a very large kitten.

Right. A kitten, he told himself, *a large kitten … with a head the size of the boat. Oh, Gods, we're all going to die.*

'What is it?' Asper asked, her whisper barely heard above its song-like noise.

'Captain Argaol told us about it before, didn't he?' Denaos muttered, sinking low. 'He gave it a name … told us something else about it. Damn, what did he say? What did he call it?'

'An Akaneed,' Dreadaeleon replied. 'He called it an Akaneed ...'

'In mating season,' Kataria finished, eyes narrowed. 'Don't make any sudden moves. Don't make any loud noises.' She turned her emerald scowl upward. 'Gariath, get down or it'll kill us all!'

'What makes you so sure it won't kill us now?' Lenk asked.

'Learn something about beasts, you nit,' she hissed. 'The little ones always want flesh. There's not enough flesh around for this thing to get that big.' She dared a bit of movement, pointing at its head. 'Look. Do you see a mouth? It might not even have teeth.'

Apparently, Lenk thought, the Akaneed *did* have a sense of irony. For as it opened its rather prominent mouth to expose a rather sharp pair of needlelike teeth, the sound it emitted was nothing at all like any kitten should ever make.

'Learn something about beasts,' he muttered, 'indeed. Or were you hoping it had teeth so it would kill me and save you the difficulty?'

Her hand flashed out and he cringed, his hand tightening on his sword in expectation of a blow. It was with nearly as much alarm, however, that he looked down to see her gloved hand clenching his own, wrapping her fingers about it. His confusion only deepened as he looked up and saw her staring at him, intently, emerald eyes glistening.

'Not now,' she whispered, *'please* not now.'

Baffled to the point of barely noticing the colossal shadow looming over him, Lenk's attention was nevertheless drawn to the yellow eyes that regarded him curiously. It seemed, at that moment, that the creature's stare was reserved specifically for him, its echoing keen directing incomprehensible queries to him alone.

Even as a distant rumble of thunder lit the skies with the echoes of lightning and split the sky open for a light rain to begin falling over the sea, the Akaneed remained unhurried. It continued to sway; its body rippled with the droplets that struck it, and its eyes glowed with increasing intensity through the haze of the shower.

'It's hesitating,' Lenk whispered, unsure what to make of the creature's swaying attentions.

'It'll stay that way,' Kataria replied. 'It's curious, not hungry. If it wanted to kill us, it would have attacked already. Now all we need to do is wait and—'

The sound of wood splitting interrupted her. Eyes turned, horrified and befuddled at once, to see Gariath's thick muscles tensing before the boat's tiny mast. With a grunt and a sturdy kick, he snapped the long pole from its base and turned its splintered edge up. Balancing it on his shoulder, he walked casually to the side of the boat.

'What are you doing?' Lenk asked, barely mindful of his voice. 'You can't fight it!'

'I'm not going to fight it,' the dragonman replied simply. He affixed his black eyes upon Lenk, his expression grim for but a moment before he smiled. 'A human with a name will always find his way back home, Lenk.'

'*Told you we should have left them,*' the voice chimed in.

The dragonman swept one cursory gaze over the others assembled, offering nothing in the rough clench of his jaw and the stern set of his scaly brow. No excuses, no apologies, nothing but acknowledgement.

And then, Gariath threw.

Their hands came too late to hold back his muscular arm. Their protests were too soft to hinder the flight of the splintered mast. It shrieked through the air, its tattered sail wafting like a banner as it sped toward the Akaneed, who merely cocked its head curiously.

Then screamed.

Its massive head snapped backward, the mast jutting from its face. Its pain lasted for an agonised, screeching eternity. When it brought its head down once more, it regarded the companions through a yellow eye stained red, opened its jaws and loosed a rumble that sent torrents of mist from its gaping maw.

'Damn it,' Lenk hissed, 'damn it, damn it, damn it.' He glanced about furtively, his sword suddenly seeming so small, so weak. Dreadaeleon didn't look any better as the boy stared up with quaking eyes, but he would have to do. '*Dread!*'

The boy looked at him, unblinking, mouth agape.

'Get up here!' Lenk roared, waving madly. 'Kill it!'

'What? *How?*'

'*DO IT.*'

Whether it was the tone of the young man or the roar of the great serpent that drove him to his feet, Dreadaeleon had no time to know. He scrambled to the fore of the boat, unhindered, unfazed even as Gariath looked at him with a bemused expression. The boy's hand trembled as he raised it before him like a weapon; his lips quivered as he began to recite the words that summoned the azure electricity to the tip of his finger.

Lenk watched with desperate fear, his gaze darting between the wizard and the beast. Each time he turned back to Dreadaeleon, something new looked out of place on the wizard. The crimson energy pouring from his eyes flickered like a candle in a breeze; he stuttered and the electricity crackled and sputtered erratically on his skin.

It was not just fear that hindered the boy.

'*He is weak,*' the voice hissed inside Lenk's head. '*Your folly was in staying with them for this long.*'

'Shut up,' Lenk muttered in return.

'*Do you think we'll die from this? Rest easy. They die. You don't.*'

'Shut up!'

'*I won't let you.*'

'Shut—'

There was the sound of shrieking, of cracking. Dreadaeleon staggered backward, as if struck, his hand twisted into a claw and his face twisted into a mask of pain and shame. The reason did not become apparent until they looked down at his shaking knees and saw the growing dark spot upon his breeches.

'Dread,' Asper gasped.

'*Now?*' Denaos asked, cringing. 'Of all times?'

'T-too much.' The electricity on Dreadaeleon's finger fizzled as he clutched his head. 'The strain … it's just … the cost is too—'

Like a lash, the rest of the creature hurled itself from the sea. Its long, snaking tail swung high over the heads of the companions, striking Dreadaeleon squarely in the chest. His shriek was a whisper on the wind, his coat fluttering as he sailed through the air and plummeted into the water with a faint splash.

The companions watched the waters ripple and re-form over him, hastily disguising the fact that the boy had ever even existed as the rain carelessly pounded the sea. They blinked, staring at the spot until it finally was still.

'Well.' Denaos coughed. 'Now what?'

'I don't know,' Lenk replied. 'Die horribly, I guess.'

As though it were a request to be answered, the Akaneed

complied. Mist bursting from its mouth, it hurled itself over the boat, its head kicking up a great wave as it crashed into the waters on the other side. The companions, all save Gariath, flung themselves to the deck and stared as the creature's long, sinewy body replaced the sky over them, as vast and eternal. It continued for an age, its body finally disappearing beneath the water as a great black smear under the waves.

'It was going to leave us alone,' Kataria gasped, staring at the vanishing shape, then at Gariath. 'It was going to go away! Why did you do that?'

'Isn't it obvious?' Denaos snarled, sliding his dagger out. 'He wanted this. He *wanted* to kill us. It's only fair that we return the favour before that thing eats us.'

'Gariath … why?' was all Asper could squeak out, a look of pure, baffled horror painting her expression.

The dragonman only smiled and spoke. 'It's not like you're the last humans.'

Lenk had no words, his attentions still fixed upon the Akaneed's dark, sinewy shape beneath the surface. He watched it intently, sword in hand, as it swept about in a great semicircle and turned, narrowing its glowing yellow eye upon the vessel.

'It's going to ram us!' he shouted over the roar of thunder as the rain intensified overhead.

'The head!' Kataria shrieked. 'Use the head!'

He wasted no time in hurling himself to the deck, jamming his hand into their stowed equipment. He searched, wrapped fingers about thick locks of hair and pulled free a burlap sack. Holding it like a beacon before him, he outstretched his hand, pulled the sack free.

The Deepshriek's head dangled in the wind, eyes shut, mouth pursed tightly. It regarded the approaching Akaneed impassively, not caring that it was about to be lost with every other piece of flesh on board. *In fact,* Lenk had the presence of mind to think, *it's probably enjoying this.*

No time for thought, barely enough time for one word.

'Scream,' he whispered.

And was obeyed.

The head's jaws parted, stretching open impossibly wide as its eyelids fluttered open to expose a gaze golden with malevolence. There was the faint sound of air whistling for but a moment before the thunder that followed.

The head screamed, sent the air fleeing before its vocal fury, ripped the waves apart as the sky rippled and threatened to become unseamed. The blast of sound met the Akaneed head-on, and the yellow gaze flickered beneath the water. The dark, sinewy shape grew fainter, its agonised growl an echo carried on bubbles as it retreated below the water.

'I got it,' Lenk whispered excitedly. 'I got it!' He laughed hysterically, holding the head above his own. '*I win!*'

The water split open; a writhing tail lashed out and spitefully slapped the hull of the boat. His arms swung wildly as he fought to hold onto his balance, and when he looked up, the Deepshriek's head was gone from his grasp.

'Oh ...'

The eyes appeared again, far away at the other side of the boat, bright with eager hatred. The sea churned around it as it growled beneath the surface, coiled into a shadowy spring, then hurled itself through the waves. Lenk cursed, then screamed.

'Down! *Down!*'

He spared no words for Gariath, who stood with arms hanging limply at his side, snout tilted into the air. The dragonman's eyes closed, his wings folded behind his back, as he raised his hands to the sky. Though he could spare but a moment of observation before panic seized his senses once more, Lenk noted this as the only time he had ever seen the dragonman smile pleasantly, almost as though he were at peace.

He was still smiling when the Akaneed struck.

Its roar split the sea in half as it came crashing out of the waves, its skull smashing against the boat's meagre hull. The world was consumed in a horrific cracking sound as splinters hurled themselves through the gushing froth. The companions themselves seemed so meagre, so insignificant amongst the flying wreckage, their shapes fleeting shadows lost in the night as they flew through the sky.

Air, Lenk told himself as he paddled toward the flashes of lightning above him. *Air. Air.* Instinct banished fear as fear had banished hate. He found himself thrashing, kicking as he scrambled for the surface. With a gasp that seared his lungs, he pulled himself free and hacked the stray streams out of his mouth.

A fervent, panicked glance brought no sign of his companions or the beast. The boat itself remained intact, though barely, bobbing upon the water in the wake of the mayhem with insulting calmness. The rations and tools it had carried floated around it, winking beneath the surface one by one.

'*Get to it, fool*,' the voice snarled. '*We can't swim forever.*'

Unable to tell the difference between the cold presence in his head and his own voice of instinct, Lenk paddled until his heart threatened to burst. He drew closer and closer, searching for any sign of his companions: a gloved hand reaching out of the gloom, brown hair disappearing into the water.

Green eyes closing ... one by one.

Later, he told himself as he reached for the bobbing wooden corpse. *Survive now, worry later.* His inner voice became hysterical, a frenzied smile on his lips as he neared. *Just a little more. Just a little more!*

The water erupted around him as a great blue pillar tore itself free from a liquid womb. It looked down at him, its feral disdain matching his horror. It wasn't until several breathless moments had passed that Lenk noticed the fact that the beast now stared at him with two glittering yellow eyes, whole and unskewered.

'Sweet Khetashe,' he had not the breath to scream, 'there's two of them.'

The Akaneed's answer was a roar that matched the heavens' thunder as it reared back and hurled itself upon what remained of the boat. Its skull sent the timbers flying in reckless flocks. Lenk watched in horror, unable to act as a shattered plank struck him against the temple. Instinct, fear, hate … all gave way to darkness as his body went numb. His arms stopped thrashing, legs stopped kicking.

Unblinking as he slipped under the water, he stared up at the corpse of the ship, illuminated by the flicker of lightning, as it sank to its grave with him. Soon, that faded as his eyes forgot how to focus and his lungs forgot their need for air. He reached out, half-hearted, for the sword that descended alongside him.

When he grasped only water, he knew he was going to die.

'*No*,' the voice spoke, more threatening than comforting. '*No, you won't.*'

The seawater flooded into his mouth and he found not the will to push it out. The world changed from blue to black as he drifted into darkness on a haunting echo.

'*I won't let you.*'

Three

ONE THOUSAND PAPER WINGS

Poets, she had often suspected, were supposed to have beautiful dreams: silhouettes of women behind silk, visions of gold that blinded their closed eyes, images of fires so bright they should take the poet's breath away before she could put them to paper.

Anacha dreamt of cattle.

She dreamt of shovelling stalls and milking cows. She dreamt of wheat and of rice in shallow pools, dirty feet firmly planted in mud, ugly cotton breeches hiked up to knobby knees as grubby hands rooted around in filth. She dreamt of a time when she still wore such ugly clothing instead of the silks she wore now, when she covered herself in mud instead of perfume.

Those were the good dreams.

The nightmares had men clad in the rich robes of money-lenders, their brown faces red as they yelled at her father and waved debtor's claims. They had her father helpless to resist as he signed his name on the scrolls and the men, with their soft and uncallused hands, helped her into a crate with silk walls. She would dream of her tears mingling with the bathwater as women, too old to be of any desire for clients, scrubbed the mud from her rough flesh and the calluses from her feet.

She used to have nightmares every night. She used to cry every night.

That was before Bralston.

Now she dreamed of him often, the night she met him, the first poem she ever read. It was painted upon her breasts and belly as she was ordered into her room to meet a new client, her tears threatening to make the dye run.

'*Do* not *cry*,' the older women had hissed, '*this is a member of the Venarium. A wizard. Do what you do, do it well. Wizards are as generous with their gold as they are with their fire and lightning.*'

She couldn't help but cry the moment the door closed behind her and she faced him: broad-shouldered, slender of waist, with not a curl of hair upon his head. He had smiled at her, even as she cried, had taken her to the cushion they would sit upon for many years and had read the poetry on her skin. He would read for many days before he finally claimed what he paid for.

By then, he needn't take it.

She began to yearn for him in her sleep, rolling over to find his warm brown flesh in her silk sheets. To find an empty space where he should be wasn't something she was unused to; a strict schedule was required to keep his magic flowing correctly, as he often said. To find her fingers wrapping about a scrap of paper, however, was new.

Fearing that he had finally left her the farewell note she lived in perpetual terror of, she opened her eyes and unwrapped her trembling fingers from the parchment. Fear turned to surprise as she saw the slightly wrinkled form of a paper crane sitting in her palm, its crimson painted eyes glaring up at her, offended at her fingers wrinkling its paper wings. Without an apology for it, she looked around her room, and surprise turned to outright befuddlement.

In silent flocks, the cranes had perched everywhere: on her bookshelf, her nightstand, her washbasin, her mirror, all over her floors. They stared down at her with wary, blood-red eyes, their beaks folded up sharply in silent judgement.

So dense they were, she might never have found him amongst the flocks if not for the sound of his fingers diligently folding another. He straightened up from his squat on her balcony, casting a glower over his bare, brown back.

'That wasn't precisely easy to fold, you know,' he said.

She started, suddenly realising she still held the wrinkled paper crane in her hand. Doing her best to carefully readjust the tiny creature, she couldn't help but notice the unnatural smoothness to the parchment. Paper was supposed to have wrinkles, she knew, tiny little edges of roughness. That paper had character, eager to receive the poet's brush.

This paper ... seemed to resent her touching it.

'None of these could have been easy to fold,' Anacha said, placing the crane down carefully and pulling her hand away with a fearful swiftness that she suspected must have looked quite silly. 'How long have you been up?'

'Hours,' Bralston replied.

She peered over his pate to the black sky beyond, just now beginning to turn blue.

'It's not yet dawn,' she said. 'You always get fussy if you don't sleep enough.'

'Anacha,' he sighed, his shoulders sinking. 'I am a hunter of heretic wizards. I enforce the law of Venarie through fire and frost, lightning and force. I do not get *fussy*.'

He smiled, paying little attention to the fact that she did not return the expression. She was incapable of smiling now, at least not in the way she had the first night she had met him.

'This is a lovely poem,' he had said, as she lay on the bed before him. *'Do you like poetry?'*

She had answered with a stiff nod, an obedient nod scrubbed and scolded into her. He had smiled.

'What's your favourite?'

When she had no reply, he had laughed. She had felt the urge to smile, if only for the fact that it was as well-known that wizards didn't laugh as it was that they drank pulverised excrement and ate people's brains for the gooey knowledge contained within.

'Then I will bring you poetry. I am coming back in one week.' Upon seeing her confused stare, he rolled his shoulders. *'My duty demands that I visit Muraska for a time. Do you know where it is?'* She shook her head; he smiled. *'It's a great, grey city to the north. I'll bring you a book from it. Would you like that?'*

She nodded. He smiled and rose, draping his coat about him. She watched him go, the sigil upon his back shrinking as he slipped out the door. Only when it was small as her thumb did she speak and ask if she would see him again. He was gone then, however, the door closing behind him.

And the urge to smile grew as faint then as it was now.

'This is ... for work, then?' she asked, the hesitation in her voice only indicative that she knew the answer.

'This is for my *duty*, yes,' he corrected as he set aside another paper crane and plucked up another bone-white sheet. 'Librarian helpers, I call them. My helpful little flocks.'

She plucked up the crane beside her delicately in her

hand, stared into its irritated little eyes. The dye was thick, didn't settle on the page as proper ink should. It was only when the scent of copper filled her mouth that she realised that this paper wasn't meant for ink.

'You … This is,' she gasped, 'your blood?'

'Some of it, yes.' He held up a tiny little vial with an impressive label, shook it, then set in a decidedly large pile. 'I ran out after the four hundredth one. Fortunately, I've been granted special privileges for this particular duty, up to and including the requisition of a few spare pints.'

Anacha had long ago learned that wizards did laugh and that they rarely did anything relatively offensive to brains from those not possessing their particular talents. Their attitude towards other bodily parts and fluids, however, was not something she ever intended to hear about without cringing.

She had little time to reflect on such ghastly practices this morning.

'Why do you need so many?'

At this, he paused, as he had when she had discovered wizards could lie.

'What is your duty?' she had asked, their sixth night together after five nights of reading.

'I'm a Librarian.' He had turned at her giggle and raised a brow. *'What?'*

'I thought you were a wizard.'

'I am.'

'A member of the Venarium.'

'I am.'

'Librarians stock shelves and adjust spectacles.'

'Have you learned nothing of the books I've brought you? Words can have multiple meanings.'

'Books only make me wonder more ... like how a Librarian can go to Muraska and afford whores?'

'Well, no one can afford whores in Muraska.'

'Why did you go to Muraska, then?'

'Duty called.'

'What kind of duty?'

'Difficult duties. Ones that demand the talents of a man like myself.'

'Talents?'

'Talents.'

'Fire and lightning talents? Turning people to frogs and burning down houses talents?'

'We don't turn people into frogs, no. The other talents, though ... I use them sometimes. In this particular case, some apprentice out in the city went heretic. He started selling his secrets, his services. He violated the laws.'

'What did you do to him?'

'My duty.'

'Did you kill him?'

He had paused then, too.

'No,' he had lied then, 'I didn't.'

'No reason,' he lied now.

'I'm not an idiot, Bralston,' she said.

'I know,' he replied. 'You read books.'

'Don't insult me.' She held up a hand, winced. 'Please ... you never insult me like clients insult the other girls.' She sighed, her head sinking low. 'You're bleeding yourself dry, creating thousands of these little birds ...' She crawled across the bed, staring at his back intently. 'Why?'

'Because of my—'

'Duty, yes, I know. But what is it?'

He regarded her coldly. 'You know enough about it to

know that I don't want you to ever have to think about it.'

'And you know enough about me that I would never ask if I didn't have good reason.' She rose up, snatching her robe as it lay across her chair and wrapping it about her body, her eyes never leaving him. 'You want to be certain of carrying out your duty this time, I can tell ... but why? What's special about this one?'

Bralston rose and turned to her, opening his mouth to say something, to give some rehearsed line about all duties being equal, about there being nothing wrong with being cautious. But he paused. Wizards were terrible liars, and Bralston especially so. He wore his reasons on his face, the frown-weary wrinkles, the wide eyes that resembled a child straining to come to terms with a puppy's death.

And she wore her concern on her face, just as visible in the purse of her lips and narrow of her eyes. He sighed, looked down at his cranes.

'A woman is involved.'

'A woman?'

'Not like that,' he said. 'A woman came to the Venarium ... told us a story about a heretic.'

'You get plenty of stories about heretics.'

'Not from women ... not from women like *this*.' He winced. 'This heretic ... he ... did something to her.'

She took a step forward, weaving her way through the cranes.

'What did he do?'

'He ...' Bralston ran a hand over his head, tilted his neck back and sighed again. 'It's a gift that we have, you know? Wizards, that is. Fire, lightning ... that's only part of it. That's energy that comes from our own bodies. A wizard that knows ... a wizard that practises, can affect other people's bodies, twist their muscles, manipulate them, make them do things. If we wanted to, we wizards, we could …

'This heretic … this … this …' For all the books he had read, Bralston apparently had no word to describe what the rage playing across his face demanded. 'He broke the law. He used his power in a foul way.'

'That's why they're sending you out?' she whispered, breathless.

'That's why I'm *choosing* to go,' he replied, his voice rising slightly. She took a step back, regardless, as crimson flashed behind his eyes.

She could only remember once when he had raised his voice.

'*What happened?*' he had asked as he came through the door.

It had been a month since he had begun paying for her, not yet to the point when he began to pay for exclusive visitations. She had lain on the bed, the poetry smeared across her breasts with greasy handprints, her belly contorted with the lash marks upon it, her face buried in her pillow, hiding the redness in her cheeks.

'*What,*' he had raised his voice then, '*happened?*'

'*Some …*' she had gasped, '*some clients prefer to be rough … I'm told. This one … he brought in a cat.*'

'*A whip? That's against the rules.*'

'*He paid extra. Someone working for the Jackals with a lot of money. He … he wanted it …*' She pointed to the hall. '*He's going down the halls … to all the girls. He had a lot of …*'

Bralston rose at that point, turned to walk out the door again. She had grabbed his coattails in her hand and pulled with all that desperation demanded. No one troubled the

Jackals. It wasn't as hard a rule then as it was now, the Jackals being a mere gang instead of a syndicate back then, which was the sole reason Bralston never had to raise his voice again. No one troubled them; not the nobles, not the guards, not even the Venarium.

Bralston pulled away sharply, left the room. His boots clicked the length of the hall. She heard the scream that ensued, smelled the embers on his coat when he returned and sat down beside her.

'*What did you do?*' she had asked.

He had paused and said. '*Nothing.*'

She had barely noticed him pulling on his breeches now. He did not dress so much as gird himself, slinging a heavy belt with several large pouches hanging from it and attaching his massive spellbook with a large chain. He pulled his tunic over the large amulet, a tiny red vial set within a bronze frame, hanging from his neck. It wasn't until he reached for his final garment that she realised he wouldn't be stopped.

'Your hat,' she whispered, eyeing the broad-rimmed leather garment, a steel circlet adorning its interior ring. 'You never wear it.'

'I was requested to.' He ran a finger along the leather band about it, the sigils upon it briefly glowing. He traced his thumb across the steel circle inside it. 'This is ... a special case.'

She watched him drape the great coat across his back, cinch it tight against his body. She watched the sigil scrawled upon it shrink as he walked to the balcony. She never thought she would get used to the sight of it.

*

'You've ... come back.' She had gasped not so many years ago, astonished to find him standing on her balcony, clad in his coat and hat. 'You said it was a special case.'

'It was. I came back, anyway.' He smiled, shrugged off his coat. 'I've already paid.'

'Paid? Why?' She pulled away from him, tears brimming in her eyes. 'I thought ... you were going to take me away when you came back. You said ...'

'I know ... I know.' The pain on his face had been visible then, not hidden behind years of wrinkles. 'But ... the case got me noticed. I'm being made ...' He had sighed, rubbed his eyes, shook his head. 'I can't. I'm sorry. I won't lie again.'

'But ... you ... you said ...'

'And I never will again. It was stupid of me to say it in the first place.'

'It wasn't! You were going to—'

'It was. I can't. I'm a Librarian. I have duties.'

'But why?' she asked then. 'Why do you have to be a Librarian?'

'Why?' she asked now, shaking her head. 'Why do you have to be the one to avenge her?' She held up a hand. 'Don't say duty ... don't you dare say it.'

'Because I have a gift,' he said without hesitation. 'And so rarely do I get the chance for that gift to be used in a way that I consider more worthwhile than duty.'

'Will I see you again?'

He paused as he opened his coat and held open his pocket.

'Maybe,' he answered.

His next word was something she couldn't understand, something no one else but a wizard could understand. She certainly understood what it was, however, for no sooner did he speak it than the sound of paper rustling filled the room.

Silent save for the rattle of their wings, the cranes came to life. Their eyes glowed in a thousand little pinpricks of ruby; their wings shuddered in a thousand little whispers. They fell from bookshelf and basin, rose from tile and chair, hung a moment in the air.

Then flew.

She shrieked, shielding herself from the thousand paper wings as the room was filled with bone-white cranes and the sound of tiny wings flapping. In a great torrent, they flew into Bralston's coat pocket, folding themselves neatly therein.

She kept her eyes closed, opening them only when she heard the larger wings flapping. Opening her eyes and seeing nothing standing at her balcony, she rushed to the edge and watched him sail over the rooftops of Cier'Djaal on the leather wings his coat had once been. And with each breath, he shrank until he wasn't even bigger than her thumb.

And then, Bralston was gone.

Four

THE PRISTINE MADNESS

'Pretty,' he whispered.

'*Hmm?*' the voice replied.

'I was simply noting the beauty of it all,' Lenk replied as he stared out over the vast, dreaming blue around him.

The ocean stretched out, engulfing him in a gaping, azure yawn. A yawn seemed fitting, Lenk decided, for the sheer uncaring nature of it all. It did not move, did not ripple, did not change as the sky did. There wasn't a cloud to mar his perfect view of the sprawling underwater world.

The sky had betrayed him too many times. It had hidden his sun behind clouds and sullied his earth with rain. The sky was a spiteful, wicked thing of thunder and wind. The ocean didn't care.

'The ocean … it loves me,' he whispered. His face contorted suddenly and his eyes went wide, not feeling the salt that should be stinging them. 'What did I just say?'

'*I wasn't listening,*' the voice said.

'No, I said the "ocean loves me." What a deranged thing to say. I said the sky was spiteful, it betrayed me.'

'*You only thought that.*'

'I thought you weren't listening.'

'*Not to your voice, no.*'

'Then …' He clutched his head, not feeling his fingers on his skin. 'It's finally happened. I've gone insane.'

'You didn't stop to think that when you realised you weren't breathing?'

Lenk's hands went to his throat. The panic that surged through him left his heartbeat oddly slow and his pulse standing still. He knew he should be terrified, should be thrashing and watching his screams drift to the surface in soundless bubbles. But, for all that he knew he should, drowning simply didn't bother him.

But it should, he told himself. *I should be afraid. But I'm not ... I feel ...*

'Peaceful.'

The voice, or rather voices, that finished his thoughts were not his own, but they were familiar to his ears. Far more familiar, he knew, than he would have ever liked. He recognised them, remembered them from his dreams and heard them every time his leg ached.

It would have seemed redundant to call the Deepshriek by name, even as it drifted out of the endless blue and into his vision. Three pairs of eyes stared at him. The pair of soulless black eyes affixed to the massive shark that served as the abomination's body was simply unnerving. He didn't truly begin to worry until he looked into the glimmering golden stares of the two feminine faces with hair of red and black, swaying upon delicate, grey stalks from the beast's grey back.

'It could always be this way, you know,' the one with the copper hair said. 'Drifting. Endless. Peace. Lay down your sword.'

'I can't,' he replied.

'Why do you want to kill us?' the black-haired one asked, her lips a pout. 'We merely wish to deliver the peace you feel now to all who have been lied to by the sky.'

'It deceives,' the red one hissed. 'Tricks. You are told to pray to it, to give your troubles to the sky.'

'It gives warmth,' Lenk noticed, seeing the beams of sun that even now sought to reach him below. It was warm down here, far too warm for the ocean he had come to know these past weeks.

'Fleeting. When you need it most, where is the light? What does the sky offer then?' the black one sighed. 'Rain, thunder, sorrows. How can you trust something that is so fickle? So changing?'

'It lied to you,' the red one growled.

'It sent you down here,' the black one snarled.

'But we embrace you,' they both replied in discordant harmony. 'We give you peace. We give you ...'

'Endless blue,' Lenk finished for them. He narrowed his eyes. 'I've heard that before.'

'Have you?'

'From every one of your demon servants, yes.'

'Demons?'

'What else would you call them?'

'Interesting question,' the black one muttered.

'Very interesting,' the red one agreed. It looked to its counterpart. 'What would you call Mother Deep's children?'

'Hellspawn,' Lenk chimed in.

'Dramatic, but a bit too vague,' the red one said. 'Deeplings?'

'A tad too predictable,' the black one replied. 'What are they, after all? Creatures returned from whence they were so unjustly banished. Creatures from a place far beyond the understanding of mankind and his sky and earth.'

'They had a word for such things,' the red one said.

'Ah, yes,' the black one said.

'Aeon,' they both finished.

Lenk felt he should ask a question at that, but found that none in his head would slide into his throat. He felt the ocean begin to change around him, felt it abandon him as he began to fall, his head like a lead weight that dragged him farther below. Above, the Deepshriek became a halo, swimming in slow circles that shrank with every passing breath.

It was getting warm, he noted, incredibly so. His blood felt like it was boiling, his skull an oven for his mind to simmer thoughtfully in. Every breath came through a tightened throat: laboured, heavy, then impossible.

Breath. His eyes widened at the word. *Can't breathe.* His throat tightened, heart pounded, pulse raced. *Can't breathe, can't breathe!*

'What a pity,' came another voice, one he did not recognise.

This one was deep, bass and shook the waters, changing them as it spoke. It drowned the sky, doused the sun with its laughter. It sent the waves roiling up to meet him.

He tilted his head, stared down into a pair of glimmering green eyes that he knew well. They stared up at him from above a smile that was entirely too big, between long ears that floated like feathery gills, as a slender, leather-clad hand reached up to beckon him down.

'But where we must all go,' she whispered, her voice making the sand beneath her shudder, 'we do not sin with breath.'

His scream was silent. Her stare was vast. The sun died above. The ocean floor opened up, a great gaping yawn that callously swallowed him whole.

*

After so many times waking in screams and sweat, Lenk simply didn't have the energy to do it this time, even when his eyes fluttered open and beheld the eight polished eyes that stared back at him through a thin sheet of silk. His scream withered and died in his chest, but the dredgespider loosed a frustrated hiss before leaping off of his chest and scurrying away into the surf.

He stared up at the sky through the gauzy webs the many-legged creature had blanketed him in. *Air*, he thought as he inhaled great gulps. He remembered air.

He remembered everything, he found, between the twitches of his eyes. He remembered the Deepshriek, what it had said. He remembered Kataria … had that been Kataria? He remembered the ocean, uncaring, and the darkness, consuming. That had all happened. Hadn't it? Was it some temporary, trauma-induced madness? His head hurt; he had been struck in the wreck, he recalled.

The wreck … They had been wrecked, destroyed, cast to the bottom of the ocean.

But he was alive now. He breathed. He saw clouds moving in a deceitful sky. He felt treacherous sunlight on his skin. He was alive. He forced himself to rise.

The pain that racked him with every movement only served to confirm that he was still alive. Unless he had arrived in hell, anyway. He doubted that, though. The tome had told him of hell. It had mentioned nothing of warm, sunny beaches.

Nor, he thought as he spied a slender figure standing knee-deep in the surf, did hell possess women. Not ones that didn't sever and slurp up one's testes, anyway. The sunlight blinded him as he squinted against the shimmering shore. He saw pale skin, long hair wafting in the breeze, a flash of emerald.

77

'Kat ...' he whispered, afraid to ask. 'Kataria?'

The gale carried a cloud across the sun that cloaked the beach with the cruel clarity of shadow. The figure turned to regard him and he saw green locks tumbling to pale shoulders, feathery gills wafting delicately about her neck, fins extending from the sides and crown of her head as she canted her head and regarded him.

'Oh,' he muttered, 'it's you.'

Greenhair was not her name, he remembered, but it was what they had given her. She was a siren, a servant of Zamanthras, the Mother. She had aided them in locating the tome. But she had fled afterwards, he recalled, fled from the duty to find the tome and slay the Abysmyths, fled from the duty she claimed was holy.

Why?

'Young silverhair is awake.' The siren's voice was a melody, a lilting lyric in every syllable. He remembered it being more beautiful before, rather than the dirge it was now. 'I feared you dead.'

'I suppose it would have been a waste of time, then, to keep the bugs off of me,' Lenk muttered, pulling the dredgespider's webbing from his body.

'They feed where they can, silverhair,' she replied. 'It has been a long time since they found something substantial and alive on this island.'

'Except me?'

'Except you,' she said, sounding almost disappointed. Seeing his furrowed brow, she forced a weak smile. 'But you live. I am glad.'

'Don't get me wrong, I'm awfully pleased, myself,' he said, trying to rise, 'but—'

A shriek ripped through him alongside the fire lancing through his leg. He collapsed back to the sand, looking to his thigh. Or rather, to the scaly green mass that had once been his neatly-stitched and bandaged thigh. The wound had been ripped open, the meat beneath the skin glistening and discoloured at the edges.

'Do not tax yourself,' Greenhair said, wading out of the surf. Her webbed fingers twitched as she approached him. 'Your wound festers. Your life flows with your protest. The scent is sweet to predators.'

He glanced out over the sea. The dredgespiders skimmed across the surface, casting eight-eyed glares at his unsportsmanlike decision to live. The pain coursed through him with such agony that he absently considered lying back and letting them have him.

Still, biting back both the agony and the obscenities accompanying it, he rose to one foot, fighting off the dizziness that struggled to bring him back down.

'Where am I?' he asked.

'The home of the Owauku,' she replied. 'Dutiful servants of the Sea Mother, devout in their respect for her ways.'

'Owa ... what?' Lenk twitched. 'No, where *am* I? What is this place?'

'Teji.'

'Teji ...' The word tasted familiar on his tongue. The realisation lit up behind his eyes, gave him strength to rise. 'Teji. *Teji!*' At her baffled glance, he grinned broadly, hysteria reflected in every tooth. 'This is where we're supposed to be! This is where Sebast is going to meet us, who will take us back to Miron, who will pay us and then we're *done*. We did it! We made it! We're ... we ...'

We.

That word tasted bitter, sounded hollow on the sky. He stared across the shore. Empty sand, empty sea met him, vast and utterly indifferent to the despair that grew in his belly and spread onto his face.

'Where are they?' he asked, choked. 'Did you find no one else?'

She shook her head. 'Teji is not where people go to live, silverhair.'

'What? It's a trading post, Argaol said.'

She fixed him with a dire gaze. 'Silverhair … Teji is a tomb.'

She levelled a finger over his head. At once, he felt a darkness over him, a shadow that reached deeper into him than the clouded sky overhead. He turned and stared up into the face of a god.

The statue looked back down at him from where it leaned, high upon a sandy ridge. A right hand wrought of stone was extended, palm flat and commanding all who beheld it. A stone robe wrapped a lean figure set upon iron, treaded wheels. In lieu of a face, the great winged phoenix sigil of Talanas was carved, staring down at Lenk through unfurled wings and crying beak.

The monolith was a vision of decay: wheels rusted and sand-choked, stone rumbling in places, worn where it was intact. Against that, the pile of skulls that had been heaped about its wheels seemed almost insignificant.

'What?' he gasped. 'What is this place?'

'It is where the battle between Aeons and mortals began in earnest,' Greenhair replied. 'The servants of the House of the Vanquishing Trinity opposed the Aeons, the greed-poisoned servants of the Gods. Ulbecetonth, most spiteful and vicious of them, was driven back before their onslaught. Her children and followers faced them down here. They died. The mortals died. And when the last drop was spilled, the land died with them.'

'Died …' he whispered. 'My companions …'

'Unfortunate' she said, moving closer to him. 'The Akaneeds are vigilant, voracious. They leave nothing behind.'

'Nothing …'

'Even if your companions survived, there is nothing here to feed them. They would die, too. They would find nothing here.'

Nothing.

The word was heavier than the whisper it was carried on, loading itself upon Lenk's shoulders and driving him to the earth. He collapsed in the shadow of the monolith, the sigil of Talanas looking down upon him without pity, as he was certain the god Himself did at that moment.

'I am sorry,' Greenhair whispered, her voice heavy in its own right as her lips drew close to his ear. 'I found nothing of them.'

'Nothing.'

'No one …'

'No one.' Lenk swallowed hard. 'The others … all of them …' The next word felt like forcing razors up through his throat. 'Kataria.'

'You survive, silverhair,' she whispered, placing hands upon his shoulders, sitting down. 'No fear for you now. There is no danger. Rest now.'

'Rest … I must rest.' He was suddenly aware of how tired he was, how his bones seemed to melt inside him. She gently eased his head in her lap. 'This …' he muttered as he felt the coolness of her ivory skin. 'This seems … feels strange.'

'Worry will cause you nothing but pain,' Greenhair whispered. Her voice seemed to rise now, the whispering crescendo to a melodic choir. 'You need only rest, silverhair. Fear for them later. Close your eyes ... You need only worry about one thing.'

'What's that?' he asked, barely aware of the yawn in his question, barely aware of the iron weight of his eyelids.

'Where is it?' she whispered, a gentle prod in his ear.

'Where's what?'

'The tome,' she prodded again. 'Where is it?'

'*This*,' another voice, harsh and cold against her melody, hummed inside his head, '*is wrong. We must search, not rest.*'

'The Akaneeds leave nothing ...' Lenk repeated, his own tone listless.

'*How does she know of the serpents? Why does she want us to sleep?*'

'You must have had it,' Greenhair whispered. 'You have read it. You know where it is.'

'*She does not know that*,' the voice growled, drowning out her whisper. '*She cannot know that.*'

'How,' Lenk muttered, 'do you know that?'

He felt her tense beneath him, even as he felt his head tighten.

'I ... I do not ...' she began to stammer, the melody breaking in her voice.

'*She's in our head*,' the voice roared, echoing off his skull. '*Get out! Get out!* GET OUT!'

'*OUT!*'

He shot up like a spear, whirling around just as she scrambled to get away from him. Her pale, slender arm was held up in pitiful defence before a slack-jawed, wide-eyed face full of terror. He was unmoved by the display, as he was unmoved by the hot agony in his leg. That pain quickly seeped away, replaced with a chill that snaked through his body, numbing him to pain, to fear.

To pity.

From beneath the emerald locks, a large, crested fin rose upon the siren's head. The same coldness that numbed his muscles now drove him forward as he leapt upon her and wrapped his hands about her throat, slamming her to the ground.

'No more songs, no more screaming.' It was not Lenk's voice that hissed through his teeth, nor his eyes that stared contemptibly down upon her. 'You ... betrayed us.'

She choked out a plea, unheard.

'All you care about is the tome! Pages! Nothing but pages of demonic filth! Kataria ... the others ...' He felt his teeth threaten to crack under the strain of his clenched jaw. 'They mean *nothing* to you!'

She beat hands against his arms, unfelt.

'Those things, the Akaneeds,' he snarled, his breath a fine mist, 'they didn't attack immediately. They didn't act like beasts at all! Someone sent them!' He slammed her head upon the ground. 'Was it you? *Did you do this to us? Did you kill Kataria?*'

She drew back a hand. Tiny claws extended from her fingers, unnoticed.

His next words were a startled snarl as she drew her hand up and raked the bony nails across his cheek. He recoiled with a shriek and she slithered out from under him like an eel. Before he even opened his mouth to curse her, she was on her feet and rushing to the sea. In a flash of green and a spray of water, she vanished beneath the waves.

'You can't run,' Lenk growled as he staggered to his feet. The agony in his leg made its presence known with a decidedly rude sear of muscle. He collapsed, reaching out for the long-gone figure of the siren. 'I'll ... kill ...'

A glint of viscous liquid upon his fingers, tinged with his

own blood, caught his eye. He brought it close, watched it swirl upon his hand even as he felt it swirl inside his cheek. His eyelids fluttered, pulse pounded, body failed.

'*Poison*,' the voice hissed inside his head. '*You idiot*.'

He made a retort, lost in a groan and a mouthful of sand as he collapsed forward and lay unmoving.

The cold, Lenk decided, when he regained consciousness, was sorely missed. When he managed to realise that he had a rather impolite crab scuttling over his face, pinching at tender flesh in search of something to devour, he also realised that his skull was on fire.

Or felt like it, at the very least.

He cast a look up at the sky, saw the shroud of clouds that masked the sun. Yet he still burned. Even the mild light that filtered through in rays that refused to be hindered seared his eyes, his flesh.

Fever.

He felt an itch at his leg, reached down to scratch and felt moist and scaly flesh under his nails. However long he had been out, the sun had suckled at his wound and left a mass of green-rimmed skin weeping tears of blood-flecked pus.

That would explain it.

He looked around for Greenhair, wondering if perhaps she might be able to make another makeshift bandage to stem the flow. He felt an itch on his cheek quickly followed by a sting of pain.

Oh, right …

The urge to chase her down and beat a cure out of her was fleeting; even if she hadn't vanished into the sea like the shark-whoring ocean-bitch she was, he couldn't very well search the whole beach on a limb that begged for a merciful amputation.

He was so very tired.

Perhaps, he reasoned, it would be better to just wait for Gevrauch's cold hand on his shoulder. Perhaps it would be better to be the final period in the Bookkeeper's last sentence on a page marked: '*Six Imbeciles who Fought for Gold and Were Eaten by Seagulls. Big, Ugly Seagulls. With Teeth.*'

Yes, he thought, *better to die here, wait for it. Wait to see the others ... wait to see my family.* Following that thought came his grandfather's words, with no voice to accompany them.

'*Gevrauch loathes an adventurer*,' he had said to him once, '*because they never know when to die. We don't return the bodies we were loaned when the Bookkeeper asks for them. Recognise when it's your time to die. Suffer it. Say a prayer to Him and maybe He'll forgive you refusing your space in His ledger all these years.*'

Sound advice, he thought.

His boat was likely at the bottom of the sea, along with the fortune he had chased. His companions likely weren't far away, drifting either as half-chewed corpses or long, sinewy Akaneed stool. After both of those images, the fact that he had no food or water didn't seem quite so worrying.

He would not like to upset the Gods and be sent to hell; he had seen what came out of *that* place. *No, no*, he told himself, *it's over now.* All the suffering, all the pain he had experienced in his life all led up to this: a few moments of heat-stricken delirium, then off to the sea to be picked clean by crabs and eels.

Sound plan.

A wave washed over his leg; he felt something bump against his bare foot. He explored it with his toes, expecting to find splintered driftwood, maybe from his craft. Or, he thought, perhaps the remains of his companions: Asper's severed head, Denaos' chewed leg. He chuckled at the macabre thought, then paused as he ran a toe against the object.

It was not so soft as flesh, not even as wood. He felt firmness, a familiar chill as blood wept from his toe.

He fought to sit up, fought to reach into the surf and was rewarded with hands around wet leather. Almost too scared to believe that he was touching what he thought he was, he jerked hard before fear could make him do otherwise.

His sword, his grandfather's sword, rose with all the firm gentleness of a lover in his hands. Its naked steel glittered in the sunlight, defiant of its would-be watery grave. The sun recoiled at its sight; there would be no angelic glow of deliverance from this sword, he thought. This was a sword for grey skies and grim smiles.

None had smiled grimmer than Lenk's grandfather.

'Remember, though,' he had finished, 'you and I, we're men of Khetashe, men of the Outcast. He has no place in heaven for his followers. He loathes us for the reputation we cast on him. So why should we die when He wants us to?'

Lenk felt his own smile grow as he struggled to his feet. It might very well be his time. The sword's arrival might have been coincidence, might have been charity from the Gods: an heirloom to take to his grave. He followed the Outcast, though, and Khetashe had never sent him a divine message he would be expected to listen to.

He turned and looked over his shoulder, toward a distant wall of greenery. A forest, he recognised. Forests were plants. Plants needed water. And so did he.

86

Water first, he thought as he stalked toward the foliage, sword clenched against his body. *Water first, then food, then find Sebast and keep him around long enough for me to find the others.*

His smile grew particularly grim.

Or at least something to bury.

Five

WHITE TREES

'*Tell me, Kataria,*' she had said once, '*what is a shict?*'
'*I learned that ages ago,*' her daughter had grumbled
in reply, . '*I could be learning how to skin a buck right now if I
wasn't here being stabbed with trivia. A buck. I could be coated
in gore right now if – OW!*'

After the blow, her daughter had muttered, '*Riffid led the
shicts out of the Dark Forest and gave us instinct, nothing else.
She would not indulge us in weaknesses and we prosper from
Her distance and – OW! No fair, I got that one right!*'

'*You told me what your father says a shict is.*'

'*Everyone agrees with him! You asked me what a shict was,
not what I thought one was! What do you want me to say?*'

'*If you could predict what I wanted you to say, you wouldn't
have gotten hit. That's what it means to be a shict.*'

'*So, violent hypocrisy makes a shict? That sounds pretty
simple.*'

'*You disagree?*'

'*I do.*'

'*Then tell me.*'

'*No.*'

'*No?*'

'*Whatever I tell you, you'll just hit me until I say what you
want me to say. If I'm saying what you want me to say, I'm not
a shict. I know that much.*'

She had smiled once.

Kataria stared up at the sky, folding her arms behind her head as she lay upon the shore. The sun was moving slowly, sliding lazily behind the grey clouds, completely unconcerned for her careful scrutiny of its progress. By the time it peered out behind the rolling sheets of cloud, as if checking to see if she were still watching, she estimated three hours had passed.

She craned her neck up, looking past her bare feet.

The shoreline greeted her: vast, empty, eager. It was all too pleased to show her the rolling froth, the murmuring surf, the endless blue horizon stretching out before her.

And nothing more.

There was no wreckage, no movement, not even a corpse.

She sighed, turning her gaze skyward again, wondering just how long it was acceptable to wait for signs that one's companions might have survived after being cast apart in an explosion of sea induced by a colossal, flesh-eating sea serpent.

What does *one look for, anyway?* she wondered. *Wood? A severed limb?* She recalled the Akaneed's gaping maw, its sharp, flesh-rending teeth. *Stool?*

Very little sign of any of that, she noted with a sigh. And why should there be? What *were* the chances of one of them washing up, anyway? And if they did, why would they wash up as she did, having lost nothing more than her bow and boots?

They were dead now, she told herself, floating in the sea, resting in a gullet, picked apart by gulls or about to wash up as a bloated, pale, waterlogged piece of flesh. They were dead and she was alive. She should count herself lucky.

She was alive.

And they're dead.

And she was not.

And he's dead.

And she was a very lucky shict.

Shict, she repeated that word in her head. *I am a shict. Shicts are proud. Shicts are strong. Shicts don't fight fair. Shicts were given instinct by Riffid, nothing more. Shicts fight to protect. Shicts fight to cleanse. Shicts kill humans. Humans are the disease. Humans are the scourge that overruns this world. Humans build, humans destroy, humans burn and humans kill. Shicts kill humans. Shicts do not trust humans.*

Nature conspired in silence at that moment. The roar of the ocean lulled, the whisper of the breeze stilled, the sound of trees swaying stopped. All for a moment just long enough for her to hear a single, insignificant thought that crept into the fore of her consciousness.

But you did.

The creeping thought became a sudden rush of memory, memories she had tried her best to shove in some dark corner of her mind until she could experience a blow against her skull and lose them.

But they came back, no matter how much she tried to block them out.

She remembered the sight of a silver mane, remembered how she thought it was so unusual to see in a human. She remembered how that had made her lower her bow, lower the arrow that had been poised at his head, a head so blissfully free of suspicions and projectiles alike. She remembered being intrigued, remembered following him out.

Shicts kill humans, she told herself, trying to drown the memory in rhetoric. *Shicts slaughter humans. Shicts cleanse the world of humans. Mother told you what shicts were.*

But she could not drown the sounds. His sounds, the sounds she had studied and learned: the murmurs that meant he was nervous around her, the griping that meant she had said something he would think about if not talk about, the sighs that meant he was thinking about something she had yet to learn about him.

Humans don't have thoughts, she growled inwardly. *Humans only have desires. Humans desire gold, desire land, desire whatever it is they don't have. Father told you what humans were.*

And through it all, she heard the distant beat of a heart. The sound of a heart that had beat fiercely enough to drown out the sound of a roaring sea. The sound of a heart that she was supposed to cut out, the sound of a heart that had fed the pulse in a throat she was supposed to slit. His heart, his pulsating, hideous human heart that she had heard before they departed. His horrific heart. His human heart. The heart she heard now.

But that's just a memory. This knowledge came without forcing, the thought resounding in her head only once. *Those are just sounds. He's dead now.*

And the memories were gone, leaving that thought hanging inside her head.

He's dead. Your problems are solved.

She rose up, stiffly. She turned from the ocean, not looking back.

He was dead. He was a dead human. Her world was restored. She didn't feel anything for a dead human. Dead humans did not have heartbeats. She was a shict once more.

This is more than luck, she told herself. *This is a blessing from on high.*

That thought gave her no comfort as she walked over the dunes and away from the shore.

She was a shict. For her, all that was on high was Riffid.

And Riffid did not give blessings.

'What is a human?' her daughter had asked.

She had paused before answering.

'Your father should have told you.'

'You said Father didn't know what a shict was.'

'I didn't say that.'

'You implied it.'

'And you wonder why people hit you.'

'If you can't answer it, just say so and I'll figure it out for myself.'

'A human is ... not a shict.'

'That's it?'

'That's enough.'

'No, it isn't.'

'Has anyone ever told you you're amazingly bull-headed?'

'Grandfather says they filed down my antlers after I was born. But that's not important. What is a human?'

She had wandered away from their village, into the part of the forest where the earth beneath their feet and the ancestors that came before them were one.

'Humans are ... not like us, but also like us. They fight, they kill, just as we do. And what we claim is ours, they claim is theirs. Our cause is righteous. They say theirs is, too. We do what we must. They do as they do.'

'Then how do we know they deserve to die?'

She had stared at a grave marked with long white mourning feathers.

'Because they knew we deserved it.'

She journeyed over the dunes, through the valleys of the beach as the sun continued to crawl across the sky. Always, she found her gaze drifting off to the distant forest and shortly thereafter to her own belly as it let out an angry growl.

The knowledge that any food to be had would be found in the dense foliage gnawed at her as surely as the hunger that struggled to wrest control over her from a frail and withering hope inside her. In fact, she knew, it would be wiser to go into the woods now, to begin the search for something to eat as soon as possible, lest she find herself too weary and starving to conduct a more thorough search later.

Still, she reminded herself, *it's not like it's hard to find something to eat in a forest. You've never had trouble sniffing out roots and fruits before. Hell, find a dark spot and you can probably find a nice, juicy grub.*

The image of a writhing, ivory larva filled her mind. She smacked her lips. The fact that she was salivating at the thought of a squishy, tender infant insect brimming with glistening guts, she reasoned, was likely a strong indicator that she should go seek one out, if only to keep herself from dwelling on how bizarre this entire train of thought was.

And yet, no matter how strong the reasoning, she continued to walk along the beach, staring out over the waves. And always, no matter what she hoped to see, nothing but empty shoreline greeted her.

Stop it, she snarled inwardly. *Forget them. They're dead. And you will be, too, if you don't find food soon. This isn't what a shict does. Look, it's easy. Just turn around.*

She did so, facing the forest.

Now take a step forward.

She did so.

Now don't look back.

That, as ever, was where everything went wrong.

She glanced over her shoulder, ignoring the instant frustration she felt for herself the moment she spied something dark out of the corner of her eye. Tucked behind a dune, bobbing in the water, she could see it: the distinct glisten of water-kissed wood.

Her heart rose in her chest as she spun about and began to hurry toward it, despite her own thoughts striving to temper her stride.

It's wood, she told herself. *It doesn't mean anything beyond the fact that it's wood. Don't get your hopes up. Don't get too excited. Remember the wreck. Remember the Akaneed.*

As she drew closer, the boat's shape became clearer: resting comfortably upon the shore, intact and unsullied. She furrowed her brow, cautioning her stride. This wasn't her boat; hers was now in several pieces and probably jammed in one or two skulls right now.

So it's someone else's, she told herself. *All the more reason to turn back now. No one with any good intentions would be out here. It's not them. It's not him. Turn back.* She did not, creeping around the dune. *Turn* back. *Remember you're alive. Remember he's dead. Remember they're dead. They're* dead.

And, it became clear as she peered around the dune, they were not the only ones.

A lone tree, long dead but clinging to the sandy earth with the tenacity only a very old one could manage, stood in the middle of a small, barren valley. She peered closer, spying rope wrapped tightly about its highest branches, hanging taut. The grey, jagged limbs bent, creaking in protest as macabre, pink-skinned fruit swayed in the breeze, hanging by their ankles from the ropes.

She recognised them, the humans hanging from the tree. Even with their throats slashed and their bodies mutilated, their blood splashed against roots that no longer drank, she knew them as crewmen from the *Riptide*, the ship she and her companions had travelled on before pursuing the tome, the ship whose crew was supposed to come seeking them after they had obtained the book.

Apparently, they had found something else.

About the base of the tree, they swarmed. Kataria was uncertain what they were, exactly. They didn't *look* dangerous, though neither did they look like anything she had seen before. She peered closer, saw that they resembled roaches the size of small deer, sporting great feathery antennae and rainbow-coloured wing carapaces that twitched in time with each other. They chittered endlessly, making strange clicking sounds as they craned up on their rearmost legs to brush their antennae against the swaying corpses.

And then, in an instant, they stopped. Their antennae twitched soundlessly, all in the same direction. A shrill chittering noise went out over them and they scattered, scurrying over the dunes before whatever had alarmed them could come to them.

But Kataria came out around her cover, unafraid as she approached the whitetree. She was unafraid. She knew its name. She knew the men whose blood-drained bodies hung from it.

And she had seen this before.

'They had swords.'

Kataria had heard such a voice before: feminine, but harsh, thick and rasping. Her ears twitched, trembled at the sound, taking it in. It was a voice thick with a bloody history: people killed, ancestors murdered, families avenged. She heard the hatred boiling in the voice, felt it in her head.

And she knew the speaker as shict.

'Humans always have swords,' this newcomer said, her shictish thick as shictish should be. 'They always move with the intent to kill.'

'You killed them instead?'

'And fed the earth with them. And warned their people with them.'

Kataria stared down at the red-stained ground. 'So much blood ...'

'This island is thick with it. That which was shed here is far more righteous.'

Kataria clenched her teeth behind her lips, stilled her heart. 'Have you found others?'

'I have.'

At that, Kataria turned to look at her newfound company.

She was a shict, as Kataria knew, as Kataria was. But in her presence, her shadow that stretched unnaturally long, Kataria could feel her ears wither and droop.

The shict's, however, stood tall and proud, six notches carved into each length, each ear as long as half her forearm. The rest of her followed suit: towering over her at six and a half feet tall, spear-rigid and steel-hard body bereft of any clothing beyond a pair of buckskin breeches. Her black hair was sculpted into a tall, bristly mohawk, her bare head decorated with black sigils on either side of the crude cut. She folded powerful arms over naked breasts that were barely a curve on her lean musculature and regarded Kataria coolly.

And, as Kataria stared, only one thought came to her.

So ... green.

Her skin was the colour of a crisp apple ... or a week-old corpse. Kataria wasn't quite sure which was more appropriate. But her skin colour was just a herald that declared her deeds, her ancestry, her heritage.

And Kataria knew them both. She had heard the stories.

She was a member of the twelfth tribe: the only tribe to stand against humanity and turn them back. She was a member of the *s'na shict s'ha*: headhunters, hideskinners, silent ghosts known to every creature that feared the night.

A greenshict. A true shict.

And Kataria knew dread.

'I have found tracks, anyway,' she said, pointing to the earth with a toe. Kataria glanced down and saw the long toes, complete with opposable 'thumb,' that constituted the greenshict's feet. 'There are other humans here, for some reason.' She stared out over the dunes. 'Not for much longer.'

'Why would they be here?'

'This island is rife with death. Humans are drawn to the scent.'

'Death?'

'This land is poisoned. Trees grow, but there is death in the roots. That which lives here feeds on death and we feed upon them.'

'I saw the roaches ...'

'Unimportant. We come for the frogs. They eat the poison. The poison feeds our blood. We feed on them.'

'We?'

'Three of *s'na shict s'ha* came to this island.'

'Where are the others?'

'They seek. Naxiaw seeks humans. Avaij seeks frogs. I seek you.'

Kataria felt the greenshict's stare like a knife in her chest.

'I heard your Howling long ago. I have searched for you since.' The greenshict fixed her with a stare that went far beyond cursory, her long ears twitching as if hearing something without sound. 'You come with strange sounds in your heart, Kataria.'

Kataria did not start, barely flinched. But the greenshict's eyes narrowed; she could see past her face, could see Kataria's nerves rattle, heart wither.

'What is your name?' Kataria asked.

'You know it already.'

She *should* know it, at least, Kataria knew. She could feel the connection between them, as though some fleshless part of them reached out towards each other and barely brushed, imparting a common thought, a common knowledge between them. The Howling, Kataria knew: that shared, ancestral instinct that connected all shicts. The same instinct that had told the greenshict her name.

That same instinct that Kataria could now only barely remember, so long had it been since she used it.

But she reached out with it all the same, straining to feel for the greenshict's name, straining the most basic, fundamental knowledge shared by the Howling.

'In ...' she whispered. 'Inqalle?'

Inqalle nodded, but did not so much as blink. She continued probing, staring into Kataria, sensing out with the Howling that which Kataria could not hide. Kataria did not bother to keep herself from squirming under the gaze, from looking down at her feet. In a few moments, Inqalle had looked into her, had seen her shame and judged.

'Little Sister,' she whispered, 'I know why you are here.'

'It's complicated,' she replied.

'It is not.'

'No?'

'You are filled with fear. I hear it in your bones.' Her eyes narrowed, ears flattened against her skull. 'You have been with humans ...'

Funny, Kataria thought, that she should only then notice the blood-slick tomahawk hanging at Inqalle's waist. She stared at it for a long time.

Amongst shicts, there were those that loathed humans, there were those that *despised* humans and then there were the *s'na shict s'ha*, those few that had seen such success driving the round-eared menace from their lands that they had abandoned those same lands, embarking on pilgrimages to exterminate that which had once threatened them.

And for those that had consorted with the human disease, slaughter was seen as an act of mercy to the incurably infected. As such, Kataria remained tense, ready to turn and bolt the moment the tomahawk left her belt.

The blow never came. Inqalle's gaze was sharp enough to wound without it.

'Kataria,' she whispered, taking a step closer. Kataria felt the greenshict's eyes digging deeper into her, sifting through thought, ancestry, everything she could not hide from the Howling. 'Daughter of Kalindris. Daughter of Rokuda. I have heard your names spoken by the living.'

Her eyes drifted toward the feathers in Kataria's hair, resting uncomfortably on a long, ivory-coloured crest nestled amongst the darker ones.

'And the dead,' she whispered. 'Who do you mourn, Little Sister?'

Kataria turned her head aside to hide it. Inqalle's hand

was a lash, reaching out to seize her by the hair, twisting her head about as Inqalle's long green fingers knotted into her locks.

'You are ... infected,' she hissed, voice raking Kataria's ears. 'Not voiceless.'

'Let go,' Kataria snarled back.

'You speak words. That is all I hear.' She tapped her tattooed brow. 'In here, I hear nothing. You cannot speak with the Howling. You are no shict.' She wrenched the white feather free, strands of hair coming loose with them. 'You mourn no shict.'

'Give that back,' Kataria growled, lashing out a hand to grab it back. With insulting ease, Inqalle's hand lashed back, striking her against her cheek and laying her to the earth. She looked up, eyes pleading. 'You have no right.' She winced. 'Please.'

'Shicts do not beg.'

'I am a shict!' Kataria roared back, springing to her feet. Her ears were flattened against her head, her teeth bared and flashing white. 'Show me your hand again and I'll prove it.'

'You wish to prove it,' Inqalle said softly, a statement rather than a challenge or insult. 'I wish to see it.'

'Then let me show you how to make a *redshict*, you six-toed piece of—'

'There is another way, Little Sister.'

Kataria paused. She felt Inqalle's Howling, the promise within its distant voice, the desire to help. And Inqalle heard the anticipation in her little sister's, the desperation to be helped. Inqalle smiled, thin and sharp. Kataria swallowed hard, voice dry.

'Tell me.'

*

'*You know you talk in your sleep,*' her daughter had said years later, long after she was gone from the world and her daughter wore a white feather. '*I could have shot you from four hundred paces away.*'

'*Lucky for me that you were only six away,*' the thing with silver hair had said in return. '*Which, coincidentally, is the sixth time you've told me you could kill me.*'

'*Today?*'

'*Since breakfast.*'

'*That sounds about right.*'

'*So?*'

'*So what?*'

'*Do it already. Add another notch to your belt ... or, is it feathers with you?*'

'*I don't have any kill feathers.*'

'*What are those for, then?*'

Her daughter had tucked the white one behind her ear. '*Lots of things.*'

'*Okay.*'

'*You're not curious?*'

'*Not really.*'

'*You've never wondered why we do what we do?*'

'*If the legends are true, your people's connections with my people tend to be either arrows, swords or fire. That all seems pretty straightforward to me.*'

Her daughter had frowned.

'*You, though ...*' he had said.

'*What about me?*'

He had stared, then, as he hefted his sword.

'*You stare at me. It's weird.*'

He hadn't told her daughter to stop. He hadn't told her daughter to leave. And Kataria never had.

*

They stretched out into the distance, over the sand, a story in each moist imprint. They spoke of suffering, of pain, of confusion, of fear. She narrowed her eyes as she knelt down low, tracing her fingers over two of the tracks. The voices in the footprints spoke clearly to her, told her where they were heading.

She knew her companions well enough to recognise their tracks.

'There are more,' Inqalle said behind her. 'They are familiar to you.'

'They are,' Kataria replied.

'They are your cure.'

She turned and saw the feather first. Inqalle held it in her hand, attached to a smooth, carved stick. She held it before Kataria.

'You know what this is.'

'I remember,' she said. 'A Spokesman.'

'It speaks. It makes a declaration. This one says that you shall not mourn until you are a shict.' She regarded Kataria coolly. 'This one will tell you when you are a shict.'

'I remember,' she said. 'My father told me.'

'This is a cure for the disease. This is a cure for your fear. This restores you.' She handed the Spokesman to Kataria. 'Keep it. Use it. Survive until you become a shict again.'

'And when I do. You will know?'

Inqalle tapped her head.

'We will all know.'

Six

CHEATING LIFE

The heavens move in enigmatic circles.

In the human tongue, this translated roughly to 'it's not my fault.' Gariath had heard it enough times to know. Those humans he knew had been happiest when they could blame someone else.

Formerly humans, he corrected himself, *currently chum. Lucky little idiots with no one to blame.*

Not entirely true, he knew. If their heavens did indeed circle enigmatically overhead, and they had indeed gone to them, they were likely hurling curses upon his head from there at that very moment. A tad hypocritical, he thought, to praise their mysterious gods and resent being sent to them.

Or is that what they call 'irony'?

But that was a concern for dead people. Gariath, sadly, was still alive and without a convenient excuse for it.

The *Rhega* had no gods to blame. The *Rhega* had no gods to claim them. That was what he wanted to believe, at least.

He had been able to overlook his inability to die, at first, throwing himself at pirates, at longfaces, at demons and at his former humans and coming out with only a few healthy scars. They might have cursed him, if he left them enough blood to choke on, but they were lucky. Death by a *Rhega*'s hand would be as good a death as they could hope for.

When a colossal serpent failed to kill him, he began to suspect something more than just mere luck. The sea, too, had rejected him and spat him onto the shore, painfully alive. If gods did exist, and if their circles were wide enough to touch him, they took a cruel pride in keeping him alive.

Now that is *irony*.

The former humans, he was certain, would have agreed. And if he had learned anything from them and their excuses, it was that their gods rarely seemed content to allow a victim of their ironies merely to wallow in their misery. They preferred to leave reminders, 'omens' to rub their jagged victories into wounds that had routinely failed to prove fatal.

And, as his own personal omen crested out of the waves to turn a golden scowl upon him, he was growing more faithful by the moment.

Like a black worm wriggling under liquid skin, the Akaneed continued to whirl, twist and writhe beneath the sun-coloured waves. It emerged every so often to turn its single, furious eye upon him, narrowing the yellow sphere to a golden slit that burned through the waves.

Just as it had burned all throughout the morning when the sea denied him, he thought. Just as it had continued to burn throughout the afternoon he squatted upon the sand, watching it as it watched him.

He wasn't quite sure why either of them hadn't moved on yet. For himself, he suspected whatever divine entity had turned him away from death thought to inspire some contemplation in watching the sea.

Humans often thought sitting and staring to be a religiously productive use of their time. *And they die like flies,* he thought. *Maybe I'll get lucky and starve to death.*

That seemed as good a plan as any.

The Akaneed's motives, he could only guess at. Surely, he reasoned, colossal sea snakes couldn't subsist purely on angry glowers and snarls from the deep. Perhaps, then, it was simply a battle of wills: his will to die and the snake's will to eat him.

Though those two seem more complementary than conflicting...

By that reasoning, it would be easy to walk fifteen paces into the surf until the sea touched his neck. It would be easy to close his eyes, take three deep breaths as he felt the water shift beneath him. It would be easy to feel the creature's titanic jaws clamp around him, feel the needles merciful on his flesh and watch his blood seep out on blossoming clouds as the beast carried his corpse to an afterlife beneath the waves.

The Akaneed's eye emerged, casting a curious glare in his direction, as though it sensed this train of thought and thoroughly approved.

'No,' he assured it. 'If I do that, then you'll have an easy meal and I'll have an easy death. Neither of us will have worked for it and neither of us will be happy.'

It shot Gariath another look, conveying its agreement in the twitch of its blue eyelid. Then, in the flash of its stare before it disappeared beneath the waves, it seemed to suggest that it could wait.

Gariath lay upon his back and closed his eyes. The gnawing in his belly was growing sharper, but not swiftly enough. Sitting still, never moving, he reasoned he had about three days before he died of thirst and his husk drifted out on the tide. The Akaneed was willing to earn its meal and he was willing to settle for this bitter comfort.

That being the case, he reasoned he might as well be comfortable.

The sounds of the shore would be a fitting elegy: nothing but the murmur of waves and the skittering legs of beach vermin to commemorate the loss of the last of the *Rhega*. Fitting, perhaps, that he should go out in such a way, shoulders heavy with death and finally bowed by the weight of his own mortality, with only the beady, glistening eyes of crabs to watch the noblest of people disappear and leave this world to its weakling pink-skinned diseases.

The Akaneed hummed in the distance, its reverberating keen rumbling up onto the shore and scattering the skittering things. The waves drew in a sharp inhale, retreating back to the open sea and holding its frothy breath as it went calm and placid. Sound died, sea died and Gariath resolved to die with it.

In the silence, the sound was deafening.

He recognised immediately feet crunching upon the sand. The pace was slow, casual, utterly without care or concern for the dragonman trying to die.

An old enemy, perhaps, one of the many faceless bodies he had torn and crushed and failed to kill, come for vengeance at the tip of a sword. Or maybe a new one, some terrified creature with a slow and hesitant pace, ready to impale him with a weapon clenched in trembling hands.

Or, if gods were truly intent on proving their existence, it might be one of his former companions. One of them might have survived, he reasoned, and come searching for vengeance. He listened intently to the sound.

Too heavy to be the pointy-eared human, he reasoned; she wouldn't attack him until his back was turned anyway. And likewise, the feet were too deliberate to be the bumbling, skinny human with the fiery hands. That one would just kill him from a distance.

He dearly hoped it wasn't the tall, brown-haired human

woman. She would likely come all masked with tears, demanding explanations in sobbing tones while righteously insisting that the others hadn't deserved to die. If that were the case, he would have much preferred the rat. Yes, the rat would come and give him a quick knife in the throat; surely that would kill even a *Rhega* suffering from a severe case of irony.

It pained him to think that the feet might belong to Lenk. The death he so richly deserved then would never come from the young man's hands.

The others knew how to kill. Lenk alone knew how to hurt.

The feet stopped just above his head. Gariath held his breath.

No blow, no steel, no vengeance. The shadow that fell over him was warm rather than cold. Even against the setting sun, the heat was distinctly familiar and embracing, heavy arms wrapped gently around him.

He hadn't felt such warmth since ...

Almost afraid to, he opened his nostrils, drew in a deep breath. His body jolted at once, his eyes snapping wide open at a scent that instantly overwhelmed his senses and the stink of the sea alike. He opened his mouth, drinking it in and at once finding it impossible that it filled his body.

Rivers and rocks.

He looked up and saw black eyes staring down at him beneath a pair of horns, one short and topped with a jagged break. The snout that they stared down from was wrinkled and scarred, but taut, each twisted line a point of pride and wisdom. The frills at either side fanned out unenthused, crimson petals of a wilting flower that had not seen rain in a long time.

It was the eyes, alone untouched by age, that seized

Gariath's gaze. They were softer than his own black stare, but that softness only made their depth all the more apparent. Where his were hard and unyielding doors of obsidian, the eyes that stared down at him were windows that stretched into endless night.

The elderly *Rhega* smiled, exposing teeth well worn.

'You know,' he rumbled, the *Rhega* tongue deep and hard as a rock in his chest, 'for someone who has such reverence for my stare, you could at *least* get up to talk to me.'

Gariath's eye ridges raised half a hair. 'You read thoughts?'

'I don't get much conversation otherwise.' The elder returned the raised ridge. 'Not impressed?'

'I have seen many things, Grandfather,' Gariath replied.

The elder considered him thoughtfully for a moment, then nodded.

'So you have, Wisest.'

The elder scanned the beach, finding a nearby piece of driftwood half buried in the sand. Lifting his limp tail up behind him, he took a seat upon it and stared out over the setting sun. The light met his stare and Gariath saw the elder's shape change as beams of light sifted through a spectral figure.

'You're dead, Grandfather,' Gariath grunted.

'I hear that a lot,' the elder replied.

Gariath looked up and down the empty beach, bereft of even a hint of any other life.

'I find that hard to believe.'

'You would,' the elder snorted. 'The fact remains that you are the only one who has come by; you're the only one who noticed. My point stands.'

'Why aren't you at your elder stone?'

'I got bored.'

'Grahta never left his stone.'

'Why would he? Grahta was a pup. He would get lost.'

'Ah.'

Gariath settled himself back on the sand, staring up at the orange-painted sky above. After a moment, he looked back to the elder.

'Grahta,' he said softly. 'Is he … ?'

'Sleeping, Wisest,' the elder replied.

'Good.'

Another silence descended between them, broken only by the sound of the Akaneed's murmuring keen rising up from below the waves. After an eternity of that, Gariath once again looked up.

'Aren't you going to ask me what I'm doing?'

'Seems a bit unnecessary,' the elder said, tapping his brow.

'Then aren't you going to ask me why?'

'You are *Rhega*,' the elder replied, shrugging. 'You have a good reason.'

'So, you won't try to stop me.'

'I might have a hard time with that.' The elder held up his clawed hand to the light, grinning as it vanished. 'What with being dead and all.'

'Then why are you here?'

'I thought you might like some company while you waited to die.'

'I don't.'

'Oh?' The elder looked at him thoughtfully for a moment. 'Was it not you who was just wishing that his humans would come visit him?'

'Those thoughts were private,' Gariath snarled, glowering.

'Then you shouldn't have thought them while I was standing right here.'

'It doesn't matter.' The younger dragonman turned his stare back up to the sky. 'They're dead.'

'Possibly.'

'Possibly?'

'*You* didn't die.'

'I am *Rhega*. I am strong. They are weak and stupid.'

'Bold words coming from a lizard hoping to starve to death so a snake will eat him.'

'Can you think of a better way to die, given the circumstances?'

'I can think of a better way to live.'

'Live?' Gariath's snout split in an unpleasant grin. 'I've tried living, Grandfather. I've tried living without my family, living without other *Rhega* and living without even humans.' He sighed, chest trembling with the breath. 'Living was fine for a time, but it was too full of death for my tastes. Maybe dying will be better.'

'There is nothing worth living for, Wisest?'

'There was. Now, I have nothing.'

'You have me.'

'Yes, I do,' Gariath grunted. 'One thing I never seem to lack is dead *Rhega*.' He waved a clawed hand at the elder. 'I do not need you, Grandfather.'

'What do you need, then?'

'It's not obvious?'

'Not to you.'

'I need to die, Grandfather,' Gariath sighed. 'I need to rid myself of all' – he waved a hand out to the sky and sea – 'this. I don't need it anymore.'

'You've had plenty of opportunities to die.'

'I haven't found the right one yet.'

'They all basically end the same way, don't they?'

'Not for a *Rhega*.'

'Ah, I see.' The elder scratched his chin thoughtfully. 'So, the right way is to lie down here and wait to die while contemplating the existence of weak, *human* gods?'

'It's a way.'

'Not the way of the *Rhega*.'

'There are no more *Rhega*,' Gariath growled in response. 'I am the last one. I get to decide what the right way to die is.'

'And what is the right way to die, Wisest?'

Gariath had an answer for that.

It was an answer that he had often dreamed of, birthed at the fore of his mind when he held two barking pups that seemed so tiny in his arms. That answer had grown along with those pups, nurtured by their experiences. When they had learned to catch jumping fish, to chase down running horses, to spread their wings and glide on the winds, that answer had grown to something that swelled with his own heart.

He would have very much liked to have that heart stop beating when they held pups of their own and watched red silhouettes gliding across the sky. He would have very much liked for them to have their own answers for the question.

Instead, two hearts had stopped beating instead of one. And with them, so did his answer die.

The elder stared at him with intent concentration, seeing it unfurl inside him. He shuddered as he and the younger dragonman shared the final thought.

An angry, agonised wail, offered to a weeping sky as Gariath clutched two lifeless forms in his arms. The same wail offered to so many wide-eyed, terrified faces as

Gariath threw himself at them time and again, hoping for and being denied a righteous death.

'That would be a good way to die,' the elder said, nodding. 'I would have liked to have left my family in such a way.'

'How did you die, Grandfather?'

'I didn't,' the elder replied with an enigmatic smile.

'You are most certainly dead, Grandfather.'

'In body, perhaps.'

'Oh, *this*.'

'What?' The elder furrowed his ridges.

'I've heard this before. Some vague philosophy about the separation of body and spirit, and it always ends the same way.' Gariath made a dismissive wave. 'Some attempt to be inspirational by suggesting the two can be resurrected alongside each other, maybe a little aside about raising spirits and being true to oneself. Then we all hug and cry and I vomit.' He snorted derisively. 'Humans do it all the time.'

'Humans have had their points, Wisest. The difference between body and spirit is one they adopted, but it is not one they thought of on their own.'

'It's all greasy, imbecilic vomit, no matter who spews it.'

'Is it? You've seen me. You've seen Grahta. Can you still deny the difference, knowing what death means to the *Rhega*?'

'I wonder if I do,' Gariath muttered. '*You* know what Grahta told me.' He stared up at the sky, frowning at its endless orange and white oblivion. 'I can't follow.'

'I know,' the elder said, nodding solemnly.

'Do *you*, Grandfather?' Gariath turned his hard stare upon the specter. 'You know death, but you know peace.

You will know your ancestors, eventually, as Grahta did. You will know rest. Me …' He sat up suddenly, brimming with anger. 'I can't follow you. Grahta said as much. I can't see my family, my ancestors …'

They shared a shuddering cringe as they both felt his heart turn to stone inside him and pull his chest low to the ground.

'I can't see my sons, Grandfather … I can *never* see them again. I can't follow.'

'It is the way it must be, Wisest.'

'*Why?*'

He leapt to his feet, the sand erupting beneath him. The earth trembled as he stomped his feet, curled his hands into fists so tight that blood wept from his claws. He bared his teeth, narrowed his eyes and fanned his frills out beside his head.

'*Every* time this happens,' he snarled. '*Every* time some-one dies, *every* time *I* don't, that's "the way it must be". Everyone sighs and rolls their shoulders and goes back to living. I've *done* that and I'm *done* living. If this is how life must be, then I choose death!'

'It is that way for a reason, Wisest. You have duties to your ancestors.'

'*More* excuses! *More* stupidity! Duty and honour and responsibility!' He howled and stomped his feet. 'All just excuses for not getting things done, for trying to excuse away life and all its pain! I have *served* my duty, Grandfather! I have *tried* to live the way the *Rhega* are supposed to. I have *tried* to be a *Rhega* when there are no more. I have *tried* and … and …'

His fist came down with a howl, splintering a hole in the driftwood beside the elder. He jerked it out with a shriek, wooden shards lodged in his fist that wept blood as his eyes wept tears. He collapsed to his knees, pressed his brow against the wood and drew in a staggering, wet breath.

'It's too hard, Grandfather. I don't know what I'm supposed to do anymore. I *can't* follow.' He punched the wood again. 'I *can't* kill myself.' Another bloody-handed blow. 'I just … can't.'

It wasn't often that Gariath flinched at a touch. All the steel and iron that had cursed his flesh in crimson words, all the scars and bruises they had left behind had never made him so much as tremble. But they had struck shoulders that were broad and proud, arms that were thick and fierce.

The hand that rested upon him now was upon shoulders that were broken and bowed, arms that hung limp and bloody at his side.

'Wisest,' the elder whispered. 'We are *Rhega*. The rivers flow in both our blood and we feel the same agonies, as we have felt since we were born of the red rock. I don't ask you to do this for you or for me …' He tightened his grip on Gariath's shoulder. 'I tell you to do it for us. For the *Rhega*.'

'What,' Gariath asked, weak, 'am I supposed to do?'

'Live.'

'It can't be that easy.'

'You know it isn't.' The elder rose up, walking toward the shore. 'You've spent so much time bleeding, Wisest, so much time killing. You've forgotten what living is like.'

'It's hard.'

'I will help you where I can, Wisest,' the elder replied with a smile. 'But there are better guides to life than the dead.'

'Such as?'

After a moment of careful contemplation, the elder scratched his chin. 'What of Lenk?'

'Dead.'

'You're certain?'

'What does it matter?'

'Consider where you would be without him,' the elder replied. 'Still where you buried your sons? Or buried yourself, if whoever killed you had enough respect not to skin you alive and wear your face as a hat? How was it you managed to get away from there?'

'By following Lenk.'

'And how was it you managed to find Grahta? To end up here so that I might find you?'

'Are you saying I need Lenk?' Gariath growled, slightly repulsed by the idea. 'He is decent enough to deserve a good death, but he's still stupid and weak ... still *human*. If he is even alive, how do I get him to lead me to where I need to go next? How can I even—?'

'Many questions,' the elder said with a sigh, 'demand many answers. For now, limit yourself to simplicity. You are caught between lives. Choose one, then make another choice.'

'What kind of choices?'

'In time, many.' The elder turned and walked toward Gariath, counting out each pace beneath him. 'The choice to seek out my elder stone is one, but that is far away in time and distance. The hardest choice' – he paused and drew a line in the earth with his toe – 'is to recognise that you will never be as alone as you hope to be.'

'I don't understand.'

'That's the point of cryptic musing, pup,' the elder muttered. 'But we don't have time to discuss it. The much more immediate choice must happen within your next fifty breaths.'

'What?' Gariath creased his ridges together. 'What choice?'

'Whether to move or not. Forty-five breaths.'

'What, like … move on? More philosophical gibberish?'

'More immediate. Forty-two breaths.'

'Why forty-two?'

'The tide comes in at twenty, it's taking me another fifteen to tell you all of this, and the Akaneed, which has been known to hurl itself upon a beach to get at its prey at distances up to twenty-six paces, has been waiting for the aforementioned tide for about five breaths, leaving you …' The elder glanced over his shoulder. 'Two breaths.'

It only took one for the water to rise up in a great blue wall, the Akaneed's eye scorching a golden hole through it. Its jaws were parted as it erupted onto the shore, bursting through the liquid barrier with a roar that sent great gouts of salty mist peeling from between rows of needle-like teeth.

It took Gariath another to leap backwards as those great teeth snapped shut in a wall of glistening white. A low keen burbled out of the Akaneed's gullet, cursing the dragonman as it might curse any man who broke a fair deal. Snarling, it writhed upon the sand, trying to shift its massive pillar of a body back into the surf.

'Huh.' The elder observed the younger dragonman's wide-eyed shock with a raised eye ridge. 'You jumped away. Nerves, perhaps. If you still want to die, I'm sure he won't think it a hassle to come back for a second time.'

Gariath regarded the spectre through narrowed eyes. Impassive, the elder stared at him without flinching. He folded his wings behind his back, raised his one-horned head up to meet Gariath's eyes with his own gaze that shone hard as rocks.

'Make your choice, Wisest.'

And, with the sound of a snort and claws sinking into wood, Gariath did.

His muscles trembled, then burst to life in his arms, great beasts awakening from hibernation. The driftwood log was long and proud, clinging to the earth. But it tore free, resigning itself to its fate.

His roar matched the Akaneed's, matched the sound of air rent apart as the wood howled. Both were rendered silent by a massive jaw cracking, teeth flying out to lie upon the earth like unsown seeds, and a keening shriek that followed the Akaneed back into the ocean. Blood leaking from its maw, it disappeared beneath the waves, sparing only a moment to level a cyclopean scowl upon the dragonman before vanishing into the endless blue.

The breath that came out of Gariath, rising in his massive chest, was not one he had felt in days. His hands trembled about the shattered piece of wood he still held, as though they had never known the life that coursed through them. When he did finally drop it, that life sent his arms tensing, his tail twitching …

His body thirsting for more.

This is what it means? He stared down at his hands. *To be a* Rhega? *More death? More violence? This is what it is to be alive?*

'Not the answer you're looking for, Wisest,' the elder chimed, his voice distant and fading. 'But good enough for now.'

When Gariath turned about, nothing but sand and wind greeted him. No footprints remained in the disturbed earth, nothing to even suggest that the elder had ever been there. And yet, with each breath that Gariath took, the scent of rivers and rocks continued to permeate his senses.

Perhaps he should be concerned that he felt alive again only when he was grievously wounding something. Perhaps he should take it as a sign that his road in life was destined to run alongside a river of blood. Or perhaps he should just take pride in having knocked the teeth out of a giant snake that had now failed to kill him twice.

Philosophy is for idiots, anyway.

His concerns left him immediately as he plucked the serpent's shattered fangs up from the earth and felt their warm sharpness scrape against his palm. He would keep these, he decided, as a reminder of what it meant, for the moment, to be a *Rhega*.

But he could not dwell on that. His feet moved beneath him as the sun disappeared behind the sea, and already his nostrils were quivering, drawing in the scent of living things.

Seven

HONEST AFFLICTIONS

No matter how hard she stared, the sun refused to yield any answers to her.

It had been a long time since she had first turned her stare upward, mouth agape and eyes unblinking. If her throat was dry or if the tears had been scorched from her eyes, she didn't care. Her breath had evaporated long ago, dissipating on the heat.

And Asper continued to stare.

The sun was supposed to reveal truth to her. This she knew. Every scripture claimed as much.

'*And when the Healer did give up His body and His skin and His blood until there was nothing left for Him to give to mankind, and only when the entirety of His being was spent for His children, then did He leave the agonies of the cruel earth and ascend to the Heavens on wings heavy with lament.*

'*He left no apologies, He left no excuses and He left no promises for those He had so freely given His body. He left but this: hope. The great, golden disc that reminded His children that He had taken only His bones and breath back to the World Above, leaving His body, His skin, His blood and His great eye.*'

She could recite the hymn until her lips bled and her tongue swelled up, and that used to be fine, so long as the words that were uttered were the words she had sought comfort in all her life.

Now words were not enough. And the sun refused to answer her.

Her arm burned with an intensity to rival the golden heat she raised it to. Flickering, twitching crimson light engulfed it, the bones blackened as over-forged sin beneath the red that had been her skin. Each bone of knuckle and digit stretched out, reaching ebon talons to the sun, seeking to wrest truth from it.

Her reach was too short. And lacking that, she could but ask.

'Why?'

The sky sighed, its moan reaching into her body and racking the bones boiling black inside her.

'*I'm sorry,*' the sun answered. '*It's my fault.*'

No room for pride in her body, no room to take pleasure or offer forgiveness. She could feel the crimson slip up over her shoulder, sliding over her throat on red fingers and crushing her breasts in blood-tinted grip. The pain shoved out all other feelings, scarring her skeleton black beneath her.

She saw the ebon joints of her knees rise up to meet her as she collapsed, pressing skeletal hands against the dirt. The sun was hot now, unbearably so. She threw back an ebon skull, cried out through a mouth that leaked red light between black teeth, pleading wordlessly for the great eye to stop.

'*I'm sorry,*' it replied. '*I couldn't. I'm sorry. I'm sorry.*'

Her screams were wasted on the pitiless sky, her pleas nothing beneath its endless, airless droning. It repeated the words, bludgeoning her to the floor and beating her into darkness.

'*I'm sorry, I'm sorry, I'm sorry, I'm sorry ...*'

*

Eyelids twitched in time with the breath that rained hot and stale upon her face. They ached as they cracked open, encrusted with dried tears. The light assaulted her, blinding.

She blinked a moment, dispelling the haze that clouded her to bring into view a pair of dark eyes rimmed with dark circles, staring vast and desperate holes into her skull as a smile full of long yellow teeth assaulted her widening stare. She felt leather fingers gingerly brush a lock of brown hair away from her sweat-stained brow with arachnid sensuality.

'Good morning,' a voice rasped.

The scream that followed was swiftly silenced.

Long-fingered hands snapped over her mouth, drowning her shriek in a tide of leathery flesh. Another hand was under the first and she felt a heavy thumb press lightly against her throat, seeking her windpipe with practised swiftness.

'Silence is sacred,' the voice suggested in a way that implied it was no impotent hymn.

Whatever threat not implicit in the voice was frighteningly apparent in the hands, coursing down the palm and into the fingers that slid across her throat. Her breath came in short, terrified gulps. Her heart pounded in her chest, eyes terrified to meet the dark and heavy stare that bore down on her like a bird of prey.

Breath after desperate breath passed and the light ceased to sting. As a face came to the eyes staring over her, breath came more swiftly and confidently. The smile ceased to be so menacing once she remembered well the crooked bent to it. And, at the look of recognition that crossed her face, the hands slipped off her mouth and neck.

'Not that I'm not thrilled to hear your melodic voice,'

Denaos whispered, 'but it does get a little tiresome after hearing it for a few days.'

'A ... few days?' Asper felt her voice scratch raw against a throat turned to leather.

'A few days, yes,' Denaos replied, his nod a little disjointed. 'You took a nasty blow to the head.' He rubbed a tender spot against her brow, wincing in time with her. 'Not surprising. Lots of wood flying this way and that. Hard to keep track of, no?'

'Wood ... flying ...' And wet, she remembered, falling like slow-moving hail, herself only one more fleshy stone descending in an airless blue sky. Her eyes widened with the realisation. 'We were attacked. Sunk! But ...' She felt the sand beneath her, smelled the sea before her. 'Where are we?'

'Island. Archipelago, maybe?' Denaos tapped his chin thoughtfully. 'Peninsula, coast, beach, shore, littoral ... left side of an isthmus. Not sure, lost the map.' He stared out at the sea. 'Lost everything.'

'And ... the others?'

'Lost *everything*.'

Everything.

The word echoed inside her mind and down her body. Her heart pounded against it, feeling surprisingly light, a familiar weight removed from her chest. She glanced down and saw her robes parted, exposing a generous amount of bosom, a patch of particularly pale skin in the shape of a bird where her pendant had once hung dutifully.

She should have been more alarmed at that, she knew. The pendant had been with her since she had first been admitted to the priesthood. It had seen everything, from her initiation as a novice, to her rise to acolyte, to her full initiation.

It saw Taire, she told herself grimly. *It saw the longface. It's seen my arm. It knows. And now it's gone.*

Perhaps it wasn't any wonder she was breathing more freely now.

'I don't wear my robes like this,' she muttered. A horrific suspicion leapt from her mind to her eyes and she turned them, wide as moons, upon the tall man. 'I was out for a few days.'

'Three.' He canted his head to the side, looking to some imaginary consultant. 'Four? Six? No … three sounds right, thereabouts.'

'You didn't …' She grimaced as she readjusted her garments. 'You didn't *do* anything, did you?'

'Seems a little pointless, doesn't it?' He sneered at her blue garment. 'I've already seen you naked.'

'What? *When?*' She put that thought from her mind, however difficult it was. 'No, don't tell me. Just … did you do anything?'

'I might have. I am well versed in Sleeping Toad.'

She opened her mouth to protest further, but something in his grin caught her eye. It was not the smooth, rehearsed split of his mouth that he so often wore like a mask. It was strained at the edges, frayed, as though the porcelain of that mask had begun to crack, exposing a desperate grin and wide, shadow-rimmed eyes.

She forced her next words through a grimace. 'You don't look so good.'

His parched lips peeled off glistening gums like leather in the sun, seeming to suggest that he was aware of as much. His hair formed a greasy frame about his strained, stubble-caked expression.

'Not so good at sleeping these days,' he whispered. 'There could be enemies anywhere.'

'All this time?'

'Doesn't seem that long now,' he replied.

She furrowed her brow; she had seen him function on three days' insomnia without any ill effects before. That he would suddenly seem so rabid didn't make any sense to her until he loosed a long breath, its stale air reeking with old barrels and barley.

'You managed to save the whisky?' she asked, crinkling her nose.

'Wasn't easy,' he grunted. 'Had to do some diving. Had the time, though. Couldn't sleep, obvious reasons.' He patted his breeches and smiled grimly. 'No more knives, see? Felt naked, insecure. Whisky helped me alert stay ...' He trailed off for a moment before snapping back with a sudden twitch. 'Stay alert.'

'You could have slept, you know.'

'No, I *didn't* know,' he snarled. '*I'm* not the healer here. I didn't know if you would even wake up.'

'So, you ...' Her eyes widened slowly this time, the realisation less horrific, but no less shocking. 'You watched over me all this time?'

'Not much choice,' he said, shaking his head. 'You were out. None of the others made it. Dread was absolutely worthless.'

'Dreadaeleon? He's alive?'

'Fished both of you out. You were unconscious. He wasn't. Had him make a raft with his ice ... breath ... magic-thing.' He gestured to the beach. 'Floated here. He stalked off to the forest shortly after, never came back out.'

She followed his finger to the dense patch of foliage over her head, saw the scrawny figure leaning against a tall tree, in such still repose as to appear dead. Perhaps he was, she thought with a twinge of panic.

'Gods,' she muttered. 'What's the matter with him?'

'What isn't?'

'You didn't *check*?' She turned to him, aghast. 'You didn't *ask*?'

'Not the healer.' The rogue sneered. 'I couldn't watch over *both* of you, and you were the one with breasts. Process of elimination.'

'How delightful,' she muttered. 'I suppose since I'm awake now ...' She made to rise, then paused as she became aware of a sudden pain in her cheek. She winced, pressing her hand to her jaw. 'My face hurts.'

'Yeah,' he grunted, scratching his chin. 'I've been hitting you for the past few days.'

She could but blink.

'All right ... should I ask?'

'I've seen you do it before. Seemed like an easy medical process.'

'You hit people who are in *shock*, idiot.'

'I was a bit startled.'

She sighed, rubbing her eyes. When she looked up again, an unsympathetic sea met her gaze with the uninterested rumble of waves.

'Lost everything?' she repeated dully.

'Does it somehow make it more believable if I say it three times?' Denaos sighed. 'Yes, lost *everything*, up to and including the derelict reptile that got us here.'

'And Lenk, and Kataria ...' She sighed, placing her face in her hands and staring glumly out over the sea. 'It ...' She winced, or rather, forced a wince to her face. 'It had to happen, I suppose.'

'It did,' Denaos grunted, casting her a curious eye. 'I'm

shocked you're taking it so well, though. One would expect you to be all on knees and hands, cutting your forehead for Talanas and praying for their safe return ... or at least safe passage to heaven.'

She scratched the spot her pendant had hung. 'Maybe it's not so necessary these days.'

'Gods are always necessary,' he replied. 'Especially in cases like these.'

She said nothing at that, instead letting the full weight of the words sink upon her. *Lost everything ... everything ...*

'The tome,' she gasped suddenly, turning to the rogue. 'The tome! Did you at least look for it?'

'Did,' Denaos grunted, then gestured up the hill to Dreadaeleon. 'Or *he* did, rather. Used some kind of weird bird magic that didn't work before running off like a milksop. Useless.'

That thought plucked an uncomfortable string on her heart. She should have been more upset about the loss of her companions, she knew. But somehow, the loss of the book carried more weight. It seemed to her that the loss of the tome, merely the topmost piece in a growing pile of disappointments, was just a spiteful afterthought to drive home the pointlessness of it all.

It was for nothing. It was futile.

Those thoughts were becoming easier to endure with their frequency.

She looked up at a hand placed on her shoulder, doing her best not to cringe at his unpleasant smile.

'Losing faith?' he asked.

'I didn't know faith concerned you.'

'Washed up on an island. No food, little water, friends dead and book lost.' He shrugged. 'Not much left but faith.'

She frowned; faith used to be all she needed. Somehow, Denaos seemed to sense that thought, however. He rose up, offering her a hand and a whisper.

'I'm sorry.'

It came back on a flood of sensation, images carried on the stink of his breath, sounds in the warmth of his grasp.

'*I'm sorry.*' It was his voice that slipped through her memory, clear and concise, stored in the fog of her mind. And he repeated it, over and over. '*I'm sorry, I'm sorry … but why? Why does this always happen to me?*'

Was it merely an echo? An errant thought emerging from her subconscious? She had been unconscious, she knew, sleeping. She couldn't have heard him. But, then, why did his voice continue to ring out in her mind?

'*This is the second one,*' he had said, she was certain. '*I didn't even do anything this time! It's not fair! First* her, *then … her.*' She could remember a hand, lovingly brushing against her cheek. '*Please, Silf, Talanas … any of you! I deserve it, I know, but she doesn't! And* she *didn't! Please. Please, I'm sorry, I'm sorry …*'

'Who was she?' The question came from her mouth unbidden on the tail of that sporadic voice that rose from her mind.

'What?' He hesitated pulling her up, looking down at her. The mask shattered completely, crumbled in thick, white shards onto the sand. What was left behind was something hard-eyed and purse-lipped. 'What did you say?'

'She … the woman you were speaking of.' Asper pulled herself the rest of the way up. 'You kept apologising.'

'No, I didn't.' He let his hand fall from hers. 'How would you even know? You were out.'

'I remember, though. I must have been awake for part of it, and—'

'No, you *weren't.*' He cut her off with a razor edge. '*I* watched over you. *You* were out and you *didn't* wake up, at any time.' He turned away from her curtly. 'I'm going to go sleep myself now. Go check on Dread.'

She watched him take all of three steps before the words came again.

'For what it's worth,' she said, 'I'm sure she forgives you.'

He turned upon her with the staggering need of a beggar two weeks starved. Considering her through expressionless eyes for a moment, he walked toward her, arms up in benediction. With more confusion than hesitation, she let herself into his embrace. There was no warmth in his arms, but an unpleasant constrictor tightness.

She gasped as she felt the knife, sliding like a snake up her tunic to kiss her kidneys with steel lips, the menace of the weapon conveyed in a touch that barely grazed her skin.

'*You,*' he whispered, his voice an unsharpened edge, 'don't *ever* speak of *her.*'

'You ...' She swallowed hard. 'You said you didn't have any knives left. You *lied.*'

'No,' he gasped, looking at her with mock incredulousness. '*Me?*'

And in a flash, he was striding away from her. His back was tall and straight, shaking off his threat like a cloak. It fell atop the shards of his mask, and as she stared at his back, mouth agape, she couldn't help but feel that he was already weaving another one to put on.

A warm breeze blew across the beach. The sun was silent. Her left arm began to ache.

*

After much careful deliberation, a lone seagull drifted down off the warm currents crisscrossing the island to land upon the sands and peck at the earth. In its simple mind, it vaguely recalled not visiting this area before. It was a barren land, bereft of much food. But in its simple eyes, it beheld all manner of debris not seen on these shores before. And thus, curious, it hopped along, picking at the various pieces of wood.

A shadow caught its attention. It looked up. It remembered these two-legged things, such as the one that sat not far away from it. It remembered it should run from them. It spread its wings to fly.

And instantly, it was seized in an invisible grip.

'No, no,' Dreadaeleon whispered, pulling his arm back. The force that gripped the seagull drew it closer to him, the bird's movement completely wrenched up in panic. 'I need your brain.'

His voice was hot with frustration. He hadn't expected it to take nearly this long to seize a stupid bird that, by all accounts, should be infesting the shores like winged rats. But that was a momentary irritation, one quickly overrun by the sudden pain that lanced through his bowels.

His breath went short, his hand trembled and the seagull writhed a little as his attentions went to the agony rising into his chest. This was not normal, he knew; pain was the cost of magic overspent, and the ice raft he had wrought to deliver his companions certainly qualified. But those pains were mostly relegated to the brain and rarely lasted for more than a few hours. This particular agony that coursed through his entire being was new to him.

But not unknown.

Stop it, he scolded himself. *You've got enough trouble without wondering about the Decay. You don't have it. Stop it. Focus on the task at hand. Focus on the seagull.*

The seagull, he thought as he drew the trembling bird into his lap, and its tiny, juicy, electric little brain.

Still, he hesitated as he rested a finger upon the bird's skull. More magic would mean more pain, he realised, and it seemed unwise to expend any energy on anything that wasn't guaranteed to find salvation from the sea. And, as magic went, avian scrying was as unreliable as they came.

Dreadaeleon had never found a bird that wasn't a bumbling, hunger-driven moron. He could sense the electricity in its brain now: straight, if crude, lines of energy suggesting minimal, single-minded activity. It was those lines that made birds easier to manipulate than the jumble of confused sparks that made up the human brain, but it also made them relatively pointless for finding anything beyond carrion and crumbs.

But carrion and crumbs were food. And, as his growling belly reminded him, food was not something they had managed to salvage.

He whispered a word. A faint jolt of electricity burst through his fingers, into the avian's skull. It twitched once, then let out a frightened caw. He could feel the snaps of primitive cognition, bursting in his own mind as their electric thoughts synchronised.

Scared, they told him. *Scared, scared, scared, scared.*

'Fine,' he muttered. 'Go, then.'

He released the bird, sending it flying out over the waters. He leaned back, closing his eyes. In his mind, he could feel the gull's presence, sense its location, know its thoughts as he felt each sputtering pop of thought in its tiny brain. All he needed to do now was wait; he could hold onto its signature for at least an hour.

A lance of pain shot through him. He winced.

Or less.

'What do you hope to achieve?' someone asked him.

'Animals search for food first. If there's any around here, I'll know about it,' he replied, his thoughts preoccupied with the gull's.

'There are many places the Sea Mother's creatures go that you cannot.'

'If I can tap into a seagull's *brain*, I can certainly figure out how to get where he's going,' he snarled. Only when his ire rose higher than his pain did he realise that the voice was not that of one of his companions.

But it was not unknown.

He turned about and saw her standing before him: tall, pale body wrapped in a silken garment, fins cresting about her head, feathery gills blended with emerald-colour hair. He looked up, agape, and the siren smiled back at him.

'I am pleased that you are well, lorekeeper,' Greenhair said. The fins on the sides of her head twitched. 'Or … are you?'

'Not so much now,' he said. He tried to rise, felt a stab of pain and, immediately afterward, felt the urge to wince.

Don't do it, old man, he warned himself. *Remember, she's tricky. She can get into your head. She can manipulate your thoughts. Stay calm. Don't think about the pain. She'll know … unless she already knows and is telling you how to feel now to further her agenda. Stop thinking. I SAID, STOP THINKING!*

'Be calm, lorekeeper,' she whispered. 'I do not come seeking strife.'

'Yes, you're quite talented, aren't you? You find it without even searching for it,' Dreadaeleon muttered. 'You tricked us into going into Irontide after the tome and abandoned us when we had to fight for it.'

'I was concerned for the appearance of—'

'I wasn't finished,' he spat. 'You *then* came back after we had it and got into my head.' He tapped his temple. '*My* head, and tried to tell me to steal it for you.'

She blinked. 'You are finished now?'

'*And* you smell like fish,' he said. 'There. Get out of my sight. I'm busy here.'

'Seeking salvation for your companions?'

'Shut up,' he muttered. He closed his eyes, attempted to seek out the gull's thoughts.

'That they might look upon you with the adoration that befits a hero?'

Don't answer, old man. She'll twist your words first, your thoughts second and probably your bits last. Focus on the gull. Focus on finding help.

He found the gull and listened intently to its electric pulse. There was a silence, then a burst, then a gentle sense of relief. A bowel movement.

Good thing you didn't waste any energy on that. Oh, wait.

'This is not the way, lorekeeper,' she whispered. 'You will find no salvation in the sea. This island is dead. It has claimed your other companions.'

'Not all of them,' he replied.

'You seek their approval? When they do not so much as care for the effort you expend for them? The pain you feel?'

'There is no pain. I'm fine.'

'You are not. Something has broken within you, lore-keeper. A well of sickness rises inside your flesh.'

'Nausea,' he replied. 'Sea air and sea trollops both make me sick.'

'And you continue to harm yourself,' she whispered. 'For what? For them?'

Dreadaeleon said nothing. Yet he could feel her staring at him, staring past his skull, eyes raking at his brain.

'Or for her?' Greenhair said.

'Shut up,' he muttered. 'Go away. Go turn into a tuna or get harpooned or whatever it is you do when you go beneath the waves. I have business to attend to.'

'As do they.'

'What?'

He turned to her and found her staring down at the beach. He followed her gaze, down to the shore and the two people upon it. The people he had extended his power for, the people that he had put himself in pain for, the people he had magically lassoed and mentally dominated a filth-ridden sea-pigeon for. He saw them.

Embracing.

'But ... he's a rat,' he whispered. 'And she's ... she's ...'

'She has betrayed you.'

'No, they're just doing ... they're ...'

'And you are not,' Greenhair said, slipping up behind him. 'As you burn yourself with impure fire, as you expend yourself for them, they roll on each other like hogs.'

'They just don't know,' he said. 'Once they see, they'll know, they'll see—'

'They didn't know when you saved them from the Akaneeds? When you kept them aloft with no concern for your own safety? Your own health? When will they notice?'

'When ... when ...'

'When you find the tome.'

'What?' he asked.

'This island has barely any food. Even the creatures of the Sea Mother avoid it. But there is something else. The gull can find it. It calls to everything. It will call to the gull. The gull will call to you.'

Her voice was a melodic serpent, slithering into his ears, coiling around his brain. He was aware of it, of her talents, of her treachery. Yet even fools occasionally had good ideas, didn't they? If he could find the tome, find it and show it to them, to her, she would know, she would know him. They would all know. They would see his power.

He closed his eyes, searched for the gull. He found it, circling somewhere out over the sea. Its eyes were down, its head was crackling as it spotted things bobbing in the water. It saw wood – wreckage, Dreadaeleon concluded, even if the gull couldn't comprehend it. It saw no food, yet remained entranced, circling lower toward the sea.

Tome.

He twitched; that shouldn't be possible. Birds had no idea what a tome was. They could not recognise it.

But it did, somehow; Dreadaeleon could feel it. It stared down into the depths, seeing it clearly as a stain of ink upon the pristine blue. It stared into the sea, past the wreckage and past the brine. It stared into the water, it stared into a perfect, dark square plainly visible even so far down as it was.

Tome.

The gull stared.

Tome.

The tome stared back.

And suddenly, Dreadaeleon heard it, felt it. Voices in his head, whispers that glided on stale air and whispering brine rather than electric jolts. A grasping arm that reached out, found the current that connected gull and wizard, and squeezed.

Where is it, the voices whispered, *where is it? It was here ages ago. It spoke. It read. It knew. Tell us where it is. Tell us where it went. Tell us how it got there. Tell us. Tell us everything. Tell us who you are. Tell us what you're made of. Tell us of your tender meat and your little mind. Tell us of brittle bones and tears that taste salty. Tell us. Tell us everything. Tell us how you work. Tell us. Tell us. We will know. Tell us.*

He trembled, clenched his teeth so fiercely that they creaked behind his lips. His breath came in short, sporadic breaths. His head seared with fire, whispering claws reaching out to flense his brain and taste the electric-stained meat, tasting it for knowledge. He could hear the tome. He could hear it speak to him.

TELL US.

And then he heard himself scream.

'Dread?'

He hadn't recalled falling onto his back. He certainly hadn't noticed Greenhair leaving. And he was absolutely positive he would have seen Asper coming. And yet he was on his back, the siren vanished and the priestess was kneeling beside him, propping him up, staring at him with concern. His voice was a nonsensical croak, his head spinning as thoughts, his own and the gull's, sizzled in his skull.

'Are you all right?'

'No,' he said, shaking his head to dispel the last sparks. 'I mean, yes. Yes, perfectly fine.'

'You don't' – she paused to cringe – 'look it.'

Steady, old man, he reminded himself. *Don't act all helpless now. Don't let her know what's wrong.* He snarled inwardly. *What do you mean what's wrong? Nothing's wrong! Just a headache. Don't worry about it. Don't let her worry about it. And most importantly, don't pay attention to the urge to piss yourself.*

That proved a little harder. His bowels stirred at her

touch, rigid with pain, threatening to burst like overfilled waterskins. Still, he bit back pain, water and screams as she helped him to his feet, resisting the urge to burst from any orifice.

'What happened?' she asked.

'Strain,' he replied, shaking his head. 'Magical strain.'

'Bird magic, Denaos said.'

'*Bird magic*,' Dreadaeleon said, all but spitting. 'Of course. It's nothing so marvellous as seizing control of another living thing's brain functions. It's *bird* magic. What would he know?' He found himself glaring without willing it, the words hissing through his teeth. 'What would *you* know?'

'Dread ...' She recoiled, as though struck.

'Sorry,' he muttered. 'Sorry, sorry. It's just ... a headache.'

In the bowels, he added mentally, *the kind that makes you explode from both ends and probably kills you if it is what you think it is.* He shook his head. *No, no. Calm down. Calm down.*

'Of course,' Asper said, sighing. 'Denaos said you'd exerted yourself.' She offered him a weak smile. 'I trust you won't begrudge me if I say I'm glad you did?'

You're probably going to develop some magical ailment where you begin defecating out your mouth and choke on your own stool and she's glad?

'I mean, I know it was a lot,' she said, 'but you did save us.'

'Oh ... right,' he replied. 'The ice raft. Yeah, it was ... nothing.'

Nothing except the inability to stand up on your own power. Good show.

'It's just a shame you couldn't save the others,' she said.

'Or … is that what you were doing with your bird magic?'

'*Avian scrying*,' he snapped, on the verge of a snarl before he twitched into a childish grin. 'And … yes. Yes, I was looking for them.'

'Did you find anything?'

'Not yet.'

'I suppose you wouldn't, would you?' She sighed, looking forlornly over the sea. 'We were lucky to escape, ourselves. Anything left by the wreck would be devoured.'

There was something in her that caused him to tense, or rather something *not* there. Ordinarily, her eyes followed her voice, always a sharp little upscale at the end of each thought to suggest that she was waiting to be proven wrong, waiting for someone to refute a grim thought. If enough time passed, she would, and often did, refute herself, citing hope against the hopeless.

But such an expression was absent today, such an upscale gone from her voice. She spoke with finality; she stared without blinking. And she looked so very, very tired.

'They … they might be out there,' he said. 'Wouldn't Talanas watch over them?'

'If Talanas listened, we wouldn't be here in the first place.'

And then, he saw it, in the seriousness of her eyes, the firm certainty in her jaw. The idealistic hope was removed from her eyes, that whimsical twinge that he was always certain indicated at least a minor form of brain damage was gone from her voice. She was a person less reliant on faith, if she had any at all anymore.

She's stopped, he thought. *She doesn't believe in gods. Not right now, at least.*

There were a number of reactions that went through his mind: congratulate her on her enlightenment, rejoice in the fact that they could finally communicate as equals or maybe just speak quietly and offer to guide her. He rejected them all; each was entirely inappropriate. And nothing, *nothing*, he knew, was a less appropriate reaction than the tingling he felt in his loins.

Stave it off, stave it OFF, he told himself. *This is the absolutely* worst *possible time for that.*

'Did you ... feel something?' she asked suddenly.

'*Absolutely not*,' he squealed.

She seemed to take no notice of his outburst, instead staring off into the distance. 'Something ... like I felt back at Irontide. Hot and cold ...'

He quirked a brow; she *had* sensed magic back then, he recalled, but many were sensitive to it without showing any other gifts. And the source at the time, a fire- and frost-spewing longface, was a bright enough beacon that even the thickest bark-neck would have sensed it.

This concerned him, though. He could feel nothing in the air, none of the fluctuating chill and heat that typically indicated a magical presence. He wondered, absently, if she might be faking it.

Her left arm tensed and she clenched at it, scratching it as though it were consumed by ants. A low whine rose in her throat, becoming an agonised whisper as she scratched fiercer and fiercer until red began to stain the sleeve of her robe.

'Dread,' she looked up at him, certainty replaced by horror. '*What's happening?*'

Eight

THE NATURALIST

The crawling thing picked its way across the sand, intent on some distant goal. It had six legs, two claws, two bulbous eyes and, apparently, no visible destination. Over the bones, over the tainted earth, over the fallen, rusted weapons it crawled, eyes always ahead, eyes never moving, legs never stopping.

Surely, Sheraptus reasoned, something so small would not know where it was going. Could it even comprehend the vastness of the worlds around it? The worlds beyond its own damp sand? Perhaps it would walk forever, never knowing, never stopping.

Until, Sheraptus thought as he lifted his boot over the thing, it became aware of just how small it was.

Then it happened: a change in the wind, a fluctuation of temperature. He turned and looked into the distance.

'There it is again,' he muttered.

'Hmm?' his companion asked.

'You don't sense it?'

'Magic?'

'*Nethra*, yes.'

'I am attuned to higher callings, I am afraid.'

'So you say,' Sheraptus said.

'You have no reason to distrust me, do you?'

'Not as such, no.' His lip curled up in a sneer. 'That provides me little comfort.'

'What is it that troubles you, if I may ask?'

'You may, thank you. A signature, a fleeting expenditure of strength. It's not what you'd call "big", but rather ... pronounced. It's a moth that flutters before the flame and disappears before I can catch it in my hands.'

'A moth?'

'Yes. They do fly before flame, do they not?'

'They do.' The Grey One That Grins smiled, baring finger-long teeth. 'You seem to be fascinated with all things insect today.'

'Ah, but did you not say that this thing—' He flitted a hand to the crawler.

'Crab.'

'This crab. It is not an insect?'

'It is not.'

'It has a carapace, many legs ...'

'It does.'

'Why is it not an insect, then?'

'Its identity is its own, I suppose.'

Sheraptus glanced down to the sand and the tiny crab. 'Why does it exist?'

'Hmm?'

'A tiny thing that moves in the same, meaningless direction as other tiny things, that looks exactly like other tiny things, but is not the same tiny thing as the others?' He quirked a brow. 'I have never seen such a thing.'

'They have no such things in the Nether?'

'None. Females are females. Males are males. Females kill. Males speak with *nethra*. This is how things are.' He sighed, rolling his eyes. 'This is what makes them so ... dull.'

'Hence our agreement.'

'Naturally,' Sheraptus said. He adjusted the crown on his head, felt the red stones inside it burn at his touch. 'And while I am not ungrateful for your donations, I have some reservations.'

'Such as?'

'This world … I have difficulty comprehending it. The Nether is dull, of course, but it is logical. It makes sense. This one …'

'What about it?'

'I suppose I'm mainly concerned with everyone's decision to do whatever they want.'

'Expound?'

'This is supposedly an island of death, yes?'

'The war between Ulbecetonth's brood and the House of the Vanquishing Trinity left the land scarred. The taint of death is embroiled in its very earth. Nothing pure grows here. Nothing pure lives here.'

'I believe you said, originally, that nothing lived here, period.'

'Did I?' The Grey One That Grins smiled. 'It likely seemed more dramatic at the time, the better to catch your interest. Apologies for the deception.'

'Please, think nothing of it. My interest is certainly caught. But as we see, things do live here.' He glanced down the beach. 'Or did, anyway.'

The earth there was a place of deeper death than even the ruinous battlefield of the beach could match. The earth was seared black, still smoking in places. Mingled amongst the burned earth were shapes consisting of two arms and two legs, their bodies twisted into ash that flaked off with each stray gust of wind. They were scarcely distinct from the blackened earth, let alone as Those Green Things they had started life as.

'Truth be told, they are among the source of my worries.'

'Go on.'

'They came down. They attacked me.'

'You were on their land.'

'Their land that nothing lives on.'

'It was still theirs.'

'But why? Why bother over such a land? Would it not make more sense to depart to a place where life persists?'

'If you'll recall, and I mean no disrespect in reminding you, they *did* have such a land. You repurposed it.'

'Your generosity is obliged, but I take no offence in the common term.' Sheraptus shrugged. 'The netherlings required their land. We took it.'

'And why did you take it?'

'Because we are strong. They are weak. Why did they not simply flee from us?'

'Ah, I begin to see your puzzlement. May I pose a theory?'

'By all means.'

'The term you seek is "symbiosis".'

'Sym … bi … osis,' he sounded it out. A smile of jagged teeth creased his purple lips. 'I *like* that word. What does it mean?'

'It is the condition in which, through mutual cooperation, one life-form supports another.'

'Ah, now I am further confused. You'll have to pardon me.'

'Not at all. Consider them …' The Grey One That Grins gestured to the burned corpses.

'Those Green Things,' Sheraptus said, nodding. 'Well, not so green anymore. What of them?'

'They did not abandon their land until they had no choice, because to abandon their land would mean their death. They cultivate the land, feed their trees, guard their waters. In return, the land provides them with fruit and fish to feed off of.'

'Mm,' Sheraptus hummed. 'One almost feels poorly for what we did to them.'

'Almost?'

'As I said, we required their land if we are to return your generous contributions.'

'Please, don't make any mistake. The Martyr Stones are our gift to you.' His companion gestured to the crown. 'You have used them wisely thus far. We trust that you will use them wisely in days to come.'

'Trust ...' Sheraptus gazed skyward for a moment, his milk-white, pupilless eyes lighting up. 'Ah. I believe I understand. Do you mind if I theorise?'

'Oh, please do.'

'Symbiosis is what you believe us to be. You give us these stones, you lead us to this new green world and in return ...'

'Go on.'

'We kill the underscum. This ... Kraken Queen of yours.'

'You seem to grasp it quite well.'

'Yet I remain puzzled.'

'Oh?'

'Indeed. I am told there is a bigger, vaster world beyond these chunks of sand floating in this ... it's called an ocean?'

'It is and there are.'

'A bigger, vaster world filled with more beasts, more birds, more trees and more people and all their vast multitudes of invisible sky-people.'

'Gods.'

'Another word for "stupid".'

'Agreed.'

'And there are ...' He looked to his companion, smirked. 'Females there?'

'Many.'

'Then why are Sheraptus and Arkklan Kaharn here on this desolate place? Why are we not out and learning more of this world?'

'I did request your presence here.'

'Ah. I suppose the question then becomes, why are we listening to you?'

His vision was painted red as the *nethra* surged through him. Crimson light leaked from his eyes, painting his companion as a dark blob against the ruby haze. The Martyr Stones in his crown blazed, the black iron they were set in growing warm with their response.

It had been the last sight Those Green Things had seen before they were reduced to ash. They had shrieked in their language, tried to crawl over each other to escape. The Grey One That Grins did not try to escape, though. The Grey One That Grins never moved unless he had to.

He thought he didn't have to move.

Sheraptus made people move.

Sheraptus was not pleased.

'Ah, but how would you make this world work for you?'

'I'd find a way.'

'You did not find a way to reach this world. It was our searching that discovered the Nether before we found heaven.'

'Heaven does not exist.'

'Many suspect it does.'

'Then they are weak.'

'Weakness rules this world, Sheraptus. They believe in things that they themselves do not understand. You cannot hope to understand it, either. Not without us.'

'And what do you provide?' Sheraptus asked, narrowing his fiery stare. 'You send us on errands against the under-scum. They are weak. The females hunger for greater fights.'

'You suggested that they were dull for their hunger.'

'What I said then and what I say now are different. I, too, tire of this pointless burning. The appeal of the Martyr Stones remains trivial, fleeting. I wish to know more of this land, and all I have discovered are useless relics from useless wars.'

'May I dispute?'

'I'd rather you didn't.'

'I must insist,' the Grey One That Grins said. 'Within these ruins lie secrets of the House, the methods they used to banish Ulbecetonth. We must seek them out if we are to destroy her.'

'You mean if *I* am to destroy her,' Sheraptus replied. 'You only seem to emerge when you require something else of me.'

'I would entreat you to have patience with me. My presence is required at many places at once.'

'The point remains, I have yet to see a reason to oblige you in this vendetta against your demons.'

'You wish to see the world beyond this one? Very well. But know that Gods are strange things. People may not understand it, but they believe that the Gods will protect them in exchange for their devotion.'

'Symbiosis.'

'Precisely. And their devotions come with spears and swords, Sheraptus, and they are many. Arkklan Kaharn numbers how many? Five hundred?'

'That is as many as we've been able to bring through the Nether.'

'Slay Ulbecetonth and you shall have more. We will put our resources behind you. We will open more doors to the Nether. We will point you to the seats of knowledge in this world. We will unleash you ... if you simply perform this triviality for us.'

Sheraptus stared at him for a time before he blinked. The stones ceased to burn. His eyes returned to their milky white.

'I suppose I can have patience for a while yet, then,' he said.

'I am pleased we could reach an agreement. All else goes according to plan?'

'It does. Yldus is scouting the overscum city you wished us to. Vashnear combs this island with the Carnassials.'

'And you?'

'I am here to speak to someone about a book,' Sheraptus said, smiling.

'I was intending to inquire as to its status.'

'I am pleased to have saved you the trouble.'

'You would take no offence if I left now, then?'

'Unless you require something else of me.'

'At the moment?'

'Or in the near future.'

The Grey One That Grins tilted his head to the side, looking thoughtful. Or as thoughtful as Sheraptus suspected his companion was capable of looking.

'I have been made aware of certain presences upon the

island,' he said after a moment. 'Peculiar creatures that should have died long ago.'

'Beyond Those Green Things?'

'Far beyond. Humans.'

'With all due respect to your awareness and attunements,' Sheraptus said, 'I suspect That Thing That Screams would have told me if any other elements arrived.'

'I do not trust that creature.'

'I would suggest, then, that you trust in my hold over her.'

'As you say. Of course, should you find trust in my reasoning, I would ask that you do your best not to slaughter these humans. They continue to oppose Ulbecetonth and have dealt blows against her before.'

Sheraptus quirked a brow. 'These are the ones that were at Irontide?'

'The very same. Does this aggravate you?'

'Not entirely, no. The females lost were … females. They'd have been disappointed if they didn't die.'

'And the male?'

'Cahulus was weak, apparently.'

'I can trust your discretion, then?'

'Discretion …' Sheraptus hummed the word. 'Judgement.'

'You can concede my judgement.'

'I will settle for that, then.' The Grey One That Grins turned to go, crawling upon his hands and feet. 'I trust Vashnear will arrange for the usual transportation?'

'Of course.'

'Very well, then. I leave things in your capabilities.' The Grey One That Grins continued for another three paces before pausing and glancing over his emaciated shoulder. 'Sheraptus?'

'Hm?'

'Symbiosis without certainty is faith.'

'Faith being?'

'The ability to move in one direction without necessarily knowing where one is going.'

'Weakness.'

'The one that drives the world.'

The Grey One That Grins said nothing more as he slinked down the rest of the beach, disappearing behind a dune. Sheraptus watched him go for as long as it took for him to feel it again: a light brushing of air against his cheeks, the faint warmth of fire screened through snow.

A moth's wings, flapping.

He recognised it as *nethra*, albeit only a faint, fleeting trace of it. Weak as it was, though, the intent behind it was clear. With whatever pitiful power they had, someone was reaching out for him.

He smiled softly, narrowed his eyes and reached back.

As one, the fire erupted from his eyes as a wave of force swept out from his body. It sped along the sand, kicking it up in small waves of dirt. In a moment, it dissipated, but the force lingered. He watched it sweep over dunes, over beach, over puddle, following a distant, unseen goal.

He waited patiently.

He heard a scream, faint in the distance.

Female.

He smiled.

Dreadaeleon turned at her howl, seeing her clutching at her arm wildly.

'*What's happening?*' Asper wailed. '*What is it?*'

He was about to ask when he was struck by it a moment later. The force shot through him, reaching up into his body with a burning hand, seizing his bowels in intangible icy fingers and giving it a sharp twist.

Keep it together, old man, he tried to tell himself. *Keep it together. She's in trouble now. Keep it together for her.* He took a step toward her, collapsed onto his knees. Breath was coming in rasping, thick gasps, the force slipping up to choke him from the inside. *FOR VENARIE'S SAKE, YOU WEAK LITTLE—*

His insult died with his thoughts as electricity gripped his skull, setting it rattling in its thin case of flesh and hair. For a fleeting moment, he was aware of the sensation, aware of what it meant. Someone was attempting to find his thoughts, to harness the electric impulse in his skull. The human mind was too complex for that, he knew, just as he knew that every experimental attempt to do so had ended in—

He screamed. He couldn't hear it. His ears were ringing. His vision was darkening.

He looked to his side. Asper was not screaming. Why wasn't she screaming? She was always screaming, always terrified. He was supposed to protect her now. Once he remembered how to use his legs, he decided, he would do just that. All he needed to do was remember how to do that, also how to breathe.

Asper was clutching her arm, obviously in pain, but speaking clearly. The certainty was still present in the set of her jaw, the determination in her face. But there was something else there, a glimmer of something in her eye. He recognised it; he wished he could remember what it meant.

With his last thought, he wondered how things could have gone so wrong. He was going to save everyone, save her. But now he was numb, barely aware of the earth moving under him. But as his vision darkened, he could see the gloved hands gripping his shoulders, pulling him along. He stared up into Denaos' face and summoned up the will for one final thought.

You dumb asshole.

Nine

PESTS

Five hundred and forty-nine patches of disease crawling on two legs, he thought as he stared down at the tiny port city beneath the setting sun.

Two hundred and sixty able to hold a weapon, with five hundred and twenty eyes that spoke of their inability to know how.

One hundred and three of them carrying fishing rods and nets instead, taking their aggressions out against an ocean that was far too kind to them.

Ninety and six of them infirm, indisposed or suffering from the delusion that their lack of external genitalia was an excuse to let others do the fighting.

Ninety remained, evenly split between visitors in short boats who believed that the glittering chunks of metal they traded for their fish and grain was what made their civilisation worthy of crushing other peoples beneath its boot, and the children ...

The children ...

Naxiaw scratched his chin, acknowledging the coarse scrawl of tattoos etched from beneath his lip to up over his skull.

Forty and five little, toddling future lamentations. Forty and five impending regrets on skinny, hairless legs. His eyes narrowed, teeth clenched behind thin lips. Forty and five future murderers, butchers, burners and desecrators.

He had counted.

Diseases all.

Naxiaw took note of them: where they stood, what weapons they carried and which ones would cower in pools of their own urine when he led the rest of them down into their streets. With a finger smeared with black dye, on a piece of tanned leather, he scrawled the city as he saw it from high on the cliff. His six-toed feet dangled over the ledge, kicking with carefree casualness as he plotted a death with each dab of dye.

Port Yonder, as the humans called it, was a city built on contempt.

It was a demonstration of stone walls and hewn wood that the *kou'ru* bred with more rapidity than could be contained. It was proof that there would never be enough flesh and fish to satisfy their voracity. It was their assertion of contempt for the land, that they would desecrate and destroy in the name of building walls to cower behind, to raise filthy little children behind.

Children, he knew, *that will grow up to consume more land, to spread the same disease.*

It was a city that proved beyond a doubt the threat of humanity.

He reached behind him, ran his long fingers down the long black braid that descended from his otherwise hairless head. He brushed the four black feathers laced into its tuft. He had earned them the day he proved that threats, no matter how unstoppable they might seem, could be killed.

The time for vengeance would be later; for the moment, he returned their contempt.

He sat brazenly out in the open, long having deemed subterfuge and camouflage unnecessary. The humans hadn't spotted him in the week he'd been there, and wouldn't. To do that, they would have to look up.

All it would take for him to be spotted would be for one of them to look up, to see his pale green skin, to squint until they saw the long, pointed ears with six notches carved into each length, to let eyes go wide and scream '*Shict!*' They would all be upon him, then; they would kill him, find his map, realise there were more of him coming, assemble their forces, pass the word to their many outliers and empires.

And then, *Intsh Kir Maa*, Many Red Harvests, and all the long and deliberate years that had gone into its planning would be foiled. The greatest collaboration amongst the twelve tribes would be ruined.

And the human disease, in all its writhing, gluttonous, greedy glory, would fester.

But for that to happen, they would have to look up.

Naxiaw couldn't help but feel slightly insulted at the ease with which the plan was developing. He had dared to venture down towards the city on more than one occasion, to slip a bit of venom into a drink or subtly jab someone from afar with a hair-thin dart. For his efforts, he had counted ten diseases cured. The venom acted quickly – a brief sickness, a swift death. That wasn't the problem.

What angered him was that the humans never seemed to care.

No alarms were raised, no weapons drawn, no oaths sworn as their companions coughed, cried and fell dead. They simply dumped the slain into the ocean and went on without sorrow, without hatred, without asking why.

He had hoped to share that with them: the anger, the fury, the pain. He hoped to return these gifts of anguish, the ones he had taken when the round-eared menace had come to his lands. But the humans would not accept it. They refused sorrow. They refused pain. They refused him.

Many Red Harvests would be a lesson as much as revenge. It would be the wailing of two people, linked forever in death.

But that would take time. That would take patience. For now, he simply sat on a cliff and continued to plot the end of a race as serenely as he might paint the sunset.

The *s'na shict s'ha* had time. The *s'na shict s'ha* had patience.

The *s'na shict s'ha* knew how to paint a scene of vengeance.

His ears suddenly pricked up of their own volition, sensing the danger long before he did. Footsteps, the details becoming clearer with each hairsbreadth by which his ears rose. Four flat, heavy feet clad in metal, heavy weapons and skins of iron making their approach loud and unwieldy.

Humans. Careless foragers or vigilant searchers for a threat. It did not matter.

His eyes drifted to the thick Spokesman Stick resting at his side; he ran his stare along the twisting, macabre design burned into its polished and solid wood.

Two more go missing, he told himself. *No one cares. Then there are only five hundred and forty-seven strains of disease to cure. Still ...* He folded up the tanned hide into a thin, solid square. With a yawn, he tossed it into his mouth and swallowed. *No sense in being careless.*

The footsteps stopped; he narrowed his eyes. They had found his camp.

'Someone else has come here,' someone grunted.

He raised a hairless brow at the voice. It was thick, sharp, grating with an indeterminate accent, like two pieces of rusted metal hissing off one another. He was not so concerned with their unfamiliarity; the disease came in all shapes, sizes and voices. What gave him pause was the distinct, if harsh, femininity to their voices.

Their females fight now? He had thought that to be a strictly shictish practice. *They are evolving ...*

'*Saharkk* Sheraptus sent others ahead of us?' the other one asked, grumbling. 'He might have said something and spared us the—'

There was the sharp crack of metal on flesh, a growl instead of a shriek.

'*His* motives are not for you to question,' the first one snarled. 'And he's called *Master* now.' The footsteps began again. 'And we'll find out who wants to stomp here uninvited.'

Yes, Naxiaw thought as he rose, the stick heavy and hungry in his hand, *we shall*.

He didn't have to wait long before the footsteps and voices were both thunder in his ears. They were behind him now; he could hear them breathing.

'Ha!' The first one, he recognised, her voice being a bit sharper than the other's. 'Look at that. They come in green.'

'A green pinky,' the other one grunted. 'I don't remember them having long ears, neither.'

His back was still turned and they hadn't attacked him yet. They were either supremely overconfident or desired a solution that ended without someone's entrails stuffed up their own nose. Either way, he thought as he turned about, they would be surprised.

Of all the things he had expected to meet his narrowed eyes, however, he did not expect to stare at these ... things.

They *looked* human, at least superficially, but were far too tall, their musculature obscene and exposed by the iron half-skins they wore. Their faces, lean and long as spears under hacked crowns of black hair, scowled at him with eyes of pure white, bereft of any colour or pupil.

The fact that they were purple was less of a concern than the swords at their waists. 'And it has a stick,' the one closest to him said. 'A *stick*. What would even be the point of killing it?'

'Fun?' the other one asked.

'Ah, yes.'

'*Sh'shaqk ne'warr, kou'ru,*' Naxiaw hissed between clenched teeth.

Even if they weren't human, they were close enough for the insult to fit. And even if he refused to speak their language, he made sure his tone carried as much threatening edge as his raised stick.

At both, the two merely smiled broad white slashes filled with jagged teeth.

'Look at that,' one said, as she shook a round iron shield loose on her gauntleted wrist. 'It wants to fight.'

'We have duties to attend to,' the other one muttered, sliding a short spike of dark iron from her belt. 'Make it quick.'

'*Sh'shaqk ne'warr,*' he repeated, hefting his Spokesman. *You don't belong here.*

If they didn't understand his words, they understood his intonation as they slid easily into rehearsed defensive stances. Their muscles trembled with constrained fury as they edged close to him, careful and cautious, every movement planned and poised, every inch of their lean bodies speaking of an iron discipline.

That lasted for all of three breaths.

'*AKH! ZEKH! LAKH!*' Her shriek was accompanied by the metal roar of her spike clanging against her shield as she charged him. '*EVISCERATE! DECAPITATE! EXTERMINATE!*'

The other one was close behind her, cursing her companion's recklessness and her own slowness. Naxiaw watched them come, watched the hate pour from their eyes over their shields, their spikes thirsty in their hands. He licked his lips, the stick resting comfortably and silently in his long fingers.

Then, he met their charge.

Tall as they were, they were compact creatures born of rocks, he recognised: too slow, too hard. He was *s'na shict s'ha*, and he was long. As they rushed, he leapt, his long legs carrying him from the envious earth as their shields went up with their alarmed cries. His long toes curled over the rim of the leading one's shield, his long fingers caught her by what hair she had, his long arms pulled him up and over her head as her sword whined in a vicious chop that caught only the stench of his feet.

He smiled at the rearmost one's baffled expression. They always wore it when he did that.

As broad as his smile was, his stick's was broader, crueller. As he descended to the earth, the stick yearned to show its wooden teeth to her, to offer a brown-and-black kiss.

Naxiaw obliged it.

His stick struck her jaw with a loud crack, sent her staggering backward. He spared enough time to drive the stick's head into her exposed belly, throwing her farther back. He could hear the other one turning around, hear her spike whining for his blood.

When that whine became a roar, he fell to the ground, heard the spike shriek iron frustrations over his head. He

157

pressed his hands flat against the sand, hurled himself from the earth as his feet curled into fists and legs lashed out like coiled vipers.

He felt skin, then muscle, a shocking amount of muscle. More importantly, he heard her stagger backward, counted off her steps. *One, two, three ...*

Then came the scream, fading as she took one step too many over the cliff face. One moment for a self-satisfied smile, then he was back on his feet, his Spokesman in hand, ready to make a final argument.

The other longface was up, far sooner than he expected, and her weapon was ready. He glowered; she was strong, resilient, but still a *kou'ru*. All that separated this monkey from the ones below was that she was too stupid to run.

Instead she settled back, waited for him to come to her. He obliged, darting past her thrust, ducking her shield and coming up inside her guard. Half a moment to savour her snarl, another to make sure she could see his large canines.

Then he struck.

The Spokesman had few words for her. It was not a weapon made for long, savoury stabs or vicious, sloppy chops. It spoke in short bursts, rapping against her jaw, then her clavicle, then her arm. Its arguments were sound, though, and reverberated inside her bones, each vibration compounded by the one that soon followed.

Naxiaw had learned well the ways of the Spokesman, heard its arguments voiced to over four hundred *kou'ru*, watched them all yield to its unwavering wooden logic. This one, he realised, was deaf. She recoiled from each blow, staggered backward, but her muscles did not fail beneath its logic, bones did not shake painfully against her blood. Each sound was solid, firm, where they should be hollow, reverberating.

Like hitting a rock, he thought.

He swung harder, sending her reeling back two steps, then retreated. *Now she falls*, he told himself. *The shock was keeping her upright. Now, she will die. Now, she will fall.*

She did neither.

Instead, the longface rolled her neck, letting the vertebrae crack within. She flashed him a smile, her jagged teeth stained with only the most meagre trace of red. All her crimson was in the malice of her narrowed eyes.

'Well,' she hissed, 'aren't you just *adorable*.'

She charged. He sprang. This time her hand was in the air, her metal fingers wrapped about his ankle. He had never truly felt the earth until she gave a sharp tug and slammed him down upon it in a spray of sand.

Strong, he thought. His eyes snapped open, body rolled as her spike came down to impale the earth beside him. *Too strong*. He swung the Spokesman up, and shock rolled down his arm as it kissed her shield. *Far too strong*. She swung her spike down and his wrist groaned under the strain as he narrowly caught it.

Another quick jerk and he was back on his feet, her turn to savour his baffled expression, his turn to see her jagged teeth. In a snap of her neck, his entire world became her teeth as she drove her head against his face. He felt bones snap under the thin flesh of his nose, blood spurt out in a great slobbery kiss.

'Ha!' she cackled. '*CRUNCH*.'

Even as he reeled back, his own crimson trickling down upon the earth, he could not help but smile. Her own smile was undiminished, even as his blood painted her face in a spattering red mask.

They always looked that way, right before it started to burn.

Her grin turned to angry befuddlement, then to anger proper, and then back to shock as her smile grew wider, skin stretching tight about her face. He savoured each twitch, each expression, each moment before it invariably ended the same way it always did …

'It burns,' she grunted. 'It … it *burns!*'

His venom-laced blood went to work with hungry zeal. Her grunt twisted to a shriek as she dropped her sword and began to claw at her face. The skin was drawn tight now, growing redder as the blood sizzled beneath the purple flesh. Her metal fingers raked wildly, drawing out great gouts as she sought to rip the poison out from under her flesh.

The long-faced creature collapsed to her knees and he saw his opportunity.

His knee led his leap, driving her gauntlet deeper into her face and knocking her to the ground. Her neck was a twisting snake, writhing as she ignored the blow and continued to shriek into her hand.

The *s'na shict s'ha* knew how to kill snakes.

His foot was up and curled into a fist in one breath, then down again in one crunching, choked gurgle. The longface ceased to writhe, ceased to shriek, but her hand did not leave her face. *Just as well*, Naxiaw thought; he had seen the seething red mass beneath those digits before. It had lost its appeal after he had earned his first feather

There was little time for it, anyway. His ears pricked up again, sensing the sound of metal scraping up sand, cursing from behind.

Oh, right …

'Clever, clever …' He turned and saw that the longface's voice matched the anger painted on her face. 'But cleverness doesn't spill blood.'

He had barely noticed her hand without the large iron spike or heavy metal gauntlet that had been lost in her near-fall. He continued to ignore it right up until it slid behind her back and came out in a flash of jagged metal, the weapon flying from her hand and chased by her shriek.

'*THIS DOES!*'

The strike was too fast to dodge; he could only angle his shoulder. Even that wasn't enough to stop the pain. The blade carved through with a beaming iron smile, ripping through green flesh and drawing great gouts of red. He shrieked, staggered backward, clutching his shoulder as the Spokesman collapsed to the earth, at a loss for words.

He could barely muster the consciousness through the pain to see her hand, which had plucked up her companion's weapon. The blow came swiftly and fiercely, and he narrowly managed to seize her by the wrist to stop it, biting back the pain lancing through his arm.

And still, the spike drew ever closer. She was spiteful in her attack, but aware enough of his condition to smile. She need only press until the pain became too much to bear. He, too, was aware of her advantage, but more aware of the vein that throbbed under her purple wrist. It pulsed, pumping all the blood she had into her hand, with an inviting wriggle.

Naxiaw was not one to disoblige.

Lips parted, head jerked, canines gnashed and the longface screamed. Her life came spurting out in short, sporadic bursts as the sword fell to the earth. Her other hand came up to strike his head with its heavy gauntlet, but he narrowly caught it before it could crack his skull open.

He had only given her frenzy a desperation that drove her to even more vicious strength. She continued to press her attack, her life leaking out with every twitch of her muscles, intent on driving him into the earth itself. She would succeed, he knew, unless he ended it quickly.

He eyed the spike on the ground.

Legs began to buckle under him, but he pushed up with them, springing off the ground and curling six long toes around her belt buckle. His other leg craned down, toes twitching eagerly, violently. The longface spared enough hatred to glance at them, her eyes going wide as she saw his foot grasp the spike by its hilt and, on a quivering green leg, bring it back up.

'No!' she screamed. Her voice grew louder as her arms pressed harder as the spike drew closer. '*No, no, no, NO! That's not fair!*'

'*Shict n'dinne uah crah,*' he replied. *Shicts do not fight fair.*

His leg twisted; he ignored the cracking sound as he brought the spike up between them. He sucked in his belly to allow his foot to pass up, past his chest, the spike angling upward sharply and aiming for a writhing, shrieking part of her.

'*CHEAT!*' she roared. '*I'LL KILL YOU! I'LL RIP OFF YOUR—*'

His leg twitched. She stopped moving. He felt blood trickle down from below her jaw and smear his foot.

His leap from her falling body was less nimble than he had hoped; his shoulder stung and his legs buckled as he hit the ground. The fight had gone on too long, his body had taken too much of a toll. If they had been humans, he would have walked away whistling a tune. But they were … These things were …

He ran a hand over his bald scalp. He did not know. But he must tell the others.

He plucked up his stick from the earth. His canoe lay

hidden in the reeds nearby. All he need do was reach it, row out until he could concentrate enough to reach the other *s'na shict s'ha* through the Howling. From there, they could make it to friendly territory, the forests of the sixth tribe, maybe. They could deliver their report; Many Red Harvests would gain a new, purple crop to reap.

Yes, he told himself as the blood seeped out of his shoulder and sizzled on the ground, *this will work. Everything will*—

'Interesting ...'

No ... no, no, no!

As fervently as he tried to deny them, as much as he tried to shut them from his sight, from his mind, every time he blinked and opened his eyes, they were still there.

A dozen long, purple faces, staring back at him.

'A rather unique approach to combat, I must say,' the one in the lead said.

If he didn't know what the other ones were, Naxiaw might have thought it to be a female surrounded by burly, hulking males. The scrawny effeminate creature swathed in violet robes looked tiny against the sea of iron skins behind him. Only his goatee gave him away, the colour of bone instead of night like the hair of the females behind him, as he stroked it contemplatively.

'It looks surprised,' the female beside him snickered.

This one stood taller and more muscular than any of the ones present, carrying a massive wedge of steel hacked and hammered into a single, haggard edge. The smile she levelled at Naxiaw's very visible shock was no less crude or cruel.

'Oh, come on,' she said, her laughter deep and grating. 'You thought we only sent two up here? Who would do that?'

163

'I am not sure it understands you,' the goateed male said, leaning forward slightly. 'I do not think it is even human.' His face twisted up, puzzled. 'What is it, anyway?'

'No idea,' the large female said, hefting her giant blade over her shoulder. 'Better kill it.'

'I suppose.'

Naxiaw did not wait for the war cry, not the tensing of muscle or the groan of iron skin. He exploded first, charging, his stick held high, his plan a dizzy, swirling collection of images inside a head that swam from blood loss.

The male leads, he told himself. *Kill the male. He looks weak. One blow. That's all it will take. Kill him, break through, run to the water, drown. The others will find you, they'll pull the map out of your stomach. Don't watch the female. Watch him.*

The male did not move at this sudden charge, instead raising a single white eyebrow. Had Naxiaw glanced to the side, shifted his eye half a hair's breadth, he would have seen the females backing away. The fear that should have been on their faces was replaced with morbid bemusement, as though they expected something bloody and glorious to happen.

But Naxiaw did not see that.

Watch him. Kill him. Kill the male.

The male's lips started to move, just barely, beginning as only a few twitches. His eyes shut, not with the tightness of panic, but with a gentleness that suggested some kind of boredom. His breath leaked from his mouth in faintly visible lines of mist.

Kill him.

The male's eyes opened, milky whites gone and replaced with a burning crimson energy that poured out of his gaze. Naxiaw's stick was up, feet off the ground. It was too late to worry about the crimson, too late to do anything about the inflation of the male's chest as he inhaled deeply, too late to do anything but strike.

One blow.

But that would come far too late.

The male's face split in half with the opening of his mouth; the mist poured from his throat on echoing words that bore no meaning to Naxiaw. The chill that enveloped his body, the frost that formed on his skin – those had meaning.

His feet struck the earth, far, far heavier than when they had left it. The blood crystallised in blackish smears, the healthy green of his skin turned quickly to a light blue. The Spokesman felt light in a hand gone numb. His muscles creaked, cracked under his skin. His jaw opened in a cry, of war or of fear he knew not, and he found he could not close it again.

Then he could not move at all.

When the mist cleared, he saw the male, eyes a disinterested white again. The longface glanced to the side, noting the Spokesman, a finger's length from his head, and clenched in a frozen blue grip. Paying little attention to that, he reached out and plucked something from beneath Naxiaw's broken nose.

'Interesting,' he muttered, regarding the tiny little crimson icicle. Separated from the shict's body, it quickly became liquid, sizzling between the longface's fingers. He hissed and shook his hand. 'Envenomed blood … curious.' He leaned forward and studied Naxiaw intently. 'That may explain why this one is still alive, despite being frozen.' He rapped a knuckle against Naxiaw's forehead, smiling at the tinkling sound. 'It is not a pink. They could not survive such *nethra.*'

'Well, I could have told you that. I mean, it's *green*.' The large female chuckled. 'No wonder you're in charge, Yldus.'

'Hush, Qaine,' the male called Yldus muttered, his voice lacking her snarling ferocity. 'Whatever it is, Sheraptus will want to look at it closer.' He glanced over his shoulder to a pair of nearby females. 'You and you, take it *carefully* back to the ship. And do be careful not to let any extremities break off.'

'The *rest* of you,' the female called Qaine growled, sweeping her white-eyed glower over the remaining females, 'retrieve ink and parchment. Remain here and take note of the city's defences: numbers, weapons, positions, *everything*. Master Sheraptus demands thoroughness.' Her eyes narrowed. 'And while I remain appreciative of a female's need to spill blood, I remind you that your duty is reconno … reconna …'

'Reconnaissance,' Yldus sighed.

'Whatever,' she snarled. 'You are *not* to be seen. Whoever objects answers to me. Whoever violates this order … answers to Sheraptus.' Her grin broadened at the stiffness that surged through them. 'Get to work, low-fingers. We return in days.'

'With an army behind us,' Yldus added, his face a long, grim frown.

There were grunts of salute, the shuffling of metal as the females reorganised themselves. Naxiaw could not turn his neck, could not even think to turn his neck. He could barely muster the worry for such a thing, either. His mind felt distant, as though whatever rime covered his body also seeped into his skull, past the bone and into his brain.

The sensation of movement was lost to him. He could not recognise the sky as two females gripped him by his arms and legs and tilted him onto his back. They proceeded to carry him down the hill, behind Yldus and Qaine, as though he were little more than a fleshy blue piece of furniture.

'*Days*, she says,' one of them muttered, her voice muted to his ears. 'How does anyone expect us to wait that long?'

'The Master demands patience,' the other replied.

'The Master demands a lot,' the first one growled. 'He never asks the females to hold their iron.' She glowered. 'Rarely does he ask *netherling* females to do anything for him, so absorbed with the pinks ...'

'No one questions the Master,' the other one snarled. 'Leave complaining to low-fingers.' She glanced over her shoulder at the remaining females. 'Weaklings.' She glanced at Naxiaw, stared into his wide, rime-coated eyes. 'This thing is hardly heavier than a piece of metal. How did it kill the other two?'

'As you said, they were low-fingers pretending to be real warriors. They should have stuck with their weakling bows instead of thinking they knew how to use swords.' She snorted, spat. 'They die first when we attack.'

'They can't even speak right. What was it she said before she died?'

'"Eviscerate, decapitate, exterminate."'

'That can't be right. It's "eviscerate, decapitate, annihilate," isn't it?'

'Right. Exterminate means to crush something under your heel and leave its corpse twitching in a pile of its own innards. It is what humans do to insects.'

'What does "annihilate" mean?'

'To leave nothing behind. Low-fingers can't even remember the stupid chant.' The other one hoisted Naxiaw higher as a sleek, black vessel drifted into view on the beach below. 'That's why they're dead.'

Ten

DREAMING IN SHRIEKS

Lenk had never truly been in a position to appreciate nature before. It was always something to be overcome: endless plains and hills, relentless storms and ice, burning seas of trees, sand, salt and marsh. Nature was a foe.

Kataria had always chided him for that.

Kataria was gone now.

And Lenk wasn't any closer to appreciating nature because of it. The moonlight peered through the dense foliage above, undeterred by the trees' attempts to keep it out. The babbling brook that snaked through the forest floor became a serpent of quicksilver, slithering under roots, over tiny waterfalls, to empty out somewhere he simply did not care.

When he had found it and drank, he had thanked whatever god had sent it. When he used it to soothe his filthy wound, promises of conversion and martyrdom had followed.

Now, the stream was one more endless shriek in the forest's thousand screaming symphonies. His joy had lasted less than an hour before he had began to curse the Gods for abandoning him in a soft green hell.

It was murderous, noisy war in the canopy: the birds, decrepit winged felons pitting their wailing night songs against the howling and shaking of trees of their hatred rivals, the monkeys.

His eyes darted amongst the trees, searching for one of the noisy warriors, any of the disgusting little things. His sword rested in his lap, twitching in time with his eyelids as he swept his gaze back and forth, back and forth like a pendulum.

None of them ever emerged. He saw not a hair, not a feather. *They might not even be there*, he thought. *What if it's all just a dream, a hallucination before Gevrauch claims me?* A shrill cry punctured his ears. *Or could I ever hope to be that lucky?*

He clenched his scavenged tuber like a weapon, assaulting his mouth with it. It was the only way he could convince himself to eat the foul-tasting fibrous matter. Kataria had taught him basic foraging, in between moments of regaling him how shicts were capable of laying out a feast from what they found in mud.

She could have found something else here, he thought. *She could have found some delicious plant. 'Eat it,' she would have said, 'it'll help your bowel movements.' Always with everyone's bowel movements …*

No, he stared down at the floor, *always with my bowel movements.*

He wasn't sure why that thought made him despair.

'But she's dead now. They all are.'

The voice came and went in a fleeting whisper, rising from the gooseflesh on his arm. It had grown fainter through the fevered veil that swaddled his brain, coming as a slinking hush that coiled around his skull before slithering into silence.

He supposed he ought to have been thankful. He had long wished to be free of the voice, of its cruel commands and horrific demands. Now, as he sat alone under the canopy, he silently wished that it might linger for a moment, if only to give him someone to talk to preserve his sanity.

He paused mid-chew, considering the lunacy of that thought.

He grumbled, continuing to chew. *It's not as though you could ever preserve your sanity talking to the others, either. If anything talking to Kat would only drive you madder in short order.*

'It matters not,' the voice whispered. 'She's drowned, claimed by the deep. They all are. They all float in reefs of flesh and bone; they all drift on tides of blood and salt.'

Lenk had never recalled the voice being quite so specific before, but it slithered away before he could inquire. In its wake, fever creased his brows, sent his brain boiling.

That isn't right, he told himself. The voice made him cold, not hot. It was the fever, no doubt, twisting his mind, making his thoughts deranged. *Of course, your thoughts couldn't have been too clear to begin with.*

There was a rustle in the leaves overhead, a creak of a sinewy branch as something rolled itself out of the canopy to level a beady, glossy stare at him. It hung from a long, feathery tail, tiny humanlike hands and feet dangling under its squat body. Its head rolled from side to side, rubbery black lips peeling back in what appeared to be a smile as its skull swayed on its neck in time with its tail.

Back and forth, back and forth …

It's mocking me, Lenk thought, his eyelid twitching. *The monkey is mocking me.* He put a hand to his brow, felt it burn. *Keep it together. Monkeys can't mock. They don't have the sense of social propriety necessary to upsetting it in the first place. That makes sense, doesn't it? Of course it does. Monkeys have no sense of comedic timing. It's not in their nature …*

He stared up, found his tongue creeping unbidden to his cracked lips.

Their juicy ... meaty nature.

His sword was in his hands unbidden, glimmering with the same hungry intent as his fever-boiled eyes, licking its steel lips with the same ideas as he licked his own rawhide mouth.

The monkey swung tantalisingly back and forth, back and forth, bidding him to rise, stalk closer to the tiny beast, his sword hanging heavily. It wasn't until he was close enough to spit on it that the thing looked at him with wariness.

'Don't look at me like that,' he growled. 'This is nature. You sit there and swing like a little morsel on a string, I bash your ugly little face open and slurp your delicious monkey brains off the ground.'

The beast looked at him and smiled a human smile.

'Now, doesn't that seem a bit hypocritical?' it asked in a clear baritone.

Lenk paused. 'How do you figure?'

'Are you not aware of how close the families of beasts and man are?' the monkey asked, holding up its little paws. 'Look at our hands. They both suggest something, don't they? The same fleeting, insignificant, inconsequential lifespan through us both ...'

'We are *not* close, you little faeces-flinger. Mankind was created by the Gods.'

'That sort of renders your point about "nature" a bit moot, doesn't it? Gods or nature?' The monkey waggled a finger. 'Which is it?'

'That *isn't* what I meant and you know it!' Lenk snarled, jabbing a finger at the monkey. 'Look, don't argue with me. Monkeys should *not* argue. That's a rule.'

'Where?'

'*Somewhere*, I don't know.'

'What is the desire to be shackled by rules, Lenk? Why

did mankind create them? Was the burden of freedom too much to bear?'

'And if monkeys shouldn't argue,' Lenk snarled, 'they *damn* well shouldn't make philosophical inquiries.'

'The truth is,' the monkey continued, 'that freedom *is* just too much. Freedom is twisting, nebulous; what one man considers it, another does not. It's impossible to live when no one can agree what living is.'

'Shut up.'

'Thusly, mankind *created* rules. Or, if you choose to believe, had them handed down to them by gods. This wasn't for the sake of any divine creation, of course, but only to make the thought of life less unbearable, so that these thoughts of freedom didn't cripple them with fear.'

'Shut up!' Lenk roared, clutching his head.

'We both know why you want me to be silent. You've already seen this theory of freedom in action, haven't you? When a man is free, *truly* free, he can't be trusted to do what's right. The last time you saw someone that was free—'

'I said ...' Lenk pulled his sword from the ground. 'Shut up.'

'He attacked a giant sea serpent and caused it to sink your boat, killing everyone aboard and leaving you alone.'

'*Shut up!*'

Lenk's swing bit nothing but air, its metal song drowned out by the chattering screeches and laughter of the creatures above. He swung his gaze up with his weapon, sweeping it cautiously across the branches, searching for his hidden opponent.

Back and forth, back and forth ...

'It's very bad form to give up the argument when some-one presents a counterpoint,' Lenk snarled. 'Are you afraid to engage in further discourse?' He shrieked, attacked a low-hanging branch and sent its leaves spilling to the earth. 'You're too good to come down and fight me, is that it?'

'*Now,*' a voice asked from the trees, '*why is it that you solve everything with violence, Lenk? It never works.*'

'It seems to work to shut people up,' Lenk replied, backing away defensively.

'*That's not a bad point, is it? After all, Gariath isn't talking anymore, is he? Then again, neither are Denaos, Dreadaeleon, Asper ... Kataria ...*'

'Don't you talk about them! *Or* her!'

He felt his back strike something hard and unyielding, felt a long and shadowy reach slink down toward his neck. He whirled around, his sword between him and the demon as it stared at him with great, empty whites above a jaw hanging loose.

'Abysmyth ...' Lenk gasped.

The creature showed no recognition, showed nothing in its stare. Its body – that towering, underfed amalgamation of black skin stretched tightly over black bone – should have been exploding into action, Lenk knew. Those long, webbed claws should be tight across his throat, excreting the fatal ooze that would kill him.

'Good afternoon,' Lenk growled.

The Abysmyth, however, did nothing. The Abysmyth merely tilted a great fishlike head to the side and uttered a question.

'Violence didn't work, did it?'

'We haven't tried yet!'

The thing made no attempt to defend himself as Lenk erupted like an overcoiled spring, flinging himself at the beast. *My sword can hurt it*, he told himself. *I've seen it happen.* Even if nothing else could, Lenk's blade seemed to drink deeply of the creature's blood as he hacked at it. Its flesh came off in great, hewed strips; blood fell in thick, fatty globs.

'Is the futility not crushing?' the creature asked, its voice a rumbling gurgle in its rib cage. 'You shriek, squeal, strike – as though you could solve all the woes and agonies that plague yourself and your world with steel and hatred.'

'It tends to solve *most* problems,' Lenk grunted through a face spattered with blood. 'It solved the problem of your leader, you know.' His grin was broad and maniacal. 'I killed her ... it. I took its head. I killed one of your brothers.'

'I suppose I should be impressed.'

'You're not?'

'Not entirely, no. The Deepshriek has three heads. You took only one.'

'But—'

'You killed one Abysmyth. Are there not more?'

'Then I'll take the other two heads! I'll kill every last one of you!'

'To what end? There will always be more. Kill one, more rise from the depths. Kill the Deepshriek, another prophet will be found.'

'I'll kill them, too!' Lenk's snarl was accompanied by a hollow sound as his sword sank into the beast's chest and remained there, despite his violent tugging. '*ALL OF THEM! ALL OF YOU!*'

'And then what? Wipe us from the earth, fill your ears with blood and blind yourself with steel. You will find someone else to hate. There will never be enough blood and steel, and you will go on wondering ...'

'Wondering ... what?'

'Wondering why. What is the point of it all?' The

creature loosed a gurgle. 'Or, more specifically to your problem, you'll never stop wondering why she doesn't feel the way you do … You'll never understand why Kataria said what she did.'

Lenk released his grip on his sword, his hands weak and dead as he backed away from the creature, his eyes wide enough to roll out of his head. The Abysmyth, if it was at all capable of it, laughed at him with its white eyes and gaping jaw.

'How?' he gasped. 'How do you know that?'

'That is a good question.'

The Abysmyth's face split into a broad smile.

Abysmyths can't smile.

'A better one, however,' it gurgled, 'might be why are you attacking a tree?'

'No …'

Words could not deny it, nor could the sword quivering in its mossy flesh. The tree stared back at him with pity, wooden woe exuding through its eyes.

Trees don't have eyes. He knew that. *Trees don't offer pity! Trees don't talk!*

'Steady.' His breathing was laboured, searing in his throat and charring his lungs black inside him. 'Steady … no one's talking. It's just you and the forest now. Trees don't talk … monkeys don't talk … people talk. You're a people … a person.' He rubbed his eyes. 'Steady. Things are hazy at night. In the morning, everything will be clearer.'

'They will be.'

Don't turn around.

But he knew the voice.

It was her voice. Not a monkey's voice. Not a tree's voice. Not a voice inside his head. Her voice. And it felt cool and gentle upon his skin, felt like a few scant droplets of water flicked upon his brow.

And he had to have more.

When he turned about, the first thing he noticed was her smile.

'We never get to watch the mornings, do we?' Kataria asked, sliding a lock of hair behind her long ear. 'It's always something else: a burning afternoon, a cold dawn, or a long night. We never get to sit down at just the right time when normal people get up.'

'We're not normal people,' he replied, distracted.

It was difficult to concentrate with every step she took closer to him. The moonlight clung to her like silk slipped in water, hugging every line of her body left exposed by her short green tunic. Her body was a battle of shadow and silver. He felt his eyes slide in his sockets, running over every muscle that pressed against her skin, counting every shallow contour of her figure.

His gaze followed the line that ran down her abdomen, sliding to the shallow oval of her navel. His stare lingered there, contemplating the translucent hairs that shimmered upon her skin. The night was sweltering.

And she did not sweat a single drop.

When he returned from his thoughts, she was close, nearly pressed against him.

'We aren't,' she replied softly. 'But that doesn't mean we must be expected to not enjoy a morning, does it? Don't we deserve to see the sun rise?'

His breath, previously stale with disease, drew in her scent on a cool and gentle inhale. She smelled pleasant, of leaves on rivers and wind over the sea. His eyelids twitched in time with his nostrils, as though something within him spastically flailed out in an attempt to seize control of his face and turn it away from her.

'This doesn't sound like you.' His whisper was a thunderous echo off her face. 'Not after what you said on the boat.'

'I regret those words,' she replied.

'You never regret anything.'

'Consider my problems,' she said. 'I am just like you. Small, weak and made of the same degenerate meat. I share your fears, I share your terrors . . .'

'This isn't you,' Lenk whispered, his voice hot and frantic. 'This isn't you.'

'And you' – she ignored him as her hands went to the hem of her shirt, her face split apart with a broad smile – 'share my meat.'

His confusion was lost in her cackle, attention seized by her hands as they pulled her tunic up over her head and tossed it aside, exposing the slender body beneath. His eyes blinked wildly of their own volition, and with each flutter of the eyelids, she changed beneath him. Her breasts twitched and writhed under his gaze for three blinks.

By the fourth, they blinked back at him.

Eels, perhaps? Snakes? He could contemplate their nature for one more blink before they launched from her chest, jaws gaping in silent, gasping shrieks forced between tiny, serrated teeth. His own scream, he felt, was nothing more than a fevered sucking of air through the hole that was quickly torn in his throat by their vicelike jaws.

His hands were iron, their bodies were water. He slapped, clawed, raked at them. They chewed, rent, ripped his flesh, brazenly ignoring his desperation. He felt blood weep from his face and mingle with his sweat in thick, greasy tears.

He collapsed under the assault of their teeth and her

shrieking laughter, curling up like a terrified, squealing piglet, marinating. He shivered through his tensed body, expecting the teeth to return at any moment and start raking his back and chewing on his spine.

The agony never came. Nor did the death he was certain would come from having one's face torn off and eaten. He reached up and touched his face, feeling greasy and sticky skin beneath. He looked up.

She, or whatever had been posing as her, was gone.

Shaking, he pulled himself to his hands and feet and crawled to the brook, peering in. His face was red, smeared with blood, but from long lines that raced down his cheeks. Long lines, he thought as he noticed his hands, that perfectly matched the strip of fingernails glutted with skin.

Though it seemed slightly redundant to say so after engaging in philosophical debate with a simian and committing bodily assault on a tree, Lenk felt the need to collapse onto his back and mutter in a feverish whisper.

'You're losing it, friend.'

'*Understatement.*'

Lenk blinked at the voice, coldly familiar after such a long and fiery silence inside his head. He fought the urge to smile, to revel in the return of a more intimate madness. It didn't matter how hard he strained to resist, though; the voice sensed it.

'*Seems pointless to try to resist.*'

'Where were you?' Lenk asked.

'*Always with you.*'

'Then you saw ... all that?'

'*Know what you know.*'

'Your thoughts?'

'*Our thoughts.*'

'You know what I meant.'

'*The point is no less valid. Nothing that has happened tonight was real.*'

'It seemed so—'

'*It wasn't.*'

'How do you figure?'

'*For one, she's dead. Fact.*'

'It's a distinct possibility.'

'*A certainty. Listen to reason.*'

'Greenhair said she didn't find any other bodies. It's perfectly sane to believe the others might be alive.'

'*One would be hard-pressed to take advice on sanity from he who hears voices.*'

'Point.'

'*Referring to your dependence on them. Why bother insisting that they live?*'

'I ... need them. They watch my back, help me during the hard times.'

'*We have each other.*'

'*We* have nothing *but* hard times.'

'*Their deaths are clearly a sign from heaven. We waste time and effort mourning them.*'

'No one's mourning anyone yet. They could still be alive.'

'*We could be back in Toha right now if not for them, the book safe and away where it belongs and our body aching to wreak vengeance upon the next blight that stains the earth. They are a hindrance.*'

'No, they aren't.'

'*It is* them *who needs us. They wouldn't survive without us. They* didn't *survive without us. They are useless.*'

'No, they aren't!'

'*We have our duties. We have our blights to cleanse. The demons fear us, fear what we do to them. We were created*

179

to cleanse the earth of impurities. These companions can only be called thus because they were considerate enough to cleanse themselves for us. They're better off dead.'

'*No, they aren't!*'

The last echoes of the voice vanished, forced out of his mind as he threw himself into a fervent rampage of thought. He sprang to his feet, began to pace back and forth, muttering to himself.

'Think, think ... you don't need that thing. Think ... it's hard to think. So hot ...' He snarled, thumped his temple. '*Think!* This isn't just fever causing the hallucinations. How do you know?' He ran a finger at one of his scratches. 'Well, it makes sense, doesn't it?

'No,' he answered himself. '*Nothing* makes sense.' He gritted his teeth, the effort of thought seeming to cause his brain to boil. 'You were hallucinating strange things, thoughts that never occurred to you before. Why is that odd?

'Because hallucinations are a product of the mind, are they not?' He nodded vigorously to himself. 'You can't hallucinate something you don't know, can you?' He shook his head violently. 'No, not at all. You can't hallucinate monkeys with philosophical ideas or trees with latent desires for peace, or ...

'Kataria.' He blinked, eyes sizzling with the effort. 'She wasn't wearing her leathers when you saw her. You've never seen her without them, have you? No, you haven't. Well, maybe once, but you always think of her in them, don't you?' He threw his head back. 'What does all this say to us? Hallucination of things that are *not* the product of your disease or your mind? Either you're dead and this is some rather infinitely subtle and frustrating hell as opposed to the whole "lakes of fire and sodomised with a pitchfork" thing, or, much more likely …'

'*Someone else is inside your head.*'

His breath went short at the realisation. The world seemed very cold at that moment.

He glanced down at the brook. Eyes cloudy with ice stared back. A thin, frozen sheet crowned the water. As he leaned down to inspect it, it grew harder, whiter, louder.

Ice doesn't talk.

But this one did, voices ensconced between each crackling hiss as the frost formed thicker, denser. They spoke in hushes, as though they groaned from a place far below the ice, far below the earth. And they spoke in hateful, angry whispers, speaking of treachery, of distrust. He felt their loathing, their fury, but they spoke a language he only barely understood in fragments and whispers.

He stared intently, trying to make them out. There was desperation in them, as though they dearly wanted him to hear and would curse him with their hoary whispers if he didn't expend every last ounce of his will to do so.

As far as events that made him question his sanity went, this one wasn't the worst.

'What?' he whispered to it. 'What is it?'

'*Survive,*' something whispered back.

'*Yo! Sa-klea!*'

'*What*?' Lenk whispered.

'*Didn't say anything,*' the voice replied.

'Not you. The ice.' He looked up, glancing about. 'Or … someone.'

'*Dasso?*'

'Hide,' Lenk whispered.

'*Sound advice,*' the voice agreed.

Too weary to run, Lenk limped behind a nearby rock,

snatching up his sword as he did. No sooner had he pressed his belly against the forest floor than he saw the leaves of the underbrush rustle and stir.

Whatever emerged from the foliage did so with casual ease inappropriate for such dense greenery. Its features were indecipherable through the gloom, save for its rather impressive height and lanky, slightly hunched build.

Denaos? He quickly discounted that thought; the rogue wouldn't enter so recklessly. Any further resemblance the creature might have borne to Lenk's companion was banished as it set a long-toed, green foot into the moonlit clearing.

Even as it stepped fully into the light, Lenk was at a loss as to its identity. It stood tall on two long, thick legs, like a man, but that was all the resemblance to humanity it bore. Its scales, like tiny emeralds sewn together, were stretched hard over lean muscle, exposed save for the loincloth it wore at its hips, from which a long, lashing tail protruded.

Its head, large and reptilian, swung back and forth, two hard yellow eyes peering through the darkness; a limp beard of scaly flesh dangled beneath its chin. It held a spear, little more than a sharpened stick, in two clawed hands as it searched the night.

Suddenly, its gaze came to a halt upon Lenk's hiding place. His blood froze; chilled for the stare, frigid for the sudden sight of red splotches upon its chest and hands.

If the creature saw Lenk, it gave no indication. Instead, it swivelled its head back to the underbrush and croaked out something in a gravelly, rasping voice.

'*Sa-klea,*' it hissed. '*Na-ah man-eh heah.*'

The brush rustled again and a second creature, nearly identical to the first, slinked out into the clearing. It swept its gaze about, scratched its scaly beard.

'*Dasso. Noh man-eh.*' It shook its head and sighed. '*Kai-ja.*' It raised two fingers and pressed them against the side of its head in pantomime of ears as it made a show of baring its teeth. '*Lah shict-wa noh samaila.*'

His eyes lit up at the word, spoken with an ire he had felt pass his own lips more than once.

Shict, he thought. *They said 'shict.' Did they find her?*

He saw the ruby hues of the spatters upon their chests. Lenk felt his heart turn to a cold lump of ice.

That chill lasted for all of the time it took him to seize his sword and tighten his muscles. His temper boiled with his brain, fevered rage clutched his head as he clutched his weapon. He made a move to rise, but the pain in his thigh was too great for his fury to overcome. He fell to one knee, biting back a shriek of agony as he did.

'*What was that supposed to be?*' the voice hissed.

'They killed her ... they *killed* her,' he replied through clenched teeth.

'*She is dead.*'

'They killed her ...'

'*Is that important? That she is dead? Or is what is important that they must die?*'

'*Ka-a, ka-a,*' one of the scaly creatures sighed as it knelt by the brook and brought a handful of water to its lips. '*Utuu ah-ka, ja?*'

'*Ka-a,*' the second one apparently agreed, hefting its spear.

'What do you mean?' Lenk muttered.

'*She is dead. We are in agreement. Now vengeance is craved.*'

'And you want to stop me?'

'*Only from getting killed. Vengeance is noble.*'

'Vengeance is pure,' Lenk agreed.

'*Ka-a,*' the first one muttered again, rising to its feet. '*Utuu ah. Tuwa,* uut *fu-uh mah Togu.*'

'*Maat?*' The second looked indignant for a moment before sighing. '*Kai-ja. Poyok.*'

The first one bobbed its bearded head and turned on a large, flat foot. It slinked into the underbrush as it had emerged, like a serpent through water. Its companion moved to follow, taking a moment to sweep its amber gaze over its shoulder. It narrowed its eyes upon Lenk's rock for a moment before it, too, slid into the underbrush.

'*Vengeance ...*' the voice began.

'Requires patience,' Lenk finished.

He huddled up against his rock, snatching up a nearby tuber and chewing on it softly, as much as in memory of Kataria as for sustenance. Tonight, he would rest and recuperate. Tomorrow, he would search.

He would search for Sebast. He would search for his companions. If he found neither, he would search for bodies.

If the lizard-things had left nothing, then he would search for them.

He would find them. He would ask them.

And they would tell him, Lenk resolved, when they all held hands and plummeted into lakes of fire together.

Eleven

THE INOPPORTUNE CONSCIENCE

Reasonable men had qualities that made them what they were. A reasonable man was a man of faith over doubt, of logic over faith, and honesty over logic. With these three, a reasonable man was a man who was prepared for all challenges, with force over weakness, reason over force, and personality over reason.

Assuming he had all three.

Denaos liked to consider himself a reasonable man.

It was around that last bit that he found himself lacking. And, as a reasonable man without honesty, Denaos turned to running.

He hadn't been intending to, of course. The plan, short-sighted as it was, was to get Dreadaeleon far away from whatever was sending him into fits of unconscious babbling with intermittent bursts of waking, wailing pain. They had done that, dragging him into the forest. From there, the plan became survival: find water for Dreadaeleon, food for themselves.

He had liked that plan. He had offered to go searching. It would give him a lot of time out in the woods, alone with his bottle.

Then Asper had to go and ruin everything.

'Hot, hot, hot,' Dreadaeleon had been whispering, as he had been since he collapsed on the beach. 'Hot, hot ...'

'Why does he keep doing that?' Denaos had asked.

'Shock, mild trauma,' Asper had replied. 'It's my second problem.'

'The first being?'

She had glowered at him, adjusting the wizard over her shoulder. 'Mostly that you aren't helping me carry him.'

'We agreed we would divide the workload. You carry him. I scout ahead.'

'You haven't found *anything*.'

Denaos had smacked his lips, glanced about the forest's edge and pointed. 'There's a rock.'

'Look, just take him for a while.' She had grunted, laying the unconscious wizard down and propping him against a tree. 'He's not exactly tiny, you know.'

'As a matter of fact, I didn't know,' Denaos had replied. 'From here, he looks decidedly wee.' He glanced at the dark stain on the boy's trousers. 'In every possible sense of the word.'

'Are you planning on taking him at *all*?' she had demanded.

'Once he dries out, sure. In the meantime, his sodden trousers are the heaviest part of him. What's the problem?'

She had glowered at him before turning to the wizard. 'You shouldn't make fun of him. He's done more for us than we know.' She glanced to the burning torch in the rogue's hand. 'He lit that.'

'I don't think he meant to,' Denaos had replied, rubbing at a sooty spot where he had narrowly avoided the boy's first magical outburst. 'And afterward, he pissed himself and fell back into a coma. As contributions go, I'll call it valued, but not invaluable.'

'He can't help it,' she had growled. 'He's got … I don't know, some magic thing's happened to him.'

'When did this happen again?'

She slowly lowered her left arm from the boy's forehead. 'It's not important.' She frowned. 'He's still got a fever, though. We can rest for a moment, but we shouldn't dawdle.'

'Why not? It's not like he's going anywhere.'

'It'd be more accurate to say,' she had replied, turning a scowl upon him, 'that I'd prefer not to spend any more time in your company than I absolutely have to.'

'As though yours is such a sound investment of my time.'

'At least *I* didn't threaten to kill *you*.'

'Are you still on that?' He had shrugged. 'What's a little death threat between friends?'

'If it had come from Kat or Gariath, it would have meant nothing. But it was *you*.'

The last word had been flung from her lips like a sentimental hatchet, sticking in his skull and quivering. He had blinked, looked at her carefully.

'So what?'

And she had looked back at him. Her eyes had been half-closed, as if simultaneously trying to hide the hurt in her stare and ward her from the question he had posed. It had not been the first time he had seen that stare, but it had been the first time he had seen it in her eyes.

And that was when everything went wrong.

Like any man who had the right to call himself scum, Denaos was religious by necessity. He was an ardent follower of

Silf, the Severer of Nooses, the Sermon in Shadows, the Patron. Denaos, like all of His followers, lived and died by the flip of His coin. And being a God of fortune, Silf's omens were as much a surprise to Him as to His followers. Any man who had a right to call himself one of the faithful would be canny enough to recognise those omens when they came.

Denaos, being a reasonable and religious man, had.

And he had acted, running the moment her back was turned, never stopping until the forest had given way to a sheer stone wall, too finely carved to be natural. He hadn't cared about that; he followed it as it stretched down a long shore, where it crumbled in places to allow the lonely whistle wind through its cracks.

Perhaps, he wondered, it would lead to some form of civilisation. Perhaps there were people on this island. And if they had the intellect needed to construct needlessly long walls, they would certainly have figured out how to carve boats. He could go to them then, Denaos resolved, tell them that he was shipwrecked and that he was the only survivor. He could barter his way off.

But with what?

He glanced down at the bottle of liquor, its fine, clear amber swirling about inside a very well-crafted, very expensive glass coffin. He smacked his lips a little.

Maybe they accept promises …

Or, he considered, maybe he would just die out here. That could work, too. He'd be devoured by dredgespiders, drown in a sudden tide, get hit on the head with a falling coconut and quietly bleed out of his skull, or just walk until starvation killed him.

All decent options, he thought, so long as he would never have to see her again.

'Do you remember how we met?' she had asked, staring at him.

He had nodded. He remembered it.

Theirs had been an encounter of mutual necessity: hers one of tradition, his one of practicality. She was beginning her pilgrimage, to spread her knowledge of medicine to those in need. He was looking to avoid parties interested in mutilating him. Their motives seemed complementary enough.

It wasn't unheard-of for people with either problem to hang on to an adventuring party to get the job done. Though, it had to be said there were a fair bit more adventurers suffering his problem than hers.

They had met Lenk and the creatures he called companions: a hulking dragonman, a feral shict. They had looked strong, capable and in no shortage of wounds to inflict or mend, and so the man and the woman had left the city with them that same day. They had gone out the gate, trailing behind a man with blue eyes, a bipedal reptile and a she-wolf.

She had smiled nervously at him.

He had smiled back.

'We met Dread not long after,' she said. He had thought he could make out traces of nostalgia in her smile ... or violent nausea. Either way, she was fighting it down. 'And suddenly I was in the middle of a pack consisting of a wizard, a monster, a savage and Lenk. I wanted to run.'

So had he. He hadn't been planning on staying with them longer than it took to escape the noose, let alone a year. But he had found something in the companions and their goals that, occasionally, helped people.

Opportunity, however minuscule, for redemption, however insignificant.

'And I couldn't help but think, through it all,' she had sighed, looking up at the moon, '"Thank you, Talanas, for sending me another normal human."' Her frown was subtle, all the more painful for it. 'Back when I had no idea who you were, you seemed to be the only familiar thing I could count on. We were the same, both from the cities, believed in the Gods, knew that, no matter what happened, we had each other to fall back on. So I stayed with them, no matter how much I wanted to run, because I thought you were ...'

A sign, he had thought.

'But you are what you are.' She had looked up to him, something pitiful in her right eye, something desperate in her left. 'Aren't you?'

'No,' he had said.

'What?' she had asked.

'Hot, hot, hot ...' Dreadaeleon had whispered.

And she had turned to the wizard.

And Denaos had dropped the torch and run.

It was a sloppy escape, he knew. She might come looking for him. He hoped she wouldn't, what with him having threatened to cut her open, but there was always the possibility. He knew that the moment he had looked into her eyes and she had looked past his, into something deeper.

She had seen the face he showed her and realised it wasn't his. And in her eyes, the quaver of her voice, he knew she would want to know. She would want to know ... everything.

And he had worked too hard for her to know. Things had become sloppy even before he beat his retreat. She had heard him whisper over her. She had seen his face slip off. She had seen something in him that didn't make her turn away.

He couldn't have that.

Better for it to end this way, he thought as he rested against the wall and took a long, slow sip from the bottle. Better for her to never know anything. If he had stayed, she would keep pushing. If she kept pushing, he would eventually break. He would come to trust her.

And she ... she would begin to relax around him, a man that no one should relax around. She would sigh with contentment instead of frustration. She would stop twitching when she heard him approach. She would give him coy smiles, demure giggles and all the things ladies weren't supposed to give men like him.

She would come to trust him.

And you remember how that turned out last time, don't you?

He blinked. Red and black flashed behind his eyelids. A woman lay beside him and smiled at him, twice: once with her lips, once through her throat.

He shook his head, pulled the bottle to his lips and drank deeply.

It was all very philosophically sound. It was better for her, he thought, that he leave. That was a lie, he knew, but it was a good lie, a sacred lie blessed by Silf. The Patron would be pleased at such a reasonable, philosophical man.

But philosophy, too, required honesty. And like any philosophical man without honesty, Denaos turned once more to drinking.

He was in a haze, but a pleasant one. The lies were making sense now. The logic was clear and, most importantly, he could close his eyes and see only darkness. The drink did that for him. It made everything quiet.

And everything was quiet. The mutter of the ocean was distant and faint. The sound of stone was earth-silent. The clouds moved across the moon without any fuss from the wind that gently hurried them along. Everything was quiet.

So quiet that he heard the whispers with painful clarity.

They began formlessly, babble rising over the grey stone without words. But as they hung over him, they coalesced, formed a spear that plunged into his head with a shriek. Accusations lanced his mind, condemnations tore at his brain, pleas punched a hole in his skull for so much hateful, violent screaming to pour. It was enough to make him drop his bottle and torch alike and fall to his knees.

His dagger was out and the whispering faded. His head pounded, his eyes sought to seal themselves shut. He strained to keep them open as he looked up and caught a glance at the far end of the wall.

And his blood went cold.

Slender fingers gripped the edge. Half a face peered from behind, locks of long and dark hair framing pale cheeks with a broad and horrifically unpleasant smile. An immense eye, round, white and knowing stared at him.

Into him.

'No ...' he whispered.

And the woman said nothing in return.

The whispering came back, grazing his skull and forcing his hands over his ears and his eyes shut tight. They dissipated again and when he was again able to look, she was gone.

He rose, plucking the bottle and dagger up from the sand and sheathing both in his belt as he stared at the space where she had just been.

Hallucination, he told himself, *or delusion or both, wrought by any number of causes, all sinful, of which you have no short-age. Paranoia, drink, sleeplessness. Reasonable, right?*

He nodded to himself.

Whatever the cause, we can agree that ... that wasn't her.

It seemed reasonable.

Then why are we following it?

Because Denaos was a reasonable man, he told himself, a reasonable man with plenty of reasons for not wanting to see a woman who he knew was already dead and none of them convincing enough to turn him back.

He rounded the corner and the land changed in the blink of a bloodshot eye. Forest and shore were conquered by a sprawling courtyard: the stone wall was joined by many, crowding the trees above, smothering the sand below. The walls bore carvings, mosaics twisted in cloaked moonlight, of faces he did not recognise, gods that no one had names for.

Those same gods rose over him, massive statues challenging the moon as they towered over the courtyard. Their robes were stone, their right hands were extended, their faces had long crumbled away and been shattered upon a floor swathed with mist, tendrils of fog rising up to shake spitefully at the moon attempting to ruin its shroud. The stench of salt scraped his throat, seared his lungs. But he could not care for that now.

Not when she was standing there in the centre of the courtyard, staring at him.

It was the same gown she had worn when he saw her last, the simple flowing ivory, now the same colour as her skin, rendering her body and the garment indistinguishable. Her hair was the same, frazzled still, undoubtedly still thick with the scent of streets and people. But he couldn't be sure it was her, not until he took a step closer.

Not until she smiled at him twice.

Once with her mouth.

'*Good morning, tall man*,' she said suddenly, her voice still thick and accented from a tongue that had no taste for lies.

He stared back at her, a silence thick as the death that seeped into the courtyard hanging between them. When he spoke, his words wilted in his mouth.

'I'm sorry,' he said.

She said nothing.

'There was no choice,' he said, weakly. 'I had no choice. There were … obligations, promises.' He swallowed a mouthful of salt. 'Threats.'

She simply smiled back.

'But … I made a choice, anyway. I made it. What would you have done?' His vision was hazy, but not with the fog. Tears were stinging his eyes, their salty stink worse than the ocean's. '*What was I supposed to do?*'

No curses, no weeping, no wailing, no whispers. She simply stared. He stepped forward.

'Please, just talk to me—'

His foot struck something soft. The sound echoed through a conspiracy of silence. He looked down. He blanched.

As though it possessed a particularly morbid sense of humour, the white blanket of mist parted to expose a face twisted in death. Black eyes glistening in a pale, bony face bereft of blood stared up at him, a mouth filled with needles open in a silent scream as wide as the wound in its hairless chest.

A frogman, he recognised, a servant of the horrific Abysmyths. It was dead. It was not alone. Other silhouettes, black against the mist, corpses gripping spears in

194

their chest, clutching wounds in their bellies with webbed hands.

Beside them, their faces contorted in unquiet death, he could see the longfaces, the netherlings. Their purple skin was painted with crimson, their iron and armour stained and battered with the battle that had just raged between them and their pale, hairless foes.

Something about the scene of carnage was unsettling, even beyond the death and decay that permeated the mist. The netherlings were dead, but not from wounds that would have been delivered with the bone spears and knives that the frogmen clutched. The injuries were universal across the dead: each one large and jagged, having wept the last of their blood just hours ago. They had all been made by the same weapons.

And the frogmen hadn't killed any of them.

Then, he narrowed his eyes, *what would make the netherlings turn upon each other?*

'It is the way of the faithless to clean itself of its sins,' a deep, gurgling voice spoke from nearby, 'in blood.'

Denaos whirled, his dagger out. The Abysmyth stared back at him, down at him, from its seven-foot height. Its eyes were vast, white voids. Its mouth hung open in its dead fish head, breathing ragged breaths through jagged teeth. Its towering body, a skeleton wrapped in a skin of shadow, stood tall, four-jointed arms hanging down to its knobby knees.

But the arms did not reach. The legs did not advance. It stared, nothing more.

The massive wedge of metal that was jammed through its chest and which pinned it to the wall might have had something to do with that.

He glanced back to the courtyard. She was gone. He was alone.

Almost.

'Before the Sermonic, the longfaces were confronted,' the Abysmyth croaked. 'Before the Sermonic, they beheld their own sins of faithlessness. She spoke to them in the dark places where they could not hide from her light. She spoke to them, she offered them salvation.'

The Abysmyth craned one of its massive arms up. A longface's corpse hung from its webbed, black claw, a sheen of suffocating ooze coating a face smothered in its grasp.

'You fought the netherlings, then,' Denaos whispered. He glanced at the weapon jammed through its chest. 'Doesn't look like it ended well for you.'

'The faithful can never find joy in the slaughter of lambs,' the Abysmyth gurgled in reply. 'Our solemn task was to follow the longfaces here, to blind their prying eyes, to silence their blasphemous questions.'

'They were searching for something?'

'It is the nature of the faithless to search. They crave answers from everything but She who gives them. In Mother Deep, there is salvation, child.' It extended its other arm, far too long for Denaos' comfort. 'Approach me. My time ends, my service endures. I can save you. I can deliver you from your agonies.'

Denaos took a step back at the sight of the glistening, choking ooze dripping from its claws. He had seen men die from that ooze, drowned on dry land, committed to a watery grave while their feet still touched sand.

'I already have a god,' he said. 'Sorry.'

'God? *God*?' It roared. The wound in its chest sizzled with acidic green venom, the same sickly sheen that coated the blade. He had seen this, too, and what it did to the demons. 'You have *nothing!* Your gods care not for you! They are deaf to your cries! They are deaf to your suffering. To *my* suffering.'

The creature looked up above it, to one of the towering, robed monoliths.

'We remember them. We remember how they were driven to us, uncaring in stone as they are in heaven. The mortals, they prayed to *them*, while *we* were the ones who protected them, who saved them. And now they mock you, child, impassive even as they drain me.'

'The statues ... kill you?'

'Merely remind us,' the Abysmyth said, 'as they will remind you of your own impotence. They take our strength. They take our faithful. It is the way of gods to take.'

'I don't know,' Denaos said. 'I've seen what that poison does to you. You're as good as dead and you can't reach me. Seems the Gods are doing fine, as far as I'm concerned.'

'And do they protect you from the whispers, my child?'

He froze, staring at the demon. As far as he knew, the creatures lacked the ability to smile at all, let alone smugly. But in the darkness, it certainly looked like the thing was trying its damnedest.

'Do they care that you live in torment? Do they hide your prying eyes from visions of your shame? Do they guard your thoughts against the sins that lurk beneath them?'

'Shut up,' Denaos whispered.

'I speak nothing but the truth. The Sermonic speaks nothing but the truth. Find salvation in her whispers.'

'Shut *up*,' he snarled, taking a step backward.

'Where will you run, child?' it croaked. 'Where will you hide? There is no darkness deeper than your soul's. She will find you. She will speak to you. You will hear her. You will rejoice.'

He resolved not to listen any further, resolved to remove himself. He was supposed to be running, to be hiding from her. And from *her*. He took another step backward, sparing only a moment to rub a spiteful glare into the dying demon's wound. He turned.

She was there. He stared directly into her smile.

Both of them.

'*Don't you scream,*' she whispered.

Denaos disobeyed.

His terror echoed through the courtyard, reverberated off every stone, every corpse, ringing clear as a bell. The woman was gone, but the sound persisted. In its wake, a thick silence settled with the mist. The world was quiet.

And he heard the whispers.

Hearyouhearyouhearyou, they emanated in his head, *comingcomingcoming* ...

At the distant edge of the courtyard, he spied a gap in the wall, illuminated by a faint blue light. It pulsed, growing brighter, waxing and waning like an icy heart beating as it grew more vivid, as it drew closer. He held his breath, stared at the light as it came around the gap.

And he beheld the monstrosity from which it emanated.

At first, all he saw was the head: a bulbous, quivering globe of grey flesh tilted upward toward the sky. Black eyes shone like the shrouded, starless void to which they stared. From a glistening brow, a long stalk of flesh snaked, bobbing aimlessly before the creature and terminating in a fleshy sac from which the azure light pulsed.

It glowed mercilessly, refusing to spare him the sight of the creature as it slithered into view. Withered breasts hung from a skeletal rib cage as it pulled the rest of its body – a long, eel-like tail where legs should be – upon thin, emaciated arms.

It wasn't until it emerged fully from behind the gap, until Denaos could see its face in full that he felt fear. But the moment he beheld it, he was frozen. Beneath the fist-sized eyes, skeletal jaws brimmed with teeth like bent needles. They gaped open, exposing another mouth between them, a pair of soft and womanly lips, full and glistening, twitching, moving.

Whispering.

'She comes, child,' the Abysmyth gurgled, its dying voice fast fading. 'She comes to deliver you ... You cannot hide ...'

Denaos disagreed.

Perhaps Silf truly did love him enough to send the clouds roiling over the moon to bathe the courtyard in darkness. Perhaps it was dumb luck. Denaos didn't intend to question it. He flung himself to the earth, finding the thickest corpse in a particularly well-armoured netherling and hunkering down behind her.

He chanced a look, peering up over his cover of flesh and iron, to see the creature, this Sermonic, dragging itself bodily into the courtyard. Its void-like eyes swept the mist as its outer jaws chattered, the sound of teeth clacking against bone heard with every twitch. All the while, the soft and feminine lips pouted behind those jagged teeth, muttering whispers that shifted from formless babble to sharp, honed daggers.

KnowyouarethereKnowyouarethere ...

He heard them keenly now, felt them rattle through his being. The urge to scream rose within him; he nearly choked on it. He averted his eyes, but he could not protect his ears, even as he pressed his hands over them.

WhereareyouWhereareyou ... comeoutcomeoutcomeout ...

He bent low to the ground, felt the blue lantern light

sweep over his position and continue past. The creature chattered, clicked its teeth in ire. He heard its claws rake the ground and pull a massive weight across the courtyard.

He dared to look up and saw the creature continue across the ground, winding between corpses, sweeping its light over the mist. Behind it, lights trailed, flashing the same blue glow that emanated from its stalk.

HearyouHearyou ... NoisythoughtsNoisyNoisy ... Knowyour-thoughtsKnowKnow ...

The whispers echoed in his mind, felt like sand on his skull. He could feel his brain twitch under them, as though the creature's claws followed them and plucked at every thought inside his head like harp strings.

Sorrowsorrowsorrow ... Hatehatehate ...

The creature craned its neck about, its lantern lighting up its inner lips in a morbid smile.

Knivesknives...Darkdarkdark...Screamingscreamingscreaming ...

He blinked and the images flashed behind his eyes once more. He saw each whisper painted on his lids, saw the knife coming down and beheld a red blossom.

Bloodbloodblood ... soMUCHbloodblood ...

He forced his eyes open and saw the creature begin to angle its unwieldy body around with some difficulty. Seeing an opportunity, he crept from one body to another, slinking low through the mist. His dagger remained far from his hand; striking the creature was not on his mind. Escape was.

He spied a rent in the nearby walls. He could make it, he thought; he could slip through it, vanish in the greenery. If the creature didn't see him now, it certainly wouldn't in the forest. From there, he could make his way to shore, he could escape.

All he had to do was reach it and—

Killedherkilledherkilledher ...

He froze.

Watchedherdiediedie ...

He fought to keep his eyes open.

Poorgirlgirl ... lovedyoulovedloved ...

It didn't help. He could see the images flashing before him now, even as his eyes stung with salt and went dry.

Killedherkilledherkilledher ...

A scream began to well up in his throat, carried on a boil of tears.

Killedkilledkilled ...

His hand fumbled for the bottle, fingers too weak to grasp it. He felt the light sweep toward him, settle on the corpse he lay behind.

KILLEDKILLEDKILLEDHER ...

He opened his mouth. A choked whimper emerged.

'Denaos?'

Instantly, the whispers retreated. He felt his mind relax, his body go slack. The images left his mind, just as the light left him. He watched it through blurry vision as it swept along the courtyard, heading for another hole in the wall through which the orange light of a torch flickered and a voice emerged.

'Are you in here?' Asper called.

Relief died in his heart. He looked up and saw the creature's twin jaws smile a pair of horrific grins as the light waned. The last thing he saw of the beast was its chattering teeth as the lantern's blue light dimmed.

And then died.

This is your chance.

It was a foul thought to think, he knew, but it was true. He could escape now. He could flee.

And she would die.

But what could he do? The creature, whatever it was, was clearly too strong for her, or for him.

But together ...

No, no. He thumped his head. There was no telling what the thing was, if it could even be killed, by a hundred or two. Where was the sense in offering it up two victims instead of one? Where was the sense in lingering behind? What would be the point of it all?

He sucked in a breath. A thought came to him, clear and concise.

Redemption, however insignificant.

He clenched his teeth and reached for his bottle.

She shouldn't be surprised, Asper told herself. She should have expected this; even something as simple as going to get water, even something as noble as easing a companion's fever was beyond the rogue. The ability to perform any act that wasn't completely selfish was beyond Denaos as a matter of nature. She knew this, as she knew she shouldn't be surprised.

Let alone hurt.

Every step, she scolded herself with a fury that burned as hot as the torch in her hand. To think that she had told him she had once relied on him, even in such a roundabout manner as she had. Undoubtedly he relived that moment, those words, revelled in them, laughed at how much power he had held over her.

She loathed him for it, but for every ounce of scorn she spared for him she took two more for herself. She was the one who had told him. And even if she told herself that she had left Dreadaeleon behind to find water herself, she knew that she searched for the rogue with equal intent.

As for what that intent was, she thought as she looked at the torch thoughtfully, she would know when she found him.

So raptly did her loathing capture her attention that she hadn't even seen where she had wandered. The rock wall she had followed had become a decaying ruin, rife with mist and silence. She swept her torch about; the darkness of the night drank her fire and offered only inky blackness in exchange.

She had taken three more steps into the gloom before the thought occurred, not for the first time, that she was wasting her time. To go searching for a man whom she had once seen evade scent hounds while doused in cherry liquor and whorestink was folly enough, but to expend so much effort on a man for whom getting doused in cherry liquor and whorestink was a frequent occurrence was simply stupid.

Let him cling to the power she had so foolishly offered him, she thought, let his laughs be black. She turned about, held her chin high and tried not to care.

The wind picked up, sending the mist roiling about her ankles and her torch's light flickering. It carried with it a stink of salt and the faded coppery stench of dried blood. The moon shifted overhead, exposing a scant trace of light over her.

And with it, a shadow.

She turned and beheld the monolith, towering over her. She did not recognise it, she did not know it. But something inside her did. Her left arm began to sear with pain, to pulse angrily. She let out a shriek, holding it tightly against her body, not daring to drop her torch. Instead, she raised the light to the statue, exposing it to fire.

A great robed figure stared back at her. Its left arm

was extended, robe open to expose a thin, skeletal limb. She recognised the arm. Just as the arm recognised itself, throbbing angrily at its stone reflection. Biting back pain, she stared farther up at the statue. Beneath the stone hood, a skull grinned back at her.

And spoke.

Cursedcursedcursed ...

Her eyes widened at the sound inside her head that echoed into her heart. She whirled about, searching for the source of the whispers.

Godsabandonedyouabandonedyou ... *hateyouhateyouhateyou* ...

'No,' she whispered. She clenched her teeth as thoughts came racing back to her, images of two young girls in a temple, a flash of bright, agonising red, and one young girl walking out. '*No.*'

Cursedcursedcursed ... *killedherkilledher* ... *TaireTaireTaire* ...

It was with the mention of that name that the pain began. Her arm ached, burned with an unbearable agony that pulsed in time with the beat of her heart.

The torch fell from her hand and its light was smothered in the mist. But even as darkness fell upon her in a thick cloak, Asper's world was still bright and blindingly crimson. The arm twitched, pulsed beneath her sleeve, and she could feel its heat through the cloth. She writhed, collapsed to her knees and moaned into the darkness.

'Stop ... *please* stop,' she whimpered, unable to hear her own voice.

TaireTaireTaire ... *deaddeaddead* ... *gonegonegone* ... *nothingleftnothingnothing* ...

'Why?' she wailed. 'Why, Talanas? Why? What did I do this time?' She held her arm up to the sky and shrieked. '*WHAT DO YOU WANT?*'

Godsgodsgods ...

The whispers came now, slowly and brimming with a bitterness where before there was only sharp malice.

Don'tcaredon'thearwon'tlistencan'thelparen'ttherewon'thelp-can'thelp ...

And slowly, the pain in her arm began to abate, to subside from agonising throb to dull and steady ache. Her pain began to seep out of her in hot breaths. The whispers, however, continued.

Weren'ttherenottheredidn'tlistendidn'thelpabandonedleftus-cursedusloathedus ...

She should escape. She should run.

But Denaos ...

No. She pushed him out her mind with hate, hatred for herself for thinking of *him* even as her body was racked and her mind on fire, for thinking of him when her arm was awakened. She fought the whispers, tried not to listen to them as they became moans in her ears.

LeftusMotherlovesustellsusspeakstousgodswon'tgodsdon'tgods-gonegonegonegonegone ...

She looked to the rent in the wall through which she had come and took two steps before becoming aware of the fact that she could see it. In an instant, she knew that made no sense; the moon was shrouded, the torch was dead.

Where had the blue light come from?

HatehatehatehatehateHATEHATEHATEHATEHATE ...

A low, chattering sound rose from behind her.

She whirled, and the scream was drowned from her as two mouths of teeth and lips opened as one, emitting a screech that overwhelmed all other senses. Pain, fear, instinct were rendered mute before the wailing. Her voice followed a moment after as she felt a pair of cold hands wrap about her throat.

She had no screams to offer the sight that awaited her,

had barely the clarity of mind to take in the full extent of the creature. Its lantern swayed between them on a long and glistening stalk, bathing its bulbous head in waves of light and shadow. She saw a pair of mouths – twisted and sharp, soft and female – torn between gaping, toothy growl and broad, wicked smile.

It did not occur to Asper to fight, to struggle against the creature or even to scream. The abomination transfixed her with horror, rendering her capable only of staring in gaping, mind-numbed abhorrence. She was aware of being lifted from the ground, drawn toward its glistening, jagged outer teeth. She was aware of the creature's vast void-like eyes dilating into tiny pinpricks of blackness against froth-coloured whites. But she was aware of nothing else.

Certainly not the shadow rising up behind the creature.

Both priestess and abomination were made keenly aware of Denaos' presence in a blink of silver, however, as the man's knife flashed out of the gloom and sank deeply into the creature's collarbone. The beast growled, rather than shrieked; more annoyed than furious. It twisted its neck to see its attacker.

Denaos pulled his blade free from the creature, and at the sight of blood pouring from the wound, Asper's senses returned to her with a fury. She began to hit, kick at the creature, pulled at its webbed claws and drove her feet into soft, rubbery flesh. The thing turned its attention to her and snarled, offended by her sudden vigour, as it tightened its grip on her throat.

Her fury was choked from her in an instant, her life quick on its heels. Denaos was quicker; his knife came up again, digging into the creature's armpit, and twisted. The beast roared this time, but there wasn't nearly enough blood to justify agony. It tossed Asper aside, sent her skidding through the mist, and turned upon Denaos, black voids bubbling with rage.

Asper pulled herself from the earth, ignored the stench of death on the ground, and looked toward the battle unfurling.

Denaos did not cringe, did not turn and run. His form was smooth and flowing, an ink stain on the mist, as he brought his weapon back up to face the creature. It, too, flowed, body swaying from side to side, its lantern illuminating only one combatant each moment.

She saw the fight in flashes of blue light. The creature twitched, hurled itself forward, claws outstretched. Denaos flowed backward; his blade leapt. The thing's lantern erupted in a burst of blue coupled by twin shrieks as it drew back, clutching a webbed hand with three fingers of steel jammed through the palm.

The lantern glowed white-hot for a moment as the creature recoiled. Then, the flashes of light became bursts and the battle raged in the darkness between them.

It lunged. Denaos reached for his belt. There was the sound of glass shattering, the odour of liquor. It growled, stretched jaws open, lashed a hand out. There was a shriek, this one male and agonisingly human. There was the sound of something heavy hitting the floor.

And then, silence.

The light returned slowly. It waxed to a pinprick; she could see it drift down to a man's face contorted in pain, breath sucked in through teeth clenched. It became the size of a fist and she saw a grey webbed hand, stained dark with blood and dripping with whisky, reach down to grab the tall man by a throat smeared with green-stained claw marks.

When it bloomed, Asper stared at Denaos hanging from the creature's choking grasp.

She rose to help him, but found her body fighting between her commands and the throbbing pain in her arm. She whimpered, clutched it, tried to stagger to her feet.

'Not now, not now, not now,' she whined, 'please, just let me ... just this once. *Please!*'

'Hot,' a voice answered in reply. 'Hot ... hot ...'

She felt Dreadaeleon beside her, the fever of his body seeping out of his glowing red eyes. His hair hung about his face, coat about his body as he swayed precariously on overtaxed feet. He stared at the monstrosity and the rogue without acknowledgement for the latter's imminent demise. Instead, he merely raised a hand, a small circle of orange glowing upon his palm.

'Hot,' he whispered, eyes suddenly blossoming into burning red flowers. '*HOT!*'

The word that followed next, she did not hear. But she did see the circle become a spark, flickering and twisting like a rose petal as it flew from his palm and wafted with an orange glow toward the two combatants. The creature took no notice of it as it sizzled over the mist, nor did it look away from its victim as the little spark drifted up and came to a rest with a hiss upon the thing's whisky-soaked brow.

HothothothotHOTHOTHOTHOTHOTHOT ...

The whispers came in short, staccato shrieks. Denaos was dropped, forgotten as the creature erupted into flames. It writhed in a pillar, blue light sputtering out in the inferno that consumed it. Asper thought she could see something in its figure, now illuminated in the blaze, that seemed vaguely familiar. The shape of its torso, a mockery of womanly figures, perhaps, or the feathery gills that were burnt away like sticks of incense as it hurled itself to the earth.

She wasn't about to try to get a closer look as the horror pulled its body across the ground, leaving a trail of ash behind it. Its wails, its whispers left her mind as the creature left the courtyard, pulling its burning body through a hole in the wall to disappear into the night.

Asper watched it for but a moment before her attentions were brought back to the scrawny boy beside her, legs giving out beneath him.

'Did it ... ?' Dreadaeleon muttered as he collapsed onto his back. 'Saved again ...'

She knelt beside him, felt his brow. The fever was no worse that she could tell; it was simply exhaustion stacked upon exhaustion. That simple spark had pushed him to a brink he was nowhere near well enough to tread upon. And like the spark, he flickered. He needed water; he needed rest.

'Stay ...' he whispered, reaching for her. 'Hot ... hurts ... but I did it ... I saved ...'

'I know you did,' she replied, smoothing the hair from his brow. 'And I'll be here, but I have to help Denaos, too.'

'Denaos?' His eyes and mouth twisted into anger. '*Denaos?* He did *nothing*! It was me! I saved you! *I'm* the hero!' He tried to rise, but fell back, gasping. 'I'm the ... the ...'

'Please, Dread,' she pleaded as she laid him back down to the stones. 'Just a moment.'

'Assholes,' he muttered as his eyes closed, mouth still contorted in a snarl. 'Both of you.'

No time to heed or take offence, she rose from his side and hurried to Denaos'. Pulling his head up to her lap, she could see the wound in his neck, the seeping green venom. She checked him over quickly, hands flying across his body. His breathing was swift and laboured, but steady. His muscles were tensed, but neither turning to jelly nor hardening with preemptive rigour. His pulse raced, but was there. He was wounded and poisoned, but he wasn't going to die.

Because of her.

'Gone,' he whispered.

'Yeah,' she said, 'it ran away.'

'I meant my whisky,' he croaked out through a dry mouth.

'Yeah. Sorry.'

'Not your fault.' He grinned. 'Not completely, anyway.' He tried to muster a brave laugh, but wound up cringing. 'It hurts.'

'The wound's not the worst I've seen,' she said with a sigh. 'I think you might—'

'Last rites.'

'What?'

'Last rites.'

'No, you're not—'

'I don't want to die without absolution.'

The hand he laid on her arm was gentle. Her arm throbbed beneath his touch, rejecting the warmth of another human being. She fought the urge to tear it away.

'I don't want to die,' he whispered.

She knew she couldn't offer him last rites; he wasn't going to die. There were no signs of a fatal poisoning; the claws had missed his jugular, and the venom likely wouldn't do much more than hurt terribly. For all the wretched things he had done, he was going to live … again.

To offer last rites would be deception, a sin.

She could have told him that.

'Absolution,' she said instead, in a gentle voice, 'requires confession.'

'I ...' His eyelids flickered with his trembling words. 'I – I killed her.'

'Killed who?'

'She was ... it ... so beautiful. Just cut her ... no pain, no screaming. Sacred silence.'

'Who was it, Denaos?' Urgency she did not understand was in the quaver of her voice and the tension of her hands. '*Who?*'

The next words he spoke were choked on spittle. The agony was plain in his eyes, as was the alarm as he looked past her shoulder, gaping. He raised a finger to the cleft tops of the walls. She followed the tip of it, saw them there, and stared.

And in the darkness, dozens of round, yellow eyes stared back.

Twelve

INSTINCTUAL SHAME

Semnein Xhai was not obsessed with death. She was a Carnassial, proud of the kills she had made to earn the right to be called such, but only those kills. Deaths wrought by hands not her own were annoying. They left her with questions. Questions required thinking. Thinking was for the weak.

And the weak lay at her feet, two cold bodies of the longfaces before her.

'How?' she snarled through jagged teeth.

'Perhaps they were ambushed,' Vashnear suggested beside her.

The male held himself away from the corpses, hands folded cautiously inside his red robe as he surveyed them dispassionately. His long, purple face was a pristine mask of boredom, framed by immaculately groomed white hair. Only the thinnest twitch of a grin suggested he was more than a statue.

'It is not as though females are renowned for awareness,' he said softly.

'They're renowned for *not* dying like a pair of worthless, stupid weaklings,' she growled. 'What did they die from?' she muttered, letting her voice simmer in her throat. After a moment, she turned to the female beside her. '*Well?*'

The female, some scarred, black-haired thing with

a weakling's bow grunted at Xhai before stalking to the corpses. She surveyed them briefly before tugging off her glove. Xhai observed her fingers, three total with the lower two fused together, with contempt. Her particular birth defect, like all other low-fingers, relegated her to using the bow and thus relegated her to contempt.

Her three fingers ran delicately down the females' corpses, studying the savage cuts, the wicked bruises and particularly well-placed arrows that dominated the purple skin left bare by their iron chestplates and half-skirts. After a moment, she nodded, satisfied, and rose up. She turned to Xhai and snorted.

'Dead,' she said.

'Well done,' Vashnear muttered, rolling his milk-white eyes.

'How?' Xhai growled.

The low-finger shrugged. 'Same way we found the others. Smashed skulls, torn flesh, few arrows here and there. Somethin' came up and got 'em right in the back.'

'I told Sheraptus you shouldn't be allowed to roam without one of us accompanying,' Vashnear muttered. 'If females are incapable of thinking that someone might *ambush* them in a deep forest, then they're certainly incapable of finding anything of worth to use against the underscum.'

'And what would you have done?' Xhai asked.

His grin broadened as his eyes went wide. The crimson light leaking from his stare was reflected in his white, jagged smile.

'Burn down the forest. Remove the issue.'

'Master Sheraptus said not to. It will infringe on his plans.'

'Sheraptus believes himself infallible,' Vashnear said.

'He is.'

'And yet he wastes three females for each hour we waste looking for means to slaughter the underscum when we have always had the answer.' He pulled a pendant out from under his robe, the red stone attached to it glowing in time with his eyes. 'Kill them all.'

'That won't work against their queen. The Master says so.'

'He cannot *know* that.'

'He has his ways.'

'And they are not working.'

Slowly, Xhai turned a scowl upon him. 'The Master is not to be questioned.'

'Males have no masters,' Vashnear replied coldly. 'Sheraptus is my equal. You are beneath him and beneath *me*.'

'I am his First Carnassial,' Xhai snarled back. 'I lead his warriors. I kill his enemies. His enemies question him.'

Vashnear lofted a brow beneath which his stare smouldered, the leaking light glowing angrily for a moment. It faded, and with it so did his grin, leaving only a solemn face.

'Our search continues,' he said softly. 'I've sent Dech out to find further evidence. We will find her before we lose a Carnassial instead of a pair of warriors.' He walked past her, his step slowing slightly as he did. 'Carnassials are killers. Nothing more. Sheraptus knows this.'

She turned to watch him go. At her belt, her jagged gnawblade called to her, begging her to pluck it free and plant it in his back. On her back, her massive, wedged gnashblade shrieked for her to feed it with his tender neck flesh. Her own fingers, the middle two proudly fused together in the true mark of the Carnassial, humbly suggested that strangulation might be more fitting for him.

But Sheraptus had told her not to harm him.

Sheraptus was not to be questioned.

'What do we do with the dead ones?' the low-finger beside her asked.

'How far behind us is the sikkhun?' Xhai asked.

'Still glutting itself on Those Green Things we found earlier.'

'It'll still be hungry. It fights better when it's been fed.' She glanced disdainfully at the corpses. 'Leave them.'

The low-finger followed her scowl to Vashnear and snorted. 'He's weak. Even Dech says so. His own Carnassial ...' She chuckled morbidly. 'If whatever's killing us kills him, no one will weep.'

Xhai grunted.

'Who knows?' the female continued. 'Maybe if we don't come back with him, we'll get a reward from the Saharkk.'

Xhai whirled on her, saw the distant, dreamy gaze in her eyes.

'What did you call him?'

'Saharkk?' The low-finger shrugged, walking past her. 'It means the same thing.'

She had taken two steps before Xhai's hand lashed out to seize her by the throat. Xhai heard the satisfying wheeze of a windpipe collapsing; she was right to listen to her fingers.

'He wants to be called *Master*,' Xhai growled. 'And *I* don't share rewards.'

The low-finger shrieked, a wordless, breathless rasp, as Xhai pulled harshly on her neck and swung her skull toward the nearest tree.

Kataria felt the bones shatter, the impact coursing through the bark and down her spine. She kept her back against the tree, regardless, not moving, not so much as starting at the sound of the netherling's brutality. She held her voice and her breath in her throat, quietly waiting for it to be over.

But she had met Xhai before, in Irontide. She could feel the old wounds that the Carnassial had given her begin to ache with every moment she heard the longface's grunts of violent exertion. She knew that when it came to Xhai, nothing painful was ever over quickly.

Her victim's grunts lasted only a few moments. The sound that resembled overripe fruit descending from a great height, however, persisted.

The sound of twitching, chittering, clicking caught her attention. She glanced at the tremendous roach standing before her, its feathery antennae wafting in her direction as it studied her through compound eyes. Long having since recognised the oversized pest for what it was, she did nothing more than raise her finger to her lips. Futile, she thought; even if the roach could understand the gesture, she doubted it could make enough noise to be heard over Xhai's brutality.

Apparently, the roach disagreed.

Its rainbow-coloured carapace trembled with the flutter of wings as it turned about and raised a bulbous, hairy abdomen to her. Her eyes widened as the back of its body opened wide.

And sprayed.

Screaming was her first instinct as the reeking spray washed over her. Cursing was her second. Turning around, dropping her breeches and spraying the thing right back quickly fought its way to the fore, but she rejected it as soon as she felt the tree still against her back.

At the other side, a body slumped to the earth with a

splash as it landed in a puddle of something Kataria had no wish to identify. The sound of Xhai's growl and her heavy iron boots stomping off quickly followed and faded in short order.

Kataria allowed herself to breathe and quickly regretted it as the roach's stench assaulted her nose. The insect chittered, satisfied, and scurried into the forest's underbrush. Still, she counted herself lucky that the only thing to locate her was a roach.

A roach that sprays from its anus, she reminded herself, wiping the stuff from her face. *And the longfaces almost found you that time.*

She grunted at her own thoughts; the longfaces were crawling over the island, roaming the forest and its edges in great, noisy droves. They were searching, she had learned from the few times they deigned to speak in a language she could understand. For what, she had no idea and she didn't care. She was on a search of her own, one that could not be compromised by the addition of bloodthirsty, purple-skinned warrior women.

The Spokesman stick in her hand reminded her of it, with a warm assurance that it had tasted many human bones before.

She stared down at it contemplatively. The *s'na shict s'ha*, her father said, often claimed that their famed sticks earned their names for the fact that each one possessed the faintest hints of the Howling. The trees they were carved from drank deeply of shictish blood spilled in their defence. They carried the memories of the dead, perpetual reminders of the duties that every shict carried.

As Kataria stared at the white feather tied to it, she suspected the power of the Spokesman was likely a lot simpler than that.

Inqalle infested her mind, in words and thoughts alike. She had slipped in on the Howling, sank teeth into Kataria's thoughts, and she could still feel them there.

But this was not such an awful thing.

Inqalle's words only persisted because truth was always like venom: once injected, it could not be removed until the proper steps had been taken to cure it. Kataria knew this, just as she knew that what Inqalle had said was true.

For too long had she been comfortable telling herself she was a shict while acting so unlike one. How could any shict call herself such when she stared for hours over the sea, watching ... ?

No. Hoping, she corrected herself. *You were* hoping *that one of them would come up on shore and you could go back to the way things were. Those days are over. You always wanted them to be over, right?*

She didn't answer herself.

Maybe ... this is *a gift from Riffid,* she told herself. *Maybe this* is *how you prove yourself to Inqalle. No, not to Inqalle. To yourself.* She shook her head. *No, not to yourself ...*

She looked down at the white feather, frowned.

Not just to yourself.

The Spokesman stick was heavy with purpose, eager to be used upon unsuspecting human skulls. It reminded her why this had to be the way. It reminded her of the sensations she had felt in the company of her companions. *Former companions,* she corrected herself.

They had infected her, deafened her to the Howling. They had taken something from her. This was how she would take it back.

She had found their trail earlier. She could follow it, descend upon them when they weren't paying attention. Two swift cracks at the base of the skull. They would die immediately. They wouldn't be able to ask her why. She could do it, she told herself. If she could avoid the long-faces' patrols, she could sneak up on them. She could kill them.

If you could, the thought entered her mind involuntarily, *you would have done it long ago.*

She shook her head, growled.

Something in the forest growled back.

She froze, hearing the footsteps. Her ears twitched, angling from left to right, absorbing each noise. Heavy feet fell upon the earth with the ungainly disquiet of a predator glutted. Nostrils drew in deep breaths, sniffing about the woods. The growl, a deep chest-born noise, became a shrill cackle. Gooseflesh grew upon her body.

The sikkhun, she thought. *They said something about a sikkhun.* She swallowed hard. *What the hell is a sikkhun?*

And in the sounds that followed, she realised she didn't want to know. She heard a sharp ripping sound; the stench of blood filled her nostrils. Slurping followed, meat rent from bone and scooped into a pair of powerful jaws. Blood dripped softly, hitting the ground with the sound of fat raindrops. A bone snapped, crunched, was sucked down.

And with every breath it could spare, the thing let loose a short, warbling cackle.

She folded her ears against her head, unable to listen anymore. Slinking on her hands and feet, she slid into the underbrush, leaving the sikkhun to its gruesome feast.

Yes, she thought without willing, *so gruesome. Good thing you're about to do something as civil as murdering your companions, you weak little—*

She folded her ears further, shutting them to all sounds, within and without, as she softly crept away.

*

Tracks told stories.

This was the accepted thought amongst her people. A person spoke to the earth through his feet, unable to lie or hide through his soles. The earth had a long memory, remembered what it was told. Earth remembered. Earth told shict. Shict remembered.

Kataria remembered finding his tracks in the forest, almost a year ago.

Long, slow strides, she recalled, heavy on the heels and the toes alike. He was a man who walked in two different directions: striving to go forward, always held back.

She had tracked him, then, certain that she was going to kill him. She tracked him now, certain that she had to.

And what's different this time? she asked herself. *You went after him, attempting to kill him. You wound up following him for a year.*

Because, she told herself, that was a time when she did not know what it was to be a shict. This time, she knew. She would prove it.

She had found their tracks shortly after. The earth was moist and dry at once, torn between whether it wished to continue living or not. It made the stories hard to hear. Those she recognised in the tracks were simple tales: anguish, pain, misery, confusion, hunger. But those were common enough, especially to those humans she had once called companions.

No matter. They all had to die, eventually. The other humans would be a nice warm-up before she stalked and killed her true quarry. She would have liked to have started with Lenk, though, suspecting that he would be the hardest to kill. He was the most agitated, the most paranoid, the most cautious.

Oh, and that's *why he's going to be hard to kill?* she asked herself. *Right. He's just so crafty and clever. This entire 'stalking' is a farce. If you showed up in front of him and waved, he'd wave back and smile and say how good it was to see you as you clubbed his brains out.*

No, she told herself, he liked her, but probably not *that* much.

Right, she agreed with herself, *but the point is, you know this is just a stalling tactic. Pretending to stalk him? Pretending to track him? Go run around the forest screaming his name if you think he's alive. Wait for him to come out and then embrace him and then crush his neck. If you* really *wanted to kill him, you wouldn't even have to try. But ...*

She snarled inwardly, opened her ears wide to let the sounds of the forest drown out her own thoughts.

You also know this forest is dead. Nothing's going to make you stop thinking, dimwit.

She sighed. No wind sighed back. And from the dead wind, no trees rustled in response. And from the quiet trees, no animals cried out in response. And all around her, the verdant greenery and blue skies and bright morning sunshine yielded no sound, no life.

Barren forests weren't unheard of. Plants, inedible and intolerable to animal palates, often thrived where those on two and four legs could not.

Except for roaches, apparently. She flicked away a dried trace of anal sputum.

But there was something different about this forest, this silence. This silence lingered like a pestilence, seeping into her skin, reaching into her ears, her lungs. It found the sound of her breath intolerable, the clamour of her twitching muscles unbearable. It sought to drive the wind from her stomach, to still the noisy blood in her veins.

She shook her head, thumped it with the heel of her

hand, scolded herself for being stupid. Silence was uncomfortable, nothing more. It wasn't a disease. *He* was. *He* was the one that needed to be cured, not *her*. It was *him* that was the problem.

So the problem is him, she told herself. *That makes sense. That's what Inqalle said. The greenshicts ... no, no. They're the s'na shict s'ha, remember? Greenshicts are what humans call them. The problem is him. Kill him and you're a shict, right? Right.*

Because that was what a shict was, she told herself, pressing forward and following the tracks. A shict killed humans. That was what shicts did. Her father said so. Inqalle said so. Her mother ...

Her step faltered. The earth heard her hesitation.

Mother, she told herself, *asked you what a shict was.*

She stared down at the Spokesman stick in her hand, at the white mourning feather tied to it.

And you said ...

Her ears twitched, still listening even if her mind was not. They rose up on either side of her head, slowly shifting from side to side as they heard a sound.

Water?

She followed it, the roar of rushing liquid growing more thunderous with every step. She glanced down at the earth; the tracks continued to it, though the earth still refused to yield the speaker of their stories, even as it became moister.

Soon, the ground turned to mud beneath as forest and river met in battle. The trees refused to yield, leaning in close over the great blue serpent that slithered through the earth. It flowed swiftly, fed by a distant waterfall thundering down a craggy cliff face not far from where she stood at its bank.

Not ten feet away from her, where the water was at its most shallow, an island of earth and stone rose like a rocky pimple. Long and wide, it defied the nature of the river with its stone-paved floors, crumbling pillars and the occasional vine-decorated statue. But the forest challenged even this, those trees and underbrush that had managed to grow over it encroaching upon it, obscuring the finer points of its decay as it strangled the island with leafy hands.

Odd, she thought, but not the oddest part about this place.

She surveyed the river, eyes narrowing. Certainly it sounded like a river ought to. The water was clear and, at a glance, clean enough and suitable for drinking. Her dry lips begged her to drink, her ears told her it was safe. Only her nose rejected it.

The scent of freshness was nowhere present in the air; the aroma of growing things fed by the flow was overwhelmed by a reek that lurked just beneath.

But surely, water was water. Even the water couldn't be tainted if it caused such plants to grow. There was no harm, she told herself, in simply taking a drink. It would enable her to hunt farther, faster, and do what must be done.

She glanced down at the water, smacking her lips. Her nostrils quivered.

Still, she thought, glancing over to the waterfall, *no sense in not taking a drink directly from the source.*

She stared up, wondering exactly where the river came thundering from. And, atop the great crags of the cliff, she found an answer pouring from great, skeletal jaws.

The skull, resembling something of a massive, fleshless fish, stared back down at her through empty eye sockets as it hung precariously over the edge of the cliff, wide as a boulder, water weeping through every empty void in its bleached surface. Liquid poured from its great, toothsome jaws, burst from each empty black eye, weeping and vomiting in equal measure.

Not that such imagery *didn't* unnerve her, but it paled in comparison to the fact that she had seen this skull before, in a much smaller form. But she had seen it, cleaned of shadowy black skin, sockets where vast, empty white eyes had once been. She remembered the teeth, she remembered the jaws, she remembered the gurgling, drowning voice that went with them.

An Abysmyth. She was staring at a demon's skull, far more massive than any she had ever thought possible.

But it was just a skull, she thought. Whatever demon it had belonged to was dead now and there was no need for her to fear. Nor was there a need to wonder where it had come from. She had tracks to follow, tracks that had to have led through the shallows, over the island and onto the opposite bank.

Rolling her breeches up to her knees, she carefully waded in. The current was swift, but not deep enough to drag her under. Still, it was a slow and steady pace that carried her across, mercilessly leaving her time to be with her thoughts.

If there are *demons here …* she thought. *I mean, I know that one's dead and all, but if they're here … you're actually doing them a kindness, aren't you? You'd be killing them before they could have their heads chewed off. Of course, you'd be eaten moments later, wouldn't you? But that's fine, so long as they die before that happens. That's just the kind of selfless person you are, right?*

She laughed bitterly.

Sure. I'm certain they'll see it my way.

Her foot caught. A root reached up from muddy ground

to tangle her. She cursed, reached down to free herself and found no rough and jagged tuber. Rather, what caught at her ankle was smooth and came easily out of the water and in her hand, the mud of the riverbed sloughing off to land in the flow like globs of great brown fat.

She might have thought how fitting that metaphor was, if it weren't for the fact that she was currently staring at a fleshless, skeletal arm in her hand.

Before she could even warn herself against the dangers of doing so, she looked down.

And the small, rounded human skull looked back up, grinning and politely asking for its arm back.

With a sneer, she obliged, dropping the appendage and scurrying out of the water. Suddenly, the vague reek made itself known to her, the familiarity of it cloying her nostrils.

The water was rife with the scent of corpses.

'Still alive.'

The sound of a voice beside the one in her head caused her to whirl about, tense and ready to fight or flee. And while she breathed out a scant relieved exhale at the sight of red flesh stretched over muscle before her, she didn't outright discount either option.

Gariath, for his part, didn't seem particularly interested in what she might do. Perched upon a shattered pillar beneath the shade of a tree, he seemed far more interested in the corpse twitching on his feet. She recognised it as one of the rainbow-coloured roaches, its innards exposed and glistening, loosing reeking, unseen clouds as he scooped out its guts.

Strange, she thought, that a dead roach should be more recognisable than the creature she had once called a companion.

It certainly looked like Gariath, of course: all muscles, horns, teeth and claws. His tail hung over the pillar and swayed ponderously, his wings were folded tightly behind his back, as they had been many times before. His hands were no less powerful as they tore a whiskered leg from the roach and guided it into teeth glistening with roach innards. His utter casualness about having a corpse at his feet and in his mouth was also decidedly familiar to her.

And yet, there was something off about him, she thought as she studied him with ears upraised. His skin appeared stretched a bit too tightly. His jaws opened with mechanical precision instead of morbid enthusiasm. The disgust on her face was plain as another wave of roach reek hit her nostrils, but he showed no particular joy at the discomfort he caused her.

This was all strange enough without considering his stare. There was intensity behind it, as ever, but it was not a fire that flickered and burned. His stare was hard and immutable, a stone that pressed against her.

'So are you,' she said, observing him coolly as he shovelled another handful of innards into his jaws.

'You sound disappointed,' he grunted through a full mouth.

She was, she admitted, if only slightly. Things certainly didn't get *less* complicated with a hulking reptile still alive. She was certainly surprised to see him, given his rather obvious intent on dying the last time she saw him.

Still, she took some satisfaction in his appearance. It merely confirmed her previous suspicions: If Gariath was alive, Lenk would be, too.

And if Lenk is alive ...

Gariath's neck suddenly stiffened. He looked up, ear-frills fanning out. She started, unsure whether to run. He made no movement beyond sitting, ear-frills twitching, as though hearing something she could not. This, noting the differences between their ears, she found disconcerting.

'Angry?' He glanced to the air at his side. 'Maybe. Probably. I don't care.'

'Are … you talking to me?'

'If I was talking to you, I'd be angry.' He cast a sidelong glare to the emptiness. 'As it is, I'm only mildly irritated.'

While there were many oddities one could accuse Gariath of, madness was not one of them. What dribbled from his mouth on insect ichor might have *sounded* like lunacy, and she wasn't ready to discount that it was, but it was uttered with such clarity that he was not possessed of even in his more lucid moments. He was serene. He was coherent. He was calm.

That unnerved her.

'You look upset,' he observed.

She said nothing. 'Concerned' and 'observant' were two other qualities one never accused Gariath of having.

'Understandable, isn't it?' she asked. 'I'm standing in front of a lizard who, up until moments ago, I thought dead and was pleased for it, because, as of a few days ago, said lizard tried to kill me by bringing down a giant snake on my head.' She sneered. 'Maybe a little upset, yeah.'

'What?'

'I just said—'

'Not you, stupid.' He held a hand up and looked to the side again, shaking his head. 'No, she always sounds like this. Stupid humans cry about things like near-death experiences.' He laughed morbidly. 'No, no. They call it "attempted murder".' He snorted. 'Babies.'

She stared at the nothingness beside him intently, straining to see what he saw. It became evident that trying to do so was as futile as trying to see what crack had split his skull from which this sudden lunacy leaked out.

She took a step back warily.

'Going somewhere?'

She slowed, but did not freeze at his growl. 'Back to tracking.'

'Tracking what? The other humans?'

'*The* humans, yes.'

'Pointless. I can't smell them. They're probably dead.'

'Given that you tried your damnedest to kill them, that's definitely possible.'

'They're always snide like this, too,' he growled to the air once more. 'Hmm? No, you wouldn't think so, but the pointy-eared one gets uppity about the other ones, too. Or at least, the other *one*.'

She felt the stab in his words surely as she felt the ire rise in her glare, seeking to leap out and impale him. The ichor on his unpleasant smile and the lunatic calm in his stare, however, convinced her to instead turn around, walk toward the opposite bank and hope he did nothing more than continue to stare.

'Never seen you run before,' he grunted after her.

'I've never seen you talk to invisible people before, so I suppose we're even,' she called over her shoulder. 'And for the thousandth time I remind you, knowing full well you don't care or can't understand, I'm a *shict*.'

The question came just as she set foot back onto damp soil, voiced without accusation, without malice, without anything beyond genuine curiosity.

'Are you?'

And she froze, turned around so slowly she heard her vertebrae creak.

'What ... what did you say?'

'You're not going about this the right way, you know,' he replied with a shrug.

'You can't possibly—'

'I do,' he replied, 'and I can tell you that more dead bodies, theirs or yours, won't make your ears any pointier.'

'And I'm supposed to listen to that?' It was unwise to snarl at him so, to bare her teeth at him challengingly, but she didn't care. It was likewise unwise to allow the tears to form in the corners of her eyes, but she could not help it. 'You expect me to believe that *you*, of all people, think violence isn't a solution?'

'I don't expect you to do much more than die,' he replied with coolness not befitting him. 'Someone else expects you to do so in a more meaningful way.' He blinked, then looked to the air with incredulousness. 'Really? How do you figure that?'

'Who—?'

'Right.' He nodded once, then turned to her. 'But this isn't it, we agree. No matter who dies, you're still what you are.'

Walk away, she told herself. *Run, if you have to. He's a long way gone and he was rather far away to begin with. Go. Run.*

Sound advice. She should have cursed her frozen feet, her eyes set against his. She should have done anything, she knew, besides open her mouth to him. But she could not help it, just as she couldn't help the genuine curiosity in her voice.

'What am I?'

'Well, *I* don't care,' he replied sharply. 'But whatever you are, whatever you're planning, it won't work.'

'You know nothing of what I'm planning, of what I have to do.'

'You don't *know* what you have to do. Isn't that why you're being such a whiny moron?' He leaned closer; the weight of his stare became oppressive, drove her back a step. 'What happens when you do it? When you kill Lenk? Your thoughts won't get any more quiet.'

'What do I *do* then?' She was far past concern for how he seemed to know her plans, far past baring her teeth or hiding her tears. 'What does your lunacy tell you? Because I've been thinking with sanity and logic, and I can't come to any other conclusion. *This* has to happen. *He* has to die.'

His expression didn't change. The stone of his stare became one of body. His tail ceased to sway, his claws ceased to twitch. He stared without words, for he had no more for her.

And she had none for him. His might be a serene madness, but it was still madness. And she still knew what she must do.

She turned about swiftly this time, stalked back to the river. She hadn't even lifted sole from stone this time before she heard him growl.

'There, see? I told you she wouldn't listen.'

She heard him rise, wings flapping, claws stretching, leathery lips creaking with the force of his snarl.

'Now, we do things *my* way.'

In an instant, the sun was drowned behind her, choked by a shadow that bloomed like a dark flower over her. She had no thought for reasons why, only instinct. She heeded it as she leapt backwards.

He was Gariath. He didn't know why. Reasons were for weaklings.

The ground shook as he fell where she had stood. His claws raked the rock and his wings flapped, sending up a cloud of granite-laced dust. She whirled, narrowing her eyes against the grit as he turned to face her, eyes bright and burning.

She wasn't surprised; sudden and irrational violence was simply what he did. Still, she felt compelled to ask.

'What's it matter to you?' She crouched, a cat ready to spring, ears flattened against her head aggressively. 'Sad that you won't get to be the one to kill them?'

'They don't matter.' He rose like a red monolith, muscles twitching, claws flexed. 'I don't matter.' His legs tensed, eyes narrowed. *'You don't matter!'*

His roar split the dust cloud in half as he hurled himself at her. Her ears rang from his fury; she felt hairs on her neck wilt under the heat of his breath as she darted low beneath him. Her spine trembled as his jaws snapped shut, a hairsbreadth over it.

She heard him crash into the foliage, but did not turn to see. Instead, she scrambled across the stones, mind racing with her limbs as she searched for options and found them desperately scarce.

Fighting was impossible, even if she had her bow and knife. Hiding was futile, for his nose guided him as surely as her ears did her. Negotiation ... just seemed stupid at this point. With nothing left, she turned to face him as he tore himself free in an eruption of soil and leaves.

And she hurled the Spokesman at him.

He lowered his head, let it smash against his skull. Such blows from a greenshict were legendary, the sticks splitting open heads as easily as they did melons. But no matter what she was, she was not a greenshict. The stick crashed against his brow, clattered harmlessly to the stones.

He stepped over it, his tail flicking behind him to snatch the stick and send it flying into the river, where it disappeared. She watched it vanish with wide eyes, the white of the feather tied to it visible for a long, horrifying moment. She forced herself to tear her eyes from it, forced the fear from her face and replaced it with snarling, white-toothed rage.

'So what is it, then?' she growled. 'Why fight me? You won't get a scratch, let alone die!'

'Dying isn't important ... not anymore,' he growled back. 'Living is.'

'You can't possibly expect me to believe you came up with that all on your own.'

'I don't expect you to do anything but die.' He stalked toward her with more caution than she expected. Or, she wondered, was that hesitation? 'And I don't care if I live, either. What's important is that *he* lives.'

'Who? Lenk?'

'I need him.'

She paused, blinking. 'Uh ... for ...'

'*I don't know!*' His roar was mostly fury, but tinged at the edges with pain. 'Some lives ... are worth more than others.'

'What of my life?' She backed away as he continued toward her. 'I killed alongside you. I fought. I thought you respected that.'

'Liked, yes. Respected, never.' He drew back a thin red lip in a sneer. 'You're still just a pointy-eared human. Still stupid, still weak, still have to die sometime.'

'And when did you reach this conclusion?' she asked. 'Was it before yet another failed attempt to kill yourself? Or after another failed attempt to kill this stupid, weak *shict*?'

'Shut up.' His ear-frills twitched. His gaze danced from side to side before settling on her. 'You should have died at sea. I shouldn't have. I see that now.'

'And what of Lenk? What if he died there, too?'

'He lives.'

'How do you know?'

'How do you?'

His lunge came swiftly, but it was half-hearted, all fury with no hate to guide it. She darted aside, but did not flee. Perhaps, though, he was giving her the opportunity to do just that? No. He would think that cowardly. The madness that possessed him couldn't have affected him deeply enough that he would be afflicted with the disease of mercy.

Still, something plagued his strikes, hindered his muscle, smothered his growl. Was he in his right mind, she wondered, or merely distracted?

There was an opportunity she could seize.

'What of the others, then?' she shouted, adding her voice to whatever assault kept his ear-frills twitching madly. 'If Lenk lives, the others might, as well.'

'I said *some* lives,' he snarled, leaning low. 'He lives because he was strong. The others died because they were weak.'

'The giant raging sea snake might have also had something to do with it.'

'It had to be done. The Akaneed was necessary. It was sent for me.'

'You seem to say that about a lot of things that try to kill you.' She took another step backward and felt unyielding stone at her back. 'Since they haven't, you think maybe whatever's sending them to you might be mistaken?'

The rage that brimmed in his eyes at the insult was neither fire nor stone. It was a bodily thunder that boiled up through his chest, rumbled in his throat and became a storm behind his stare, vast, unrelenting and hungry for carnage.

'The *Rhega* do not make mistakes,' he growled, fingers tightening around something on the ground. 'The spirits do not make mistakes.' He rose, a fragmented stone head from a nearby decapitated statue in his hand. 'The beast was sent not to kill, but to teach. And I have learned from it. I thought you and the others weak, stupid. I thought you dead. And now ...'

His arm snapped, sending the granite skull hurtling like a meteor toward her face.

'I'M RIGHT TWICE!'

She dove, felt the impact on the pillar behind her as the head burst into fragments and powder that settled over her like a cloak; she took advantage of its cover, crawling on her belly into the foliage and disappearing amongst the greenery.

Futile, of course; he would sniff her out. But between the futility of hiding and the futility of attacking a seven-foot-tall slab of muscle with nothing but her fangs and harsh language, this seemed modestly wiser.

Still, she couldn't help but search for other options. Desperately scarce before, every strategy fled at the dragonman's roar. She heard him clearly, the breaths laden with anger, the feet heavy with hate, his claws twitching impatiently for bones to break and flesh to rend. Above the sounds of his hatred, it was near impossible to hear anything else. But she heard a sound regardless, faint and quiet. Between the flickering of his fury and the rumble of his growls, his nostrils twitched, searched the air.

And found nothing.

He can't smell me. The thought raced with the beating of her heart. *Or is he just drawing it out? No, he's not that patient. But it makes no sense. Why can't he—?*

The answer came on an invisible cloud of reek, filling

her nostrils with knowledge and the pungent stink of roach innards. She glanced up, peered out of the foliage and saw the roach's corpse loosing its incense onto the sunbeams filtering through the canopy.

And an idea came.

She could barely keep from laughing. The dragonman, the terror of all things that walked on two legs and four, laid low by a stinking *bug*. He had a weakness after all. And, if one of the many curses about shicts was true, it was that they knew weaknesses could be exploited.

Shicts, she thought with obscene pride, *don't fight fair*.

The sole obstacle to capitalising on this pride was the expanse between her and the dead insect, dominated by a mass of red flesh and eager claws.

But that suddenly did not seem so grievous an obstacle anymore. He was *only* flesh and claws ... and teeth, she admitted, but she was a shict. She was cunning, she was stealth, she was hunter. These were things the Howling taught her, reminded her of in faint echoes as she fell to all fours and crept about the bush.

'What's that?'

She froze.

'What?' he growled again. 'No, I never said I couldn't learn.' Gariath sighed, unaware as she pressed on through the brush around him. 'It's just that the humans, round or pointy, have nothing to teach me. They know few things: desecration, degradation and indignation.'

He laughed blackly, a sound that made her skin crawl as it never had before.

'No, it means she thinks she's claiming some sort of victory here ... no, an *invisible* victory,' he growled. 'It's as stupid as it sounds. She pretends she's avoiding me because she doesn't deserve to be splattered on the ground. *That* is indignation, something humans claim to possess when everything else is taken from them.

'In this case,' he continued, 'it's stupid of her to think she's going to die with anything more than mud in her teeth and a rock in her skull. That's as invisible as victories get, I suppose. Eh? No, it makes sense to them *morally*.'

He's speaking to you, she told herself, *not the air ... maybe both.*

'It basically means she's lying to herself. Really, all we're fighting over is killing rights, which is acceptable.' He snorted disdainfully. 'But she wants to kill the others, the stupid weaklings, to prove she's less stupid and weak. This is a lie ... sorry, a *moral victory*.'

He's taunting you, trying to lure you out. Keep going. Don't fall for it.

'And this is why they look at her with hatred, why Lenk feared to turn his back to her.'

She froze.

'She is a liar, a schemer. She tells herself they have to die for reasons she thinks will help, that she'll stink less like a human after rubbing against their soft skin for so long. They know this. They hate her. What?' He grunted. 'Yes, *I'd* kill them, but only because I don't like them. Honesty is an admirable trait.'

She was not prepared for this. Claws, fists, bellowing roars she had steeled herself against. But when he spoke with confidence, not rage, when his words were laced with cunning rather than hatred, she was stunned into in-action.

'Ironic? Yes, I know what the word means. That's different, though. I don't *protect* Lenk. If he needed protection, I would laugh as he died. I give him the respect and honour of a fair fight by killing her first. He's a stupid bug, all wings and stinger, that will leap into the jaws of a snapping flower because he can't tell that the pollen stinks. He knows there's something foul about the stench, but he sniffs it, anyway. *She* is the pollen. I'm just clearing his nostrils.'

Well? she demanded of her body. *What are you upset about? That's what you wanted, isn't it? Lenk's hatred, his fear ... if you've got that, it's all so much easier, isn't it?*

It was supposed to be, anyway.

'No, no ...' Gariath's voice drifted softly over the leaves like a breeze. 'That's not the funny part. The real humour is that she's running away when I'm doing her a favour she doesn't deserve. If she does fear, as you say she does, not being so pointy-eared, then how is what I'm doing a bad thing? Eh? No, I disagree. The kindest thing here ...'

She felt the shadow on her back, looked up into hard black eyes.

'Is a swift and fair death.'

Move.

She did, too late.

His claws raked her, dug into the tender flesh of her back. She felt blood weeping down her skin, shallow muscles screaming, but not the numbing agony that would suggest a crippling blow. She tried to ignore the pain and scrambled away. She leapt to her feet, heard him fall to his feet and his claws as he charged. The bug grew large in her eyes, its stink brilliantly foul in her nose.

He lunged; she jumped.

He caught her ankle in a grasping claw; she seized a handful of pasty yellow innards.

She twisted and saw his teeth looming forward. With a growl to match his, she thrust the glistening, guts-laden fist at him and smeared the insect's ichor into his nostrils.

Though he didn't let go, he did howl. The roach's juices

vengefully filled his nostrils, seeped over his snout to sting his eyes. He threw his head back enough that she could pull her ankle from his weakened grip, claws scratching at her heel as she did.

He sprang to his feet, swung his fists out, lashed his tail out, stomped the earth in a blind, anosmic rage.

His roar filled her ears, as did the sound of his nostrils futilely searching the air for her. Such sounds continued as she ran into the forest, leaping over the river's shallows and leaving him far behind. Without direction, without stopping, she ducked branches, leapt over logs. And through his howling and snarling she could hear his words, spoken with such venomous clarity. She could feel them continue to seep into her, as she could feel her eyes brim with tears.

She ran, and lied to herself that she wept because of the pain in her back.

She flew past a roach, the rainbow-coloured insect's antennae twitching curiously as she sped past it without so much as a glance. It chittered quietly, confused. She did not look back at it.

Perhaps if she had, she might have noticed the pair of wide yellow eyes peering out of the foliage. Perhaps, if she had, she might have heard the sound of long, green footsteps that set off after her.

Thirteen

SCORN

Bralston, like most wizards, resented the term 'magic' as it pertained to his gifts.

Magic, in the accepted application of the word, was a dismissive means of explaining the inexplicable. The word 'magic' was uttered, whispered and squealed at everything from stars falling across the sky to a flower blooming in snowfall.

Wizards did not practise 'magic.' Wizards channelled *Venarie*. And as Venarie was the soul of the wizard, so too was reason the soul of Venarie.

'Magic' was no more mystical than a fever in the blood, the moisture in one's breath, the faint shock that occurred when one touched a doorknob or the force that kept a man's feet on the ground. Venarie was simply an added quality that allowed wizards to channel fever to flames, to freeze the moisture in their breath, to twist a shock to a bolt of lightning and to defy the earth itself.

This had been explained before, in countless theses, debates and lectures to the gifted and the unenlightened alike. Met with too many slack-jawed stares and the inability of the unenlightened to even fumble with these concepts, let alone grasp them, the Venarium had turned their efforts to more worthwhile studies.

Without the guidance of wizards, the unenlightened

had turned to the only other source of explanation: their priests. And the priests offered only one explanation.

'Magic.'

Venarie was the domain of wizards.

'Magic' was the practice of priests.

The explanation wasn't always 'magic.' Just as frequently it was 'fate,' or 'the will of the Gods,' or 'apologies that your son died in a war we told him was just; perhaps if you had just given a few more coins in the dish when it was passed your way.' Whatever the explanation, priests lived to undo what wizards did.

The reasons for the Venarium's enmity for priesthoods of all faiths had roots that sank into the earth of history, the greatest one taking years to explain in full every slight and grudge the wizards had meticulously recorded.

Bralston did not have years, so he simply settled for scowling across the table at Miron Evenhands.

'I don't like you.'

For his part, the priest seemed unfazed by this. He simply smiled, a sort of smile that irked Bralston to admit reminded him fondly of his grandfather, and brought a cup of steaming tea up to a long face beneath a white cowl.

'I'm sorry,' the Lord Emissary said.

'Apologies suggest that there is something you can do to alter my opinion,' Bralston replied sharply. 'I assure you, my reasons remain steeped far enough in history and philosophy that any such suggestions are ultimately a frivolous, and borderline insulting, waste of time and attention on your part and mine.'

'That's one interpretation.' The priest bobbed his head. 'There are others. For example, it can also imply a deep lament that history and philosophy have more to do with an opinion than character and personal experience do. It can also imply a subtle desire that said relations could be repaired, if only through two open minds meeting at the right time with the right attitude.'

Bralston snorted, crinkling his nose in a sneer. 'That's stupid.'

'I'm sorry.'

'Look,' the wizard said, rubbing his eyes. 'I get my fill of arguing philosophical trivia in Cier'Djaal. I was hoping that this mission would heighten my appreciation for simplicity.'

'You hoped that a mission to track down people who shoot fire from their fingertips and don't soil themselves with the effort due to glowing red stones would be simple?'

'What did I *just* say?'

'I'm sorry.' Miron smiled and held up a hand for preemptive peace. 'Excuse me. In truth, I had hoped that summoning you here would result in a greater enhancement of your desire for simplicity.'

Bralston merely grunted at that. Thus far, the two hours of contact that he had shared with the Lord Emissary had been anything but simple.

He had arrived in Port Destiny shortly after dawn broke on the blue horizon of the sea, as scheduled, planning only on lingering for as long as it took to find a meal. He had been surprised to find a bronze-clad, fierce-looking woman with raven hair and a long sword, standing exactly three feet from where he landed, wearing an expression as though she had been waiting there specifically for him.

His surprise had turned to suspicion when she, one Knight-Serrant Quillian Guisarne-Garrelle Yanates, had revealed that she was doing exactly that. That suspicion had convinced him to follow her lead to the luxurious temple in the city, and from there to the table where he now sat, across from a priest of Talanas – an apparently high-ranking priest of Talanas – who somehow seemed to know everything about his mission.

And, he thought with a twitch of his eyelid, *who just won't ... stop ... smiling.*

'You'll forgive me for being less than willing to nod my head dumbly and accept whatever you say, *Lord Emissary*.' Bralston all but spat the title on the table. 'But given that the Venarium acts with at least a modicum of secrecy, I must be more than a little suspicious at how you know what my mission concerns.'

'Suspicion is a wise policy, even in times of peace.' Miron shook his head and sighed. 'In times of turmoil ... well ...'

'That doesn't explain anything.'

'No appreciation for dramatic segues, I see.' The priest smiled, took another sip. 'I can see why, of course. Drama tends to be a word in a forgotten language that roughly translates to "long-winded, unimportant babble purely for the sake of entertaining idiots."'

'I would not disagree.'

'When "long-winded and unimportant" tend to be the exact opposite of the concise and sharp-witted pride of the wizard, no? Curtness, forthrightness, everything explained, everything understood. That is what you believe, is it not?'

'Priests believe. Wizards *know*.'

'Indeed. However, what you apparently don't know is that everything is not quite so neatly explained as you might think. This supposed rivalry between the churches and the Venarium, for example.' The priest's smile seemed to grow larger with every mounting moment of Bralston's ire. 'It would cast such *knowledge* into doubt to learn that there might be one or two wizards out there who find the company of priests tolerable, would it not?' He smiled and winked. 'Even to the point of sharing the details on missions conducted with a modicum of secrecy?'

Bralston's eyes went wide, mouth went small.

'You're saying ...' he uttered. 'We have a leak.'

'Now who's being dramatic?' The priest's laughter was dry, like pages turning in a well-read book. 'No, no, my friend. I simply meant that, where our concerns coincide, Lector Annis and myself are not above violating enmities steeped in philosophy and history.'

'Coincide?' Bralston raised a brow. 'The Lector mentioned nothing.'

'I suppose he wouldn't, for fear that you might believe what I am about to tell you is an order, rather than a humble request, something you would no doubt resent.'

'And that request is?'

Miron's smile faded, and a look of concern, so familiar as to have been etched on the face of every soft-hearted grandmother and hard-working grandfather that Bralston had ever seen, spread over his face.

'I would like you to find my employees.'

'Surely,' Bralston replied, 'agents of the church are more than capable of performing your will, given the funding and support you undoubtedly boast.'

'*True* agents, perhaps.' Miron nodded. 'However, for want of those, I instead hired adventurers.'

Bralston rolled his eyes and placed a finger to his temple, the reasoning suddenly becoming all too clear. 'You hired some vagrant lowlifes to do your bidding, they broke their contract and they made off with your money or your daughter or whatever you wear under your robes, if not all three, and you want me to get them back?' He sat rigid in his chair, uncompromising. 'I'm not a mercenary.'

'No, you're a Librarian,' Miron replied, unfazed by the sarcastic assault. 'But more than that, you're a good man, Bralston.'

'I didn't tell you my name.'

'Annis did, amongst other things.' The priest leaned forward in his chair, propping his elbows on his table. 'He told me many things about you, many foul things you did for the right reasons.'

The Librarian had prided himself on being difficult to surprise. But it wasn't the words emanating from the Lord Emissary's mouth that caused him to feel so small in his chair. Rather, it was the intensity, that instinctual concern that played across the priest's face that suggested he had known Bralston all his life.

Only one person had ever looked at him in such a way before …

'You know …' the Librarian whispered.

'I know that you love a woman,' Miron replied. 'That you spilled blood to protect her, blood that nearly brought the Venarium to war with the Jackals. I know you burned two men alive without question for the agonies they inflicted on a poor woman. I know that your duties go far, far beyond whatever the Venarium claims they do in the name of their laws.'

Bralston expected to feel cold, expected that such a revelation should seize him by the heart and twist. Instead, he felt warm, comforted by the reassuring smile that the priest wore. He felt a familiar urge, the same urge that when young would cause him to run crying to his mother when he had skinned his knee, or to hug his father's legs when a dog had growled at him.

An urge that he thought he had hardened himself to.

'That is why, Bralston,' Miron whispered, 'I want you to find my employees. There are six of them, four men and two women.'

'And ...' Bralston swallowed hard. 'You want me to protect the women.'

'If it is in your power, I would ask you to protect them all. As it stands, these adventurers are a capable lot. The men are well-armed, and one of the women, a shict, is possibly even better-equipped to handle herself.' Miron's face wrinkled with concern. 'The sixth member, however ... she is not weak, by any means, but she is ... untested.'

'I see.' Bralston scratched his chin contemplatively. 'This woman ... I assume she's one of your own.'

'Do you?'

'As compassionate as even a Lord Emissary is, I doubt his charity extends so low as to reach adventurers. They live to die, do they not, to be used and disposed of?'

'Perhaps some hold that attitude.' For the first time, Miron betrayed a hint of sadness in his face. 'Though you are right. She is sacred to Talanas, serving her pilgrimage with the others. A priestess.'

The Librarian didn't feel the usual cringe that accompanied such a word. Enmity steeped in years was forgotten, replaced by a sudden surge through his being, the same surge that had called him to burn men alive.

'A priestess ...' he whispered.

'I know you do not agree with her calling. But she is not yet hardened enough to know that anything beyond her faith exists.' Miron smiled. 'She is the one I wish to preserve the most. I fear the horror that was inflicted upon the woman in Cier'Djaal would shatter her completely.'

The woman leapt to his mind, and he felt that cringe return. He recalled the bruises on her face, the way she folded into herself to escape the room. He recalled her eyes, so empty and distant as she watched two men burn for what they had done to her. He tried to picture what she might have been before the wizard, the heretic, had shattered her.

He found he couldn't bear to.

'Perhaps, if rhetoric does not sway you, we might see if personal experience truly does trump age-old loathing?' Miron asked as Bralston looked up. 'I am told you were one of the few members of the Venarium that assisted with transporting the wounded during the Night of Hounds.'

He nodded, slowly, loath to remember the event. A lesser man would have remembered images and sounds: fire, screams, felons running in the street, women begging for their lives, looting, carnage. Bralston, however, was a Librarian and had no choice but to remember the horror with precise chronology.

One hour after dawn: the Houndmistress, bane of the Jackals and champion of the citizenry, before there were statuettes of her in every place of business in Cier'Djaal, had been found in her bed with her throat cut, her adviser missing from his chambers and her child missing from hers.

Two hours: a man named Ran Anniq, small-time Jackal thug, had thrown the stone that struck the herald announcing her death.

Three hours: Bralston was strongly reconsidering his denial that hell, as men knew it, existed.

The Venarium had not been petitioned by the fashas of Cier'Djaal to aid until seven hours after dawn, when the wounded had become too great for the healers of the city to tend to. Bralston had not stepped away from the window of his study for all seven of the hours, save to file a request to visit a brothel, which was promptly denied. He had spared that building, still unblackened by the flames engulfing the city, only a glance as he and several other wizards filed onto a ship to use their magic to propel it toward Muraska and the healers there.

They arrived seventeen hours after dawn, exhausted. The priests of Talanas had offered succour to the wizards, in addition to the wounded they had brought over, and many had grudgingly accepted. Bralston declined with no thought to why he should; he simply could not sleep for fear that the brothel had been razed, its women defiled.

Twenty-two hours in, he had felt a hand on his shoulder. He had looked up into bright eyes, into a smile offering comfort. Hands flecked with dried blood had offered him a cup of tea. A woman in blue robes had placed her right hand around him and asked him what the matter was.

At twenty-three hours, he wept. At twenty-four, he slept. At forty-three, he watched her from his ship, taking her words with him. Two weeks later, he had returned to the brothel, still thanking her quietly.

Seven years later, he now thought of her again, of her god, of what she had done for him.

'I know not much about the specifics of your mission,' Miron continued. 'Only that you seek a violator of laws, both wizardly and godly, and in this we coincide. I know what direction you head, and I know what direction I sent my employees … what direction I sent her.'

'I … will do it,' Bralston replied softly without looking up. 'If I can find her … I will return her.'

'I am sure you can find her … if someone else has not found her first.' Miron cringed. 'But I am not asking you to go without aid on my part. Your coat flew you here from Cier'Djaal, did it not? A journey that takes weeks by ship done in only a day and a half … its power must be exhausted.'

'It will take some time to replenish itself, yes,' Bralston replied.

'Time, I fear, she does not have. A ship, however, is what I have.' Miron pointed out the window of his room, toward the city's harbour. 'Seek a ship called the *Riptide*; you will find its captain not far away. Tell him that his charter requests that he deliver you to your destination.'

'Our intelligence suggests that the outlaw is based near the Reaches,' Bralston said. 'But beyond that, we know little.'

'There may be someone who knows more,' Miron suggested. 'A man by the name of Rashodd. He was involved in certain … peculiarities before my employees brought him low. We entrusted him to the care of authorities at Port Yonder.'

'I shall seek him out, then. Your assistance is duly noted and will be reflected in my report.'

'I trust that you will,' Miron replied, nodding sternly. 'Godspeed, Librarian.'

Bralston rose swiftly and stiffly from his chair and cast a look over the table at the priest. He sniffed, then placed his hat upon his head, running fingers along its brim.

'I don't need gods.'

The door shut with a resilient slam, as though the Librarian sought to make his discontent known through the rattle of porcelain as the impact sent Miron's teacup stirring on its saucer. The Lord Emissary let it settle, listening for the sound of the Librarian's determined footsteps over the hiss of the brown liquid.

When all was quiet once more, he gently took his cup in hand and smiled at the door through a veil of steam.

'Idiot.'

The harbour of Port Destiny was lax, only a few ships bobbing in blue waters that kissed blue sands, rendering city and sea indistinct from one another. Their cargoes had been unloaded, their crews vanished into the city for wine, dice and women. Most would return destitute and broken, ready to serve at sea for further wages. A few would not return, usually paying for debts they had racked up with either their service or their kidneys.

That was a problem for a captain, Argaol thought as he lay back and shut his eyes against the morning sun. He would be one of those again someday, a captain with problems of unruly men and hostile seas and obligations to greedy men. But today, he was a man whose long, dark legs hung bare over the docks, a fishing line tied to his big toe.

His titanic ship, the *Riptide*, lounged as lazily as her captain did, bobbing up and down in the water beside him. They would both be called away before too long. But for now, each was content to lose themselves in their shared insignificance between the vast city and the boundless ocean, each content in the knowledge they could ask for no better company.

'It just goes on and on, doesn't it?'

He never *asked* for worse company. It always just seemed to find him.

'Vast ... endless ...'

Argaol stifled a groan, attempting to pretend he couldn't hear her. He remembered many an awkward conversation that had begun with this particular clichéd pseudo-insight.

'I can't even begin to fathom how enormous it is ...'

Any moment now, this would turn to some horrible confession, probably one involving a pelvic rash or a request for help removing a fishing hook from a particularly tender area. He clenched his teeth, hoped quietly that she would give up before she said—

'On and on and on and on and—'

'Zamanthras' loving bosoms, *all right*,' he finally spat out. '*What* in the sweet hell that I so dearly prefer to listening to you is on your wretched little mind?'

Quillian looked down with disdain as he cracked one eye open from his lounging on the dock. Her face was hard, barely any more femininity revealed in it than was revealed in her bronze-swaddled body. She brushed a lock of black hair aside, exposing the red line of an indecipherable oath written beneath her eye.

'What makes you think something's on my mind?'

Argaol stared at her with disbelief that bordered on offended. 'I suppose I'm just the sensitive type.'

Her befuddlement was short-lived, concern etching its way across her features as she turned her gaze back out past the docks and over the sea.

'I heard what the Lord Emissary plans,' she said, 'before he met with the heathen.'

Argaol chewed his lower lip thoughtfully. 'Is it wise to use the word "heathen" in reference to someone who can spit icicles into your face?'

'Perhaps your faith extends only as far as your fears,' she replied coldly. 'The Knights-Serrant cannot afford such luxuries of sloth. Our sins do not allow it.'

Your sins apparently don't allow anything less than a gods-damned theatre production whenever you say something, either, he thought with a roll of his eyes. To hear her speak would lead anyone else to believe she was more than human. He had seen the flesh underneath her bronze, however. He had seen the red ink that was etched into her side. He knew not the language of sin, but whatever hers had been, they had been many.

That fact made the Serrant's temperament at least somewhat understandable, even if nothing else about her was.

'You're not concerned?' she asked.

He glanced down at his naked foot, the fishing line tied to his big toe as the rest of his slight, dark build sprawled out across the dock. He shrugged, folding his hands behind his bald head as he did.

'I suppose I don't look it, do I?'

'His plan is to head for Port Yonder.'

'Yonder's fine enough,' Argaol replied. 'A little light on entertainment, but a bit of sobriety is good for the soul.' He snorted, spat over the edge of the dock. 'One would think a Lord Emissary's duties would demand his presence here in Destiny, though.'

'They do,' Quillian muttered.

That caused Argaol to turn a glare upon her.

'Aye? The Lord Emissary's not coming?'

'Not unless something has changed since he went to speak with that heathen.' Quillian shook her head. 'He means for us to act as … as *aides* to the vile creature.'

'Ah.'

'Surely you can't be well with that.' The Serrant turned an incredulous glare upon the captain. 'I was assigned by the Master-Serrants to protect the Lord Emissary, *not* some … some …'

'I wouldn't bother finishing that thought,' Argaol interjected curtly. 'For someone who likes spewing them as much as you do, your repertoire of insults is surprisingly short and boring. And' – he held up an authoritative finger – 'as I recall, you were assigned to *obey* Evenhands, which protection most certainly falls under. And I was *hired* to do the same. No one's violating any sacred oaths of red ink here.'

Her glare turned violent, face contorting with the audible grinding of teeth as she levelled a bronze finger at him.

'Don't you *dare* speak of oaths like you know any beyond your own to coin, you chicken-legged, cowardly, purse-fornicating, wheel-raping, hairless *eater of broken meats*!'

'Uh … all right.' Argaol rose up, scratched the back of his head. '*That* one I haven't heard before, I'll grant you.' Rather than anger, it was with a furrow-browed curiosity that he cast his gaze at the Serrant. 'So … what's *really* on your mind?'

The Serrant turned her bronze shoulder to him. 'It's complicated.'

'To you, doorknobs are complicated.'

'Why would you be interested?'

'Perverse fascination is not interest.'

She stared at him for a moment, expression teetering between appalled and murderous. Like two panes of glass grinding against each other, her face cracked in short order and revealed a look that Argaol had not yet seen on her normally stolid, firm-browed face.

Fear.

'I worry,' she said, 'about the adventurers.'

Argaol blinked. 'Do they owe you money?'

Her face screwed up. 'Ah, no.'

'So …'

'Well, just one of them, really.'

'Which one?'

Quillian stared into the waters lapping at the dock. 'I shouldn't say.'

'Asper, then.'

'What?' Her head snapped back up with a look of alarm on her face.

'Don't look so damned shocked,' he said, rolling his eyes. 'You think you're the first woman to worry after another woman? It was either her or the shict.' He furrowed his brow. 'It's not the shict, is it?'

'*No.*'

'Didn't think so,' he replied. 'That would have been far, far too interesting to hope for.' He lay back down upon the dock, folding his arms behind his head. 'Makes sense, though; the priestess is the only decent one amongst them.'

'Then you share my concern.'

'Not especially, no. Sebast is due to meet with them any day now. From then, he brings them back to us, they collect their pay and you get to be content that a woman who thinks you're a fanatical lunatic is safe.'

'But she's ...' Quillian paused, looking a little more alarmed. 'Wait, did she tell you she thinks I'm a fanatical lunatic?'

'I'm assuming she thinks it. It's sort of your thing.'

'My *thing* is atonement through service to the clergy,' the Serrant snapped. 'If I am zealous in this pursuit, it's only because I'm truly repentant, truly devoted.'

'Well, wait for her to come back and you can show her your thing yourself. The trip from Teji to Destiny takes only a week or so.'

'So you say,' Quillian said, folding her arms. 'But Teji is part of the Reaching Isles.'

'Aye.'

'They're not called that because they're convenient. They've been lawless and beyond the grasp of Toha's navy for ages.'

'What military force can't solve, gold can. Teji's a trading outpost. It's always been a trading outpost. It'll always be a trading outpost. No pirate is going to attack it if they can save themselves the energy by trading.'

'Given that we only barely held off Rashodd when you swore you could deal with him and his brigands, I trust you'll see why I'm not confident in your opinion on pirate thought processes.' She frowned, staring out to the distant horizon. 'Have you heard any news, then? From either Teji or Sebast?'

'None,' Argaol said. 'But he'll get the job done.'

'If he was going to,' Quillian muttered, 'why would the Lord Emissary send a heathen after him?'

'Ask him,' Argaol muttered, closing his eyes as he dangled his leg back over the edge. 'Confess your sinful thoughts about the priestess while you're at it. I'm not interested anymore.'

The next part was fairly routine: the moment of frustrated silence, the flurry of grunts as she sought to come up with a retort and, finding none, the rattle of metal as she reached for her sword. He didn't bother to open his eyes, even when he heard the steel slide back into its sheath and the heavy, burdened slam of her feet as she skulked down the dock.

He had just begun to get settled, ready to entice a curious fish with the dark flesh of his big toe, when the footsteps began to get louder.

'I told you,' Argaol said with a sigh, 'I'm not—'

'You are Argaol.'

The voice was deep, resonant, full of presumed authority. He cracked one lid open.

The other shot up like a crossbow bolt.

There was no doubting the man for a wizard: the long

coat with many pockets and heavy book hanging from his belt left no room for doubt. But the size of the man, his broad shoulders and healthy frame, contradicted any impression he had ever had of the faithless magic-users. Whereas the other wizards he had known were thin and sickly, the tan vigour of this one, a Djaalman, he thought, suggested at least normal vitality.

Then again, he reminded himself, *you've only known the one.*

Apparently unwilling to wait for a reply, the man turned his head, atop which sat a rather impressive-looking hat, to the massive three-masted ship not far away. He squinted a pair of blue eyes at the bold black lettering on its hull.

'That is the *Riptide*,' he said.

'You can read,' Argaol replied, his shock fading and general contempt seeping back in. 'I'm thrilled for you, really. Run along home and tell your mother.'

'The priest told me to seek you out. We are to leave for Port Yonder at once.'

'So I hear,' Argaol muttered, easing back. He made a gesture in the general direction of the city. 'The crew's out on leave. They'll be back tomorrow morning.'

'I will go out and find them,' the man said sharply. 'Be ready to leave when I return. My duties demand a swift departure.'

'I have duties of my own,' the captain replied coolly. 'Chief among which is catching my lunch today.'

He wiggled his toe and added, silently, *As well as making a point that I won't be cowed by any overzealous bookworm.* Too late, Argaol tried to remember if mind-reading was a wizard trick.

'You're not a man that visits Cier'Djaal much, are you?'

'I've been once or twice.'

'Not enough to know that the Librarians are the arm of the Venarium.' His eyelid twitched. Crimson light poured out in flickering flames. 'The duties of the Venarium supersede the necessity of lunch.'

'Yes, I've seen that trick before.' Argaol waved a hand dismissively. 'I know enough of wizards to know they have limits. Tell me, Mighty and Terrifying Librarian, do you know how to pilot a ship?'

'No.'

'I see. And do you have enough wicked hoojoo, or whatever it is that makes your eyes do that, in you to move a ship the size of the *Riptide* by yourself?'

'I do not.'

'Then it would seem the duties of the Venarium can wait until I catch something scaly and full of meat, then,' Argaol muttered. 'Round up the crew, if whatever weird stuff you do allows you to do that, but neither the *Riptide* nor myself are moving until I get some nice, salted fish in my gut.'

'Terms accepted.'

The sound of footsteps did not come, as Argaol anticipated. Rather, there was the sound of cloth shuffling. It was unusual enough that it demanded the captain open his eyes again in time to spy the man pulling a piece of paper folded to resemble a crane from his coat pocket.

It rested daintily in the man's dark palm for a moment before he leaned over and muttered something, as if whispering a secret to it. His eyes flashed bright, as did the tiny smear upon the crane's parchment. It fluttered briefly in his palm, imbued with a sudden glowing life, and leapt into the air.

Argaol watched it, at a loss for words, as it glided on a trail of red light, descending into the waters of the harbour.

It vanished without a splash, its glow dimming as it slid beneath the green-and-blue depths.

Behind him, he heard Bralston take two steps backward.

The water erupted in a vast pillar of foam, forcing up with it a cacophonous explosion that tore the harbour's tranquility apart. The fish, their mouths gaping in silent screams, eyes wide in unblinking surprise, tumbled through the air like falling stars. They seemed to hang there for a moment before collapsing, flopping in their last throes of life, upon the deck and into the sea.

Argaol blinked, saltwater peeling off his brow, and turned to Bralston. The wizard smiled back at him, then gave a gentle kick to the flopping creature at his insultingly dry feet and sent it skidding to Argaol.

'I'll be back within the hour,' he said. 'I'll see if I can't find you some salt.'

Fourteen

THE MANY CORPSES

When he discovered it, Lenk christened his vessel the *Nag.*

It seemed fitting enough to name it after a dying beast of burden, anyway. Though he couldn't quite recall any diseased mare he had ever seen in as pathetic a condition as his former ship, spared no indignity by the Akaneeds or whatever god had sent them, was in.

Its two pieces had washed ashore together, lying upon the beach like wooden skeletons of long-deceased sea beasts. Their shattered timbers reached up, as if in plea to an unsympathetic sky, desperate for something to pull them free of the sand they sank farther into with every rising wave. Their reeking, rotting ribs clouded the air with unseen stench, and what remained of a sail flapped in the breeze, trying to escape this crumbling hell and flee upon the wind. Through the dunes, a dying river snaked from the distant forest to serve as a resting place for the wreckage, slipping through its shattered wood as it emptied into the sea.

Lenk could take some macabre solace in the fact that it had found a use as a battlefield for beach vermin. Crabs and legged eels slithered and scuttled in and out of its cracks and holes, desperately trying to avoid the watching eyes of seagulls and screaming in salty, silent breaths when they were caught by probing beaks.

Unable to bear their tiny despairs, Lenk turned his attention to scanning the wreckage, searching for anything of value. He supposed it would have been too much to hope that some supplies might have run aground with the *Nag*'s corpse. Of course, if anything edible had come ashore, it was likely devoured by one of the many combatants that crawled around the rubble.

Or, far more likely, Lenk thought, *spirited away by some god who isn't content to smite me with disease and despair. Any divine favour I might have enjoyed came exclusively from Asper's presence, and she's ...*

He winced, trying not to finish that thought.

'*Dead?*' the voice finished for him.

'I was trying to avoid that conclusion,' Lenk muttered.

'*What purpose is born through denial of the inevitable?*'

'Hope?'

'*Purpose, not delusion.*'

'I find myself hard-pressed to argue.' Lenk stalked closer to the ruined vessel, ignoring the resentful glares the seagulls shot him and the sword he carried. 'Still, there might be something here ... some clue ...'

'*What could you possibly find here that would make you realise anything you don't already know?*'

'I don't know. Maybe they left something for me to find.'

'*Such as?*'

'I said I *don't know.*'

'*One would think that clueless futility is also a delusion.*'

'One would think.'

'*The indulgence can't be healthy, you know.*'

'Given that my leg is a festering mass of disease and I'm having a conversation with a symptom of insanity, I'd say I'm well beyond concern for health, mental or otherwise.'

'*Did you ever stop to think that perhaps my presence is a blessing?*'

'In between you causing me to look like a lunatic in front of people and telling me to kill people, no, that thought hadn't occurred to me.'

'*Consider this: You're currently searching through rotting timber when you should be seeking medicinal aid. The captain sent his mate to pick you up. You and the tome, do you recall?*'

'I recall the giant, man-eating sea snakes that complicated matters a bit.'

'*Regardless, even if you've lost the tome, there would be medicine, supplies aboard the ship they sent. We could recuperate, recover, and then search—*'

'For the others ...' Lenk muttered, scratching his chin. 'You're concerned about them and my well-being. Does the fever affect you, too?'

'*The tome. We must find the tome. As for the others ... stop this. They are weak. They are dead. We must concern ourselves with our well-being.*'

'You don't know that.'

'*I know that this ship was wood and metal and the snakes destroyed it. What chance does flesh and bone have?*'

'I survived.'

'*Because of me, as you continue to do. Because of me. Now take heed and listen.*'

'There's still a chance. There has to be something here. Something that can—'

'*There is something here.*'

'Where?'

The voice didn't have to reply. Lenk didn't have to look hard. He spied it, struggling to break free in the flow and flee into the ocean. His eyes went wide, a chill swept over his fevered body. Suddenly, the sun dimmed, his blood ran

260

thin in his body, and his voice could barely rise from his throat.

'*No ...*' he whispered.

Kataria's feather, floating in the water, pulled by the flow as the smooth stick attached to it held it captive.

'No ... no, no. *No!*' Lenk swept up to it, cradling it in trembling hands as though it might break at any moment. 'No ... she ... she'd never leave this behind. She always wears them.'

'*Wore them.*'

'*Shut up! YOU SHUT UP!*' Lenk snarled, bashing his fist against his temple. 'This can't be it. She wouldn't have left this. She ... they ...' He swallowed hard, a lump of boiling lead tumbling down his throat. 'All ...'

'*Dead.*'

The word was given a sudden, heavy weight. It drove him to his knees, pulled the sword from his hand, crushed the blood from his face like dirty water from a sponge.

'Dead ...'

'*Dead,*' the voice repeated. '*Another blessing you will come to realise in time.*'

'Please ...' Lenk gasped, his voice wet and heavy in his throat. 'Please don't say that.'

'*She would have killed you, you know.*'

'Don't say that.'

'*She said as much.*'

The voices flashed through his mind, as hot and tense as his fevered brow. All he had left to remember them by – her by – was the scorn that had dripped from her lips when they last spoke. The memories, the pleasantries, faded into nothingness and left one voice behind.

'*I want to feel like myself.*'

'*And you can only do that by ignoring me?*'

'*No, I can only do that by killing you!*'

It continued to ring, cathedral bells of cracked brass. He clenched his skull, trying to stop it from echoing inside his head. He could not let go of the noise. It was all he had left.

'Kill you ...' he repeated to himself. 'Kill you ... kill you ...'

'*She would have,*' the voice replied. '*But that's not important now. Now, we must rise up, we must—*'

It faded, drowned in a flood of logic and reason that swept into Lenk's brain on a hatefully reasonable tone.

Of course she would have, he thought. *She's a shict. You're a human. They live to kill us.* This voice, familiarly cynical and harsh, he realised was Denaos' own, seeping up from some gash in his mind. *What, you thought she'd give up her whole race for you?*

Maybe it's a blessing, a voice like Asper's said inside him. *The one favour the Gods will show you. You don't have to worry about her anymore, do you? You don't have to worry about anything ...*

Well, it's just logical, isn't it? Dreadaeleon asked, more decisive and snide than ever. *Put two opposing forces in the same atmosphere and one destroys the other. You can't change that. It's just how it works.*

Your life only became more meaningless when you centred it on her, Gariath growled. *You deserve to die.*

'I deserve it ...'

'*Self-pity is also a ...*' The voice paused suddenly, its tone shifting to cold anger. '*What are you doing?*'

'I deserve it.'

Lenk reached up and took the feather, the last action he took before he rose without compulsion from his body. He turned to stare out over the sea, clutching the white object close to him. Then, his feet beginning to move with numb mechanic, he walked toward the hungry, frothing sea.

'*What are you doing?*' The voice's demand didn't penetrate the numbness in his body. Whatever eyes it had, it must have seen the shore looming up. '*Stop! This is not our purpose!*'

'You were right,' Lenk said, a smile creeping across his face. 'She's dead. They're all dead. We'll be together again, though. Companions forever.'

'*Listen to me. LISTEN. Something is wrong.*'

'It's over.' The young man shook his head. 'I can't do this anymore. Not without them. Not without her.'

'*Sacrifice isn't noble if it hinders everything else. We have much to do. What of purpose? What of vengeance?*'

No more words. No more arguing with them, any of them. His willpower seeped out of his leg on weeping pus. Hope could no longer carry him. Futility could no longer fuel him. Surrender, the promise of an end to the blood and the pain, drove him forward, inevitably toward the sea.

'*Resist,*' the voice commanded. '*Fight. We are stronger.*'

No more words. The waves rose up to meet him. He would never stop walking until his lungs burst with salt and his flesh was picked clean by hungry fish.

'*You do not get to die here,*' the voice uttered, cold and commanding. '*That is not your decision.*'

No more words.

He felt a sudden, overwhelming cold, his fever coursing out of him on a frost-laden breath. His legs locked up beneath him; ice water coursed through his veins and sent him to the ground.

'*I won't let you.*'

So close to release, Lenk reached out with fingers trembling to grasp the earth and pull him into sweet, blue freedom. Freedom from Miron, from Greenhair, freedom from anyone and everything that had made him think she should have died for leather and paper.

'Why ... ?' He felt his tears as ice on his face as his body trembled and folded over itself. 'I can't do this. Just let me die ... I want to ...'

'*It does not matter what you want,*' the voice replied, unsympathetic. '*All that matters is what you must do.*'

The pounding in his head faded, freeing his ears to the sound of feet scraping against sand, alien voices rising over the sandy ridge. Alien, but familiar.

'*Hake-yo! Man-eh komah owah!*'

'*And what you must do ... is hide.*'

'But I—'

'*You don't get to make that decision.*'

He could barely feel the sand beneath his feet or his spine bending as he plucked up the sword. He barely noticed; his entire willpower, what didn't ooze out of him, was concentrated in his fingers as he held desperately onto the feather. He wasn't even aware of moving behind the sandy dune until he was finally there, his numb body forced to the earth as whatever force moved his legs suddenly gave out.

No sooner had his belly pressed against the dirt than the first green scalp came rising over the opposite ridge. A pair of wide, amber eyes shifted across the wreckage. A satisfied snort emerged from a long, green snout. Two long, clawed feet slid down the sand and into the valley, their tracks concealed by the long tail dragging behind it.

That the creature didn't notice his presence spoke more of its inattention than his subtlety. Even amidst the beach scrub, a head of silver hair couldn't have been hard to spot. He lay still; his body bore obedience for only one voice.

The lizardman turned about, cast its glower over the ridge and snarled.

'*Nah-ah. Shii man-eh.*'

'*Shaa?*' came an indignant hiss from beyond the dune.

Three additional green bodies came clambering over the ridge. Lenk took greater note of them now, particularly the clubs studded with jagged teeth and savage machetes hanging from their loincloths. A decidedly vicious improvement from the sharpened sticks they had carried last night, but that only brought a grim smile to Lenk's face.

Their weapons were so sharp, so brutal-looking. They could eviscerate him in the wink of an eye, end the suffering in a horrific chop and smattering of red and fleshy pink chunks on the sand. It would be so quick, so easy.

His felt his leg spasm on the sand.

Despite his mounting excitement, he thought it odd that they hadn't carried those tools last night. Even more curious was the fact that they seemed taller than before, their lanky musculature packed tightly under taut green flesh. Tattoos as ferocious as their weaponry ran up and down their bodies in alternating hoops, jagged bands and cat-like strips of red and black ink. Still, it wasn't until Lenk noticed the space under their long snouts that the realisation dawned upon him.

'Beardless,' he whispered. 'These aren't the same ones.'

'*These are warriors. Look at the way they move.*'

Lenk took note immediately. No step was uncalculated, no amber scowl was wasted. They stalked around the wreckage of the *Nag* with gazes far more predatory than the lizards from the other night.

Killers' gazes, Lenk thought. *They can smell my blood. They hunger for it. They're violent, bloodthirsty creatures.* His grin grew so large that he had to bite his lower lip to stifle it. *Gods, but they're going to kill me so quick.*

He felt his hands tighten around the scrub grass in ecstasy. If the voice could feel the plants, too, it made no indication.

'*That one,*' it muttered. '*The one with the bow. That's the leader.*'

Scarcely a revelation. *That* one lingered behind the three others with the cool casualness of command against its companions' predatory vigilance. Its polished black bow hung off its shoulder with the easy relationship of a master and his weapon. Any remaining doubt was quickly dispelled by the fact that its tattoos covered more of its flesh than any other lizard present.

'*Cho-a?*' it called out, apparent disinterest in its voice.

'*Na-ah!*' One of them, the one that had first arrived, looked up with a snarl. '*Man-eh shii ko ah okah!*'

'*Shaa,*' the leader said, waving its scaly hand. It jerked its head back toward the ridge they had come from. '*Igeh ah Shalake. Na-ah man-eh hakaa.*'

The other two lizardmen looked up from their own inquiries into the wreckage with nods. They grunted once, then stalked away from the debris, past the leader and up the ridge, vanishing behind it. The leader sighed and folded its arms over its inked chest as it stared at the obstinate one expectantly.

'*Mad-eh kawa yo!*' it snarled, jerking its head back to the ridge. '*Kawa!*'

'*Sia-ah!*' the other one hissed, scanning the wreckage with desperate intensity. '*Shii ko a man-eh!*'

'They look agitated,' Lenk whispered, unconsciously slithering a little closer. He eyed the quiver of brightly coloured arrows hanging off the leader's back and his voice took on a hysterical edge. 'Absolutely irate, even. How close do you think we'd have to be?'

'For what?'

'For him to put one of those arrows right between my eyes.'

'It won't happen. They're leaving now, look.'

Lenk bit back a despairing shriek, or it was bitten back for him by whatever numbed his throat. He didn't care about anything save for the fact that the insistent lizardman's tattooed body shrank with a sudden sigh. Looking dejected, it turned to go and follow the leader back up the ridge.

Until something on the ground caught its eye.

'Yes,' Lenk squealed, 'yes, yes!'

'No!' the voice countered with a chilling anger.

Lenk followed the creature's yellow gaze past the gutted timbers and scampering crabs, onto the moist sand.

To the perfectly preserved indentation of his footprint.

'Don't move,' the voice warned. *'They haven't seen us yet.'*

'Well, we can fix *that.*'

'No! DO NOT—'

The voice's command was lost in his laughter. Its control vanished in a fevered surge as Lenk rose to his feet. He spread his arms wide in a deranged welcome, his sword flashing in the sunlight and catching the attention of the creatures below.

From atop their heads, large crests fanned up. Lenk caught a glimpse of the many colours painting the webs of the green protrusions. Murals of blood and steel and teeth stretched from brow to backbone.

The obstinate one pointed a scaly finger up, opened its jaws in a shriek.

'MAN-EH!'

267

'Yes, yes!' Lenk cried back. 'Welcome, gentlemen, to the butchery! If you'll just hoist those fancy-looking weapons, we can finally get down to the gritty process of spilling my guts onto the dirt!'

'This isn't your decision!'

'You keep saying that, but here I am,' Lenk replied. His eyes went wide as the leader unslung his bow, nocked and drew back an arrow in short order. 'If it makes you feel any better, you can say it was *your* decision.'

'Down, fool!'

It was not a suggestion. Lenk's legs gave out the moment the bowstring hummed; he teetered backwards in time to loose a whining curse as the arrow shrieked just over his face. His hand seized up, clenching his sword as he tumbled down the dune and onto the beach.

'No matter,' he sputtered through a tangle of sand and steel, 'no matter, no matter. I can still do this. It's just going to be a bit messier.'

He felt the vibrations through his feet as he clambered upright, of legs thundering across the sand, long clawed toes kicking up earth as it shot toward him. He smiled, the same sort of grin he might have had for a fond relative, as he looked up at the ridge.

He did not have to wait long.

'SHENKO-SA!'

The war cry came on the eruption of sand and a shiny emerald flash as the lizardman came leaping over the dune. For an instant, Lenk saw the majesty of his impending demise: the teeth glittering in the creature's war club, the enraged circle of its stare, the tensing muscles in its body.

'Oh,' Lenk gasped, 'this is going to be *good*.'

'No,' the voice uttered. *'Fight.'*

'I don't want to.' The protest of Lenk's voice was a

sentiment not shared by his body, however, as his sword came up regardless. '*I want to die.*'

'*Fight,*' the voice commanded.

Refusal was mute against the creature, which slid down the dune in a cloud of sand and screams, swinging its club in wide circles over its head. Lenk watched the tattooed flesh, saw the mural painted on its crest foretelling his own bloody demise.

'*FIGHT!*'

'I don't—'

Lenk did.

His sword jerked up spastically, was seized in hands not his own. The club sputtered a spray of splinters as it bit the blade, steel grinding against teeth. Lenk felt the shock rattle down his arm, shake his heart in his rib cage. Gouts of fire lanced his leg as he felt himself being pushed backwards.

Let it drop, he told himself. *Let the sword drop and let him smash your head in. You won't even feel it. Then all this will be over.*

Against this, his body had one reply.

'*Fight.*'

'I said I won't!' Lenk shrieked back.

'*Man-eh shaa ige?*' the lizard snarled.

'*I wasn't talking to you!*' Lenk roared

The lizard's body twitched in response. It slid backwards, breaking the deadlock as it spun about wildly. His dumbfounded stare lasted only as long as it took the creature's tail to rise up and smash against his jaw.

A heavy blow, but not enough that it should make him as dizzy as he felt. He reeled, feet giving out beneath him. The world spun into darkness, banishing his opponent and his body. He did not strike the earth as he fell, but tumbled through, twisting in the dark.

'This is it, then?' He heard his voice echoing in the gloom as a gasp. 'This is what it is to die?'

'*No,*' the voice answered.

The world came rushing back to him in new eyes. The sand was soft. His sword was clenched in his hands, *his* hands. The club crashing down upon him was slow, weak. He stared up at what had been his enemy. What he saw was a corpse waiting to fall.

'*This,*' the voice said, '*is what it is to kill.*'

'*SHENKO-SA!*' the lizard screeched.

Lenk's sword replied for him. There was no shock, no strength behind the lizard's club as it met his blade. Or if there had been, Lenk did not feel it. He could barely feel anything, even the foot he rammed into his foe's groin. The creature merely hissed, recoiling with composure unbefitting the injury.

That was unimportant. The earth was unimportant. He rose to his feet, easily. There was weeping from his leg, he knew, but he could not feel it. It was cold in his veins, cold as the steel he raised against his foe. From the corner of his eye, he caught his own reflection in the weapon's face.

Two blue orbs, burning cold and bereft of pupils, stared back.

That was wrong, he knew in some part of him that faded with every frigid breath. His eyes should have pupils. He should feel hot, not cold. He should fear the voice, fear the chill that coursed through him. He should scream, protest, fight it.

He stared at his opponent over the sword.

No more words.

They sprang at each other, arrows of flesh in overdrawn bows. Their weapons embraced in splinters and sparks, crushing against each other time and again. He could only feel the metallic curse of his sword as it searched with the patience of a hound for some gap in the creature's defence. Every steel blow sent the lizardman sliding back, every breath grew more laboured, each block came a little slower.

Only a matter of time, Lenk and his sword both knew. Only a matter of time before a fatal flinch, a minuscule cramp in the muscle, something that ...

There.

The lizardman raised its club, too high. Lenk's sword was up, too swift. The creature's eyes were wide, too wide.

Then the sword came down.

Skin came first, unravelling like paper from a present. Sinew next. Lenk watched as the cords of muscle drew taut and snapped as lute strings too tight. Bone was sheared through, cracking open to expose glistening pink. There might have been blood; he was sure the creature's arm hit the earth, but didn't stop to look.

The lizardman looked up, mouth agape, eyes wide as it collapsed to its knees. It mouthed something that his ears were numb to. Threats, maybe. Curses.

All silent before the metal hum of Lenk's sword as it came up.

No more words.

The sword slid seamlessly, over the arm that came up too meagre to serve as any defence and into the creature's collarbone. Lenk pushed down, his sword humming happily and drowning out the screaming and muscle popping beneath it. He pushed it down until he felt it jam.

By then, the creature was lifeless, suspended only by Lenk's grip on the sword that impaled it.

'*This*,' the voice uttered, '*is what we do.*'

It should feel wrong, the young man knew. He should

feel the rush of battle, the thunder of his heart. He should feel terrified, worried, elated, relieved.

He should, he knew, feel something, *anything* other than calm, whole.

Even as the voice faded, the cold going with it, the sense of wholeness remained. His purpose, he realised, was gripped in his hands and knelt lifeless at his feet. His breath came easy, even as the fever returned. The desperation and fear had fled, leaving only a young man and his sword.

His bloody, bloody sword …

His senses came flooding back to him with the sound of a bowstring being drawn. He looked up, mouth parted in a vaguely surprised circle.

'Oh, right,' he whispered, 'there's two.'

It happened too fast: the string humming, the arrow shrieking, the flesh piercing. He felt it impale itself deep into his thigh, near his wound. He collapsed to his knees, falling with the other lizardman's corpse as he lost his grip on his sword.

'Ah,' he squealed through the pain. 'Khetashe, but that *hurts.*' He looked up at the inked lizard stalking toward him. 'I think you missed, though. It didn't hit bone.'

The lizard didn't seem to hear or care as it casually nocked another arrow.

'It's funny, though,' Lenk said, giggling hysterically. 'Moments ago, I was wishing for this, *hoping* for it. Now, I've killed your ugly little friend here and I want to live so I can kill you, too. But …' He let loose a shrieking peal. 'But *you're* going to kill me. Is that irony or poetry?'

No answer but the drawing of a bowstring.

'I shouldn't be afraid,' he whispered, 'but … I can't help but feel that I learned something a little too late.'

'Too bad for you,' the lizard replied in perfect, unbroken human tongue.

'Oh,' Lenk said, blinking. 'Two things, then.'

Voice and bow spoke with one unsympathetic voice. 'Shame.'

Lenk had no reply; pleading seemed a little hypocritical, what with the creature's companion dead at his knees. Still, stoicism seemed hard to achieve in the face of the arrow. With nothing left, he desperately tried to come up with a final thought to ride into the afterlife.

And all he could come up with was, *Sorry, Kat.*

A shriek hit his ears. Not of a bow, he realised as he watched the creature spasm, but of a long, sharpened stick that ended its swift and violet flight in the lizardman's shoulder. The arrow fell to the earth, and the lizardman shrieked and scampered backward, groping at the make-shift spear in its flesh.

'Lenk,' a voice said, distant. 'Move.'

'What?' he asked in a trembling voice.

'*Down, moron!*'

The shape came tearing over him, hands on his shoulders and pulling itself over his head. In a flash of brown and white, it struck the creature in a tackle, pulling both to the ground.

Lenk blinked, unable to make sense of the frenzy of movement before him. He caught glimpses of green, brighter than the lizard's flesh, amidst a whirlwind of pale white and gold. The creature shrieked under the other shape, swatting at clawing hands and biting teeth.

The shriek arced to a vicious crescendo. There was a flash of bright ruby.

Blood, Lenk realised, then realised his own leg was warm and wet. *Blood!* It poured out of his wound in rivulets from the jagged rent the arrow had left, spilling across his leg and onto the sand. *How long have I been bleeding? Why didn't anyone tell me?*

That thought was fleeting, as were the rest as he felt himself grow dizzy.

He heard, faintly, the sound of a tail slapping against skin and an agonised grunt. The pale figure toppled to the earth as the creature scrambled up, clutching a face painted with glistening red. It howled curses, incomprehensible, as it scrambled away, dragging its bow behind it.

'I got its eye,' the figure laughed as it rose up. 'Reeking little bleeder.'

A familiar voice, Lenk thought, though its features were unfamiliar. Even as it rose and stood still, its face was blurry, its figure hazy as it approached him. It leaned closer; he thought he could make out some mass of twisted gold and emerald, a mouth stained with red.

'Lenk?' it asked, its voice feminine. It twitched suddenly. He felt a hand on his leg. She had found his wound. 'Oh, *damn it*. Was it too much to ask that you survive on your own for two days?'

Hands wrapping around his torso, arms under his, sand moving under him. The sensation of being dragged was not as visceral as it should be, but he was quickly learning to forget what it should be.

'Poetry,' he gasped, breath wet and hot.

'What?'

'If I had just died quickly after I realised I didn't want to, that would be irony.'

'You're not going to die,' she snarled, tightening her grip. He made out other voices, alien languages behind him. 'Help!' she cried to them. 'Help me pick him up! *Move!*'

'I am,' he laughed on fading whimsy. 'It's beautiful poetry now; I see it. I'm going to die.'

'You're not,' she snarled as another pair of hands picked up his legs. Green hands. 'I won't let you.'

He rode those words, off the stained earth and into oblivion.

Fifteen

PREFERABLE DELUSIONS

'*That could have gone better.*'

'Really? I thought it went rather well. In hindsight, I suppose we should have killed the one with the bow, first.'

'*Hindsight.*'

'Yes. I could have done with a bit more planning, couldn't I?'

'*Planning.*'

'Look, if you're just going to repeat everything I say, I can really have this conversation by myself.'

'*There was no PLAN.*' His head trembled, brains rattling against bone. '*There was only you indulging your madness and nearly ending us.*'

'I'm … I'm sorry, I just felt—'

'*Feeling is a corruption of the mind and body. Feeling is what we eradicate from ourselves before we eradicate whatever did this to us.*'

'Whatever did this … to us?'

'*Something was in our head. Something is interfering with our duty, my commands. Something … we must kill it.*'

'We must kill something.'

'*Not just kill it. Maim it. Burn it. Eviscerate it. Rip it apart and press its meat between sharp rocks. Cleanse it.*'

'What is it?'

'*Unknown.*'

'So ... do I just start eviscerating and hope I get lucky?'

A frigid silence consumed him.

'*Do not grow smug.*'

'I didn't mean to—'

'*Do not grow confident. Do not grow comfortable. Do not let anything stewing in the tepid mush boiling in your skull convince you that you are in control.*'

'What do you—?'

'*I saved you from your suicidal madness. I saved you from the demons. I continue to preserve your life in the name of our duty.*'

'But what is it? What *is* our duty?'

'*That you do not know is only further proof that you do not deserve the legs you are allowed to walk with. I save you only that we may fulfil our duties. What I preserve, I can destroy.*'

'That would seem a little contradictory, wouldn't it? Destroy me and you die, too ... don't you?'

'*I did not say,*' a gentle breeze caressed his mind, '*that I would destroy you.*'

'What does that mean?'

The wind died.

'*What does that mean?*'

Warmth returned.

'*What are you?*'

'I'm here,' said another voice. 'I'm right here.'

'What? Where?'

'Here, Lenk. I'm right here.'

A swift, erratic beat of a drum: certain of nothing.

It reached her as she pressed her ear against his chest, rising up from some deep place inside him. It had come to her before in fleeting whispers, murmurs, the occasional frantic scream. Now his heart hummed softly, sighing inside his body.

And though she knew she should try to resist it, her smile grew with each beat.

'He's alive,' she whispered. She let her head rest upon his chest, felt it rise and fall with each breath. Her eyes closed. 'Damn.'

It would have been easier if he had died, if he had *stayed* dead. She could have shed a tear, said a few words of memory, and called herself a shict again. She looked to the bandages covering his wounds, smelled the aroma of their salve. She could rip those off right now, she thought, and he would be dead and her problems would be solved. It was another opportunity, another chance to prove herself. And again, she couldn't kill him.

You couldn't even watch him die, she scolded herself. *You couldn't even have just sat back and let him die. Why couldn't you do at least that?*

Kataria sighed in time with his heartbeat; it was never that easy.

Her ears twitched as his muscles spasmed under his skin. Bones moaned, blood began to flow unhindered; he was waking up. She pulled back, heard his eyelids flutter open and held her breath as they peeled back fully. He groaned, turned his head and stared at her.

Two blue eyes, brilliant with the moisture that flooded them, looked up. *Two blue eyes*, she released her breath in a relieved exhale, *with pupils in them*. It was Lenk looking up at her, and not whoever else dwelt inside him. It was Lenk's eyes blinking, Lenk's lips twitching.

Lenk's trembling hand, reaching up to touch her.

You could go now, you know, she told herself. *You could run away and he would tell himself it was all a dream. You could*

*find another way off the island and never see him again. Then,
at least, you could say you didn't sit there and let him touch you.
It would be easy.*

She saw the bleariness clear from his eyes, tears drying
in the sun seeping through the thatched roof. She felt
his fingers on her cheek, felt her shame straining to be
heard as she pressed her face into his palm. She could feel
his heartbeat through his fingertips, growing faster, and
sighed.

It was never that easy.

'You ...' he whispered, his voice choked.

'Me,' she replied. She saw her canines reflected in his
eyes. She saw her own smile. 'Damn.'

He didn't seem to hear her, barely even seemed to see
her. His sole sense was touch, and he explored her with it.
She felt the ridges of his fingers, the calluses of his palm
on a skin of sweat as his hand traced her face. His fingers
creased under her nose, traced the ridges of her lips. She
could feel her breath break upon his fingertips, feel its
heat.

He's just mindlessly probing, she told herself. *Groping like
a monkey. He* is *a monkey, remember? He probably thinks he's
still asleep ... or dead. You can still run, or you can push him
away.* When she felt herself leaning into his touch again,
she all but screamed at herself. *For Riffid's sake, at least* bite
him or something!

'You're real,' he whispered.

His hand slid farther up, plunging into her hair. She felt
the sweat of her scalp under it mingle with his skin, felt his
hand gentle upon her.

It's not gentle, she reminded herself. *Remember how many
people he's killed. Remember how easily he killed them. He's not
gentle. Stop thinking he is.*

279

A sensation cold and hot at once, like a chill breeze on sweat-kissed skin, lanced through her body, causing it to shudder. She drew in a sharp breath as his fingers found the notches in her right ear, tracing them carefully.

Oh, you can't be serious, she all but shrieked. *Those are your ears! Shict ears, stupid! He can't touch those! They're ... they're sacred! They're precious ... they're ... he ...*

'You're alive,' he whispered. His smile was easy, bereft of the malice and confusion she had seen in him before. 'You're alive ... you're ...' She felt his hand stop suddenly, something brushing against his hand. 'Your feathers.' He blinked, as if remembering. 'You never leave your feathers behind.'

'Not usually, no,' she replied. It felt easy to tell him now, the words spilling from her lips. 'But this time I—'

She felt his fingers wrap around her locks, pull hard. She felt the sudden stab of pain as the shriek escaped her lips.

It was easy to punch him after that as she brought her fist against his jaw and sent his head snapping to the side.

'You stupid little *kou'ru*,' she snarled, baring fangs. 'What the hell was that for?'

And when he brought his face back, rubbing his jaw with the hand that was still slick with her sweat, it was easy to return the broad, stupid grin he gave to her.

'I had to know,' he said, his laughter harsh and parched.

'You couldn't have just *asked*?'

'If you were a hallucination, you'd have said "yes".' He looked thoughtful, his grin growing broader. 'Then again, if you were a hallucination you'd probably be ...' His eyes drifted lower, widening. 'Um ... nude.' He rubbed the back of his neck, clearing his throat. 'So, ah ... not that I don't have more impressive things to say, but I feel I must ask.' He levelled a finger at her chest. 'Why are you wearing that?'

She followed his finger to the scanty garment of brown fur wrapped about her breasts. From there, she followed his eyes down to her naked midriff and to the loincloth hanging off her sand-covered, pale thighs.

'For the same reason,' she said, prodding his bare, wiry chest, 'you're wearing *that*.'

Up until that point, she never thought that humans were capable of leaping nearly so high or turning such a shade of red. He slapped at his body, naked but for a similar garment tied about his hips, as if wondering if his clothes had perhaps seeped under his skin.

The panic fled after a moment of desperate slapping, leaving him staring thoughtfully at his new garb and the bandage wrapped tightly about his thigh.

'So …' He looked from his loincloth, then up to her. 'Did I miss something fun?'

'Well, the fun only started *after* you passed out from blood loss,' she replied.

'As usual,' he grunted, looking about. 'So, where *are* my pants? Where's …' His eyes widened, scanning the sandy floor intently. 'Where's my sword? I had it! I had it right—'

'It's elsewhere,' she replied, putting a hand on his shoulder. 'Calm down. Your pants, what remained of them, were filthy and covered in piss.'

Lenk blinked, turned a leery eye on her.

'*Whose* piss?'

'Your piss.' She cringed a little at his visible relief. 'You may have been unconscious, but your other … parts were still working despite you. The smell became unbearable after the third time.'

'I suppose that explains this.' He fingered his loincloth. 'But why did you dress yourself that way, too? And not that I don't appreciate your enthusiasm for cleanliness, but couldn't you have just cleaned my pants?'

'You think *I* did this?' She slapped her torso. 'Listen, you demented little shaven mole, if I wanted to see so much scrawny flesh I could have just plucked a chicken.' She sighed and leaned back on her hands. 'I passed out on my way here and woke up like this. They're not too big on modesty here.'

Lenk raised an eyebrow.

'They?'

'They.' She gestured over his head with her chin. 'Specifically, him.'

And it was at *that* point, as he turned his head to his other side, that she realised how high humans could jump. She grinned, studying him even as he studied the creature squatting beside him, reliving the moments she had experienced when she had awakened under their tremendous yellow gazes.

Bulbous eyes, larger than overripe grapefruits and apparently desperate to escape the green, short-snouted skull they were ensconced in, were undoubtedly the first thing he noticed. From there, he would see the creature's squat and scaly body, the apparent horrific crossbreed of a gecko and an ale keg, with four stubby appendages ending in three pudgy digits.

He would then find the most unsettling fact that it wore clothes. The creature absently scratched its furry loincloth and adjusted the round black hat, too small for its large head. One eye remained locked on Lenk while its other independently swivelled up over a pair of smoked-glass spectacles to look at Kataria.

"S'the matter with him?' the creature asked in a voice bass enough to make Lenk jump again.

'Fever,' Kataria replied. 'He's just a little strange right now.'

'*I'm* a little strange?' Lenk replied, voice hoarse with surprise.

'Oh, hey, 's'not polite, cousin,' the creature said, shaking its massive head. 'King Togu always want politeness in Teji, y'know.'

'King ... *what?*' Lenk asked, grimacing at the creature. He held up a hand. 'Wait, wait ...' He turned back to Kataria. 'First of all, what the hell *is* it?'

'*He* is not an it,' the shict shot back with a glare. '*He* is an Owauku and *his* name is Bagagame.'

'That's an Owauku?' Lenk looked back at the creature. 'And his name ... is ...'

'Bagagameogouppukudunatagana-oh-sho-shindo,' the creature said, a long and yellow grin splitting his face apart as he tipped his hat. 'M'the herald o' King Togu, welcomin' you to Teji.'

'So ... Bagagame.'

'Sure, cousin.' His head sank considerably, smile disappearing behind dark green lips. 'Go ahead and call me that. Not like I got a name that means anything special as my father might have given me to boil down my entire lineage into a single word. No. Bagagame 's'fine.'

'Oh, ah ...' Lenk rubbed the back of his neck. 'Listen, I never really expected a lizard to have ancestry that I *could* insult, so ...'

'Yeah,' Bagagame grunted. 'M'just so damn pleased you're up and awake and not babbling anymore in your sleep.'

'I was babbling?' Lenk's curiosity swiftly became shock,

and he turned to Kataria. 'You let him *watch* me sleep?'

'Well, he wasn't really interested until you pissed yourself,' she replied, shrugging.

'*Why did you let him do that?*'

'I couldn't very well say no; it's his house. He volunteered before any of the others could.'

He swept his eyes about the reed hut, the thatched roof, and mats of woven fronds on the floor. 'There are more? They have *houses*? What do lizards need houses for?'

'Oh, fantastic,' she sighed. She rolled her eyes in the direction of Bagagame. 'He's doing it again.'

'W'sat?' the Owauku asked, tilting his head.

'He does this sometimes, starts repeating everything in the form of a question.' She tapped her temple. 'He wasn't too right to begin with and the fever hasn't helped. You'd better go get *ah-he man-eh-wa*.'

'I kuu you, cousin,' Bagagame said, bobbing his head and rising up. 'M'had a fellow once, acted like way, kuuin' things that weren't there. W'beat him over the head a bit.' He turned a bulging, thoughtful stare to Lenk. 'Y'sure that wouldn't just be easier?'

Lenk blinked.

'Yes. Yes, I'm sure.'

'Do things the hard way, huh? Yeah, I'll grab *ah-he man-eh-wa*.' He hopped to the leather flap serving as a door. 'Togu's gonna be wantin' to talk with you after.'

Kataria watched the flap open and saw the various green shapes moving about in the bright sunlight beyond, the errant burble of their alien languages drifting into the hut. They were silenced as Bagagame slid out and she turned back to Lenk, eager to see another layer of horrified shock on his face.

What she saw instead was him lying supine on the sand,

his arm draped over his eyes. She studied his wiry body, the slight twitch of his muscles as he drew in deep breaths and exhaled them as stale, weary air. His body had become tense, trembling with every sigh he made.

For as much as he seemed to enjoy being grim and silent, Lenk was not the most difficult human to read, she thought. Even if he never spoke his feelings, his body told her enough. He seemed to compress as he lay upon the sand, some great weight pressing him down upon the earth.

She opened her mouth to speak when her thoughts leapt unbidden to the fore of her mind.

Don't, she told herself. *Don't ask him what's wrong. You know what he'll say. He's thinking about what you said on the boat before the Akaneeds attacked. He'll ask you why you said them, why you said you had to kill him to feel like a shict again. Then he'll ask you why you're still here, having said all that, why you didn't kill him. Don't ask him. Don't tell him. He's just now recovering; he can't handle the answer.*

Yeah. She sighed inwardly, rubbing her eyes. *He's the one that can't handle it.*

'How long?'

'What?' She looked up with a start. 'How long what?'

'Have I been out?'

'Oh,' she said. 'About two days.'

'Two days,' he muttered. 'I've been out for two days and on the island for two days. Four days total, three days past the time we were supposed to meet Sebast so he could take us back.' He cracked a smile. 'I'm assuming we lost the tome, too?'

'It hasn't been found, no,' Kataria said, shaking her head. 'The lizardmen have been fishing things out of the ocean for a while now, but no book.'

'Well,' he sighed, folding his arms behind his head. 'I suppose it doesn't really matter if we don't get picked up, then, does it?'

'Not necessarily,' she offered. 'The Owauku haven't said anything about a ship arriving in the past few days. Sebast might just be late.' She shrugged helplessly. 'I suppose that isn't much comfort, though.'

It would certainly be *less* comfort, she reasoned, to tell him that Sebast might not be coming because his search party was currently being digested and excreted by roaches. She held her tongue at that, knowing that the loss of the tome would likely be too much for him to bear.

It didn't appear to be, for his smile didn't diminish. Even when his lips quivered, it only grew a little larger. His eyes didn't grow any colder, their blue suddenly seeming less like frigid sheets of ice and more like the sea, endless and peaceful.

And even as she stared back at him, he didn't turn them away from her.

That, she knew, was unusual. He had stared at her many times before through many different eyes. She had felt his curiosity, his anger, his yearning all hammered upon her back through his stare. And always, he had turned away like a sheep before a wolf when she turned to meet his stare.

Now, it was she who felt the urge to turn away. It was she who felt her smile as sheepish upon her face. To see him so ... pleasant, without his sword and without blood spattering his face, was so unusual she couldn't help but feel as though it were somehow wrong, as though he were naked without violence and anger.

As if you needed any more reason to run.

'We're trapped here, you know,' she said, 'for the

foreseeable future, at least. We have no weapons, no tome, no *clothes*. We're stuck amidst a bunch of walking reptiles and you just *barely* survived an arrow through your leg.' She sneered, leaning back onto her hands. 'So, just in case you'd forgotten, there really isn't anything to smile about.'

'I suppose not,' he replied, 'but things are a lot better than they were two days ago.'

'Things will get worse.'

'They always do,' he agreed, nodding. 'But for now …'

For now, she told herself, *you should be dead. It should have been me to kill you. For now, I'm sitting here feeling like a helpless idiot because* I'm *the one turning away from your* stare. *For now, I let you …* touch *me like that. My father thinks a human touch can infect a* shict, *and you touched me* that *way. You touched my ears! For now, I should kill you, I should run, I should kill myself so I don't have to think about you and your horrible diseased race and your round ears.*

As the thoughts ran through her head, only two words made it to her lips.

'For now?' she asked.

'For now,' he said, smiling. 'We're alive.'

'Yeah,' she sighed, returning her smile. 'All of us.'

He blinked, his face screwing up in confusion.

'Did you say all of us?'

'She did,' came a familiar voice from the leather flap.

A smile crossed both their faces at the sight of a head full of thick brown locks over a hazel stare peering through the doorframe. The smile beneath it was slight, but warm, genuine and comfortably familiar.

'All of us,' Kataria repeated, gesturing to the door. 'Including *ah-he man-eh-wa* here.'

'I see,' Lenk said, smiling.

'You can still call me Asper,' the priestess replied. 'The Owauku are fond of long names, apparently.'

'I noticed.' A long moment of silence passed awkwardly before Lenk finally coughed. 'So, uh, are you going to come in?'

'Yeah … sure, just …' The priestess fidgeted behind the door. 'Just don't rush me.'

'Ah, yes,' Kataria said, smirking. '*Ah-he man-eh-wa* apparently means "shy when near-nude."'

'*You're* near-nude, too,' Asper spat through the door and tilted up her nose. 'And those of us *without* the physique of an adolescent boy have something to be considered worth concealing.'

'Is that right?' Kataria snarled. 'Maybe you can pray some clothes up, then? Like you prayed us to have a safe journey?'

'Physique *and* wits to match,' Asper growled at her. 'It's those prayers, and the faith that accompanies them, that are keeping me from bashing you in the head.'

'With what? Those colossal *haunches* of yours?' Kataria bared her canines at the priestess. 'I'd like to see you try.'

'So …' Lenk shifted his stare between the two of them. 'Did I miss something *really* fun, then?'

'It's nothing.' Asper's bashfulness apparently disappeared as she stormed into the hut, a bulging waterskin pressed against her torso. She thrust it into Lenk's hands as she knelt beside him. 'I need to check your injury. Drink.'

He did so, greedily, as Asper ran practised hands over his bandaged thigh, applying pressure to certain locations.

'You tore your stitches open when the Akaneeds attacked,' she said, not looking up. 'It wasn't easy to close you up again. Not to mention clear out the infected skin *and* salve and stitch up the arrow wound you so charitably left me to work with.'

'I suppose I should be grateful you didn't just put me out of my misery, then,' he replied between gulps.

She hesitated suddenly, spine stiffening. Absently, she rubbed an itch on her arm and returned to work.

'Yeah,' she muttered, 'I guess so.' She pressed on part of his leg. 'Did you feel that?'

'A little,' he replied, 'but it didn't hurt.'

'Good, good,' she said, nodding. 'It wasn't *too* bad an infection, thankfully. The Owauku had the medicine and the Gonwa knew how to use it.'

'Gonwa?' Lenk arched a brow.

'The other lizards here,' Kataria replied. 'Taller, skinnier ... and apparently good with medicine.'

'Not that their help was all that necessary,' Asper interjected. 'Most of the work I did on your wound before held over, so you shouldn't have been in too much pain.'

At that, Lenk sputtered on his water.

'Wait, what?' he asked, gasping for breath. 'It hurt like *hell*.'

'Well, yeah, but not too much, right? You could still walk. Your fever was only mild.'

'*Mild?* It felt like my brains were boiling! I was hallucinating! I saw ...'

Kataria's own eyes widened as he turned a cringing, moon-eyed stare at her. She met his gaze for a moment, the sudden quiver in his eyes allowing her to scrutinise him carefully. He turned away.

'I saw things,' he muttered.

'With this infection? I doubt it,' Asper replied. 'It was probably just exhaustion.'

'But I—'

289

'You didn't,' she said, curtly.

'He says he did,' Kataria interjected.

'Well,' Asper said, turning a heated glare upon the shict, 'how nice of you to be concerned for a lowly human.'

At that, Kataria felt her anger quelled only by the shame that blossomed within her like an agonising rose. *She's right*, she told herself. *I shouldn't be concerned.* She rode that thought to the sandy earth, turning her gaze away.

'Just eat something,' Asper said, rising up. 'You'll be fine. I'll check on you later.' She stalked to the door, heedless of Lenk's befuddlement of Kataria's scowl. And yet, she hesitated at the frame, standing in the door flap. 'Lenk ... you know I wouldn't ever put you out of your misery, right?'

'Sure, I know.'

'Good,' she said. She cast a smile over her shoulder, small and timid. 'I'm glad you're all right.'

And then, she swept out of the hut, leaving Lenk blinking and Kataria flattened-eared and hissing at the space left behind.

'So,' he said, 'what was that?'

'She's been agitated ever since she started working on you,' the shict replied, never taking her glower off the door. 'She started screaming one night, telling everyone to get out ... went mad for a while, I don't know. Denaos certainly hasn't been a help in calming her down.'

'Denaos? He's alive?'

'And here, as well as Dreadaeleon.'

'And Gariath?'

She blinked, opened her mouth to reply, then shook her head.

'Not yet,' she muttered before quickly adding, 'if at all.'

'If at all,' he echoed, and the weight seemed to return to him.

'Don't think about it,' she said, smiling and placing a hand on his shoulder. 'It'd be rather anticlimactic if you worried yourself back into a coma. What say we find you something to eat?'

'That'd be nice,' he said, rubbing his belly. 'I haven't had anything but tubers and roots.'

'Ha!' She clapped her hands. 'You remembered how to forage just like I taught you! And they said humans couldn't be trained!' Laughing, she rose up from the sandy floor. 'I'll go hunt something down for you.'

'I appreciate it,' he replied.

'You won't once you find out what they eat out here.'

She walked to the door, feeling no eyes upon her back and taking great relief in that. She could hear his breath coming in short, steady bursts. His heartbeat no longer plagued her ears. She smiled as she pulled back the leather flap.

Just a passing fascination, she told herself. *He was just thrilled to be alive and awake. All his attentions were focused on you because you happened to be there … watching over him.* No! She had to resist thumping her temple. *No, no. Don't start. He was … was just like a pup.* Yeah. *He's momentarily happy. Once he gets some food, he'll forget about everything else, about how you were there … about how he touched your ears …*

She reached up and tugged on her earlobe. The sensation of his finger, the scent of his sweat mingling with hers, still lingered.

He'll forget all about it, she told herself, *and then so can you.*

'Kat?'

Don't turn around. Don't look. Don't even acknowledge him.

'Yeah?' she asked.

'I'm happy you're alive.'

'Yeah,' she said.

She emerged into the daylight, waited for the leather flap to fall so that she could no longer hear him breathing. Then, she let her heavy chin fall to her chest and let her breath escape in a long, tired sigh.

'Damn,' she whispered, stalking off across the sands, 'damn, damn, damn ...'

Sixteen

THE SIN OF MEMORY

He found he could not remember his name.

Other memories returned to him, vivid as the city that loomed in the distance.

Port Yonder. He remembered its name, at least.

He had lived there once. He'd had a house on the land, back when dry earth did not burn his feet. It had been made of stone that had seemed strong at the time and bore the weight of a family once. He had known the witless, bovine satisfaction of staring up at a temple and praying to a goddess that priests said would protect him. He recalled living through each night, when such knowledge was all he needed.

He had known what it meant to be human once.

But that was long ago. That was a time before he knew the weight of humanity could not be set on flimsy, shifting land. That was a time before he knew that stone, trees and air all gave way before relentless tides. That was a time before his goddess had found his devotion and offerings not enough and had spitefully taken his family to compensate. His name, too, was from that time.

Before he had become the Mouth of Ulbecetonth.

'Do you desire to know your name, then?'

The Prophet's twin voices lilted up from the deep. He looked over the edge of the tiny rock he squatted upon, saw the black shadow of a tremendous fish circling his outcropping. He remembered when he had first seen that shadow and the golden eyes that had peered up at him. There had been six of them, then; now there were only four, two of them put out forever by heretical steel.

'I desire nothing,' he answered the water, 'save that the Mother is liberated.'

The *real* Mother, he reminded himself, not the Sea Mother.

The Sea Mother was a benevolent and kindly concept, one that took pity upon the land-bound folk and blessed them with the bounty of the deep. The Sea Mother was a concept that rewarded thoughtless prayer, asked for nothing more than humble sacrifice and protected families in return.

The Sea Mother was a lie.

Mother Deep was mercy.

'Liberation is a just cause, indeed,' the Prophet replied. 'And it is because of that cause that we ask you to return to the prison of earth and wind once more. The Father must be freed for the Mother to rise.'

He found a slight smirk creeping upon his face at the naming of the city a prison. Truly, that was what it was, he knew – nothing more than thick walls constructed by fear, doors made of ignorance and the key thrown away by unquestioning faith.

That smile soured the instant he remembered that they were sending him back there, to feel cruel stone beneath his unwebbed feet and languish in the embrace of air. His brow furrowed and he could feel the hairs growing back even as he did, tiny black reminders that the Prophet commanded and the Mouth sacrificed.

And for what?

As if summoned by his thoughts, he heard the sound of flapping wings. He looked up and saw the Heralds descending from the unworthy sky, their pure white feathers stretched out as they glided to the reefs jutting from the surface. Upon talons that had once been meagre webs, clutching with hands that had once been pitiful gull wings, the creatures landed silently upon the risen coral.

He remembered what they had been before: squat little creatures, wide-eyed crone heads upon gull bodies, incapable of even the slightest independent thought. The faces that stared at him now, still withered, were set upside down upon their crane-like necks above sagging, vein-mapped teats. Their bulging blue eyes now regarded him with a keen intellect that had not been present before. The teeth set in mouths that should have been their foreheads were long yellow spikes that clicked as they chattered relentlessly.

He had once looked upon them as evidence of Mother Deep's power, the ability to effect change where other gods were deaf and powerless. Now, he saw them only as items of envy, proof that even the least of Her congregation evolved where he stood, painfully and profoundly human.

'Do we sense uncertainty in you?' the Prophet asked, stacking accusation upon scorn.

'Uncertainty?' the Heralds echoed in crude mimic of the Prophet. 'Doubt? Inability? Weakness?' They leaned their upside-down heads thoughtfully closer. 'Faithlessness?'

'My protests are unworthy,' the Mouth replied. 'All that matters is that the Father is freed. I have no other desire.'

'Lies,' the Heralds retorted with decisiveness.

'Irrelevant,' the Mouth replied. 'Service is all that is required. Motive is unimportant.'

'Ignorance,' they crowed in shrill chorus.

'What great sin is desire, then? What is the weight that is levied upon my shoulders for my want of vengeance? Mother Deep's enemies are my enemies. Her purpose is my purpose.'

'Blasphemy,' the voices hissed from below.

The Prophet's twin tones contained a wailing keen, the subtlest discordant harmony that shook his body painfully and caused him to wince. How he longed to abandon his ears with what remained of his memories. How he longed to embrace the Prophet's shrieking sermon with the same lustful joy as the others.

Mother Deep demanded sacrifice, too, however.

'You suffer doubts, then,' the Prophet murmured, four golden eyes regarding him curiously.

'Intolerable,' the Heralds muttered. 'Inexcusable. Unthinkable.'

'I had not expected to be asked to return here,' he replied, staring out over the walls. 'I left this place, and all its callous hatreds, on land where it belonged.' He hugged his legs to his chest. 'I found reprieve in the Deep.'

But not salvation, he added mentally. He had been granted gifts: the embrace of the water, freedom from the greedy liquid hands that sought to steal air and quench it, and the loyalty of Her children. But the true mercies of Mother Deep had been withheld from him, for the moment.

And yet, he lamented, that moment had lasted for years that only made his awareness of the passage of time more profound.

He gazed down into the water, below the swimming shadow of the Prophet, and saw the faithful congregate in pale flashes as they boiled up from below. The fading sunlight shifted on the water hesitantly, wary to expose the creatures bobbing below it. And, as the golden light speared through the waves, a great forest of hairless flesh, swaying on the waves, met his eyes as hundreds of glossy stares incapable of reflecting the light looked up.

They floated so effortlessly, bodies lent buoyancy with the absence of memory. They were oblivious, ignorant to what their lives might have been when their feet lacked webs and could abide the feel of land beneath them. They were blind to the meaning of the rising and setting of the sun. They were deaf to the world, save the wailing chorus of the Prophet's twin mouths, which he could not abide, and the distant call of Mother Deep, which he could not yet hear.

And, he thought resentfully, *they sacrificed nothing*.

They gave themselves fully, ate of the fruit of the Shepherd's births, and were freed from their memories and the embrace of greedy, lying gods. He had abstained, at the Prophet's request. He had become the Mouth and was denied their serenity, their bliss.

Their freedom ...

And he ... *he* had given everything. He had abstained from the embrace of Mother Deep's children, and for what? That he could be tormented still with his own ignorance? Taunted with the years he had wasted on a goddess that spared not his family? Agonised with the visions of their faces, the memories of their laughter?

And *now*, now they asked him to return to the land, to bear the stain of solid ground and recall the memories they had promised to take away from him. What he saw when he looked up across the channel at the docks he had walked off of, following three voices in the night, was a return to sinful memory and the company of ignorant airbreathers.

Not the salvation he had been promised.

'And for what?' he muttered. 'This brings us no closer to the book.'

'An ocean is a vast and tremulous thing,' the Prophet replied coolly. 'Its sheer magnitude makes it incomprehensible to view with mortal eyes. Where a gale blowing from the west may seem separate from a wave roaring in the east, they meet in the middle as a raging maelstrom.' The shadow of the fish's body paused thoughtfully. 'And even then, it cannot be fully fathomed unless viewed from below.'

He could see flashes of white in the darkness as two broad mouths split open in wide, fanged smiles.

'She sees where we cannot,' the Heralds burbled in agreement. 'Thinks in ways we cannot comprehend. The maelstrom whirls, swirls chaotically, inexplicably.'

'But it is nonetheless felt,' the Prophet added quietly. 'The Mouth should not concern itself with the book. Mother Deep has seen to its return.'

He might have asked how. How could any creature, even one that made such promises and delivered such freedom as Mother Deep, affect anything beyond the bonds of her prison? How could she promise the salvation so freely, knowing that hers was a hand still wrapped in chains?

He might have asked, but recalled too keenly the wisdom of the Shepherds, delivered from their gaping jaws to the unworthy grasped in their oozing claws.

Memory was a burden. Knowledge was a sin.

'A key, after all,' the Prophet continued, 'is but one part of a door. There must be hinges upon it to swing and hands to turn the knob.' Golden gazes drifted toward the distant city. 'If those hands should be freed from unjust bondage, so much the better.'

'Better,' the Heralds echoed. 'The sons need a father. The faithful need a leader.'

Beneath the waves, something stirred in agreement.

Below, he saw the thousand glossy stares of the faithful turn in unison toward the city, as though something had called to them in a great, echoing call. Darkness stirred beneath them, where the light did not dare to touch, and he saw the great white stares of the Shepherds rise to add their attention.

It angered him that he could not hear what they heard, see what they saw. Before them loomed a prison in their eyes, an unjust and foul dungeon of stone and wind wherein lay the salvation he could not claim. All he could see was the lies and hate that had driven him to the deep in the first place.

What they heard, he could only make out faintly. Even as far away as he was, through the roiling waves and over the murmur of wind, he could hear it. Slowly, steadily, with a patience that had outlasted mountains and earth, it droned like small hands upon a large door.

A single heart, beating.

He supposed, he thought dejectedly, he should be thankful that he was blessed enough to hear even that. His ears burned enviously with thoughts of what the congregation might hear, what bliss it might bring minds wiped clean of memories and lies.

'Impatience does not become the position She chose you for,' the Prophet said coldly, as though sensing his thoughts.

'At times, the reason for my choosing becomes obscured,' he replied just as brusquely.

'Is devotion no longer reason enough?' the Prophet asked.

'Recall the maelstrom,' the Heralds agreed. 'It is—'

'I *cannot* subsist on metaphors,' the Mouth snarled suddenly, his patience lost in a sudden surge of grief. 'Words do *nothing* to diminish the memories, to make me forget that *I* am denied the gifts of Mother Deep that are promised to the less faithful!'

'In time!' the Heralds squawked in protest. 'In time, there will be—'

'Will be *what?*' His frustration inspired words that he knew he should not speak, gave force to will that he knew was sinful. 'All your promises, all your great plans have availed us nothing! The tome is *lost*, the longfaces drive back the faithful time and again, even desecrating the Shepherds with their vile poisons! And now, while they sniff out the book like landborne hounds, *you* sit here and point me toward the very city I turned to you to free myself of?'

He drew in a sharp breath whose saltless taste was yet not foul on his lips. He narrowed eyes that were not glossed over, clenched fists that were not webbed, as weak, sinful emotion came flooding into him.

'Occasionally, Prophet,' the man hissed, 'gales and walls of water are nothing more than mere winds and waves, each without substance.'

Satisfaction was something he knew he should not feel. It was, like all sensations outside of unrelenting devotion, a sin, and he made himself stern with the knowledge that it would be punished. He imagined himself being torn to shreds by the Prophet's shriek, the same wailing doom that had wrought ruin upon the faithless and blasphemers that stood in the way of the faithful.

Perhaps, he thought, that was as close to hearing the harmony in its words as he would ever come.

The Prophet circled his outcropping silently. The Heralds' relentless crowing had fallen silent; they tilted their heads right side up in curiosity. The golden eyes were dark below. The congregation was still, suspended motion-less in the water. Even the white stares of the Shepherds had vanished, as though afraid of what wrath awaited their former preacher, Ulbecetonth's Mouth.

But after several painful breaths, all that emerged from below was a pair of melodic whispers.

'Our pity is well given to you,' the Prophet said softly. 'Perhaps we have become too much like the Gods that ig-nore your cries. But we are not deaf …' The voices snaked up like vocal tendrils, caressing him with slender, shim-mering sound. 'Your agonies are heard. Your faith shall be rewarded.

'You wish your sinful memories to be absolved, the trag-edy of your life to be eased inside your mind,' the Prophet continued. 'It shall be done. Yours will be ears closer to the Mother's song than any of the faithful. All that is asked of you is that you grant Her one more favour.'

He drew in another deep breath, felt his heart pound with anticipation.

'Free the Father,' one Herald whispered, its voice car-ried on the wind.

'End the injustice of his imprisonment,' another hissed.

'Lead the faithful to salvation,' more crowed.

'Free him,' they burbled. 'Free him … free him … free him …'

'Let him crush the earth beneath his feet again.' The Prophet's voices silenced the chorus. Gold eyes turned up-ward again, burning with purpose. 'Liberate Daga-Mer.'

As the Prophet's voices echoed, fading with each moment, another sound grew stronger. As if in the moment before a great drawing of breath, it echoed from the deep and carried to his ears.

A heartbeat.

The Heralds scattered at the sound, taking wing on shrieks of ecstasy as they twirled and writhed in feathery columns stretching toward the sun-stolen sky.

Another beat, louder.

The faithful stared up, their mouths splitting open in broad, toothy grins. Their eyes quivered in the rising starlight, as though they might add their own joyful salt to the sea.

Another.

The Shepherds dropped their jaws open, exposing sharp teeth as they howled some ancient hymn that went unheard, rising to the surface on bubbles that popped soundlessly.

Another beat, loud and clear as if it were that of the Mouth's.

And he felt himself smile to hear it.

The water called to him and he obeyed, sliding in. It embraced him like a family that would never leave him, never deny him. He swam silently upon its tide towards the distant prison of earth and air. He swam, sliding through the waves as a world of dark flesh, dark eyes and glorious faith moved beneath him.

He swam, dipping his head below the surf.

And through it, he heard the Father calling.

ACT TWO
Island of Hope and Death

Seventeen

BETTER OFF IGNORANT

The Aeons' Gate
Island of Teji
Summer, pleasantly so

One of the more sobering realisations I have stumbled across since I first picked up a sword is that society, at least as we know it, does not exist.

Of course, I'm actually a little disappointed to put it down on paper. After all, I had rather enjoyed the ideas behind civilisation: linking together against common enemies, joining like-minded trades and arms for mutual prosperity, the coalition of many single gods for the benefit of all and, of course, the keen urge to keep one's neighbour close so that, when he finally did knife one in the kidneys and steal one's sheep, at least one couldn't claim they didn't see it coming.

Regardless, my most horrific discovery has been that society is nothing more than a series of carefully calculated choices based solely around economics. That's it. No like-minded philosophies, no common gods, not even healthy distrust made it possible.

Just gold and greed.

Any other thoughts I've had about this were quickly banished once I arrived on Teji and was subjected to the curious company of the Owauku. As far as I've been able to tell from as far as I've been able to understand their language, Teji was a thriving trading post, as Argaol informed me ... once, anyway.

Humans used to live here. That much is clear by what has happened to the locals. I'd seen some of the more remote societies on the outskirts of Toha when we first began looking for the Aeons' Gate, as Miron originally hired us to do. They tended to have both a keen distrust for me and a keen intent on putting something sharp in my guts.

Or an arrow in my shoulder, as the case may be.

The tall, tattooed lizardmen ... they're called 'Shen', the Owauku tell me: raiders, scavengers, generally as uncivilised as one would expect loincloth-clad reptiles to be. Of them, I know not much else, save that the Owauku have driven them off. They're gone.

So they tell me.

The Owauku ... are friendlier than most. Almost too much. They offer us freely their meat and drink, at least what passes for meat and drink, but with the subtle gleam in their eyes that suggests something would be appreciated in return. That gleam, anyway, is what I deduce from the times I can stand looking in those giant melons they call eyes. They do this ... thing ... where they look at me with one eye, then look at something else with the other, and they keep moving in different directions and ...

Never mind. It's too disgusting to recount. It does make one yearn for the company of the Gonwa, though. Those taller, bearded things that I saw in the forest apparently share the village with the Owauku. I can't imagine why; the Gonwa are tall and stoic where the Owauku are short and spastic. The Gonwa are reserved and distrustful where the Owauku are almost offensively open. The Gonwa only look at me when they think I'm not looking at them, and sometimes with murder in their eyes, while the Owauku look at me ...

No. No. Disgusting.

The point is that the Owauku have and love and the Gonwa

lack and loathe everything one might find in a city: gambling; smoke, in both cigar and hookah form; alcohol, from their own making; and various other sundries and goods remnant from when humans still traded with them. The little ones adore the idea of trade, and constantly ask us if we have anything to put forth in that regard.

What they think we have, I really can't even begin to wonder. They've already taken our pants ...

Anyway, as I was saying, the idea of everything important being driven by economics does not apply solely to society. In the age we live in, it's become a healthy substitute for instinct. If something costs more to get than it's worth, then it's not worth the effort. It's that easy.

And, with that in mind, I've decided to follow my instincts ...

And give up.

I'm through. I'm through with everything. I don't want to have anything to do with Miron, with books, with bounties or monsters or netherlings or demons ever again. Especially nothing to do with books. I nearly lost all my companions, and did lose at least one, searching for the stupid thing.

Once, long ago, that thought wouldn't have seemed so bad. But ... that was before. Before I stopped fighting, before I put the sword down and had a chance to breathe. It wasn't by choice that I stumbled across this realisation. On Teji, there's nothing to fight, nothing to kill, nothing to worry about killing me.

And ... I find that I kind of like it.

Without anything's entrails to spill upon it, I find myself doing a lot of walking on the ground instead. I spend most of my days walking down the beaches with Kataria, listening to her tell me about the various plants, shells and driftwood we find. At least half of the stuff she spews, I'm certain she's making up, but every time I feel like accusing her, she smiles and ... looks at me.

Not look looks at me, but ... looks at me, like I'm something

307

she wants to look at. She stares at me, not in the way that suggests she's looking for something beneath my skin, but like my skin is fine as is. She stares at me and I don't mind. There's nothing screaming in my head.

I'm ... not hearing the voices anymore so much.

I'm even starting to remember my old life, before this all happened. I can remember my family. Not their names, but their faces, the colour of my grandfather's beard, the feel of the calluses on my father's hands, the smell of the tea my mother brewed in the morning. I can remember cows I've milked, dogs I've fed, barns I've swept ...

All while I'm around her.

It's not all great, to be perfectly honest. I still dream, and when I do, I dream of flames, of big blue eyes without pupils. And while I'm at ease with the Owauku, their taller, bearded friends, the Gonwa, eye me with distaste. Perhaps they knew, at one point, I planned to kill them? I don't see why they would take offence at that, really. I didn't know them at the time; it was going to be a perfectly honest killing.

And ... I'm still hearing the voices.

That's another thing. I did just write 'voices', with an 's'. There's another one, I think ... a fainter one than the first one, not so loud, not so demanding. The first one was like a fist: jabbing, pounding at the door to let it in. This one ... is subtler, like a wiggle of the knob, a hand pulling at the sheet around me, someone moving a cup of tea from where I set it down.

And sometimes, it's not so subtle. It tries to break the door down, tears the sheet off, slips and breaks the cup. It gets so loud ... so ANGRY ...

But let's not think about that. There's more important things to worry about.

For example, Sebast is now almost a week overdue. The ship that Argaol promised to send to pick us up has never been seen, even when Kat and I wait on the beach for any sign on the horizon. The Owauku assure me that if any did arrive, they would tell me. Frankly, I believe them, since any boat that came would be instantly harried by them as they sought to trade with it.

I should be more worried about this than I am. But I've since decided that Argaol wasn't as good as his word. It's really not that big a surprise; he managed to get six bloodthirsty lunatics off his ship. Why would he send anyone to go get them back?

Still, I'm not too worried. Even if it's fallen into disuse, this is still a trading post. It's still close to the shipping lanes. There's no reason to expect that a ship won't eventually come by. If all that means is a few weeks stuck in a loincloth walking down the beach alongside Kat, who I must say looks pretty smashing in her own, then I'm fine with that. Naturally, I'm a little disappointed that there are no more humans on the island.

Strange, though, I don't recall if Togu ever told me what happened to them.

Not that I go out of my way to spend time with Togu, actually. Amongst the Owauku, or even amongst all the horrible things I've seen, he definitely ranks as one of the worst. He is living proof that the Gods exist and that their sense of humour appeals only to themselves. It's as though they made some dwarfish, scaly creature with giant gourds for eyes and a horrifyingly strange accent and decided he just wasn't irritating enough without having the insufferable speech prowess of a six-headed politician crossbred with a forty-handed merchant.

I'm content to mostly spend time with my companions, even if the reverse isn't true.

Asper has nothing but harsh words and ire for me, though I gather she's short with everyone these days. Why, I cannot say. I know something ... occurred when she was tending to my wounds, something that is largely accredited to the stress of the situation and her lack of clothes. Denaos tells me something similar occurred shortly after she woke up and spoke to Dreadaeleon. He didn't have any time to check on her, of course, since shortly after, he made the acquaintance of the Owauku and became wise to their insatiable voracity for human pants.

Either way, his attentions are solely on her, in the same way a voyeur's attentions are solely on a lady's unguarded window. Dreadaeleon isn't much better. His conversation is curt and brief and, every time, he always scampers behind a hut or a bush to avoid me. If I wasn't so trusting, and if I didn't care so little, I'd say he was hiding something. And every day I thank Khetashe that pubescent wizards are as loath to share their problems as I am to hear them.

We've kept eyes open for signs of Gariath, albeit not very widely. Perhaps it's just the peace that Teji has infected me with, or perhaps it's the fact that he's a deranged, flesh-eating lunatic, but I can't say there's much of a reason to look very hard.

In short, I have to say that Teji might be the best thing that happened to me. Despite the disappearance of my sword, the tome and all my clothes, I'm ... almost happy.

A ship will come, eventually. We'll get new pants. We'll get new boots. We'll clean the sand from our buttocks, wash our faces in fresh water, read books with real words and never have need to pick up a sword again.

Hope ... doesn't seem such a bad thing.

Eighteen

THE BENEFITS OF SWAYING GENITALS

On the very small list of upsides that came with wearing a loincloth, Dreadaeleon counted the ability to urinate without adjusting the garment to be somewhere between gross exposure to insects with a taste for his flesh and the persistent sensation of having a dead rodent lodged up one's rectum.

Though he had been enjoying all in obscene measure since his arrival on Teji, he found the former to be the one most practised.

Of course, he told himself, it wasn't his fault. Venarie was not a precise art. Even the most careful practitioner could find himself strained too much, his spells improperly channelled, and end up with the occasional premature liver spot or loose bladder.

Surprisingly enough, the boy didn't take much comfort in that.

Instead, he pressed his hands against the reed wall of a nearby hut and attempted to convince himself that clenching his teeth and grunting would pass as casual behaviour amidst a plethora of lizardmen. If they had taken notice of this the first dozen times he had done it, they had long since ceased paying attention to the scrawny fellow with the trail of yellow dripping down his leg.

'Come on,' he whispered, 'finish, finish ...'

Even knowing this was far beyond his physical control now, let alone his verbal control, he couldn't help but urge it along. Thus far, he had been able to convince himself that such commendations were all that kept his companions from finding out. Relief had come when Kataria began tending to Lenk, and Denaos had never really taken an interest in him before.

It was Asper's outburst that caused him conflict. On the one hand, the doubtless endless inquiries as to his health that she would have usually hurled at him were better off avoided. Fortunate, he considered, for he hadn't yet figured out a way to make loss of bladder control sound like the kind of thing she would want to concern herself with. But at the same time, she was snappish and curt with him, as well as everyone else, and did her best to avoid them all.

And, he thought with a sigh, he had indeed grown fond of the sight of her in Teji's native garb.

The stream ended with a shudder as he carefully wiped himself down with a handkerchief one of the Owauku had offered him in exchange for a brief display of fire dancing along his fingers. Not quite an even trade by his reckoning, since that display had likely been the reason behind his sudden breakings of the dam.

He found himself hard-pressed to stay mad at the creatures, though, if only because he found himself hard-pressed to even look them in their tremendous, rotating eyes. This became doubly difficult due to the fact that he was especially hard-pressed to find any way to avoid the creatures.

He looked down from the lip of the sprawling, spiralling valley that was their village. Sandy paths topped the concentric rings of stone that formed their streets and held their reed huts. Tiny, swift-moving streams flanked each road. And walking upon these roads, swimming in these streams, dozens of little green blobs scampered about.

Scampering was apparently one of their very few ambitions in life, haggling and yelling at each other being the others. But above both of these, they seemed very fond of lounging. Under the shade of their lean-tos, amongst the pools fed by the waterfalls dripping in from the forest that loomed over their valley, in the half-drowned sandy bottom of their village; it didn't matter where they happened to fall, the Owauku had turned laziness into an art form.

And because of this, Dreadaeleon found himself wondering, once more, where this particular village had come from. The stone circles were far too smooth, far too orderly to be anything born from nature. The waterfalls did not trickle of their own accord, but were fed into their streams and pools from aqueducts and trenches that undoubtedly had required many very patient men a long time to carve from the rock. But the creatures scarcely seemed to have the attention span required to carve a slur into a coconut, much less hew this marvel of sand and stone and stream.

He studied for as long as he dared until he heard the unmistakable cry of greeting. He assumed it was greeting, anyway; the Owauku's language tended to blend salutations, curses and propositions into remarkably similar words. The dozens of green blobs became dozens of pairs of bulbous golden globes as they all looked up at him, yellow smiles splitting their faces and stubby appendages waving at him. His grin and wave were equally meek as he noted with no undue relief that only the Owauku demanded such a reaction.

The Gonwa were mercifully curt.

There was no shortage of the lankier bearded lizards walking amidst the sandy pathways, either. Very rarely did the more stoic creatures even deign to notice their companions' presence, and when they did it was only with a mutter in their own language and a downturn of their eyes.

Side by side with the Owauku, they didn't look *particularly* strange, and their smaller cohorts didn't seem to mind their presence one bit. Together, they soaked in the dozens of pools that lined the rising sandy ridges in the valley, each one fed by gently trickling waterfalls, flowing swiftly from the forest above to splash in the pools below, sending cascading droplets against the damp earth and …

His eyes widened as he felt a sudden warmth cascade down his inner thigh.

'Oh, come *on*,' he whispered, turning back to the hut's wall.

The effects of an overuse of Venarie were random and imprecise, ranging anything from pink sweat to instantaneous internal combustion, swiftly followed by external combustion. Horror stories lingered about the occasional bout of extreme overindulgence that resulted in spontaneous hermaphrodite transformation combined with the sudden growth of tails, fins, horns and extra mouths.

Dreadaeleon supposed he ought to be pleased that an uncontrollable bladder was all that he suffered.

And he was, indeed, pleased up until the moment he heard a familiarly unpleasant voice behind him.

'Well, well,' the distinctly masculine voice muttered, 'watering your garden, are you?'

He whirled about, seeing his horrified visage reflected in Denaos' broad, white grin. The tall man folded his arms over his naked chest and canted his head to the side at the boy, the wrinkled lines in his face suddenly giving him a decidedly sadistic visage.

'I'm not sure what you know of botany,' the rogue said, stifling a chuckle, 'but you won't be growing any daffodils with the fertiliser you're using.'

'How long have you been standing there?' Dreadaeleon demanded, painfully aware of the startled crack in his voice.

'You're never happy to see me anymore.'

'Possibly because you watch people while they urinate for purposes I cannot begin to even summon the will to fathom.'

'Intimidation, mostly,' the rogue replied with a shrug.

'I don't follow.'

'Well, see, a fellow who can sneak up on you and put steel in your kidneys while you're not looking is just unpleasant. A fellow who can do all that while you're indulging your glittering wine?' His grin took on an exceedingly unpleasant quality. 'Well, there's a man to be scared of.'

'I suppose I should have clarified,' Dreadaeleon muttered, waving a hand, 'I don't *want* to follow. Go away.'

'I don't see why I should,' Denaos replied. 'You're doing well enough.'

'Did you take me for the type that would lock up while being watched?' the boy growled.

'Well, no.' The rogue chuckled. 'That would be *weird*.' He cleared his throat. 'Anyway, mind telling me?'

'Telling you what?'

'Why, precisely, you go wherever you please? Being amongst half-naked reptiles is hardly an excuse to cast modesty to the wind.'

'It's not your place to know.'

'It *is* my place to ask,' Denaos retorted. 'Frankly, if you're going to go explode in some magical blaze of fire, I think I have the right to know.'

'You think it's magical, then?' the boy asked, sneering.

'Don't get me wrong, there are plenty of things wrong with you that *aren't* magical, but this ...' He gestured to the soaked earth. 'This seems more in the realm of "things that could go horrifically awry."'

'It's just a little loss of control,' Dreadaeleon replied as calmly as he could. 'Magic needs fuel. I am that fuel. I don't get to decide which muscles it eats away.'

'That doesn't seem much like a muscle you should be gambling with,' Denaos said. 'What was it that caused it? Too much magic stuff?'

'Yes, exactly. All the wondrous thought and power that goes into my gift and you've boiled it down to "too much magic stuff,"' the boy snarled. 'You have a promising future as an archivist for the drunk and simple.' He glowered disdainfully at the sleepy look in the rogue's eyes, sniffed at his foul breath. 'Mostly the drunk.'

'Well, there's hardly any need to be snide about it,' the rogue replied. 'Really, though, I am a bit curious.'

'And I'm a bit uncomfortable with where this is heading.'

'Hush, I'm pontificating.' The rogue leaned back with an air of scholarly ponder, tapping his chin. 'Why in Silf's name, or whatever gods you don't happen to believe in, would you still be suffering magic-related ailments if you haven't had need, cause or want to continue using magic for all the time we've been here?'

He knows. He knows about the tome, about the scrying, about the stone ...

The thought came almost unbidden, and the stiffening of his spine and sudden dripping halt of his flow came completely unbidden. The rogue's eyebrow rose so slowly, with such arrogant curiosity, that Dreadaeleon could almost hear the muscles behind it creak like a door.

No, he told himself. *He knows nothing. How could he?*

How could he not? the boy countered himself. *It's not like you've been particularly subtle about it. And he has a penchant for sneaking up on people …*

That made sense, the boy had to admit. He should have known he couldn't get far enough away to avoid Denaos.

Still, he told himself, *he can't know much. What could he know? He doesn't understand how scrying works.*

But he could have learned. He could have found out, watched the wizard in his meditations long enough to have discerned that he was sniffing about the island, that he was pulling down more and more seagulls for purposes beyond getting covered in bird stool.

His heart started to beat quicker. How much *did* the rogue know? Was he aware of the tome's location? Was he aware that the boy knew? Had he surmised the boy's plan, to delay their discovery until he could bring himself up to his full strength and find it himself?

He must know; he's not an idiot, Dreadaeleon told himself. *Maybe I should just tell him. He can be persuaded to keep a secret …*

No, fool! He reprimanded himself with a mental snarl. *Tell him, and he'll tell Lenk. Lenk will get it and what will you have done? Tattled like a child? They'll be the great heroes again, adored by her, and you'll be nothing more than a whiny little brat who had to go running to the men again.*

He paused, frowning. *Maybe I'm overreacting. They can't possibly see me like that.*

But when have they not? The irritation came flooding back into him with a scowl. *They treat you like a match, sparking*

*you and throwing you away at their convenience. You set the fires
and they enjoy the warmth. It's time you proved that your fires
shouldn't be ignored so lightly. You've conquered bigger obstacles
with magic before. You can do this.*

Right, he told himself. *I can do this.* He grimaced. *Right?*

'You're hiding something,' Denaos said, angling the
accusation like a knife.

'What makes you so sure?' the boy replied as smooth as
he could manage.

'You just froze while I was talking you, likely disappearing into some bizarre stream of thought that you'd rather
I was not privy to.' The rogue sniffed. 'Also, your piss is
on fire.'

The smoke filled his nostrils before Dreadaeleon could
even think of a reply. He stared down with twofold horror:
once to see the stream renewed and twice to see the yellow
taint ending in a small blaze that smouldered angrily on
the ground. His cry, too, came twice as he leapt backward
and sprayed fiery soil across the earth.

'Good Gods, how do you explain *this*?' Denaos leapt
from the errant stream.

'It's ... it's perfectly natural,' Dreadaeleon stammered.
'Well, all right, not natural, but not uncommon. Sometimes
fluids get crossed when a wizard channels them through
his body, resulting in urine that explodes when exposed to
air. Nothing to worry about.' He nodded sternly, placed
his hands on his hips, then looked up at the rogue. 'So, uh,
what do I do?'

'How should I know what to do about your fluids?'
Denaos said, cringing away. 'How often does this happen?'

'Not enough that I know what to do,' the boy shrieked,
gesturing wildly. 'How do I stop it? *What do I do?*'

'Well, don't *point* it at me!' Denaos angled himself sharply behind the wizard, seizing him by the shoulders and directing him toward a nearby bush. 'There! Just … just close your eyes and think of Muraska. It'll wear itself out.'

Damn, damn, damn, Dreadaeleon scolded himself mentally. *This!* This *is what happens when I don't rest! I knew this was going to happen. Well, not this, specifically, but something like this! Oh, I'm so bad at this …* His hands twitched about his loincloth, fearful to touch and aim the suddenly lethal spewer. *Well … no, it's fine. Denaos can keep a secret, right? He'll make me pay for it later, but for now, all that matters is that no one sees—*

'What's going on?' a familiarly feminine voice lilted to his ears.

He nearly broke his neck as he contorted it to see over his shoulder. Asper stood, hands on bare hips, her expression a blend of concern and irritation that drifted between the wizard and the tall man standing between them. Dreadaeleon felt his blood run cold, even as he felt a sudden, fiery spurt.

Damn, damn, damn, damn, DAMN!

'Watch my back,' he whispered his plea to Denaos.

'Better than your front, surely,' the rogue muttered in reply.

'Is there something going on here that I should be informed about?' Asper demanded again, crinkling her nose as she witnessed Dreadaeleon's activity. 'Or is this actually as foul as it appears?'

'Foul?' Denaos mimicked her indignant stance. 'What's foul about it?'

'He appears to be urinating on a burning bush,' she replied, fixing him with a suspicious stare. 'Why?'

'Dry season.'

'And Dreadaeleon is …'

'Performing his humanitarian duty by putting it out.' The rogue sighed dramatically. 'Listen, this is rather a personal aspect of a man's life, so is there something we can help you with?'

'Lenk has something to say to us,' she said. 'He has a hard time climbing the rings with his injury, so I went out to find you.'

'Well, injured or not, he'll have to come to us,' Denaos said with a shrug. 'Dread's going to be a while.' At her confused stare, he nodded sagely. 'It was a *very* dry season.' Following that, he thrust his own curious stare at her. 'Interesting that you should come this far just to find us, though … Almost out of character, isn't it?'

Even over the crackle of the blazing bush, Dreadaeleon could hear the accusation intoned in Denaos' voice. He lofted a brow, then lofted it higher as he heard Asper's feet slide aggressively across the sand and her hand clap on the rogue's naked back. An instant of remembered pain flashed through his mind, memories of the rogue's arm around the priestess, the sensation of impotent fury that followed.

He hid his scowl, strained to stifle himself and hear the harsh whispers emanating between her clenched teeth.

'You say *nothing* of what happened,' she snarled to him, pulling him closer. '*Nothing.*'

'Ashamed?' Denaos muttered in reply.

'Secretive,' she growled. 'You know the difference.'

'I don't know why it matters so much.'

'No, you don't.'

By the time he heard her break away from him, listened to hear feet tramping down the sandy hill, the blood boiled in his ears with enough fury to render him deaf to all else, save the thunder in his own head.

You fool! You FOOL! What was she doing while you *were scenting out the tome? What was* he *doing while* you *were preparing to save them all? Of course, why wouldn't they? Filthy, god-fearing animals acting in decidedly filthy mannerisms* ...

'She's gone now,' Denaos said, glancing down the hill. 'How's the progress over there?'

Maybe it's not like that ... Maybe she's talking about something else. Let's remain calm here. It's the fumes that are making me like this ... burning urine can't be good for the sinuses.

'Really, though,' the rogue continued without his reply, 'I'm not sure why it needed to be a secret. Chances are she'd be impressed that you could pull off something like this.'

She doesn't need to know anything, he muttered inwardly. *She doesn't need to know that you can't even control yourself while he* ... He felt his teeth threaten to crack under the strain of their clenching. *She knows all about* his *bodily functions, doesn't she? No ... no, stop thinking like that, old man. He's a cad ... a liar ... a rat.*

He probably seduced her, tricked her ... I'm still the better man.

The stream sputtered and died out, leaving a fire that gave no heat that Dreadaeleon could feel. His head throbbed, but he didn't mind. His fingers ached, but he didn't feel them. All feeling poured into his stare as he felt the crimson light flicker behind his eyes.

The better man with all the power.

Too late, Kataria realised that not everything could be learned from the wisdom of the elders. For years, she had been content to accept their categorisation of the human menace as a disease. It had made sense when she had only four notches in her ears.

Humans contaminated, infected, multiplied, spread. It was how they had bred to the point where they threatened land and people, where they began to require a cure. Still, she was forced to admit, certain aspects of the elders' wisdom left out key information.

Such as onset time.

Perhaps one year was enough, she thought as she stared down at the strain that sat against the reed hut. Perhaps one year and six days was enough to be infected beyond the point of a cure. That made sense now that she had six notches in her ears.

After all, she thought resentfully, *how long has it been since you felt the urge to kill him?*

'Six days.'

'What?' Her eyes went wide, as though fearing he could hear her thoughts with those puny little ears.

'Six days since we landed,' Lenk elaborated.

'Shipwrecked,' Kataria corrected.

'I was trying to be optimistic.'

'It doesn't suit you.'

'Fine,' he grunted. '*Six days* since we were shipwrecked on an island forgotten by man and abandoned for dead by the very people we so foolishly trusted to come and rescue us from a slow, lingering death surrounded by an impenetrable wall of salt and wind.' He turned a glare upon her. 'Happy?'

'Well, now you're just being negative,' she replied. 'What's your point, anyway?'

'My point is that I've had enough of it,' he said. 'Enough loincloths, enough lizardmen, and enough forbidden islands.'

'Better than berserker purple women, giant fish demons and gaping, diseased wounds, surely.'

'I haven't forgotten those.' He rubbed the bandages upon his leg thoughtfully. 'And I've had enough of that, too.'

'Enough adventuring?' Her tone was as sly as her smile. 'I thought it was all you wanted.'

'No one *wants* to be an adventurer. They just do it when they can't get any other work.'

'Your grandfather was an adventurer,' she offered. 'He wanted to be one.' She frowned at his puzzled expression. 'Or so you said.'

His face twitched, an expression of doubt flashing across his features like sparks off flint. She held her breath at the sight, waiting for the question that would inevitably follow. He didn't ask it, didn't have to. The doubt upon his face twisted to an all-telling despair in an instant as he undoubtedly realised he couldn't remember his grandfather ever having been such a thing.

His memory was improving. He had said that, but he was human. Humans lied. He had little to offer in regard to his past, save for brief flashes of memory in a deep and smothering darkness: a name of a girl he once knew, an image of a tree struck by lightning, the sound of cocks crowing. Even those days he spoke of slid by swiftly, into memory and out, back into darkness.

To look at him struggling to recall brought her own memories to the surface. When she looked upon him out of the corner of her eyes, his silver hair was a pelt, his eyes were faded and cloud-covered, his breath slow and stagnant. In those brief glimpses, he was no longer Lenk; he was a beast, and he was sick.

When she looked at Lenk, it was difficult to see him as

a man anymore. More and more, he resembled something dying, struggling with the symptom of his own memories.

And you know what happens to sick beasts.

She closed her eyes, trying to forget the sound of shrill whimpers fading under the crunch of pitiless boots.

'Yeah,' Lenk suddenly whispered, 'he was, wasn't he?'

She opened her eyes and he was smiling at her, and caring not if it was for her sake or his own, she returned it.

'So,' she said, 'no more adventure?'

'No more near-death experiences,' he grunted.

'No more sharp pieces of metal aimed at your vitals.'

'No more fervent pleading to gods.'

'No more waiting to be eaten in your sleep.'

'Or stabbed or crushed or otherwise maimed,' he said, nodding. 'No more adventure.'

'No more,' the words spilled from her mouth unconsciously, 'companions.'

It was a slow and heavy dawn that rose on their faces, a long and jagged frown that was shared between them. Neither could find any words of the same weight. None were exchanged. They turned away from each other; she fought back both her sigh of relief at the knowledge that passed between them and the urge to turn and look at him.

No, she told herself, *don't look. The solution is easy ... Now you don't even have to worry about anything else. No one has to die. You're still a shict. He's still a human. All you need to do is not turn around and stay—*

'So ...' she muttered.

Silent. Damn it.

'If not adventure, what?'

'Back to my roots, maybe,' Lenk replied, rolling his

shoulders against the reed wall. 'Find some land, build a farm, hack dirt, sell dirt. Honourable work.'

'Alone?'

Damn it, she immediately scolded herself, *don't ask him that! Why do you keep doing that? WHAT'S WRONG WITH YOU?*

She turned to look, couldn't help it, and saw him staring at her thoughtfully. Whatever she screamed at herself next, she couldn't hear. Whatever he was about to say next, he didn't say.

'Cousin!'

Another sigh of relief was bitten back before they both looked up to see the massive yellow stare above a massive yellow grin set in a massive green head. A three-fingered hand went up, tipping a round black hat upon Bagagame's scaly crown as he sauntered toward them.

'Y'farin' well, guests of Teji?' He kept one eye upon them, the other circling in its socket to look at the bandage upon Lenk's leg. 'Sun feelin' mighty fine on your meat, no? No cure better.' He drew in a long breath through his nostrils and twisted his other eye up at the sun. 'Too bad it never actually makes things stop hurting.'

'Medicine does,' Lenk replied, rubbing his leg. He glanced up at the Owauku's rotating eyes and shuddered. 'Do … do you always do that?'

''S'yeah, cousin,' he said, bobbing his great head. 'M'always extendin' the warmest of welcomes all the damn time.' He tipped his hat again. 'King Togu's always pleased to have humans on Teji, always pleased to share his medicine and hospitality.' His scaly lips split in a broad, banana-coloured grin. 'All for the smiling faces.'

'That wasn't what I was talking about, but—'

'Oh.' If such a thing were possible, the creature's eyes

seemed to grow even larger, threatening to erupt from their sockets with despair. 'Oh no … you ain't happy.' His hands, trembling, reached up to clutch his face. 'Oh, sweet spirits, I knew 's'would happen. Was it me?' He jabbed at his shallow green chest. 'W'did I ever do to you?'

'It's … it's nothing, it's just—'

'You're hungry.' His head nearly came toppling off with the force of his nod. 'That's it. Sunshine and happy thoughts can't heal. M'get you a nice gohmn, cousin. A fine, fat one.'

Before anyone could protest, Bagagame had spun on his heel and scampered toward a nearby pool ringed by several rainbow-coloured carapaces. Another Owauku wearing a leather hood and wielding a crooked stick looked up as Bagagame began hooting something in their high-pitched babble. A dozen feathery antennae twitched, a dozen compound eyes looked up from their drinking pools, and even from such a distance, Kataria could see her distaste reflected back at her over a hundred times.

'Gohmns,' she muttered disdainfully.

'You don't like them?' Lenk's lip twisted in a crooked grin.

'We have a history.' She tried not to remember, but a sudden itch on her face prevented her from doing so. No matter how many times she washed it, she doubted she'd ever get her face clean again. 'Stupid insects.'

'It doesn't seem a little odd to hold a grudge against an insect?' he asked.

'I'm entitled.' She growled. 'Anything that sprays anything from its anus I dislike on principle. Anything that sprays anything from its anus on *my face* I'm obligated to hate.'

'Really,' he mused, 'I would have thought you'd admire them.'

'For what?'

'Well, you're always boasting about how shicts ate every part of their kill, right? I thought you'd appreciate them for versatility alone. The Owauku use them for everything: food, milk ...'

'Clothes,' she added, scratching her loincloth. 'It's one thing for a deer or a bear to fulfil those needs. If it comes off a giant rainbow roach ...' She moved her hand up, scratching an errant itch on her belly. 'They don't even taste good. What I need is venison stewed in its own blood ... maybe a nice, hairy flank right off a pig. *Something* made of meat.'

'Insects are made of meat.'

'It doesn't seem a little odd to defend an insect so vehemently?'

'A little.' His smile was broad, if no less crooked. 'Maybe I'm not so averse to the various oddities that surround me anymore.'

His lips twitched, something tremulous scratching his mouth, straining to find a place where it could break out. She recalled how many times she had seen his gaze before, bereft of the softness it bore now. His gaze had been something hard and endlessly blue before, something to be avoided.

Quietly, she longed to see those eyes again. They would at least be easier to turn away from. Instead, she was bound by his stare, forced to look at him as he stared back at her with an expression that was terribly human.

'Maybe,' he whispered, 'I don't want to leave all of them behind.'

Why do you keep doing this? Her voice was growing ever more faint in her mind, but still returned to gnaw at her heart with sharp teeth. *Why do you encourage him like this?*

Even if you wanted this, even if you wanted *to be infected, this can't last. It can't even last as long as you think it can.*

Lenk didn't see the fear on her face as he looked up. His smile diminished only slightly as he stared at the three half-naked figures approaching them. His wave was weak, his eyes lost their softness; it only reminded her painfully of how he had just looked at her.

'Other oddities, I'll be glad to be rid of.'

'The same could be said of you,' Denaos muttered as he slunk forward. 'At the very least, don't expect me to leave flowers on your grave.'

'And don't expect me not to leave something brown and steaming on yours,' Lenk replied sharply. 'But I didn't call you out here to just insult you.'

'*Just* insult me? Were you going to kick me, as well?'

'Not today.' Lenk patted his leg. 'I had something to—'

'You should kick him.'

Dreadaeleon's voice was as sullen as his frown was long. His eyes shifted irately toward Denaos, who merely sneered in reply.

'Some gratitude,' the rogue muttered. 'This is the thanks I get from you?'

'For what?' Asper asked, cocking a brow.

'For . . .' Whatever it was that flashed across Dreadaeleon's face, only Denaos seemed to catch it. 'A secret.'

'Secrets,' the priestess repeated quietly. 'I suppose he knows all about that, doesn't he?'

This time, something flashed across Denaos' face. His visage shifted, as though he tried on and discarded a mask in a single breath many times over. When he finally chose one, the blankness on his face was as cool as his tone of voice.

'Everyone knows something about them.'

His eyes flickered and Kataria's breath caught in her throat, as though he had hurled that sentence like a dagger and struck her squarely in the heart. Her ears lowered, flattened against her head as a thick and awkward silence smothered the air between them, even if it could do nothing to hide the scowls darting from face to face.

And, like the baffled eye of a half-naked storm of scorn, Lenk turned a single raised brow to his companions.

'Something wrong?'

'Not at all.' Kataria spoke up with a swiftness that made her want to kick herself. 'Nothing, really. Nerves are … you know, worn, from having sand up our collective rear ends for a while.'

'Six days,' Dreadaeleon said, nodding, 'since we arrived.'

'Since we were shipwrecked,' Asper pointed out.

'Yes, we've been over this,' Lenk snarled, rubbing his brow. 'And now, it's over.'

A panoply of furrowed brows and confused looks met him.

'Did I miss something?' Denaos asked. 'We don't have the tome, don't have a boat, we certainly aren't *paid* and, in fact, seem to be poorer by about three pounds of clothing, give or take, since we started.'

'Not to mention the fact that Kataria has, in fact, told you that netherlings are on the island,' Dreadaeleon pointed out.

'And I think Denaos mentioned something about demons, didn't he?' Kataria asked.

'Yes, but when you found them, they were busy killing each other,' Lenk replied. 'And none of them saw you, did they?'

A choral attempt at inconspicuousness assaulted Kataria's

ears: Dreadaeleon cleared his throat and appeared to study the sky overhead, Denaos sniffed and spared a momentary sneer, Asper shuffled her feet briefly before reaching for a holy symbol that wasn't there and resigning herself to casting her eyes downward. The shict couldn't afford to furrow her brow at them for long before Lenk turned the same scrutinising, expectant stare upon her.

She blinked, then shook her head briefly.

'No one,' she replied. 'The netherlings were busy with the demons, as you say.'

'And likely the same can be said of the other fish-things,' Lenk replied, rolling his shoulders. 'So what's the problem?'

'Well, basically, *everything*,' Asper interjected. 'Between the presence of the longfaces, the demons, the lizardmen and the noted *absence* of the presences of the tome, our clothes—'

'The gold,' Denaos added, 'our dignity, and so forth ...'

'Point being,' Asper said after shooting the rogue a silencing glare, 'things certainly don't *look* over.'

'Because you're not looking at it with the proper perspective,' Lenk replied. 'What you're seeing is the broth, not the meat.'

'The what?'

'I wrote about it earlier.'

'How does that help any—'

'*As I was saying*, you're only seeing what we don't have: the tome, the gold. We didn't have a lot of dignity to begin with, so that's no great loss.' He offered a weak smile around the circle. 'But we do have each other. We have our lives. We should hold on to them.'

Kataria wasn't quite certain what he expected, be it a raucous chorus of cheering approval or a weary sigh of resignation and agreement, but she could guess by the sudden narrowing of his eyes that he wasn't expecting the choked snort Denaos forced through a crooked grin.

'You *girl*,' the rogue cackled and held up his hands for peace. 'No, no, sorry, I meant to say something far less insulting to our female cohorts and far more insulting to you, but ... you *girl*.'

'Don't feign bravery now, you roach,' Lenk snarled at him. 'You were the most eager to run when we started this.'

'And I still am. I agree with your philosophy, but not your reasons. Let's not go acting like you give a damn over everyone's lives at this point, not after we've nearly died ... how many times now?'

'Roughly thirteen since we left the *Riptide*,' Dreadaeleon interjected. 'Those are only the potential deaths by injury, of course. Taking into account factors such as accidents, disease and premeditation sans follow-through, the tally rises considerably.'

'All of which you remained conspicuously silent through until now,' Denaos said, scratching his chin. 'What's changed?'

Lenk made no reply for the rogue to hear, nor did he offer one to anyone. Still, Kataria saw it in the brief flash of blue as he cast her a sidelong glimpse. It was only the barest sliver of azure, but she could see his answer in the sudden softness of his stare, the quiet thaw of his eyes. Something had changed; what it was, he would not say to her or any of the others.

And so, as he stood silent, she ignored the feeling that she should follow and spoke up.

'The longest-lived rat doesn't ask why a crumb comes his way,' she snarled at the rogue. 'The fact that *this* one standing in front of me is suddenly so interested in why he's *not* getting stepped on should be more questionable than anything else.'

She had expected anything from the rogue: a sneer, a snide comment, a veiled threat, even the sudden appearance of a dagger he had somehow unnervingly concealed. These she was prepared for; these she had retorts for. Thus, when he angled his eyes away from her stare and said nothing more, she was struck dumb.

'As always,' Lenk continued, sighing, 'I don't expect anyone to follow me where they don't want to. If any of you wish to stay here, carve out whatever life you care to amongst the lizards and count the days before something – purple, black or otherwise – rips off your head and eats it, feel free to.' He sniffed. 'Anyone else is free to listen to my plan.'

Another chorus of begrudging coughs brought a grin out on his face.

'How swiftly the tide turns, eh? Was it the mention of escape or the promise of having your head digested, then?'

'I'm more curious about how, exactly, you plan to get off this island, given our circumstances,' Denaos interjected. The sullenness from his face was banished and reinvigorated with snidery. 'Did we or did we not miss our trip back to Port Destiny?'

'We haven't missed it.' Kataria looked pointedly at the ground. 'Sebast might still show up.'

'If he doesn't arrive soon, I still have a plan,' Lenk replied.

'Does it include a way to leave the Owauku,' Asper began sharply, 'who, I feel the need to point out, saved *our lives* and who, I feel again the need to point out, we are about to abandon as they are caught in the cross between the netherlings and the demons?'

'Yes,' Lenk said. He coughed discreetly. 'In a way.'

'In *what* way?'

'If we tell them, they're not going to help us escape, so I figured we'd ... I don't know, leave a note or something.'

'Good,' the priestess said, nodding. 'Maybe they can use it to stanch the blood when their intestines get spilled out on the ground.'

'They took our stuff,' Lenk replied with a shrug. 'Seems a fair trade.'

She blinked. 'They made us slightly sunburnt and uncomfortable ... so we're being reasonable in condemning them to a slow, agonising death.'

'Stop being dramatic,' Denaos said. 'You know as well as we do that the longfaces kill their prey quickly.'

'Oh, so now you're *for* this?' She whirled, snarling at the rogue. 'What was that momentary conscience growing out of your mouth a moment ago?'

'Indigestion, probably,' he replied. 'Upon further consideration—'

'You mean three breaths long?'

'*Further* consideration,' he replied forcefully, 'it's rather clear we aren't going to make any money or avoid an imminent disembowelment any longer by staying here. Prudence dictates we leave, maybe come back later when everyone's dead and sift through the innards until we find something.'

Kataria glowered at the distant gohmn herd sipping from a pool. 'If there's anything left.'

'What?'

'Nothing.'

'Well, it's all moot, isn't it?' Dreadaeleon suddenly chimed in. 'I mean, we can't just *leave* yet.'

'At least someone has a sense of decency,' Asper muttered.

'Not a person in this circle is in a position to lecture anyone on decency, young lady,' Denaos replied. 'He probably just wants to stay as long as he can to catch a glimpse of all the flesh on display.'

'Clearly,' Dreadaeleon said, sneering. 'But I was more referring to the fact that we're, as yet, incomplete.' His expression was half-beseeching and half-curious as he swept it about the circle. 'I mean, what about Gariath? If the rest of us are alive, he probably is, too.'

'He seemed fairly determined not to be when we last saw him,' Asper said.

'He's alive,' Kataria said softly.

'How do you know?'

The shict felt a sudden unease as the human eyes turned toward her, scrutinising her slowly. She felt the urge to flee, to escape both their stares and the memory of her encounter with Gariath. She had done a good enough job over the past days, she thought, trying to trick herself into thinking that the dragonman was dead and her secret was safe.

In her heart, though, she knew he was alive. There was no way she could be so lucky for anything else to be true.

'She knows because she's not an idiot,' Lenk replied before she could. 'He's stronger than all of us. He would survive. And I suppose we can delay our plans until we find him.'

'A thought occurs,' Denaos interjected. A thoughtful look crossed his face and he inhaled sharply, as though about to deliver a stirring conclusion. 'Why?'

'What do you mean, why? He's part of our group, isn't he?'

'Well, we're not really a "group", are we? And he's really more of a hanger-on that chose to insinuate himself into our loose coalition … a parasite, if you will.'

'Parasites don't so abruptly try to kill us,' Kataria muttered.

'Well, he's been doing it for the past year,' Dreadaeleon retorted. 'I thought we were past holding that against him.'

'Yes, but he came awfully close this time,' Asper said. 'It's probably wiser to abandon him now after his … what, eighteenth try?'

Denaos chuckled. 'Stick up for the lizardmen that you just met, but abandon the one you've known for ages? Is that sort of behaviour condoned in the Talanite faith?'

'I sleep easy,' she replied. 'Do you?'

'I'm sure there's some lovely backstory that I don't care about between you two,' Lenk interjected, 'but I'll have to interrupt to put this to a vote.' He swept a careful stare around the circle. 'Acknowledging full well what it means to say so … how many of you want to leave Gariath behind?'

Denaos' hand shot up with swiftness, Asper's followed with only enough hesitation to display a minor internal struggle. Dreadaeleon glanced at them both with a frown that went slightly beyond disapproval. It wasn't until Lenk looked to his side and saw the pale, slender arm in the air that he quirked a brow.

'Really?' he asked Kataria. 'I would have thought you to be his only supporter.'

'Wouldn't be the first time you were wrong, would it?' she growled at him.

He frowned. 'I … guess not.' With a sigh, he rubbed his eyes. 'Well, that's that, then, isn't it? If he is alive and we go through with this, I suppose we've got one more thing that can and will kill us.'

'All the more reason to leave,' Kataria agreed.

'Which you still haven't explained how you intend to do,' Denaos pointed out.

Whatever Lenk had to say in response was suddenly drowned out by the sound of a heavy breathing, heavy footsteps and a heavy stick being dragged through the sand. It was hard to ignore the sight of Bagagame approaching the group, and outright impossible to miss the sight of the screeching writhing roach he dragged by its antennae alongside his stick.

'Okay, cousin,' he gasped, pulling his twitching prize before Lenk. 'Ol' Bagagame got you covered. Took some whacking, but m'found you a nice slab to chew on.' With a grunt, he hurled the insect forward. 'Eat hearty.'

'That's ... nice?' Lenk said. 'But there's something else you can do for us.'

'Ah, right. Rude.' The Owauku's tiny muscles strained as he hoisted his stick high above his head and brought it down in a shrieking splatter of foul-smelling ichor. His tongue flicked out from behind his grin to slurp up a glistening gob on his mouth. 'Juicy enough for a king, eh?'

'I was thinking the same thing,' Lenk said as he turned his smile from the lizardman to his companions. 'Bagagame, show us to Togu.'

Nineteen

MEN OF VIRTUE AND THE NOOSES THEY SWAY FROM

He crept quietly through the city's backstreets, hood drawn up, cloak held tightly about him. He navigated them quickly, quietly, the sins of his memories still embedded in the stones when he walked without webs on his feet, when he could bear the sensation of earth on his soles. He once had done so. He once had walked among them and they had called him neighbour.

And what do they call me now, I wonder, he thought. *Monster? Heretic? Betrayer? Demon worshipper.* He paused at the mouth of an alley, glancing about before sliding through the sunlight and back into shadow. *And what slurs I could level at them. Sheep. Cattle. Blind, ignorant masses that feed themselves into the furnaces stoked by the lies of the Gods and their servants. If they want it so bad, they deserve to die. They deserve to—*

No, no, he chastised himself. *Remember what this is all for.*

He glanced down at the vial in his palm, the thick, viscous liquid swirling with a nebulous life all its own. Mother's Milk. The gift of Ulbecetonth. The agent of change.

Change, he reminded himself, was what it was all about. Change needed to lift the blinders from mortalkind, to show them that their gods were deaf and uncaring. It would be violent, he knew. People would die. More would live, guided by a matron that heard them and spoke to them in return. But they would never understand.

They would call him a monster.

He called himself the Mouth.

But before that, he had called himself something else, he recalled. He'd had a name. He'd had a home. He'd had memories; he still did. The Prophet was cruel to keep him from being absolved of them, but perhaps there was a point to their withholding. Perhaps he needed to remember why he forsook name, home, land and sky alike.

And so, when he came to the rotting doorframe of a house long abandoned, when he felt his heart begin to ache as he laid a hand upon the splintering door marked with a large red cross, he fought against the urge to turn away. He pushed it open. He went in.

Shadows greeted him. They still knew him. They had been around for a long time, ingrained into the wood of the house itself. They had seen all. They remembered all. And he read their lightless testimony as he drew his hood back and walked across the rotting floorboards.

He walked past a doorway; the shadows told him of a kitchen that had never been stuffed, but had enough to make stew every night. He walked past a rotting table; the shadows spoke of three bodies seated there, breaking a single loaf of bread to share. He walked to the decrepit stairs at the edge of the house.

And the shadows asked him to turn away. They remembered what happened. They told him he would not want to see again.

But he went up, regardless. The stairs knew him, offering the same creak of complaint they had offered him for years. He paused beside them, staring at a barren spot upon the wall where the shade was a tad lighter than the rest of the decay. A holy symbol had hung there once, the great cresting wave of Zamanthras, the Sea Mother, as a ward against the woes of life and an invitation for the goddess' boon.

He remembered that symbol. He remembered when he had hung it up. He remembered when he had taken it down. He remembered when he had screamed questions at it, demanded answers and received nothing. He remembered when he had hurled it into a dying fire. He had forgotten to stoke it that night. Someone else usually did that.

But there had been no one else left that night.

He glanced back to the door, frowning. A lesson learned, he told himself; he knew that the Gods were impotent and did not care. Surely, nothing more could be gained from venturing farther upward.

Nothing ...

But he went, anyway. The shadows lamented his return and told him of the long hallway he had once paced back and forth across. They warned him against going to the room at the far end. But he went, anyway.

And he saw the shadows in a small, decrepit room. And he saw the shadows of a small, decrepit cot. It had been a tiny thing, one that he had built hastily when the girl who lay in it grew too big for her crib.

He smiled. The shadows did not have to remind him of when he sat beside that cot and told stories. He remembered them all on his own: the Kraken and the Swan, Old King Gnash, How Zamanthras Stained Toha's Sand Blue. He remembered the promises made beside it: how the girl who lay in it and he would go to Toha one day and she would see the blue sand, how she would one day captain a ship that would dwarf his little fishing skiff, how he would build her a bigger bed in a few months, at the rate she was growing.

But it was only a few days later that the girl who lay in it stopped growing altogether.

The shadows didn't have to tell him that. He remembered it all on his own.

But the shadows were not silent. The shadows spoke of the healer who had knelt beside the little cot. The shadows spoke of heads that shook, eyes that closed, condolences offered and arrangements advised. The shadows spoke of threats, of pleas, of prayers he had offered to the healer, to their Talanas, to his Zamanthras, to anyone who would listen.

No one answered. No one ever answered.

The shadows spoke of the day when that little cot lay empty. The shadows spoke of the day when he sat beside it and cradled his head in hands. The shadows spoke of the day when he pressed his hands against his ears to drown out the sound of the waves. The waves that the girl lay in.

That was where their memory stopped. That was where his stopped. That was where he was no longer neighbour, no longer father, no longer slave to the Gods.

He narrowed his eyes; that was the day when, in the silence, he had heard the voice of Mother Deep. That was the day when he forgot his name. That was the day the Mouth had left the shadows and the wood and the city behind entirely, swearing he would not return until he could change the world.

And now, he had. And now, he could.

He stared down at the vial of Mother's Milk, narrowing his eyes. This was what it had come to. This was how the world would be changed. The Mother would be free. But for Her to reign properly, to guide mankind from their blind darkness, She would need a consort.

The Father must be freed.

And this was the key, this was what would draw Daga-Mer from the prison he had been so cruelly cast into. This was what would call to Mother Deep, to free Her from the Gate, to let Her guide her children and through them mortalkind. And this would all happen … through him.

He knew where Daga-Mer's prison lay; he heard the Father's call, he heard the distant beating of his heart as he slumbered. He closed his eyes, let the memories slip from his mind, let the sound of the heartbeat, the sound of change waiting to happen, fill his thoughts.

And all he heard was a door slamming shut, feet across the floor.

Fool, he scolded himself. *They know. They're coming for you. You wasted too much time. Run!* In his other hand, the weight of a bone dagger made itself known. *No … no, you can't run. If anyone knows you're here, they must be eliminated. They can't tell anyone you were here. They can't know … not yet.*

With the blade in his hand, he crept to the stairs, narrowed his eyes. He was unrepentant as he searched for the life he would snuff out; change was violent, after all. He saw the intruder now: a mess of wild black hair atop a thin body clad in a poor person's linens. A spy, maybe? A beggar, probably. No matter; he was going to die, regardless. This was no sin. If one had to die so that the others might live, then that was just …

His thoughts were interrupted by the deafening sound of the stairs offering their familiar creak.

The intruder's head snapped up. Wide, brown eyes took

him in. A thin, dark-skinned face went slack with fear at the sight of him. And he could feel his own face go slack, his own eyes go wide, his own lips speak words.

'A ... girl?'

'I'm not doing anything!' she spoke up. 'No one's lived here for years.'

'I used to,' he replied without thinking.

And her response was to turn swiftly and bolt, the door swinging in her wake.

He was leaping over the railings in a moment, following after her. It was only after a hundred paces that he realised he had dropped the knife back in the house. It was only after a hundred fifty that he realised he didn't mind. He didn't want to kill her. He just wanted to ...

To what, he asked himself. *Look at her? Think of duty! Think of change!*

But he could think of nothing else, he realised, but her face. Her thin face, her wide eyes. He had to see her again. He had to look into her face again.

He saw the back of her head as she twisted through the alleys, trying to lose him. His cloak flew wide open as he pursued, trying not to be lost. His body, pale white and fingers webbed, was plainly visible. He did not belong amongst these dark-skinned island people. They would know him. They would call him monster. His mission would be over. Change would never come.

But he had to see her.

'Wait! *Wait!*' he called after her. 'I'm not angry! I just want to talk!'

She said nothing. She twisted down an alley, disappeared. He followed, twisting down the same alley and coming to a sudden halt as he slammed into a broad, leather-bound chest.

He looked up. Fierce, dark eyes looked down. He saw himself reflected: ghostly white, black-eyed, hairless. He panicked, turned about and fled down the alley.

And Bralston stared after him.

'Does Port Yonder have a habit of degenerates running unrestricted through the streets without a care for whom they collide with?' he asked his guide.

'Port Yonder, of late, is no longer a city of habits.'

Mesri was his name, priest of Zamanthras and speaker for the tiny abode. He had met Bralston at the docks, he had explained, out of custom. Bralston gave him a quick glance: portly, robes that had once been nice now frayed at the hem, a thick dark moustache and a bright, cresting wave medallion hanging about his neck. All in all, he looked like the type of man that a fishing city would send to meet a man who arrived on a giant, three-masted ship.

'Granted, we *used* to be,' Mesri explained. 'But since the fish have stopped coming around, the sight of people running in and out of the back alleys have become more common.'

Bralston glanced up, surveying the decaying, crumbling buildings that rose up around them.

'And these?'

'Have always been here,' Mesri replied. 'Long ago, someone discovered that the fish migrated through these waters. Yonder was founded shortly after and enjoyed a brief time of ostentatiousness, back when we had a lord-admiral of our own.' He chuckled, smoothing out his robes. 'Said lord-admiral gave these fine robes to me, in fact. But the fish caught wise and the merchants shortly thereafter. These homes were abandoned, but most of us get by ... well, I mean, not lately, but we did.'

'You no longer have a lord-admiral?' Bralston quirked a brow. 'Then the Toha Navy does not govern this city?'

'Not actively, no. A patrol ship still comes around every month, if you're concerned about our capacity to deal with the prisoner you've come to speak with.'

'I am.'

'What? You don't trust a tiny, impoverished shell of a city commandeered mostly by women, children and men with pointy sticks to take care of a titanic, bearded Cragsman?' Mesri chuckled. 'I suppose wizards have their reputations for a reason, don't they?'

Bralston simply stared at the man, stern-faced. Mesri cleared his throat, looking down. A distinct lack of a sense of humour was another reputation wizards had earned, one that Bralston did absolutely everything in his power to nurture. The priest shuffled his feet, waving for the Librarian to follow as he continued down the winding streets of the abandoned section of the city.

'Truth be told, it was our pleasure to take the Cragsman,' he said. 'If only to keep him away from decent society.' Mesri looked thoughtful. 'Further truth, he's been remarkably docile, considering his reputation. I like to think we might have encouraged that. We did what we could for his wounds, but—'

'Wounds?'

Mesri paused, giving no indication that he had even heard the Librarian. A shudder, small and clearly not intended to be seen, coursed through his body. After a moment, he resumed his pace, Bralston keeping up.

'What manner of wounds?'

'You're going to see him,' Mesri muttered. 'See for yourself. Perhaps it's more common in the cities. But cities have Talanites to deal with it. I'm a Zamanthran. I can deliver children and tell where the fish are going. Not handle ...' He sighed, rubbing his eyes. 'Any of this.'

Bralston did not inquire; he did not have to. Even for a city half-abandoned, he had noticed the scanty population of Port Yonder. Most accredited it to poor fish harvests, though few could explain the lapse in the seasonally bustling migrations. Some explained it as most of the population being ill from some manner of disease, a very select few raving about shicts being behind the whole thing.

Those not ill or in exceeding poverty were doing well enough, Bralston had been told, but his concerns were not for this city and its people. He had a duty that went beyond poor fish harvests, illnesses or anything that a priest might claim to be able to cure.

They emerged from the abandoned district, setting foot on sand. Undeveloped beach, marred only by scrub grass and two small buildings stretched as far as the cliffs where the island ended entirely. Apparently, when development of Yonder had stopped, it had stopped swiftly.

'The prisoner is in the warehouse,' Mesri said, pointing to the closer of the two buildings. 'I guess it's a prison now? We had to move a few spare skiffs and a crate or two ... or three. He's an immense man. Ask the two boys we assigned to guard him if you require protection.'

'It will not be necessary,' Bralston said. He glanced to the more distant of the buildings, a crumbling work of stones and pillars to which a small, beaten path of haphazardly laid stones led. 'What's that, then?'

'That?' Mesri followed his gaze and sighed. 'That is our temple.'

In that instant, as much as he might have loathed to admit it to himself, Bralston knew he liked the man. As far as priests went, it was difficult to find fault with him beyond the obvious. He was a man who clearly cared about his people; that much was obvious by the *many* delays they had suffered on their trip through the city, Mesri insisting on stopping to hear every problem and plea. He had considered them all carefully and offered each one, from a sick child to a broken net, a clear and logical answer. Never once had the man even uttered, 'The will of the Gods.'

Bralston had suffered each delay, each problem, in silence, no matter how trivial he had considered it. But it was only now, now that he saw the crumbling, run-down temple, barely any more noticeable than the buildings of the decayed abandoned district, that he deigned to look at the man with admiration.

'Is it not an insult to your gods that it remains in such a shape?' he asked.

'I wager They'd be more insulted if I used the few coins it would have taken to feed one of Their starving followers on a new rug.'

Bralston clenched his teeth behind his lips, looking thoughtful. After a moment, as if in defeat, he sighed.

'The Venarium has a policy of paying stipends for research purposes,' he said. 'If we are forced to repurpose a settlement without its own standing government for our means of research' – he paused, coughing – 'such as studying the cause for a change in fish migrations ... we are bound to offer a stipend.'

'Such as one that might put food in hungry bellies and blankets over cold shoulders,' Mesri replied, a smile curling beneath his moustache. 'The offer is appreciated, Librarian.'

'We do, of course, insist on a policy of extreme secularism,' Bralston said, eyeing the decaying temple. 'Given the general laxity of upkeep, though, I don't foresee this as being too objectionable an—'

'It is,' Mesri answered, swift and stern. 'The offer *was* appreciated, Librarian, but I must decline. I cannot ask the people to part with their matron.'

'It's a simple request,' Bralston muttered, heat creeping into his voice. 'Worship in your own homes, if you must. Simply keep it out of sight of the Venarium and no one needs to know. It's a generous offer.'

'It is, sir,' Mesri said. 'But I must decline, all the same. We are men of Yonder. Men of Yonder are followers of Zamanthras. She is a part of the city and us.'

'Faith cannot feed the hungry.'

'Money cannot define a man.'

'So you say,' Bralston sneered. 'I will never understand your profession, Mesri – you or the priest who guided me here.'

'No one mentioned a priest.' Mesri's brows furrowed. 'Who was he?'

'Evenhands. Miron Evenhands. Lord Emissary, so-called, of the Church of Talanas.'

'Evenhands?' Mesri's face nearly burrowed back into his skull, so fiercely did it screw up. 'How is that—'

'*Mesri! Mesri!*'

The priest's attentions were seized by the young, dark-skinned man that came barrelling out of the poor district. He did not even look at Bralston as he rushed up to the priest.

'Another fell ill,' the young man panted. 'Swears it was shicts.'

'Of course,' Mesri sighed. 'It's always shicts … or ghosts … or whatever fell spirit has been thought up.' He turned to Bralston. 'Sir Librarian, please—'

'Time is limited,' the Librarian replied curtly, shoving past young man and priest alike. 'Those endeavours that cannot be pursued must settle behind those that can.'

Mesri was calling something after him, he realised, as he walked toward the warehouse. But he shut his ears to the sound, all the same. It was foolish to have offered; a stipend would require paperwork, endorsements, evaluations. He had a job to do.

One that led him into a dark, dank place.

Twenty

THE SOUND OF SICKNESS

Shicts were created from Riffid, the Huntress. Shicts had been birthed from Her blood, given Her voice in their ears and nothing more. Shicts were created. Shicts were born. Shicts were meant to be here on this world.

This was fact.

Naxiaw knew this.

Humans were born from no gods, despite the misguided fanaticism they tried to justify their infectious presence with. Humans, instead, began as monkeys that learned how to pick up swords. Humans adapted. Humans evolved. Humans did not belong here on this world.

This was fact.

Naxiaw was convinced of it now.

From their humble origins when the first monkey stabbed his brother and called himself human, the round-ears had shed their body hair, built houses over stone and birthed the corruptions of politics and gold and found more productive uses for their feces. They had evolved.

Logical, Naxiaw told himself. *Sickness is a predator. It mutates, learns to resist medicine and bypass immunities to spread its infection. That the human disease should learn to become more efficient at killing and destroying should be no surprise.*

And truthfully, he admitted, when he had been brought amongst the longfaces and witnessed their brutal devastation, their efficient destruction, their utterly gleeful murder, he had not been surprised.

Shocked, of course.

Horrified, naturally.

And, he thought as he peered through the bars of his cage, *ever more curious* ...

From high atop the crumbling stone ruins upon the sandy ridge that overlooked the valley in which they crawled, he watched them. For the past six days, he had studied them as they crushed the earth beneath their iron-shod feet, as they blackened the sky with their forges, as they broke their scaly, green servants with whip and blade.

Horror and repulsion for the purple-skinned brutes had long ago faded. He scolded himself now for wasting time on indulgent loathing. What he was watching was no longer something disgusting, something vicious and cruel to be loathed. What he was watching was something ominous, something miraculous, something wholly terrifying.

He had thought them to be one more aberration on an already-tainted world, one more threat for the shicts to destroy, one more disease to cure. But as he continued to watch them, to study their cruelty and monitor their rapaciousness, he realised they were no new illness. They were merely one strain of the same sickness he had been at-tempting to purge since he could first carry his Spokesman stick.

They might have been purple instead of pink, thicker of bone and harder of flesh, long of face and white of eye, but he recognised them all too swiftly. And the more he watched them as they spread across the island, purple patches of disease contaminating a pure and pristine land, the less ridiculous it seemed.

After all, he reasoned, *if humans could evolve once, they could surely do it again.*

More aggressive and violent than the human strain had ever been, the longface infection continued to amaze him, even after six days of being held prisoner by them, watching them boil across the sands.

The females were the dominant infection, the true ravagers of flesh and blood. That much was obvious from watching them, tall and muscular, chewing the earth beneath their feet, staining the sand red with the blood of their slaves and themselves, filling the air with the iron challenges and grinding snarls they hurled at each other like spears.

They were the sickness that drove the green lizard-things to do what they did, the fever that boiled their minds and forced them to act in ways unwise. Under the cracks of their knotted whips and the threats from their jagged teeth, the pitiful, scaly creatures worked with broken backs and dragging feet as the females drove them forward. They hewed down the trees from the forests that flanked the beach, dragging the logs to feed the forge pits and build the great black ships that bobbed in the roiling surf.

The land was thick with iron, the sky was thick with smoke. Those females who worked the forge pits, fire-scarred and shorn-haired, relentlessly thrust and pulled glowing iron rods from the embers, tirelessly hammered them into cruel-edged wedges and vicious-tipped spikes, eagerly sharpened their edges to jagged metal teeth.

Not a grain of sand remained undisturbed amidst the activity. The disease swept across the land as the females worked tirelessly. They drilled in tight, square formations under the barking orders of their white-haired superiors. They brawled and attacked each other in impromptu displays of dominance that quickly turned fatal. They hauled the bodies of those scaled slaves too exhausted to work to a pit ringed by iron bars, tossing them in and filling the air with screaming as the denizens of the massive hole let out eerie cackles through full mouths.

And through it all, Naxiaw watched, Naxiaw studied, Naxiaw noted.

This was not the first time he had witnessed such a scene. Voracious greed, heedless industry, the smell of blood and sweat so thick the violence was a collective hunger in the belly of every female present. He had seen these sensations in the round-ears many times before, if never to such an extent.

He knew a war when he saw one.

For what, he did not know. For why, it did not matter. These things, these evolutions of disease, were preparing to spread their infection.

The sole comfort he took was in their numbers. He had counted no more than two hundred since he had first been thrown into his cage. Theirs was nothing like the teeming masses of the smaller, pinker strain.

And, he thought as he lowered his head and raised his ears, *it falls to the shicts to make certain that they never will have such numbers.*

He closed his eyes. His ears went rigid. Through the carnage below, he attempted to hear.

It began quickly, as it always did, with a sudden awareness of sounds without meaning: feet on sand, breeze in sky, air in lungs, snarls in throats. This awareness amplified, sought specificity in noise: trees shuddering under blunted axes, black-bellied ships bobbing in the surf, muscles stretching and contorting under purple flesh.

Close to its goal, the awareness pressed further, reduced

the world to nothing but those few sounds that bore significance, the essence of life. Splinters falling in soft, pattering whispers in tiny droplets of sweat-kissed blood. Breezes colliding with clouds of smoke. A crab's carapace scratching against grains of sand as it stirred in a hibernating dream beneath the earth.

And then, silence: the sound with the most meaning, the sensation of his own mind blooming into a vast and formless flower within his head. No more sound, no more thought. The flower stretched out silently, instinctually, reaching out, muttering wordless sounds, whispering unheard speeches. Somewhere beyond his mind, he felt something stir.

The Howling had heard him.

The Howling had found him.

Had he the consciousness to feel his heart stop, he still would not have been afraid of it. The Howling had long ago ceased to be something strange and mystical, long ago ceased to even be the instinctual knowledge that all shicts shared. He had spent many years within it, listening to it, learning it. It was a part of him, as it was a part of all shicts. As he was one with the Howling, so too was he one with all shicts.

And they would hear him as they heard their own thoughts.

Emptiness passed in an instant; then his head filled. Images of sand and blood consumed him, swirled together with sea and ships, purple faces, clenching teeth, red iron, bleeding bodies, fallen trees. War, disease, mutation, danger, anger, hatred. Through these things, coursing as blood through his thoughts, his intent boiled over.

Find.

Rescue.

Kill.

Harvest.

The intent flowed across the emptiness, dew across the petals of the flower. It would reach his people, he knew: a whisper in their ears, a sudden chill down their spines as they knew what he knew in an instant. They would hear him, they would feel him, and they would come with their blood and Spokesmen and hatred and—

Wait.

His ears went taut of their own volition, sensing something he had not the consciousness to. A sound without meaning? No, he realised, a sound craving meaning. It ranged wildly, whimpering quietly one moment, snarling angrily the next, then letting out a terrified howl and searching for an answer beyond its own echo.

Impossible to listen to. *Too loud, too painful.*

Impossible to ignore. *Too close, too familiar.*

His people? *No.*

No *s'na shict s'ha.* Then ... *what?*

'Oh! Look, look, look! He's doing it again!'

Another voice. Distant, meaningless.

'What is it that he's doing, then?'

Words for those without minds, terrified of emptiness.

'No idea. He always does this, though. Never says a word, just ... sits.'

Words for those without thought, terrified of silence.

'Well, it's boring. Wake him up.'

An explosion of sound.

His eyes snapped open as the flower of emptiness wilted in his mind; he turned to see the iron blade rattled against the bars of his cage. Behind it, white hair, white eyes and jagged teeth set in a long, purple face. He recognised this one, gathered her name long ago, associated it with her ever-present, ever-unpleasant grin.

Qaine.

The longfaces behind her, the male with the wispy patch of hair beneath his lower lip, the male with the long nose and red robe, the female with the long, spiky bristles of white serving as hair, he recognised too.

Yldus, Vashnear, Dech.

Behind them, standing with arms crossed over her chest, taller and more powerful than any male or female assembled, face drawn so tight it appeared as though it would split apart and bare glistening muscle underneath at any moment ... This one, he knew only by the venom with which the others spewed her name.

Xhai. Carnassial.

He repeated their names to himself whenever he felt his anger towards them slipping. He collected their names like flowers and wore them about his neck in something fragile that he would pluck, petal by bloody petal and crush under his six toes. Names for now, targets for later. Just as soon as his people heard, just as soon as they knew ...

'Must you really do that?' the one called Yldus asked, making a look of disapproval that seemed perpetual.

'It's not fair,' Qaine replied, peering into the cage. 'I caught him, I should get to kill him.'

'*I* froze him, thank you. I suppose the irony is lost on you that we are gathered here to discuss the ways in which you can kill more than just one overscum and you're barely paying attention for want of killing this one?'

'He killed *two* females! I didn't even get a chance to fight him!'

'Two?' Dech asked, raising an eyebrow. 'I didn't think they were that hard.'

'Did you not also say he bled all over them?' The one called Vashnear, long of nose, red of robe, twisted his upper lip in disgust. 'Filthy creature. Keep it in its cage.'

'It's obvious by now that the overscum won't infect you with anything,' Yldus replied, rolling his eyes.

'You cannot know that,' Vashnear snapped back.

'Just a moment out of the cage,' Qaine whispered. Her hands drifted, one toward the lock on his cage, the other toward the blade on her belt. 'It'll be quick. Those others were weaklings. He can't be *that* strong.'

Naxiaw held his belt, already calculating how he would kill her, then leap to the spike-headed one and rip her throat out, seize her sword and move to the males. They were small, delicate – one stroke would finish them both. The big one with the taut face … he would have to flee and come back for her later. Just as well, though; shicts didn't fight fair.

His breath came slow and steady as her fingers drifted closer to the lock. He was prepared for this. He was ready to spill their blood. He was *s'na shict s'ha*. He would kill them all as soon as she just drew a little closer and—

'No.'

There wasn't even enough air left to gasp with after the voice spoke. There was no threat in it, Naxiaw discerned; threats implied uncertainty, conditions that must be met. The voice spoke with nothing of the sort. It was a word full of certainty, a sound full of meaning.

This one sat so still at the edge of the ruined terrace, demurely seated upon a hewn brick, idly drumming his long fingertips on a crumbling trellis, staring down at the valley with what Naxiaw was sure was extreme boredom, even if he couldn't see the male's long face.

This one had no name as far as Naxiaw knew. His was

whispered so softly, with such quiet reverence, that it escaped even the long reach of his ears. It seemed, rather, that the other longfaces took great care not to mention his name within earshot of the shict. They turned their eyes away from him, and even Naxiaw felt the urge to look away, to avoid the sight of his void-black robes and long and stiff white hair.

But he forced himself to look, to give this one a name, one more flower to the necklace. This one would bleed. This one would die. This one, Black-clad, would suffer most of all.

After a moment, the sound of fingers drumming resumed. Air returned to their lungs, meaninglessness to their voices.

'As I was saying,' Yldus continued, 'the subject of the invasion is of some concern to me.'

'As to us all,' Vashnear replied with a sneer. 'The fact that *you* were chosen to lead it is a decision of unending concern.'

'I suppose you have a better idea?' Qaine replied, stepping in front of Yldus, returning his sneer.

This, Naxiaw gathered, was their function – to be hounds to the males. To bare their teeth and snarl at those who looked at them without their express approval. These tall, white-haired ones, the Carnassials, were the fiercest and most protective of their charges. And Naxiaw waited with morbid anticipation for the spike-headed Dech to return Qaine's aggression with the grim hope that one of them would die shortly after.

'Granted, given the company,' Yldus said before Dech could make a move, 'I know that to request an end to your female posturing and snarling is to ask the impossible, but I was hoping we could get at least a little business done before you start tearing each other apart.'

'The Master's decision,' Xhai uttered, 'was made.'

A long silence trailed her words, suggesting that any event of tearing apart, as far as she was concerned, would end with her in possession of all her limbs and possibly one or two extra. The remaining females met her gaze briefly before snorting derisively and stepping back to their respective males.

'If *Sheraptus* has anything to tell us,' Vashnear snarled, 'then he can speak without the use of females. Until then, nothing is decided.' He glanced fleetingly at Black-clad. 'I still advocate overwhelming force. The males lead, use the *nethra* to burn the city to cinders without having to set foot in it and risk contamination.'

'The cost would be enormous,' Yldus protested.

'You act as though we do *not* possess the stones.' Vashnear tapped the red sphere dangling from his neck, smiled as it glowed brightly at his touch. 'The cost is trivial.'

'You aren't considering the resources spent.'

'Oh no,' Vashnear moaned, rolling his white eyes. '*More* dead slaves? If only we had some inexhaustible source of working flesh and …' He blinked suddenly, holding up a finger. '*Oh wait.*' His thin hand made a dismissive gesture. 'Ours is the right to take. We can always get more over-scum.'

'Really?' Yldus strode to the edge of the ridge and stared down at the valley below. 'We've already rounded up every green thing on the island and killed half of them already. Attempts to collect and subjugate the painted lizards have gone …'

Naxiaw peered through his bars, following the longface's stare to the valley. Two females below dragged an unmoving compatriot by her ankles. Naxiaw's eyes widened as he spied the female's head, or the red pulp that used to be the head. He had but enough time to make out a miasma of colour, red-stained grey porridge rolling around in bits of exposed, glistening bone held together by a web of tattered purple flesh.

Then the two females tossed their fellow unceremoniously into the spike-lined pit. Shadowy figures moved beneath, stirred with sudden, violent movement. Naxiaw caught flashes of red and brown fur, bright teeth against black lips. An eerie cackle rose from the pit, to be drowned out by the sound of chewing and ripping.

'Not as well as we had planned,' Yldus finished.

'If the worst that comes from our attempts is that the sikkhuns eat a little better and we lose a few females, so be it.' Vashnear spoke with a very pleased smirk he was certain to swing toward Qaine. 'Of course, we have an entire wealth of green-things that will *not* fight back readily, just waiting for—'

'Not them.'

Black-clad's voice lingered for just a moment this time, a spear instead of a cloak that he aimed directly at Vashnear. The red-robed longface nodded briefly, his smile disappearing.

'Of course.' He turned his stare back toward his fellow male. 'But it is not as though there is a shortage of overscum in this world. We will use what we have to ruin their city and eliminate the need for this useless chatter or for useless females. The three of us. Burn them out. Burn them up. The problem is solved.'

Dech snorted. 'What would be the point in just burning them, though?'

'That's what I was beginning to illuminate,' Yldus replied. 'The specifics simply have to be—'

'Specifics?' Dech frowned deeply. 'You have a city full

of pinkies. Stomp their faces in, cut their heads off, and if you want to get *really* specific, rip their arms out of their sockets and stab them in their throats with them.'

'Stab them,' Yldus repeated, 'in the throat.'

'With their arms, yeah.'

A silence settled over the assembly. Yldus stared at the Carnassial for a very long, unblinking moment before pursing his lips together and taking a deep breath through his nose.

'At any rate,' he continued, clearly biting back words far more suited to his mood, 'burning will not work. The considerable resources that such a plan would utilise aside, our goal is not actually to burn as many overscum as possible, you will recall.'

'Right,' Qaine chuckled blackly. 'Just a bonus.'

'*Rather*,' Yldus continued, shooting her a scowl, 'I am hoping to *minimise* the amount of casualties needed, at least as far as our forces are concerned. Every female we lose in this battle will be a female we will not have for further conflicts. Hence, I will need more to attack the city.'

'I don't follow,' Dech grunted.

'Really.' Yldus rolled his eyes. 'The logic is simple. The overscum has a sizable presence. Not enough to hold my current force back, of course, but enough to take a toll that would make future conflicts with the underscum more of a difficulty than they need be.'

'You have been given three *venri* to use,' Xhai growled curtly. 'More than enough for any true warrior.'

'Females are warriors,' Yldus countered. 'I am not. And if we hope to have any warriors to fight the underscum with—'

'The underscum are yet to be a problem.'

'Really?' Vashnear eyed her, noting the mass of thick

360

purple tissue near her collarbone. 'How did you get that mark again, unscarred? Or are we still able to call you that?'

'*This* was given to me,' she snarled, thumping the scar, 'from no black-skinned, slime-spewing piece of *krazhak*.'

'From the overscum you reported, then?' Vashnear asked, smirking. 'Perhaps you should have kept that to yourself, no?'

'I have plans for that,' she uttered, rubbing the scar with an intensity that went far beyond grudge-filled memory.

'Could we perhaps get back to *my* plans?' Yldus asked. 'You know, the important ones?'

'Proceed.'

Yldus shuddered slightly at Black-clad's voice, gritting his teeth before continuing.

'We ...' He paused to inhale. 'We are in agreement that the overscum city must be sacked, yes? The relic must be procured. Our allies demand it. However, our knowledge on the subject's location is as delicate as our allies' patience is. We lack the time to spend sifting through ashes. Hence, burning is not an option.' He glanced toward Xhai. 'Neither is failure. To that end, it would be easier to crush them in one overwhelming force, rather than bleeding them, and our forces, over a longer period.'

'And what are you asking for, exactly?' Xhai asked. 'How many more *venri*?'

'One.'

'One?'

'The First.'

At this, a collective inhale of breath, a collective call to objection and insult, coursed through the longfaces. Naxiaw saw that even Black-clad's head tilted slightly at the mention.

'Unnecessary,' Qaine growled. 'I'm going with the invasion. *One* Carnassial is more than enough to kill a bunch of pinkies.'

'Stupid,' Dech snarled. 'Those stupid high-fingers get all the fighting already. Why give them more?'

'Weak,' Vashnear scoffed. 'The First are there to break backs and crush heads *only* when the backs are too stiff and the heads too high. And you think you need them to take a single ... whatever it is you are seeking?'

'No,' Xhai uttered. 'The First cannot be commanded by you. They answer only to the Master, only to—'

'Yes.'

Of all the eyes that swept toward Black-clad, Xhai's were the widest, lingered the longest, boiled with the most anger. Though she doubtlessly desired to erupt in a violent torrent of her grating, snarling language, she kept her voice low, language clear and neck so rigid it appeared as though her spine had turned to iron.

'*He* doesn't have the authority to command the First,' she whispered harshly. 'It undercuts you, makes you look ...' She clenched her teeth together. 'I already told him—'

'Leave.'

She recoiled, to Naxiaw's surprise, with a look of shock. He hadn't thought any of the longfaces capable of any expression beyond varying degrees of anger. Thus, it was with particular interest that he watched her face melt slightly, whatever force holding her visage so taut snapping and sloughing off to reveal a look of parted lips, quivering eyes.

He certainly hadn't thought that any longface could look so hurt, least of all this one.

'As you wish,' Yldus replied. 'We will depart swiftly and return all the more quickly for it.'

Slowly, one by one, they began to dissipate from

the ridge. Yldus strode as tall as he could beside Qaine. Vashnear skulked with Dech following reluctantly. Xhai was the last to leave and took the longest, stopping to turn and look behind with each step.

But she, too, left, as did they all, without so much as looking at Naxiaw, leaving the shict and the black-draped longface alone.

And no sooner did they than Naxiaw made ready to leave, as well. He lowered his head and closed his eyes, prepared to withdraw into his mind, to touch the Howling and send out his panicked warnings, his fevered shouts to his kin.

Longfaces coming, his thoughts ran like terrified deer. *Poison soon. Let them all die together, purple and pink alike. Kill the human evolution before it begins again. Cleanse all diseases.*

A good list, he thought, one he would eagerly relay once he vanished into sounds without meaning, once he reached his people, once they heard—

'Not answering, are they?'

He felt cold, the words echoing through his ribs to clench at his heart. Black-clad's face had not turned, yet there was no doubt who he spoke to.

'You're shocked,' the longface said, chuckling softly. 'Your kind typically is. Overscum, that is. I like that about you, though.' He made a long gesture over the valley. 'Everything with netherlings is always a foregone conclusion. When they're born, they know what they're going to do. Males use *nethra* to lead the females, who use iron to kill each other. Low-fingers use bows, high-fingers use swords, bridge-fingers become Carnassials. Those with black hair die; those with white hair kill. It's so …'

His sigh drained the air from the sky, left Naxiaw breathless, helpless, staring in astonished silence.

'And what's more,' Black-clad continued. 'They don't just *know* what it is they do, they *love* doing it. Males love leading, females love killing, none of them knowing they could do something different. But these … *humans*, if you'll pardon the mention of their race, these are fascinating creatures. They never know what's going to happen, the females, especially. And when they find out …'

Naxiaw felt the longface's smile, even without seeing it. He could feel the stretch of lips, the baring of teeth, the long, slow drag of a long pink tongue across them.

'Really, I'm surprised you don't think more of the females. You seem to be of similar mindsets: both always thinking about killing, both always thinking about death. Though you don't think of it as death. You think yourself to have medicine, to cure.' His fingers drummed. 'Lying … we've never had reason to, what with everyone knowing everything about themselves and each other. What a fascinating creation.'

Naxiaw opened his mouth, urged his voice into his throat even as it fought to stay down, stay hidden from this creature, to avoid matching itself against his sounds full of meaning. Before the shict could even squeak, though, Black-clad continued.

'No, I can't read your thoughts. Not the ones you keep to yourself, anyway. But whenever you bow your head and start thinking … well, it's so loud, I can hardly hear anything else. Even then, I can't garner much besides some general information, bits and pieces, mostly. I know you hate us, but that's hardly surprising, what with you being our prisoner and all. I know you're looking to kill … apologies, "cure" the humans, but who isn't? And I know you can understand me, even if you never speak.'

Naxiaw felt his eyelids begging him to blink, his breath

begging him to suck in more, but he had the wits to do neither.

'No, I don't particularly care, really. You want to kill them, kill Yldus and Vashnear, kill Xhai … kill me, even. I could put an end to that right now, you know. But then, that would be just one more foregone conclusion, wouldn't it? I rather like the idea of something new and interesting happening if I let you live. If you kill a few females, that's fine. I have more than enough to spare. Will you kill me, though?'

He chuckled again.

'I'd really like to see if you could come close, actually. Everything I learn about you … you people and your bright red sun fascinate me. Your lying, your railing against truth, fighting against what you know. I must know more … Perhaps you'll tell me eventually?'

Naxiaw had not the voice to reply.

'Eventually, of course. For the moment, I'm not interested in much else … except that voice. You heard it, too, didn't you? Whining, whimpering, and then … screaming. What was that, anyway? One of your people? But not one you were trying to reach … I can sense that much. But it was trying to reach you, even if it didn't know it. How curious it was, though. So lost, so alone, so blind. I can't know if you can tell or not, but I, for my opinion, think it sounded strange, unique … *female.*'

The words rolled off his tongue like a dagger, hanging in the air, its echo the smooth and relentless edge that pierced Naxiaw's heart. Was the voice, that lost and whimpering voice, a female? He could not know. But it was a shict, this was fact, and it was a shict he must warn. But how? If he could not use the Howling without this longface knowing, what would he do?

'It is a confusing dilemma, isn't it?' Black-clad asked. Slowly, he turned to face the shict, his grin broad and white. 'I might have an answer, though. This thing you use, your loud thoughts. It can't be too hard for me to figure out. Why don't you just relax ...'

Naxiaw swallowed hard as he met the longface's eyes, bright crimson and burning like pyres.

'And let me have a look inside?'

Something reached out, slid past Naxiaw's brow and into his brain. He threw his head back, pricked his ears up. In a word without sound, a noise without speech, he let out a long, meaningless scream.

Twenty-One

THE KING OF TEJI

'*She did it again.*'

The voice came subtly this time, without cold fingers of rime. It came this time as soft as snow falling on his brow, accumulating and growing heavier.

'*She thinks you don't see her.*'

Growing impossible to ignore.

'*Thinks* we *don't see her.*'

Still, Lenk tried.

He focused on other distractions in the hut: the oppressive moisture of sweat sliding down his body, the stale breath of the still and humid air filtered through the roof of dried reeds, the sounds of buzzings, chirpings, the rustling of leaves.

And her.

He could feel her, too, just as easily as the sweat. He could feel her body trembling with each shallow breath, feel her eyes occasionally glancing to him, hear her voice bristling behind her teeth, ready to say something. He could feel the brief space of earth between them. When her hand twitched, he felt the dirt shift beneath his palm. When his fingers drummed, he knew she could feel the resonance in hers.

He felt her as he sat, felt her smile as easily as he felt his own creeping across his face.

'*She isn't smiling.*'

He furrowed his brow suddenly, resisting the urge to speak to the voice, to even acknowledge it. Try as he did, though, he couldn't stop the thought from boiling up in his head.

She isn't?

'*Look.*'

Out of the corner of his eye, he saw her for the first time since they had entered the hut. She was not smiling, not even looking at him. Her stare was tilted up to the roof, along with her ears, rigid and twitching with the same delicate, wary searching that he had seen before, once.

But she had been looking at him, then.

'*She listens.*'

That makes sense. He was distantly aware of a voice in the room. *Someone else is talking.*

'*Not to them.*'

Why wouldn't she be listening to them?

'*You aren't.*'

Point.

'*Watch carefully. She searches for something that you can't hear.*'

But you can ...

'*Only fragments of ... wait, she is going to hear it again.*'

As if she had heard the voice herself, she suddenly stiffened, her chin jerking. Her neck twisted, face looking out somewhere, through the stone walls and beneath the soil. He followed her stare, but whatever it was that she saw, he obviously could not.

'*She does not see it, either. She hears. It is loud.*'

And at that cue, her ears trembled with a sudden violent tremor that coursed down her neck and into her shoulders. He saw her lips peel back in a teeth-clenching wince, as though she sought to hold on with her jaws to whatever it was she had found with her ears. He felt her shudder, through the soil, as she clung to it.

And he saw her release it, head bowing, ears drooping and folding over themselves, seeking to drive it away with as much intensity as she sought to hold on to it.

He listened intently and heard nothing but the frigid voice.

'Didn't like the noise. Pity.'

You ... did you hear it?

'Mmm ... are we on speaking terms again?'

Did you or did you not?

'Heard, not so much. Sensed, though ...'

Sensed what?

'Intent.'

What intent?

No reply.

Whose intent?

Silence.

'Whose?'

It was only after the snow had flaked away, after the numbing silence in his head passed and was replaced with the distant ambience of the village outside, that Lenk realised he had just spoken aloud.

She turned to regard him with a start, eyes more suited to a frightened beast than a shict.

'What?' she asked.

'What?' he repeated, blankly.

'You said something?'

'We didn't.'

'We?'

'Well, you didn't, did you?'

'Nothing.' She shook her head a tad too vigorously to be considered not alarming.

'Are you … ?' He furrowed his brow at her, frowning. 'You looked a bit distracted just now.'

'Not me, no,' she said, her head trembling again with a tad more nervous enthusiasm. Just before it seemed as though her skull would come flying off, she stopped, her face sliding into an easy smile, eyes relaxing in their sockets. 'What about you?'

'What about me?'

'Are you well?'

'I'm …'

'*Calm.*'

What?

'*When was the last time we felt like this? No concerns, no fears, no duties …*'

'You're what?' Kataria pressed.

He opened his mouth to reply, but became distracted by the sudden, fierce buzzing that violated his ears. A blue blur whizzed past his head, circling twice before he could even think to swat at it. And as he felt a sapphire-coloured dragonfly the size of a hand land on his face for the twenty-fifth time, he was far too resigned to do anything about it.

'I'm a tad annoyed, actually,' he replied as the insect made itself comfortable in his hair.

'You could always swat it off, you know,' she said.

'I could and then its little, biting cousins would flense me alive,' he growled, scratching at the red dots littering his arms and chest. 'The big ones, at least, command enough fear that the little ones will flee at the sight of them.'

'Perhaps it's for the best that we're leaving,' Kataria said, 'if you've been around long enough to figure out insect politics.'

'It's not like I've got a lot else to do,' he growled. He cast a glance over her insultingly pale flesh, unpocked by even a hint of red. 'How is it that they're not biting you, anyway?'

'Ah.' Grinning, she held up an arm to a stray beam of sun seeping through the roof and displayed the waxy glisten of her skin. 'I smeared myself in gohmn fat. Bugs don't like the taste, I found.'

'Is *that* what that smell is?'

'I'm surprised you didn't notice earlier.'

'Well, I noticed the smell, certainly, I just thought it was all the gohmns you were eating.'

She grinned broadly. 'Every part is used, you know.'

'Yeah,' he said, scratching an errant itch under his loin-cloth. 'I know.'

He could feel her laugh, seeping into his body like some particularly merry disease. And like a disease, it infected him, caused him to flash a grin of his own at her, to take in the depth of her eyes. He could scarcely remember when they had looked so bright, so clear, unsullied by scrutinising concern.

'It is nice, isn't it?'

It is.

'It could always be this way.'

It could?

'Is that not why you wish to leave?'

It is, yes, but ... well, you hardly seem the type to encourage that sort of thing. In the back of his mind, he became aware of an ache, slow and cold. *In fact, you're being awfully polite today. That's ... not normal, is it?*

It should have occurred to him, he supposed, that it would take a special kind of logic to try and ask the voice in one's head what constitutes normalcy, but his attentions were quickly snatched away by Kataria's sudden exasperated sigh.

'How long have we been sitting here, anyway?' she asked.

Lenk gave his buttocks a thoughtful squeeze; there was approximately one more knuckle's worth of soil clenched between them, as far as he could sense.

'About half an hour,' he replied. 'You remember how we're going to go about this?'

'Not hard,' she said. 'Tell Togu we're leaving, ask on the progress of our stuff, get it back, find a sea chart, ask for a boat, head to shipping lanes, quit adventuring and the possibility of dying horribly by steel in the guts and instead wait to die horribly by scurvy.'

'Right, but remember, we aren't leaving without pants.'

'Are you still on about that?' She grinned, adjusting the fur garment about her hips. 'You don't find the winds of Teji ... invigorating?'

'The winds of Teji, muggy and bug-laden as they may be, are tolerable,' he grumbled. 'It's the subsequent knocking about that I can't abide.'

'The what?'

'Yours don't dangle. I don't expect you to understand.'

'Oh ... *oh!*' Her understanding dawned on her in an expression of disgust. 'They knock?'

'They knock.'

'Well, then.' She coughed, apparently looking for a change of subject in the damp soil beneath them. 'Pants, then?'

'And food.'

'What about your sword?'

Not the first time she asked, not the first time he felt the leather in his hands and the weight in his arms at the thought of it. The image of it, aged steel, nicked from where he and his grandfather had both carved their professions through anything that would net them a single coin. His sword. His profession. His legacy.

'Just a weapon,' he whispered. 'Plenty more to be had.'

He could feel her stare upon him, feel it become thick with studying intent for a moment before he felt it turn away, toward the opposite end of the hut. She leaned back on her palms and sighed.

'Chances are it might be here,' she said, sweeping an arm about the hut, 'given all the other garbage he seems to collect.'

He followed her gesture with a frown; it was a bit unfair to call the possessions crowding the hut 'garbage', he thought, especially considering that most of it was stuffed away in various chests and drawers. He did wonder, not for the first time, how a monarch who presided over lizards with little more to their collective names beyond dried reeds and dirty hookahs managed to assemble such an eclectic collection of antiques.

The hut's stone walls looked as though they might be buckling with the sheer weight of the various chests, dressers, wardrobes, braziers, model ships, crates, mannequins sporting everything from dresses to priestly robes, busts of long-dead monarchs and the occasional jar of ... something.

And over all of them grew a thick net of ivy, flowers blooming upon flowers, leaves twitching as insects crawled over them. They seemed a world away from the dead forests beyond with no life.

'*All that grows on Teji,*' the lizardman Bagagame had said as he escorted them in, '*grows for Togu.*'

Of course, the reptile hadn't bothered to say why,

amongst the various pieces of furniture, there wasn't a chair or stool to spare the honoured guests the uniquely displeasing sensation of having soil crawl up one's rear end. Then again, he hadn't bothered to say why the king never moved or spoke before he vanished behind the throne … and presumably stayed there.

'We'll ask him if we can sift through this' – he paused – 'collection.'

'You were going to say "garbage".'

'You don't know what I was going to say.'

'Whatever,' Kataria grunted. 'It's all moot since I'm pretty sure he's not going to wake up in this lifetime.'

He glanced up towards the throne at the end of the hut, overpolished to a lumpy, greasy sheen. Squatting in its seat, as he had done for the past half hour, the past four conversations and the past two conversations that included discussions of itches in strange places, Togu sat, impassive, unmoving and possibly dead.

He was likely very impressive under the brown cloak, Lenk thought, if bottle-shaped and narrow-necked counted as kingly features in Owauku society. He blinked, considering; that seemed to fit the kind of persona that would be cultivated by a race of heavy-smoking, bug-eyed, bipedal reptiles who ate, raised and wore bugs.

But electing a corpse seemed a bit too eccentric even for them.

He was giving heavy consideration to the idea, though, considering King Togu didn't even appear to be breathing, much less moving, at the moment.

Probably a concern.

'Why worry about it?'

Why worry about the fact that we've been waiting half an hour to talk to a dead lizard?

'*Well, when you say it like* that ...'

A noise crept through his head. It began softly, then rang with crystalline clarity: cold, clear and mirthful. His eyes went wide.

Did you just ... laugh?

'Ah, honoured guests!'

The bass voice of Bagagame boomed with the ache that rose in Lenk's neck whenever the Owauku made his presence known. He looked up to see the stout lizardman waddling in from the small hole in the stone wall that formed the hut's back entrance. His yellow grin broad, he bowed deeply, doffing his hat.

'May Bagagame present, on behalf of y'most pleased hosts of Teji ...' He stepped aside, pulling back the portal's leather flap. 'King Togu!'

Lenk turned a baffled stare from the hole to the figure seated upon the throne. Seeing no movement from the shrouded figure seated upon the throne, he glanced back to the portal and instantly had to choose between greeting, screaming or vomiting at the sight of the creature creeping out of the shadows.

It was difficult to decide, however; there was no clear way to regard the amalgamation of green flesh, fine silk and dirty feathers that came out and regarded the companions with its yellow stare, for, truly, Lenk really had no idea what the hell King Togu was.

Superficially, at least, it resembled an Owauku: stout, green, with a belly as round as his massive, gourdlike eyes. But this one sported a pair of long, fleshy whiskers that hung so far from his blunt snout as to dangle about his stubby feet.

Still, the silk robe he wore open, so that it formed a purple frame to the bright jewel he wore in his belly, suggested something that had been digging in a nobleman's trash. The feathered headdress he wore about his prodigious skull and the nauseating blend of flowers, vines, feathers and leathers he wore as decoration ... well, Lenk really had no explanation for that.

Quietly, the creature surveyed them, his eyes swivelling from Lenk to Kataria, then fixating one on Kataria while the other rolled with uncomfortable slowness to stare at Lenk. Eyes split apart, his face soon followed suit as a large, yellow-toothed smile neatly bisected the green visage into two equal segments of scaly flesh.

'Cousins,' King Togu spoke in a voice earth-deep and flower-sweet, 'be welcome.'

'Uh ... thanks,' Lenk replied. Possibly not the best greeting in the presence of reptilian royalty, he thought, but he found that the creature's presence robbed him of coherent thought for anything more elegant. 'I'm ...' He searched for a word and settled, reluctantly. '*Glad?* Glad that you've given us your time today.'

'*Glad? Glad?*' Both yellow eyes swivelled to regard Lenk incredulously. '*Merely* glad?' He whirled upon Bagagame, face twisted into a frown. '*Merely* glad. Why not great? Why not fantastic? Why not in need of a drink, so viciously does the excitement inspired by Teji's majesty seep out of their mouths?'

'I don't know!' Bagagame offered, shrugging helplessly. 'Maybe they came to complain? The sun don't shine that brightly these days and maybe—'

'The sun *always* shines on Teji!' Togu drove his point home at the end of a stubby backhand against the shorter Owauku's cheek. '*You* are the one that diminishes our great reputation! Look!' He smacked his subject again, sending one eye spinning towards Lenk. 'A giant *bug* is sitting on his head! Is this how we will be remembered?'

'Oh, right,' Lenk said, suddenly feeling the dragonfly as it, suddenly frightened by the noise, scurried down onto his face. He reached up to brush it away. 'It's really no—'

'Sorry! Sorry! M'fix that right up now!' Bagagame came bounding over, eyes fixated on the sapphire-coloured insect.

'It's not necessary!' Lenk's hand moved away from the bug and out in a futile attempt to stop the Owauku as his lips slowly parted. 'No! *No, don't*—'

His words were lost in the subsequent squishing sound and he blinked dumbly, unable to find any others. He didn't feel this was at all inappropriate; it was, after all, quite difficult to form the proper thoughts to express one's feelings at feeling the thick, sticky end of a lizardman's three-foot-long tongue plastered to one's cheek. Even as Bagagame drew it back, winged prize twitching as he yanked it into his grinning mouth, he was at a loss.

He remained in that dumbstruck silence for a moment, blinking through the veil of saliva dribbling down his eyelid as he slowly, calmly licked his lips.

'Right,' he said, 'so, anyway, we're leaving.'

'Leaving.' Togu levelled a scowl at Bagagame. '*Leaving*. Why leaving?'

'I don't—'

The king made a sweeping gesture back to the portal he had emerged from. 'Go and get the coals.'

Bagagame offered a bob of his head, scurrying off to the shadows and leaving the larger Owauku to sigh and stalk toward his throne, keeping one large eye upon the companions. Lenk watched him with some befuddlement;

he wasn't quite sure how he expected the king to take the news, but he wasn't anticipating such calmness.

Then again, he wasn't sure he had ever actually anticipated having to explain anything to a feathered lizardman.

'Naturally, I'm a bit curious,' Togu said. 'Have we not done all we could to establish our hospitality?'

The quality of the king's speech should likely have provided some comfortable familiarity, Lenk thought. Contrasted against the other Owauku, it merely made him seem all the more peculiar.

'Well, yes,' Lenk replied, 'but surely, you must have known we'd have to leave sometime.'

'Of course.'

The king deftly leapt onto the armrest of his throne, nearly slipping from the wax before sliding up to perch on the velvet-lined back. His position, combined with his feathers, lent him an avian appearance that was only made more ominous as he reached down with a foot to slide the cloak off the stout figure seated in the throne. A truly massive waterpipe was revealed, seated smugly on the red velvet as Togu reached down to pluck up the hose and bring it to his scaly lips.

'I suppose I was hoping that, against better judgement, you would linger for a while. It has been nice to have humans about in the village again.'

'And your hospitality has been ...' *Don't say 'horrifying'.* '—lovely,' Lenk said. 'But we've got other places to be.'

'And there is nothing I can say to convince you otherwise, I'm assuming, or you would not have come to me.'

A great yellow eye swivelled to the portal, regarding Bagagame sourly as the smaller Owauku came teetering out with a tiny censer full of smouldering coals. He quickly applied them to the waterpipe, the rich scent of flavoured tobacco filling the air almost instantly as the water burbled inside its vase. Togu drew in a breath that lasted for ages, his chest inflating to a size preposterous for a creature his size. When he did speak again, his words came out on a cloud of smoke that made him resemble some great, fire-breathing beast.

'Which does make old Togu wonder why you *have* come.'

Bagagame cringed at even the brief, dismissive wave Togu offered him and quickly ran, bowing apologies to both of the companions as he scurried between them and out the door. Lenk watched him go only until he was exactly three and a half feet out of earshot then turned back to Togu.

'Well, as you may have noticed, we aren't in much shape to be getting anywhere,' he explained. 'We *had* been expecting a ...' *Don't say 'hired peon.'* '—friend to come retrieve us, but we haven't seen any sign of a black ship lately.'

'Have you?' Kataria chimed in.

Togu coughed slightly, apparently choking on a stray ash that had crept its way into his hose. He shook his head, thumping his chest gently.

'Not as such, no,' he said. He appeared to furrow his scaly ridges in thought, Lenk thought, but that might just be some other emotion too deep for eyes the size of grapefruits to convey. 'No ... no ... the Gonwa would have spoken of such a boat.'

'Ah, well, that seems—'

'*Lies.*'

A cold ache crept through him, a frosty hand wringing his spine for a moment before releasing it. He shook his head, as he might shake snow from his hair.

'Discouraging,' Lenk finished, his voice degenerating

into a mutter. 'I suppose it might have been helpful if the Gonwa had actually told *us* first, though.'

'They are … a complex people,' Togu replied, scratching his chin. 'They come from Komga, an island with too many trees, not enough sun and, as such, they lack our "sunny" disposition.' He grinned at his own joke. 'They must be more than a little irritated at having moved here, anyway, but Teji will grow on them.'

'And why did they move here, exactly?' Kataria asked, drawing a glance from Lenk.

That does seem important … Should … shouldn't I have asked that?

'Why would you?'

That's usually my thing.

'Worrying? Let someone else do it.'

Togu's eyes rotated to regard her carefully. 'Feel free to ask them.'

She accepted the retort with what would appear, to anyone else, as a cool silence. Lenk, however, could see the faint tremble of her upper lip, the minuscule twitch of her eyelid, and a tiny, distinct quiver of her ears.

'Sees. Hears. Lies.'

'What?' he whispered inwardly.

'Point being,' Togu continued, 'Teji warms all and all warm to Teji, in time.' He settled back, taking another deep puff of his pipe. 'I'm sure you could find your place in it, if you wished.'

'Point being,' Lenk retorted, 'that we don't. We appreciate the hospitality inasmuch as we *can* appreciate having loincloths slapped on us, but—'

'We are mending your clothes. It takes time when we lack thread.'

'That, too, is appreciated, which brings me to my next

point,' he continued. 'We were wondering if we could ask a little more of you.'

Togu's eyes shifted to him. 'Ask away.'

'A sea chart to find the nearest shipping lanes to the mainland, a boat to take us there, food to make it there and—'

'*Sword.*'

'And ...'

'*Sword.*'

'Something ...'

'*Need.*'

'Pants,' Kataria interjected. 'We want our pants back.'

'Pants?' Togu began to mutter, clouds of smoke roiling out of his nostrils. 'Pants, pants, pants ... It's *always* pants with humans, isn't it?'

'What *is* it with lizardthings and calling me human? I'm *not* human!' She took her ears in her hands, pulling them out for display. '*Look at these things!* They're *huge!*'

'Can you get us that sort of thing or not?' Lenk asked with a sigh. 'You can keep whatever it is you found from our wreckage in payment or we can work something out.'

'What sort of something?' Togu asked.

'We can do ... things.'

'Such as?'

'Kill stuff,' Kataria said, sniffing, 'mostly.'

'We do other things,' Lenk countered with a glare.

'Like what?' she asked, sneering.

'*Things*, you know ...' He leaned back, twirling his hand in what he hoped was at least vaguely thoughtful. 'Such as ... well, Denaos, I know, can play the lute. You probably have something like that, right?'

'Ah, yes, the tall one,' Togu said, inclining his head

approvingly. 'My people are quite fond of him. Does he have anything to say about your decision to leave?'

'Nothing worthwhile,' Kataria replied. 'The only thing missing by him, or the rest of them, not being here is a bunch of whining and probably some attempt at innuendo or something stupid like that.' She frowned, shrugging. 'So can we have the boat or not?'

Before Togu could even open his mouth, Lenk whirled upon her.

'What are you doing?'

'Negotiating.'

'No, you're just speaking loudly. You don't understand negotiation.' He tapped his chest. 'That's what *I* do.'

'So … don't this time,' she replied, regarding him curiously. 'Is that such a problem?'

'*It isn't, you know.*'

'*You* be quiet,' Lenk snarled.

'Who be quiet?' Togu asked.

'*Why even negotiate? Why leave? Everything you need is right here.*'

'Everything we need …' Lenk whispered to himself.

The words seeped into him on the silence inside his head, sowing his mind with seeds of comfort. In his brain, they began to bloom, a calm logic spreading over him. Why was this important? he wondered. Why go back to the fighting and death on the mainland? What was the point of it all?

Everything he needed was here: sun, water, food, and though she may have been regarding him with a stare that twitched between confusion and worry, she was here, too. He smiled, not knowing why, not caring why.

'*No.*'

It came back, a sudden frost that swept over his mind, killed the blooming calm. His skull throbbed with fear, anger, contempt, all swirling about his mind, all carrying the voice through.

'*Cannot leave now.*'

'Cannot leave now,' he whispered.

'What?' Kataria asked.

'Then,' Togu muttered, hope rising in his voice, 'you wish to stay?'

'*Need to stay … need to kill …*'

'Kill,' he uttered quietly.

'What was that?' Togu asked.

'Lenk …' she whispered, leaning close.

'*Lies all around us. Surrounded by worthlessness. Need to kill. Need to stay.*'

'Need …'

'*Sword.*'

'Sword.'

'Sword?' Kataria asked.

'*Need sword.*'

'Need it,' he whispered.

'Need what?' Togu asked.

'*Sword.*'

'Sword.'

'*Sword!*'

'Not again, Lenk …'

'*SWORD!*'

'*WHERE IS IT?*'

Togu recoiled, threatening to teeter off his throne as Lenk leapt to his feet and flung an icy stare at him. Lenk could feel his lids narrowing to slits, feel himself freezing despite the sun, but did not care. His head throbbed with need; his hands hungered for leather and steel.

'Where is it?' he demanded, not hearing the rasp of his

voice. 'Where is my sword? I need it … I …' He took a step forward, leg trembling. '*Need it.*'

It was cold at that moment. He could feel his flesh prickle, hairs standing on end, feel the departure of buzzing insects, as though his skin was suddenly unhallowed ground. All of nature seemed to follow their example: the sun averted its warmth, the air was strangled into a crisp chill.

'No.'

Even he would not have heard himself whimper if he didn't know he had said the words; his voice was throttled, frozen in his throat. He did not dare to speak louder for fear of what might emerge instead.

He stared into Togu's ever-widening eyes and knew that such a thing was wrong, not merely because such a feat seemed impossible for the creature's already tremendous stare. Rather, he was familiar with such an expression, familiar with the fear embedded in a face rendered speechless by a voice not his own.

Familiarity turned to pain the instant he felt her eyes upon him. Clearness gone, softness gone, now hard, scrutinising, studying, watching, peering, probing.

'*Staring.*'

'Stop …' he whispered so softly only he could hear it.

Or so he thought.

'Mad.' Togu may have whispered; the king's voice was deep enough that such an effort was futile. His head trembled back and forth, as though refusing to acknowledge what he saw. 'You're … *you* …'

'He's fine.'

Her hand was warm on his shoulder; that should not be. But it was, and strong, effortlessly pushing him past. Not past, he recognised, but behind. She stepped in front of him; he could not see the hardness in her eyes, but in her body, it was undeniable. She was tense, her spine rigid under her skin, muscles glistening with sweat, feet planting themselves solidly on the ground, neck rigid and eyes staring forward.

'Just stressed.'

'But he—'

'*Stressed.*'

Her canines flashed ivory white in the sunlight, her lip curling back to bare them menacingly. The meaning behind their sudden appearance, the inarguable fact that there would be no more discussion on the matter, was received by Togu and displayed in the slow and subtle tilt of his head.

'These times are stressful, yes,' the king muttered, nodding. 'It is understandable that ... people are on edge.'

'It is,' she said with an air of finality. 'Now, then, about our request?'

'A boat is no particular problem,' Togu replied. 'We had many before and the Gonwa only brought more. But—'

'But what?'

'I still dislike to waste one. What can you do with a boat? Sail out and hope for the best?' He tilted his head to the side thoughtfully. 'Not that we are not so very pleased that you managed to find your way, but ... *how* was it you managed to arrive on Teji again?'

Her body rippled slightly with swallowed ire, Lenk noticed, and undoubtedly Togu did as well. She was not a creature of subtlety. She must have known this as well as he did.

So why did she step in? A resolve, fragile as glass, welled up meekly inside him. *I should be the one to do this, the one to*

... And that resolve threatened to crack as he took a step forward.

'Well, we wouldn't be asking if our information was correct in the first place,' she growled. 'We were *told* this was a trading post, not a lizard den.'

Snideness, Lenk thought. *Lovely. How long until the threats?*

'Trade implies something that is *not* me giving you a boat that you may or may not destroy with nothing more than goodwill and a kiss on the cheek, cousin,' Togu said.

'No one's denying that you will get something in return,' she replied, eyes narrowing, 'and, in this case, what you are getting is whatever *won't* be happening with regards to your cheek.'

That took a bit longer than I'd have thought.

'Beyond the potential hazards of this trade, both before and after you hypothetically launch your boat,' Togu said, 'there is the matter of expenses.'

'Expenses?'

'Supplies? Food? Charts? These things we are in no certain supply of.' He shrugged, taking a long puff of his pipe. 'A difficult thing to ask.'

'Ah, of course,' Kataria said, folding her arms. 'Forgive me, I should have asked the *other* king lizard with a house full of garbage.'

'*These*,' the king said, sweeping an arm about his collection, 'are investments for when the humans return.'

'So ... this *was* a trading post.'

'Was, yes,' Togu said, nodding. 'Not so long ago, in fact, which would account for your information.' He eased back as far as he could without tipping over, groaning a smoky sigh. 'They came from Toha, seeking trading routes. They had not expected to find partners, and we had not expected

386

that we would enjoy their company. But, like all trade, this was driven by necessity.'

'You seem to have everything you need,' Kataria said, glancing over the crowding collection, 'and more.'

'I have many things, but nothing I need, no. The humans came with food, food we desperately needed. We found you in Teji's jungles, yes? You saw.'

Lenk furrowed his brow at that. He *had* seen Teji's jungles, and even through the fever that had swept over him, he could see things growing: greenery, leaves, wildlife. There looked to be no shortage of food. The moment he began to say this, however, Kataria spoke.

'It's a barren forest,' she said, 'lots of trees, but no fruit.'

'No *nothing*,' Togu replied. 'Nothing but roots and tubers. Food for the moment, but not for the people.' He shrugged. 'Thus, when the humans came with fruits, meats, wines, grain to make the gohmns larger and more hardy ... we traded. From there, we continued to trade. Our needs sated, we could take things we wanted: brandy, tobacco ...'

And yet no one thought to trade for pants, Lenk thought sourly.

'Don't mistake me for a fool, my people for simpletons,' Togu said. 'I was not made leader because they didn't know any better. I looked out for them, I learned the human language, the human ways.' His face seemed to melt with the heat of his frown. 'I learned they move on.

'And, as I said, I am no fool. I knew you would have to leave, eventually, and I suppose my people did, too.' He tried to offer a smile, but it was an expression with fragile legs, trembling under the weight that stood upon him. 'But we wanted you to stay ... if only so we could remember those times again.'

Lenk regarded the creature thoughtfully. He tried his hardest not to be suspicious, and indeed, Togu's story gave him no ready cause to be distrusted. And yet …

Something in the creature's eyes, perhaps: a little too intent to be reminiscent. Or maybe the long, slow pause that followed: a moment intended to reflect the severity of the memory, or a moment to gauge their reactions? He distrusted the lizard, but, for the life of him, he couldn't really think why.

'*He's a liar.*'

Oh, right … that's why.

Lenk wasn't sure if the voice did have moods, but he suspected that none of them were of the kind to humour him. And so, he felt the cold creep over him with greater vigour, greater ferocity.

'Surrounded *by liars. Everywhere. He lies. They lie.* You *lie.*'

Me, he tried to think through the freezing throb of his head, *what do you—?*

'*Listen. Listen to nothing else. Only to us. Only to ourselves. Realise.*'

No, no more listening. This is supposed to be over. This is supposed to be—

'*THROUGH the lies! Do not be tricked! We cannot afford it! We need to stay! Need to fight! Need our sword! See through them! Do not listen! Do not trust!*'

'Not trust …' he whispered, finding the words less reprehensible on his lips.

'Something the matter, cousin?' Togu asked.

'What happened to them, King?' The question sprang to Lenk's lips easily, instinctually. 'Where are they?'

'What?' Togu's smile was crushed under his sudden frown. 'Who?'

'Lenk ...' Kataria placed a hand on his shoulder, but he could not feel it.

'The humans,' he said, 'where are they now? Where did they go?'

'They are' – Togu's lips trembled, searching for the words – 'not here. They ...' He swallowed hard, a sudden fear in his eyes. 'They are ...'

'*Shi-i ah-ne-tange, Togu!*'

The voice rang out through the hut like a thrown spear, its speaker following shortly through the front door. While it was impossible to slam a leather flap, the Gonwa that emerged, tall and limber with the ridges on his head flaring, certainly gave it his all.

Lenk could only guess at the thing's gender, of course, and that came only from his booming voice as he shoved his way between the two companions, sparing a glare for both of them. With an arm long and lean like a javelin, he thrust a finger at Togu, using the other hand to pat at a satchel strung about his torso.

'*Ah-ne-ambe, Togu! Sakle-ah man-eh!*'

Togu spared an indignant glare for the Gonwa, which quickly shifted to Bagagame as the littler lizardman came scurrying behind, gasping for air.

'*Bagagame!*' the king boomed. '*Ah-dak-eh mah?*'

Bagagame made a reply, his voice going far too rapidly to be discerned. In response, the Gonwa stepped up the tempo of his own voice, his ire flowing freely through his words. Togu tried to dominate them in speed and pitch both, roaring over them as they blended into a whirlwind of green limbs and bass rumbles.

'Who's the big one?' Lenk asked, glancing sidelong at Kataria.

'How am I supposed to know?' she growled, fixing him with a very direct scowl. 'What was that?'

'What was what?'

'That. What you just did.'

'I asked him—'

'*You* didn't ask him anything.'

He strained to keep the shock beneath a stony visage hardened by denial. *She couldn't have heard, she can't hear that, her ears aren't that long ... are they?*

The argument between the lizardmen seemed to end in a thunderous roar as Togu shouted something and thrust a hand to the rear door. The Gonwa swung a scowl from him to the companions before nodding and stalking off to the back, Bagagame following with a nervous glance to Togu. The king himself hopped off of his throne and grunted at the two non-scaly creatures in the room.

'Forgive the interruption,' he said as he disappeared into the gloom. 'This won't take long.'

'Huh,' Lenk said. They were gone, but their voices carried into the hut, only slightly diminished by the walls between them. 'What, exactly, do you suppose reptiles argue about?'

He turned to her and saw her lunging toward him, hands outstretched. Before he could even think to protest, question, or squeal and piss himself, she took him roughly by his head, pressing her fingers fiercely against his temples and pulling him close. Their foreheads met with a cracking sound, but they were bound by shock and narrow-eyed anger, neither making a move to resist.

'Stop,' she said swiftly.

'What?'

'*Stop.*'

'I don't—'

'No, you *do*. You *are*. That's the problem.'

'I really don't think—'

'Then *don't*. No more thinking; no more speaking. Don't listen to anyone else. No one else.'

He felt his temples burn, warm blood weeping down in faint trickles. He saw a bead of sweat peel from her brow, slide over her snarling lip as she bared her teeth at him.

'*Only. Listen. To. Me.*'

The warmth from her brow was feverish, intense, as though his skin might melt onto hers and come sloughing off when she pulled away. His whole body felt warm, hot, unbearable yet entrancing, all-consuming. It swept through him like a fire, sliding down his body on his sweat to send his arms aching, shoulders drooping, heart racing, stirring his body as it drifted lower and lower until it boiled his blood away, leaving him light-headed.

And, as such, he could only nod weakly.

'It's going to be over, soon.'

She sighed, the heavy breath sending her scent roiling over him, filling his nostrils, one more unbearable sensation heaped upon the other that threatened to send him crashing to the earth. Her grip relaxed slightly, her hands sliding down to rest upon his shoulders.

'I'm going to take care of everything.'

She stepped away from him, turning her attentions back to the portal as the Gonwa came storming out first. Togu and Bagagame emerged from behind, looking alternately weary and shocked. The taller creature paused in front of the companions, whirling about to level his bulbous, yellow-eyed glower upon them.

'*Togu*,' he uttered softly, '*Shi-ne-eh ade, netha.*'

He raised his hands slowly, deliberately dusting his palms together.

'*Lah.*'

And with that, he spun again, the companions having to step aside to avoid his whipping tail as he stalked out the front door. They turned to Togu, each baffled. The king merely sighed.

'Hongwe,' he said, gesturing at the vanished Gonwa. 'Proud boy. His father was, too.'

'And that was ... what?' Lenk asked.

'A disagreement,' Togu replied. He looked up with a weary smile. 'So ... you truly wish to leave, then?'

They both nodded stiffly.

'Then you and Hongwe agree,' he said, nodding sagely. 'And so, I must respect the wishes of my guests and my people. Tomorrow, you depart. Tonight, we offer you a *Kampo San-Bah.*'

Lenk frowned at the word. It sounded ominous in his ears.

'And that is?'

'A party, of course!' the king said, grinning.

'Ah.'

Funny, he thought, that the word should get even more menacing with the definition.

Twenty-Two

WISE MEN REMEMBER TO STOMP FACES TWICE

Gariath had never particularly understood the reverence for elders that some weaker races seemed to possess. Celebrating the gradual and inevitable weakening of body and mind that ultimately ended in a few years of uncontrolled bodily functions and a mound of dirt just didn't seem all that logical.

Of course, it was different for his people. A weakened *Rhega* mind was still sharp; a frail *Rhega* body was still strong. And while weaker races praised senility as wisdom, the *Rhega* undoubtedly grew craftier with their years. Taking these traits, and only these traits, into account, he could see how an elder might be revered and respected.

However, when he factored in how incredibly annoying elders, particularly dead ones, could be, he figured he was justified in regarding them with a level of contempt just a hair above 'intolerable'.

'How long has it been since you saw the sun shine like this, Wisest?'

He growled in response, not looking up. 'Is that rhetorical?'

'Philosophical.'

'There are an awful lot of words to say "pointless", I've found.'

The fact that he didn't even have to see the elder's teeth to know he was grinning, with a profound smugness that only someone who had died and come back could achieve, was just number eleven on an itemised list of irritating traits that was quickly growing.

'Have you not noticed your surroundings, Wisest?' the grandfather asked. 'There is beauty in the land.'

Senseless optimism. Number five.

Gariath stopped in his tracks and looked up, regarding his companion, the grandfather growing slightly translucent as a beam of light struck him. Narrowing his eyes, he looked up and out from the river, its stream reduced to a shallow half-a-toe high. The forest rose in great walls upon the ridges of the ravine he stood in, fingers of brown and green sticking up decisively to present a unity of arboreal rude gestures at him. Sunlight seeped through them, painting the ravine in contrasting portraits of black smears and golden rays.

'Dying rivers,' he snorted. 'Broken rocks. This land is dead.'

'What?' The spirit looked at him ponderously. 'No, no. There is life here. We spoke to it, once. We heard the land and the land … the land …'

His voice drifted into nothingness, his form following soon after, disappearing in the sunlight. Gariath continued on, unworried. Grandfather would not stay gone. Gariath was not *that* lucky. His sigh was one of many, added to the snarls and curses that formed his symphony of annoyance.

The river's bed of sharp rocks was not to blame, of course. His feet had been toughened over six days, searing coastal sand, twisted forest thorns and, more recently, a number of ravines home to sharper rocks than these.

It was the repetition, the endless monotony of it all, that

drove him to voice as he did, if only to serve as reprieve from the forest's endless chorus. The island's dynamic environs *might* have pleased someone else, someone simpler: a leaf-brained, tree-sniffing, fart-breathing pale piece of filth.

The pointy-eared thing would enjoy this, he thought. *She likes dirt and trees and things that smell worse than her. This sort of thing would fill her head with so many happy thoughts.* He paused, inhaled deeply and growled. *As good a reason as any to spill her brains out on a rock.*

'Really? Thinking about brains *again*?'

The voice came ahead of him. He looked up and growled at the grandfather crouching upon a large, round boulder. The elder's penchant for shifting positions wildly did not do anything to impress the dragonman anymore.

'You're getting predictable, Wisest,' the elder chided.

'It weighs heavily on my mind,' he grunted. 'And hers will weigh heavily on the ground.' He stalked past, trying to ignore the grandfather's stare. 'Once I pick up the scent again.'

'It's been days since you last had it.'

'It's important.'

'Why?'

'Because she will lead me to Lenk.'

'Which is important why?'

'Because Lenk is the key to finding meaning again.'

'How?'

'Because ...' He stopped and whirled about, not surprised to see the rock empty of residence, but growling all the same. 'That's what you told me.' He turned and scowled at the elder leaning against the ravine's wall. 'Were you lying to me?'

'Not entirely, no,' the grandfather replied with a roll of

effulgent shoulders. 'I had simply thought you might lose interest by now, as all pups do.'

'Pups aren't big enough to smash heads, Grandfather.'

'Size is relative to age.'

'No matter how old you are, I'm still big enough to crush your head.'

'All right, then, size is irrelevant to someone with no head to crush, which is a benefit of being very old.'

'And dead.'

The grandfather held up a single clawed finger. 'Point being, I had thought you would have found something else to do by now.'

'Something else …'

'Something else.'

He spared a single, hard scowl for the grandfather before shouldering past. 'Something *other* than finding a reason to live? I suppose I could always die.' He snorted. 'But *someone* had a problem with that.'

'I meant finding a reason that doesn't involve killing so many things. You've tried *that* already. Has it brought you any closer to happiness?'

'I'm not *looking* for happiness. I'm *looking* for a reason to keep going.'

'The sun? The trees? There is much here, Wisest, far away from the sorrows that have made you unhappy. A *Rhega* could live well here, wanting for nothing, without humans of any kind.'

'And do what? Listen to you all day? Have pleasant conversations about the weather?'

'Would that be so bad?' The grandfather's voice drifted to his ear frills softly. 'It is rather sunny, today, Wisest … Have you noticed?'

The whisper in the elder's voice quelled the roar rumbling

in Gariath's chest, so he merely snorted. 'I've noticed.'

'When did you last see this much life?'

Gariath glanced around. The forest was silent. The trees did not blow. 'There is nothing but death here, Grandfather.'

He didn't bother to look up to see. He could feel the elder's frown as sharp as any rock.

'The stench is hard to miss.' His nostrils quivered, lips curled back in a cringe at the scent. 'The trees are trying to cover it up, but there's the stink of dead bodies everywhere. Bones, mostly, some other smellier things ...'

'There is also life, Wisest. Trees, some beasts, water ...'

'There's *something*, yeah. I've been smelling it for hours now.' Gariath took in a deep breath, glancing over his shoulder. 'Broken rocks, dried-up rivers, dead leaves and dusk.'

'There was so much before ... so much,' the spirit whispered. 'I used to hear it everywhere. And now ... death?' He sounded confused, distracted. 'But why so much?'

'There would be more,' Gariath growled. 'Good deaths, too. But someone distracted me from killing the pointy-eared one.'

'Would that be me or the roach she shoved up your nose?' The grandfather chuckled. 'If it means there's one less dead body on this island, I won't object to it.'

'*You* were the one to tell me she was going to kill Lenk!' Gariath snarled in response. 'If she hasn't already, she's still planning to.'

'And if she has? Then what?'

'*You're* the elder. You're supposed to know!'

'My point remains,' the grandfather said. 'What do you suppose happens when you find the humans again? Given it any thought?'

'By following him this far, I've found Grahta and I've found you. That's a start.'

'But where is the end? Will you just go chasing ghosts your whole life, Wisest?'

He glanced up, regarding the elder with hard eyes. 'What are you trying to tell me, Grandfather?'

He blinked and the elder was gone. He turned about and saw him perched on the lip of the ravine, staring down the river.

'I want you to know, Wisest,' he whispered, 'that what you find may not be what you're looking for.'

Gariath raised an eye ridge as the elder's figure quivered slightly. The sunlight seemed to shine through his body a little more clearly, as though golden teeth seeped into his spectral flesh and devoured his substance, bit by bit.

'So much was lost here, Wisest. Sometimes I wonder if anything can really be found. But the scent, since you mentioned it ...'

There was reluctance in Gariath's step as he walked toward the elder. 'Grandfather?'

'This place was not dug,' he said. 'Not by natural hands, anyway.'

'What?'

'Suffering was more plentiful back then,' the grandfather replied, his voice whispery as his body faded briefly and re-appeared in the river. 'Swift death was the sole mercy, and a rare one, at that. Many more died in agony ... *many* more.'

'Back *when?*'

'We didn't want any part of it,' the grandfather continued, heedless of his company, 'but maybe that's just how the *Rhega* are destined to die ... not by our own hands, our own fights. What is it we were even fighting for? I can't remember ...'

Gariath stopped and watched as the elder trudged farther down the river, growing hazier with each step. Every twitch of the dragonman's eyelid saw the grandfather fading more and more, leaving a bit of himself in each ray of sunlight he stepped into and out of.

Gariath was tempted to let him go, to keep walking that way until there was nothing left of him, nothing heavy enough that he would have to drop, nothing substantial enough about him that could ache.

He watched the grandfather go, watched him disappear, leaving him in the riverbed …

Alone again.

'Grandfather!' he suddenly cried out.

The outline stopped at the edge of a sunbeam, all that remained of him being the single black eye he turned upon Gariath. The younger dragonman approached him warily, head low, scrutinising, ear frills out, wary.

'Grandfather,' Gariath asked, barely louder than a whisper, 'how long have you been awake?'

'For … quite some … no! *No!* You won't send me away like that!'

This time, when Gariath noticed the elder beside him again, he was defined, flesh full and red, eyes hard and black. The elder gestured farther down the river with his chin.

'Up ahead.'

'What?'

Gariath glanced up, saw nothing through the beams of light. When he looked back to his side, the water stirred with a ripple and nothing more. The grandfather was up ahead, trudging through the river, vanishing behind each beam of light.

'What's ahead?'

'A reason, Wisest, if you would follow … and see.'

Gariath followed, without particularly knowing why, save for the urge to keep the elder in sight, to keep him from fading behind the walls of sun. With each step he took, his nostrils filled with strange scents, not unfamiliar to him. The chalky odour of bone was prevalent, though that didn't tell Gariath much; he doubted that he could go anywhere on the island without that particular stink.

Thus, he was not particularly surprised when he spied the skeleton, its great white foot looming out of sunlight. It was titanic, the river humbly winding its way beneath the dead creature, flowing with such a soft trickle to suggest it was afraid the bleached behemoth might stir and rise at any moment.

Gariath found that not particularly hard to believe as he stalked alongside it, ducking beneath its massive splayed leg, winding between its shattered ribs, approaching the great, fishlike skull.

His eyes were immediately drawn to the massive hole punched through its head, a jagged rent far wider than the smooth round sockets that had been the creature's eyes. Its bones bore similar injuries: cracks in the ribs, gashes in the femur, the left forearm bent backward behind a spine that crested to challenge the height of the ravine as the right one reached forward.

Towards what, though?

The great dead thing, when it had been slightly greater and not so dead, had stopped with its arm extended, skeletal fingers withered in such a way to suggest that it had reached for something and failed to seize it.

He stared back down the ravine, noting the cut of the rock: too rough to be wrought by careful tools and delicate chiselling, too smooth to have been made by any natural spirit. Rather, it was haphazardly hewn, as if by accident, as though some great thing had fallen ...

And was dragged, he thought, looking back to the cracked skull, *or dragged itself through until* ...

'This land is not our land. Not anymore.'

Gariath looked up and saw the elder crouched upon the fishlike skull, staring at the rent in the bone intently.

'This island is a cairn.'

'Those dark stains upon the rock,' Gariath said. 'They are—'

'Blood,' the elder answered. 'Flesh, spilling out, sloughing off, tainting the earth as this thing's screams tainted the air when it dragged itself away from the weapons that had shattered its legs and broken its back.'

Gariath looked to the gaping jaws, the rows upon rows of serrated teeth, the shadows cast in the expanse of its fleshless maw.

'What did it scream?'

'Same thing all children scream for ... its mother and father.'

He did not ask if they had come to save their titanic offspring, did not even want to think what kind of creatures could have sired something akin to this tremendous demon. He knew he should have looked away, then, away from the mouth that was suddenly so pitiably silent, away from the eyes that he could see vast, empty and straining to find the liquid to brim with tears. He tried to look away, forced his stare to the earth.

But it was impossible. Impossible not to hear the cries of two voices moaning for their mother. Impossible not to wonder if they had died screaming for their father. Impossible not to see their eyes, so wide, so vacant, their breath vanished in the rain. Impossible not to—

'*No.*'

His fist followed his snarl, striking against the skull and finding an unyielding, merciful pain that ripped through his mind, bathing vision and voice in endless ringing red.

'Why this, Grandfather?' he asked. 'Why show me?'

'I have heard it said,' the elder replied coldly, 'that all life is connected.' His laugh was short, unpleasant. 'Stupidity. From mouths that repeated it over and over so that no one may speak long enough to point out their stupidity.' He crawled across the skull, staring down into the skull. 'It's *deaths* that are connected, Wisest. Never forget that. One life taken is another one fading, one life gone and another one vanishes because of its absence. Each one more horrible, more senseless than the last.'

'I don't understand, Grandfather.'

'You do, you're just too stupid to realise it, too scared to remember it.' He stared down at the dragonman, eyes hard, voice harder. 'Your sons, Wisest.'

Gariath's eyes went wide, his hands clenched into fists.

'Don't.'

'They died, horribly.'

'Shut up.'

'Senselessly.'

'*Grandfather …*'

'And you would so willingly follow them. A senseless, pointless, *worthless* death.'

No reply came this time but a roar incomprehensible of everything but the anger and pain melded together behind it. Gariath flung himself at the skeleton, scaling up the ribs, pulling himself onto the spine and leaping, vertebra over giant vertebra, toward the skull.

The grandfather regarded him quietly before he tilted

just slightly to his left and collapsed into the rent, disappearing into shadow.

'You brought me here to mock me? *Them?*' Gariath roared, approaching the cavernous hole. 'To show me this monument of death?'

'A monument, yes,' the grandfather's voice echoed from inside, 'of death, yes … but whose, Wisest?'

'Yours …' Gariath snarled, leaning over and into the hole. '*AGAIN!*'

The elder gave no reply and Gariath did not demand one, did not have the sense to as he was struck suddenly, by the faintest, lingering memory of a scent, but recoiled as though struck by a fist. He reeled back, blinking wildly, before thrusting his face back down below and inhaling deeply, choking back the foul staleness within to filter and find that scent, that odiferous candle that refused to extinguish itself in the dark.

'Rivers …' he whispered.

'Rocks …' the elder replied.

'A *Rhega* died here,' he gasped.

He felt the rent beneath his grip, felt the roughness of it. This was no clean blow, no gentle tap that had caved in the beast's skull. The gash was brutal, messy, cracked unevenly and laden with jagged ridges and deep, furrowed marks.

Claw marks, he recognised. *Bite marks.*

'A *Rhega* fought here.' He stared into the blackness. 'Who, Grandfather? Who was it?'

'Connected,' the elder murmured back, 'all connected.'

'Grandfather, tell me!'

'You will know, Wisest … I tried so hard that you wouldn't, but … you will …'

A sigh rose up from the darkness, the elder's voice growing softer upon it.

'And the answer won't make you happy …'

'Grandfather.'

'Because at the end of a *Rhega*'s life … there is nothing.'

'What are you talking about?'

'All you are missing, Wisest … is darkness and quiet.'

'Grandfather.'

Silence.

'*GRANDFATHER!*'

Darkness.

His own echo returned to him, ringing out through the skull and reverberating into the forest. It seemed to take the scent with it, the smell dissipating in his nostrils as the sound faded, dying with every whispered repetition as it slipped into trees that had suddenly gone quiet, leaving him alone.

Again.

That thought became an echo of its own, spiralling inward and growing heavier on his heart with every repetition.

Alone. Again, again, again.

No matter how many spirits he found, how many rocks he stomped, how many soft pink things he surrounded himself with. They would leave him, all of them, leaving him with nothing, nothing of weight, nothing of meaning.

Except that word.

'Again, again,' he whispered, smashing his fist against the bone impotently with each repetition. 'Alone again and always … always and again …'

'*Again …*'

It was not him who spoke this time, nor was it the grandfather's voice. It certainly was not the scent of either of them that filled his nostrils and drew his head up. His lip quivered at the odour: pungent, iron, sweaty, familiar.

Longface.

The creature appeared farther down the ravine, black against the assault of sunlight, but unmistakable. Its frame was thick, tall, laden with the contours of overdeveloped muscle and the jagged ridges of iron armour. A thick wedge of sharpened metal was slung over its shoulder as a long-jawed face scanned the rocks. He recognised the sight immediately, his eyes narrowing, lip curling up in a quiet snarl.

Female.

'And again and again and again,' she snarled, her voice grating. 'Until you tell me what I want to know, you green filth.'

'*Shi-neh-ah! Shi-neh!*' the creature at her blood-covered feet spoke a language he did not understand. '*Maw-wah!*'

At a glimpse, it resembled something akin to a bipedal lizard … or it had been bipedal before both its legs had been crushed. It now strained to crawl away on long, lanky arms, leaving the sands of the cliff they stood upon stained red. Over the corpses of other creatures, identical to it but for their severed limbs, split chests and lifeless eyes, it crawled towards Gariath.

It caught sight of him, looked up. Its yellow eyes were wide, full of fear, full of pain, trembling with a life that flickered like a candle before a breeze. It reached out a hand to him, opened its mouth to speak. He stared back, anticipating its words to the point of agony.

They never came.

'I don't have *time* to learn how to speak *your* language.' The longface seized the creature's long tail, hauled it up with one hand. 'You have exactly two breaths to learn how to speak overscum!'

'*MAW-WAH! MAW-WAH!*'

The sounds of its shrieking mingled with the sound of claws raking against the sand stained with its own life, straining to find some handhold as it was hoisted up by its tail. Gariath saw its eyes wide as it looked to him, saw the pleading in its eyes, the familiar fear and pain that he had seen in so many eyes before.

'RHE—'

One breath.

Her thick blade burst out the creature's belly, thick ribbons of glistening meat pouring out. She paused, twisted it once, and dropped the creature. The blade laughed a thick, grisly cackle as it slowly slid from the creature's flesh.

Gariath continued to stare at the creature's eyes, at its mouth. He saw only darkness. Heard only silence.

'Hey.'

It was the sheer casualness with which she spoke that made him look up to the longface. Her expression was blank, unamused and only barely interested in him. She slammed the blade down, embedding it in the sand as she dusted blood-flecked hands together.

'They come in red?' she asked. Narrowing white eyes at him, she snorted. 'No. You aren't one of them, are you?'

'No,' he said.

'That's fine,' she said. 'You want to fight, yeah?'

He wasn't sure why he nodded.

'That's fine,' she said again as she sat upon a rock with a grunt. 'Just give me a moment.'

He wasn't sure why he waited.

'What are they?' he asked, at last.

'Those Green Things?' she replied with a shrug. 'They don't have names, as far as I know. They don't need names.'

'Everything has a name.'

'You?'

'Wise—' He paused, grunting. 'Gariath.'

'Dech,' she said, slapping her shoulder. 'Carnassial of Arkklan Kaharn, chief among my people, the netherlings and—'

'I know what you are,' he replied. 'I've killed a lot of you.'

'No fooling?' She grinned at him. 'Yeah, I've heard of you. The Ugly Red One, they called you. You cut open a lot of warriors, you know. I knew a few of them.' Her lips curled back, the grin evolving from unpleasant to horrific. 'You're good at what you do.'

'You're calm about that.'

'Why wouldn't I be?' she asked. 'Don't get me wrong, I'm still going to kill you, but it's not going to be personal or anything. It's just what I do. It's what you do. Just like dying was just what those warriors did.'

'I don't follow.'

'Yeah, I don't blame you. A lot of overscum have trouble understanding it, which is why they're always rushing around. They don't know what they're supposed to do.' She gestured to the eviscerated lizard-creatures. 'Take These Green Things. We got plenty of them back at our base. Slaves. Some of them try to fight against us, some of them pray to some kind of sky-thing, some of them beg for mercy, some of them try to run, some of them talk about how things were ...' She looked up at him. 'And some of them cry. Big, slimy tears come pouring down their faces when we kill one of them. That's what baffles me.'

'They mourn.'

'Why?'

'To honour their dead.'

'The dead don't care.'

'They do.'

'You talk to them?'

'Sometimes,' he replied.

'Huh ... well, they shouldn't. What do they got to ask for once they're dead?'

'Honour. Respect.'

'You and I both know that's ... what's the word? *Shnitz*?' She shrugged. 'If you believed that, you wouldn't have watched this ugly thing' – she kicked the eviscerated corpse – 'do what he did.'

'He didn't do anything. You killed him.'

'Ah, see, this is where the overscum stop learning,' she said, smirking. 'You all talk about death like it's a sole decision. It takes two to die. The person with the sword does the least amount of work.'

He furrowed his eye ridges.

'See,' she elaborated, 'these dumb things are quick. I only caught them because there was no other place to run.' She gestured to the river rushing beneath the cliff. 'Now, when I grabbed one, the others could have run away. They all stood and fought, though. They made the decision to die.'

She looked up at him disdainfully. 'You could run now, too. I've killed plenty today. I can kill you later, if you want.'

'You could run, too,' he replied.

'No, I couldn't. There's nothing for a female but death. I kill or I die.' She spat on the ground. 'You?'

He stared at her, unblinking. He closed his eyes. Darkness. He inhaled sharply. Quiet.

'Nothing,' he replied.

'Didn't think so,' she said. She rose from the rock, pulled her blade from the sand and slung it over her shoulder. 'You ready, then?'

He nodded. She furrowed her brow at him.

'No weapon?'

'Unnecessary.'

'Don't know what that means.'

'It means—'

'Don't care, either.'

She howled, iron voice grinding against jagged teeth as she rushed him. Her blade came out in an unruly swing, adding its metal groan to her roar as it clove the air, hungry for Gariath's neck, or torso, or head. A blade that big couldn't be picky.

He ducked, more from reflex than desire, and dropped to all fours, meeting her rush with horns to her belly. It was impossible not to shudder at the blow, not to marvel at the rock-hard muscle he pressed against as he shoved, driving her back only one minuscule, agonising step.

As he extended his last weary breath, his muscles giving out at the futility and his mind fighting hard to remember a time when this had been easy, it was impossible to think of a reason to keep going … and even more so to keep from listening to her long, loud laugh.

'Come *on*,' she whined. 'How are you going to kill me this way?'

It shouldn't have hurt as much as it did. He remembered shrugging off blows like this before. Yet her first came down upon his neck and sent him buckling to his knees effortlessly. She made a clicking sound of disapproval, which he noticed less than the second strike she delivered. It was an intimate blow, all three metal-bound knuckles of her hand digging into his red flesh, finding a tender, affectionate spot between his shoulder blades.

Not possible. His thoughts ran wild, leaking out of his mouth as he hacked wildly, *I don't have tender spots.*

His spine disagreed. His vertebrae rattled against each other, sinew bunched up painfully at the force that ran up his back and into his skull, sending brain slamming against bone and sending body crashing to the earth.

That's never happened before ...

That it *had* happened should have shocked him. It was difficult to feel shock, fear, pain, anything. Every scrap of consciousness was devoted to keeping his eyes open, to resist the urge to sleep into darkness, though he didn't know why. At least if he fell now, he wouldn't have to see the long, purple face leering down at him.

'You're doing it wrong.' Her voice was clear and sharp as a knife.

Funny, but he hadn't expected there to be a right way to die. The fact that he had been doing it wrong *did* explain a lot. He might have mentioned this to her, had his throat not been swelling up.

'It's fine for us to do this, you know,' she said. 'But we're netherlings. We come from nothing. We return to nothing. We live. We breed. We kill. We die. This is all there is in life.' She reached down and tapped his red brow. 'Note that third part, though, **about the killing. That's important.**'

Her throat loomed over him. His hand would just about fit around it, he figured, but it trembled, refused to rise.

And why should it? he asked himself. *Whatever your body knows, you didn't. Now you're both done. There's nothing left.*

'But overscum are supposed to have bigger things on their minds, yeah? They talk to invisible people, spend their whole lives hoarding bits of metal instead of making them into weapons; they do stupid stuff like plant crops and store food and leave it all to wailing whelps who did nothing to deserve it. Point being … you've got reasons to scream, don't you?'

His breath came in shrill whispers, leaking through a closing throat, just enough to breathe, just enough to think.

Kill her and then what? What's left? Kill more, kill more, live in death. Die, live in nothingness … but with nothing to think about, to speak about, no one left to disappear.

'But that's what's so *fascinating* to us. To Carnassials, that is.' She glanced over the cliff. 'And some males. We've never seen this before, a breed that worries about so many stupid things and lives in complete fear of whatever invisible thing they talk to and is concerned with things other than breeding and killing. It's like … watching ants. That's the correct animal, right? Yeah … ants that run around and cling to every little piece of dirt like it's the greatest piece they've ever seen, even as a thousand more lie around. Take that piece away, and what do they do? Some grab new ones, but most sit there … like you.'

And how much dirt have you been clinging to? Grahta, Grandfather, the humans … they're all gone. How much more can you pick up?

'You're not going to get up, are you?' She rose up, took her sword in both hands.

This won't be so bad.

'No more dirt, huh?'

No more hurting; no more being alone.

'Too bad.'

She raised the weapon, angled the flat edge of it at his throat. It would be messy.

No more rivers; no more rocks.

'Hey, maybe you're right about the whole invisible thing, yeah? If so, I'm sure you'll see your pink friends there with you by tonight.'

No more anything ... It'll be so great ...

'Anyway ...'

'*SHENKO-SA!*'

He blinked. Those words weren't said by the longface. That shrill, shrieking sound didn't emanate from her, either.

The loud, angry roar as she staggered away, clutching at the arrow embedded in her side, however, certainly did.

Gariath was almost afraid to look across the river, afraid that he would see the pointy-eared one. If *she* had placed the timely arrow and saved him, he resolved he would die right then and there, hopefully taking her with him. He was prepared for that possibility, prepared for the idea that it might have come from nowhere and given him an opportunity to take one last breath before lying down and dying.

What he saw, however, he was not prepared for.

Not *Rhega*, but definitely not human, the creature stood, tall and covered in green scales, at the other side of the river. His long, black bow was in a powerful, clawed hand. His body, ringed by black-and-red tattoos, was tensed and muscular. Behind his long, lashing tail, more like him – more reptilian creatures – stared at Gariath with broad, yellow eyes down long, green snouts.

The one in front raised his hand, regarded Gariath through his single yellow eye, and spoke.

'*Inda-ah, Rhega.*'

'What?' he breathed.

'I knew it! *I knew it!*' He looked to see the longface pulling the arrow free without wincing, as though she were simply scratching an itch with a jagged, biting head. 'Xhai said you all got up when someone started mocking you! I didn't believe her!'

He swept his stare across the river again. The creatures were gone; nothing but greenery remained where they had once stood. Perhaps he had imagined them; perhaps they hadn't ever been there ...

But that arrow on the sand, covered in blood, was impossible to imagine. And it lay there now. He looked from it to the longface staggering toward him, dragging her weapon.

Good enough.

'I didn't think it would work. I owe Xhai a—'

If she saw the fist coming, she didn't move away.

A possibility, Gariath conceded, but one he was willing to accept as he and his arm rose as one, his knuckles connecting with her chin and sending her head snapping back. She was all skull – that much was apparent from his aching fist, if not her conversation.

She, too, was ready to accept. She accepted his punches as he followed with two more in rapid succession, feeling bones shake, but not break, under his fists. She accepted the ground lost as he drove her back. She accepted his horns again, accepted the broken nose as he drove his head against her face.

Only when he stepped back, waiting for her to fall that he might end it with a foot to her skull, did she refuse to accept. She pulled her face back up to stare at him, neck creaking as she did, teeth flashing in a grin that had only grown more wild as blood from her spattered visage dripped over her lips.

'Yeah ...'

She came howling again, no concern for strategy, position or anything but the imminent and immediate desire to bring her blade swinging up to lop off his head. A moment of nostalgia swept over him at the sight of such recklessness, followed by a moment of swift panic as he saw the blade just as eager as her, sweeping up towards his head.

He caught it on his wrist, the metal gnawing at the metal bracers there. She drove the blade harder, straining to chew through and cleave his hand from his wrist, his head from his neck. He pushed back just as hard, reaching up to place his free hand on the edge. It was an effort tinged in blood as the weapon bit into his palm, making his grip slick as he shoved back, but an effort that sent the blade swinging wide and leaving her open.

He wasn't sure if he was roaring or laughing, didn't bother to think which it might have been, just as he didn't wonder why his muscles suddenly felt so easy, so strong. There was blood on the ground, blood in his nostrils, anger in his veins and a purple neck beneath his claws.

Good enough.

He clenched, clawed, heard her gurgle as her blood seeped out over his palms, blending with his own. He refused to release her as she groped at him with one hand, dropped her massive, suddenly unwieldy weapon to punch at him with the other. Blows rained upon his head, one after the other. He felt the agony, felt his skull want to crack, but refused to succumb to either.

Instead, he swung his body to the side and she followed, like a purple boulder. Releasing, he sent her crashing into the ridge. The earth cracked before she did, but she stood there, bleeding from nose and neck, murder flashing in her eyes, breath coming hot and hateful from between jagged teeth.

'That's it,' she snarled, 'that's *it*. This is how it's going to happen. This is how it *has* to happen. From nothing, to nothing.'

'And no one will remember you,' he uttered. 'I won't leave enough of you for it.'

'Fine, that's just fine,' she gasped. Her hand slipped behind her belt. 'Good to know you've got a plan. Thinking ahead, grabbing your pieces of dirt ...' Her hand whipped out, sent the green vial spinning toward him. '*STUPID!*'

He had smelled it before she pulled it out, recognised it. Poison, the same that had felled Abysmyths, ate their flesh like fire ate paper. He wasn't sure if it worked similarly on things not demonic, but he was hardly willing to see for curiosity's sake.

He darted aside; the vial smashed against the rock and he felt a few sputtering instances of pain as droplets spat out and licked his back. His flesh burned; the scent of it sizzling filled his nostrils. It hurt, he admitted as he clenched his teeth, a lot.

'*QAI ZHOTH!*'

So did the spinning blade that followed Dech's screech. He remembered this weapon, the curved knife with its cruel, jagged edge. And it certainly remembered him, it seemed, as it sank into his shoulder and bit deeply, metal prongs slaking themselves on his blood. Pain racked him, coursing through his body in such excessive quantity that it screamed to be shared.

'Gnaw, bite, gnash,' Dech snarled as she took off charging toward him. '*AKH ZEKH LAKH!*'

He met her, muscle for muscle, fury for fury. They gripped each other about each other's throats, turning, twisting, staggering as they fought for control for their respective tracheas. Gariath slipped his hands up, releasing her throat, seizing her by the temples. Her smile was momentary, lasting only as long as it took him to slip his clawed thumbs into her eyes and push.

He had heard her scream in fury and hatred, but the sound of her pain was enough to make him step away momentarily. It lasted only as long as it took her to lash out blindly, searching for him, snarling for him. He roared in reply, seizing her by the wrist, spinning her about and twisting it behind her back. His limbs worked in furious conjunction, his spare hand grabbing her by her hair, his free foot slamming onto her back, driving her to her knees, then her belly.

There his foot remained, wedged firmly between her shoulder blades as he narrowed his eyes, tightened his grip on her wild white spikes of hair and pulled.

Stubborn as the rest of her, it came slowly, hair clinging to her with such vindictiveness that scarcely any came off in his hand. But he did not stop pulling, as her neck craned. He did not stop pulling, as she screamed in panic and beat at his ankle in bloody blindness. He did not stop pulling, as he heard her flesh begin to rip.

By the time he stared down at a glistening red pate, a mop of crimson and white clenched in his claw, it seemed pointless to keep going.

He tossed it aside, taking only enough time to see that she had stopped moving, before turning away and looking back over the cliff. The other side wasn't too far, he saw, and the scent of the creatures, their dead leaves and dry rivers, was still there, despite the blood seeping into his nostrils. He could keep going downriver, find a fallen tree or a narrow gap, and from there he could—

'QAI ZHOTH!'

She struck him from behind, wrapping arms about his torso. Blind and scalped, nothing remained of her save arms and feet, the latter of which pumped furiously, edging him towards the cliff.

'Nothing else, nothing else,' she babbled behind him as he lashed out, seeking to dislodge her with an elbow, 'there is nothing else but *this*.'

They staggered toward the edge, the riverbed and its sharp rocks waiting just below a surface of deceptively pristine blue. Gariath had no fear for that, no mind to think of anything but his enemy, thick in his nostrils, heavy on his back. He reached behind him as they tumbled over, seizing her blood-slick pate and twisting, tail lashing, wings flapping.

They plummeted, a brief struggle in the air, her shrieking, him roaring, until they finally righted themselves. She, the heavier in her iron skin. He, on top of her like a red anvil, hands wrapped about her face.

They hit the water in an eruption of red and white froth. Gariath, too, was plunged into blindness like his foe. But the battle was his, he knew, as she lay unmoving beneath him.

When the water settled and she lay beneath the water, skull neatly bisected like a rock, it was unnecessary to do more than rise, snort and stagger away.

'Any happier now, Wisest?' The grandfather was there, seated on the rocks jutting from the river. 'Find a good reason to keep going?'

'No thanks to you,' Gariath snorted. 'You didn't tell me about them.'

'Who?'

'The creatures, the green things. They called me *Rhega*.'

'You have not been called that before?'

'Not by anything that looks like me.'

'You said they were green, not red.'

'Closer than pink,' he growled. 'Tell me, then, Grandfather, who are they?'

'They are … lost, Wisest,' Grandfather replied. 'They will lead you to nothing.'

Gariath regarded the spirit for a moment. His eyes narrowed as he saw something in him. *No*, Gariath thought, it was at this moment that he saw *through* him. The spirit waxed, his shape trembling, becoming hazy as the sunlight poured through him. In this light, there was nothing to Grandfather, nothing hard, nothing blooded, nothing fleshy.

And Gariath turned his back to the spirit, stalking down the river.

'Where do you go, Wisest?' Grandfather called after him.

'To nothing,' he replied.

Twenty-Three

QUESTIONS OF A VISCERAL NATURE

'If he asks for water, don't give him any,' the young man posing as a guard said, waving his key ring like a symbol of authority. 'And I wouldn't look at him directly, if I were you.' He sneered. 'It's a mess.'

Bralston nodded briefly as the young man cracked open the reinforced door to the converted warehouse room that served as a prison. It opened into shadow, which Bralston stepped into.

The door swung shut behind him, the cramped quarters swallowing the echo. He turned on his heel and walked deeper, taking a moment to scratch the corner of his eye as he removed his hat. The room had likely been storage for the least important objects, possibly the least important members of society, if the smell was any suggestion. The walls were as tall and wide as two men, the only source of light a dim beam seeping in from a grated hole above. Dust swirled within it, flakes clawing over each other in a futile bid to escape.

Against the pervasive despair, the figure huddled pitifully against the wall was scarcely noticeable.

Bralston said nothing, at first, content only to observe. Taking the man in – at least, he had been *told* it was a man

419

– was difficult, for the sheer commitment with which he pressed himself against the wall.

The Librarian could make out his features: scraggly beard that had once been kempt, a broad frame used to standing tall now railing against its owner's determination to hunch, a single, gleaming eye cast down at the floor, heavy-lidded, unblinking.

'I am here to speak with you,' Bralston said, his voice painful in the silence.

The man said nothing in reply.

'Your assistance is required.'

Bralston felt his ire rise at the man's continued quiet.

'Cooperation,' he said, clenching his hand, 'is compulsory.'

'How long, sir, have you been seeking my company?'

The man spoke without flinching, without looking up. The voice had once been booming, he could tell. Something had hollowed it out with sharp fingers and left only a smothered whisper.

'Approximately one week.'

A chuckle, black and once used to herald merry terrors. 'I lament my lack of surprise. But would it surprise you that I was once a man whose presence was fleeting as gentle zephyrs?' He leaned back, resting a hand on a massive knee. 'I once was, despite the shrouded sorrow before you.' He drummed curiously short, stubby fingers. 'I once was.'

A closer glance revealed both the fact that the man's fingers were, in fact, fleshy stumps, and that the hairy backs of his hands were twisted with tattoos. Consequently, any sympathy or desire to know what had happened to the man passed quickly.

Cragsman.

Whatever cruelties had been visited upon this man by

whomever was undoubtedly kindness compared to the blood he had shed, the lives he had defiled. Bralston felt his left eyelid twitch at the fate of the last Cragsman he had known.

'Your … days of zephyr, as it were, are the object of concern,' Bralston said curtly.

'No gentleman would accuse another of lying,' the Cragsman replied smoothly, 'and whilst I am possessed of the most gracious inclination to benefit you the title of man most gentle, I can quite distinctly detect the odiferous reek of a lie dribbling out of your craw. Were I bold enough to declare, I would that you did not come all this way to discuss the seas I've plied and the women I've loved.'

That last word sent Bralston's spine rigid, his fist tight.

'I am concerned with the past month of your life,' he said, 'nothing more.'

'Ah, now *that* bears the sweet, tangy foulness of truth to it,' the man replied, chuckling. 'I would still hesitate to commit fully my conscience to your claim, sir, for any man interested in the latest chapter of the script of a man named Rashodd would likely be here with the express intent of doing things more visceral than polite conversation and pleasant queries.'

His great head swung up, grey hair hanging limply at a thick jaw. His eye fixed itself upon the Librarian. Through the gloom, the yellow of his smile came out in golden crescents.

'So I ask the man who has displayed tact towards my innards by not ripping them out through my most fortunate nose,' Rashodd said. 'Who sent you?'

Bralston considered carefully answering. Somehow, the words he spoke seemed tainted by the man's presence the moment they left his mouth.

'The Venarium.'

'Sought by a circle of heathens, I am reduced to? From being pursued by the greatest navies of the seas? Perhaps such a degradation is fitting, having been laid low by that most meanest and crudest of callings.'

Adventurer, Bralston recognised the universal description. *He did have contact with them, then.*

'I digress, though,' Rashodd continued. 'What can I do for you, sir?'

'I am on an extended search,' Bralston replied. 'The location of one party will lead to the other, I am certain.'

'The ultimate goal being?'

Bralston studied him carefully, wary to divulge the answer. 'Purple-skinned longfaces.'

'Ah.' Rashodd smiled. '*Them.*'

'Your tone suggests knowledge.'

'You may safely conclude imprisonment has done little to tarnish my talents and predilections towards the coy. My knowledge of the netherlings is from the second hand of a second hand.'

'Nether ... lings?'

'*Your* tone suggests our initial comprehension of their title to be mutual. The nomenclature would lend itself to the conclusion that they are descended from nether; that is, from nothing at all. I could not assure you that they do not live up to the name, sir, for I have never seen one, knowing they exist only through their anger towards my former allies.'

Bralston nodded. 'Continue.'

'On which subject? My allies or their violet foes? Of the latter, I know little but what I have heard: rumours of relentlessness, viciousness and faithlessness blended into one.' Rashodd raised a brow at the Librarian. 'Something akin to yourself, except with less fire and more yelling, I'm told.'

'The Venarium has charged them with heresy.'

'The practice of a heathenry that differs from yours,' Rashodd said, nodding. 'Ironic, is it not, that the faithless should steal a term used by the faithful to condemn those of a different faith ... or is it just obnoxious? Regardless, I know as much of the netherlings as I knew of my allies, and you would do well to avoid both, lest you, too, find yourself embroiled in their deceits and find us with more in common' – he held up his hand and wiggled his stumps – 'than you would like.'

'What I find is that my incredible patience is gradually, but wholly, stretched thin with your delusions of eloquence.' Bralston allowed ire to sow his voice, fire to spark behind his stare. 'My mission, my order, my *duty* has no concern for your need to waste my time with pretence. My questions are swift and to the point. You will answer them in kind.'

'It is a sad day I live every day that the language of poet-kings is considered delusional,' Rashodd replied with a sneer. 'But I will answer your questions with as much open eagerness and hidden loathing as I can manage.'

That was enough, Bralston reasoned, to avoid resorting to anything fiery. 'I have been informed, roughly, as to the nature of your "allies". I do not hold the opinion that they are entirely factual.'

'Factual, sir? One would assume that if you had been granted even the loosest of information regarding my former persons of association, you would recant.' He canted his massive head. 'Have you, sir?'

'Thirty-six sailors of the *Riptide* have attested to the encounter.'

'And you cannot consider the account of thirty-six good and honourable men trustworthy?'

'There have been mass hallucinations before, often much grander in scale.'

Rashodd's laugh gained a horrible enthusiasm. 'Of course. The Venarium's unwavering stance of discrediting the Gods and strangling decent men and women with their smugness is not unknown to me. Spare me the rhetoric, sir. I am well informed on the subject, and I humbly disagree with your theory.'

'Well informed enough to infer our stance on the idea of demons?' Bralston asked sternly. 'Even if we were to ignore the idea that they are stories made up by priests to cow people into coercion, we cannot, and *do not*, accept the idea of an incarnation of evil, as we do not accept the idea of "evil" or "good". We acknowledge human nature.'

'I see ... and what do *you* believe, sir?'

Men would feel anger at the Cragsman's words, men would let their composures crack. Librarians were not men, Bralston reminded himself. Librarians answered to higher authorities. Librarians might *possess* the power to compel forthrightness through any manner of burning, freezing, crushing or electrocuting, but such would be a flagrant, wasteful demonstration of superiority that *should*, ostensibly, require no establishing.

Still, it would be satisfying ...

Far more satisfying than uttering coldly, 'There is no belief. Only knowledge.'

'And you *know* your knowledge to be superior over that of thirty-six people? You *know* that demons do not exist?'

'I *accept* that there are *unknowns* typically explained by frivolous imaginations by branding them "demons". But, as stated, I didn't come to exchange arguments.'

'Of course not, sir,' Rashodd replied. 'You came seeking purple-skinned longfaces, foes inveterate of demons theoretical. The former pursues the latter for reasons unknown whilst, for reasons incomprehensible, the demons evade them. You hope to find the former by locating the latter. To find the latter, you seek a seeker.

'And to have come this far, being a man of decencies and honorifics as befits his education, you undoubtedly know who you seek. Six members, of a band most foul, which I would conclude to be the second object of your search, would fulfil such a purpose. And, most importantly, the location of their precious cargo would put you in a fine position to locate all parties desirable, regardless of skin colour.'

Rashodd's smile was filled with piercing congeniality.

'But of course, you already knew that.'

Bralston took a deep breath, the first phase of a common meditative technique, taught to apprentices and used by Librarians. He raised a hand, the second phase, to hone the flow of Venarie and tune the senses.

The spark of crimson, the arcane word, the sound of a heavy body crunching against the wall that followed were part of no meditation. Yet, Bralston couldn't deny that the sight of the man crushed between the force and stone was decidedly therapeutic.

'Where the Venarium is concerned,' he said, 'there is no definition of the word "request". You are not free to refuse what we require. You are not free to wallow in the safety of a cell when you possess what we require.' His fingers twitched; he could feel a fleshy throat across the room tighten in his hand. 'Not with *both* lungs, anyway. Gurgle if you will comply.'

The sound that boiled out of the man's lips was particularly thick and moist.

'Good enough,' the Librarian said, relaxing his magical grip only slightly. 'Speak quickly and curtly. What cargo do the adventurers carry?'

'A tome,' Rashodd gasped. '*The* tome. I overheard on the *Riptide*. A book to establish contact between earth and heaven ... or hell. The demons want it for the latter ... I assume.'

'Pointless. Neither place exists.'

'I saw the beast. I've seen the demon. It could come from no other place.'

'The priest mentioned no tome.'

'Sent the adventurers after it. Needs it back.'

'And these ... demons pursue it?'

'Also need it. It's the key.'

'To the door to take them back to hell?'

'No, sir,' Rashodd gasped. 'To let their brethren in.'

Bralston narrowed his eyes. 'And the longfaces chase the demons ...'

'Demons chase the tome. Adventurers seek the tome. If they found it, you'll find the longfaces and demons with them.'

'How long ago did they set out?'

'Two weeks, roughly. Not much supplies for the Reaching Isles. Probably dead now, or mostly.' Rashodd found the strength to sneer through the strangulation. 'Chase their trail to Ktamgi, north. Find whatever hell you deserve.'

Bralston pursed his lips, eased his fingers. The air ceased to ripple. The Cragsman collapsed to the floor, expelling great hacking coughs.

Bralston offered no particular apology for the treatment; the only error he had committed was, perhaps, a small expenditure of power wasted where a little patience would have been prudent. No reason for guilt, though. His course was clear.

The Reaching Isles at the edge of Toha's empire were, as far as the atlases and charts suggested, uninhabited, the Tohana Navy outposts having long since been rendered economically unviable. Locating a rabble of desperate, half-dead vagrants should prove no great challenge; if they were *completely* dead, the task would be only slightly more difficult.

'Describe the adventurers,' he said, replacing his hat.

'Six,' Rashodd replied. 'Three men, one woman, two … *things*. One, a shict. The other …' He grimaced. 'But they aren't important. It's the men, one in particular. There are two runty little things, but the other, a tall and evil—'

'The woman.'

'What?' Rashodd shook his head. 'No, it's the tall man, the Sainite you're interested in, he—'

'*What of the woman?*' Bralston pressed. 'Was she in good health? Did you harm her?'

'Ah, that's it, is it? I am certain it is no uncertain blasphemy that you should lust after a woman of the Healer, sir, but I must wonder whose faith, or lack thereof, it offends more.' At the Librarian's scowl, he chuckled. 'Rest assured, she was well, no matter what happened.'

Bralston kept the man's single-eyed stare for a moment. A moment was all it took for him to breathe in, raise a hand, mutter an incomprehensible word, and swiftly lower his hand.

Rashodd's face followed its arc, an invisible force sending him to kiss the stone floor with a resounding crack. He lay there, unmoving but for the faint breath that sent his body, broad and unwashed, shivering.

Not dead, then, Bralston thought. *Pity.*

But it was no longer his concern. Restraint, wisdom, prudence were the watchwords of the Venarium; bravado, haste, fury, its anathema. He had spent enough energy on the Cragsman, wasted enough words. He sneered at Rashodd; there wasn't even a splatter of blood to suggest his nose was broken. He would live until he was delivered to whomever would lower the axe on his head. That pleasure was not to be his.

Lesser men had pleasures. Librarians had duties.

He had just turned away from the Cragsman when he heard the chuckle. He turned, hardly astonished to see the man rising. Bralston was prepared for that, prepared to put him back down if need be, and more likely prepared to let him retreat and subsequently rot in the shadows.

Bralston, however, was not prepared for the sight of him in the yellow, pitiless light.

'Is your aim to inflict suffering, sir?' A pair of hands, three fingers between them, splayed their fleshy stumps, hoisting up a great, tattooed bulk. 'I lament your lateness, my friend. *Lament* it.' He levelled a single eye at Bralston as the other one, a colourless mass surrounded by tiny lines of scar tissue, stared off into nothingness. 'You see, kind sir ...'

His smile was all the broader for the flesh that had been neatly sliced from the left side of his lip, baring dry, grey gum beneath a mass of scab. His grey hair was matted all the more from the dried crimson where his left ear had once been. His face all the more akin to a slab of flesh and sinew for the two gaping punctures where he had once bore a nose.

'I've nothing left to feel it with.'

Bralston's veneer of indifference cracked; he did not

notice, did not care that the shock was plain on his face, the horror clear in his eyes. Rashodd's black humour dropped, as though he were suddenly aware of the great joke and no longer found it funny. He shuffled backwards, back into the gloom, but Bralston's mouth remained agape, his voice remained a whisper.

'You ...' he said softly. 'Someone ... *spited* you?'

'You've seen this before,' Rashodd replied, gesturing to his face. 'I somehow thought you might. You are ... a Djaalman, yes?'

'That's ... yes ...' Bralston said, struggling in vain to find his composure again. 'During the riots, the Jackals ... they spited people, spited everyone they could. There were ...' His eyes widened. 'When did you meet a Jackal? Are they active outside of Cier'Djaal?'

'Enough questions from your end, sir,' Rashodd said, and Bralston did not challenge him. 'You are an observant Djaalman, yes? Touched your eye in reverence for the Houndmistress. Lady most admirable, she was ... culled the Jackals, restored the common man's faith in the city.'

'Until she was murdered,' Bralston said. 'Her husband and child likely dead, too.'

'Likely?'

'They disappeared.'

'Disappeared, sir? Or fled?'

'What do you mean?' Bralston's eyes flared to crimson light. 'What do you know?' He stepped forward brashly at Rashodd's silence, scowl burning without care. 'Her murder started the riots, killed over a *thousand* people. *What do you know?*'

'Only what I've read, sir,' Rashodd said, 'only what I've seen, sir.' His vigour left him with every whispered word. 'I have heard rumours, descriptions ... her husband ...'

'A Sainite,' Bralston replied. 'I met him, when the Houndmistress formalised relations with the Karnerians. Tall man, red hair, dark eyes.' He stared intently at the Cragsman. 'You … have you seen him?'

'Seen him …' Rashodd repeated. 'Yes. I saw him …'

He ran a ruined hand over a ruined face.

'And I didn't scream.'

Before the Librarian had even set foot upon the docks, Argaol could sense the man's presence. An invisible tremor swept across the modest harbour of Port Yonder, sending tiny ripples across the water, dock cats fleeing and the various sailors and fishermen cringing as though struck.

They parted before the wizard like a tide of tanned flesh, none eager to get in his way as he moved toward the captain with rigid, deliberate movements and locked a cold, relentless gaze upon him.

'What happened?' Argaol asked, questioning the wisdom of such an action.

'Many things,' Bralston replied. 'Ktamgi. How far is it?'

'What?'

'I am unfamiliar with the lay of this area. Enlighten me.'

'You're looking for the adventurers?' Argaol shook his head. 'They went that way, but if they survived, they'd be at Teji by now.'

'And how far from Ktamgi is that?'

'A day's travel by ship,' Argaol said. 'My crew is already in the city, but I can have the *Riptide* up and ready to go by then if you need—'

'I do,' Bralston said. He purposefully shoved the man aside as he strode to the end of the docks. 'But I don't have that long.'

'What are you doing?'

'Leaving.'

'What? Why? What happened?'

'That information is the concern of the Venarium alone.'

'And what am I supposed to tell the Lord Emissary?' Argaol demanded hotly. 'He instructed me to help you!'

'And you have. Whatever you do next is the concern of anyone *but* the Venarium.' He adjusted his broad-brimmed hat upon his head, pulled his cloak a little tighter about his body. He glanced at Argaol briefly. 'Captain.'

Before Argaol could even ask, the wizard's coat twitched, the air ripped apart as its leather twisted in the blink of an eye. A pair of great, birdlike wings spread out behind Bralston, sending Argaol tumbling to the dock, and he left with as little fanfare as a man with a winged coat could manage, leaping off the edge and taking flight, soaring high over the harbour before any sailor or fisherman could even think to curse.

Something was happening outside, Rashodd could tell. People were excited, shouting, pointing at the sky. He could not see beyond the thick walls of his cell. He could not hear above the nearby roar of the ocean slamming against the cliffs below. But he knew all the same, because he knew the wizard would act.

'Just as you said he would ...' he whispered to the darkness.

'*Those without faith are convinced of their righteousness,*' a pair of voices whispered back from a place far below. '*Faith is purpose. To admit a lack of purpose is to admit that they possess no place in this world. Understand this and the faithless become beasts to be trained and commanded.*'

'It is with a fond lamentation that I make audible that which stirs in my mind,' Rashodd sighed, 'but speaking as a man with only time and darkness to his name, I cannot help but wonder if you're capable of making a point without a religious speech to accompany.'

'The point lay in the speech,' the voices replied. *'You are no beast, Rashodd. Not a beast, but a prisoner, and not much longer.'*

'So you say,' Rashodd growled. 'Of course, and it is with no undue distaste that I point this out, I am only a prisoner because you failed to live up to your end of our prior bargain.'

'Lamentable,' the voices said. *'But your presence here serves our purpose further. You shall be free.'*

'The door is scarcely more than sticks bound with twine,' Rashodd replied. 'I can be free as soon as I wish to strangle the boy outside. I remain only on your promises.' His voice became a throaty snarl. 'In days of darkness, though, I must confess I find them less than illuminating.'

'And yet, your faith compels you to stay.'

'For a time longer.'

'We find our own faith in the Mouth falters. The praises we heap upon him are no longer enough to compel his service. He wavers. He wanes.'

'And you wish my service,' Rashodd whispered. 'You wish me to free this ... Daga-Mer.'

'For Mother Deep to find her way, the Father must also find his.'

'And if I do ...'

'We grant you what you wish.'

Rashodd's thick fingers, what remained of them, ran across his face. No matter how many times he did it, no matter how many times he knew they wouldn't be there, he continued to anticipate pieces of himself still in their proper place: a nose, an eye, part of his lip. And no matter how many times his fingers caressed jagged rents where those parts were missing, his rage continued to grow.

'My face ...' he whispered.

'We can return it.'

'My fingers ...'

'We can bring them back.'

He stared down at his hand. He could still feel the kiss of steel, the dagger's tongue that had taken his digits. He could still see the hand that had held it. He could hear the voice that had told him not to scream. He could remember the tall man, the felon clad in black with the tears in his eyes.

'My revenge ...' he whispered hoarsely.

With a melodic laughter, the Deepshriek replied.

'It will be yours.'

Twenty-Four

NAMING THE SIN

The water is cold today.

Lenk let that thought linger as he let his hand linger in the rush of the stream. Between the clear surface and the bed of yellow pebbles below, he could see the legged eels, their vast and vacant eyes staring out from either side of their gaping mouths as stubby, pinlike legs clung to rocks and streamweeds to resist the current.

He mimicked their expression, staring blankly into the water as he waited for a reply to bubble up inside his mind. He did not wait long.

'*Mm.*'

The Steadbrook was never this cold.

'*You remember that?*'

It was what the village was named for. It powered the mill that ground the grain. It was the heart of the village. My grandfather told me.

'*Memories are returning. This is good.*'

Is it?

'*Should it not be?*'

You never seemed concerned with that before.

'*You never spoke back before.*'

Do you suppose there'll be more?

'*More what?*'

Memories.

He waited, listening patiently for an answer. All that responded was the stream, burbling aimlessly over the rocks. He furrowed his brow and frowned.

Are you still there?

The sun felt warm on his brow, uncomfortably so. Someone, somewhere else, muttered something.

'Memories,' it replied with a sudden chill, '*are a reminder of what was never meant to be.*'

He blinked. Behind his eyes, shadows danced amidst flames in a wild, gyrating torture of consumption. Against a pale and pitiless moon, a mill's many limbs turned slowly, raising a burning appendage pleadingly to the sky before lowering it, ignored and dejected. And at its wooden, smouldering base, bodies lay facedown, hands reaching out toward a warm brook.

'*Remember*,' the voice said with such severity to make Lenk wince, '*why we do not need them.*'

'No,' he whimpered.

'Well, *fine*,' someone said beside him. 'Refuse if you want, but you don't have to look so agonised at the suggestion.'

He opened his eyes, glowered at the stream and the quivering reflection of a stubble-caked face staring down at him.

'If I'm looking pained,' he said harshly, 'it's because you're talking.'

'Feel free to leave. I don't recall inviting you here, anyway.'

Denaos was no longer one singular voice, not so easy to ignore as he had once been. Rather, every noise that emanated from him was now a chorus: complaint followed by a loud slurping sound, an uncouth belch as punctuation and the sound of half a hollowed-out gourd landing in a growing pile of hollowed-out gourd halves to serve as pause between complaints.

He looked down at the young man and grinned, licking up the droplets soaked in his stubbled lip.

'They can't figure out the concept of clothing that keeps one's stones from swaying in the breeze, but they can make some fine liquor.' He held out the fruit-made-cup to Lenk. 'You're *sure* you don't want any?'

'I'm sure I don't know what it is,' Lenk replied, rising up.

'Drinking irresponsibly is a time-honoured tradition amongst my people.'

'Humans?'

'Drunks.'

'Uh-huh. What's it called?'

Denaos glanced to his left and cleared his throat. Squatting on stubby legs beside the stream, fishing pole in hand, the Owauku took one eye off of the lure bobbing in the water and rotated it slowly to regard the rogue with as much narrowed ire as one could manage with eyes the size of melons.

'*Mangwo*,' he grunted, slowly sliding his eye back to the bobber.

'And ... what's it made of?' Lenk asked.

'Well, now ...' Denaos took a swig, swished it about thoughtfully in his mouth. 'I'd say it's fermented something, blended with the finest I-don't-want-to-know and aged for exactly who-gives-a-damn-you-stupid-tit.' He smacked his lips. 'Delicious.'

'I suppose I should be pleased you're making such good friends with the reptiles,' Lenk said, raising an eyebrow. 'Or do they just find your sliminess blends well with their own?'

'Jhombi and I are getting on quite well, yes,' the rogue replied as he plucked his own rod and line from the ground and cast it into the stream. 'Probably because he barely understands a word of the human tongue and thusly isn't as prone to be a whining silver-haired hamster.' He grinned to the Owauku. 'Am I not right, Jhombi?'

Jhombi grunted.

'Man of few words,' Denaos said. 'Speaking of, I trust negotiations with Togu went well?'

Lenk stared blankly for a moment before clearing his throat.

'Yes.'

'So he'll—'

'*I said yes.*'

'Oh …' The rogue blinked, taken aback. 'Well, uh, good.' He slurped up the rest of his drink and tossed it aside. 'When do we leave, then?'

'Tomorrow.'

'Delightful.'

'After the party.'

There was something unwholesome in Denaos' grin.

Lenk growled. 'I hate it when your eyes light up like that. It always means someone is about to get stabbed or molested.'

'And yet, you have now inadvertently invited me to an event that is conducive to both.' Denaos chuckled, shaking his head. 'My gratitude will best be expressed in the generous offer that I will save you for last in either endeavour. How's that sound, Jhombi?'

Jhombi grunted.

'Jhombi agrees.'

'How would you know?'

'How would *you*?'

'How is it that he can't speak the tongue? Every creature on this island does.' He glowered as a thought occurred to him. 'Well, except for Hongwe.'

'Who?'

'Tall Gonwa, looked irritated and important.'

'Ah.' Denaos furrowed his brow. 'They all look irritated, though. What made this one look important?'

'Well, he had a satchel.'

'A satchel, huh? I suppose that does count as sort of a status symbol amongst a people for whom the concept of pants is an incomprehensible technology.' The rogue glanced at Lenk with worry on his face. 'You negotiated all our terms, right? We've got pants?'

'We've got pants, yes,' Lenk said, nodding. 'Kataria said—'

'Kataria was there?' Denaos asked, blanching.

'She was, yeah.' He glared at the rogue. 'Why wouldn't she be?'

'Well, was there any trash to root around in? Filth to roll in? Perhaps a bone with a tiny piece of meat on it?'

Lenk's neck stiffened. 'I thought we settled this.'

'Settled what?'

'You talking about her like that.'

'We did settle, but on different things. What *you* settled with was a willingness to ignore the fact that a woman – called such only in theory, mind you – threatened to *kill* you.'

'She saved my life.'

'I'm not finished.' The rogue pressed a thumb to his own chest. '*I* settled with the idea that I should cease trying to help a man intent on ignoring that this "woman" has fangs and that he wants them near tender areas.'

438

'If she was planning on killing me, she would have done it already, wouldn't she?'

'So you're honestly trying to rationalise your attraction to a woman a step above a beast with the excuse that she hasn't killed you *yet*.'

'I am.'

'And nothing about that seems insane to you?'

'Like you've never threatened to kill someone and not gone through with it.'

'There's no time limit on murder oaths.'

'Point being, things change, don't they?' Lenk replied. 'Oaths are forgotten—'

'Delayed.'

'Even so ... things change. Things happen.' Lenk stared at the stream intently, his mind drifting back to so many nights ago. 'Something ... something happened.'

Denaos cast a suspicious glare at the young man. 'What *kind* of something?'

Lenk sighed and rubbed the back of his neck. 'It's going to sound insane.'

'Coming from *you*?' the rogue gasped. '*No*. Not the man who's been spotted, on more than one occasion, talking to himself, yelling at nothing and possibly eating his own filth.'

'I *told* you, I wasn't *eating* it, I was—'

'*No!*' Denaos flung a hand up in warding. 'Stop there, sir, for there is no end to that thought that will not make me want to punch you in the eye.'

'Just listen—'

'*No, sir.* You've given me the excellent news that we are soon to be off and that we're having a celebration tonight. My life is going exceedingly well right now. I have food, drink, and the comforting company of a surly green man-lizard. Tomorrow, I'm going to start heading back to a world where undergarments are not only invented but *encouraged*. I tried to talk you out of this deranged bestiality plot you've cooked up, and I defy you – *defy* you, sir – to say anything to lure me back in.'

In the wake of the outburst, the stream burbled quietly. Neither Denaos nor Jhombi looked up from their lures. A long moment of silence passed as Lenk stared and then, with a gentle clear of his throat and two words, shattered it.

'Eel tits.'

Denaos blinked twice, cringed once, then swiftly snapped his rod over his knee and sighed deeply.

'Gods *damn it.*' He plucked up one of the empty half-gourds and stalked to a nearby mossy rock, taking a seat. 'All right ... tell me.'

'Well, it happened days ago, before Kataria found me with the Shen.'

'Go on.'

'I was in the forest and I was ... hallucinating.' Lenk stared at the earth, the images returning to his mind. 'I felt a river cold as ice, I saw demons in trees, I ... I ...' He turned a wild, worried stare upon Denaos. 'I *argued* with a *monkey.*'

The rogue blinked. 'Did you win?'

Lenk felt his brow grow heavy, his jaw clench. Something spoke inside his head.

'*Not important.*'

'Not important,' he growled. 'I saw ... *Kataria* there. She said things, tempted me and she peeled off her shirt and ... eels.'

'Eels.'

'*Eels!*' Lenk shouted. 'She was there, speaking to me, saying such things, telling me to stop—'

'Stop what?'

'It doesn't matter. The fever was eating at me, cooking my brains in my skull.'

'Are ... you sure?' Denaos' face screwed up in confusion as he stared at the young man curiously. 'I was there when Kataria dragged you in, and I should note that I saw nothing writhing beneath her fur. I was there when Asper looked you over. She said your fever was mild.'

'*What would she know?*' the voice asked.

'It was *my* head, *not hers!*' Lenk snarled, jabbing his temple fiercely. 'What would Asper know about it?'

'Considering the years she's spent to studying the physical condition? Probably quite a bit.' Denaos tapped his chin. 'She started screaming and ran us out a moment later, but I remember clearly—'

'*He knows nothing.*'

'Remember what? How could you know? You and Kat have *both* now said she went mad and drove you out like ... like ...'

'*Heathens.*'

'Heathens!' he spat. 'How could you know what she knew? What happened after she drove you out? Why did she do it in the first place?'

Denaos remained unmoving, glaring quietly at the young man with the same unpronounced tension in his body that Lenk had seen before, usually moments before someone found something sharp embedded in something soft. The fact that there was scarcely anywhere on the rogue where he could keep a knife hidden was small comfort.

'That,' he said, 'is no business of anyone's but hers. I believe her word over yours.'

'*Liar.*'

'A good point,' Lenk muttered.

'What is?'

'Why so defensive over her?' the young man asked, raising a brow. 'You're always the first to suspect, yet you so willingly take her word over mine?'

'*She* has the benefit of not being visibly demented,' Denaos replied.

Lenk wanted to scowl, to snarl, but the pain inside his head was growing unbearable. On wispy shrieks, the voice was agonisingly clear.

'*Traitors. Liars. Faithless. Ignorant. Unnecessary.*'

'Just ignorant,' Lenk muttered, shaking his head. 'Just … just …'

'Look,' Denaos said, his tension melting away with his sigh. 'I'm not sure what kind of message is entailed by displaying the object of your attention with sea life replacing her anatomy, but it can't be good.' He leaned back and looked thoughtful. 'The Gods send visions to speak to the faithful, to reward them, to guide them,' his eyes narrowed, 'to warn them.'

'I didn't think you were religious.'

'Silf's creed is silence and secrecy. It's probably a mild blasphemy even telling you about this.'

'So why do it?'

'Greed, mostly,' the rogue replied. 'Averting a man from imminent mutilation of heart, head and probably genitalia seems a deed the Gods would smile upon.' He glanced at the young man. 'Tell me, what were you hoping to do once this whole bloody business was over and we stood on the mainland again?'

'I'd given it some thought,' Lenk replied, rolling his shoulders. 'Farming is as good a trade as any. I figured I'd get some land and hold onto it as long as I could. Just a cow, a plough …'

'And her?'

Lenk frowned without knowing why. 'Maybe.'

'Do you remember how she smiles?'

Lenk stared at the ground, a slight grin forming at the corner of his mouth. 'Yeah, I remember.'

'Remember her laughter?'

His smile wormed its way to the other side of his face. 'I do.'

'You've probably seen her truly happy a few times, in fact.'

He stared up at the sun, remembered a different kind of warmth. He remembered a hand on his shoulder, a puff of hot air between thin lips, heat that sent tiny droplets of sweat coursing down muscles wrapped under pale flesh. He remembered smiling then, as he did now.

'I have.'

'Good,' Denaos said. 'Now, of those times, how many had come just after she shot something?'

His smile vanished, head dropped. The rogue's words rang through his head and heart with an awful truth to them. Surely, he realised, there were some moments between the shict and himself where she had smiled, where she had laughed and there hadn't been a lick of blood involved.

But had she really smiled, then?

'So she … ?'

'Was around for the violence? It's a possibility, really. Nature of the beast, if you'll excuse the accuracy of the statement.' Denaos sighed. 'Perhaps it wasn't what you wanted to hear, but it's the truth.'

'It's not.'

'*It is,*' the voice hissed.

'It's not!' Lenk insisted.

'*Her motivation is pointless. She is a distraction, useless. He,*

443

as well, but less so if he makes our purpose that much clearer to foggy minds.'

'Well, it's not like you'll have to stop seeing her,' Denaos offered. 'Just keep killing things and she'll continue to follow the scent of blood.'

'He is right.'

'He is *not!*' Lenk muttered.

'Ours is a higher calling. We are not made for idle farming and contemplating dirt. There is still too much to do.'

'What happened to you?' he whispered. 'Why do you speak like this now?'

'Too much to cleanse. A stain lingers on this island. Duty is clear.'

'Well, you *asked* for my opinion,' Denaos replied, raising an eyebrow. 'It's hardly my fault that your thoughts run so contrary that you find sanity offensive, but the fact remains ...' He held out his hands helplessly. 'Adventuring or the shict. You can embrace both or give up both, but never dismiss either. And you've got divine reinforcement for that fact, not that godly visions are necessary.'

'Or real.'

The sudden appearance of what appeared to be a pale, talking stick drew both men's attentions up to the stream bank. Dreadaeleon stood there with skinny arms folded over skinny chest, nose up in the air in an attempt at superiority that was made unsurprisingly difficult given his distinct lack of clothing, muscle and dignity.

'How long have you been standing there?' Denaos cut him off with a direct swiftness. 'It's weird enough to be wearing a loincloth, talking to another man in a loincloth, without a third *boy* sitting and staring ... *in a loincloth.*'

'I had come by to talk to you. Fortunately, I arrived just as the delusional talk of gods came up.' Dreadaeleon waved a hand as he sauntered toward them. 'It's irrelevant as pertains to the subject of hallucinations.'

'It is?' Lenk asked, quirking a brow.

'Wait,' Denaos interjected, 'don't tell me you're going to listen to *him*.'

'Why shouldn't he?' Dreadaeleon replied smugly. 'Insight based on reason and knowledge is far superior to conjecture based on ignorant superstition and … well, I suppose you would probably cite something like your "gut" as credible source, no?'

'That and the fact that, between the two of us, I'm the only one who's managed to talk to a woman without breathing hard,' the rogue snapped. 'You're aware we're talking about women, right? Nothing even remotely logical.'

'Everything is logical in nature, *especially* hallucinations, which you were also discussing.' The boy turned to Lenk. 'To credit one hallucination to one delusion is preposterous.'

Lenk frowned at the boy. 'You … *do* know I'm a follower of Khetashe, don't you?'

'And yet, gods' – Dreadaeleon paused to look disparagingly at Denaos – '*and* their followers don't seem to be doing much for you. I once believed in them, too, when I was young and stupid.'

'You're *still*—'

'*The point I'm trying to make*,' he said with fierce insistence, 'is that hallucinations are matters of mind, not divinity. And who is more knowledgeable in the ways of the mind than a wizard? You know it was the Venarium that discovered the brain as the centre of thought.'

'Being that this is also a matter of attraction,' Denaos muttered, 'brains have shockingly little to do with it.'

'Then we should introduce a little more to the situation.'

Dreadaeleon folded his hands with a businesslike air of importance as he regarded Lenk thoughtfully. 'Now, the hallucination you experienced, the … ah …'

'Eel tits,' the young man replied.

'Yes, the eel … *that*. It was a sign, make no mistake.' He tapped his temple. 'But it came from up here. Wait no …' He reached out a hand and prodded Lenk's forehead sharply. 'In *there*.'

The young man growled, slapping Dreadaeleon's hand away. 'So … what, you think it's madness?'

'Madness is the result of the rational coming to terms with the irrational, like rel—'

'*Sweet Khetashe*, I get it!' Lenk said exasperatedly. 'You're incredibly enlightened and your brain is big enough to make your neck buckle under it.'

'That may just be the fat in his head,' Denaos offered.

'Regardless, can we please remember to focus on *my* problem here?'

'Of course,' Dreadaeleon replied. 'Your hallucination is just that: your rational mind, what you know to be true and real, is struggling with your irrational mind, what you desire and hope. The hallucination was simply an image manifestation of that. That she was not there was rational; that she was there was irrational; the eels represent—'

'There are precious few ways one can interpret eel tits, my friend,' Denaos interjected.

'Can we *please* stop saying that?' Dreadaeleon growled. 'The eels are simply the bridge between, the sole obstacle to what you hope to accomplish, hence their characterisation as something horrifically ugly.'

'Couldn't that also suggest an aversion or fear to what lay under her shirt? Or sexuality in general?' Denaos mused.

The boy whirled on him with teeth bared. 'Oh, was

446

it a group of smelly thieves and rapists who uncovered the innermost machinations of the organ driving human consciousness? Because here I thought it was the most enlightened body of scholarly inquiry in the world that figured it out. But if Denaos said it, it must be the other way, *because he's so great and he's right about everything!'*

Lenk had never thought he would actually see a man will himself to explode, much less a boy, but as Dreadaeleon stared fiery holes into the rogue's forehead, chest expanding with each fevered breath like a bladder filling with water, he absently felt the urge to take cover from the impending splatter.

'Right,' Dreadaeleon said, body shrinking with one expulsion of hot air as he returned to Lenk. 'The correct thing to do, then, would be to embrace the urge and simply … you know … have at it.'

Lenk regarded the boy curiously for a moment. There was something different in him, to be sure. The burning crimson that heralded his power seemed to be present, if only in brief, faint flickers behind his dark eyes. And yet, all his being seemed to have sunk into those eyes, the rest of him looking far skinnier than usual, his hair far greasier than it should be, his cheeks hollow and his jaw clenched.

'Well, ah … okay, then.' Lenk blinked. 'Thanks?'

'My pleasure,' Dreadaeleon said, leaning against a tree. 'I'm a little curious as to where you managed to find a girl on this island to hallucinate over, though. Or was this someone prior to our departure?'

'What?' Lenk asked. 'Didn't you hear?'

'Bits and pieces. I didn't catch the identity.' Dreadaeleon's eyes flared wide, the fire behind them bursting to faint embers. 'It's not Asper, is it?' Before the young man could answer, he leaned forward violently. '*Is it?*'

'No, no,' Denaos spoke up from behind. 'Our boy here has decided that romancing within his own breed is a bit too dull.'

'Oh … one of the lizards, then? Tell me, how can you tell the difference between the males and—'

'It's *Kat*, you spindly little freak!' Lenk snarled suddenly.

'Oh … what, really?' Dreadaeleon blanched. 'I mean … ah. No, I don't think that'll work at all.'

'See?' Denaos said.

'What?' Lenk frowned. 'A moment ago you were telling me to follow my hallucination!'

'Hallucination and delusion are two different things,' Denaos replied. 'This isn't a matter of heart or mind, but of instinct. I mean, she'll *kill you*.'

'That's what *I* said,' Denaos muttered.

'She hasn't yet,' Lenk replied, 'and I'm sure I won't be the first one she does.'

'Who can say when or why an animal attacks? Perhaps she's just waiting to show you her true colours, like a cat stalking. Or maybe she's waiting until she's hungry enough?'

'Now wait just a—'

Denaos interrupted. 'See, I hadn't considered that. Here, I thought it was right until she got bored.'

'She's not going to—'

'That's a good point, but I think it may be biologically spurred,' Dreadaeleon offered. 'Like her instincts will only come to light when he spots her demiphallus.'

'I'm not going to …' This time, Lenk cut himself off as he stared at the boy with wide eyes. 'Wait. Her what?'

'All female shicts have them, it's theorised. Granted, our necropsies haven't catalogued enough to—'

'No, shut up. What's a demiphallus?'

'Pretty much what it sounds like,' the boy replied. 'Used to show dominance over males, it's … well … it's …' He appeared thoughtful for a moment. 'All right, remember when we saw those exotic pets being unloaded in Muraska's harbour?'

'Right.'

'Right, and remember the hyenas?'

'Some noble in Cier'Djaal had shipped them up, I remember.'

'Remember the *female* one?'

'Yes, I—' His eyes suddenly wide at the memory. 'Oh … *no*.'

'Really?' Denaos asked, gaping. 'She has one, you think? That would make *perfect* sense.'

'I know!' Dreadaeleon replied, grinning. 'Wouldn't it?'

'How would *that* make perfect sense?' Lenk demanded, eyes narrowing. '*How*?' He glowered at the boy. 'And how are you in any position to be commenting on any part of a female south of her neck?'

'I've … read books.'

'Books?' Denaos asked, chuckling.

'Books, yes,' Dreadaeleon replied. 'I'm … familiar with the basic process, anyway. It's not like it's particularly difficult to perform, let along conceptualise.'

The two men stared at him, challenging. He cleared his throat.

'See, uh.' The boy scratched the back of his neck. 'See, a lot of it has to do with the maidenhead. The, er, hymen, if you will, per se.'

'Oh, I certainly will,' Denaos said.

'This isn't helping me with my—' Lenk muttered and was promptly ignored.

'Right, well, this provides a form of ... tightness ... a sort of barrier that provides difficulty to the expeditious party. That ... that makes sense, doesn't it?'

'Entirely, yes,' Denaos confirmed through a grin.

'All right, then ... so, the only thing *really* necessary is some manner of ... of ...'

'Penetration?'

'No, see, because it's a barrier. It ... uh ... needs a sort of crushing.' He made a fist and thrust it forward demonstratively. 'A punching motion.'

'Punching?'

'Yes. Punching.' He turned to Lenk. 'See? It's a matter of nature, physical and mental. There's no way you can possibly—'

'Shut up,' the young man said.

'You *did* ask—' Denaos began.

'I said *shut up!*' Lenk roared, fists trembling at his side as he impaled the two men with his stare. 'I can't believe I asked either of you. *You*' – he levelled a finger at Denaos – 'who would leap at the chance to rut a sow so long as you were drunk enough or *you*' – he thrust it at Dreadaeleon – 'who divides his time between alienating every woman in sight with his pretentious sputter and staring holes in Asper's robe and trying desperately to hide the chicken-bone swelling in his trousers.'

'Asper?' Denaos asked, glancing at the boy. 'Really?'

'Did I speak too softly or did you hear me when I told you to *shut up?*' Lenk demanded, his scowl growing more intense, his voice harsher. 'I don't care what you, you or *any* voice says. *I'm* the leader, and even if what I decide to do is at *all* mad, it's still a damn sight better than any of you cowardly piss-slurpers could think of. Rest assured that no matter who I walk away from this with, their presence will be a small blessing against the fact that I am leaving *both* of you to rot in filth, get sodomised in an alley and otherwise *die alone*.'

He turned away from them, forcing his eyes on the stream, forcing himself to control his breathing. It tasted warm in his mouth, cold on his lips. He could feel their stares upon him, feel their shock. As though there were something wrong with *him*.

'We are going to turn around,' he uttered. 'Do not be there.'

They left. He did not turn around. He didn't have to. He could feel their fear seeping out of their feet and into the earth. They hadn't even waited until they were out of earshot to start running.

Scared little animals. The very kind of animal they accused her of being. The very kind of beast they saw when they had looked at him.

They were the animals. Fearful, weak, squeaking rodents. Useless. Pointless.

He was strong. He saw it in his reflection in the stream. His face was hard. His eyes were hard. No apology, no weakness.

No pupils. He blinked. *That can't be right.*

Falling to his knees seemed a bit too easy; his head pulled the rest of him to the earth. He rested on his hands and knees, staring at himself in the river. His breath poured out of him in great, unrestrained puffs that stirred the water, blurred his face in it.

The legged eels below the surface released their grips on the rocks, went drifting down the stream. Lenk ignored them; his image was no more clearer with them gone. He could make out flashes of grey, blue, each one a stark and solid colour that he had rarely seen in his hair or eyes before. Slowly, he leaned down farther, breath pouring out of his mouth to kiss the water.

And freeze it into tiny, drifting chunks of ice that were lost down the stream.

'That ... that *definitely* is not right.'

'One would suspect,' a deep voice spoke, 'that you are a poor judge of that.'

He looked up immediately and saw no one to match the bass, alien voice. He was alone in the forest, even the birds and chattering beasts of the trees having fled to leave him bathed in silence. Just him, the stream, and ...

'Jhombi?' he asked.

The squat reptile made no immediate answer, did not even look up from his lure bobbing in the water. Then, slowly, his massive head began to twist towards Lenk, staring at him with two immense eyes.

Lenk stared back, mouth gaping open; of all the words he could have used to describe the Owauku's gourdlike eyes, 'gleeful' and 'malicious' had rarely come to mind. And 'terrifying', not at all.

'Hello, Lenk.' His ... or its voice was like sap: thick and bitter in the air. 'I see you're experiencing some difficulty with your current plan? Perhaps I could be of help.'

Lenk shook his head, dispelling his befuddlement. 'I'm sorry, I didn't think you spoke the tongue.' He cast a glare into the forest. 'I suppose I shouldn't be shocked. Denaos has lied to me before.'

'He has,' the lizardman said, 'but he didn't this time.'

'He said Jhombi didn't speak the human tongue.'

'Jhombi does not.'

Lenk stared as the lizardman's green smile grew a bit larger and eyes shrank a bit narrower.

'So,' the young man said breathlessly, 'you would be ...'

452

'I'd say that my name was unimportant, but that would be a lie. You've had far too many of those lately, haven't you?'

'I'd agree with you, but any bond of trust we might have would probably be shattered by the fact that I am speaking to someone wearing Jhombi's skin like a costume.'

The creature laughed, not joylessly. Rather, there was plenty of mirth in his deep, booming chuckle, and all of it made Lenk's skin crawl.

'You *are* clever, sir. A bit macabre, but clever.' He held up a hand. 'Jhombi is fine, my friend. Not present, but certainly still alive and possessing all his skin. He was lured away long ago by a gourd of his people's wicked brew. Not half as clever as you were, that one, not half as determined.' He quirked a scaly eye ridge. 'Or perhaps now that you're giving up, you're roughly on par?'

Lenk could but stare, tongue dry in his gaping mouth. 'Are ... you another one?'

'A hallucination?' The creature shook his bulbous head. 'Would a hallucination admit to being such? After all, they only linger as long as you consider them real. I must linger, Lenk; not long, only enough to speak with you, but I must. After that, you can imagine me away.'

'All my hallucinations want to speak with me, lately. My mind must have a lot to say ... Or is it the Gods that are trying to tell me something?' Lenk dared a smile at the creature. It could hardly hurt, he reasoned. He would hate to gain a reputation for rudeness amongst his growing collection of mental problems.

'Good to see you've kept a sense of humour about it. I can hardly blame you. Lunatics have a reputation for laughing uncontrollably for a reason.'

'So you *are* a hallucination.'

'No, but you are going mad.' The creature sighed. 'Mad and clever, I suppose you could answer me this question: do you suppose it will stop?'

The young man blinked. 'Will what stop?'

'All of it. All the madness, the suffering.' The creature looked at him intently. 'The *voices*.' It nodded slowly, all mirth gone from its face. 'I know. I can't hear them, but I know. I know how they torment you, running endlessly: hot, cold, soothing, frightening, day in, day out, screaming, shrieking, demanding, whispering, whining, *talking all the time*.'

Lenk, having nothing else to respond with, leaned forward, unblinking, unbreathing, unmoving.

'Will they?'

The creature stared back at him and shook his head. 'One will.'

'One? There are ...' *Should have realised that, should have known that.* He stopped cursing himself long enough to breathe. 'Which?'

'Scarcely matters. One whispers lies, the other whispers what you don't want to hear. You think either of them will stop?' It sighed deeply. 'Or is it that you think the one with the sweet lies will be correct? The one that tells you that everything will be fine, that you'll go back to the mainland and leave all this behind you, grow fat on a field with your slender shict bride and watch the sunset until your lids grow too heavy to keep up and you die feeding the horseflies.

'And yet, everything isn't fine, is it? You are still here. Your companions fear you to the point that they have difficulty following you even back to their precious civilisation. You feel sick without your sword, angry in the company of

454

those who smile at you, experience silence from one voice only when the other speaks …'

The creature shook its head.

'No, not fine, at all, I'd say. One could scarcely be blamed for fleeing, especially when the alternative is to stay here, amidst the intolerable sun and rivers that turn to ice.'

'There is nothing here,' Lenk replied, 'nothing but lizard-men and bugs. What purpose is there in staying here?'

'When was the last time you found a purpose by looking behind you? What awaits you there? Burned ruins of your old home? The graves of your family?'

'What would you know of it?' Lenk snarled, feeling his hands tense, restrained from strangling the creature only by curiosity and dread for the answer.

'I know they will not be there when you return,' the creature replied. 'Just as I know what little family you've scraped together you only have by coming this far.' It grinned broadly. 'Go farther and who knows? Blood, yes. Death, most certainly. But in these, you find peace … Perhaps you'll find the kind that lasts? The kind that lets you know who it is that speaks in your head and who it was that sent you on a road that began with the blood of your family? The kind where everything is fine at the end?'

Lenk swallowed hard.

'Will I find it?'

'Are you asking me if things will get better or if things will turn out the way you hoped?'

'I don't know.'

'Just as well. Much of the future is uncertain, save for this …' It leaned forward slowly, eyes widening, mouth widening. 'None of that matters.'

'My happiness does not matter?'

'You were not *bred* for happiness. You were *bred* to do your duty.'

'I ... wasn't bred! I was born!' Lenk nodded stiffly, as if affirming to himself. 'My name is Lenk!'

'Lenk what?'

'Lenk ... Lenk ...' He racked his brain. 'I had a grandfather.'

'What was his name?'

'He was ... he was my mother's father! We were all born in the same place! The same village!'

'Where?'

'A ... a village. Somewhere. I can't ...' He thumped his head with the heel of his hand. 'But, I knew! I *remembered!* Just a moment ago! Where ...' He turned to the creature, eyes wide. 'Where did they go?'

'It hardly matters. They won't be coming back ... not on the mainland.'

A long silence persisted between them, neither of them breaking their stare to so much as blink. When Lenk spoke, his voice quavered.

'But they will here?'

'I did not say that. What I *implied* was that there is nothing to gain upon returning to the mainland.'

'And what is here, then?'

'Here?' The creature grinned. 'Death, obviously.'

'Whose death?'

'A meaningful one, be certain.' It twisted its yellow gaze toward the distant edge of the forest and the village beyond. 'Ah ... sunset will come soon and your precious farewell feast with it. I would be wary of these green creatures, Lenk. You never know what might be lurking behind their faces.'

The creature's saplike voice felt as though it had poured

over Lenk's body, pooled at his feet and held him there staring dumbfoundedly at the creature as it strode away like a thing much larger than its size would suggest. Dumbstruck, the young man found the voice to speak only as the creature began to slip into the foliage, green flesh blending with green leaves.

'Wait!' Lenk called after it. 'Tell me ... something! Anything! Give me a reason to keep going!' As the creature continued on, he took a tentative step toward its fading figure. 'Tell me! Will Kataria kill me? Who killed my family? Who is it in my head? You never told me!' He growled, his voice a curse unto itself. 'You never told me *anything!*'

'I know ...'

Whatever pursuit Lenk might have mustered further was halted as the creature turned to look over its shoulder with a face not its own. Its jaws were wide, impossibly so, to the point that Lenk could almost hear them straining under the pressure.

Gritted between them, reflecting his own horrified visage that shrank with every horrified step he retreated, a set of teeth, each tooth the length and colour of three bleached knucklebones stacked atop each other, glittered brightly.

'Ominous, isn't it?'

The words echoed in his thoughts, just as the polished, toothy grin embedded itself in eyes that stared blankly, long into the sunset, after the creature had vanished and drums began to pound in the distance.

Twenty-Five

CONFESSIONAL VIOLENCE

Pagans had certain enviable qualities, Asper decided after an hour of lying in the mossy bed and staring up at the sun, enjoying the sensation of it as it bathed her.

First among those qualities was the confidence to lounge around in skimpy furs beneath the sun for hours on end, she decided. That was certainly a practice she'd have to abandon upon returning to decent society. Not too hard, she thought as she scratched a red spot on her belly, especially if meant fewer bug bites.

But she was possessed of the worrying suspicion that she would have more difficulty leaving behind the second quality she found so enviable: the complete confidence they had in their faiths. She had often wondered what it was about people with limited grasps of homesteading and hygiene that made them so sure of their heathen beliefs.

Only recently, though, was she wondering what it was they had that she lacked.

Perhaps, she reasoned, her faith permitted her a unique position to come to the conclusion. The creed of Talanite was to heal, regardless of ideological difference. The occasional attempt to convert the barbarian races from their shallow, false gods were largely carried out by the more militant faiths of Daeon and Galataur. The most she had ever seen of such attempts was the gruesome aftermath: the hacked bodies of shict, tulwar or couthi who had refused to give up their gods and chose to meet them instead. The most thought she had ever expended for them was a brief prayer and a silent lament for the futility of dying in the name of a faith that made no sense to her.

Of course, she reminded herself, *you worship the sun. That seems pretty silly at a glance, doesn't it?* She sighed, wondering if those barbaric races had ever asked themselves the same question. *Does Kataria ever wonder that? She doesn't look like she does ... then again, she doesn't look like she ever pays enough attention to anything deeper than food ... or Lenk.*

She instantly cursed herself for thinking his name. The memories always began with his name. Like a river, they flowed from his name to that night when Kataria had dragged his unconscious body into the hut. The memories never got any easier to digest. Her heart never ceased to beat faster with every recollection.

It was seared into her mind, its heat every bit as intense as the one that ran through her arm that night.

Funny, she had almost forgotten about her arm, at least for a moment. She had almost forgotten the night prior to that, when it burned at the sight of that hooded face and skeletal grin, the confusion of waking up amidst a tribe of sentient reptiles, she could hardly think of anything else.

Of course, *he* changed that entirely.

Naturally, she had fallen to her knees beside him, running practised hands over his body, checking flesh for wounds, bones for breaking, skin for fever. She had ignored it all at that point: Kataria's shrieking demands, Denaos' cautious stare, the Owauku's incomprehensible babble. All that mattered, at that point, was her charge, her patient, her companion. At that point, she could ignore everything.

Everything except her arm.

She was too well-used to it: the aching, the burning. She could feel it coming, feel it tense, feel it hunger beneath her skin. The scream that had torn itself from her lungs had been cleverly disguised, the pain concealed beneath a command that they all leave. They might have suspected something by the second and third screams, too shrill to be commanding.

But they left, left her alone.

With him.

The arm might have been merciful in waiting until the others had gone to erupt. Or it might simply not have been able to contain itself. She didn't care any more now than she did then; thinking on it brought far too much fear now, far too much pain then. There was no slow eating away this time; the arm simply burst into crimson, the bones black beneath the suddenly transparent red flesh, pulsating, throbbing, burning.

Hungering.

It had pulled itself of its own volition, for a reason she could not bring herself to fathom, towards Lenk. And try as she might to tell herself there was likewise no fathoming why she let her body follow its burning grasp, she had to live with the fact that, at that moment, she had simply let go.

There was no thought for what might have happened next, had her hand clenched on his throat, had he become twisted and reduced to nothing, like those who had felt the crimson touch before. There was no thought for what her god, his god or any god might have said of it. There was only pain, only hunger.

And a blessed, unconscious meal before her. A relief from pain, from the agony that racked her.

But where her hand had slid slowly and carefully towards

him, his was swift and merciless. It snapped out suddenly from the sand, without a snarl or curse or even any indication that Lenk had known what was about to happen. Her body went from burning to freezing in an instant as his fingers wrapped about her throat. Her arm fell at her side limply as he opened eyes that weren't his and spoke with a voice that belonged to someone else.

'*Do not think*,' it had said, '*that it will ever stop if you do it.*'

It could have been Lenk, she thought, probably was him. He *was* feverish, if not enough to cause a hallucination, and he *was* starved and beaten. Trauma was known to cause such changes in personality, she knew from experience, and the fact that he remembered nothing of waking up would support this. But the eerie sensation that it was something more, some madness that gripped him, gripped her, too.

Fear had made her recoil and hold her arm away from him as his slipped from her throat and he fell back into feverish slumber. Or maybe it was compassion, a sudden shock of shame that made her spare her friend. Maybe she had finally claimed some victory over the arm.

Maybe.

The pain was too intense to think, though, the burning from her arm and the cold from his grasp conspiring to plunge her into agony. There she remained, huddled against the hut's wall, choking on her sobs so that no one outside would hear her.

The pain passed, after it had thrust her into agonised sleep and she had awoken to find her arm whole again and Denaos standing over her. She had no idea what he had seen. He stared at her with what looked like concern, but that was a lie.

It had to be.

It was greed, she was sure, the presence of an opportunity to gain an advantage over her for whatever vileness he was planning that kept him around. It was greed that made him lean down and brace her up and offer her water. It was greed that made him ask with such feigned tenderness if she was all right. It was greed that she used to justify cursing at him and driving him out again that she might tend to Lenk and go through the ordeal of forgetting everything.

She had not forgotten, of course. She never would.

She spoke of the event often, posing questions and theorising answers with brazen frequency, but never to anyone with a mouth to reply with. Any time she was alone for a moment, she asked the same questions, as she did now.

'Why?'

And answers now, as they had then, did not come.

'Why him?' Her tone was soft, inquisitive; all her previous indignant, tear-choked anger had long boiled out her mouth and soaked into the earth. 'What is it about him that you want?'

That seemed a fair question to her. It had never really sought anyone with the unerring grip that it had sought Lenk. Of course, fair or not, it didn't answer. Perhaps it had heard that one before. Or maybe she wasn't asking the right question. And, in its silence, she furrowed her brow as a new thought occurred to her.

'Who sent you?' She held her hand up to the sun, as though the light would finally deign to give her an answer she had been asking for all these years and shine through the flesh to reveal its purpose. 'Why is it you wanted him? What did he do to … ?'

And she remembered his eyes, his voice, his cold grasp. And so, she asked.

'Did he … ?' she whispered. 'Does he deserve it? Should he die?'

A sudden breeze struck. Clouds shifted. Branches parted. The sun shone down with more intensity than it had before, focusing a great golden eye upon her. She gasped, beholden, and stared back at the eye, unblinking.

'Is that it?' she whispered. 'Is that the answer? Is what I'm meant to do with this?' She bit her lower lip to control the tremble that racked her as she raised her head and whispered with a shrill, squeaking voice. 'Please, I just want to—'

A shadow fell. Light died. She blinked. Giant green orbs and bright white angles assaulted her senses, narrowing and twisting into horrible shapes as greasy yellow strands dangled down and pricked at her skin.

She recognised Kataria too late. Too late to keep herself from starting and far too late to avoid the shict's forehead as it came down upon her own with a resounding crack. She cried out, clutching her throbbing brow and scrambling to get away. She raised herself on her rear, staring at the shict, caught between shock and anger.

Kataria's own expression seemed settled on a grating, irritating grin.

'Hey,' she said.

'Why did you do that?' Asper shrieked.

'Do what?'

'You *headbutted* me.'

'Yeah, you looked busy.'

Asper stared intently at her. 'How … how does that even—?'

'You seem like you're going to dwell on this for a while and leave me no opportunity to give you the present I brought you.'

'What?'

The question was apparently enough of an invitation to spur the shict into action. She snapped her arm, sending a brown, multilimbed body into Asper's lap. The priestess looked down at the gohmn, aghast; it was browned from cooking and, if the sticky substance dripping onto her legs was any indication, basted in something of origins she fiercely fought the urge to inquire over.

Instead, she merely scowled up, her distaste compounded as the shict brought a barbed roach leg to her teeth and tore a tough chunk from it.

'Like venison,' she said with a grin, her teeth white against the brown smear on her mouth, 'except a tad roachier.'

'I'm ...' *'Leaving' would be a good thing to say*, Asper thought, *or 'furious' or 'about to strangle you.'* 'Not hungry.'

'Eat while you can,' Kataria said. 'You don't know how much you'll miss basted bug meat when there's no room for them on the boat.'

'There's a boat?' Asper asked, eyes widening. 'Sebast! He's all right? He's come?'

'No, no,' Kataria said, shaking her head. 'Togu is lending us one to take back to the mainland ... well, *giving* us one, since we can't bring it back, obviously. We'll set out tomorrow, Lenk says, after the party tonight.'

'There's a party now?'

'A farewell celebration, I guess? Togu was insistent on it, so we figured it'd be less irritating to simply glut ourselves tonight and spend tomorrow defecating over the railing than arguing about it today.'

'How ... pleasant,' Asper said, blanching. 'Why would he be insistent?'

'Neediness, maybe? Loneliness? A fierce desire to see half-clad pink skin instead of half-clad green skin?' Kataria growled, taking another bite from the leg. 'How am I supposed to know what goes on inside a lizardman's head?'

'Well, are they at least going to give us back our clothes?' Asper asked, gesturing to the aforementioned pink skin. 'If it's a choice between coming back to the mainland dressed like *this* or staying here …' She paused and frowned. 'I suppose drowning would be preferable.'

'I feel like you're worrying a lot about trivial things,' Kataria said, licking the bug juices from her lips. 'It's quite annoying. You're starting to sound like Lenk.'

Asper went rigid, fixing a hard stare on Kataria.

'What,' she asked, 'do you mean by that?'

'Nothing,' Kataria replied, canting her head to the side. 'I'm merely suggesting that you're being overly stupid about things that don't matter and very rude when I bartered, slaughtered, cooked and slathered a twitching roach for you.' She sneered. 'You're welcome, by the way.'

'There are *just* enough things offensive about that sentence that I don't feel bad for it.' Asper rose up, futilely trying to wipe the juices from her skin. 'Or for leaving. Good day.'

She fought the urge to recoil as the shict leapt in front of her, but could do nothing to prevent the sudden beating of her heart. Kataria's muscles tensed as she regarded the priestess with an unflinching stare.

She heard me, Asper thought. *She heard me ask if I should kill Lenk. She heard me. And now she's going to …* Asper's face screwed up in confusion as the shict's softened, her green eyes quivering. *Cry?*

It certainly looked that way, at least. The savage humour, the feral grin, the bloodlust always lurking: all evaporated in an instant. Kataria's mouth quivered wordlessly, fumbling for words to defeat this expression to no avail as she rubbed her foot self-consciously upon the moist earth.

Asper found herself unable to leave for the painful familiarity of it all. She hadn't seen such a display since …

Since I saw myself in the river today.

'I need …' Kataria spoke hesitantly, shaking her head and summoning up a growl. 'I *want* to talk.'

'Oh.' Asper glanced over the shict's shoulder. 'Lenk went into the forest, last I saw.'

'*Not to Lenk*,' Kataria snarled suddenly, then clenched her teeth, as though it pained her to spoke. 'To you.'

'What?' Asper looked incredulous. 'What did *I* do?'

'What is that supposed to mean? I just … I want that thing that priests do.'

'The last time I tried to bless you, you *bit* me.'

'I don't want that. I want the other thing; the one where we talk.'

Asper looked at her curiously. 'Confession?'

'Yeah, that.' Kataria nodded. 'How's it work?'

'Well, with people of the same faith with something they seek atonement for, we usually sit down, they tell me their sins or their problem, and I listen and help if I can.'

'Yes, yes!' Kataria's nod became one of vicious enthusiasm. 'We need to do that!'

'I'm not sure it's—'

'*Immediately!*'

'Look, we're not even of the same faith!' Asper replied hotly. 'Besides, your problems always seem to be the kind that are solved by shooting someone in the eye. What makes this one so special?'

'*Fine, then*,' Kataria spat as she turned away. 'I'll figure it out myself, *as usual.*'

The shict's impending departure should have been a

relief, Asper knew. After all, any problems Kataria was like to share were equally likely to be foul, unpleasant and possibly involving the marking of territory.

And yet, she couldn't help but catch a glimpse of Kataria's face as she turned away. A choked expression, confused, lost.

The shict had a question without an answer.

And the priestess had an oath.

'Wait a moment.' Her own words should have been a worry, Asper knew, but she forced a smile. 'I can listen, at the very least.'

Kataria turned and stared as Asper took a seat upon a patch of moss, gesturing to the earth before her. With a stiff nod, Kataria took a hesitant seat before her. For an age, they simply sat, staring at each other with eyes intent and befuddled respectively. After waiting long past what would be considered polite, Asper cleared her throat.

'So,' she said, 'what did you want to—?'

'This is supposed to be anonymous,' Kataria interrupted, 'isn't it?'

'What?'

'I thought there were curtains or something.'

'In a proper temple, yes,' Asper replied. 'But ... look, even disregarding the fact that we're in a forest, disregarding the fact that *you* asked *me* to do this, I've known you for a *year* now. Kat, I know you by voice and by smell both.'

'What *I* smell is a loss of principles,' Kataria replied, far more haughtily than someone clutching a roach leg should be able to. 'And you, my friend, are *reeking*.'

'Oh Gods, *fine!*' Asper loosed a low grumble as she shifted about in the earth, turning her back to Kataria. 'There, is that better?'

A sudden jolt was her answer as Kataria pressed her own back against the priestess'.

'Sort of.' The shict's hum reverberated into Asper. 'Is there any way you could do this in a different voice so—'

'No.'

'Fine.'

The shict's snarl was the last noise she made for a long moment. In the silence that followed, it occurred to Asper with some mild dismay that she had never actually wondered what her companion felt like. She had always suspected that Kataria would be more relaxed, her muscles loose and breath coming in slow and easy gulps of air.

Someone who cuts wind with as much abandon as she does would have *to be relaxed, right?*

But there was nothing but tension in the shict's body. Not the kind of nervous tremble of dismay at having another woman's bare flesh touching her own that now enveloped Asper, Kataria's tension was muscle-deep, her entire body feeling like she had been twisted so tightly that she might explode in a bloody, stressful mess at any moment.

One more regret for ever having agreed to this, Asper thought.

'So, did you want to talk about?'

'What's it like?' Kataria interrupted.

'What's what like?'

'Being a coward.'

'What?' Asper began to rise. 'Did you get me to sit down just so you could insult me? Because it seems like a lot of work for something you already do standing up.'

'Wait.' Kataria's hand shot out and wrapped with a desperate firmness about Asper's wrist, yanking the priestess back to the earth. 'I mean ... I've watched you. When we fight.' Her grip tightened. 'You're scared.'

Asper opened her mouth to retort, but found precious little to say by way of refuting the accusation, and even less to say to pull her hand back.

'I suppose,' she said, pressing her back up against the shict's again. 'It can be a frightening thing, combat.'

'But you don't run,' Kataria continued. 'You don't back away.'

'Neither do you,' Asper replied.

'Well, obviously. But it's different with me. I know how to fight. If I *can* kill it, and I usually can, I do kill it. If I can't kill it, and sometimes I can't, I run away until I *can* kill it and then I come back, shoot it in the face, tear off its face and then wear its face as a hat … if I can.'

'Uh …'

'But *you*,' Kataria said, her body trembling. '*You* look so terrified, so uncertain … and really, sometimes, I'm uncertain when the fight breaks out. I don't know if you'll make it out of this one or that one and I expect you to run. I would, were I you.'

'But,' Asper said softly, 'you're not.'

'No, I'm not. I don't stick around if it's not certain.' The shict leaned back, sighing. 'It was all certain when I left the forest to follow Lenk, you know? I knew I couldn't stay there because I didn't know what was going to happen. But everyone knows what a monkey will do. Even one with silver fur just fights, screams, hoards gold and tries to convince himself he's not a monkey.'

'Fighting, screaming and hoarding gold is all we've done since we left on the *Riptide*,' Asper said. 'Come to think of it, it's all we've done since I met you.'

'So why doesn't it make *sense* anymore,' Kataria all but moaned as she slumped against the priestess' back. 'This was all so much *fun* when we started. But now we're just sitting around in furs, *talking* instead of killing people.'

'And ... that's bad?' Asper asked. 'I'm sorry, I really can't tell with you.'

'That's bad,' Kataria confirmed. 'I should be running.'

'But you're not.'

'And *why* am I not? Why don't *you* run when you feel like it?' The shict scratched herself contemplatively. 'Duty?'

She swallowed the question, and Asper wondered if Kataria could feel her own tension as it plummeted down to rest like an iron weight in her belly. Why *did* she stay? she wondered. Certainly not to protect her friends. *I need it more than they do.* To survive, then? *Maybe, but why get involved at all with them, then?* Duty?

That must be it.

Yeah, she told herself, *that's it. Duty to the Healer. That's why you fight ... that's why you kill. It's certainly not because you've got an arm that kills people that you can't possibly run away from. No, it's duty. Tell her that. Tell her it's duty and she'll say 'oh' and leave and then there will be two people who hate themselves and don't have answers and you won't be alone anymore.*

'Is it your god?' Kataria asked, snapping the priestess from her reverie. 'Does he command you to stay and fight?'

'Not exactly,' Asper replied hesitantly, the question settling uneasily on her ears. 'He asks that we heal the wounded and comfort the despairing. I suppose being on the battlefield lends itself well to that practice, no?'

Is that it, then? Are you meant to be here to help people? That's why you joined with them, isn't it? But then ... why do you have the arm?

'You have your own god, don't you?' Asper asked, if only to keep out of her own head. 'A goddess, anyway.'

'Riffid, yeah,' Kataria replied. 'But Riffid doesn't ask, Riffid doesn't command, Riffid doesn't give. She made the shicts and gave us instinct and that's it. We live or die by those instincts.'

And what of a god who gives you a curse? Asper asked herself. *Does he love or hate you, then?*

'So we don't have signs or omens or whatever. And I've never looked for them before,' Kataria continued with a sigh. 'I've never needed to. Instinct has told me whether I could or I couldn't. I've never had to look for a different answer.'

Is there a different answer? What else could there be, though? How many ways can you interpret a curse such as this? How many ways can you ask a god to explain why he made you able to kill, to remove *people completely, to your satisfaction?*

'So ... how do you do it?'

It took a moment for Asper to realise she had just been asked a question. 'Do what?'

'Know,' Kataria replied. 'How do you know what's supposed to happen if nothing tells you?'

How would a woman of faith know if her god doesn't tell her?

'I suppose,' Asper whispered softly, 'you just keep asking until someone answers.'

'That's what I'm *trying* to do,' Kataria said, pressing against Asper's back as she pressed her question. 'But you're not answering. What do I do?'

'About your instincts?'

'About *Lenk*, stupid!'

'Oh,' Asper said, blanching. 'Ew.'

'Ew?'

'Well ... yeah,' Asper replied. 'What about him? Do you like him or some—'

The question was suddenly bludgeoned from her mouth into a senseless cry of pain as something heavy cracked against her head. She cast a scowl over her shoulder to see Kataria resting the gohmn leg gently in her lap, not offering so much as a shrug in excuse.

'Did … did you just hit me with a roach leg?' the priestess demanded, rubbing her head.

'Yeah, I guess.'

'*Why* did you just hit me with a roach leg?'

'You were about to ask something dangerous,' Kataria replied casually. 'Shicts share an instinctual rapport with one another. We instantly know what's acceptable and unacceptable to speak about.'

'I'm *human!*'

'Hence the leg.'

'So you've graduated from insults to physical assault and you expect me to sit here and listen to whatever lunacy you spew out? What happens next, then? Don't tell me.' She started to rise again. 'How many times have *you* been hit in the head today?'

Kataria's grip was weak, her voice soft when she took Asper by the wrist and spoke. Asper could feel the tension in her body slacken, as though something inside her had clenched to the point of snapping. It was this that made the priestess hesitate.

'I'm asking you to listen,' the shict whispered, 'so that I don't find out what happens next.'

Uncertain as to whether that was a threat or not, Asper settled back into her seat and tried to ignore the feeling of the shict's tension.

'The thing is, we're not even supposed to *talk* to humans,' Kataria explained. 'We only learn your language so we can know what you're plotting next. Originally, I thought that being amongst your kind would be a good way to find that out.' She sighed. 'Of course, within a week, it became clear that no one really had anything all that interesting going on in their head.'

Asper nodded; an insult to her entire race was slightly more tolerable than an insult to her person, at least.

'I should have run, then,' Kataria said. 'I should be running now ... Why am I not?'

'Is it' – Asper winced, bracing for another blow – 'just Lenk that's keeping you here?'

'I protected him today,' the shict said, a weak chuckle clawing its way out of her mouth. 'He was going into one of his fits, so I stepped forward and did the talking. I *protected* a human.'

'You've done that before, haven't you?'

'I've killed something that might have killed a human before, but I never did ... whatever it was I did,' Kataria said. 'He just needed help and I ...'

'Uh-huh,' Asper said after the shict's voice had trailed off. 'And you did it because of his ... fits did you call them?'

'Have you noticed them?'

Asper closed her eyes, drawing in a deep breath. She wondered if Kataria could feel her tension growing, if she could feel the chill racking her body.

Fits, she thought to herself. *I have noticed no fits. I have noticed what Denaos whispers, how he accuses Lenk of going mad, slowly. I have noticed the emptiness of Lenk's eyes, the death in his voice, the words he spoke.*

'Tell me,' Asper said softly, the words finding their way to her lips of their own accord. 'Do you listen to your instincts?'

'Of course.'

'Even when they tell you something you don't want to hear?'

'What do you mean?'

'Let's talk about Lenk for a moment.'

'All right,' Kataria replied hesitantly.

'We don't know where he came from aside from a village no one's heard of, we don't know who his parents are, what his lineage is or even where he got his sword.'

'That's not fair,' Kataria protested. 'Even *he* doesn't know that.'

'And does he know who taught him to fight?'

'What?'

'I learned from the priests, Dreadaeleon was taught by his master, even Denaos likely learned all that he knows from someone,' Asper pressed. 'Who taught you to fire a bow? To track?'

Kataria's body tensed up again, the kind of nervous tension that Asper had felt many times before. Uncertainty, doubt, fear. It ached more than she thought it might to put Kataria through them. But her duty, too, was clearer than she thought it might be.

'My mother,' Kataria said. 'But what—?'

'Have you ever known,' Asper spoke silently, 'anyone who fights, who kills as naturally as Lenk does?' At Kataria's silence, she pressed her back against her. 'Have you seen him after he kills?'

Her question was not delivered with the cold, calculating tone she thought would be befitting. It was choked, quavering, but she could hardly help it. The realisations were only coming to her now, with swift and sudden horror. But perhaps that wasn't so bad, she reasoned; perhaps Kataria would be comforted to know someone shared her plight, someone that was trying to help her.

And she *would* help the shict, she resolved. Helping people, regardless of what kind of people they were. That was why she had taken her oaths.

'I … I have,' Kataria replied with such hesitation that Asper knew the same images filled her head.

'I've seen everyone kill,' Asper whispered. 'I forced myself to, to know how it was done, if … if I ever had to. Denaos boasts, you exult, Dreadaeleon pauses to breathe, even Gariath took the time to snort. But Lenk … does nothing. He says nothing, he doesn't react, but he looks … he looks …' The dread came off her tongue. 'Satisfied. Whole.'

She could feel Kataria tremble, or perhaps that was herself, for she frightened herself as much as she tried to frighten her companion. But perhaps both of them needed to be frightened, she reasoned, both of them needed to be scared in the face of this new realisation that, in the absence of any demon or longface, Lenk might be the greatest threat.

'Who looks like that?' she asked. 'What would make a man act like that?'

Trauma? Madness? Something else? Whatever plagued him, whatever threatened him, threatened them all, Asper knew. And as she felt Kataria tremble, felt her go limp against her back, she knew her friend knew it as well.

'Your instincts were confused,' Asper said softly. 'You wanted to run, as would anyone, but you want to help and only a few can say they would want that.'

But in this knowledge, Asper found peace, as demented as it sounded to her. In Kataria's sinking body, she found the urge to rise up. In her friend's suffering, she found a strength that allowed her to reach down and take Kataria's hand in her own, a strength that would carry her to the peace the priestess felt, a strength that would carry Lenk.

This was her purpose, her duty.

'And we will help him,' Asper said, giving her hand a gentle squeeze. 'It's not gods or instinct that make us do it.'

'Then what is it?' Kataria asked, her voice weak.

'You,' Asper said gently. 'You will do it, because you're in love.'

This was the moment she lived for, the moment that had been far too rare in coming lately. The face of a child told they would walk again, the exasperated gasp of a moments-old mother told their infant was healthy, the solemn nod and sad smile of a widow who heard the blessings said over her husband's grave.

And now, she thought, the embrace between races supposed to be enemies, the long road to helping a friend recover.

This was it.

This was her purpose.

This was why.

She released Kataria's hand and turned around. Her companion did not, at first, but she waited patiently. It would come slowly, with great difficulty. It always did, but the reward was always greater in coming. And so she waited, watching as Kataria tensed, as Kataria clutched the gohmn leg in trembling fingers, smiling.

She continued to smile.

Right up until the leg lashed out and caught her in the face with such force as to snap her head to the side.

'Wh-what?' she asked, recovering from the blow with a hand on an astonished expression. 'I didn't mean to say—'

'I'm not.'

The leg whipped out again, struck her in the side with more force than a leg should be able.

'Okay, you're not, but—'

'I'm not.'

Again it lashed out, found her elbow. It snapped, leaving a red mark upon Asper's flesh covered by the stain of its basting juice. She didn't even have time to form a reply before Kataria whirled, hurling what remained of the leg at her.

'I'm not.'

She lunged, took Asper by the shoulders and hurled her to the earth. No anger in her face, no sadness, no tears. Nothing but something cold and stony loomed over her, a face as hard as the fist that came down and cracked upon her cheek.

'I'm not, I'm not, I'm *not*, *I'm not*, *I'm not*, *I'm not*, *I'm not*—'

No protests from Asper, no denial but for the feeble defence she tried to muster, raising her hands to protect her face, futilely, as the shict blindly lashed out and struck her over and over, once for each word, each kiss of fist to face a confirmation, each bruise that blossomed a reality.

And then, it stopped, without gloating, without a reason, without even a noise. Asper heard the shict flee, heard her running with all the desperation one flees for their life with.

The sound faded into nothingness. The trees whispered as the sun began to set behind them. In the distance, toward the village, a whoop of celebration rose. Their feast was starting.

She should rise, she knew, and go to it. She should rise, even though her body was racked with pain. She should go, even though her legs felt dead and useless beneath her. She should see the others, even though her eyes were filled with tears. She should see them, they who had beaten her, lied to her, disparaged her faith and tried to throttle her.

She should.

But she could not think of a reason why.

ACT THREE

Feast among the Bones

Twenty-Six

WHISPERS IN DARK PLACES

The Aeons' Gate
The Island of Teji
Fall, early ... maybe?

Of my grandfather, I don't remember much. Of my father, even less. He was a farmer, a quiet man, always tithed. Even as I'm able to remember more here on Teji, that's roughly all I recall.

Well, that's not entirely true. I do remember what he said to me, once.

'There are two kinds of men in this world: those who live with war and those who can't live without it. We can live without it. We can live a long time.'

I remember he died in fire.

I had always wanted to believe I could live without war. Even after I picked up my grandfather's sword, I wanted to know of a time when I could put it down again. I had always wanted to say that this part of my life was something I did to survive and nothing more. I wanted to be able to tell my children that we could live without war.

I wanted children.

And for the past few days, I was certain I would have them and that I could tell them that.

Maybe I was wrong. Maybe father was wrong.

I tried. I really did. Khetashe knows how I did, how I tried not to think about my missing sword or the tome or that life I left at the bottom of the ocean. I tried to do this 'normal' thing, to be the kind of man who isn't obsessed with death – his or someone else's.

It's harder to do than I thought.

The bones are everywhere on Teji. I can't take a step outside the village without stubbing my toe on someone's bleached face. The reek of death is always present, and so the Owauku light fires to scare away the spirits. They survive off their roaches. The roaches thrive off the island's tubers. The tubers are the only edible growing things here.

And here, amidst the bones and the death, I thought I would become normal. I thought this was where I could sit back and stare at the sunset and not worry over whether or not I was going to live tomorrow.

Days ago, I was ready to leave this life behind.

Maybe I was wrong.

Things are tense. It must be the water … the air … whichever one paranoia breeds in. Crooked stares meet me wherever I go. People go quiet when I pass. I hear them whisper as I leave.

The Owauku try to hide it, forcing big grins, friendly chatter before they slip away from my sight. The Gonwa aren't nearly so interested in my comfort. They stare, without shame, until I leave. They speak in their own tongue, in low murmurs, even as I stare at them. And now, they've started following me.

Or one has, anyway. Hongwe, they call him, the spokesman for the Gonwa. I don't know if he's been doing it for a while and I just caught on or what. But when I walk through the forest, down the beach, he follows me. He only leaves if I try to talk to him. And even then, he does so without excuse or apology.

Granted, if he were going to kill me, he probably wouldn't bother with either. But then, if he were going to kill me, he's been taking his time.

Teji is one of the few places I've been able to sleep soundly, without worry for the fact that my organs are almost entirely on display for stabbing. And I happen to know from the many, many times Bagagame has told me Hongwe's watched me sleep that the only thing standing between my kidneys and a knife is a thin strip of leather and a wall of reeds.

So far, he's done nothing. And as strange as it sounds, I'm not really that worried about a walking lizard that brazenly stalks me and possibly watches me sleep. One wouldn't think I'd have bigger concerns than that, but it would seem poor form to start questioning it now.

My companions ...

I don't think I've ever truly trusted them. Really, I've just been able to predict them up to this point. Their feelings are easy to see; their emotions are always apparent. And while I'm not a man who considers himself in touch with – or interested in – such things, I can tell that all of them are holding back something.

Dreadaeleon skulks around the edges of my periphery, almost as bad as Hongwe. I say 'almost' only because he spooks and flees the moment he even gets a whiff of me. I may have been harsh with him in the forest, but he's never ... well, rarely been this jittery before.

Denaos tells me, in passing, that Dread is going through some changes. That's about all he'll ever tell me. It's interesting: of all the sins I've tallied against Denaos, drunkenness was not one until now. If I don't speak to him before breakfast, I'll never understand him before the slurring, assuming he doesn't go spilling his innards in the bushes. Each time I try to talk to him, he's got an alcohol-fuelled excuse that I cannot argue against. It almost seems like he's planning each drunken snore, each incomprehensible rant. Or maybe he just likes his list of sins well rounded.

In such cases as this, Asper can usually provide insight, but she's been just as silent. And when I say silent, I mean exactly that. Dreadaeleon flees, Denaos drinks, Asper doesn't even look at me. I might get the occasional nod or rehearsed advice she's said to a hundred different grieving widows, but she won't look me in the eyes. I pressed her once; she screamed.

'Ask your stupid little shict if you're so Gods-damned concerned about everything! Pointy-eared little beast knows everything, anyway!'

'Humans, eh?' was the extent of Kataria's explanation when I did consult said beast. Of all of them, Kataria is the one who doesn't flee, who will look me in the eyes. I should be happy with this. But she's the most tense of all, even when she smiles. Especially when she smiles.

She seems at ease, but her ears are always high on her head. She's always alert, always listening to me just a bit too closely, waiting for me to say ... something.

She doesn't stare anymore.

I never thought I would be worried by that.

I never considered them honest, but I did consider them open. Some more than others. Sometimes I wonder if Gariath, and his constant threats, kept all our tension directed toward him. These bipedal lizards just don't have the same appeal that he has.

Sorry. Had.

If he's alive, he's not coming back. He's wanted to be rid of us for ages, so he said. Of course, he didn't seem to want to live very badly to begin with, so perhaps he's found a nice cliff to leap from. Either way, I hope he's happy.

I want them all to be happy. I do. I want them to be able to live without war. I want us to part ways and be able to forget that our best memories together were born in bloodshed.

And maybe it's up to me to help them with that. I am the leader, after all. I should be there for them, help them with this, no matter how drunk, skittish, silent or paranoid.

It won't be easy. For any of us, least of all me. I hear the voice. Not always, not often, but I know it's there. I'm likely the one man who shouldn't be looking into someone else's life.

But I can do this.

I can do this for all of us.

Tonight is Togu's celebration, a 'kampo', he calls it. It's something of a joint feast to herald the end of summer and remember the day humans came to their island with salvation from starvation. To hear the other Owauku speak of it, it's an excuse to drink fermented bug guts and rut.

Sounds like fun.

As good a time as any to gather everyone together, to tell them all that I've been thinking, to tell them what we can do, that we can live without war. From there? I suppose I'll find out.

Hope is not going to come easy.

But I can do this.

Twenty-Seven

AN INVITATION WITH FISTS

'*KAMPO!*'

The collective roar of jubilation rose from the village's valley into the night sky like an eruption from a volcano too long dormant.

The Owauku had come exploding out of their huts and lean-tos in waist-high green tides, setting bonfires alight to challenge the black sky overhead. Their drums had followed shortly after, pounding relentlessly without concern for rhythm. And, as though it were some honoured guest arriving to mark the official beginning of the festivities, the *mangwo* had been rolled out in tremendous hollowed-out gourds, dispensed into smaller cups for the patient. Those lizardmen not possessing such restraint simply buried their heads in the drink and came out barely alive but wholly satisfied.

Once Lenk had seen enough to know that he was quite annoyed by the whole affair, his attentions turned to the Gonwa. To a lizardman, they abstained from the merriment, keeping out of the paths of the exuberant Owauku, lingering near fires only long enough to cook gohmn. Against the throngs of their squat, joyous hosts, they stood in groups of three or five, with only three or five groups amongst them.

Only now, as he walked along the edge of the upper lip

of the valley, did Lenk truly notice how few and how silent they were.

'They aren't going to join?' he asked the brightly coloured creature to his side, gesturing to a nearby throng of Gonwa.

'The Gonwa come from Komga,' Togu explained. 'They have always had enough, so they don't think it cause to celebrate when you no longer have nothing.' He sniffed. 'Also, they're just *weird*.'

'Right, but weren't they invited? You said this was for *us*, didn't you?'

'That might have been a lie.'

'Might have been?'

'They get hard to keep track of when you have a position of authority,' Togu replied. 'You know … well, of course *you* know. You lead, don't you?'

'Yes, but I don't really lie.' Lenk's eyebrows rose appreciatively. 'Is that what I've been doing wrong?'

'Probably,' Togu said. 'At any rate, it's not a *complete* lie. This time twenty years ago, humans came to our starving island and brought with them all we needed to become what we are today: coin to collect, grains to make the gohmns grow strong …'

'*And all the brandy needed to forget when we didn't be havin' 'em!*' a passing Owauku cried out, to the roaring amusement of his companions.

'I've been curious,' Lenk said, glancing to the distant forest. 'If your forests are barren, how have you survived this long?'

'Barely,' Togu replied. 'Our numbers reached a point where we could subsist off of the occasional fish caught. But they swam so far from our shores that we could only bring back so many. We survived by starving.'

'Until the humans came.'

'Yes,' Togu continued, 'and the *Kampo* is here to remind us of what the humans have done for us, and to celebrate what we came from. In a way, it is a celebration of you.' He flashed a broad grin at the young man. 'Of course, there was some hope that you'd be smitten by our native charm and be convinced to stay and convince more humans to come.'

Lenk blinked, pondering if the intent fixation of both of the Owauku's eyes was supposed to be expectant, speculative or possibly slightly nauseous. Hedging his bets, he simply shrugged.

'Sorry,' he replied. 'We're hoping to leave tomorrow.' He glanced over the ledge, deeper in the valley, where he spied Denaos adding another half-gourd cup to a growing pile. 'Most of us, anyway. In fact, I was hoping to see the boat.'

'The boat?'

'The one you're lend ... giving us,' Lenk replied. 'If I can figure out how it works now, it'll save the time of learning it tomorrow.'

'Of course ... tomorrow ...' Togu waddled to the edge and stared down at the jubilant masses. 'My people have forgotten the word, it sometimes seems. A few down there likely remember the barren forests we came from, but they have plenty now, so why should they remember?' He sighed deeply, and then looked to Lenk. 'Have you ever had this problem in your position? Sparing your friends the harshness so that they might continue to laugh and smile?'

'As far as most of them are concerned, the laughing and smiling tends to come from killing, which in turn seems to come from being honest,' Lenk replied, shrugging. 'But that's killing. It's done when it needs to be done.'

488

'And you leave Teji? Will you not return to more killing?'

'I don't plan on it. I've seen plenty of it.'

'I see ...' Togu said, looking back down at his people. 'You would say it is fair, then, to avoid spilling blood when need be?'

'I would say,' Lenk replied slowly, 'that bloodshed is something that gets very tiring, quickly. If it's at all possible to live without it, I don't think it's a ridiculous idea.' He offered a weak smile. 'So can't some things just come without it?'

He laughed a vacant laugh. Somehow, he didn't feel quite convinced by his own words.

'I am glad you see things that way,' Togu said, bobbing his head as he turned about and began heading back up the valley's edge toward his stone hut. 'Apologies, cousin. The *Kampo* is tiring to people in my position. I will see you at the end of it all.'

Lenk nodded stiffly. Somehow, Togu didn't sound convinced, either.

It was quickly forgotten, however, as he watched Togu fight against the tide of Owauku pouring into the deeper levels of the valley. The king's words lingered in his ears, the uncertainty in them infecting his thoughts.

He wasn't much of a liar, he admitted to himself. Honesty had been bred into him. But when it came to his companions, it was really more a matter of practicality; lying to them simply wasn't feasible.

Asper had taken enough confessionals to know them before they even began. Dreadaeleon asked too many questions for any to hold up against him. Gariath claimed to be able to smell lies and proved to be able to beat the truth out of people he suspected it of. Denaos would hear them, nod slowly, and then grin knowingly. And Kataria …

She believes you, he told himself. *She follows you, anyway, doesn't she? The others threaten to leave if they don't get their way and you tell them you don't care if they do and that's the truth. But she's never tried to leave …*

He swallowed hard. His mouth felt dry. The bonfires were suddenly unbearably warm.

'*So what are you going to tell her when she does?*'

'Hey!'

He turned and saw her wading through the green herds towards him. He blinked.

'Hey,' he replied.

'*Not as earth-shattering as you'd hoped, is it?*'

'I thought you'd be with the others,' Kataria said, stepping over a staggering, laughing Owauku.

'Probably not a good idea,' Lenk said, glancing down to the pink shapes in the valley below. 'They …'

'*What are you going to tell her? That they looked at you like she* does *and you wanted to strangle them?*'

'Annoyed me.'

'*Not quite honest, but that hardly matters.*'

'I'm sure you could join them, though,' he offered, ignoring the voice.

She shook her head. 'Asper and I had a disagreement.'

'What kind of disagreement?'

'I beat her with a roach leg.'

'Ah.'

Through the din of festivities rising from the valley, a silence hung between them that felt unfamiliar. Even amongst the roiling green stew below, even as she stood beside him, he could not help but feel as though he were alone.

'*A thought occurs.*'

Almost alone, anyway.

'*Why bother telling her anything? Is that not how all your problems start?*'

I can't deal with you right now.

'*Why not simply enjoy the celebration? Can't some things come without strife?*'

I ... suppose that makes sense.

'*You said it yourself, did you not?*'

I did. It made sense, then, too. He smiled. *I should relax, shouldn't I?*

A cold wind swept over the ridge.

'*Idiocy.*'

He trembled at the sudden chill. That her hand then fell upon his shoulder should have stopped such a quaking, he knew, yet it didn't. Not until he turned and looked into her eyes.

After that, he felt himself about to shudder, shatter and fall apart.

There was a certainty in her stare that pained him to see. In her eyes was reflected that which he had feared, that thought that had consumed him since morning. She stared at him with a knowledge of who she was, *what* she was.

She knew how this was going to end.

He knew it now, too.

'Hey,' she said again.

'Hey,' he replied.

He waited for the confirmation, the declaration as to how it would all happen, how it would all end. He braced himself, wondering if it might be easier just to hurl himself off the ledge right now. She spoke.

'Let's get drunk.'

'Oh!' His eyes went a bit too wide for anything other

than tumbling screaming over a ridge. 'That's what you want to do.'

'Yeah.' She eyed him cautiously. 'What did you think I wanted?'

He glanced down into the throngs below. *Not too steep*, he noted. *Probably wouldn't have killed you, anyway, not with your luck.*

'Nothing,' he said, sighing. 'Let's go.'

'Huh …'

Asper had done many services for the Healer in her time, tending to the wounds of many different people. Absently, as she felt a pair of fingers prod the bruise under her cheek, she wondered if others felt as uncomfortable as she did when she tended to them.

'Yeah, this isn't anything to be particularly concerned about,' Denaos said, giving her cheek a light pat.

'She beat me with a basted leg from a giant bug,' Asper growled, slapping away his hand. 'How is that *not* worth concern?'

'She does a lot of things,' Dreadaeleon offered with a shrug. 'She spits, farts, snorts …'

'And I have a strong suspicion that she once left a steaming pile in my pack,' Denaos added.

'I liked that pack,' Dreadaeleon said.

'It will be missed.' the rogue replied, sighing. He glanced Asper over and took another sip from his half-gourd. 'At any rate, she wasn't *trying* to hurt you. I'd say she was likely pulling her punches, probably just to scare you.' He eyed her curiously. 'What'd you say to her, anyway?'

'Nothing that's worth repeating to someone who gives his medical opinion while drinking,' she replied sharply.

'It's not like there's a lot of other options.'

'Well,' Dreadaeleon said meekly, taking a step forward and extending trembling hands, 'I ... I could take a look, I suppose.'

'It's fine, thanks,' Asper said, waving his concern away.

'Well, no! I mean ... are you sure?' the boy asked, swallowing hard. 'It's not that much of a problem, really. I'm familiar with ...' His eyes quivered. 'Anatomy.'

'Yes, very familiar,' Denaos agreed. 'Particularly the relationship between fists and genitalia.'

'That's not—' The boy's anxiety boiled to ire as he whirled upon the rogue, glancing at his drink. 'That's what? Your fourth tonight?'

'Astute.'

'I think you have a problem.'

'I agree.' Denaos downed the last of the liquid and leaned in close to the boy, his words tumbling out on a tangy reek. 'Though I'm hoping that if I drink enough, you'll go away.'

'You *are* drinking quite a bit,' Asper said, furrowing her brow. 'How is it you're even still standing?'

'This stuff is tasty, indeed,' Denaos replied, smacking his lips, 'but not that rough to anyone who's ever drunk stronger than wine.' He cast a sidelong glare at Dreadaeleon. 'Or milk.'

'I've drunk before,' the boy protested.

'You had *one* sip of ale and started crying,' Denaos replied. 'Perhaps you should preserve your dignity now and flee before you find a sip of *this* stuff and add involuntary urination to the problem.'

Dreadaeleon somehow managed to find a healthy medium between fury and astonishment at the insult. Asper felt the passing – swiftly – urge to question the rogue's sudden and frequent interest in the boy's bladder, but something else about the tall man drew her attention.

He had made it clear from the moment she had met him that liquor was second on his list of great loves, wedged neatly between cheap prostitutes and portraits depicting expensive prostitutes. And he had taken great pains to make it clear that there was never any excuse for a rush when enjoying any of those three.

Thus to see him imbibe so, with such reckless desperation, made her pause.

'Why *are* you drinking so much, anyway?' she asked.

The swiftness with which he turned to regard her was not half as startling as the look upon his face. It lingered for only a breath longer, but she saw it clearly, the same slight slackening in his jaw, the same subtle sinking in his eyes.

And then, even swifter, it was gone, replaced with a grin too fierce to be convincing to either of them.

'It's a party, is it not?' he asked, laughing weakly. 'Who doesn't have fun at a party? Besides you, I mean.'

'I'm not having fun because of the fact that I was violently assaulted and I'm surrounded by drunks' – she paused and edged away from a flailing, cackling Owauku – 'of various sizes and pigments.'

'Perhaps you could try, possibly?' he suggested. 'I mean, before *too* long, you'll be back in cold temples, reciting stale vows and flagellating yourself whenever you even think of something mildly amusing. This might be your last chance to do something interesting.'

'Wait, what?' Dreadaeleon glanced at Asper, worry plain on his face. 'You're leaving?'

'What did you expect was going to happen when we reached the mainland?' Denaos answered before the priestess could.

'I don't know … find more work or something?' Dread-aeleon replied. 'That's what adventurers do, isn't it?'

'Adventurers take the opportunities they're given,' the rogue spat back. 'And given that only one of us has the opportunity and reputation to return to decent society, why wouldn't they take it?'

Asper made no response to the tall man beyond a look of intent scrutiny. There was something to his eyes, she thought, a quaver he sought to bury beneath snideness and sarcasm that continually dug its way out. It was as if the minute cracks to his visage had begun to spread, seeping into his voice, exposing something dire and desperate beneath.

'And what,' she asked him softly, 'will you do when we part ways, Denaos?'

She had barely expected to be heard through the din of drumming and raucous cheer that echoed off the valley walls. And yet the expression on his face made it quite clear that he had. It didn't so much crack as fall off in one great, pale sheet, leaving behind a wild, sunken stare and a long, sleepless face.

He merely stared at her, hollow, as though he weren't certain whether to search for words or a knife.

'I don't know,' he whispered.

His words were lost on the smoke of the fires, vanishing into the night air. And he, too, vanished, turning and staggering through the green jubilation. And she simply watched him go.

Against the chaotic festivities and imbibings in the valley, she was starkly aware of Dreadaeleon's impassiveness. And against his cold expression and folded arms, she was suddenly aware of her own furrowed brow and open mouth.

'You look calm,' she said with a hint of envy.

'Should I not be?' he asked, glancing over to her.

'You weren't at all … confused by what just happened?'

'A drunken lout is doing things drunken and loutish,' the boy said, shrugging. 'He'll wake up tomorrow with a headache and a desperate desire that we all forget what he said tonight. Shortly after that, we'll be back to hearing snideness, cynicism and sarcasm until his neurosis demands him to try and drown himself again.' He glanced over the woman's shoulder. 'Speaking of …'

She followed his gaze to a nearby puddle fed by a thin trickle of water, in which an Owauku was passed out face-down, a rapidly fading line of bubbles emerging. She made a move to rise up and help the creature, but Dreadaeleon's lips were quicker. At a muttered, alien word, the lizardman was flipped over by an invisible force and unceremoniously dropped on his back. Apparently heedless of the rough-ness, he looked up through eyes as bleary as those the size of fruits could be and grinned.

'Oh, *cousin*,' he burbled through liquor-stained teeth, 'someone loves me tonight.'

She couldn't help but smile at the boy. 'That was rather nice of you.'

'Oh,' he said, looking a little surprised. 'Yes, I suppose it was.'

'I thought wizards didn't waste power, though.'

'Well … he was probably going to die,' Dreadaeleon said, rubbing the back of his neck. 'I suppose we *could* have pulled him out ourselves, but by then he might have inhaled a lot of water and you'd feel compelled to give him the kiss of life and …'

'Ah,' she said, laughing. 'How noble of you to save me from having to mouth a lizard.' Her laugh faded, but her smile did not as she regarded him intently. 'How did you know?'

'I suspected that it was worth it to spare you having to resuscitate him and—'

'No, how do you *know*?' she interrupted. 'How are you always so sure?'

'What?' He cast her a baffled look. 'I'm not sure I—'

'Yes, you are,' she replied. 'You always are. You were certain that you could get us to shore when the ship was destroyed, you know Denaos will be fine, you knew you had to save that lizard ... how?'

He studied her intently and she suddenly understood that her face mirrored his own; somewhere, her expression had gone from smiling curiosity to careful scrutiny. His voice, however, bore none of the uncertainty of hers.

'Why,' he asked, 'do you wish to know?'

'Because I'm not sure,' she blurted out, the answer writhing on her tongue. 'I haven't been sure for a long time.' She glanced down at the earth. 'It wasn't always like this. I used to know, because the Gods had to know, and I was content with that.'

'I know you don't want to hear it,' Dreadaeleon replied, 'but I don't think you'll find any answers in gods. I don't think anyone ever has.'

She should have grown angry, indignant at that. Instead, she looked at him again and frowned. 'When did you first know?'

'What?'

'That you didn't believe in the Gods?'

'Ah,' he replied. Now he stared at the earth. 'About a year after I was indoctrinated into the Venarium. I was about eleven, then, my parents having said good-bye to me when I was ten.' He sighed. 'They were Karnerian immigrants to Muraska, strict followers of Daeon.'

'The Conqueror,' she said.

'Indeed. They raised me to believe that their horned god would descend one day, subjugate the Sainites and lay waste to the bestial races, ushering in a new age of progress for humanity. When I learned of my power by accidentally setting my bed on fire, my father wasn't furious, nor did he sing praises to Daeon. Instead, a week later, the man who would become my tutor took me away and my father had a thick pouch at his belt.'

'They *sold* you?'

'It's not an uncommon practice,' he replied. 'The Venarium has the right to demand children who show talent – to preserve the Laws, of course – but an incentive is offered for people who turn theirs in before it comes to hunting them down.'

'So it was then …'

'No. I was still saying my prayers as I practised my spells, not taking meals I hadn't earned, still cursing Sainites. It wasn't until my indoctrination …' He stared up at the sky. 'We all do a task with our mentors to realise our duties to the Venarium. Mine was to hunt down a heretic, someone who practises magic outside our influence.

'We learned he was a priest, a Daeonist, who had thought to put his talents to help his church: repairing roofs, warding off Sainites, that sort of thing. We tracked him down to his home and burst in, demanding that he come with us. He was weak, having no control over his powers had drained him. So his wife stepped before us, my master and I, and threw her arms out to stop us, saying we could not take him, that Daeon needed him.

'We followed protocol, of course. We cited precedent,

the agreement between the Venarium and all civilised nations to respect our Laws. After that, a verbal warning, and then finally, a demonstration of power.' His face grew hard, bitter. 'She refused to abide by all three.' His voice was a whisper. 'We ... I burned her alive.'

Asper stared at him intently. The shock in her gullet was choked by sympathy; she edged closer to him.

'So that did it?'

'That only made me wonder,' he replied. 'If a god did exist, and he did love us to the point that we would die for him ... why did my parents give me up so easily?'

When he had finished speaking, she saw him differently and was certain it was his face, and not her eyes, that had changed. By faith or nature, she strove to see him softer, more vulnerable. She scrutinised his eyes for moisture, but found only hardness. His body had become more rigid, as though it ate and found sustenance from his words as he folded his arms and stared past the crowds of lizardmen.

It was neither faith nor nature, she told herself, that made her reach out a hand and place it upon his shoulder.

'Have you ever ... told anyone else about this?'

She expected him to tremble, as he occasionally did in her presence. It was with utter calm that he turned to her, however.

'It is not a problem of the Venarium, hence not a problem of my mentor, hence no.'

'There are others to talk to, you know,' she offered.

'I find no solace in priests, obviously,' he replied coldly. 'And who amongst the others would listen, even if I wanted to talk to them?'

'Me?' she asked, smiling.

Now, he trembled, as though the thought were only occurring to him now. 'I ... already said about priests—'

'I'm also a friend,' she replied, her smiling fading as she glanced down. 'And I've been considering my position as to the Gods.' She awaited some considerate word, some phrase of understanding from him, perhaps even a little reassurance. When he merely stared blankly at her, she continued, regardless. 'It seems … sometimes that no one's listening. I mean, up there.

'Well, how could they, right? Even if you don't believe that the Gods watch over *everyone*, they're supposed to watch over their followers, aren't they? So how come I'm frequently surrounded by people obsessed with causing injuries that I'm supposed to cure? And half the time, they're inflicting said injuries on *me*. I've thought it over, wondered if this was just all a test, but what kind of test just doesn't end? And what about gods whose messages conflict with others'? If there are so many, and not all of them can be right, who is?'

She sighed, rubbed her eyes, heard him take in a deep, quivering breath.

'You've probably thought about this before, haven't you? I mean, maybe you've wondered if there was anything beyond just this. So, if anyone has some insight, I'd wager you—'

Empty space greeted her when she looked up, the boy vanished amidst the crowd.

'Do.'

No sigh followed; she was out of them, almost out of sources for answers, as well. She muttered angrily, reaching out and snatching a *mangwo*-filled gourd from a passing Owauku who scarcely noticed. She stared down at it with more thought than liquor likely deserved.

Almost, she told herself as she tipped her head back and drank, *but not yet.*

Feasts, fetes and parties were foggy memories in Lenk's mind. He could recall food, lights, people. He could not recall tastes, warmth, faces. Disturbing, he knew, cause for great alarm, but he could not bring himself to care. The world was without chill memories and cold fears. The bonfires burned brightly; the liquor had long since drowned any concern he had for the sweat peeling off his body and the loincloth precariously tied about his hips.

No sense in worrying about it, anyway, he thought. After the *Kampo*, he determined that no other parties would ever matter. Even if he could have remembered them, Steadbrook's humble festivities would be a world behind the Owauku's riots.

And, to hear from her, at least six worlds behind a shic-tish party.

'So, anyway,' Kataria said through a voice thick with re-strained giggling, 'there are pretty much only three things worth celebrating.' She counted them off on her fingers. 'Birth, death and raids.'

'Raids,' Lenk mused, his mind seeming to follow his tongue rather than the other way around. 'You typically kill humans during them, don't you?'

'Sometimes, and only because they're the most numerous. But Tulwar, too, and Vulgores, Couthi … well, not Couthi, anymore, obviously, but only because they had it coming.'

'So, you celebrate birth, death … and more death?'

'If you want to dumb it down like a dumb … dumb, yeah,' she grunted, slurring at the edges of her speech. 'But it's the whole *atmosphere* that makes it special. See, we bring back all the loot … er, reclamations back to camp and eat and drink and sing, *and* if there was one who was particularly bothersome, we drag his body back to camp – never alive, see – and make a *whitetree*. That's when we take them by their legs and … and …'

She looked up, the fierce glow of her green eyes a contrast to the sheepish smile she shot him.

'It's a tradition,' she said, chuckling. 'Even if it is violent, you aren't in any place to pass judgement.'

'I never did,' he replied, offering a grin of his own.

'Yeah, but you were thinking it.' She made to step closer and wound up nearly toppling over, her face a hairsbreadth from his. 'I know. I can smell your brains.'

That statement, at the moment, was the least offensive thing about her and, no matter what she smelled, brains certainly weren't what filled Lenk's nose. Her breath reeked of liquor, roiling out from between her teeth in a great cloud. This was challenged only by the smoky odour of her body, her usual musk complemented by the copious amounts of sweat painting her flesh.

He was not intoxicated, not by the sight or scent of her, at least. His fifth empty cup lay in the sand behind him, forgotten and neglected. His head was swimming, his body quivering; it felt as though the *mangwo* coursed through his veins. Drums were still pounding, song still roaring, but the idea of crashing down onto the sand and waiting for the morning to come seemed quite appealing.

Or it had, anyway.

Her presence invited a quick and ruthless sobriety. It was not likely that she could smell his brains anymore, since he could feel them threatening to leak out of his ears as she swayed closer to him. Thought faded, leaving all focus for sight and sound … and smell.

The firelight bathed her sweat-slick skin in gold, battling the pervasive moonlight's determination to paint her silver, both defeated by the smudges of earth and mud that smeared her pale skin from where she had fallen more than a few times. Her breath was an omnisensed affront: a reeking, heavy, warm cloud. Her smile was bright, sharp, lazy like a sated predator. The typical sharp scrutiny of her eyes was smothered beneath heavy lids. Her belly trembled, a belch rising up out of her mouth. He blinked, stared, heard, smelled.

Arousal, he reasoned, was possibly the *least* sane, and – given his attire – most awkward, response imaginable.

It hurt, if only slightly, to take a step back.

'So,' he said, 'do you miss it?'

'Miss what?' she asked with a sneer. 'My family? My people?' She raised a brow. 'Or the killing?'

'Is that all you have to go back to?'

She turned her frown away and asked the ground instead of him. 'What else is there?'

'Other things.'

'Oh yeah?' she asked. 'What is it you're going back to?'

A good question, he thought, as he stared at her. He had no family to go back to, and while, technically, his 'people' were in no short supply, he had no particular group of humans he wished to call by that name. She stared at him expectantly, as though waiting for his eyes to offer an answer his lips could not.

'To a place where I don't have to kill anymore.'

Her expression was unreadable. It might have been, anyway, if he had been staring at it. Instead he met her eyes, the same eyes that he had squirmed under, that he had shouted at her over, that he had turned away from, feeling the chills that followed the stare, hearing the voice that followed the chills.

Turn away now, he told himself. *Better to not know her*

answer. Even if she doesn't kill you right now, even if she doesn't say she'll go back to the killing even after all of this, you can't live with this. Not the staring. Not the question if she ever really means what she's going to say. You can't live with this, just as she can't live without the killing. Better to turn away now.

Drums thundered. Her ears twitched. She didn't blink.

Better to turn away.

Fires smouldered. He breathed deeply. He stared back.

Turn away.

Her lips twitched. He held his breath.

She smiled at him.

All at once, heat seemed to return to him, his blood turning to *mangwo* again. He smiled back, strained to smile harder than she was, to show her he felt the same as her. Of course, he thought, if he could read past the pained smile and know exactly *what* she was feeling, that would have been helpful, too, but he resolved to make do with what he knew.

He knew he wanted this bloodless moment, this voiceless silence, this stare he could not turn away from to last for the years to come.

And as he stared at her – at the sad, pitying smile she gave him – he knew he had only one more night.

'So!' she said swiftly, lids drooping, smile widening. 'Why aren't we still drinking?' *If that.*

'It's a party, right?' she asked with a quavering laugh. 'We're going to be at sea for who knows how long by to-morrow. Best not think about anything but tonight, right?' She jerked a nod on his behalf. 'Of course right.'

He said nothing as he followed her farther over the ridge, her eyes furtively searching for any sign of the drink. Any drop visible, however, was fast disappearing down gaping, green gullets. He noticed that her ire seemed to rise with every moment her lips were left dry, a growl rumbling through her body. He could almost see the hackles rise on her naked back.

Denaos was probably right, you know, he told himself. *She thrives on the violence. She can't even go this long without getting angry. How long could you possibly take that in? It's the right decision, then. Say nothing. Try not to even think about her. That's wisest.*

It occurred to him, not for the first time, that he rarely took the wisest course of action. And as he walked behind her, eyes drawn to her slender, sweat-kissed back, he began to develop a theory as to why that was.

Desperate to turn his attention to anything else, he glanced at the rapidly thinning throngs of various green bodies. The lizardmen were vanishing, either collapsing into dark corners or wandering off, leaving only the echoes of their laughter and their aromas behind.

'Where the hell are all of them even going?' he muttered to no one. 'Is … is it us? Do we smell or something?'

'Who knows?' she said, chuckling. 'Maybe there's some ancient code of conduct for drinking with lizard-things that we're not adhering to.'

'Of course. Maybe if we ate insects we'd be fine.'

She laughed a long, obnoxious laugh. The very same noise that he had once loathed now put him at ease. Whatever he might be feeling, all the tragic and inconceivable thoughts he might have, she felt none of them. That much was clear by the ease with which she carried herself around him, how swift she was to laugh, how very much unlike him she appeared to be.

Good, he thought, glancing at a nearby fire, *that's good. If she's not feeling anything, then there's nothing to talk about. I mean, if she was going to feel anything, she would have done it with a lot of drink, wouldn't she? The worst is behind you, my friend. Well done. Well done, ind—*

His brief self-congratulatory mood was quashed the moment he collided with her. She had turned about, regarding him with an intent stare. Enraptured, he was only aware of their proximity as he felt their sweat mingle between their skin, the rise of her belly pressing against his as she breathed deeply. His pulse raced, far too swiftly for him to feel hers, as blood quickened through his body.

'Sorry,' he muttered and moved to step away.

He hadn't made it another step before she lashed out her hands and seized him. The blood had rushed out of his head, leaving him far too slow-witted to realise what was happening, let alone resist it. Her nails sank into his skin with predatory possessiveness as she drew him against her body and leaned out to press her lips against his.

There was no patience in her embrace, no sense of tact and certainly no hesitation. Her tongue slid past his lips in hasty, urgent fury. His thoughts were left far behind as his senses raced ahead on a thundering heartbeat. He could taste the *mangwo* on her tongue, feel the need in her breath and hear the growl that welled up inside her, quaking through her body and into his.

Breathless and blind, his mind finally caught up to his senses, barely conscious of what was happening. By the time he realised it, however, his body had already acted. His arm had snaked around her, feeling the tension in her as he pulled her close. His hand had woven into her locks, pressing her lips farther against his, and a feral need that he hadn't even realised was inside him burst out through his mouth. It matched her vigour, matched his pain, fingers clenching her hair where hers sank into his skin, drawing her firmly against him as she pulled at him with animal fury.

And when he finally had the space to think, it was without words: a short, fleeting sense of overwhelming satiation that threatened to bring him to his knees.

And it was made all the shorter when her hands snaked out, parting from his skin in an instant to come up between them. His chest nearly ruptured against the force with which she shoved him, sending him toppling upon his rear to the sand. He stared up, agog and slack-jawed, only to find the same expression staring back at him.

'Hey,' she said softly. 'Sorry about that.'

'No, it wasn't—'

'It was,' she interrupted, shaking her head. 'It … it really, really was. Sorry. Sorry.' Her face contorted in agony as she whirled about, fleeing past the throngs of lizardmen, past the smouldering fires, into the night. 'Damn, damn, damn, damn …'

And he, sitting on his rear, staring at the darkness into which she had vanished, finally found the time to think.

Well done, indeed.

'Not fair, not fair, not fair.'

Dreadaeleon's words churned into his mouth on acrid bile. His breath was clogged with the taste of acid; his mouth felt packed with a tongue twice its actual size. With every step he took as he scurried behind Togu's stone house, his stomach pulled its knot a little tighter.

And he still spoke.

'She was about to … about to …' He collapsed beside the hut's wall, gasping for air as he felt the nausea roil in his throat. 'About to do *something*. And now this happens? *NOW?*'

His indignation was punished with a painful clench within his belly that sent his hands to the earth, his mouth gaping open with a retching noise that stripped his throat. Something was brewing inside him, fighting its way through his knotted stomach with thick, sticky fists. His eyes bulged, blinded by tears. His jaw craned open, stretched painfully wide in anticipation of what clawed its way out of his throat.

The vomit came out on a gargling howl, tearing itself free to douse the nearby shrubbery. Dreadaeleon knew not how long it lasted; his attention was focused on keeping all other orifices shut.

It did end, however, and Dreadaeleon lay gasping on the sand, the bile dripping past his lips to pool on the earth. The pain subsided in diminishing throbs, but not slowly enough to spare him from his own thoughts and his regrets and his anger.

This was something to be worried about. This was something to be terrified about. These reactions were not normal, not to anyone not suffering the Decay. Now was a time for prudent thought, careful concern. At any rate, he certainly shouldn't have felt the rage that he did.

But he had been so *close*.

It had been a graceless exit, naturally; there was no graceful way to run away to spill one's intestines out on the earth. He would have very much liked to have stayed, to discuss philosophy with Asper. She had been so open, enough to make him open, as well. He had told no one of his parents, of his initiation into the Venarium. She had listened so thoughtfully; she had looked at him so eagerly; she had *touched* him. He could still feel her fingers on his shoulder.

And then he had gone and ruined it all. She loathed him now, he was certain. How could she not? She had reached out to him, he had bared his past to her, and when she sought answers, when she recognised that *he* had them, he had run away to paint the shrubbery with his supper.

It was better that she *hadn't* seen that, of course, but not by much.

He would have spared himself more thought for self-loathing if not for the pungent scent of smoke drifting up to his nostrils. He glanced up at what had started as shrubbery, now resembling some sort of half-digested salad. His vomit was hungrily chewing on it with a thousand tiny, semiliquid mouths, belching steam with every moment it reduced the plant to a brown, messy blob.

Suddenly, the days of fiery urine seemed not quite so bad.

His condition was worsening.

Whatever offences he might have committed were forgotten as that phrase echoed in his head. His body was acting, amplifying its functions, functions that should not *be* amplified, of its own accord. It had likely been that little display in the valley, pulling the Owauku from the puddle, that had done it. It was a stupid thing to do, he reminded himself.

But she had been so impressed . . .

A small compensation. Too small. As he struggled to rise, he found his muscles weak, even weaker than they had been moments before. His magic was going awry, applying itself to all his bodily functions, and he paid for it as he paid for any other exertion of power. Of course, flashes of lightning and fire were far more impressive than flaming urine and acidic vomit.

The stone . . . he had to retrieve it.

A violation of Laws, perhaps, but there was no other option. It was the stone of the longfaces – that chipped, red sphere – that had kept his body in check, that had kept it from being overwhelmed. He had to retrieve it; he had to return to the sea, search the wreckage, find the damn thing and return to normal.

But how? More scrying would mean more magic. More magic would kill him sooner than later, it was becoming clear.

Voices burbled out of the hut.

Togu.

Of course, he thought as he staggered toward the door. He would beseech the king, convince his companions to delay the voyage. He *needed* the stone; they didn't need to know why beyond the fact that it gave him the power to move their ship. The lizardmen had trawled the sea for their belongings and found nothing, Togu had said, but that simply meant they weren't looking *hard* enough. He could convince them. He could *force* them.

He would have believed it, too, if he hadn't paused outside the king's door to retch again.

'What was that?'

He pulled himself up from his spewing, holding his nausea-soaked breath at the sound of voices burbling out of the king's hut.

'There is someone out there,' Togu's deep voice spoke.

'Soon to be many more,' another voice replied, a lilting, lyrical phrase that flooded into Dreadaeleon's ears on a song that would be soothing if the recognition didn't shock him into wide-eyed silence.

Greenhair, he thought. *The siren ... here?*

'The longfaces have just arrived, Togu,' she continued from within the hut, 'ahead of their master. He will arrive shortly and he will expect you to be there to greet him with the human offering.'

'They haven't arrived yet, Togu,' another voice, this one

gruff and hissing, spoke. 'There is still time to avert this. The forests are dense and the longfaces are not given to caution. You can flee.'

'And they will burn the forests down,' Greenhair replied sharply. 'They *will* find you, Togu, one way or another. Embracing this way means that your people live. Hongwe *should* understand this better than even I.'

'I do understand this,' the speaker identified as Hongwe snarled, 'and that is why I know what it is you're sending the humans to. I saw it happen on Komga, to *my* people. I will not watch you do this to others.'

'You intend to stop this?' Greenhair's voice contained an edge of harmonious threat.

Hongwe muttered in return. 'They are your people, Togu. I can only ask that you see the stupid villainy in this plan.'

Dreadaeleon, heedless of the vomit hissing on the sand or the lancing pain in his stomach, held his breath, listening intently to the long silence that followed. In the valley below, the sound of drums were dimming, the noises of jubilation quieting. In the quiescence, Dreadaeleon could hear the king's body rise and fall with the force of his sigh.

'I do what is best for my people. Do as you must to make the humans ready to give to the longfaces.'

Dreadaeleon turned, bit back a shriek as he stepped in the pile of his sizzling bile, dragged his foot on the earth as he made to run down as fast as his cramping body would allow him. The pain shot through him in great spikes that he forced himself to ignore. He had to get below, to warn his companions, or at least one of them.

He collided suddenly with a bare chest and looked up, frowning. This wasn't the one he had hoped for, but still ...

'Denaos,' he gasped, 'we have to get below. Togu, he's—'

'Who cares?' the rogue asked, on a reeking chuckle that sent him swaying. 'Who gives a flying turd what's going to happen anymore?'

He wasn't sure how much the tall man had actually drunk to push him over the edge and he hardly cared. The man's only purpose now was to perhaps stall Togu and his conspirators when they emerged. Thus, Dreadaeleon wasted no more words and tried to push his way past, only to find a long arm in his path.

'You don't see what's going to happen, do you?' Denaos said, laughing. 'Not as smart as you thought you were, huh? Can't see we're all damned without Asper following us, without the Gods on our side.'

'No one's following anyone if you don't get out of the way,' Dreadaeleon growled. 'The longfaces are—'

'I said *who cares?*' Denaos emphasised the question with a hook that sent the boy sprawling to the earth. 'Don't feel bad, Dread. I'll be punished for that. For a hell of a lot more.' He held a hand to his temple, pointing to eyes that had gone from sunken to two fevered, black-lined pits. 'I can't ... I can't stop *seeing* her. The whispering just doesn't stop. I thought it was the demon, but ... but it's something inside me. Something *I* did, can't you see?'

'I can't, and I don't care,' Dreadaeleon's words were laced with wincing whines as he struggled to regain his feet. 'I ... I'm having a hard time moving. Denaos. You have to get down there and warn the others that—'

'Not important,' Denaos replied. 'Asper's leaving. She was going to hear my sins, tell me it was fine, but not yet, not now. She'd never forgive me now. Neither would They.' He pointed to the sky. 'Whatever happens now is just ... just ...'

As his voice crumbled on his tongue, the music sliding through them could be heard. He recognised the siren's song in the same instant that Denaos did not. One clapped his hands over his ears; the other collapsed to the earth. Dreadaeleon spared a glance for his fallen companion before looking up as he felt a presence beside him.

Greenhair's alien expression was indifference laid thick to try to choke the pity in her eyes, to no avail. Dreadaeleon shot back a scowl intent on conveying all the curses and venom his mouth could not produce. The siren said something he dared not hear; an apology, perhaps, or a brief explanation, or an insult.

Though whatever she said could have only been half as insulting as the fact that she turned from him as she might a gnat and strode away, towards the mouth of the valley.

He snarled, reached out a hand to wrap about her pale ankle and pull her back, only to find the reason for her disregard. No sooner had his fingers stretched out than they were forced to clench. The pain that ripped through him was extraordinary, bludgeoning breath from his lungs, tearing vigour from his body, sending blood from his head as though it were split open. He collapsed into a quivering, curled position on the ground, unable to form even a sentence through the agony.

Through eyes vanishing into darkness, he stared at Greenhair as she walked down the valley, toward his companions, leaving him coiled in a pile of his own uselessness.

Drums dying with leathery gasps. Unseen liquor vapours wafting out on snores. Gohmns chittering to each other in the night.

'So loud,' she whispered, clawing at her ears.

Futility. Trees groaning, shedding leaves. Rivers muttering curses to those who defecated in them. Gonwa jaws clenching together in ire.

'Shut up,' she fervently whimpered, 'shut up, shut up, shut up.'

The sounds were impossible to tune out, impossible to ignore. Every last one rang angrily in her ears, the soft ones intolerably loud, the moderate ones deafening. She couldn't hear her thoughts, couldn't hear her tell herself to breathe, couldn't hear herself chant over and over.

'It'll pass,' she was barely aware of telling herself, 'it'll pass, it'll pass. It's just a symptom, just a symptom, just a symptom.'

It was a symptom, she confirmed to herself, a symptom of the round-eared disease. It had to be, she reassured herself, because it had come from *him*.

She cursed him, spewed a torrent of verbal venom into the sand as she trudged across it. She didn't hear her own curses. She hoped they were good ones.

It had been brewing all afternoon in her head, coming in flashes of clarity: a mutter of resentment from the bottom of the valley, a wistful sigh on the breeze, feet dragging heavily on sand exactly four-hundred and twenty-six paces away from her. The sounds, sounds usually too insignificant to be worth hearing, had reached her ears with crystalline clarity.

She hadn't worried when she had sat beside Asper, heard the twitches in the priestess' back and felt the blood flowing with ire, with fear, through her body. That was good. Humans were supposed to feel fear around shicts. Shicts were supposed to hear.

But then, Asper had taken her hand. Kataria had heard the muscles in her body relax, had felt the fear turn to

514

concern, the ire turn to some maladjusted form of affection. That was not good. Humans were not supposed to feel that. Shicts were not supposed to hear that. She was a shict. She had heard that.

And *that* was cause for worry, for violence. She hadn't regretted what she had done to the priestess. It was a natural response. It was treating a symptom before it became an infection. It was a cure.

The noises hadn't stopped, though. She had tried to dull them with liquor, tried to ignore them with chatter. That might have worked, she reasoned, if not for him.

He had ruined everything by making it all quiet.

Standing beside him, the sounds slowly went soft, became mute. Staring into his eyes, her ears stopped throbbing. Breathing in his liquor-stained breath, smelling the stink of his sweat-laden flesh, watching him smile with crooked sheepishness, she had just begun to stop hearing altogether.

That was not good. She knew it as much then as she did now, but it was difficult to recall why she had not worried at that moment. The noise was so inoffensive, suddenly; the world's noises ceased to press upon her in intangible walls of racket. No more worries, no more weight, just lightness, just her, and ...

And then he had *done* what he had.

And she had heard him.

She had heard things in him that humans were not supposed to feel, that shicts were not supposed to hear. And she had *felt* ...

Well, there was really no other way she *could* feel.

The howl was what had coursed through her, a sourceless noise that did not obey the laws of noise, starting in her brain, clawing its way out and tearing through her ears.

It lasted for but a moment, all the time it took her body to realise what she had pressed her lips against, but it hadn't needed more. It had ripped its way free, rang in her skull.

She had heard him. She had heard the Howling.

And then, she heard *everything*.

Instinct had told her to run, and she did, fleeing far into the forest, into the night. It was the right thing to do, she knew, because it was the voice of her body. What had happened before, what had made her quiver when he snaked his arm about her middle and press her body against his, what had made her slide her own arms around him and draw him tighter, what had made her think she enjoyed it …

No, not her body's voice. Something from somewhere else inside her. Not her body.

Her body had told her to run; her body had howled at her. It was a natural defence, a rejection of the disease, of the infection that had plagued her and made her do those things. The noise – the unbearably, agonisingly loud *noise* – was just a side effect, the lingering symptoms of which were the last go.

That made sense, she told herself as she trudged to the nearby brook. It was a symptom; it just needed to be cured. She splashed the water gently over her face, ears ringing with the ensuing splash. That would pass, she told herself; it would all pass. She had been tested, passed, survived the disease, for that's what he was.

'He's a disease,' she tried to hear herself say, 'he's a disease, he's a disease …'

The water settled. She stared down at her reflection. The face staring back at her didn't look convinced.

A realisation dawned on her just as the entire island conspired against her, the forest and creatures all falling

516

silent so that she might voice it and hear it ring through her ears and heart with one painful echo.

'He didn't come after me.'

She found herself surprised that the face in the water frowned back at her at that. She found herself surprised that she didn't bother to lie to herself and say it was because she missed the silence. But found herself surprised it hurt.

What, then, she asked herself as the noises began again, *is left? You can't do this,* she silently told the reflection. *You've tried – I know you've tried – but you just can't do what you need to do, what shicts do. If you could, you would have killed him when you first saw him, when you knew you had to, when you were given no choice. But you didn't, so what else is left?* She leaned forward. *No, the water's too shallow to drown yourself. Once more, what else is left?*

But to live with the disease?

Footfalls crunching on sand. Soles sinking with shoulders heavy with dried blood. Breath short and irritated, gasped out.

Him.

She sat up on her knees, pulling her spine erect, staring into the water, saw herself biting her lower lip and forced herself to stop. Dignity, she reminded herself; she could afford a little of that when she said what she knew she had to, what a shict never would. The world fell silent again as the footfalls came upon her; she would hear every word she said. One more cruel joke she resolved to be defiant in the face of.

She closed her eyes, whispered as softly as she could.

'You came after me, Lenk.'

'What's a "Lenk"?'

Iron on iron.

Her eyes snapped open, spied a leering face in the water:

long, hard, purple. She whirled about just in time to see the boot's toe coming up to kiss her jaw.

Twenty-Eight

BESIDES THE OBVIOUS INTERNAL BLEEDING

It was cold enough to freeze his lungs, dark enough to weigh his eyelids shut with gloom. Lenk thought he was drawing in deep, steady breaths, but found the air thick and oppressive enough that he couldn't be sure.

Dead?

In the gloom, a voice on a warm and fevered wind whispered. That wasn't right, Lenk thought; the sensation here should be cold, not hot.

'*You're safe … not quite dead.*'

The voice should not be nearly so comforting.

'*Yet.*'

There it was.

Yet?

'*We've got time.*'

I can't see.

'*For the better, one would think.*'

I feel sand.

'*A warm and pleasant beach.*'

I can't move my hands.

'*They are bound.*'

What happened?

Something without words answered.

Echoes of a panicked sorrow sounded in his mind, the question 'why' resounding off the walls of his head, accompanied by muttered self-deprecations and a thousand 'should haves'. Through the thicket of noise, he could see himself: sitting, alone, the crowds of Owauku dispersed, not a slender body in sight, as he stared into a cup of *mangwo* blankly.

I remember that part, not the bit that ended with me here, though.

'*Wait.*'

They came flooding into the valley, sweeping through the fog of his mind and into memory: purple-skinned, long-faced, iron-voiced. He saw himself look up, saw them through eyes not his own.

Another emotion: fury without echoes, a long, keening wail of rage as he launched himself at them. The first at the pack, the first that would die, recoiled, stunned at the sudden assault. She looked to her cohorts for assistance, found his hands wrapped around her throat a moment later. She did not fight back as he drove her to the ground and slammed her head against the earth, over and over; she stared at him, aghast, the breath to voice her fear not found.

'*What?*' one of them grunted. '*Do they all do that?*'

'*It's getting back up!*' another shrieked.

He had risen, leaving the creature motionless beneath him. He lunged at another, reaching out hands. She met him with hesitant challenge, eyes wide over her shield as she raised it before her. He spoke words that were not from his tongue, reached out on hands that felt like ice wrapped in skin the colour of stone.

What happened then?

He felt cold all of a sudden; the voice shifted to something frigid and sharp.

'This happened.'

They looked worried.

'They were right to feel fear.'

They don't fear anything, I'm told.

'They fear us.'

That can't be right. Were those my hands?

'Hands of the willing.'

But were they mine?

'*Are yours?*'

My head is hurting. It probably wouldn't do that if I were dead.

'Not dead.'

Are you sure?

'This one isn't moving,' a voice, distant and harsh spoke. 'Give it a kick.'

A blow erupted against his ribs. He felt a scream tear through his throat.

'*Yes.*'

His eyes snapped open, blackness replaced with a blinding flash of red. His breath returned to him slowly, his sight even more so. When both finally came to him easily, his vision was a field of purple, broken only by the milky white eyes and the deep frown scarred into a long face.

'Yeah,' the netherling grunted, flashing a jagged sneer. 'It's still alive.' She peered intently at him. 'And it turned back to pink.' She glanced over her shoulder. 'You want me to kill it?'

'It strangled a low-finger earlier,' another voice snarled in reply. 'Not worth killing over that, really.' The sound of a black chuckle emerged over iron sliding from a scabbard. 'Still …'

The sound of grating metal brought his attention to the shore. Longfaces gathered there in a knot of iron and purple muscle, some watching Lenk, some hauling a boat hewn of black wood onto the shore. One emerged from the crowd with a snarl and a sword, only to be stopped by a sudden iron gauntlet cracking against her jaw. She staggered, then stalked back into line, herded by the scowl of a larger female.

'No one kills anyone,' the larger female grunted, 'until the Master says so.'

A collective sigh of disappointment swept the gathered females, including the one standing over Lenk, who quickly lost interest in him and stepped back to rejoin her companions. His attention swayed on them, his focus lost as he felt his eyes rolling in his head, desperately trying to retreat back into his skull and plunge him into a soothing dark.

He might have heeded their wishes, as his head swivelled from them on a rubbery neck to survey the beach, but shutting his eyes to the sight that greeted him quickly became impossible.

If the skeletons could still make noise, he reasoned, they would be screaming. Their mouths gaped open, bone-white jaws turned skyward, black eye sockets vast and empty. And, he further reasoned, the screams that emerged from their colossal maws would have shook the earth.

They lay on the sand in dozens, titanic hills of arching spines and reaching claws, held fast to the ground by chains that refused to release, heedless of the rust that threatened to break or the fact that their prisoners were long dead. They lay in silent agony, bound, heads stoved in, ballista missile shafts jutting from empty eye sockets and temples, screaming.

They were Abysmyths, he recognised, from their titanic fishlike skulls. They were giant Abysmyths. What could they have to scream about? What could have caused them such pain? What had pulled them to the earth?

'*Something cruel and pitiless,*' the voice uttered with a warm whisper. '*They died screaming.*'

Ah.

'*And we made them scream,*' it laughed coldly.

What? We killed them?

'*You didn't have to.*'

But . . .

'*We did.*'

You're not making sense.

'*More important problems.*'

He blinked, suddenly aware of his hands tied behind his back, suddenly feeling the agony in his flank, suddenly hearing the sounds of very violent, very muscular women with very sharp swords. So taken by the ancient carnage on the beach was he that he almost forgot he was probably going to die.

Against that, he supposed he should consider himself lucky he noticed Dreadaeleon, similarly bound beside him, at all.

'Awake,' the boy noted with a characteristic lack of concern. 'Good.'

'What's going on?' Lenk asked.

'Difficult to figure out, is it?' Dreadaeleon's sigh was heavy enough to bludgeon Lenk. 'The convenience of the longfaces' arrival following the fact that we were plied with copious amounts of unregulated alcohol? The fact that the only things tied up on this beach have pink skin instead of green?'

Even with his head swimming, it was obvious to Lenk that the unpleasant situation had done nothing to temper Dreadaeleon's snideness, but that was all that was obvious.

His thoughts were too scattered for comprehension, let alone retort. Punching, he thought, would have been suitable, if not for the obvious.

'We were betrayed, Lenk,' Dreadaeleon said, 'and if you ask by whom, I swear I'm going to vomit on you.'

The temptation to ask anyway was banished as Lenk caught a shiver of movement from the corner of his eye.

At the edge of the shore, great white knucklebones rose from the moist earth, the great skeleton they belonged to far behind, the claws attached to them so very far from the sea the dead beast had tried to crawl into. Atop it, the figure of Togu was insignificant, a gloomy little growth staring distantly over a vast ocean.

'Togu …'

The word crawled out of Lenk's mouth, uncertain. He searched the lizardman with desperate eyes, for explanation as to how this had happened, for elaboration as to why it had happened. Answered with nothing but impassive silence, uncertainty shifted to anger, and the next words charged from his mouth on wrathful legs.

'You slimy piece of diseased stool,' he snarled, trying to ignore the impotency of his words and muscles as he pulled at his bonds. 'You *sold us*, you green little sack-sucker! You betrayed us, you … you …'

'He's not going to answer,' Dreadaeleon spoke, preventing any further displays of futile fury. 'I tried the same thing, with better insults.'

The answer was unsatisfactory; anything short of leaping up and strangling the lizard-thing before chewing out his withered throat would be, Lenk knew. Togu didn't so much as flinch, his head hanging from shoulders that looked too small for him. He was burdened, by guilt, regret, something else; Lenk wasn't satisfied by that, either.

Short of strangulation, another round of verbal hate seemed futile, yet came rampaging up to Lenk's lips all the same. And there it died, frozen to death as a cold realisation struck the young man firmly across the face. He swept wide, fevered eyes about the beach, saw nothing but sand, bones, netherlings. Plenty of flesh, none of it pink. Plenty of teeth, all of them jagged and frowning. Plenty of ears ...

'Where are they?' Lenk asked in a halting, breathless voice, terrified to ask each word, horrified of the answer, scared pissless of not knowing. 'Where is *she*, Togu? Where's Kataria?'

'He won't tell you,' Dreadaeleon said, 'about her.' He paused, choked. 'Or Asper. I ... I tried, Lenk.'

'*Hardly matters*,' a voice echoed in his mind. '*Did us no favours, no harm.*'

'He ... he betrayed us,' Lenk whispered back, his voice strained. 'He ... he ...'

'*Will be punished. Betrayers die along with abominations.*'

'Too calm,' Lenk muttered. 'You're too calm.'

'*You brought this on yourself. You could have fled.*'

'She is ... she's ...'

'*Most likely. Maybe not. She can be saved.*'

He breathed in, feeling overly warm.

'*Does not matter. A task is at hand.*'

'What task?' he asked, shivering.

'*They have waited for this moment. They have waited for it to arrive. They have come. They are close.*'

'Who?'

There was no explaining how he instantly knew beyond the sudden well of dread that sprung inside him, rising up through him on oily darkness as it tried to choke the breath from him.

Tried, and failed. His breath came to him, regardless, creeping from his lips, sharp, crisp. Cold.

'*They are close.*'

Lenk knew exactly of what the voice spoke, knew it did not lie.

'*Tonight, we will kill.*'

That, too, was inevitable.

'My father told me, as his father did, that the Owauku were born without life.'

Togu was speaking, his bass voice tinged with more weariness than sorrow. Lenk looked up without fury, without hatred, saw only the throat from which the words emanated, the blood pumping underneath. He knew that he would watch it spill upon the earth.

'We were born in death,' the lizardman continued, unaware of what the young man saw. 'This land was alive when we did not have it, dead when they gave it to us. They fought here, the servants of the Gods and the brood of Mother Deep. For us, they fought here, they said, to keep us free from slavery. They killed one another for days. When only one stood, he gave us this dying land and abandoned us. We were born in death, we lived in death, we survive in death ... betrayed.'

'I know how you feel,' Dreadaeleon replied, 'poor dear.'

'*We* were betrayed,' Togu said, turning on the boy with bright, angry eyes. 'By *everyone* who claimed to love us. The servants of the Gods gave us a dying land, the Gods themselves refused to heal it, the humans ...' He muttered, turning back to the sea. 'We do what we can to survive, cousins. You will help us. I do not like it, but I cannot shed tears for you. You would do the same thing.'

'She ...' Lenk whispered, voice a hiss of air. 'Where is she, Togu?'

'A place I do not want to know.'

'And the others? Where is—?'

The answer came in the hollow sound of flesh struck, the agonised groan that followed. Lenk struggled to look behind him and spied the a long, lanky body on the earth, hands bound behind him, unmoving as the ability to writhe in pain had apparently been beaten from him.

The answer to that, too, was evident in the towering mass of purple muscle, white hair and grey metal standing over him.

'I expected a struggle,' Xhai said, her voice following an iron-shod toe to the man's ribs. 'I expected wit. I expected the man that cut me to be one who spoke more.'

'I expected that I was going to be sailing home tomorrow,' Denaos replied through a voice thick with pain, 'wearing pants and *not* having various fluids being bludgeoned out of me.' He cleared his throat, looked up at her and grinned. 'That,' he said, 'was wit.'

'This,' she replied, 'is my foot.'

The force of her kick lifted him off the earth, sent him rolling away from her, his groan tinged with red fluid. His attempt at escape, however unintentional, did not go unpunished as she stalked after him and seized him by his scalp, pulling his eyes up to the level of her neck.

'And *this*,' she gestured to a wound still mending upon her collarbone, 'is your doing. Before *you*, the little weakling I sent to the earth with *one* blow, I was untouched by metal, unmarked.' She pulled his gaze upwards, towards her snarling, jagged teeth. 'They called me Unscarred.'

'Well, they'll no longer call *me* un-pissing blood,' Denaos replied, 'but I suppose you're not willing to call it even at that?'

A resounding answer came upon the back of her hand.

'You don't even realise the insult, the *unnaturalness* of it all,' she growled. 'I've killed more overscum, underscum and netherlings than you will ever know, and you, filthy little piece of pink, scar *me*, after I laid you low?'

'That,' he said, 'is irony.' He paused. 'Wait, no, that might just be coincidental. Let me ask Lenk—'

'*NO ONE*,' her roar silenced him as she hauled him to his feet, 'scars a Carnassial and lives.'

'And yet ... here I am.'

'Only because no one,' she whispered sharply, 'scars Semnein Xhai and dies swiftly.'

The face that stared at Denaos, it was evident, was a face used to rigid, expressionless demands for obedience. The trembling of her lips, the clenching of her teeth, was something her face struggled, and failed, to contain. Rage boiled beneath her skin like a purple stew of skin, bone and hate.

Lenk assumed it was rage, anyway, not possessing the unique brand of insanity that accompanied the ability to guess at a longfaces' emotions. How Denaos remained calm in the face of them was likewise a mystery. He was used to seeing Denaos as a trembling, scurrying thing, not the kind of man that would stare down a tower of quivering muscle and iron without so much as flinching.

The sight, Lenk thought, was impressive enough that he would remember the rogue as this, instead of the splattered mess of quivering red chunks he was undoubtedly about to become.

'You *cut* me,' she all but squealed, her voice brimming with something beyond anger.

'It's what I do,' he replied, without blinking.

That the man was thrown to the earth, Lenk expected. That the longface's foot rose up was likewise predictable.

That Xhai stepped over the rogue and stalked towards her fellow netherlings instead of bringing the foot down in a spray of bone shards and porridge spatters, however, threw him.

'*Get me my scumstompers,*' she roared to the longfaces. '*The big, spiky ones!*'

That was more like it.

'Denaos,' he grunted.

'Oh, I'm just fantastic, thanks,' Denaos groaned back. 'What's that? You didn't ask? No. Why would you? I'm just getting my meadow muffins kicked out of me. *You* have to sit on the cold hard ground. How are *you* doing, Lenk?'

No time to humour him, Lenk made his question swift. 'Where are they?'

'He didn't see, obviously,' Dreadaeleon replied. 'If he was drunk enough to start showing remorse, he didn't see anything but a pool of his own vomit before he passed out.'

'I didn't have enough time to do something nearly so satisfying before that fish-woman put me under,' Denaos grunted.

Lenk blinked, the echoes of a fading song bleeding in his mind. *The siren*, he thought, *Greenhair. She's responsible for this? For knocking me out?*

'*Tried to be,*' the voice chuckled blackly. '*Was not. Took iron and fists for that.*'

'She likely put the others out, as well,' Denaos muttered. 'Thank goodness we had someone who could shoot lightning out of their asshole on-hand to *not do a gods-damned thing about it.*'

'As though it's my fault,' Dreadaeleon snarled. 'I was as powerless as you!'

'You cannot *piss fire* and be powerless!'

'You're not even supposed to be talking about this! You said you wouldn't!'

'Oh no! Denaos *lied*? *Really?*' The rogue gasped, rolling his eyes. 'Is this still even a surprise anymore?'

The boy made a reply, shrill and whining. Lenk could hear the tall man growl back. He could see the longfaces looking anxious, tending to blunted weapons with whetstones. He felt Togu's presence, breath leaking from a quivering throat begging to be cut. He knew he had been betrayed, that he was likely to be killed, very soon, very messily.

Somehow, that seemed so … unimportant.

'I'm not afraid,' he whispered. One of the two prisoners beside him replied; he ignored them both. 'Why is that?'

'*Fear is useless to us. It is for other … things. Not us.*'

'I am concerned, though … for her.'

'*Also useless.*'

'I wish I knew she was safe.'

'*Why?*'

'I left things … unsatisfied.'

'*Satisfaction is important.*'

'I need her to be safe.'

'*She does not feel similarly.*'

'You know this?'

'*Yes.*'

'You can sense her?'

'*No.*'

'Then how do you know?'

'*Inevitable.*'

'I … need …'

'*We do not.*'

He had no more words for the voice; they, too, were

unimportant. He knew no words would convince the voice. He knew he could say nothing to deny the voice. He knew nothing would make the voice wrong. He knew this, without knowing it.

He knew this, because the voice knew it.

And the voice sighed, or seemed to, for it, too, knew something of him.

'*She is not dead.*'

'No?'

'*You don't need her.*'

'I need her to be—'

'*She will.*'

'How do you—'

'*BRING HIM FORWARD.*'

A shudder through the sand, feet charging forward; Denaos put up no particular resistance as a pair of netherlings hoisted him up and brought him toward Xhai.

And her scumstompers.

She still possessed feet, but he was only fairly certain. The amalgamations of metal wrapped about her ankles, forged with enough care to only passingly resemble boots, belonged on something that used them to crawl out of hell. They brimmed with spikes, rough and jagged, no space left uncovered.

He saw it, widened his eyes. Dreadaeleon saw them, all but squealed. Denaos undoubtedly saw them, said nothing, did nothing.

The voice answered the question before he asked it, slowly, softly. '*He is at peace. He knows his sins, did what he could for them. His life is complete.*'

'It isn't,' Lenk whispered. 'Is it?'

'*His duty is to accept the inevitability.*' It spoke firmly, swiftly. '*Ours, no different.*'

'You're not making sense,' Lenk said, eyelids twitching. 'You say one thing, then another, and they contradict each other and I don't know which to listen to.' He swallowed hard, gritted his teeth, almost afraid to ask the question that plagued his mind. 'Are … you alone in there?'

'*We are not.*'

'Do you mean "we" as you and I or—'

A groan of agony drew his attention back.

The netherlings dropped Denaos before Xhai. He fell to his knees and no farther, staring up at the female impassively. She stared down at him, cruel, contemptuous, trying to hold back the rage trembling beneath her face.

'Why don't you scream?' she asked.

'No reason,' he replied.

'I'm going to kill you.'

'I've had worse.'

'I'm going to stomp you into the ground, stomp your bones into jelly, stomp the jelly into pulp and stomp the pulp until there's nothing left. I'm going to spill you out on the earth and splash in your entrails.'

He stared up at her, grinned.

'I scarred you.'

She shrieked, raised her foot, the spikes glistening in the moonlight.

And nothing more came of it.

Something happened: a shift in the night breeze, a calm of the waves, a collective twitch through a dozen purple faces. Suddenly, milky white eyes turned upwards; the fury that fuelled each of them leaked out of their mouths as they opened and turned out towards the ocean. A strange placidity settled over them, a pack of purple hounds scenting meat, stilling their barking maws and wagging tongues in anticipation.

'*Coming*,' the voice whispered.

'Them?'

'*He*.'

'He always comes like this,' Togu whispered from his perch. 'The world knows when he arrives. The sea knows it first. The sky knows it next because the sea is quiet. We know it last, because the night is too dark and the world is quiet. It doesn't want him to see. Nothing good wants him to see.'

He hopped off his perch, glanced at Lenk with eyes too narrow for anything but fear.

'Don't look into his eyes, cousins. You don't want him to see, either.'

The netherlings cleared a space at the beach, parting as though bidden by a wind unfelt and hauling Denaos with them. That same wind seemed to continue to blow through, cut across his flesh and chill him.

'I can feel it, Lenk,' the boy said on weakening breath, 'a power … constant … *wrong*. It doesn't stop. It should stop. It *needs* to stop.' He grimaced, in pain. 'Hot, cold, cold, hot. *Why won't it stop?*'

Lenk, too, felt it; not the wind, but the leaves it picked up, the scent of smoke on it, the humidity it carried. A taint, one he was familiar with.

'A demon?'

'*Their servant.*'

'Ulbecetonth?'

'*Her enemy.*'

'Our friend?'

He knew the answer as soon as he saw the shadow upon the water.

A ship, he recognised, pulling itself through the water, towards the shore, with no oars, no sails, no source of

533

motion. At the prow, a pillar of gloom. A man, tall and black, crowned by three pinpricks of red light, fire upon shadow upon shadow.

Him.

It came to a perfect halt, barely grazing the sand. The figure waved a hand, dismissed everything, demanded everything. Everything complied.

The netherlings backed away. The earth quivered; the sand drew itself together, smoothed itself out and made itself presentable to him. It rose to meet him in a perfect staircase. His foot hit the step with no sound, and the netherlings took not a breath, dared to utter the word.

'Master,' bubbled out amongst them.

'Sheraptus,' Togu said, silent as the figure descended the stairs and regarded him.

The three red lights swung back and forth, tiny fires in a halo of black wrapped around a long, purple brow. His sigh crept out of a pair of thin, purple lips. Long, silky white hair rested on thin, drooping shoulders. Seas were silent, skies were still; the world held its breath, for fear that it had angered him.

'And all that greets me,' he whispered on a voice long and dark, 'is death.

'I have seen death before.' He tilted his head up towards the distant forest. 'But in my land, Togu, I have never seen green. I have seen no rivers and blue skies, no birds and insects, no rain clouds ...' He shook his head. 'And you meet me in the dark, on a clear night, on a beach laden with death. Death, I have seen before.'

A pair of eyes opened. Bright. Crimson. Fiery.

'I will see more of it.'

The voice was languid, liquid, the threat inherent in it ebbing away as soon as it passed his lips, wasted. Or rather,

Lenk thought, unnecessary. There was something inherently threatening about the man, something that went beyond the black robes, the glowing red jewels and the black crown about his brow.

'Power ...' Dreadaeleon whispered, his voice pained. 'He's *leaking* it.'

Magic, perhaps, Lenk thought; that wasn't hard to believe, given that the characteristic crimson pyres that lit up a wizard's eyes were perpetually burning in his stare. But what Lenk sensed was not magic. It was the unseen, unmoving breeze about him, the unscented stench about him.

The taint all too plain to both Lenk and the creature inside his head.

'*Sense it,*' the voice muttered. '*He's killed many. Demon, mortal ... child, mother ... he's watched them suffer; he's drunk their pain.*' It shifted, becoming hard and rigid. '*He will again if we do not do our duty.*'

'Who ... ?' he asked. 'Whose pain?'

Cold sigh. Warm sigh. Two answers.

'*You know.*'

'Where is it?'

Another voice, neither warm nor hot, brimming with boredom and hatred. Him again. Sheraptus.

Togu did not bother defiance against his question, did not bother to interpret it as anything other than the demand that it was. He glanced over his shoulder, spoke a word in his native tongue. From around a standing skull, a quartet of Owauku approached, bearing a wooden palanquin upon their shoulders with Bagagame, head heavy and eyes thick, at their head.

They passed Lenk, keeping their gazes low. He paid them no mind, watching instead the objects heaped upon

535

the wooden platform: all of them his or his companions'. He spotted Denaos' knives, Asper's pendant, Kataria's bow. His sword was up there, too; he supposed that should have galled him. The fact that his pants were right next to it should have enraged him.

Neither of those was the reason for the sudden flash of icy heat that seared through his head on a pair of voices.

'*NO!*'

'What?' he asked, wincing.

'*He cannot be allowed to have it! It does not belong to him! It belongs to … no one … no, to YOU! TO NO ONE!*' His head pounded, seared with fever, frozen with cold before the voice finally howled in twisting cacophony. '*HE CANNOT HAVE THE TOME.*'

Sheraptus glanced over to the boat, raised a white eyebrow. The netherlings followed his gaze, reverence shifting to scorn the moment their gaze left his face. The male seemed to take no notice, though, as he glanced to the bound companions.

'This is them?' he asked.

The shape that rose up from his vessel was instantly recognisable. The skin, white even in darkness, and the crown of emerald-coloured hair were extraneous detail. The palpable aura of treachery denoted the siren's presence long before she showed her gills.

'That is … most of them, yes,' she replied, shaking her head. 'There was another with them … a beast on two legs with red skin.'

'Dead,' Denaos muttered. 'Thankfully.'

'If that is the case, then they are all here and—'

'You three,' Sheraptus said, pointing to a trio of netherlings, 'search the island for signs of this thing. If this is the same red thing that netherlings could not kill, I doubt he was slain by anything else.' He ignored Greenhair's stammered protests as the trio grunted and set off down the coast, instead turning his gaze to the palanquin. 'Now, then ... where is it?'

'That is it,' Greenhair replied, arriving beside Sheraptus and pointing a finger at the palanquin. 'It is in there.'

He swept his burning gaze back to the objects. His hands rose, the air quivering between them as he gently separated his palms, an invisible force parting the clothes and weapons to expose a pair of books resting gingerly upon the wood. The first one was musty, old, well-worn pages trembling in the breeze, as if taking the cue to quiver before the man's eyes. The other ...

Too clean, too black, too shiny, too still and smug and noticeable while the rest of the world darkened for fear of being seen by a pair of bright red eyes. The tome met the man's gaze fearlessly, sparing only enough time to look at Lenk with papery eyes and wink. Or so it seemed to, at any rate.

Surely, Sheraptus must have seen it, too. What could escape that stare? What sense did it make for him to reach down and pluck the musty, frightened book up first?

'*It does not call to him*,' a voice, he wasn't sure which, answered. '*He cannot hear it. His ears are cloyed with pride, arrogance. He will never hear it. Will never hear us before we take his head.*' He glanced to Greenhair, biting her lip, not daring to say anything as he plucked up the wrong book. '*She ... betrayed us. Those who betray ... die.*'

Warmth, then cold. Agreement.

If Sheraptus saw the intent in Lenk's stare, he made no comment. Instead, he thumbed through the pages of the musty tome, heedless of Dreadaeleon's whimper. *Ah, right*, Lenk realised. *His spellbook*. He hadn't seen it ever unattached to the boy's hip. He guessed that watching another man thumb through something that had been attached so long would be unsettling, at the least.

'Humans use *nethra*,' he hummed thoughtfully. 'I wasn't entirely sure I believed it.' Idly, he flipped page by page, his frown deepening. 'They scrawl their words on parchment, learn to burn, to scorch.' He glanced up. 'How many trees were rent asunder by such? How much green turned black?'

His eyes narrowed as he thumbed towards the end of the book. 'Possessed of everything, you ruin it all. Spill more blood over imaginary things, like gods and ideologies, never once deigning to fight over the bounties surrounding you.' He looked up, thoughtful. 'You're so concerned with these false notions of higher powers that you never once realise it's all within your grasp.'

'Merroskrit,' Dreadaeleon whispered, 'merroskrit … that's another wizard he's touching, another person and he's just … he's going to …'

He took a thin, white page and rubbed it gingerly between two fingers. The flinch of his lips, the ripping of the paper was short, bitter. Dreadaeleon's scream was longer, louder. And at that sound, the longface's lips twisted into a wry smirk.

'But that's part of your charm, isn't it?'

'Sheraptus …' Greenhair spoke, then immediately stammered out: 'M-Master … that is just a book of lore, nothing important. The true object is—'

'Not moving, for the moment.' He reached down and took a severed head from the palanquin, staring at its closed eyes, golden locks and frowning. 'And they even carry death around with them … fascinating.'

538

The head, Lenk recognised. *The Deepshriek's head. The lizards kept it.*

'They know nothing of its importance. It will be ours again soon. Patience.'

'There is a word for this sort of thing …' Sheraptus hummed, tossing the head away. 'It is either "macabre" or "deranged", but it's unimportant. I came for something else. Where is it?'

'There, Master,' Greenhair said, pointing to the palanquin. 'The tome is there.' Her glance flitted towards Dreadaeleon for a moment. 'It will be safer with you.'

Sheraptus, however, merely stared at her, as unexpressive as a man with flaming eyes could be, before he looked over her to Xhai.

'Where is it?' he asked the Carnassial.

She shot him back a look, as wounded as a woman with spike-encrusted shoes could. 'The Grey One That Grins only wants the tome. The other things are—'

'I would very much like to have it … them,' Sheraptus said. 'It would make me very happy.' He pursed his lips, furrowed his brows; beneath the fire, he looked almost hurt. 'Xhai … do you not want me to be happy?'

She recoiled, as if struck. An emotion, close to but not quite the fury that was present earlier, shook her features. After a moment, her face settled into one of cold acknowledgement. She turned her head away and barked a command.

'TCHIK QAI!'

There was a scrabble of boots, a few muffled curses from behind a massive, jutting ribcage half-buried nearby. Lenk's ears immediately pricked up, his attention drawn towards the movement, his heart beating faster at the noise. The reaction did not go unnoticed.

'*Ignore that,*' a cold voice snarled.

'*The enemy is before you,*' a hot voice growled.

'*Duty first. Betrayers die.*'

'*They will all die. They all betrayed you. Forget everything else.*'

'*Kill.*'

'*Listen.*'

He did not hear them, felt them as nothing but flashes of hot and cold in his body. His eyes were locked upon the twitches of movement between the bones. He spotted glimpses of purple, but did not pay attention them. Before them, glimpses of colour, white and silver under the moonlight, moved swiftly, but erratically.

The movement stopped momentarily. There was another shout of protest, this one louder but not clear enough to be heard well. It was met with a snarling iron retort and a faint cracking sound. Lenk found himself surprised that he was wincing at the unseen blow, found himself surprised that he was leaning forward, craning his neck to see what emerged from behind the bones.

And despite the fear that had been growing in his chest since he had awoken, he found himself surprised to see a pair of emerald eyes, wide, terrified and searching.

He tried to cry out, tried to scream when he found he couldn't. His throat was constricting, voice choked.

'*No,*' another voice answered his unspoken question, '*speak not. Draw no attention. Not yet. He does not need you, does not want you. Survive first. Kill later.*'

She looks hurt. She needs help. I need to—

'*Soon. Tome first. Duty first.*'

No! Not duty first, she's more important. She—

'*Fled. From you.*'

What?

'Fear was in her eyes. She was right to show us.'

No, she—

'Does not understand.'

'Cannot understand.'

'Your duty ... our duty ... more important. She cannot see that. Looks away from it.'

She isn't looking away now.

No response came; he wouldn't have heard it, anyway. His eyes were locked on Kataria's, and hers on his, as she was marched forward by ironbound hand and guttural snarls from purple lips. She put up minimal resistance to such, not that her bound hands would allow her much, in any case. Still, Lenk found himself surprised by her passiveness as she was ushered towards the knot of netherlings; he had expected her to be snarling, thrashing, biting and cursing.

To see that anticipated furious resistance emerge from the pale form emerging behind Kataria, however, was slightly more surprising.

'And after I've chewed *those* off, because I'm sure you things only *claim* to be females,' Asper snarled at the netherling shoving her forward, 'I'm going to rip your eyes out and eat *those*, too!' She dug her heels in, shoved back at her captor, tried to break away. All futile efforts, their failures doing nothing to curb her tongue. 'Get *back*, you slavering, sloppy little cu—'

'I know maybe three of those words,' the netherling snarled back, raising an iron fist. 'And I don't know what to *say* to make you shut up, but I do know what to hit you with.'

'No.'

Bones shook in skin, sea retreated from shore, all eyes looked up and instantly regretted doing so. Sheraptus' eyes were narrowed to fiery slits as they swept up to the

541

netherling holding the priestess. Like a flower before fire, the females' resolve withered, hands trembled, gaze turned towards the sand.

Asper's did not, however. And from the sudden widening of her eyes, the slackness of her jaw, the very visible collective clench of every muscle in her body, it wasn't clear if she even could. Nothing had seemed to leave her, least of all her fight. Rather, it was apparent that the moment she had met his eyes, something had instead entered her and had no plans of leaving.

And, judging by his broad smile, it was more apparent to no one than Sheraptus.

'This is it,' he whispered, stalking closer to her. 'This is what I came to see, what I continue to see. This ... utter rejection of the world.' He lifted a long purple hand to her, grinned as she flinched away from it. '*That*. What is that? Why do you do such a thing? You know you can't flee, know you can't escape, but you still try. Instinct *dictates* that you sit there and accept it, yet you refuse to. Why?' He glanced up towards the sky. 'I had once thought it was your notion of gods, with how often you pray to them, but I see nothing up there.'

His voice shifted to something low, something breathy and born out of his heart. Yet as soft as it went, it remained sharp and painful so that none could help but hear him. His eyes drifted from Asper's horrified stare, searching over her half-nude body. Slowly, his hand rose to follow, palm resting upon her belly, fingers drumming thoughtfully on her skin.

Her choked gasp, too, could not be ignored.

'It's not gods, though, is it?' His hand slid across her abdomen, as if beckoning something to rise from the prickling gooseflesh and reveal it to him. 'No, no ... something more. Or less?' His smile trembled at the edges, trying and failing to contain something. 'I just ... can't tell with your breed.' His gaze returned to hers, a lurid emotion burning brighter than the fire consuming them. 'But I dearly look forward to finding out.'

He turned away from her, his stare settling on Kataria for a moment, white brows furrowing. 'And this one ... doesn't even put up a fight?' He gave her a cursory glance, then shrugged. 'I like the ears, anyway. Load them up.'

'W-what?' Asper gasped. Vigour returned to her as she was forced towards the black vessel, and she struggled against her captor's grip. 'No! *NO!*' At that moment, she seemed to notice the others, bound on the sand. 'Don't let him do this to me. He's going to ... to ...' Tears began forming in her eyes. 'Help me ... *help me, D—*'

A rough cloth was wrapped about her mouth, tied tightly as she was hoisted up and over the netherling's purple shoulder and spirited to the boat.

'*Asper!*' Dreadaeleon cried out. 'I can help you ... I ... I can.' He gritted his teeth as crimson sparked behind his eyes, the magic straining to loose itself. 'It's just ... it's ...'

'Intimidating, isn't it?' Sheraptus shot a fire-eyed wink at the boy. 'I felt the same way when I first beheld it ... well, sans the pitiful weakness, anyway.' He ran a finger along the crown upon his brow, circling its three burning jewels. 'One can't help but behold it, like a candle that never snuffs out.' He considered the boy carefully for a moment. 'Which, I suppose, would make you a tiny, insignificant moth.'

As soon as he said the word, the boy collapsed, tumbling backwards with his eyes shutting tightly as if to ward against the burning. Immediately, his breathing slowed, his body went still. Lenk couldn't help but widen his eyes in fear.

Nothing he had known – human, longface or otherwise – could kill with a word.

'Dread?' he whispered.

'*Ignore it.*'

'He's …'

'*Unimportant.*'

'Should we … do something?'

'I, for one,' Denaos interjected, 'fully intend on rising up and enacting a daring rescue, as soon as I finish crapping out a kidney.'

'Plenty of time for that when I take you to the ship,' Xhai snarled as she seized the rogue by his hair and hoisted him up. 'This is better, in fact.' Her smile was as sharp and cruel as the spikes on her feet. 'Now, I can take my time.'

'Semnein Xhai.'

She looked up with an abashed expression that had no business on a face so hard. Sheraptus' befuddled dismay was just as out of place and somehow even more disturbing as he canted his head to the side.

'Do I not make you happy?' he asked. 'You require this … pink thing?'

'But you …' She bit her lower lip, the innocence of the gesture somehow lost in her jagged teeth. 'We are taking prisoners, aren't we?'

'It's necessary to understand the condition of humans, yes,' he replied. 'But it's only ever seen in females, and two is more than enough. We have no need for males. Leave this one behind.'

She glanced from Sheraptus to Denaos, gaze shifting from confused to angry in an instant. With a snarl, she hurled the rogue back to the earth and swept her scowl upon the remaining netherlings.

'If *any* of you kills him,' she growled, 'you will do it quickly and you will *not* enjoy it. Or I'll know … and I *will*.'

'We have what we came for, in any case,' Sheraptus said. He made a gesture, and the tome flew from the palanquin to his hand. He spared a smile for Togu. 'As promised, we leave your island in peace.'

'Good,' Togu replied bluntly.

Lenk was aware of movement, netherlings returning to their vessels, chatter between them. He paid attention to none of it, his eyes locked, as they had been for an eternity, on Kataria's.

Her lips remained still, her ears unquivering. It was only through her eyes that he knew she wished to say something to him. But what? The question ripped his mind apart as he searched her gaze for it. A plea for help? An apology? A farewell?

He was likewise aware of his inability to do anything for her. His bonds would not allow him to rise, to escape. The searing heat and freezing cold racing through him would not allow him to weep, to speak. And so he stared, eyes quivering, lips straining to mouth something, anything: reassurances, promises, apologies, pleas, accusations.

'Take that one to the ship, as well,' Sheraptus ordered the netherling holding her.

It was only when Kataria was hoisted up onto a power-ful shoulder, only when her eyes began to fade as she was hauled through the surf, only when her gaze finally disap-peared as she was tossed over the edge of the black boat that he recognised what had dwelled in her gaze.

Nothing.

No words. No questions. Nothing but the same utter

lack of anything beyond a desperate need to say *something* that he had felt inside of him.

And only then did he realise he could not let her disappear.

'Very well, then,' Sheraptus said, pointing to a cluster of netherlings. 'You five. You have ... pleased me. I think you deserve a reward.' He barely hid his contempt at their unpleasantly beaming visages. 'The tome is all we require. Everything else can be destroyed.'

'What?' Togu spoke up, eyes going wide. 'We had a deal! You said—'

'I say many things,' Sheraptus replied. 'All of them true. It is my right to take what I wish and give as I please. And really, you've been quite rude.'

'Sheraptus ... Master,' Greenhair spoke, 'I gave them my word that—'

'*Bored,*' the male snarled back. 'I am leaving. Come or stay, screamer. I care not.'

Confusion followed as netherlings hurried back to their boats, Sheraptus idly shaping his earthen staircase and returning to his own vessel. Greenhair reluctantly followed him aboard. Blades were drawn, cruel laughter emerging from jagged mouths. Togu shouted a word and his reptilian entourage fled. White, milky eyes settled on helpless, bound forms.

Lenk cared not, did not hear them, did not look at them. He watched the boat bearing Kataria slide out of view, vanishing into the darkness. He swallowed hard, felt his voice dry and weak in his throat.

'Tell me,' he whispered, 'can you ... can either of you save her?'

No more heat. No more fever. Something cold coursed through his blood, sent his muscles tightening against bonds that suddenly felt weak. Something frigid crept into his mind. Something dark spoke within him.

'*I can.*'

Twenty-Nine

THE SCENT OF MEMORY

The grandfather wasn't speaking to him anymore.

Unfortunately, that didn't mean he wasn't still there.

Gariath could see him at the corner of his eyes, held the scent of him in his nostrils. And it certainly didn't mean he had stopped making noise.

'We had to have known,' he muttered from somewhere, Gariath not knowing or caring where. 'At some point, we had to have known how it would all end. The *Rhega* were strong. That's why they came to us. They were weak. That's why we aided them. That was what we did, back then.'

Of all the aimless babble, Gariath recognised only the word *Rhega*. How far back, who 'they' were, when the *Rhega* had ever helped anyone weak was a mystery for people less easily annoyed. He wasn't even sure who the grandfather was speaking to anymore, either, but it hadn't been him for several hours, he was sure.

The shift had begun after they had left the shadow of the giant skeleton and its great grave of a ravine behind them. The grandfather suddenly became as the wind: elusive, difficult to see, and constantly flitting about.

He talks more, too, Gariath thought, resentfully. *Much more annoying than the wind.*

He had long given up any hopes for communication. The grandfather vanished if Gariath tried to look at him, met his questions with silence, nonsensical murmurs or bellowing songs.

'We used to sing back then, too,' the grandfather muttered. 'We had reason to in those days. More births, more pups. We killed only for food. Survival wasn't the worry it is today.'

Granted, Gariath admitted to himself, he wasn't *quite* sure how the effects of senility applied to someone long dead, but he was prepared to declare the grandfather such. The skeleton had obviously been the source, but further details eluded both Gariath's inquiries and, eventually, his interest.

The grandfather had faded from his concerns, if not from his ear-frills, hours ago. Now, the forest opened up into beach and the trees lost ground to encroaching sand. Now, he ignored sight and sound alike, focused only on scent.

Now, he hunted a memory.

It was faint, only a hint of it grazing his nostrils with the deepest of breaths, an afterthought muttered from the withered lips of an ancestor long dead. But it was there, the scent of the *Rhega*, drifting through the air, rising up from the ground, across the sea. It was a confident scent, unconcerned with earth and air and water. It had been around longer, would continue to be when earth and air and water could not tell the difference between themselves.

And he wanted to scream at it.

He craved to feel hope again, the desperate yearning that had infected him when he had last breathed such a scent. He wanted to roar and chase it down the beach. He resisted the urge. He denied the hope. The scent was a passing thought. He dared not hope until he tracked it and felt the memories in his nostrils.

There would be time enough to hope when he found the *Rhega* again.

'Wisest,' the grandfather whispered.

Gariath paused, if only because this was the first time he had heard his name pass through the spirit's spectral lips in hours.

'Your path is behind you,' he whispered. 'You will find only death ahead.'

Gariath ignored him, resuming his trek down the beach. Even if it wasn't idle babble, Gariath had been told such a thing before. Everyone certain of his inevitable and impending death had, to his endless frustration, been wrong thus far.

And yet, what his ears refused to acknowledge, his snout had difficulty denying.

Broken rocks, dried-up rivers, dead leaves, rotting bark – the scents crept into his nostrils unbidden, tugged at his senses and demanded his attention. The scent he sought was difficult to track, the source he followed difficult to concentrate on.

Each time they passed his nostrils, with every whiff of decay and age, he was reminded of the hours before this moment, of the battle at the ledge.

Of the lizard …

His mind leapt to that moment time and again, no matter how much he resisted it, of the tall, green reptile-man coated in tattoos, holding a bow in one hand, raising a palm to him. He saw the creature's single, yellow eye. He heard the creature's voice, understood its language. He drew in the creature's scent and knew its name.

Shen.

How could he have known that? How could he *still* know that? The creature had spoken to him, addressed him, called him *Rhega*. How was that possible? There weren't enough *Rhega* left on the mainland, let alone on some forsaken floating graveyard, for the thing to recognise him. And he was certain he had never seen *it* before.

And yet, it had intervened on his behalf, saved him from death. Twice, Gariath admitted to himself; once with an arrow and again with the surge of violent resolve that had swept through him afterwards. That vigour had waned, dissolving into uncomfortable itches and irritating questions.

Questions, he reminded himself, *that you have no time for. Focus. If you can't feel hope, you sure as hell can't feel confusion until you find them.*

'Find what, Wisest?' the grandfather murmured. 'The beach is barren. There is nothing for us here.'

'There must be a sign, a trace of where they went,' Gariath replied, instantly regretting it.

'There are no *Rhega* here.'

'You're here.'

'I am dead.'

'The scent is strong.'

'You have smelled it before.'

'And I found Grahta.'

'Grahta is dead.'

The grandfather's words were heavy. He ignored them. He could not afford to be burdened now. He pressed on, nose in the air and eyes upon the cloud-shrouded moon.

Thought was something he could not carry now. It would bow his head low, force his eyes upon the ground and he would never see where he was going.

'The answer lies behind you, Wisest,' the grandfather said. 'Continue, and you will find something to fear.'

The spirit was but one more thing to ignore, one more thing he couldn't afford to pay attention to. So long as he had a scent to track, answers to seek, he didn't have to think.

He wouldn't have to think about how the beach sprawled endlessly before him, how the clouds shifted to paint moonlight on the shore. Still, he made the mistake of glancing down and seeing the shadows rising up in great, curving shards farther down the beach.

Bones, he recognised. More great skeletons, more silent screaming, more shallow graves. How many, he wasn't sure. He didn't have the wit to count, either, for in another moment, the stench of death struck him like a fist.

It sent him reeling, but only that. What made him stop, what made his eyes go wide and his jaw drop, was the sudden realisation that he had been struck with no singular aroma. Another scent was wrapped up within the reek of decay, trapped inside it, inseparable from it.

Rivers. Rocks.

Rhega.

No.

That was not right. The scent of the *Rhega* was the odour of life, strong, powerful. He seized what remained of his strength, throttled it to make himself stagger forward. He would get a better scent, he knew, smell the vigour and memory of the *Rhega* that undoubtedly lingered behind it. Then everything would be fine. He would have his answers. He could feel hope again and this time, he'd—

He struck his toe, felt a pain too sharp to belong to him. A white bone lay at his feet, too small to belong to a great beast, too big to be a hapless human corpse. Its scent was too ... too ...

'No ...'

He collapsed to his knees; his hands drove themselves into the dirt and began digging. He sobbed, begging them not to in choked incoherencies. Thought weighed him down, fear drove his hands, and with every grain removed, white bone was exposed.

No.

An eye socket that should have held a dark stare looked up at him.

No!

Sharp teeth worn with use and age grinned at him.

NO!

A pair of horns, indentations where ear-frills had been, a gaping hole in the side of its bleached head ...

He was out of thought, unable to think enough to rise or look away or even touch the skull. He knelt before it, staring down.

And the dead *Rhega* stared back.

'That's why the scent is faint.'

Gariath recognised the voice, its age and depth like rocks breaking and leaves falling. He didn't look up as a pair of long, green legs came to stand beside him and a single yellow eye stared down at the skull.

'It's in the air, the earth.' He squatted beside Gariath, running a reverential hand across the sand. 'So is death. No matter how many bones we find and return' – he paused to sigh – 'there are always more.'

Gariath's stare lingered on the skull, afraid to look up, more afraid to ask the question boiling behind his lips.

'Are they ... ?' he asked, regardless. 'All of them?'

The Shen's head swung towards him, levelled the single eye upon him. 'Not all of them.'

Words heavy with meaning, Gariath recognised, made

lighter with meaninglessness. 'If a people becomes a person, there are none left.'

'If there is one left, then there is one left. Failure and philosophy are for humans.' He glanced farther down the beach. 'They have been here.'

Gariath had not expected to look up at that word. 'Humans?'

'Dragged through here, earlier, by the longfaces,' the lizardman muttered, staring intently at the earth. 'We had hoped Togu would take care of their presence, but not by feeding them to purple-skinned beasts. He encourages further incursions.' He snorted. 'He was always weak.'

'You have been tracking them? You are a hunter, then?'

'I am Yaike. I am Shen. It matters not what I do, so long as I do it for all Shen.'

'You can hunt with one eye?'

'I have another one. I am still Shen. Other races that teem have the numbers to give up when they lose one eye.' He hummed, his body rumbling with the sound. 'Tonight, we hunt longfaces. Tonight, we kill them. In this, we know we are Shen.' He glanced at Gariath. 'More bones tonight, *Rhega*. There are always more.'

'There is a lot of that on this island.'

'This?' Yaike gestured to the skull. 'A tragedy. The Shen were born in it, in death. We carry it with us.' He ran a clawed finger across his tattooed flesh. 'Our lives are painted with it, intertwined with it. In death, we find life.'

'In death, I have found nothing.'

'I am Shen.' Yaike rose to his feet. 'I know only Shen. Of *Rhega*, I know only legends.'

'And what do they say?'

'That the *Rhega* found life in all things. I am Shen. For me, all things are found in death.'

Yaike's gaze settled on Gariath for a moment before he turned and stalked off, saying nothing more. Gariath did not call after him. He knew there was nothing more the Shen could offer him, as surely as he knew the name Shen. And because he was not sure at all how he knew the name, he felt no calm. Thought felt no lighter on his shoulders.

Answers in death, he thought to himself. *I've seen much death*.

'And you haven't learned anything, Wisest,' the grandfather whispered, unseen.

Death is a better answer than nothing.

There was no response to that from the grandfather. No sound at all, but the hush of the waves and the sound of boots on sand.

'Is that it?' a grating voice asked, suddenly. 'It's pretty big, isn't it?'

His nostrils quivered: iron, rust, hate.

He turned and regarded them carefully, the trio of purple-skinned longfaces that had emerged from the night. They clutched swords in hands, carried thick, jagged throwing knives at their belts. How easy it would be, he wondered, to stand there and let them carve his flesh. How easy would it be to find an answer in his own blood, dripping out on the sand.

He hadn't learned anything that way so far.

'You have humans,' he grunted. 'I will take them.'

'They yours?' one of them asked. 'How about we burn what's left of them and what's left of you in a pile? Fair?'

He stepped forward and felt refreshed by an instant surge of ire welling up inside him. It might not have been the most profound of solutions, but then, this was not the most difficult of problems.

For this question, for *any* question, violence was an answer he understood.

The netherlings shared this thought, bringing their swords up, meeting his bared teeth with their jagged grins.

Humans were nearby, he knew, and they were likely dead. Netherlings were closer, he knew, and they would soon be dead. He would find answers tonight, answers in death.

Whose, he wasn't quite sure he cared.

Lenk felt the chill shudder through his body, seizing his attention.

'*They have come to a decision.*'

The sight of drawn swords and grins of varying width and wickedness confirmed as much. The netherlings' brief argument over who was going to kill whom had lasted only as long as it took for words to give way to fists, with the least battered picking their prey. The one most bloodied settled with a grumble for Dreadaeleon's unconscious form, still beside Lenk.

The one with the broadest grin and the bloodiest gauntlet advanced upon him, pursued by scowls from the ones with the most knuckle indentations embedded in their jaws. There were many of those, he noted. She had wanted him badly.

'*She shall never have us,*' the voice muttered. '*We will find her first, show her revelation, show them all.*'

'Revelation,' Lenk whispered, 'in blood, steel. We will show them.'

'Show us what?' the advancing netherling asked, tilting her head to the side.

'He could show us his insides,' one of the longfaces offered.

'Rather, *you* could,' another replied, kneeling beside

the prone form of Denaos. 'I intend to make this one die slowly. Xhai is going to be *pissed*.'

'*Die?*' the voice asked of Lenk.

Lenk shook his head. 'Not us.'

'*Not if she is to survive.*'

A sudden heat engulfed Lenk, bathed his brow in an instant sweat. '*And what of your survival? Save her, even try to, and you'll die, you'll rot and she'll be—*'

The sweat turned cold, froze to rime on his skin. '*Meaningless. Duty above survival. Duty above life. Duty above all. They are coming. They will die, as these ones here die.*'

'As all die,' Lenk murmured.

'Now you've got it,' the netherling said, grinning as she levelled her sword at the young man's brow. 'This is just how it is, as Master Sheraptus says. The weak give all, the strong take all.' Her grin grew broader. 'Master Sheraptus is strong. We are strong.'

'*Weak enables strong. Strong feed on weak. Not incorrect.*'

'Her perception is wrong, though,' Lenk muttered.

'What?' The netherling smiled with terrible glee. 'Oh, wait, are you going to do one of those dying monologues that pinkies do? I've heard about these! Make it good!'

His stare rose to meet hers. Instantly, her smile faded, the wickedness fleeing her face to be replaced with confusion tinged by fear. His eyes were easy as her sword arm tensed, his voice emerging on breath made visible by cold as he stared at her and whispered.

'We are stronger,' he said evenly. 'We will kill you first.'

She recoiled at that, as if struck worse than a fist could. 'I hoped to enjoy this,' she growled, drawing her blade back, ready to drive it between his eyes. 'But you *ruined* it, you stupid little—'

A roar split the sky apart, choking her voice in her throat. Her arm steadied as a new kind of confusion, fear replaced with curiosity, crossed her face. She looked over her shoulder, milk-white eyes staring down the beach, seeking the source of the fury.

'That's …' another longface hummed, squinting into the gloom, 'that's one of the low-fingers, isn't it? That the Master sent out?'

'*It is,*' the voice answered in Lenk's head, '*what we have waited for.*'

He felt his eyes drawn to the beach. Movement was obvious, even in the darkness: purple flesh shifting beneath moonlight as a netherling charged down the beach. But her gait was awkward, bobbing wildly as she rushed forward. The peculiarities grew the closer she drew: the jellylike flail of her arms and legs, the hulking shadow behind her body.

By the time Lenk saw the longface's head lolling on a distinctly shattered neck, it was clear to him and everyone else what was about to happen.

'Oh, hell, it's that … that red thing!' a netherling snarled. 'What are they called?'

'It was supposed to be dead, wasn't it?' another snarled. 'The screamer said!'

'It's not,' the third laughed, hefting her jagged throwing blade. 'This day just gets better and better.'

'What about the pink things?'

'Kill 'em if you want. Don't expect any scraps.'

A cackle tore through the longfaces. A chorus of whining metal followed as jagged hurling blades flew, shrieking to be heard over the war cry that chased them.

'*QAI ZHOTH!*'

With each meaty smack, the longface's corpse shuddered

558

as the blades gnawed into lifeless flesh and stuck fast, leaving the creature behind it unscathed. It rushed forward, trembling as a roar emerged from behind the shield of sinew. Lenk saw flashes of red skin, sharp teeth and dark, murderous eyes. He found he could hardly help the smile creeping upon his lips.

And behind the corpse, Gariath's grin was twice as long, thrice as unpleasant.

'*AKH ZEKH LAKH!*' the longfaces threw chants instead of knives, hefting their swords and shields as they charged forward to meet the dragonman's fury with their own.

'*Distracted. Escape possible. Death inevitable. Duty will be fulfilled.*'

'My hands are tied,' he whispered.

'*Move or die.*'

'Fair enough.' He pulled at the ropes; he knew little of knots, but it seemed reasonable that the netherlings would not plan to hold prisoners any longer than it took to gut them. With a little guidance, he was sure he could break free. 'Denaos, can you—'

'*He can,*' the voice replied. '*He did.*'

The slipped bonds on the earth where the rogue had lain was evidence enough of that.

'*We did not need him. Do not need any of them. Focus. Time is short.*'

A challenging howl confirmed as much. Gariath had dropped his corpse to the earth, seizing it by its ankles and dragging it to meet his foes. Their anticipation was evident in the gleam of their swords, the grin on their faces.

'*QAI ZHOTH!*' the leading one howled, leaping forward. '*EVISCERATE! DECAPITATE! ANNIHILA—*'

The chant was shattered along with her teeth as two thick skulls collided. He swung the corpse like a club of muscle and flesh. Limp arms flailed out to smash ironbound hands into chanting jaws. Bones cracked against bones, casting the attackers back as Gariath grunted and adjusted his weight for another swing.

'*Ignore*,' the voice hissed, its freezing tone bringing Lenk's attention back to his wrists. '*Duty is at hand. We must free ourselves. We must kill.*'

'I can't,' he snarled, tugging at his wrists. 'I can't!'

'Can't what?' Dreadaeleon replied. 'Gariath seems to have the matter in hand.'

'*If you cannot, then she dies. All die. Because of you.*'

'I can't help it … I can't get free!'

'*I can.*'

'You … can?'

'Who can?' Dreadaeleon asked, glancing at the young man. 'Lenk … really? *Now*?'

'*Say it.*'

Somehow, within the icy recesses of a mind not his own, he knew what he must say. And somehow, in the shortness of his own breath, he knew the consequences of saying it.

'Save her,' he whispered.

The voice made no vocal reply. Its presence was made manifest through his blood going cold and a chill sweeping over him. His skull was rimed in ice, numbing him to thought, to fear, to doubt. His muscles became hard, bereft of feeling or pain as he pulled them against the rope. They did not ache, did not burn, did not protest. They were ice.

He should worry, some part of him knew.

His hands pulled themselves free. He felt blood, cold on his skin, could not find the thought to hurt. He rose up on numb legs and staggered forward. The palanquin was before him, his sword upon it, its leather hilt thrust toward him invitingly. He clutched it and for a brief moment felt a surge of vigour, a piece he had been missing thrust violently into him and made whole.

'*You have a sword to defend yourself, the means to escape,*' another voice whispered feverishly. '*Escape! Run now! Save yourself! You don't need to die here!*'

Words on numb ears; he would not die here. He staggered forward, the blade dragging on the earth behind him. Gariath swung the corpse back and forth wildly; he was unimportant. The netherlings darted about him, seeking an opening in his defence; they were insignificant. One of them hung back, the one that had failed to kill him, the one that would enable him.

She was first.

She heard him approach, felt his breath on her neck, knew his presence; that was all so unimportant. She whirled about, the blade in her hand, the curse on her lips, the shield rising; that was just insignificant.

His own blade rose swiftly. He could see himself in its reflection, see the dead, pupilless eyes staring back at him. Then, he was gone, vanished in a bath of red. He couldn't remember when the blade had found her neck. He couldn't remember what he had said that made her look at him with such pain in her mouth, such fear in her eyes.

But he remembered this sensation, this strength. He had felt it in icy rivers and in dark dreams, in the absence of fever and the chill of wind. He remembered the voice that spoke to him now, as it melted and seeped out of his skull. He remembered its message. He heard it now.

'*Strength wanes, bodies decay, faith fails, steel breaks.*'

'Duty,' he whispered, 'persists.'

Life returned to him: warm, burning, feverish life. The body fell to the ground, the netherling gurgling and clutching at the gaping wound in her throat. The others whirled around, staring at her, then turning wide eyes up to Lenk.

'*Shtehz*,' one of them gasped, 'the damn thing just turned grey ag—'

The ensuing cracking sound would have drowned out the remark, even if the netherling's mouth wasn't reduced to a bloody mess as a red claw seized her by the back of her head and smashed her skull against her companion's.

Gariath stepped forward, regarded Lenk curiously for a moment. He snorted.

'Still alive?' he grunted.

'Still alive,' Lenk replied.

'I thought *you'd* be.' Gariath reached down and took one of the netherlings by her biceps. 'The others are dead?'

'Still alive,' Lenk repeated. 'For the moment, at least. There was another longface, Sheraptus, he took the women.'

'A problem,' Gariath replied as he placed a foot between the moaning female's shoulder blades. 'What do you want to do about it?'

'They took them by boat, to a ship,' Lenk replied, gesturing over the sea. 'It can't be far away.' He quirked an eyebrow at the dragonman. 'Why do you care, though?'

'I killed two of these things earlier. Didn't find any answers. I'll give it a little more time.'

'I see … Should I ask?'

Gariath didn't reply. His muscles tensed as he drove his foot downward, pulling the netherlings' arms farther behind her. She screamed, long and loud, but not nearly loud enough to disguise the sound of arms popping out of their sockets, not nearly long enough to drown out the deep cracking sound borne from her chest. She drew in several sharp, ragged breaths that quickly turned to gurgling, choking noises before collapsing into the sand.

'I wouldn't,' Gariath grunted.

'Fine ... that's *fine*.' They both glanced to see the remaining netherling, staggering to her feet, growling as she raised her sword towards the two. 'It doesn't matter if I die here. It's *never* mattered. It doesn't mean you won't still die; it doesn't mean the Master won't—'

In a flash of motion, a dark stripe appeared across her throat framed by two trembling fists. Her sword dropped, her eyes bulging out of their sockets as she reached up to grope helplessly at the garrotte's thick, corded kiss. A grin appeared at her ear, brimming with far more malice than Lenk thought Denaos could ever have mustered.

'It's an ideal situation,' the rogue explained to no one in particular. 'The more you struggle, the tighter it goes, faster it's over. Perfect for putting down animals. It's all but useless against someone who just sits tight and thinks.' He gave her a quick jerk, silencing her choked gurgling. 'As I said, for the circumstances, ideal.'

She collapsed to her knees, but he refused to relinquish his grip on the garrotte, stalwartly absorbing each elbow she thrust behind her. It was a valiant effort, Lenk thought, awestruck by the rogue's tenacity, though not enough to avoid a sudden thought.

Wait ... where'd he get the rope?

The question lingered only as long as it took for the hate to leak out of the netherling's eyes, whereupon Denaos loosed his grip and let her drop. Lenk stared down at the rope, recognising it as far too furry to be anything but what the man had been wearing moments ago.

It took a strong perception for Lenk to realise the

imperative need to not look back up. It took a decidedly stronger resolve not to scream when he invariably did.

Denaos certainly didn't help matters by placing his hands on his naked hips and setting a triumphant foot on the netherling's back.

'Take it all in, gentlemen,' he replied, gesturing downward and tapping his foot. 'What do you suppose? The biggest one here?'

Gariath stalked past him, casting a glance and offering a snort.

'I've seen bigger.'

'Well, this is all *highly* disturbing,' came a shrill voice. They glanced over to see Dreadaeleon sitting upright, looking at them inquisitively. 'I assume, once someone sees fit to untie me, we'll be giving chase?'

'Were you not dead a moment ago?' Denaos asked.

'Coma,' Dreadaeleon replied, pausing only to sit still long enough for Gariath to shred his bonds and hoist him to his feet. 'A momentary overwhelming of the senses, not unlike deeply inhaling a pot of mustard.'

'Mustard doesn't do *that*,' Denaos pointed out.

'Surprisingly enough, I use these childish metaphors for the benefit of your diminished comprehension,' the boy spat back, '*not* so we can waste time. We have to go after the renegade … the longface.'

'They're out at sea,' Lenk muttered. 'We don't know where.'

'We will shortly,' Denaos replied.

Before anyone could ask, the rogue slipped behind a nearby bone and returned, shoving what appeared to be a walking, bound, bruised melon before him. Togu did not raise his head, his yellow eyes cast down. Shame, Lenk thought, or perhaps just out of a sense of protection as

Denaos drew his loincloth-turned-garrotte tightly between his hands and looked to Lenk for approval.

'No,' Lenk said, sighing. 'We've got to find out what he knows first. The sea is a vast place, his ship could be anywhere and—'

'Two leagues that way,' Dreadaeleon interrupted, pointing out over the shore.

'Huh?'

'He leaks magic,' the boy replied. 'He's a skunk in linens to me.'

'Oh.' Lenk glanced over at Denaos and shrugged. 'Go nuts, then.'

'*STOP!*'

The Gonwa chased his own voice, emerging from the gloom before Denaos' wrists could even twitch. They regarded him as warily as he did they, though he seemed to be under no delusions that the sharpened stick in his hand was any match for the bloodied sword in Lenk's. Still, his eyes carried a suspicious forthrightness that Lenk instantly recalled.

'Hongwe,' he muttered the creature's name. 'If you're here to finish the betrayal ...'

'He's not,' Gariath grunted.

'I'd believe that if *anyone* else had said it,' Denaos replied.

'What makes you so sure?' Dreadaeleon asked, quirking a brow.

'I know,' the dragonman said.

'The *Rhega* speaks the truth, cousins,' Hongwe said softly. 'I am no friend to the longface.' He gestured to Togu. 'And neither is Togu.'

'He *sold* us to them,' Denaos growled.

'For survival,' Hongwe replied sharply. 'He had choices … He made the wrong one.'

'How is this not reason enough to kill him again?'

'Because I can't watch him die,' Hongwe replied, 'and don't ask me to look away. Togu saved the lives of me and my people. I trusted him, and if you want my help, I ask you to spare him.'

'What help?' Denaos asked, sneering. 'We know where the ship is. We've now got our weapons back *as well* as our monster – no offence, Gariath – so the only thing lacking is a loose end which I've already tied up and am about to strangle with my loincloth.'

Hongwe shrugged. 'You got no boat.'

'He has a point,' Dreadaeleon replied, eyeing Denaos. 'What do you care, anyway? Death is nearly assured. Not really your ideal situation, is it?'

'Prepubescent men in loincloths,' Denaos replied, 'are in a universally poor position to choose their help.'

'*Post*pubescent.'

'So you say.'

'Shut up, shut up, *shut up*,' Lenk snarled. He whirled a scowl upon Hongwe. 'You can get us to the ship?' At the Gonwa's nod, he looked to Gariath. 'You coming?'

'People will die,' Gariath replied.

'They will.'

'Then yes.'

'Great, fantastic, good,' Lenk muttered, waving an arm about in swift instruction. 'Get the boat. Get ready. We sweep in, start killing, hopefully come out of this all right.'

'That's a plan?' Denaos asked. 'Not to prove the boy's point, but a fire-leaking wizard *is* something to take a moment about in regards to how we're going to attack this.'

'Faith fades, steel shatters, bodies decay,' Lenk replied, hurrying to the palanquin. 'Duty remains.'

'What does that even *mean*?'

'Khetashe, I *don't know*, you stupid protuberance! Just shut up and help me get my pants on,' he snarled, tearing through the palanquin's array. 'If I'm about to go charging onto a ship brimming with purple psychopaths who worship someone who *leaks* fire, I'm not doing it with my balls hanging out.'

'That's a good first step, at least,' Dreadaeleon replied. 'What next?'

Lenk's fingers brushed against something thick and soft. He plucked the severed head from the assorted tribute, holding it by its golden locks and staring into its almost serene, closed eyes.

'I'll think of something,' he said softly.

Thirty

BURIED IN SKIN

A ll shicts knew how to deal with predators.

It was a matter of instinct. Those who lived in the wilds shared them with predators; those who knew how to deal with them possessed the talent for doing so. Those who did not lacked the instinct, thus they had not been given the talent by Riffid, thus they were not shict.

Kataria was a shict.

She reminded herself of this. Her breathing was slow and steady, fear kept hidden deep, far away from her eyes. She sat up straight, resting on her knees, back rigid: Those with weak stances were easy prey; those who drew attention to themselves provoked sharp teeth. Her wrists were relaxed in their rawhide bonds: Struggle suggested weakness, weakness invited attention. She forced herself still, daring no movement beyond quick breaths and subtle darts of her eyes.

She glanced at Asper, kneeling beside her, similarly bound. The priestess had only ceased to struggle against her captors when she had been forced into the cabin, placed in the corner with Kataria. Without fury to hide it behind, fear had set in quickly. She cowered in her bonds, bowed her head, breathed quietly, choking back sobs.

'Talanas protect me,' she whispered. 'I've doubted so much, I've feared for everything, I can't take this anymore, you've denied me my whole life, please don't let him do this, please, please, please ...'

'Stay calm,' Kataria muttered, 'stay still. Don't speak.'

'Shut up,' Asper whimpered, 'shut up, shut up, shut up. You don't know what's going to happen. You can't know.'

Kataria narrowed her eyes, her ears folding over themselves. She tried to ignore the priestess' fervent whispering, tried to ignore the truth of her words to no avail. For as much as she reminded herself that she was shict, that she knew how to deal with predators, she could not shut out the doubt, the fear entirely.

Nor could she ignore the sound of long purple fingers drumming on wood. Nor could she recall any predator she had seen whose eyes burned like flame.

Predators were creatures of simple motive: fear, hunger, anger all plain in their gazes. Nothing about Sheraptus was plain on him, least of all his eyes burning fire. Instinct told her to fear him, yet he had not so much as looked at them since ushering them aboard the great, black vessel. His power was obvious, but he had done nothing more than whisper quiet orders to his netherlings to prove it.

Of him, all she could be certain was that his stare, brimming with fire, was not on her. For that, she was thankful.

Sitting lazily in a massive, blackwood chair beside a matching table, he weighed the tome heavily in his hands, staring at it with varying levels of disinterest, drumming his fingers on the armrest contemplatively. Occasionally, he reached up and ran a finger along the crown of black iron upon his brow, relaxing as soon as he touched it, suitably convinced that it was still there.

The crown was his sole distraction, all he seemed to truly notice in the room. It shared his enthusiasm, its three crimson jewels glowing all the brighter at his touch, speaking in a wordless, glimmering language only he could understand. More often than not, Kataria noticed him grinning at the crown's unheard jest, the wrinkles at his lips giving the impression that his mouth stretched far longer than any mouth could or should.

At those moments, Kataria found it difficult to keep the fear buried.

'What is paper made of, anyway?'

It was both the suddenness of and genuinely curious tone behind the question that caused her to start.

'Wood,' a voice grated.

She heard Sheraptus shift in his chair, dared glance up to see him a bit surprised by the sudden voice. Xhai, leaning against the wall with arms folded across her chest, met his gaze and shrugged.

'Hacked down, pressed ... I don't know.'

'Wood ... from trees.' Sheraptus hummed thoughtfully, staring at the book. 'They have thousands of trees.' He glanced out the cabin's great bay windows. 'Water, salted and pure, they have in abundance. They have fertile earth to grow food to feed themselves *and* four-legged things they turn *into* food. There is absolutely nothing to fight over on this world.' He lifted the book up to the overhanging oil lamp, as if hoping to divine some secret from it by fire. 'But they fight ... over this.

'No, no.' He suddenly shook his head. 'Not even this: what's *inside* this.' He flipped the book open, thumbed through the pages with a sneer painted on his face. 'Ink, letters, words I can't even read.' He glanced over at Xhai. 'The Grey One That Grins ... he said that no overscum could read it, either, didn't he?'

'He did,' the female replied.

'And yet so many creatures want it,' he whispered,

astonished. 'The overscum wish to keep it out of the underscum's hands. The underscum desire it for reasons I can't even fathom. The Grey One That Grins wants it for reasons he wants us *not* to fathom. And those green things wanted it to protect them ...'

'From us,' Xhai finished, grinning.

'No, not those green things. The other ones ... the tall, tattooed ones.' He shook his head. 'So much worth fighting for ... and they choose *this*.'

'Are you going to read it?' Xhai asked. 'If the Grey One That Grins wants what's in it, we should know.' She narrowed her eyes. 'I don't trust him. Or the screamer. We should have hurt her a little. I don't think she should—'

'Of course you don't,' Sheraptus said, sighing. 'That's what makes you a netherling. You come from nothing, you return to nothing. Your entire life is set: your actions, your fate, your ...' His gaze drifted towards Kataria, causing her head to duck sharply, drawing a grin from him. 'Instincts.'

She cursed herself instantly; the movement was too sharp, too sudden. It had drawn his attention. She heard his chair slide as he rose from it, his feet scraping softly on the wood floor. She heard Xhai's teeth grind, felt the milk-white scowl levelled at her like a weapon. She tried to swallow, finding it difficult to do so with her heart lodged in her throat.

She heard his hand before it reached her, heard the quiet moan of the air as it parted in fear before his fingers. It did not stop her from cringing when it cupped her beneath the chin.

'But these things ... these creatures ...' He whispered, a farce of gentility in his voice. 'Nothing is certain. They do things that make no sense, worship creatures that don't exist,

fight over ink, scream in pain when pain is a certainty ...'
He tilted her face up, stared into her with burning eyes.
'Why?'

Her eyes wanted to burst from their sockets, to let tears boiling behind them come flowing out. Her lips twitched with the scream that sought to pry them open and be heard. She buried them with her fear, or tried to.

But his eyes of fire searched her face, searing away masks of confidence and burning down walls wrought by defiance. He sought her fear, caught it in fleeting glimpses, and bid it to emerge within her stare as his fingers slid down her chin, brushing lightly against her throat, trying to coax out the scream inside.

She trembled, a shudder that rose in the pit of her stomach and coursed through her body, up to his fingers. He sensed it, a smile tugging at lips too long, eyes brightening wickedly. The jewels on his crown shone, wordlessly squealing, whining, suggesting, pleading, demanding that she stare into his eyes, that she loose her terror and fold over and tremble and weep and feel his eyes and teeth upon her, sinking into her flesh, drinking her fear.

Do not.

She heard it. Not a voice, but a confirmation not from her own thoughts. It did not rise in her head, but in her heart.

He is a predator. All predators are the same.

It did not inform her of this. She found she knew it. It was not a message. It was simply a reinforcement of knowledge, of instinct.

Do not scream. If you scream, you will never stop.

And she knew she would not.

'This one, I think,' he whispered through his grin.

The moment he rose and stepped back, Xhai swept

forward in great, angry strides. She seized Kataria by her arm and hauled her towards the cabin's support pillar. She felt her muscles tense, protest welling up inside them, only to be quashed by the sudden knowledge that rose within her.

They are all base creatures, uncomplicated. They know weakness and kill it. They know defiance and kill it. Be as the air: light, unconcerned. They do not know the air. They cannot kill the air.

The fear did not abate, but it suddenly felt less pertinent, if no less certain. Something had intervened itself between her and the longfaces, buried the fear deep behind its shadow. She felt her breath returning slowly, even as Xhai slammed her body against the pillar and swiftly bound her wrists to it. He was a predator; she knew how to deal with predators; she could survive.

She knew this because someone else knew this. Someone else told her this through their mutual instinct, their common, racial voice. Someone told her through the Howling.

Another shict. Close enough to hear. Close enough to smell.

'Not knowing ... makes me uncomfortable.'

Her eyes were drawn back to Sheraptus as he stood over the table, running long fingers over a smooth, blackwood case. His hand lingered on it with unnerving sensuality.

'It's not right that the pursuit of knowledge should be hindered, that wisdom should be kept from the mind that thirsts for it.' The case opened at his touch with a bone-deep creaking noise. 'This is the flaw of most creatures, I find: overscum, underscum, netherling alike. They are all satisfied by what they think they know.'

His hands went to his brow, fingers digging beneath his

crown. It parted with him after some hesitation, the glow burning brightly in protest, and then going dark as he set it next to the open case.

'How is progress made, then, if everyone is sated with gods, with theories, with instinct? No. Progress ... true progress ...'

From red silk lining, it slid out: a jagged sliver of a blade, as long and thin as two of his purple fingers. Its metal was polished to a high sheen. He turned. The fires in his eyes had been extinguished with the removal of the crown. Behind them, in that milk-white stare, a sadistic glee that had been hidden in crimson was reflected in the blade.

'Is found deeper.'

Bury your fear deep, the Howling told her. *Show him nothing.*

It was difficult for her to comply with that as he drew closer, the blade hanging at his side, dangling limply from his fingers. She took it in, along with his stare, his grin, with equal dread as he came upon her.

'And look at how you look at me,' he whispered, his voice an edge itself, 'with such judgement. I've seen it before, of course, and it strikes me as so hypocritical. That is the word, isn't it? Wherein you deny one truth because it seems inconvenient? Yes, hypocritical. It is hypocritical for you to think that the pursuit of knowledge can ever be second to anything. If you think the pursuit of it cruel, then clearly, you don't know enough, do you?

'The netherlings know. We were born in nothing. We expected nothing. But this world ... it's so brimming with ... *everything*.' His tongue flicked against his teeth with each word, unable to be contained. 'And we owe it to ourselves to know, to find out. We cannot be content with instinct, with what we suspected we knew. It would be disingenuous. We would never progress.

'This, I believe, is why I arrived here. Certainly, the Grey One That Grins opened the door in his search, but it had to happen for a reason. Divine happenstance, as you might suspect? No, no ... it was natural. It was inevitable. Someone had to come, to understand this world so that netherlings and overscum as a whole might progress.'

Show nothing. Say nothing. Do not look away. Do not give him reason.

She felt a bead of sweat form at her temple. It felt her fear as it felt his stare upon it. It fled, sliding down her brow, over her jawline, rolling across her chest, through the fur garment to drip down upon her belly. As it chased the centreline of her abdomen and hung above her navel, his finger shot out, pressed against her skin. At her gasp, the shudder of her stomach, his grin grew as broad and sharp as his knife.

'But to know, we must dig, we must seek, we must pry and we must cut.' He lifted his finger, studied the bead of sweat upon it. 'We must go into the base and find out what makes you work, what makes your heart beat and belly tremble. And you will show me.'

He pinched his fingers together, a brief flash of fire behind his eyes as the sweat sizzled into steam. Grinning all the broader, he reached out to seize her by the jaw, running the tip of his blade down her body, gooseflesh rising in the wake of the gentle, razor grazing.

'You will show me *everything*.'

The urge to indulge him rose inside her, the urge to wail and scream in the hopes that someone would hear her before that knife angled just a hair and slid into the tender flesh of her abdomen. In his grins, real and reflected, was a suggestion to do just that, to obey if she sought to survive.

DO NOT. The Howling rang out inside her head. *He perverts instinct, destroys reason. Do not scream. Do not show fear. Do not even think.*

And as soon as she knew this, her breathing stilled, her eyes dimmed, the fear seeping out of them. His own grin diminished slightly, seeing such a thing. She knew then that he could not succeed, that he could not exploit fear as he had hoped.

'Get away from her!'

Not hers, anyway.

They both looked to the corner: she with a quick, fervent glance, he with a slow, lurid stare. Asper had found her nerve, sitting up straight in her bonds, staring fire through tear-stained eyes, trembling against the ropes that held her. Her lower jaw was clenched tightly as she leaned forward, baring teeth at him.

'Don't you touch her,' she hissed.

Damn it, Asper, Kataria growled inwardly.

She looked back to Sheraptus. He apparently sensed her thoughts, offering her a lurid grin. The malicious glimmer in his eyes was as unmistakable as the swell of his breeches. Kataria was more horrified than she suspected she ought to be to know that neither were meant for her.

'Close your eyes, if you want,' he whispered. 'Shut your ears as best you can. Just know …' He swept his stare to the bound priestess. 'You could have stopped this.'

Asper's resolve seemed to melt with every step forward he took, her fear becoming more apparent, every quiver on her flesh bare to his pervasive stare, every lump disappearing down her throat heard with painful clarity. Kataria desperately wanted to turn away, to not hear, but found herself bound by his words as surely as the ropes.

She had caused this. Asper would suffer.

For me.

'It never lasts long, does it?' Sheraptus almost cooed as he descended upon her. 'The defiance, the hope, the anger, the sorrow ... You can always come back.'

He shrugged. His robe fell from his shoulders. Kataria beheld purple muscle; red lines from which blood had once wept painted a picture of hate and fury upon his flesh.

'They fight back, at first, but that's only one of two constants. After that, it becomes so many things: pleading, persuasion, bargaining until finally ...' He sighed. 'The second constant. Nothing. No more fear, no more noise. They're ... broken.'

'S-stay away from me,' Asper whimpered, pulling back. Kataria noticed her shifting to one side, tucking her left arm behind her as she did. 'Don't touch me.'

'Yes, that's usually how it starts.' He canted his head to the side. 'But ... not with you, no. You're wearing a mask, aren't you? You only want me to think you're like the others. There's something within you ... something I have felt before.'

'I don't know what—'

'You do. I know you do, because I do.' Sheraptus raised a brow. 'Some qualities go deeper than breed. Some qualities, as loathsome as it is to admit it, are inherent. In you, I sense our instincts ... that which drives us to kill, to cause anguish and suffering with no reason other than that's what we do.'

'You're wrong,' she gasped, her voice a whimper. 'You're *wrong*!'

'Never.' His eyes flared to crimson life. '*Never* wrong.'

He uttered the alien word, his hand rose and she followed, suspended by an invisible force. She shrieked, the sound ringing in Kataria's ears, drawing Sheraptus' smile wider. His hand extended, he took a step forward and staggered. His spare hand went to his brow as he swayed on his feet.

'Master,' Xhai said, stepping forward with hands outstretched. 'It's the crown. The Grey One That Grins slipped it to you to weaken you. You don't need it.' A needy whine slipped into her voice. 'These overscum women, you don't need them, either. They're both making you weaker.'

'Weaker?' He turned to her with an expression of hurt on his face, though the fraud behind it was obvious. 'Xhai … do you think I'm … weak?'

Obvious to almost everyone.

'N-no, Master!' she said, shaking her head violently. 'I am just concerned for—'

'Unnecessary, Carnassial,' he hissed with sudden fury, turning back to Asper. 'I don't like using magic for this. It dulls everything. What can be learned when all qualities and variables are dashed?'

He growled another word, shoving his hand forward. Asper was flung against the wall of the cabin, her scream choked in pain, her struggling impotent as he strode forward. His eyes were wide, white. His lips trembled, shifting between grin and animal need.

'Knowledge gained through *nethra* is nothing. It's too swift, too open to doubt. True knowledge is found through observation, through experiment. Slowly.'

He waved his hand. Asper's shriek was cut short as she was flipped about by the unseen force, her belly pressed against the cabin wall, her bound arms presented to him. He reached out and placed a hand upon her naked left shoulder.

'And here is where it all starts ... This is the source of it, the beginning.' His hand slid down her arm, tightening here, pinching there, counting off each knuckle in her fingers. 'Such pain in it ... I can feel it in you, feel them screaming. But this ... this is merely a vessel.' His hand slid lower, rested upon her buttock. 'Show me, little creature, where the true suffering lies.'

Kataria didn't understand his words, didn't even hear him. She could only hear Asper's whimpering, the screams choked inside her, the shuddering dread in her flesh. She could only see Asper's tears pouring from her eyes, over her red cheeks and into her clenched teeth as she tried to shut them against him, against everything.

She could only feel Asper's fear, her rage at how little she could fight against him, how she could do nothing as his fingers slid up past her loincloth.

To his sigh of contentment, she wished she could shut her ears ... and then tear out his throat.

'Ah ...' he whispered. 'There it is.' He smiled, pressing his body against hers. 'Just takes a bit of trauma, doesn't it? Everything with your breed does. It's the catalyst that makes you shift so constantly. Yours will emerge, I think, only after more, only after ...'

He paused, looking up and away from her, staring into nothing. Xhai seemed to pick up on this instantly, stepping forward with a furrowed brow and clenched fists.

'Master?'

'We,' he whispered, 'have company.'

Before she could even form a suspicion, a chorus of screams rang out from the ship's deck and assaulted Kataria's ears. The sound of metal clanging, voices chanting, a thunderous roar, alien words. Through it all, barely audible through the wood, she heard a voice screaming itself hoarse with her name.

Lenk.

A human, the Howling answered. *Not important.*

'We're under attack,' Xhai snarled. She stalked to the wall, seizing her massive metal wedge of a sword. 'Nothing but worthless high-fingers out there. I'll be back.'

'No, no,' Sheraptus said. 'That will take a bit longer than I'd like. I'll handle this personally. Stay here and guard them.'

'Guard,' she growled in indignation. 'I'm a Carnassial. The *First* Carnassial. *Your* Carnassial. Let me do this for you; let me—'

'Unnecessary,' he replied. 'Besides …'

He glanced at his fingers, disdainfully wiping them clean upon his robes.

'I'm in a bit of a mood.'

He withdrew his other hand, his power dissipating and letting Asper slide dejectedly to the floor. He swept across the floor, beckoning robe and crown to his hand with a wave. Slowly, he affixed both and turned to the cabin's door, pausing only to spare a smile for Xhai.

'Come now, Xhai, if I trusted anyone else …'

'I would kill them,' she grunted.

'Absolutely.' He swept his burning eyes back to Asper. 'I shall return shortly.'

He was gone in an instant. Only then did Kataria look at Asper, lying motionless upon the floor, not enough breath left in her to sob, not enough life in her to stir. Kataria stared at her, the woman who was rendered so still, so lifeless, because she had spoken up for the shict. Kataria stared, mouth hanging open, unable to find words to comfort she who had spoken the words that had condemned her.

The din of battle outside grew louder. Not loud enough to drown out the Howling.

She is a human. Her actions are a symptom of her disease. You owe her nothing.

Not loud enough to convince Kataria.

Thirty-One

SUBTLETY IS FOR THE DEAD

I was supposed to have given this up ...
There was no doubt in his step as he darted low under
a wild swing from a purple arm, shoving his blade up into
purple skin, stared up into a purple face. The light leaked
out of her white eyes in swift order, the last moments of
her life spent spewing a blood-slurred curse from her teeth
before she collapsed to the deck of the ship.

Wasn't I?

'*Unique circumstances.*'

He felt his hands driven of their own accord, twisting
the blade inside her to extinguish the last sparks.

You're not supposed to be so chatty, either.

'*You're supposed to deny us more powerfully.*'

And yet ...

'*Clarity is a wonderful thing. Behind you.*'

'*QAI ZHOTH!*'

He whirled and saw the pair of longfaces charging.
While he might not have heard Dreadaeleon's arcane verse
over their war cry, he certainly heard the roaring crackle of
fire that followed. A great red plume preceded the boy like
a herald as he strode forward, arm outstretched to sweep
his fiery harbinger over the pair. They writhed, shrieking
as they attempted to press forward, then fall back, before
they simply fell, blackened and smoking.

'Nice work,' Lenk remarked.

'Well, I do it all for your approval,' Dreadaeleon replied, panting. 'This wasn't a good idea. I'm strong enough to do that, but not for much longer. Not without ...' He glanced at Lenk, then grunted. 'We should have opted for another strategy.'

'The other strategy was to leave Kat and Asper to die.'

'We could have tried something else. Subtlety, perhaps.'

'We are a pubescent magic-spewing freak, a man with a disembodied screaming head and four hundred pounds of angry reptile. What about that suggests "subtlety" to you?'

A thunder of boots rumbled through the ship's black hull; alien war cries rose through the planks of the deck. At the bow of the ship, the purple shapes of the netherlings began to emerge from the shadows of a companionway.

The shriek that met theirs was shrill and terrified.

A green shape came hurtling over Lenk's shoulder like a scaly meteor, colliding with the lead longface with a resounding cracking sound. She collapsed into her companions as Togu, bound and squealing, rebounded from her chest and rolled along the deck.

Lenk *had* wondered why Gariath had insisted on bringing him along up until now.

Gariath followed, charged on all fours, complementing Togu's strike with one from his own horns. He struck the longface's purple torso, rose to his feet and continued to press her back into her fellows, choking their rush in the companionway's darkened throat.

'Five hundred pounds, maybe. He's looking healthy today,' Lenk said, cringing at the flurry of claws and teeth and noting the wisdom in keeping his distance. 'Subtlety is where Denaos comes in.'

'Pointless,' Dreadaeleon muttered. 'The moment the heretic even looks at him sideways, he's dead and we'll follow. Did you not see what he can do? What he *did*?'

'I saw,' Lenk replied. 'If I was duly frightened of everything that makes *you* faint, however, I'd never get anything done. This is the only chance we have.' He shoved the boy forward. 'Now, do something useful.'

The boy's eyes narrowed and, whether because of Lenk's command or in spite of it, blossomed with crimson light. He swept his hands toward the companionway, the fire in his palms blooming with the murmur from his mouth. He placed them both upon the deck and, with a resounding word, sent serpentine flame racing to meet in the companionway and erect a wall of crackling orange to segregate the dragonman and the netherlings.

Gariath stared at the sudden obstacle with undue contemplation, as though wondering whether to leap through the fire and continue the assault or perhaps just break Dreadaeleon's hands to bring it down first.

Lenk was more prepared for either of those than to see the dragonman reach down, scoop up Togu's bound form, and drag him back with unnerving patience. At Lenk's apparent surprise, he shrugged.

'I've killed a lot so far,' he said. 'I can wait for a few more.'

'The point is not to kill them,' Lenk replied, 'but to distract them until Denaos can do what he needs to.' He glanced over the edge of the ship. 'Then we leap off, reunite with Hongwe and paddle off before anyone can kill us.' He glanced to Togu, wide-eyed and squealing behind a gag. 'What'd you bring him for, anyway?'

'He caused this, as you say. He should see it to the end,'

the dragonman replied. 'The end being that you all die, of course.'

'Not you?'

'Not yet.'

'You seem in good spirits. How have you been, anyway?'

'Not dead yet.'

'Nor us.'

'Yet.'

'Right, yet. It's a bit strange to see you so enthusiastic.'

'I could leave, if you want.'

'Not yet.'

Gariath said nothing in reply, sweeping his gaze up and down the ship. Aside from Dreadaeleon's murmuring chant holding the flames up and the netherlings back, the deck was quiet from companionway to the looming cabin at the ship's stern.

'And you're waiting for what?'

It happened in an instant. Sound died, wary of being heard. Clouds covered the moon, terrified to be seen. Pressure settled over the deck as the sky sank low and tried to hide beneath the sea.

'That,' Lenk whispered.

Dreadaeleon's voice was choked from him, his chant and the flames it conjured extinguished in an instant. The netherlings emerged from the companionway slowly, all their bloodlust and hatred still present in their white stares, but restrained behind shields and nocked arrows.

Keeping baleful stares on the companions as they defensively backed up against the ship's great mast, the netherlings filed out silently, uttering no more than a curse or growl as they took positions, surrounding their prey, but making no move to raise blade or draw bow. The yearning to do so was frighteningly plain on their faces, but they were restrained by some unheard command, a cautious calm settling over them that Lenk found unsettling.

He had seen this before.

'Can I help you?' a voice, deep and rolling, bade Lenk to turn.

Against the purple pillars of muscle and iron that flanked him, the longface didn't look too imposing at a glance. It didn't take long for Lenk to become reacquainted with the eyes ablaze and the halo of black iron wrapped about Sheraptus' brow, however. It took even less time for him to raise his sword cautiously and slip a hand to his belt and the burlap sack hanging from it.

'If he's got only one arm,' Gariath whispered, 'that will keep him busy, right?'

'Yes, but—'

The dragonman didn't wait. Hurling Togu at the longface, he howled and fell to all fours, charging after the squealing green projectile. The females made no movement to intervene as Sheraptus lifted a hand and casually waved it.

The air quivered with force. A gale unseen and unheard spawned from nothingness and swept over the deck, striking both Togu and Gariath from sky and deck alike and sending them hurtling over the ship. Lenk stared in astonishment as his companions' roar ended in a brief splash. Sheraptus didn't spare nearly as much shock, glancing disinterestedly over the ship's edge and then back to Lenk.

'Well?' he asked. A moment later, recognition dawned on his face. 'Oh, it's you. Still alive?'

Lenk nodded weakly, only just beginning to pull himself from his shock.

'I assume my females are dead, then?'

Another nod. Sheraptus regarded them carefully before canting his head to the side.

'And?'

Lenk recoiled, having expected nearly any other response.

'And ... what?' he asked.

'Did you need something else?'

'What? We ...' He shook the confusion from his face, replaced it with as steely a resolve as he could manage. 'We came for our friends.'

'That hardly seems fair,' Sheraptus said, looking of-fended.

'Fair?' Lenk asked, the incredulity of the statement shocking him into inaction.

'I left close to two fists of females on the beach and you killed them all,' Sheraptus said before gesturing to the deck. 'You killed three more here and who knows how many more in Irontide.' He frowned. 'I take *two* of yours and you come onto my ship and make such a ruckus as to draw me out of enjoying them?'

'Of ... of course we did.'

'Fascinating. Why?'

'Because ...' Lenk blinked, his face screwing up. '*What?*'

'Kindly don't live up to your stereotype. You know exactly what I mean. To have come here, you would have to be led here, thusly you knew what awaited you. It would have been more pragmatic to flee ... yet you came here, into a ship brimming with my warriors under my limitless control, into certain death. For what? *Two* females? You could have found more somewhere else.'

Kataria, he thought.

'*Duty*,' the voice insisted.

'What is it you hoped to accomplish, then?' Sheraptus asked.

'Realistically?' Lenk replied.

'Of course.'

The young man shrugged, seeing no particular point in lying. 'The idea was to keep you busy until the other fellow who was with us could sneak into your cabin and escape with the females.'

Sheraptus nodded, seeing no particular point in reacting. 'And ideally?'

'Kill you and render the rest of the situation something akin to making gravy.'

'I apologise to say that the metaphor is lost, though I grasp the meaning,' Sheraptus sighed. 'No matter how lofty the goals, no matter how staunch the ideal, it always ends in base instinct: eat, breed, die. It's so ...' He glanced at a nearby female and frowned. 'The sole difference between you and them is that you try so hard to deny it.'

He waved his hand. Bows creaked, arrows levelled at the companions as his eyes smouldered with burning contempt.

'I'm not sure there's anything to be learned from you, sadly.'

'*Now*,' the voice said inside Lenk's head. '*NOW!*'

Lenk's hand slipped into the burlap sack, fingers wrapping around thick locks as he pulled the object within free. Strings sang, arrows flew as he held the severed head aloft and spoke a word.

'Scream.'

And it obeyed.

The air shuddered in an explosion of sound as the mouth found a macabre life and sprang open, eyes flaring with golden awareness. The arrows found no soft flesh, but a wall of noise that shuddered out of him and tore the air apart, sending the missiles twisting away, scattered like rats before a flood.

With a shriek unheard, Dreadaeleon hurled himself to the deck as Lenk turned, levelling the head and the quavering wail tearing itself free from its mouth towards the surrounding longfaces. In great waves, it swept over them. Hands were clenched to bleeding ears, shields rose in futile defence, the truly unprepared were sent sprawling over the railings, their screams lost in the shrieking onslaught.

Unable to bear it any longer himself, he lowered the head. His ears rang; his heart throbbed as the echoes of the shrieking lingered in the sky on distant, fading thunder. Dreadaeleon rose on shaking legs, breathing heavily. The longfaces rose not at all as they groaned and bled on the deck.

All save one.

'You didn't mention that in your plan, I note,' Sheraptus said, twisting his little finger inside his ear.

'Surprise?'

'You are adorable.'

Sheraptus flung his hand out, the wave of force rippling from his fingertips to strike Lenk and hurl him towards the mast. He struck it with an angry cracking sound, letting out a breathless cry before he collapsed, unmoving.

As Dreadaeleon stared at his companion's unconscious body, he began to feel it. His breath sought to flee his lungs, his eyes his head, his legs out from under him, regardless of whether or not the rest of him decided to come. It was painfully familiar: the same sensation that had driven him into darkness a week ago, rendered him helpless only an hour before, showed him to be nothing more than an impotent weakling …

In front of Asper, he added mentally, *twice.*

He felt it now – that sensation of power, that great light that never extinguished, that unnatural presence that made nature go still. He felt the burning stare, from eyes and stones alike, and knew that the curiosity behind it was all that kept him conscious at the moment.

'Little moth?' Sheraptus asked, a smile tugging at his lips. 'I *thought* that might be you. Apologies, between the screaming and the distraction, I hardly noticed you.'

'Don't talk to me,' Dreadaeleon hissed, painfully aware of his breaking voice.

'That would make me a terrible host.'

'You're a heretic, a renegade,' the boy snarled. 'You disregard the laws of magic, the laws of the Venarium. You will be stopped.'

Sheraptus stared at him for a moment. 'By you?' He held up a hand. 'No … no, don't answer that. Don't even think about it, if you can help it. The strain might put you under. *Again.*'

'That last time, you … you cheated,' Dreadaeleon growled. 'Somehow, I don't know. That's why you have to be stopped.'

'I have to be stopped because you don't understand how I did it? How will you ever learn?'

'Shut *up*,' Dreadaeleon snarled.

His voice came with all the conviction of a constipated cow, the pressure around him threatening to shatter his jaw. Breath came harder; standing came with great difficulty. But he still breathed. He still stood. He forced his fingers straight, levelled them at Sheraptus. He forced his eyes open through the sweat dripping down his face. He forced the words to a mind that sought to shut itself down, into lips that sought to seal themselves shut. Electricity,

590

however faint, danced in blue sparks on his fingertips.

'Really?' Sheraptus asked, levelling fingers of his own. 'You know how this will end.'

'I do,' the boy grunted.

'You want to go ahead with it?'

'I do.'

'For your ... Venarium?'

'Not them.'

Sheraptus glanced over his shoulder, towards his cabin, and smiled. 'Ah, I see. The tall one?'

'If you touched her ...'

'I did,' he said, turning his smile upon the boy. 'There's more to her than you could know, little moth. There's more I will learn from her. And I will do it slowly.'

It was a scream that tore itself from Dreadaeleon's lips: unfocused, angry, wild. The electricity that launched from his fingers was no different, snaking out in a wild, twisting tongue. It was only the sheer inaccuracy of his aim that allowed the sparks to fly past a purple hand meant to ward it off and lash against a shoulder.

The longface hissed and recoiled. It had done no damage that Dreadaeleon could see: barely anything more than a black mark, barely visible against the longface's ebon robe. He supposed it was the indignity of the blow, an electric slap in the face, that caused Sheraptus' visage to screw up in fury, his eyes to become two angry miniature suns.

'Pity,' he hissed as he raised a hand and levelled it at the boy, 'that she didn't see that.'

It occurred to Dreadaeleon that such a blow shouldn't feel quite as satisfying as it did. Even if it *had* done any discernible damage, his victory was dampened by the groans heralding the rise of the netherlings.

Slowly, shaking blood from their ears, grinding curses

591

between their teeth, those remaining staggered to their feet with murder in their eyes. His companions remained lost to unconsciousness and the sea respectively. Sheraptus' fingers began to crackle with blue sparks just as his eyes went alight with red.

He was going to die, Dreadaeleon realised. And all he had done was sully a robe a little.

Still, he thought with a smile, considering he had been in a coma induced by the man's stare alone just moments ago, this didn't feel like such a bad note to end on.

His only concern was why it was taking so long.

Sheraptus' face twitched, neck jerked, as though a gnat were buzzing in his ear every moment he thought to discharge the lethal electricity and reduce Dreadaeleon to a smouldering husk. That same buzzing lingered in the boy's head, too annoying to allow him to feel fear or a need for flight. It chilled him, burned him, alternating and intensifying with each breath.

Even before he felt the shadow sail over the deck, he recognised the presence of another wizard.

That hardly kept his jaw from going slack as his eyes rose to the sky, followed by a dozen wide whites and two narrowed orange slits. The presence of the newcomer felt an anathema to Sheraptus' power, bidding the seas to churn and the moon to peer out from behind the clouds and shed light on him.

Beneath a broad-brimmed hat, a pair of hard eyes stared down at the deck from high in the sky. A coat fanned out into leathery wings behind a tall and slender body, flapping to keep him gracefully aloft above the carnage on the deck. At his hip hung a dense tome supported by a silver chain, its cover marked with a sigil of authority.

A sigil of the Venarium.

'Oh, hell,' Dreadaeleon whispered, 'a Librarian.'

'It's quite rude to come announcing yourself with that particular presence, sir,' Sheraptus snarled to the man. 'Come down and let us speak without you buzzing in my head.'

Not possible, Dreadaeleon recognised. The power roiling from the Librarian was faint, but constant, worn like the easy mantle of authority that settled about his features. It was a power that came from no crown or stone, but from years of practice and merciless discipline.

'Bralston,' the man spoke by way of callous introduction. 'Librarian under the authority of Lector Annis of the Cier'Djaal Venarium branch, unlimited jurisdiction, all treaties foregone, lethal force authorised and pre-absolved.' His eyes ran over the scene with cool surveillance. 'I have come seeking a violator of the laws of Venarie. A heretic.'

His gaze shifted from the sweaty boy in a filthy coat before settling on the purple creature with electricity dancing effortlessly on his fingers and the fire burning on his brow and in his eyes. Sheraptus recoiled, offended.

'What makes you so sure it's me?' he asked.

'Violators are offered a singular chance for absolution,' Bralston said, descending to the deck. 'Surrender your body for research and your crimes will be considered absolved.'

'*No one*,' a nearby netherling snarled, stalking to impose herself between Sheraptus and the Librarian, 'speaks to the Master like—'

'Offered and declined. Noted.'

With one smooth movement, Bralston doffed his hat and uttered a word before tossing it gently at the longface. The steel ring within instantly sprouted several glistening thorns that gnashed together with harsh, grating noise. It caught the netherling in the face, her screams muffled behind the leather as its brim wrapped about her head and the headgear's teeth began to noisily chew.

'Carnivorous hat,' Sheraptus noted as the female staggered off, clawing at the garment. 'Impressive.'

'Librarian!' Dreadaeleon called out, finding his nerve and voice at once. 'Wait!'

'All involved parties will be questioned pending execution,' Bralston replied, his eyes burning with crimson as he extended an arm glistening with flame.

'I recognised *two* of those words,' Sheraptus said, matching the Librarian's burning gaze and hand alike. 'Oh, my friend, I have so much to learn from you.'

Thirty-Two

MERCY IS FOR THE DENSE

The din outside the cabin was enough to shake the ship. There had been the clash of metal and the roar of battle, a brief moment's pause before the shuddering wail that caused the panes of glass to crack in their portholes and the doors to threaten to buckle under the pressure. Now, the snarling, roaring, grunting, clanging, hissing ruckus of fighting had resumed in earnest.

Each noise clamoured to be heard over the others, and each told Kataria nothing in their haste to tell her everything.

The din inside her head was still more aggravating. The fear, the doubt and the frustration that twisted inside her skull like so many screws were bad enough without the voice of instinct, of the Howling, of the shict she knew to be speaking to her through it, echoing in her brain.

Survive, it told her. *Shicts survive. Shicts preserve. Shicts cure. You are a shict. You have a duty to your people.* She found it hard to ignore the voice. *Ignore the human. Her duty is to live and die. Your survival is worth more.*

Especially when she couldn't find the will to agree with it.

The will of the unseen shict came with nearly every breath, and was as impossible to ignore as it was to stop breathing. Yet for every time it bade her to look within herself, she found her eyes all the more pressed on the pale, bound figure in the corner.

Asper was still alive, though her shallow breathing and still body did not do much to support it. The priestess did not move, did not speak, did not so much as shiver anymore. The soft weeping and violent trembling had left her body and left her nothing more than a pile of limp bones and skin that muttered the same thing on soft, silent breaths.

'You let it happen,' she whispered. 'I gave everything. I did everything right. You just let it happen.'

What could I do? Kataria thought to herself. *How could you not have known what he was? How could you not have known to stay silent?*

She is human, the Howling answered her. *There is no instinct in her. She survives through other methods that she does not have now. You are a shict. You have instinct. You survive so that all shicts may survive. You have a duty to your people.*

The thought was hers and not hers, a dormant, feral logic awakening within her. And it came more and more frequently, with more and more urgency. It was no longer shared knowledge. It was no longer instinct. The Howling was all her people condensed into a single thought.

It was impossible to ignore, yet impossible to grasp. The unseen shict's will brushed her only in fleeting thoughts, prodding the Howling to awaken and tell her of his location. Nothing more was offered, no advice given or instructions handed down. She racked her mind, searching for a possibility for escape, to reach him.

And then, she would look at Asper, and forget everything.

She would hear the priestess' sobbing, see the priestess' agonised tears. She would forget that she stared at a human, one of many. She would forget that Asper should mean nothing to her, forget that she should think of herself, her people, her duty. She would remember Asper was her friend.

That Asper was the reason she was not lying on the floor and sobbing.

And nothing more than that: she recalled no words of comfort, remembered no reassurances of safety. The Howling would speak to her in these moments of lapsed clarity, and it would begin anew.

Survive, it implored as it knew she should. *You must survive. We must survive. You must—*

Her bones rattled in her flesh as the wooden pillar trembled with the force of the purple fist slamming against it. A harsh, grating growl filled her ears and drowned all other thought.

'What's taking so long?'

Kataria felt slightly comforted to know she wasn't the only one wondering.

It seemed too mild a comparison to think that Xhai paced the cabin like a nervous hound as she stared at the door. Hounds, as far as she knew, didn't show nearly so many teeth when they growled.

Hounds, too, had instinct. When they sensed danger, they acted, even in spite of their master's orders. Xhai clearly sensed danger, clearly wanted to act, but remained in the cabin. She had been given an order and was determined to obey it. As vague as that order might have been, she rigidly clung to it as though it were the word of a god, or whatever equivalent longfaces worshipped.

Him, she reminded herself. *They* ... she *worships* him.

'What do you think it is, then?' Xhai grunted at her. 'Your pinkies come to take what the Master owns?'

Kataria did not answer, for it was clear Xhai didn't want one.

'We should have killed all of you,' she muttered. 'Netherlings don't need pink things.'

Whatever caused Kataria to speak up, she was certain it was no instinct.

'He seems to disagree,' she said.

'The Master *needs* nothing,' Xhai snapped. 'He wants. He wants everything.' Her gaze became hard and looked straight through Kataria. 'He deserves everything.'

'If he had everything he needed,' Kataria replied, 'he would want nothing.'

While she had known she should have stopped long before saying that, Xhai's incoming fist only confirmed that. She jerked her head to the side, saw Xhai pull back knuckles red and embedded with splinters.

'If he needed any of you,' she snarled, 'I wouldn't have watched all the cold, weak bodies of those he wanted fed to the sikkhuns when he was done with them.' She sneered. 'When I drag your body to the pits, overscum, I'm going to make sure you're still warm.'

'I'll go laughing,' Kataria replied, meeting her scowl with an even stare. 'Because the thought of a longface who desperately wants to lick her Master's feet being relegated to garbage removal is just *hilarious*.'

Xhai's hand shot out and caught her by the throat as her fist cocked back. Kataria made certain to smile broadly at the longface, knowing this would be the last time she would do so with all her teeth.

'*I DON'T CARE!*'

They both glanced to the side as Asper threw herself onto her back, her scream hurled at the ceiling from a face stained by tears.

'*I DON'T CARE ANYMORE!*' she shrieked. '*YOU LET IT HAPPEN! YOU ABANDONED ME! LET IT HAPPEN AGAIN, THEN! TAKE IT! TAKE ALL OF IT! I DON'T CARE!*'

'So soon?' Xhai released Kataria and stalked over to the prone woman. 'You're not supposed to snap this early. Wait until the Master can do more.'

'Get away from her,' Kataria growled after the long-face.

Think of yourself, the Howling insisted. *Think of your kin. Think of your duty. You have to—*

'Leave her alone!' Kataria howled, jerking at her bonds.

She is nothing. You have to survive. You have a duty.

'Asper!'

'I don't care, I don't care, I don't care, I don't care, I don't care,' the priestess sobbed, shaking her head violently. 'I want it all to end. I don't care for who.'

'It doesn't end now,' Xhai muttered, rising up and nudging her with a toe from her spike-covered boots. 'The Master doesn't want it to. His is the right to—'

She paused suddenly, then leapt backward, astonishment on her angular features.

'What,' she grunted, 'the hell is wrong with you?'

Asper's arm looked as though it had suddenly contracted and gone through the worst bouts of an infection, the blood pooling in it and painting it red as sin. It was far too deep a crimson to be anything normal, Kataria thought, all the more disturbing as it throbbed, pulsed and tensed even as the rest of the priestess' body lay unmoving.

'Take it,' Asper whispered. 'Take it all.'

Xhai could muster nothing beyond an alarmed stare, looking to the door with a newfound longing for her master to return. Kataria's eyes were locked on Asper, struggling to find the words to speak, the question to ask through the murmurings in her head. And yet, even as the Howling spoke with urgent fervour, she could still hear the sound.

Hinges without oil creaked. Something slid through a narrow frame. A pair of feet hit the floor.

She saw the porthole's window swinging on its hinges and the shadow sliding beneath it, into the darkness at the edges of the overhanging lamp's light. She only barely saw him, a shadow within a shadow in his black leathers, and only barely recognised him. His face was too long, his eyes too hard. And the smile he gave her as he noticed her staring had never unnerved her before.

Denaos raised a finger to his lips. She nodded, saying nothing, as he slunk about the halo of light. A rope slid into his hands like a snake, his fists drawing it tight. He rose up behind Xhai like a black flower and angled the garrotte over her head, his hands unnaturally steady.

He had only just begun to lower it when an eerily gentle smile split her long face.

'I knew you'd come,' she whispered.

His eyes widened just a fraction before he struck. The garrotte snapped down swiftly, finding the tender flesh of her throat and drawing tight. She snarled, thrusting her elbow back and into his ribs. He reeled, but refused to let go, pulling himself closer, hands shaking as he strained to pull the rope against her windpipe.

'I knew it,' she said, her voice only slightly raspy, 'because I know you, because I know me. I know *I* wouldn't leave my foe with just scars to remember me.'

He suffered another elbow, gritted his teeth. It was frustration and not pain that was evident in his face as he pulled so hard that the garrotte creaked in protest.

'What the hell are you *made* of?' he snarled.

'And I knew they couldn't kill you,' Xhai continued, ignoring his words and his rope alike, 'I knew you weren't dead ...'

Her hand lashed up and over her shoulder, gripping his throat in a vice of purple fingers.

'Because I hadn't killed you yet.'

His cry was a weak and pitiful thing against her roar as she yanked hard. He flew out from behind her and out before her with such swiftness as to suggest that, at some point, his innards had been replaced with soft wool.

That theory, and his all-too-fleshy body, were mercilessly dashed as he came crashing down upon the wood.

That should have worked, shouldn't it? he asked himself, not certain who would answer. *I was certain it would.*

Everyone makes mistakes, he reassured himself.

Is that her foot above me?

It is.

I should move, shouldn't I?

He needed no answer to spur him into a roll. Her spike-encrusted boot came smashing down where he had just lain. He sprang to his feet in time to see her pull her foot out, chunks of wood still clinging petulantly to its twisted spikes.

'That's fine,' she said calmly. 'We'll take our time with each other, get to know one another.' She smiled with something that was obviously intended to be warmth. 'When one of us kills the other, I want it to mean something.'

She leapt at him, just as the knife leapt to his hand. With surgical precision, he slashed it up and against her brow. Like a shattered dam of purple flesh, the blood came weeping out in great rivulets, pouring into her eyes and rendering her blind. She shrieked, swung a fist, seeking

601

him. He sprang backwards and continued to do so as she flailed too wildly.

His retreat came to a sudden halt as he felt his back meet the pillar his companion was tied to.

'Not a lot of room to move here,' he muttered.

'You talk like it's *my* fault,' Kataria snapped. 'Kill her quick and it won't be an issue.'

'I'm not getting near those hands of hers.'

'Then what are you going to do?'

'Run, maybe? Probably die. I'm not sure yet.'

'You didn't think of a backup?'

'I didn't.'

'*Why not?*'

'Oh, come on! What were the odds that strangulation wouldn't work?'

Anything she might have replied was lost in a howl of metal and a wail of cloven air. He looked and leapt just in time to avoid the massive wedge of metal that served as her sword from taking off his head. It bit deeply into the pillar instead as he scurried around it and the shict bound to it. He grabbed Kataria about her midsection, glancing around her and avoiding her offended scowl, much more concerned with the white eyes painted red narrowed at him.

'I'm assuming she won't kill you,' he said, darting behind the shict as Xhai shot out a fist at his left, 'or she would have already.'

'You can't know that!' Kataria shouted to be heard over the sword being wrenched free.

'It's an educated gamble,' Denaos said, twisting back behind her as Xhai lashed her blade out to catch him on his right. 'If she can't kill you, then you make a very good shield.'

'I can hear you, you know,' the longface said.

She swung again. He leapt again. The blade did not so much strike the pillar as shatter it completely. The ropes were slashed, sending Kataria falling to the ground. Splinters sprayed in all directions, a haze of dust and shards assaulting Xhai's already stinging eyes and sending her into a blind, howling fury.

When he looked down, Kataria was staring at him with vast and empty eyes.

'I could have died,' she whispered. 'And if I had, there would be no one left to help you.' She shook her head. 'I can't let you die.'

'Then help me find my knife.'

'Asper isn't well,' Kataria said, rising to her feet and slipping her rent bonds. 'You have your people. I have mine.'

Before he could protest, she sprang to her feet and darted past the flailing longface, shoving the cabin door open and disappearing. Though he knew he ought to feel it, the urge to curse her as a coward was decidedly faint.

The pang of regret at not having fled first: decidedly not.

A snarl seized his attention. Xhai kicked the last remnants of the shattered pillar out of her way, advancing toward Denaos, her eyes shining through a face painted with blood and adorned with splinters. Her smile was one of contentment, unconcerned with the red dripping over her lips to stain her teeth. His face was one of fervent panic as he backed away and searched for any way past her that didn't end in disembowelment.

'No,' she answered his wild gaze. 'No more chases, no more interruptions. This is where one of us dies.' Even reflected in the blade she levelled at him, her smile was possessed of macabre affection. 'I'm glad it ended this way, Denaos.'

The rogue did not cry out as he was backed up against the wall, did not think to beg or plead or make deals. There was no room in her face for that. What else he saw in there – the tinges of joy, of desire, of lust – he was determined not to take as the last thing he saw before being gutted.

Thus, when he saw the slender form of Asper stalking towards the woman on shaking feet, her body trembling, her arms still bound behind her, he focused on her immediately.

'I fought for so long,' the priestess whispered, though to who was unclear. 'I wanted so badly to believe there was a reason I should.' There was a sizzling sound; a wisp of smoke rose from behind her. 'I wanted to believe that the Gods wanted me for something other than this.'

Xhai glanced over her shoulder at the woman and snorted before returning her attentions back to the rogue.

'There are no gods,' the longface said.

'There are,' Asper whispered.

An arm extended from her shoulder: a black, skeletal limb bound in a red glow that pulsated like a decaying heart.

'They just don't care.'

The sword fell from Xhai's grasp the moment Asper laid that red-and-ebon hand that belonged to something that was not her upon the longface's neck. It was a gentle grasp, no more force behind it than that a wife would use to rub her husband's shoulders. Five fingers rested lightly upon the netherling's neck.

And Xhai screamed.

The longface fell to her knees, every muscle visible bunching up and tearing beneath her flesh. Her jaw threatened to snap off with the force of her wail, her eyes threatening to boil out of her skull and dribble in thick yolks into her mouth.

'*NO!*' she shrieked. '*NO!*'

'I told myself that, too,' Asper replied, shaking her head as tears poured down her cheeks. 'I tried. But there's nothing to be done.' She choked on a sob. 'They abandoned me. I did everything for the Gods and They just let that … let *him* happen to me. What's the point in resisting now? What does anyone care?'

'I … won't …'

Xhai's arm rose up as if to stop her. There was a loud snapping sound as an invisible force very visibly shattered her hand, causing her fingers to seize up in agonised curls. Asper's arm reacted immediately, fed on her suffering. The flesh of her shoulder seemed to dissipate into sizzling wisps as the crimson spread farther up her arm.

'This hasn't happened before,' she said, 'but why wouldn't it? Why wouldn't everything be taken from me, flesh and soul?'

'S-stop …' Xhai whimpered.

'I can't … I told them to take it,' Asper whispered. The crimson light spread like a stain of paint. The fur wrapped about her chest sizzled and fell off, her left breast bathed in translucent crimson, exposing blackened ribs below. 'To take it *all*.'

'And … I … said …'

Xhai howled, lashing out her uninjured fist that struck Asper against the jaw like a purple sledge.

'*Stop!*'

She continued to howl, to hammer, flailing wildly behind her and screaming even as her forearm trembled and shattered like her hand had.

'*STOP! STOP! STOP! STOP!*'

Asper did, her grasp shattered under the hail of blows. She collapsed, weeping, heedless of the looming purple shape as she rose up. Xhai stared at her through trembling eyes, looking from her to her ruined arm. Her face quivered, jaw hung open, as though on the brink of asking why, of demanding how, of weeping along with the priestess.

Instead, when her mouth found her voice, it was only a scream that came out.

'*QAI ZHOTH!*' she howled.

And nothing more came of it as a force exploded across her back.

She buckled under the attack, tried to look over her shoulder and caught a glimpse of the tall man in black leather holding up her master's chair. Her eyes, and her face, were driven back down as he smashed the chair against her back again and again. It cracked, splintered, shattered in his hands, and still he brought it down upon her until she no longer moved and he was left holding two hewn chair legs.

He set them down six blows later.

Panting, Denaos spared only as much attention for the netherling as it took to confirm that she wouldn't get up. Once that was clear, and after he had given her rock-hard flesh a kick for good measure, he turned his attentions to his companion.

'Asper,' he whispered gently.

She was curled in on herself, trying to bury her left arm under the whole of her shuddering body, weeping violently. With some trepidation, he knelt beside her, wary to touch her after what he had seen, wary to even look at her.

Kataria had run. He could, too. Asper was safe now. There was no reason to stay here. He could escape now, too. She wouldn't want him around, either, when she finally looked up. He was a coward, a thief, a brigand. She had called him these before. He had run from her before. He could do so now. It would be easy.

That was what he told himself.

That was not what he did.

He placed a hand gently on her, paused as she recoiled from his touch. Undeterred, he gently rolled her over.

And resisted the urge to scream.

She stared up at him through one tear-stained eye. The other was nothing more than a black socket bathed in crimson light. Her naked breast rose and fell with each breath as the ribs where the other one should be shuddered. Half a pair of lips whispered in shuddering words to him as half a black jaw moved up and down with mechanical certainty.

'I think …' she said. 'I think there's something wrong with me.'

Thirty-Three

TO OUR PEOPLE

His head was burning. If he knew nothing else in the darkness that he had been plunged into, he knew this.

And the voice that accompanied it, hot with emotion.

'*Could have been so easy ...*' it sizzled on his skull, '*it all could have been so easy. You could have been away now and we could all have been happy. You could have forgotten her, forgotten* everything. *It would have hurt, but you would have survived. Now?*'

The darkness became bright, angry red inside his head.

'*Now I'll watch you die.*'

Lenk's eyes snapped open. He knew they were open, even if he wasn't quite sure whether he was awake or even alive. His eyes swam and his head rang. He could see purple shadows moving through great red sheets. He could hear the distant cracking of the sky. His head was still burning, his face still dripping with sweat.

That might have been because of all the fire, though.

The wave of heat that rolled over him returned him to his senses. The wave of crackling orange flame came rolling shortly after. He scrambled to his hands and knees, crawling hurriedly behind the mast before he could feel anything more than the vague sensation of a branding iron tickling his rear end.

Ample reason to figure out what was going on, he thought.

He peered around the mast and was greeted with a sight of carnage. The great red tongues that came lashing out of thin purple palms had long forgotten Lenk. Behind the veil of fire, his face painted orange with the heat, Sheraptus snarled and drove the flames skywards, leaving the deck charred beneath him.

His target, the source of his fury-screwed face, became apparent as the night sky was set alight.

A man, he was at least *vaguely* sure it was, sailed over-head, the fire licking at his heels as leathery wings carried him over the deck. Those netherling females not lying in various states of cinders, icicles or both surrounded their master protectively, angling drawn bows towards their target.

The man's hand flashed, in and out of his coat, and pro-duced three scraps of paper. Only when he hurled them did Lenk realise that they were folded into the angular shapes of cranes. That realisation was not quite as interest-ing, Lenk thought, as the fact that their little papery wings were flapping of their own accord.

The man spoke a word. Whatever language, whatever command, the folded cranes heard and obeyed. Instantly, they turned from white to silver, from dull to shining, from angular to wickedly sharp. Spinning through the air, they found three purple throats and dipped steel beaks into tender flesh.

Bows clattered to the deck. The ensuing gasps and breathless screams as the netherlings clutched at severed windpipes went unheard. Sheraptus appeared less than concerned with the females, thrusting his fingers, and the ensuing whip of lightning, at his elusive prey.

'Why is this such an issue for you?' he cried to be heard above the crackling electric blast. 'I've never heard of you before. Why are you so obsessed with me?'

'Your eradication is a service to more than one power. You are a violator,' the man replied sharply. 'In every sense of the word.'

'Meaning?'

'I met your victim.'

'Which?'

'You took everything from her, including her name.'

'It comes down to females *again*?' Sheraptus snarled, thrusting a finger and sending a jagged blue arc over the man's bald, brown head. 'Are vaginae truly so scarce on this world as to be worth this much trouble?'

Lenk took it as his good fortune that the longface's attentions were so focused elsewhere. His eyes were drawn past the robed figure to the doors of the cabin, just as his thoughts were drawn to Kataria, undoubtedly inside. It would be a simple matter of crossing, infiltrating and retrieving with Sheraptus so distracted.

As simple as matters involving wizards can be, at least.

As if on cue, he felt a familiar hand, far too scrawny and sweaty as to be particularly worrying, on his shoulder. He turned to see Dreadaeleon's sweat-slick visage and purple-circled eyes staring intently at him.

'You've been busy,' he noted.

'It's incredible.' The intensity of the boy's grin raised some concern in Lenk. 'All of a sudden, the weakness … it was gone! I … I can cast again, Lenk. I can channel it. It feels …'

His eyes went unnervingly wide as he rose up. His pelvis, Lenk noted, was far too close to Lenk's face *before* the boastful thrusting began.

'Look! Not a drop of moisture, not a trace of fire, not a wisp of smoke!' the boy proclaimed loudly. 'Look! Look!'

'No! *No!*' Lenk seized him by his belt, pulling forcibly down. 'Now, listen, the longface is distracted and you're feeling ...' He paused, shook his head. 'We're not talking about that anymore. Denaos very clearly didn't make it or he'd have let us know. We've got to go in and—'

'Save them,' Dreadaeleon said, nodding. 'I can feel it, just thinking about it. The power ... I can feel the surge. Isn't that fascinating? Venarie is internal, to be sure, but it's ruled by thought and logic, not emotion. For it to work this way is—'

'Can you go out and get burned alive or something distracting?' Lenk asked. 'That ... bird-man-thing can't hold him off forever.'

'The Librarians are trained to great feats of endurance and power, Lenk,' the boy replied. 'He can do more than you or I could.' He winced. 'And, you know, I'm technically obligated to help him as a member of the Venarium.'

'*Treason, treachery, betrayal,*' the voice, frigid and sharp hissed inside Lenk's head. '*They are useless. We are—*'

'*Dead,*' the voice, feverish and burning roared inside Lenk's brain. '*You're dead. You had your chance. You're going to—*'

'*Ignore that. Focus on duty. Focus on—*'

'*Her. She's dead, too. You're all dead and—*'

'Enough, enough, *enough,*' Lenk growled to all assembled. 'I can do this without any of you.' He glared at Dreadaeleon. 'If you're going to be useless, I can do it without you, too.'

'Useless?' The boy mopped sweat off his brow, flicked it at Lenk. 'Do you think I got this from jogging in place all this time you've been unconscious, vulnerable and oh-so-stabbable? I've been setting on fire, freezing into ice, frying into blackness and otherwise *harming* the longfaces. There were ten more on this deck before you woke!'

'Eleven.'

The longface came shortly after the word, leading in with a purple fist that drove into Dreadaeleon's jaw and sent him sprawling to the deck. Lenk had scarcely enough time to blink before her hand jerked backward and slammed him against the mast while she took a moment to drive a foot into the writhing boy's ribs.

'He's already—' Lenk began to protest.

'No,' the longface interrupted, smashing her fist into his face.

He felt the bone-deep quake, felt his skin ripple across his flesh with the force of the blow. His vision did not so much swim as struggle to keep from drowning, eyesight fading as he saw first the remorseless, uncaring long face, then blackness, then her drawn-back fist, then darkness again.

He felt the knuckles connect with his jaw, even if he didn't see them.

Perhaps he was still dizzy from his previous awakening, he thought. That's why this was so easy for the longface to beat him so savagely. Perhaps this one was just particularly strong, or perhaps they had all been stronger than he suspected. Or had he always been weaker than he thought?

By the fourth blow, and the torrents of glistening red pouring from his nose, his thoughts shifted to something else.

Sword, he told himself. *Need my sword. The head ... where is it? Sword, head, sword, head ... someone ...*

'*We need no one,*' the voice rang across rime.

'*No one will come for you,*' the voice hissed across fever.

And they, too, faded, with every blow the longface rained on him. His neck felt like a willow branch, his head like a lead weight. His arms were impotent as he tried to shield himself from her attacks. He felt bruises blossoming under his skin, cuts opening on his brow, his jaw. Eyelids fluttering, he stared at the longface as she stared back, appraisingly.

'Huh,' she said. 'Don't stop to talk before you kill 'em and they just fold right up, don't they?'

She might have had a point, as the only words he could muster were vain pleas – whether to her or someone else, anyone else, he didn't know – through blistered lips and a tongue swelling with coppery taste. She didn't seem to be listening, in any case, as she knelt down before him and pulled a jagged, short blade from her belt and brought it down in a vicious chop.

He caught her arm as a tree branch catches a boulder. His wrist threatened to snap under the pressure, trembling as she strove to bring the blade down towards his soft throat, which twitched so invitingly.

Out of the corner of his eye, Lenk took a quick, despairing stock. Dreadaeleon lay fallen. Gariath was still far over the edge. Denaos was dead, Asper likely with him and Kataria …

Kataria was standing there, not twenty feet away.

She was scrambling across the deck hurriedly, pausing only to snatch up a fallen bow and a pair of arrows. Her eyes were on the companionway at the opposite end of the ship, ignoring Sheraptus hurling curses and fire at the sky, the Librarian spewing frost back at him.

She didn't even see Lenk.

'Kat!'

Not until he screamed, anyway.

She skidded to a halt, looking at him with worrying confusion. She seemed to recognise him in another instant and frowned, either at him or his situation, he wasn't sure.

'Kat! *Help!*'

His plea for aid twisted in his throat and became a shriek of agony as the longface's blade came crashing down into the tender meat of his shoulder. He fought back against her still, but even as he kept the blade from biting deeper into his flesh, the jagged teeth sawed at him. His ears were filled with the sound of each sinewy strand snapping under it so that he was only scarcely sure he was still screaming.

'*KATARIA!*'

'*Gone,*' a voice said sorrowfully.

It was right. He saw, in fleeting glimpses, the shict cringing, then turning and fleeing into the confines of the companionway. She didn't even look behind her. She hadn't even heard him.

'*She did,*' a voice hissed angrily. '*She betrayed us.*'

'*Betrayed you,*' another said. '*Abandoned you.*'

'What now?' he gasped through blood and tears. 'What … ?'

'*Fight back.*'

'*Give up.*'

With a blade in his shoulder, his companions gone and the very reason he came to this ship of blood vanishing into shadow, one option seemed much more tempting than the other.

He never got to make the choice, however, as Dreadaeleon staggered to his feet and, from there, staggered into the longface. Kneeling as she had been, she toppled over with a grunt of surprise, releasing the blade and focusing her attentions and fists on the boy.

He, however, was just as focused on her. And only one of them had crimson light in their eyes.

His hands, pitifully scrawny, clutched her throat, indomitably thick. The word, soft in his throat, went unheard through her snarling. The blue electricity that raced down into his fingertips, however, demanded her attention.

Crackling became sizzling became sputtering as her snarling became screaming became frothing convulsion. Her teeth all but welded together as the lightning coursed from his fingers into her body, snaking past purple skin and into thick bone. As though she were some blackening bull, Dreadaeleon fought to hold on as she seized violently on the deck, his fingers digging into flesh growing softer, eyes turning to red spears as they narrowed.

When it was finally over, he slid his fingers from well-cooked meat, wisps of smoke whispering out from ten tiny holes. He clambered off, exhausted, but not spent as he looked to Lenk accusingly.

'You could have fought back,' he said angrily.

'No point ...' Lenk said. 'She's gone, she's gone.'

'Who? Asper?'

'Kataria.'

'Oh ... well, yeah, why wouldn't she? She's a—'

'Yeah,' Lenk said, reaching up to clutch his bleeding shoulder. 'Yeah.'

'So ... what now?'

Lenk made no reply, but an answer came to him as a great red hand appeared at the railing. They heard the grunt, saw Gariath haul himself up and over onto the deck. He spotted them just as quickly and rushed over, panting heavily, ignoring the battle raging between the two wizards.

'Up,' he snarled. 'Get *up*.'

'What's the problem?' Dreadaeleon asked.

'Big problem,' Gariath muttered. '*Big* problem.'

'Where's Togu?'

'Dead, maybe? I don't know. Now get up. We've got a big problem.'

'You've said that already but—'

There was the sound of a distant voice shouting commands in a deep, rolling tongue, audible even over the carnage on the deck. They looked out to see the ocean alight with a swarm of fireflies, dozens of little orange dots reflected upon the waters.

'Are those … ?'

At another distant command, the fireflies rose. One more and they flew. By the time Lenk and Dreadaeleon realised the lights were no insects, they heard nothing but the shrieking of shafts and the sizzling of fire.

'Get *down!*' Gariath snarled, shoving the two of them behind the mast.

The arrows came plummeting, singing mournful dirges accompanied by crackling fire. Sheraptus glanced up just in time to throw his hand out, the air rippling as the missiles struck an unseen wall and went quivering. Those females surrounding him that had not noticed in time to bring shields up became smouldering porcupines in an instant.

The entire ship seemed to shudder with the sound of heads biting deeply into wood and flames snarling angrily as they passed through sails. After an eternity of waiting, Lenk dared to peer around the mast.

Across the sea, he saw them, their green faces and yellow eyes aflame as they lit fresh arrows. Their tattoos of red and black were stark against the firelight, causing them to resemble ghouls fresh from a grave, rotted wrinkles and throbbing veins bright on their dire expressions.

Shen, he recognised. Three long canoes full of Shen. Drawing arrows back.

'That ...' he whispered, 'that is a problem.'

Gariath shook his head. 'No, moron. I said we had a *big* problem.'

'That's *not* big?' Dreadaeleon said, astonished.

He was answered as the sound of a distant horn rose from the canoes.

And in the next moment, the horn, too, was answered.

In the eruption of the sea and the violent vomit of froth, a resonating roar tore through the sea and ripped into the sky. Combatants and companions alike were thrust to the deck as the ship rocked with the force of a violently disturbed wave. Black against the night sky, a creature rose into the air, a great, writhing pillar topped with two menacing yellow eyes.

The Akaneed stared down at the deck as those upon it stared back up at the titanic snake. Its head snapped forward, jaws parting to expose rows of needlelike teeth, a roar tearing out of its throat on sheets of salty miss.

'*That,*' Gariath roared over it, '*is big.*'

You served your people.

Kataria heard it over her own footsteps.

Yours was a duty to all shicts.

Kataria heard it over her own thoughts.

You did the right thing.

Kataria did not believe it.

And yet, she continued down the stairs of the companionway, all the same. She may have doubted the quality of the Howling's message, but was driven forward by the frequency and urgency of its insistence. It spoke inside her a dozen times with each step she took.

You did the right thing. You did the right thing. You did the right thing.

By the time she reached the end of the stairs, she knew it was right, because the shict who spoke to her knew it was right. It had ceased to be reassurance, ceased to be a message. It was knowledge now, as primal a knowledge as knowing how to swim and to hunt.

But with the next step, between the two hundred and forty-first time and the two hundred and forty-second time she heard it, she knew she still didn't believe it.

Perhaps it was that doubt that no shict could ever feel for the Howling that brought the tears to her eyes. Perhaps those came from a different instinct altogether. She didn't dare think on it. She brushed them from her face with the back of her hand. If she began weeping now, over a human, over the doubt, that knowledge would become shared.

And she could not bear the thought of descending and finding her kinsman weeping as well.

The sight that greeted her in the vast ship's hold, however, was one of emptiness. Benches and cots lined the hull, presumably for the netherlings to sleep upon when they weren't fighting, crushing, killing, shoving jagged blades into throats from which her name emerged on blood-choked screams ...

Stop it, she told herself.

Stop it, the Howling agreed.

And she did. It was powerful here, speaking to her with greater clarity, greater urgency. It needed only to speak once, and she knew it to be true. She felt her eyes drawn to the darkness at the end of the cabin, the great void that ate the light of overhanging oil lamps. She could see the shadows of a cage's cold iron bars, and while she could see nothing beyond that, she could hear something; she could feel something.

A heartbeat. A thought. A knowledge that was hers. A knowledge that was theirs.

A shict.

She had barely taken another step when she noticed the lone netherling in her path, and then only after she noticed the jagged blade hurtling towards her. She fell to the deck, hearing the blade's frustrated wail as its teeth sheared only a few hairs from her head.

'Just how many colours do you things come in?' the longface grunted.

Kataria's answer came with a growl.

The arrow was up and in the bow, drawn back as far as she could force the rigid thing to go, and launched a moment later. A moment was all it took, however, for the longface's shield to go up, sending the missile ringing off.

Stupid piece of ... Kataria thought irately, glowering at the weapon. *Who the hell would call this stick a bow?*

The netherling, apparently, agreed, if the broad grin with which she raised her sword was any indication. Still, she refused to advance, holding her shield up defensively as she watched Kataria draw her final arrow back. Such lack of a willingness to have a piece of iron wedged in one's brow, the shict figured, was likely what led this one to be below.

And yet it served her frustratingly well as Kataria aimed and launched, slipping past the longface's shield to find an unyielding iron breastplate below. It was clear, then, that what the black bow lacked in accuracy it made up for in power. The longface was driven back a step, nothing more than an inconvenience before she readied to charge upon the now-defenceless shict.

Still, Kataria smiled. A single step was all she had needed.

The green fingers that came slithering out between the bars would handle the rest.

The longface's cry was brief as the long fingers, attached to longer hands and longer arms still, wrapped around her throat in five tiny pythons. They scarcely trembled as they intertwined and pulled her back towards the bars, possessed of a cold passionlessness that suggested this was just one more neck, like all the other necks that had been strangled. Cold hands. Killer hands.

Shict hands.

Kataria forced herself to watch as the crown of the long-face's head was pulled between the bars, her screams choked as she was fed head-first into an unyielding iron mouth. There was nothing to silence the sound of bone groaning and popping as, hairsbreadth by agonising hairsbreadth, she was pulled between bars that would not accommodate her thick skull.

This, she reminded herself, was what shicts did. Shicts did what they had to. The world, filled with diseases of pink and purple, left them no choice.

The long, purple face was consumed in the void of the cage. Her body twitched soundlessly for but a moment before her legs went slack, bending her back at an awkward angle as she lay still, thick neck wedged between the bars and suspending her in standing, artificial rigour.

Cold, killer fingers slipped out and calmly reached into a pouch at the longface's belt. A few moments of deft search revealed a wrought-iron key that was drawn out neatly between two green digits. A faint clicking noise emerged after those fingers vanished back into shadow. The cage door groaned as it swung open, dragging the corpse frozen in its grip across the deck with it.

He stepped out of the void, a great green plant out of dark earth, stepping lightly on feet bearing thumbs. Countless time in a cramped cage had done nothing to stunt his stature as he rose high enough for his bald pate to scrape the underside of the oil lamp above him. From his groin up, a long line of symbols ran the length of his body, each one a story.

And each one a death. Of wife. Of child. Of their murderers.

Each symbol was no bigger than a thumbprint, but each sorrow and every hatred was condensed into a pattern of lines that only a shict would know.

Kataria knew.

'What is your name?' she asked.

He stared at her with even blue eyes.

'You already know.'

Upon his lips, the shictish tongue, *their* tongue, sounded so eloquent. She wondered absently if he could hear the dust on her own tongue.

She searched herself, listened to the Howling.

'Naxiaw,' she said, looking up at him. 'I am … pleased you are well.'

'Pleased?' His lips peeled back into a broad smile, his canines twice as large as hers. Long arms parted in a gesture almost warm enough for her to forget they had just been used to pull a longface through bars. 'Sister. We are not strangers.'

She would have been shocked to find herself laughing, possibly a little worried to find the sound so hysterical. That thought was lost in a sea of emotion that carried her on running feet to leap into him. His arms wrapped about her, drew her close to a broad chest. A great weight had fallen from her, evidenced by how easily Naxiaw drew her up off her feet.

In his arms, she found memory. She found a hand on her shoulder, reassuring her after her ears were notched. She found the scent of rabbits cooking and fires. She found the dirge of bows and the song of funeral pyres. She found memories of her father, his sternness, his words, his speeches, his memories. Of her mother, she found only lightness.

She found everything the Howling said she would find.

'Little Sister,' Naxiaw said, holding her closely, 'you are far from home.'

'The world is our home,' she replied. 'No matter what round-ears say.'

'It heartens me to hear such words.'

Her father's words.

'The creature above,' the greenshict said, 'that caused you such sorrow. I felt him. Is he dead?'

No, she thought, *he wouldn't die so soon. He's above, bleeding out under a rusty knife. Right where I left him.*

Not that *creature, stupid,* she scolded herself.

'You are worried,' Naxiaw said.

Watch what you think, moron, she hissed mentally. *And don't look at him! If he can't tell through the Howling, it'll be obvious once he sees your face.*

'I was,' she replied, keeping her voice steady. 'But I draw strength from my people.'

'As all shicts should.'

Her grandfather's words.

'It is well now, Sister,' Naxiaw said, easing her down and laying her head upon his chest. 'I live. You live. We are safe.'

Her ear against his chest, she could hear the sound of memory in his heartbeat. Slow and steady, purpose resonating with every pump of blood through it. It was comforting to hear, at least at first.

The more she listened, however, the more she was aware that she had never heard such a thing before. She had heard nothing so slow, so certain, so sure. And it caused her to pull away, her ears attuned to her own body. There was no more thunder in her ears; there had been, she was certain, when the Howling spoke to her, had urged her to hear it.

Now, she heard her own heart. It was swift, erratic, uncertain, conflicted.

Light.

Unpleasant.

Terrifying.

'Sister,' Naxiaw said, furrowing his brow. 'What is wrong?'

You, she thought. *You're wrong. Your heartbeat is too steady. You're too sure of yourself. You know everything a shict should know and you hear the Howling like it was another shict. You're probably hearing this right now because the Howling is ... isn't it?*

She said none of that. Instead, she shook her head and spoke words that none of her family had ever said before, that came from her light, erratic heart.

'I don't know.'

Naxiaw looked certain, as though he were about to speak with the voice of the Howling and whatever he were to say next would assure her of everything. She watched eagerly as he stared back at her, then said nothing, looking down at the floor of the hold.

'Ah,' he said, 'they are almost here.'

'Who?' Kataria asked, confusion overriding despair.

'You cannot hear them?' Naxiaw asked. He released her, knelt down on long legs to stare at the floor thoughtfully. 'They have been following this ship for hours now. They are waiting for something.'

His fingers ran over the wood. His ears, six notches to a lobe, perked up. She heard it, too: the groaning of wood, a cry of protest that it knew was useless as something insistent pressed up against it. Naxiaw looked up at her, his eyes keen and his face dire.

'And now,' he whispered, 'it has come.'

The boat rocked suddenly as something struck it from below, sending tremors through the floor, past Kataria's feet and into her heart. The ship's groan became a scream as jagged rents veined the wood and bled saltwater.

Naxiaw leapt up and back, putting himself between her and the rapidly spreading crack in the floor. *He's trying to protect me*, she realised. *Who ... no one's done that for me before*. The thought should have caused her less distress than it did.

She herself took a step backwards as another great blow shook the ship. From beneath the widening crack, she heard them: voices, proclamations, hymns, chants, urges, each one brimming with purpose, each purpose rife with death.

Another blow and the floor erupted into a spray of splinters, the crack became a wound leaking clear, salty blood onto the floor. And at the centre, like a black knife, the arm rose: titanic, emaciated, jointed in four places and ending in a great webbed claw.

'Not them,' Kataria whispered with what breath she had left.

'What are they?' Naxiaw asked.

His question was answered as another webbed fist

punched through the hull, ripping the wound into a great, gaping hole. Claws sank into the wood, gripped tightly and hauled an immense black shape onto the floor.

A skeleton wrapped in shadow, crowned with a wide head sporting vast, gaping jaws, it pulled itself free from a womb of water and wood. Its flesh glistening under a cowering flame, it rose from its knees, each vertebra visible beneath its black skin as it rose to its full, imposing height. On webbed feet, it slowly turned about and levelled the head of a black fish upon the two shicts.

The Abysmyth stared at Kataria, its eyes wide, white and empty.

'At the midpoint on the pilgrimage,' it said, its voice choked with the voices of the drowned, 'I looked upon the pristine creation and saw a floating blight. Mother bade me to act on her behalf, unable to bear the agony of the faithless longfaces upon her endless blue. And within the black boil, I found the lost and the lonely.' It extended a great webbed hand, glistening with thick, viscous ooze. 'Come to me, my children. I will take the agony of this waking nightmare from you.'

'Run,' Kataria said as much to herself as to Naxiaw, 'run.'

'What is it?' the greenshict asked.

'Salvation,' the Abysmyth answered.

'The Shepherd has come,' a chorus of voices burbled on the rapidly rising water. 'The faithless tremble. The faint-hearted cower. Fear not, fear not ...'

'For I am here,' the Abysmyth continued, 'to ease your agony.' It gestured to the wound. 'Rejoice.'

And, as one, they came boiling through the hull like a brood of tadpoles. Glistening bodies, bereft of hair or pallor, rejected by the great blue body of the sea and vomited out in a mass of writhing flesh, gnashing needle teeth, colourless eyes. The frogmen came in numbers immeasurable, pulling themselves out of the rising water in a gasping, rasping choir.

'We have come,' the great black demon said, 'to deliver. Messages. Sinners. Everyone.'

'Run,' Kataria said, grabbing Naxiaw by the arm. '*RUN!*'

Naxiaw heard and did not question, following her as they sprinted for the stairs leading to the deck. Struck breathless from fear, they spoke in short gasps of air.

'How do we escape?' the greenshict asked.

'The shore isn't far from here,' she said. 'Shicts can swim.'

'Those things ... they came from the water. Is it wise to go in?'

'We don't have a whole lot of choice, do we? The ship will go down in a few moments and we'll be drowning, anyway.'

'Then we swim. I trust you, Sister.'

Someone else trusted me once, she thought with a pain in her chest. *I ... I need to. I have to go back for him.*

'Wait!' she cried as they neared the companionway. 'I have to ...'

He paused, looked at her curiously. What could she say? That she had to stay on this sinking tomb, now rife with demons as well as longfaces, for the sake of a human? The great disease? How could she tell him that? How could she tell herself that, after all the time she had yearned to feel this knowledge, hear this comfort, feel this lightness?

How could she ask herself why her heart beat different than his?

She could not say that, any of that.

'I have to do what I must,' she said instead, continuing up to the deck, 'for my people.'

Someone's words.

Not hers.

Thirty-Four

MOTHER AND CHILD

Gariath was not dead yet.

Not for lack of opportunity, of course. He darted through a web of iron and curses, batting away clumsy blades, suffering the blows of those too cunning or lucky for him to avoid. Every metal favour bestowed upon him he reciprocated with claws and teeth, forcing his assailants back.

He was vaguely surprised that he could feel the many cuts on his body. He didn't remember the longfaces being quite so strong as they had been when he first encountered them. But Irontide, and the flesh he had rent in suicidal frenzy, had been many eternities ago.

He was less aware of death this time, and so was aware of many more things as he caught an errant blade in his hand and tore it free from the offending longface's grasp.

Pain was among them, but so, too, were the humans.

What had began as a chaos of fire and thunder on the deck had since degenerated into a chaos of fire, thunder, steel, cursing, spitting and screaming.

Arrows fell from the sky in intermittent fiery drizzles, longfaces scrambling to seek cover from them or return fire with hasty shots. Those few who simply couldn't be bothered to hide had either sought another target or clung by their master's side, occasionally intervening between him and a lightning bolt thrown from the dark-skinned human.

Of their sacrifice, the longface with the burning eyes took no notice, consumed wholly with his target. Whatever bemusement had been present on his face had been consumed in the vivid anger with which his eyes flared. He was no longer even making an attempt at appearing as though he was swatting a gnat. Now, he displayed the anger appropriate to a man swatting at a gnat that spewed fire and frost at him.

Those netherlings that had decided to seek easier prey had found them in the leaking weaklings pressed against the deck. Lenk refused to move, clutching his shoulder and staring quietly into nothingness, murmuring something equally stupid. The squeaky little human seemed torn between uselessly trying to get him on his feet and uselessly trying to assist the flying human, apparently by squealing and occasionally hurling something limp-wristedly at the longface.

Impotent, drained, useless and otherwise weak; they deserved to die, he knew.

What he didn't know was why the netherlings seeking to kill them found him imposed between them. Such a thought rose to him again as he caught a rampaging blade in his palm and snarled, shoving the wielder back and meeting her grin with a scowl. After all, it wasn't as though there weren't bigger problems to handle.

Bigger problems with tremendous teeth.

Such a problem made itself known in a shadow that blossomed like a flower over the netherling, blackness banished by the resounding thunder of blue jaws snapping, a scream leaking out between teeth, purple legs flailing wildly as a great serpentine head swept up and shook back and forth to silence its writhing, shrieking prisoner.

No guttural roar that boiled behind its teeth could drown out the noise of flesh rending as an errant leg went flying before the rest of the sinewy mass disappeared behind fangs and down a throat.

The Akaneed, far from sated, levelled its yellow stare at Gariath. The dragonman forgot his other foes in that instant, as the great serpent seemed to forget its other meals. Their gazes went deeper into each other, curiosity turning to respect turning to anger in an instant. In each other, they saw something familiar.

In the great serpent, Gariath saw sharp teeth stained with blood, narrowed yellow slits glowing in the night. He saw in them now what he had seen a week ago, upon a beach he had intended to be his grave: hunger, hatred, an end.

To everything.

In Gariath, the Akaneed saw something distinctly different.

This was made violently clear as its neck snapped, sending gaping jaws hurtling towards him. The dragonman lunged backwards as the serpent's snout speared the deck, shattered the wood and scattered the living and the dead.

The ship shook and groaned as the serpent tried to pull its maw free from the ship's hull, sending combatants rolling about the deck as they struggled to keep their footing. Gariath clung to the deck, his claws embedded in wood as he swept a fervent gaze about the deck.

A good chance to escape, he noted. *Lenk won't move. The runt won't leave. You could make them, though. They're small, stupid. You want to protect them, don't you? Life is precious now, right? Worth saving and all that. The snake is distracted. The longfaces are distracted. The Shen are …*

Watching, he noticed, dozens of yellow eyes staring from canoes.

Waiting, he realised, their bows lowered, bodies tense.

For him, he knew, as he found a single amber eye in the throng of lizardmen and met Yaike's gaze.

They were watching him. Waiting to see what this red thing was. Waiting to see if what they knew of *Rhega* was true or if they had all died long ago.

He would show them.

He rushed forward, striding over the dead, trampling the living, sliding on claws as the Akaneed pulled itself free, its jaws tinted red and brimming with shards of wood. He leapt, flapped his wings to pull him aloft and towards the creature's snout. He fell upon it with a snarl, sinking claws into blue flesh.

In an eruption of splinters and a thunderous roar, the dragonman became an angry red tick, clinging tenaciously with claws dug firmly into the tender flesh of the creature's nostrils as its serpentine neck twisted and writhed like a whirlwind as it struggled to dislodge this clawed, fanged parasite.

Gariath could not let that happen. His path became all the clearer as he clawed his way, arm's length by arm's length, up the creature's snout, hands digging fresh wounds, feet thrust into old ones. Each time, for a moment, he knew it would be easy to let go and fly into dark water, to sink until he could see, feel, breathe no more. Each time, he continued to claw forward.

He was *Rhega*. They would see. They would know.

'I haven't met you,' he growled to the Akaneed. 'There was another one. I took much from him. Eyes, teeth …' It replied with a roar and a futile attempt to shake him off. 'You, you're going to give me more. The fight, the blood … it means a great deal more than eyes and teeth.' He clawed his way up to eyes which burned yellow hate. 'Thank you.' He drew back a fist. 'I'm sorry.'

Through the squelch of membrane and the ensuing, wailing howl, Gariath's first thought was that an eye was very much like a hard-boiled egg, in both texture and the way yellow crumbled into sopping goo. His second thought was for the feeling of air beneath him and the ocean rising up before him as the Akaneed threw him from its head.

He flapped furiously, found a writhing blue column as he fell and twisted himself to meet it. His claws found rubbery skin, shredding it and drawing forth red blood and echoing howls from the beast as he slid down the Akaneed's hide, struggling to slow his fall. His hands tensed to the point of agony, claws threatening to rip from his fingers.

When he slowed to a halt, the beast had no more agony to spew forth, its roar becoming a low growl. It swayed dizzily upon the waves, fighting the pain inside it, struggling to stay awake, afloat, alive.

Gariath felt a pang of sympathy. It was only momentary, though, as he turned to face the dozens of yellow eyes fixated upon him. They were wide with appreciation … or he thought, or he *wanted* to think. It was so hard to see their stares at this range, swaying on the serpent's hide, his own eyes veiled by pain and weariness.

'I am alive,' he cried to them, his voice hoarse. 'The *Rhega* is alive. The *Rhega* still live.' He slammed a fist to his chest. 'I am alive. Look. Look at me.' He couldn't hear the shrill desperation in his voice, couldn't feel the tears welling up in his eyes. 'I am *Rhega*. Answer me!' He forced the words through a choked throat. '*Talk to me!*'

They said nothing, showed nothing behind their yellow stares. One by one, the fires of their arrows were snuffed into darkness. One by one, each Shen disappeared into gloom, bodies lost among the shadows.

'No!' Gariath roared at them. 'You can't leave now! Not when I'm so close!'

They continued to wink out, ceasing to exist as their flames did, giving no sign that they heard him, or cared what he had to say. He continued to shriek at them, as though they might provide an answer, any answer, before they vanished completely.

'How do you know the *Rhega*?' he howled at them. 'Where are they? How do you speak the language? Where are they? What happened to them?' His voice became a whining, wailing plea. *'WHY WON'T YOU ANSWER ME?'*

They continued to say nothing, continued to disappear until all that remained was a single, flickering flame, illuminating a single yellow eye. Yaike stared, expressionless, the ruin of what had once been his eye seeming to stare far deeper, speak far louder, than his whole eye or his rasping voice.

'Jaga, *Rhega*,' he spoke. 'Home. All that we do, we do for it.'

'And what does a *Rhega* do? Tell me.'

And the last light sizzled out, cloaking the lizardman in darkness, leaving nothing but a voice on lingering wisps of smoke.

'I am Shen.'

Gariath stared at the darkness, listening for the sound of oars dipping into water through the distant carnage of the deck and the flesh-deep groan of the Akaneed. And through it all, he could hear the voice of the grandfather, speaking with such closeness as to suggest the spirit was right next to him.

'What does a *Rhega* do, Wisest?'

His answer came slowly, his eyes and voice cast into the darkness.

'Life is precious,' Gariath whispered. 'A *Rhega* lives.'

'Is it, Wisest?'

Gariath became distinctly aware of the two creatures alone on the ship behind him, so weak, so helpless. He had fought to defend them moments ago. He had chosen them, moments ago. He had been one of them moments ago.

Now, he was *Rhega*.

'Life is precious, Wisest,' the grandfather reminded him.

Without looking back, Gariath muttered, 'To those who earn it.'

And then hurled himself into the water, pursuing the darkness.

Dreadaeleon couldn't think.

Ordinarily, he would chastise himself for such a thing. He was, theoretically, the smart one and took an immense amount of pride in living up to that expectation.

Still, between the lingering crackle of electricity and the deep-throated groan of the wounded Akaneed, the stench of brimstone caked with the coppery odour of blood and the vast, *vast* number of corpses on the deck, he found himself hard-pressed to assign himself any blame.

His senses were overwhelmed, not merely blinded and deafened by the chaos of the deck, but struck dull in the mind. The continuous clash of magical energies of lightning, fire, frost and the occasional exploding paper crane had bathed his brain in a bright crimson light that he sought to force a thought through.

Moments ago, he had felt something else: a surge of

something that he had never felt before, a bright inky black stain on the endless sheet of red. It was new, carrying a stinging, clean pain that always came attached to unknown agonies.

And yet ... had he *never* felt this before? he wondered.

He recalled vague hints of it, here and there: errant black patches in his vision that came, agonised, and left instantly. He recalled it in Irontide before, on the beach with Asper ...

Asper, he thought. *I should be saving Asper, shouldn't I? That's what we came here to do ... Where is she? What was the plan? Damn it, why can't I think straight?*

He cursed himself, despite the fact that he knew only an insane person could think straight in these conditions and Gariath had already leapt overboard. Lenk, however ...

Where was he, anyway? There was something wrong with him, surely, but what had it been?

Clearly, if anything was to be done, it was going to have to be done by someone with a rational mind, keen intellect and preferably enough power to level a small ship.

Bralston, however, seemed a tad preoccupied, if the sudden shape of his cloak-clad body hurtling towards Dreadaeleon was any indication.

He darted to the side as Bralston struck the mast bodily, his form, singed and smoking, sinking to the deck. The fire in his eyes waned and flickered as he struggled to keep them and the power within them conscious.

Dreadaeleon nearly jumped when the Librarian turned them upon him.

'Your thoughts?' Bralston asked.

'Run,' Dreadaeleon said.

'Venarium law permits no retreat.'

'He ... uh ... he's not getting tired.'

'Confirming my hypothesis. The stones feed him.'

'Their power can't be limitless.'

'They seem to be.'

'No,' Dreadaeleon said, shaking his head. 'That can't be right, I've seen them—'

'Seen them what, concomitant?'

It was too late to lie, Dreadaeleon knew the instant he saw the subtle, scrutinising narrowing of the Librarian's eye. It would have seemed a good time to tell everything about the red stone, how it drained him of his power, how it had tainted his body, how he, too, had broken the Laws by using it.

That might have been a matter to discuss when there were decidedly less flaming-eyed wizards approaching, however.

Truly, aside from an added slowness to his step, Sheraptus looked no worse for wear as he strode toward them. *Of course*, Dreadaeleon thought, *that's probably just how he always moves, all slow and confident, the asshole.*

'I find myself running out of things to learn about your breed,' the longface said calmly.

Whether Bralston saw an opportunity in the longface's easy stride, or was merely desperate and stubborn, he acted regardless. His hand whipped out, sending a paper crane fluttering from his grasp.

Even if Sheraptus hadn't seen the movement, someone else had. A longface previously motionless upon the deck rose suddenly with a wordless cry of warning for her master. The paper crane found her, latched upon her throat and began to glow bright red, a tick gorging itself with blood. In one moment, it sizzled upon her flesh. In one more, she whimpered another meaningless phrase to Sheraptus.

And in less than a moment, she came undone.

636

Sinew unthreaded, bones disconnected, flesh segmented itself in a spray. With only a sound that resembled the pop of a bottle, the longface erupted into pieces.

They flew into the air, and stayed there.

Sheraptus, unblinking, simply waved a hand, causing the air to ripple and suspend the remains of his warrior in an eerily gentle float. Slowly, the dead stirred under his feet. Bodies trembled, weapons clattered, all rising up to float around him like bleeding flowers upon a pond.

'Your denial of the obvious is charming,' he whispered sharply, 'but only to a point. To know why you do this, futile as it is, requires a certain kind of patience.' He narrowed his stare to thin, fiery slips. 'I dearly wish I possessed such a thing.'

At another word, an incomprehensible alien bellow, the dead came to horrific, swirling life. The bodies flailed limply, heedless of swords rending their dead flesh, as flesh, sinew and iron enveloped him in a whirlwind of purple and grey.

A hurricane of the dead, with him the merciless and unblinking eye, he began to approach the wizards.

'Suggestions?' Bralston asked in a way Dreadaeleon felt far too calm for the situation.

Perhaps such a calm was infectious enough to keep Dreadaeleon from hurling himself screaming overboard. Perhaps it was infectious enough to allow him to see the careful slowness to the longface's step, his face screwed up in concentration as he strove to keep the whirlwind under control. He may be able to perform such a feat forever, but he couldn't do it quickly.

His power isn't limitless, then.

And that realisation made Dreadaeleon look with a clear mind to the wounded Akaneed, swaying and only now recovering from its bloodied stupor. Its agony turned to fury as it turned an angry single eye upon the deck.

'Frost,' he muttered, unsure to who.

'What?'

'Give me cold!' he said with sudden vigour. 'Lots of it!'

Sparing no more than a curious glance for the boy, Bralston complied. His chest grew large with breath before it came pouring out of his mouth in a great, freezing cloud. Dreadaeleon looked within it, seeing each shard of ice, each flake of frost, and the potential within them.

He extended his hands, fingers making minute, barely visible movements as he began to shape the cold within the cloud, drawing freezing particles into flakes, flakes into crystals, crystals into chunks. He could feel the wind of Sheraptus' cyclone, the scorn of the longface's stare as he looked upon his prey. He could feel the roar of the Akaneed rumble through the deck as the serpent lurched forward.

But the feel of cold was stronger, kept him focused as he melded chunks together, breaking them down and rejoining them in an instant, forcing them into one immense whole. His coattails had just begun to sway from the wind of the cyclone when he finished his creation, forming the frost into a freezing blue spear the size of a large hog.

And with a thrust of his hands and a shouted word, he let it fly.

Flakes tailing behind it, the icicle fled through the sky, screeching against the night. The Akaneed had just opened its mouth to let out a thundering howl when the freezing spear's wailing flight was punctuated with a gut-wrenching sound.

Dreadaeleon watched with more glee than was probably appropriate as the spear punched through the back of the creature's head, its red-stained tip thrusting out through blue flesh. He held his breath as the Akaneed swayed, first away from the ship, teetered precariously as it seemed likely to fall back into the ocean, and then …

His eyes widened, heart raced.

'Move,' he said.

'Agreed,' Bralston confirmed, seeing the same thing.

Dreadaeleon felt himself seized by powerful hands as the Librarian wrapped his arms about his torso. He then felt the sensation of his feet leaving the deck as Bralston's coat became wings, pulling them both aloft.

From above, the boy beamed as his plan took shape. The joy he derived from Sheraptus' scowl was compounded for the sheer fact that the longface's eyes were upon him.

And not on the immense weight of a dead, serpentine column that came thundering down on his ship.

Dreadaeleon thought he might break out cackling when the longface turned about in time to see it.

Whatever happened next was lost in a crash of waves and the thunder of splinters as the Akaneed's head smashing down upon the deck like a blue comet, punching through the wood, ploughing through the hull, vanishing beneath the waves that rose up to claim the ship.

'Well done, concomitant,' Bralston said.

'That probably did it,' Dreadaeleon said, smirking to himself as he watched the corpse of the ship groan and begin to sink. 'He's dead.'

'We must assume so, for lack of any better information.'

'Then let's go down there and be certain.'

'When the Laws are violated, there are no certainties.'

'What do we do now, then?'

'The Venarium will want a report,' Bralston replied. 'My orders,' he paused, '*our* orders will dictate the next course of action, my immediate discretionary input accounted for.'

'We won, then,' Dreadaeleon whispered. 'Or … wait, there was something I was supposed to do, wasn't there?'

'There were others on the ship, I believe. I see them back on the beach,' Bralston replied. 'Associates?'

'Yes, but there were …' Dreadaeleon shook his head. 'It's still hard to think.'

'There were tremendous amounts of energies released tonight, more than most members are equipped to handle. Take some pride in the fact that you are still conscious, if not totally aware, concomitant.'

'Right …' Dreadaeleon nodded. 'Right, I feel …'

That phrase lingered on the night wind as Bralston swept about, leather wings flapping and bearing the two wizards towards the shore, neither of them taking any note of a pair of solemn blue eyes staring at them from a great wooden corpse.

'I guess,' Lenk whispered, 'that's that.'

Through the groan of wood, the splintering of the ship's ribs and the roar of great, gushing wounds filling with salt, he could hear a reply.

'*You're surprised?*'

Was the night cold or hot, he wondered? Should he feel as warm as he did at the sound inside his head?

'I … came for them, didn't I? I came for her. And she just—'

'*Left you. But it wasn't just her.*'

'No, they all did, didn't they?'

'*Distractions.*' The night turned freezing. '*As we already knew.*'

'I remember … I trusted them, once, didn't I? Towards

the end there, I was enjoying their company. We were going to go back to the mainland together. Things were going to be all right, weren't they?'

'*Not your fate.*'

'*Not our duty.*'

'I suppose not.'

Water was seeping up around him, licking at his boots. The mast behind him started to groan; its foundations shattered, it protested once, then came crashing down to smash into the ship's cabin. The world was crumbling beneath him and he stood facing the cold darkness below, alone.

'So what now?' he asked.

'*We kill.*'

'*It ends.*'

'Conflict.'

'*Tell me,*' the voice, fever-hot whispered. '*How far has killing gotten you?*'

'*Do not listen,*' another, bone-cold, protested.

'*All fighting ends eventually.*' Fire-hot. '*And by the end, what have you got but a heap of corpses? No one left to speak to, to lay your head upon, and it grows so heavy ...*'

'*Trickery. Lies.*' Snow-cold. '*We have survived before. We survive, always.*'

'*You've been killing for so long, fighting for so long. Even when you had the option to leave, you turned to fighting, and this is where it has brought you: alone, abandoned but for voices in your head. It's time to listen to reason. It's time to give up. It's over.*'

An inferno.

'*Ignore. Do not listen. Survive.*'

A mild chill.

His hands fell to his side, sword from his hands, clattering to the drowning deck. The air turned to iron in his lungs, forced him to his knees. The water was not as cold as he expected, rising up around him and embracing him, a thousand tiny, lapping little hands, welcoming him into their fold, assuring him that *they* would never abandon him.

'*Rest now. Your wounds are great. Your head is heavy. You've done enough.*'

A blanket of shadow, warm and comforting, fell over him, bidding his eyes close, bidding him to ignore the pain in his shoulder. He felt numb of his own volition, burrowing into his own body, leaving the rest of him senseless to a pair of massive hands being laid gently upon his shoulder.

'*You've fought so hard and for nothing. Let this be the end.*'

He felt the fingers on his face, but could not feel the cold of the palms that pressed against either side of his head. The water was up to his waist now, the shadow engulfing him completely. Soon it would be over. Soon it would end.

And there would be no more pain.

'*NOT OUR TIME.*'

Blood cold, brain frozen, muscles spasmed. His sword came to his hand, arm flew from his shoulder, found flesh and bit deeply. The screams were a disharmonic chorus, ringing from within and without a head that boiled and a body that froze.

He leapt to his feet, turned around.

And they were everywhere.

Bone-white hands, grasping railings and hauling up glistening hairless bodies onto the deck. Rivers of flesh pouring out from the companionway, glistening black eyes wide and needle-filled mouths gasping. Boiling out of the ship's wounds, knotted clots of skin and teeth on salty, dark blood.

And among the frogmen, their masters walked. Three of the Abysmyths dominated the rapidly sinking deck, striding over their charges on skeletal black legs, pulling their emaciated bodies through the splintered wood. And before him, a great ebon tree leaking sap, the demon clutched the wound at its flank that Lenk's sword had carved. Its vast, empty eyes strove to convey agony, just as its reaching, webbed claw strove to find Lenk's throat.

'Mother give me patience for the weak of heart,' it croaked through a drowning voice. 'I do what they cannot, through Your will.'

'*SURVIVE.*'

Advice or command, it was all that the voice told him, and it was all he needed.

The webbed claw grasped the air where his head had been as he darted low and swung his sword up, driving it into the creature's spear-thin midsection. It ate a messy feast, ichor dribbling from its metal maw and chewing through ribs as the blade and its wielder ignored the screams of the dying.

And yet, Lenk's brain was set ablaze with another wailing scream.

'*STOP IT!*'

As fervent and fiery as the command was, Lenk fought against it. When the voice's words were not obeyed, it lashed out, searing his brain and boiling the blood in his temples. He staggered, rather than darted away, from the towering demon as it collapsed to its massive knees and then landed face-first in the water.

A wall of pale white flesh greeted him, broken only by the four wide white eyes that stared at him from above. The frogmen pressed toward him, feral hisses slithering from their gaping, needle-lined mouths, webbed glistening hands outreached. The Abysmyths towering over them picked their way carefully towards him, gurgling in the voices of men long claimed by the sea.

'Absolution in submission,' one of them croaked. 'Atonement in acceptance.'

'Mercy at the Shepherd's crook,' the other one said. 'You cannot continue like this, lamb, wallowing in despair and in doubt.'

'Mother bids us,' the frogmen echoed in twisted, echoing harmony. 'The Prophet commands us. All for you.'

They reached for him with free hands, clenched bone knives in the other. The Abysmyths' jaws gaped, webbed claws open as if to invite him to get in. He saw his death reflected in every black, glossy stare and his life vanishing down every gaping gullet.

And, with no other plan, he heard the voice that spoke on freezing tongues.

'*Kill.*'

And he obeyed.

He lunged forward, swinging the blade as he did. It gorged itself, cleaving through rubbery white flesh and spilling fluids into the water indiscriminately. Those frogmen that fell he used as stepping stones across the drowning deck, cleaving into more and more still as he made his way towards the railing, ignoring the fever-hot voice screeching at him.

'*PLEASE! THEY HAVE DONE NOTHING! SPARE THEM!*'

They knotted at the railing, preventing him from hurling himself over before he could reach it. He didn't care; there would be more of them under the water, anyway, in their element. His target was closer, taller and decidedly darker.

The Abysmyth reached for him, its four-jointed arm extending to snatch him from the deck in an ooze-covered claw. He ducked low beneath it, wrapped his arm about it and lashed out with his sword, gnashing at the creature's shoulder. Its arm flailed with a shriek, pulling him up and over its skeletal body.

He bit back the pain in his shoulder and his head alike as he scrambled across the demon's body, narrowly avoiding its many jagged teeth as he grabbed at the loose folds of leathery skin in its throat and swung himself onto its back. His sword went up, a fervent scream echoing through his head.

'DON'T YOU TOUCH MY CHILDREN!'

It came down again.

The pain was agonising, the shrieks of the Abysmyth and the one in his skull making his ears ring. But he drove the blade into the creature's back again and again, forcing it as deep as he could atop his precarious perch. Such a task only became harder as the creature flung itself into a flailing frenzy, swinging its arms in an attempt to remove the silver parasite from its back and succeeding only in smashing away those frogmen that rushed to its aid.

'I tried! I tried!' it wailed as it flailed wildly with one arm and clutched at its blossoming wounds with another. 'Mother, I tried! But he won't listen! He's hurting me! *It hurts!'*

'STOP IT, STOP IT, STOP IT, STOP IT!' the voice shrieked, pounding on his skull with fiery fists and sending waves of burning pain through his head.

He clung to the beast for as long as he could, despite the pain, but it took only another breath for him to feel the grasping water again. When he could see through the pain, he saw the deck vanished completely, swallowed by the rising tide. The frogmen stood calmly, their black eyes fixed on him as their heads slowly slipped beneath the water, glittering like onyxes even as their white flesh disappeared.

'*Survive*,' the voice whispered frigidly.

Between the two voices, there was no room in his head for contemplation about how infeasible such a command was quickly becoming. There was no room left for anything but a compulsion that pulled his eyes to the side, to the sole wooden salvation.

Blackened and splintering as it might have been, the sloping mast reached out like a pleading hand, the ship's last, desperate attempt to keep above water. Fleeting as any salvation might have been, Lenk leapt for it anyway, leaving his demonic mount to sink beneath the waves.

It was far away, only growing smaller as it continued to slide under the water. He swam in a violent frenzy, kicking up froth as he struggled to bite back the pain in his shoulder and hold onto his sword as he did. Still, beneath his body, he could feel the presence of eyes staring, arms reaching.

Out of the corner of his eye, he caught a glimpse of something. A soft, blue light pulsing beneath the waves in a trio of azure heartbeats moved steadily towards him. Through the waves, through the pain, he could hear the whispers as they drew closer.

'*Noescapenoescapenoescapenoescape* ...'

'*Mercyathandmercyisheremercyforall* ...'

'*SheknowsSheseesShesympathisesgiveingiveingiveingivein giveingivein* ...'

'*No!*' the voice and he spoke as one as he found the mast and pulled himself out of the water, tumbling and facing the black water below.

The Abysmyth came rising up, its white eyes wide and stark in the gloom as it crept out, black claw glistening, reaching out of the water. He swung at it, the sword heavier in his hand than it had been, the pain in his limbs more pronounced. The beast accepted the blow, gurgling from below as it hauled the rest of its body onto the mast as he scrambled backwards.

The frogmen behind it moved with a similar inevitable purpose, staring at the blood-slick blade that had already seen its brethren, its masters spilt upon salt, without fear. They boiled up behind the Abysmyth, climbing over its body, onto the mast, reaching their webbed hands for Lenk.

He could feel the fear in his eyes, if not his head. He could see his wide stare reflected in the blade's face. He could feel the blood seeping out of his shoulder, the fire searing his skull. What he couldn't feel was the numbness, the callous cold that had swept over him and seized control before and delivered him. The voice was shrieking still, but it was faint, fading, disappearing behind a veil of fire and drowning in a sea of darkness.

He was alone. Abandoned.

'Your song is ending, lamb,' the Abysmyth croaked, reaching for him once again. 'Fleeting sounds and errant voices offer no sanctuary. Things made of paper flesh and wooden bones provide no redemption.'

'*Forsakenforsakenforsaken ...*'

'*Abandonedabandonedabandoned ...*'

'*Noonenothingnobodyleftleftleft ...*'

'But Mother hears you,' the Abysmyth said, its eyes growing wider at the mention. 'Mother wishes you to hear Her, to know what we know, to feel what we feel. Let Her speak. Let the pain end. Let the sinful thought end.' Its

647

claw reached out not to seize, but to offer, to beckon. 'Let yourself hear.'

'I ... no ...' For lack of thought to do anything else, for lack of voice to say anything better, he shook his burning head. 'I can't ... I can't.'

'*Nolongeryourchoice ...*'

'*Nolongeranychoice ...*'

'*Letushelpyou ...*'

He heard the water rip apart beneath him, an eruption of froth at his back. He managed to see them in glimpses: soft lips within gaping needle jaws, bulging black eyes set in bulbous grey heads, long grey stalks of flesh pulsing with soft blue light. He managed to feel them as they wrapped scrawny grey claws around him, coiled eel-like tails about him, pressed withered breasts against his body.

He managed to scream only once before the mast shattered under their weight and they pulled him below.

Drowning wasn't so bad.

Lenk absently wondered what the fuss was all about, really, as he continued to drift, pulled lower by liquid hands. The water was not as cold as it looked, enveloping him in a gentle warmth. It wasn't as dark as he had suspected it would be, either. The creatures saw to that.

To call them 'demons' seemed a little insulting. Demons were twisted beings, foul things that found the natural world intolerable. These creatures, circling the waters far above him, their azure lights forming a bright halo, did not look so twisted. They were emaciated, true, with their bulbous heads at odds with their bony torsos, their slithering eel tails in place of legs. Below the surface of the water, though, they looked delicate instead of underfed, graceful instead of writhing.

And their whispering had become song.

He could hear it more clearly the deeper he drifted: lilting, resonating, wordless songs that carried through water and skin, seeping into him. They sang everything at once, lullabies and dirges, love and agony. It was a familiar song, one he had heard before. But he could not think of where, could not think of anything. With the song in his ears, there was no room left for any other sound. He found comfort in that. He found peace in the deep.

So much so that he didn't know he shouldn't be able to breathe.

That didn't seem so important, though. There was no fear in the warm, welcoming depths, for drowning or for the corpses that sank around him. Down here, the anger was erased from the netherlings' long faces, their eyes open and tranquil as they sank softly, shards of the ship drifting around them like unassembled coffins. Down here, the creatures that swam around him, with their black eyes and white skins, didn't seem so menacing.

Down here, for the first time in weeks, he felt no fear.

'Enjoying yourself?'

The voices came from nowhere, clear as the water itself. He caught a glimpse in the shadows surrounding him as something swam at the edges of the halo of light. A grey hide shifted, an axe-like fin tail swept through the water, manes of copper and black wafted like kelp in the water.

He remembered the Deepshriek.

She appeared. *No*, he reminded himself, *it's not a she*. Rather, a face appeared, a soft and milk-white oval, framed by long and silky hair the colour of fire. Its eyes were golden and glittering above soft lips set in a frown. It drifted closer to Lenk and he saw the rest of it, the long grey stalk that served as its body snaking into the darkness.

Another head emerged, black hair lost in shadow, attached to an identical stalk. They circled him, as the hulking grey-skinned fish that the stalks crowned circled him. There was another stalk, hanging limp and bereft of a head. He remembered there had been another head. He remembered taking it.

He remembered the Deepshriek wanted to kill him for that.

That thought prompted the realisation of his lungs working. That realisation prompted his question.

'Why am I alive?'

'There was a time when sky and sea were not the petty rivals they are today,' the Deepshriek answered in disjointed chorus. 'They shared all. We remember that time. Ulbecetonth remembers that time.' Their eyes narrowed to four thin slits. 'This is Her domain.'

'No, that wasn't what I meant. Why am I not dead?'

'Not because of us,' the creature said. 'We wanted you to die.' The heads snaked around him, golden scowls and bared fangs. 'You took our head. You destroyed our temple. You took the tome. You ruined *everything*. We wanted you to drown, to die, to be eaten by tiny little fish over a thousand years.'

'And yet ... here we are,' he said, no room in the depths for fear.

'We were overruled.'

'By whom?'

The heads glanced at each other, then at Lenk, then through Lenk. He felt himself turning, spinning gently in the halo as unseen hands turned him upside down to face the sea floor. He stared for a moment and saw nothing.

And then, he saw teeth.

He tried to count them at a glance, absently, and found

the task tremendous enough to make his head hurt. Rows upon rows of them opened, splitting the endless sandy floor into a tremendous smile.

'Lenk.' They loosed a voice, deep and feminine. 'Hello.'

He stared into the void between them, vast and endless.

'Hello,' he replied, 'Ulbecetonth.'

It laughed. *No*, he thought, *it's a she*. And her voice was far more pleasant and matronly than a demon's ought to be, he decided. Then again, he only knew the one. It was a comforting warmth, a blanket of sound that soothed the ache in his head, banished chill from his body.

He remembered this voice.

'You're not real, are you?' he asked the teeth. 'You're in my head, just like your voice was.'

'Voices inside your head can be entirely real,' Ulbecetonth replied. 'Have you not learned this by now?'

'It's simply a form of madness.'

'If you hear voices, you're mad. If you talk back, it's something far worse.'

'Point,' he replied. 'So are you real, then? Or am I dead?' He glanced around the shadows. 'Is this—?'

'No,' she replied. 'This is a far too pleasant to be hell; your hell, anyway. Murderers of children go to far darker, far deeper places.'

'I have killed no—'

'I told you to stop,' the teeth said, twisting into a frown. 'I *begged* you to spare my children. You killed them, regardless. Both of you.'

'There was only one of me.'

'There is never only one of *you*.'

He took in a deep breath that he should not have been able to.

'You've heard it, then?'

'Many times,' she replied. 'I remember your voice well. Both of them. I heard them many times during the war that cast my family into shadow. I heard them on blades that were driven into my children's flesh. I heard them on flames that burned my followers alive in their sacred places. When I heard them in your head again ...'

The teeth snapped shut with the sound of thunder, sending his bones rattling. The echo lasted for an age, after which it took another for him to muster the nerve to speak.

'Then I ask again, why am I alive?'

'Pity, mostly,' Ulbecetonth said. 'I have seen your thoughts, your desires, your cruelties and your pains. I have seen what you have. I have seen what you want. I know that you will never have it and it moved me.'

'I don't understand.'

'You do,' she said. 'You don't want to, though. We both know this. We both know you desire something resembling peace: sinful earth to put your feet on, blasphemous fire to warm your hands by, a decaying thing of tainted breath and aging flesh to call your own. But not just any flesh ...'

'I've heard this rhetoric before,' he snapped back, finding resolve somewhere within himself. 'They say that I'm mad to want her.'

'And we have established that you are not mad,' she replied smoothly. 'You are something worse, and that is why you cannot have—'

'Her?'

'Any of it. Your earth will always be soaked in blood. Your fire will always carry the scent of death. There will be many things made of flesh that you call your own, but they will all die, and before they do, they will look into your eyes and see what I have heard in your head.'

'You're wrong.'

'You don't want to admit it. I cannot blame you. Nor can my conscience let you cling to harmful delusion.'

In his mind flashed the ship, the fire, his companions. He saw the dragonman who had leapt into the water after sparing him a glance. He saw the wizard who took off without even looking in his direction. He didn't see the rogue and the priestess, for they never so much as looked at him before they disappeared. Those were fleeting, though.

The eyes, the emerald stare that had seeped into his, and then turned away …

That image lingered.

'She left me,' he whispered. 'She looked into my eyes … and left me to die.'

'It hurts. I know.' Ulbecetonth's voice brimmed with sympathy, sounding as though she might be on the verge of tears if she were more than just teeth. 'To see those who you once loved betray you, to know the sorrow that comes with abandonment. I've seen the fear grow inside you. I know the times you felt like weeping and could not. I wept for you, despite your countless sins against me. I saw your grief and your sorrow and knew I could not give you the death you deserved. Not now.'

'What?' he asked, shaking the images from his eyes.

'I am offering you a generosity,' Ulbecetonth said. 'Return to your world of petty sea and envious earth. Forget about my children, as surely as we will forget about you. Go elsewhere and cling to fire and stone and whatever flesh makes you happy. Find someone else to kill. Your voice will be satisfied all the same.

'Between the longfaces and the Shen,' she continued, 'I have far too many enemies for my liking. The green heathens are an ancient enemy. The purple ones serve a foe older still. I have no need or wish to worry about a misguided creature with misguided desires. Take my offer. Leave these waters. I will not try to stop you. I will never again speak your name if I can help it. You need never feel the anguish you felt tonight again. All you need do … is leave.'

'I can't leave,' he whispered, shaking his head. 'There's more to do. The tome …'

'Will be safe, its terrible knowledge far from any who would use it for ill.'

'In your hands?' he asked. 'That's not right. Your Abysmyths—'

'*My children*,' she snapped back, 'are without their mother. They long for family, for my influence. They seek to use the book to return me to their embrace. Afterwards, we will have no further use for it or for bloodshed. Let us live in peace beneath the waves. Forget about us.'

'All you want … is your family?'

'What does any mother want?'

'But Miron said—'

'*PRIESTS LIE.*'

The ocean quaked. Sand stirred below; light fled above. The song of the creatures died. The swimming frogmen vanished into engulfing shadows. Corpses fell like lead; wood fell upon them in cairns. Lenk felt his breath draw tight in his chest, unseen fire searing his body.

'*Priests send children to die, condemn them to death, sit too high for the ashes of the burned to reach them and wear hoods to mute the screaming.*' The teeth twisted, gnashed, roared. '*Priests betrayed me. Betrayed you.*'

'Betrayed me? How? I don't—'

'*NO.*' The ocean boiled around him, the comforting warmth turning horrendously hot. '*No more explanations.*

654

No more answers. No matter what they call me, I am still a mother. My pity spares you this once. But remember this, you tiny little thing: This is my *world. You have a place in it only as long as I will it.'*

And with that, his breath was robbed from him. His lungs seized up, throat closed as it fought to keep out the water that flooded his mouth. He clenched at his neck, started thrashing desperately for air that was far too far above him now.

The teeth parted, loosing a long, low bellow, a command in a language far too old for mortal ears to hear. The seas obeyed, rising up to drive Lenk towards the surface. Struggling to hold his breath, he watched the teeth grow faint as he was sent hurtling above.

And yet, her voice only grew louder.

'A final kindness, mortal. Follow the ice to see what I tried so hard to protect you from. Follow it ... Follow that wickedness inside your head and realise that I was only trying to protect you from yourself and everything else. This is all I can offer you. Happiness is far out of your reach. Truth and survival is all you can hope for. Take them while you can.'

In the darkness below, two great golden eyes opened and stared at him with hate.

'Before I take them back.'

Thirty-Five

THE SINS IN THE STONE

The statue of Zamanthras was well tended. Her high, stone cheeks had been polished. The waves of Her flowing hair were lovingly carved so that each granite strand was distinct and apparent. Her bountiful breasts, uncovered by the thin garment about Her hips, were perfectly round and smooth.

The rest of the temple was in decay, ignored. It had been easy enough to sneak into, unseen. The pillars that marched the crumbling walls were shattered and decayed. Those tapestries that still hung from their sconces were frayed and coated in dust. Supplies, crates and boxes had been stacked beneath them. It appeared that the church had lost its original purpose and had been resigned to storage and other practical needs long ago. He would have accepted that. He would have smiled at that.

If not for the statue.

Zamanthras stared down at the Mouth through stone eyes, smiled at him through stone lips. She was confident in Her own care, smug in Her own polish. They still worshiped, She told him. No matter how deaf She might be, no matter how long their prayers went unanswered, the people would still polish Her statue. The people would wait for Her to save their dying children, to give them enough wealth to buy a loaf of bread. It would never come.

They would die and praise Her name even as She watched them languish.

'No more,' he whispered. 'No more wasted prayers. No more dead children.' He glanced at the vial in his hand, the swirling liquid of Mother's Milk. 'It ends here. In Your house.'

Resounding through his skull and the temple alike, a distant heartbeat voiced its deep, droning approval.

Stretching between the Mouth and the Goddess, the temple's pool stretched as long as ten men in a vast, perfect circle. The waters upon it were placid, unstirred and quiet, not the silvery flow of a lake. This water was dense, heavy, like iron.

A door to a prison.

As he leaned over the edge, staring into the water, the heartbeat grew faster, louder. The Father sensed his presence, sensed the scent of his consort, his mistress, in the Mouth's hand. Through whatever prison held him, Daga-Mer scented the faintest trace of Mother Deep.

And beneath the iron waters, Daga-Mer railed against his liquid bonds.

Free him, an urge spoke within him, born of anger, tempered by sermon. *The Father must be freed before Mother Deep can rise. Mother Deep must rise before this world can change. Remember why She must.*

Change, he reminded himself. Change that mortalkind might not tremble in fear. Change that mortalkind might not waste their words on deaf gods. Change that children would not die while their parents languished in doubt.

He stared back up, saw the statue of Zamanthras looking back at him, smiling, challenging him to do so.

Mocking him.

They would tremble, She knew. Change was terrifying.

They would pray to Her when Mother Deep rose, She said with a stone voice. Change bred a need for the familiar. She would watch children die, parents die, all in darkness, all in doubt. Change was violent.

Then ... A doubt spoke within him, blooming in darkness and watered with despair. *What's the point?*

He heard a scrape of feet against stone floors. His own heart quickened; had he been seen? He reached for a knife that wasn't there. Where was it? He had left it elsewhere, in another life, another house, when he had seen ...

He paused, noting the silence. No one was emerging. No one came out to stop him. He glanced about, spying a shadow painted upon the walls by the dim light of the hole in the ceiling.

'I know you're there,' he said. The shadow quivered, shrinking behind the pillar. 'You shouldn't be here, you know.'

A bush of black hair peered out from behind the pillar, the girl staring at him with dark eyes that betrayed wariness, caution. She was not panicked. He shouldn't have smiled at her, he knew. His smile shouldn't have been intended to reassure her, to coax her out. Change was coming. Many would die. She would likely be among them.

And yet ...

'Neither should you,' she said to him, leaning out a little more. 'Mesri says that no one should be in here.'

'In the city's temple?'

'There's less call for prayer these days,' she said, easing out from behind the pillar. 'More call for medicine and food.'

The Mouth eyed the crates stacked against the walls. 'So they are left here to rot?'

'Don't be stupid,' she sneered. 'If we had any, Mesri would have distributed them.'

'Priests serve the Gods, not man.'

'Well, if there were any in *here*, I wouldn't be scrounging in dark, abandoned houses with weird, pale-skinned strangers,' she replied sharply. 'This' – she gestured to the crates – 'is what was left behind when the rich people left Yonder.'

He glanced to a great, hulking shape beneath a white sheet. 'And that?'

The girl traipsed over to it, drawing it off to expose a well-made, untested ballista mounted on wheels, its string drawn and bolt loaded. 'They bought it when fears about Karnerian and Sainite incursions were high.' As if she suddenly remembered who she was talking to, she tensed, resting a hand on the siege weapon's launching lever. 'I know how to use it, too.'

Hers was the look of childish defiance, the urge to run suppressed because someone had once told her that running was for cowards. It was familiar. He fought the urge to smile. He fought the urge to point out that the ballista was pointing at least ten feet to the right of him.

'I'm not going to hurt you,' he said.

'And I'm sure you're telling the truth,' she replied snidely. 'Because, as we all know, only *reasonable* hairless freaks chase young girls through alleys with knives, screaming like lunatics.'

'I left the knife in the house,' he said. '*My* house.'

'Not fair,' she snapped back. 'Squatters can't claim the houses. It's a rule.'

'I'm not a squatter. I used to live there.'

'Liar.'

'What?'

659

'If you used to live there, you'd be a Tohana man. If you were a Tohana man, you'd be like me.' She tapped her dark-skinned brow. 'I'm not quite convinced that *you* aren't some kind of shaved ape.'

'I could have been from another nation,' he pointed out.

'If you were, you'd have been rich and you wouldn't live in a little shack.' She eyed him carefully. 'So ... who are you?'

'There is no good answer to that.'

'Then give me a bad one.'

He glanced from her to the pool. 'I lived here with my family once. They're dead now.'

'That's not a bad answer,' she replied. 'Not a good one, either. Lots of people have dead families. That doesn't explain what you're doing here.'

He knew he shouldn't answer. What would be the point? When the Father was freed, people would die. That was inevitable. How could he possibly tell her this? There was no need for him to even look at her, he knew. He didn't have to kill her or anything similar. All he need do was open the vial, pour the Milk into the water, free the Father. It didn't even need to be poured – he could just hurl the whole thing in and the objective would be achieved.

Change would come.

People would die.

He had tried to bite back his memories, to quash the pain that welled up inside him. He had served the Prophet to achieve oblivion, as the rest of the blessed had. And yet, gazing upon the girl roused memory in him, nurturing instincts that he had not felt since he sat beside a small cot and told stories.

Chief among these was the instinct to lie.

'I'm here to help,' he said.

'Help?'

'This city was my home once. I raised a child here. I want to help it return to its former glory.'

'Glory?' She raised a sceptical eyebrow.

'Prosperity?'

'Eh ...'

'Stability, then,' he said. 'I'm going to change this city.'

'How?'

He smiled at her. 'I'll start with the people.'

She stared at him for a moment, and as he gazed upon her expression, he knew an instinctual fear. Doubt. It was painted across her unwashed face in premature wrinkles and sunburned skin. It was the expression of someone who had heard promises before and knew, in whatever graveyard inside of her that innocence went to die, that some lies, no matter how nurturing, were simply lies.

He had seen that expression only once before. He remembered it well.

And then, her face nearly split apart with her grin.

'That's pretty stupid,' she said. 'I like it. I don't believe it, but I like it.'

'Now, why wouldn't you believe it?' He grinned back. 'If a shaven monkey can sneak into a temple unseen, why wouldn't he be able to change people?'

'Because everyone tells the same story. I'm too old to believe it now.'

'How old?'

'Sixteen.'

'What's your name?'

'Kasla,' she said, smiling. 'What's yours?'

He opened his mouth to speak, and the moment he did, her grin vanished, devoured by the expression of fear and

661

panic that swallowed her face. He quirked a brow at her as she turned and fled, scampering behind a pillar and disappearing into the shadows of the temple. He was about to call after her when he heard the voice.

'I'm not going to ask how you got in.'

He turned and saw the priest, portly, moustached and clad in fraying robes. The man eased the door shut behind him, making a point of patting the lock carefully. He turned to face the Mouth, his dark face dire.

'I'm not going to ask who you were talking to,' he said, taking a step forward. 'Nor will I inquire what you're doing here. I already know that.' A hand slipped inside his robe. 'All I wish to know is how a servant of Ulbecetonth thought he could walk in my city—'

His hand came out, clenching a chain from which a symbol dangled: a gauntlet clenching thirteen obsidian arrows. Mesri held it before him like a lantern, regarding the Mouth evenly.

'—without a member of the House knowing.'

The Mouth tensed, precariously aware of his position by the pool. He glanced down, all too aware of the vial clenched in his hand. He looked back to Mesri, painfully aware that he hadn't thrown it in yet.

'How much else do you know?' he whispered.

'Only what you do,' Mesri replied. 'We both know what's imprisoned beneath this city. We both know you're carrying the key to that abomination's release.'

'The Father is—'

'An abomination,' Mesri insisted. 'A beast that lives only to kill, only to destroy in the name of a cause that exists only to do more of the same. We both know that if he is released, that's all we'll see. Death. Destruction.' He stared at the Mouth intently. 'And yet ... we both know you've had opportunities in abundance to do so. And we both know you haven't.

'This is where my knowledge ends,' Mesri said. 'Why?'

'Just ...' The Mouth hesitated, cursing himself for it. 'I'm just taking my time, making certain that when the change comes, when the Father is freed, he—'

'Stop,' Mesri commanded. 'I know now why you haven't thrown it in.' His stare went past the Mouth's hairless flesh, plumbing something darker, deeper. It seized something inside him that was supposed to have been starved to death, banished into gloom. It seized that thing within him and drew it out. 'We both know.'

The Mouth cringed, turning away from the man's gaze.

'What I want to know is why,' Mesri said. 'Why you turned to the Kraken Queen and her empty promises.'

'Mother Deep's promises are not empty,' the Mouth hissed back. 'She demands servitude. She demands penance. Only then are the faithful rewarded.'

'With?'

'Absolution,' the Mouth said, a long smile tugging at the corners of his lips. 'Freedom from the sin of memory, oblivion from the torments of the past, salvation from the torture inflicted upon us by the Gods.'

'The benevolent matron does not demand,' Mesri retorted. 'The benevolent matron does not reward you by stealing what makes you human.'

'I am *not* human,' the Mouth snarled, holding up his webbed fingers. 'Not anymore. I am something greater. Something advanced enough to see the hypocrisy within you.' He narrowed his eyes to thin slits. 'You speak of benevolence, of rewards. What has your goddess brought you?'

The Mouth gestured wildly to the statue of Zamanthras,

her smug stone visage and self-satisfied stone smile.

'Your city is in decay! Your people lie ill and dying! The seas themselves have abandoned you!'

'Because of your matron,' Mesri snapped back. 'The fish flee because they sense her stirring. Your presence here confirms that.'

'We won't *need* fish,' the Mouth snarled. 'We won't need bread, we won't need healers and we won't need *gods*. Mother Deep will provide for us, absolve us all so that we need never suffer again. We'll live in a world where someone hears our prayers and guides us! We'll live in a world where we can talk to our gods and know they love us! We'll live in a world without doubt, where no one has to spew empty words at empty symbols while his child dies in her bed!'

The Mouth liked to think himself as in control of his emotions, his memories. Perhaps he wasn't. Perhaps they had been building up all this time, behind a dam of hymns and rehearsed proclamations, waiting for the tiniest breach to come flooding out. Perhaps Mesri's stare went deeper than he thought, pulled things up that even the Mouth didn't know he had inside of his skin. None of that mattered; the Mouth had said what he said.

Only now, when tears formed in his eyes, did he realise what it was he had just spoken.

'How long ago?' Mesri asked.

'She would have been sixteen now,' the Mouth said, aware of how choked his voice sounded. 'Plague got her. No healer could help. She would be too old for stories now. Too old for gods. They're one and the same: lies we tell each other to convince ourselves that our fates are beyond our own control.'

'That was roughly the time I gained these robes,' Mesri

sighed, rubbing at his temples. 'I believed, at the time, it was a blessing. Port Yonder thrived and I thought it was the will of the Gods.'

'The Gods have no will beyond the desire to be worshiped and do nothing in return,' the Mouth spat. 'They don't hear us. They don't do anything except fail us, and we keep coming back to them, scrounging at their feet!'

'I believed,' Mesri whispered, 'that we need simply continue to pray, to receive the blessing. I was wrong.'

'Then you see? This is the only way …' The Mouth looked to the vial. 'The Father must—'

'I was wrong in thinking that the Gods would treat us like sheep.' Mesri seized his attention with a sudden chest-borne bellow. 'I was wrong to think that we need simply to graze upon the blessings they gave us. The Gods gave us wealth and we squandered it. The Gods gave us prosperity and we wasted it. This temple could have been tremendous, like the church-hospitals of the Talanites. We could have helped so many people …'

'But the wealth vanished. The ill and hungry are everywhere. The Gods failed us.'

'The wealth is gone and the ill and hungry are as they are because of what we did. The Gods did not fail you.' Mesri closed his eyes, sighed softly. 'I did.'

The Mouth was at once insulted and astonished, unable to find words to express it.

'I could have helped your child. I could have saved her.' He tugged at his garments. 'These robes commanded respect. I could have brought the finest healers.'

'You wouldn't have.'

'I wouldn't have, no,' Mesri said, shaking his head. 'I would have languished in my gold and my silks and thought that the Gods would have solved it. But that is not their

665

fault. It is mine for believing that it would happen. If I had knowledge, if I had opportunity … we wouldn't be in this situation.'

'But we are,' the Mouth snarled. 'And we are left with no recourse but the inevitable.'

'Inevitability does not exist,' the priest spat back. 'There is only mankind and his will to do what's right. What we have here is knowledge. What we have here is opportunity.' He held out his hand. 'Give me the vial.'

There were a thousand replies the Mouth had been conditioned to offer such a demand, most of them involving some form of stabbing, all of them involving a total denial. What he did, what he hadn't expected to do, was to stare dumbly down at the vial, the key to change, the key to freedom.

To absolution.

'What will they say when you free Daga-Mer?' Mesri asked. 'What will they do when he destroys their lives, their homes, their families? They will do as you did: plunge themselves into a darkness deeper than sin. They will suffer as you have. They will try to convince themselves that they need no memory, that they need none of that torment.

'What we cannot count on is that they will be in a position to do as you have,' Mesri said softly. 'We cannot count on them to realise the value of memory, the treasure that is the image of their daughter's face.' He stared intently at the Mouth. 'You can hurl it into the pool. You can hurl her face, her life, with it.

'Or you can give it to me. And we can spare a thousand people what you're feeling right now.'

The Mouth had no desire to inflict what he currently felt on another. The Mouth wasn't even certain what it was that he was feeling. Despair, of course, blended with anger and frustration and compulsion, but they churned inside him, whirling about so that he received only glimpses of them. And at each glimpse, a memory: his daughter's laughter, his daughter's first skinned knee, his daughter's first toy, his daughter's death …

And he wanted them to be gone forever.

And he wanted to cling to them always.

And he wanted the world to see how false the Gods were.

And he wanted no one to go into the dark places he had gone to.

'I don't know your name,' Mesri said. 'I don't know your daughter's name. But I know the names of every person in this city. I will tell you all of them so that you know whose lives you hold in your hand.'

'Do you know Kasla?' he asked.

'Her parents are dead. She refuses to come to me for help. She is proud.'

'My daughter was proud.'

He looked up. He saw Mesri smile at him.

'Then I think you've made your decision.' He took a step closer. The Mouth did not retreat. He raised his hand. The Mouth raised the vial. 'It is a wise one, my fr—'

'*QAI ZHOTH!*'

The howl rang out over the city sky: an iron voice carving through the air, cleaving through a chorus of screams that reverberated off every wall.

'*WE'RE UNDER ATTACK! RUN! RUN!*'

'*ZAMANATHRAS, WHAT ARE THEY?*'

'*MESRI! WHERE'S MESRI?*'

And for every scream, a war cry answered.

'*AKH ZEKH LAKH!*'

'*EVISCERATE! DECAPITATE! ANNIHILATE!*'

'*WHERE IS IT? WHERE IS THE RELIC, SCUM?*'

Mesri did not have to ask what was happening. The sounds of fire, of pain, of death filled his ears. He did not have to ask who was invading. He did not care. And he did not have time to.

He turned. The Mouth had vanished, fled into some dark recess of the temple and of his own thoughts. He cursed, sparing only a moment to look at the pool. It was still there. Still untainted. Still holding its prisoner.

A muttered prayer was all he could spare for the Mouth as he turned and rushed into the city.

In the temple behind, fate lay in the hands of a troubled servant of demons.

In the city ahead, fate lay in the reek of smoke and the screams of the dying.

Thirty-Six

A SETTLING OF DEBTS

Dreadaeleon had begun to consider the theories behind the purifying quality of fire lately.

Of course, he didn't believe any of the nonsense of fire burning away sins. Rather, he suspected the appeal was something far more practical in nature. Theoretically, any problem could be solved by fire. If two friends fought over, say, a piece of property, setting it on fire would immediately diminish its desirability. If they still fought afterwards, setting each other on fire would quickly take their minds off of their dispute.

People are only upset, he mused, *until they can burn something. Then everything's fine.*

A shaky theory, he recognised, but if the sight of Togu's hut licking a smoke-stained sky with orange tongues was any indication, his companions would serve as excellent evidence.

'Explain to me the reasoning behind this again,' Bralston said, watching the burning hut with intent.

'It's typically referred to as "Gevrauch's Debt",' Dreadaeleon replied.

'Named for the theoretical divine entity that governs the dead.'

'Exactly. As you can probably deduce, it's never anything pleasant. Adventurers typically use it as a means of drawing payment from employers who cannot or will not pay them for their services. Looting is frequently involved.'

'And if the employer does not have anything of value?'

'Burning.'

There was a loud cracking sound as the hut's roof collapsed, sending embers flying into the air. Bralston sniffed, the faintest sign of a disapproving sneer on his face.

'Barbaric.'

'He deserves worse.'

Asper's voice was barely audible over the crackling fire. She did not look at the two wizards, her expression blank as she stared into the flames.

'He betrayed us,' she said softly. 'He should be in that hut.'

Perhaps you should ask her, he thought to himself. *She hasn't said anything about what happened, true, but that doesn't necessarily mean she won't. Is she simply waiting for someone to do so? Maybe that's why she's so moody and dark since she got back. No, wait, maybe you shouldn't ask. Maybe she needs something more physical. Put your arm around her. Or kiss her? Probably not in front of the Librarian ... then again, he might take one look at that and—*

'I've seen what the longface is capable of,' Bralston said to her. 'I've seen what he does.'

'I don't care what he does to your laws or your magic,' she replied without looking at him.

'The Venarium is concerned with the Laws only as they affect people. The longface was a deviant in more ways than one. His death was warranted.'

'You said he might not be dead, though,' Dreadaeleon put in.

Bralston whirled a glare upon him. The boy returned a baffled shrug.

'Well, I mean, you *did*.'

'Do you think he's dead, Librarian?' Asper asked.

'Certainty with any kind of magic is difficult,' he replied. 'With renegade magic, especially.'

'Well,' Dreadaeleon interjected. 'We brought down the ship. We sent it to the bottom with all his warriors. There's at least a strong chance that he's—'

'It wouldn't surprise me if he wasn't,' she interrupted.

'Well … I mean, he was quite powerful,' Dreadaeleon replied, 'and he cheated! He didn't obey the—'

'Nothing ever works out as it should, does it, Dread?' she asked, her tone cold. 'If gods can fail, so can everyone else.'

'Well, yeah,' Dreadaeleon said, 'because they don't exist.'

He had said such before to her. He anticipated righteous indignation, possibly a stern backhand, as he had received before. He hadn't expected her to remain silent, merely staring into the fire without so much as blinking.

Huh, he thought, fighting back a grin. *Got off easy there. Nice work, old man.*

The smile became decidedly easier to beat down once Bralston shot him a sidelong glare. The Librarian said nothing more, though, his attention suddenly turning back to the fire with a rapt interest that hadn't been present in his stare before. Asper's gaze, too, became a little more intent at the tall figure emerging from behind the burning building.

He wasn't quite sure what about Denaos either of them found so fascinating, but Dreadaeleon instantly decided he was against whatever it was.

The tall man paused, tilting the remnants of a bottle of whisky, pilfered from the hut, into his mouth and then tossing the liquor-stained vessel over his shoulder, ignoring the ensuing sputter of flame. His smile was long and liquid as he approached them, smacking his lips.

'And with that,' he said, 'his debt is paid in full.'

'He betrayed us,' Dreadaeleon replied. 'Violated our trust. There is no price to be put on that.'

Denaos shot the pyre an appraising glance. 'I took a quick estimate when we went rifling through his stuff. I think trust is worth about a hundred and twelve gold coins. Maybe eighty-two in eastern nations.'

Dreadaeleon's glance flitted down to the man's wrist and the wrapped leather gauntlet that hadn't been there before. He caught a glimpse of Bralston's eyes, narrowed to irate scrutiny, upon the glove.

'The spoils?' he asked.

'This?' Denaos held it up, admiring it. 'I prefer to call it an honest day's pay for an honest night's work.'

'Hardly anything honest about it,' Dreadaeleon said. 'You never once stepped out to help us on the deck. You didn't even give us the signal that you were safe.'

'And you sank the ship without making certain we were safe,' Denaos said, shrugging. 'I figure we're even. Everyone made it out unscathed, anyway.'

'Not Lenk,' Asper pointed out.

They fell silent at that.

It was only when they had returned to the shore, the ship long since sank, that anyone noticed the absence of their silver-haired companion. Bralston and Dreadaeleon had met up with Denaos standing over a blanket-wrapped Asper. Togu, having been picked up by Hongwe, stood beside the Gonwa nearby. Gariath and Kataria came to join them, without a word from either of them, only a few

672

moments later. They collected their clothes from the offering to Sheraptus and left in silence.

Lenk hadn't emerged until early the following morning.

No one had searched for him.

Dreadaeleon told himself now, as he had then, that it was not his fault. Searching for Lenk would have been pointless in dark water, if it was even an option. It was only when they had all stood upon the beach that he realised he had left Lenk behind. He suspected, if their sunken expressions were any indication, the others also shared similar guilts.

Yet, he didn't ask. Nor did anyone ask him. There had been no words exchanged between them. Each companion's expression suggested that even the meagerest of sounds would be agony. And so they had parted, the sight of each other suddenly too much to bear, without even asking about their lost companion.

And then, Lenk had come crawling back into the village the next morning, without a word, without a sword, and with a heavy gash in his shoulder. He sat himself before Asper, whose shock was abolished long enough to stitch up his wound.

After that, he had staggered to Togu's hut, where his companions and the chieftain stood assembled. He, like the others, didn't think to ask how Togu had survived after being hurled bound into the ocean. Instead, he stared for an eternity into bulbous yellow eyes that refused to meet his own before he looked up at the creature's hut and uttered the words.

'*Gevrauch's debt.*'

They had taken to the task with varying amounts of enthusiasm. Yet even Asper did it without complaint or scorn, helping herself to what medicine Togu had stockpiled. Kataria had taken arrows; Lenk had taken a shirt of mail; Dreadaeleon had taken a new pair of boots; Denaos had taken everything else. Gariath acknowledged that his grudge against Togu wasn't as great as theirs, so he contented himself with urinating on the lizardman's throne.

When the torch had come out, it was Hongwe who had protested and it was Togu who had gently silenced him. Perhaps the weight of his guilt demanded the resignation, or perhaps he was pleased that the companions limited their revenge to looting and burning. The lizardman had stared at his house burning until Lenk had whispered a few unheard words and stalked off.

Togu had said only ten words.

'*All that grows on Teji,*' he whispered, '*once grew in that house.*'

And he had sighed and he had shuffled down the stone circles as the last fragrances of flowers were consumed by fire.

Granted, there were a few odd glances shot in the direction of their beloved leader's smouldering hut. The Owauku had yet to ask a question as to why it was burning. Of course, Dreadaeleon acknowledged, they had yet to come within fifteen feet of the companions, let alone ask anything.

'Any idea where Lenk went?' Dreadaeleon asked.

'No clue, no cares,' Denaos replied. 'Maybe he wanted to try on that armour he picked up. It looked nice. Might keep him from getting cut up again.'

'That's a concern amongst you?'

Bralston spoke with a sudden depth to his voice that none had heard before. The question commanded their attentions instantly.

'Cutting?' the Librarian pressed, his hard stare never leaving Denaos.

'Hazard of the job,' Denaos replied coolly.

'Adventuring is not considered a job,' Bralston said. 'It is long thought to be the last haven of scum, criminals and murderers.'

It wasn't the first time those three words had been used to describe the profession. And by Dreadaeleon's count, that was around the sixty-fifth time those three words had been used to describe Denaos specifically. The rogue had never had anything for the accusation beyond smiles and snidery.

The sixty-sixth time, however, he merely stared back at the Librarian.

'From Cier'Djaal?' he asked.

'It is with pride that I confirm that,' Bralston replied.

'Nice city,' the rogue said.

'It once was.'

It was there for an instant, the briefest twitches across their faces, perfectly synchronised. Dreadaeleon watched their reactions with a quirked brow, as unsure as to what had just happened between them as he was unsure why Denaos turned and stalked off towards the forest.

'What was that about?' Dreadaeleon asked the Librarian.

'I don't like the look of that man,' Bralston replied, following the rogue's shrinking form.

'I think that's intentional on his part.'

'You are mistaken.' Bralston's voice and eyes carried an edge. 'That is a man too comfortable in masks. What we see is what he wants us to see. What he doesn't want us to see is what lurks beneath. A coward ... a predator.' He looked to the forest and his voice became a spiteful razor. 'A murderer.'

Dreadaeleon suspected absently he should speak up in

defence of his companion. He did not, though; mostly because he had often thought the same thing about the rogue. Besides, before he could open his mouth, someone else beat him to it.

'And what would you know of predators?' For the first time, Asper turned to them. Even if her eyes had left the fire, however, the angry flames had not left her eyes. 'What would you know of *him*?'

'I have ...' Bralston hesitated, apparently taken aback by the outburst, 'seen his type before.'

'And there is no lack of types to be used in deciding who is who, is there, Librarian?' she pressed, stepping towards him.

Dreadaeleon felt vaguely astonished at the audacity. Even if she weren't facing a man who had aptly proven his penchant for and ability to turn things into ash, he was still a powerful physical specimen, standing nearly as tall as Gariath. Beyond that, he was a *Librarian*, an agent of the Venarium charged with destroying all threats to the Laws of Venarie and with extreme leeway in what he deemed threatening.

'Asper,' he said softly, 'he didn't mean—'

'No, you great thinkers of the Venarium just have the answer to everything, don't you? You can just *look* at a man and decide what he is, using those gigantic fat heads of yours to summarise an entire person in a few words.' She scowled up at him. 'Such as the type of person who, with the kind of power that makes him feel entitled enough to look down on another person, leaves other people to *suffer* in some ship's cabin when he could just as easily lift a *finger* and help, but that's just not *fiery enough*, is it?'

He blinked, glancing from her to a shrugging Dreadaeleon, then back.

'Granted,' she said coldly, 'I could sum up *that* type of man in a single word.' She shoved past him, stalking off and muttering under her breath. 'But I'm far too polite.'

Bralston's gaze lingered on her with equal intent as it had on Denaos as she skulked away. Dreadaeleon, too, followed her with a different sort of intent on his face and a different thought in his head.

Something's wrong, he thought, immediately scolding himself. *Well, obviously, you moron. She was held captive for how long? And you didn't move to help her? Well, you stuck to the plan. Denaos was supposed to help her* ...

But you're *the wizard. You've got the power. It should have been you to help her. You could have done something* ... *right? Right. You were feeling strong, then. Incredibly so. You didn't even need the stone, or anything else. You recovered. But how?*

She glanced over her shoulder, shooting him a pained expression. His eyes widened as the realisation struck him fiercely across the face.

Of course. It was her. It was all for her, wasn't it? That's what you've been doing wrong. You keep thinking of power for power's sake, for the Laws, for the Venarium, for yourself, and all it's gotten you is flaming urine and acid vomit. Those were pretty impressive, of course, but they weren't power. You did something for her, *though, and you recovered.*

Purpose. That's what's been missing, of course! It's not nearly as mystical as it sounds, either. A focus is often used in magical exercises, why not in magical practice? Why couldn't another person lend a wizard their strength, theoretically, just by existing? By focusing on them, everything could come so much easier. This is brilliant! You've got tell Bralston! Better yet, tell ...

He emerged from his own thoughts to find a long, barren stretch of sand.

'Where'd she go?' he asked, frowning.

'To tend to her own wounds, I suspect,' Bralston said, sighing. 'Women frequently do so in privacy.'

'But ... she wasn't hurt. Denaos got her out unscathed.'

Bralston turned to regard Dreadaeleon with a look that, in the few brief hours he had known the Librarian he had learned to dread. It was a cautious, cold scrutiny, better used on items lining a merchant's stall than a person. And as though Bralston were appraising merchandise, Dreadaeleon got the very ominous feeling that the Librarian was considering if he was worth the price.

Damn, damn, damn, damn, damn. He swallowed hard, fighting his nerves' insistence that he would feel better once he vomited on himself. *He's staring at you again. Quick, say something to throw him off!*

'So ...' Dreadaeleon said, grinning meekly. 'Did ... did you want a loincloth?'

WHAT THE HELL WAS THAT?

'You concern me, concomitant,' Bralston replied.

'Well, it's just that it's sort of the common style around here, and *we* were offered, or rather forced when we—'

'Believe it or not, your crippling lack of vocal judgement is not the issue,' the Librarian said. He turned on his heel and began walking down towards the village, his very posture demanding that Dreadaeleon follow. 'You have been amongst these ... adventurers for how long, concomitant?'

'Roughly a year.'

'And you can still recall the lessons that enabled the practice of your studies?'

'My master taught me much before I left him.'

'Ah, so you are tutored instead of academy-trained.' Bralston sniffed. 'There are few like you anymore. Tell me, did your master teach you the Pillars?'

'Of course. We covered them the moment I set foot in his study: Fire, Cold, Electricity, Force ...'

'Those are the Four Noble Schools,' Bralston replied, 'the ends of what the Pillars are taught to control and use properly.'

'Aren't ... aren't they the same thing?'

Bralston paused, fixing that scrutinising stare upon Dreadaeleon.

'This is the problem,' he said, the despair evident in his voice, if not his eyes. 'Venarie is a subject of law. Law is a matter of discipline. Discipline is made possible by the Pillars.' He counted them off on his fingers. 'Rationality, Judgement and ...'

There was a long pause before Dreadaeleon realised he was awaiting an answer. The boy shook his head and Bralston's eyes narrowed.

'Perception, concomitant. Rationality grants us the clarity to recognise threats and potential alike. Judgement is what permits us to act as we must in the name of the Laws. Perception bridges the two, acting as recognition of the situation and rationalisation of the proper response.'

'How can my perception be called into doubt?' Dreadaeleon replied. 'Did you *see* what I did last night? Who else would have thought to destroy a heretic by bringing a *giant sea snake* down on him?'

While Dreadaeleon couldn't *see* the childishly eager smile spreading across his face, he was made instantly aware of it by Bralston's quickly deepening frown.

'It's *not* about spitting ice and hurling fire,' the Librarian said. 'The difference between using them as a means of enforcing the Laws and using them as means in themselves is—'

'Perception?'

'The difference between a member of the Venarium and a heretic,' Bralston corrected. 'Your time amongst these adventurers is what concerns me. How much have you done to enforce the Laws?'

'I've ... I've been enforcing them.' Dreadaeleon rubbed the back of his neck. 'I was the first one to encounter the longfaces.'

'And yet you continued on with your companions instead of notifying the Venarium of their violation instantly?'

'There wasn't enough time.'

'Time is a hindrance of the unenlightened. Wizards cannot claim the handicap.'

'But I've done so much. The tome we're chasing is—'

'This tome,' Bralston replied. 'You say a priest sent you after it?'

'Well, he hired us to—'

'Gold is for the unenlightened, as is religious zealotry. We are concerned with higher matters. Venarie is as vast as it is ever changing. In exchange for the gifts we have, we dedicate our lives to furthering knowledge, to understanding how we, as vessels, relate to this. How have you done that, concomitant?'

'I would argue that we can only understand how it relates to us by understanding how we, as vessels, relate to others. In fact, just last night I discovered—'

'Any discovery made in the company of these vagrants is irredeemably tainted by—'

'*Stop interrupting me.*'

Bralston's eyes narrowed at the boy, but Dreadaeleon, for the first time, did not look away, back down or so much as flinch. He met the Librarian's stare with a searching scowl of his own, sweeping over the man's dark face.

'This is far too insignificant a point for a Librarian to

harp on,' Dreadaeleon said firmly. 'I'm hardly the first wizard to extend his studies through adventuring and I'm sure I won't be the last, yet you act as though I'm committing some grievous breach of law just by being in these people's company.'

Bralston's eyebrow rose a little at that, his lip twitching as if to speak. Dreadaeleon, forcing himself not to dwell on the stupidity of the act, held up a hand to halt him.

'You have another motive, Librarian.'

'You are certain?' Bralston asked, a sliver of spite in his voice.

'I am more perceptive than you suspect.'

For all the ire he had been holding in his stare alone, for all the disappointment and despair he had seen in the boy, it was only at that moment that Bralston's shoulders sank with a sigh, only at that moment that he looked at the boy with something more than scrutiny.

'Perceptive enough,' he whispered, 'to know you've contracted the Decay?'

With a single word, Dreadaeleon felt the resolve flood out of him, taking everything else within him with it and leaving him nothing to stand on but quivering legs that strained to support him.

'I don't have it,' he replied.

'You do,' Bralston insisted.

'No,' he said, shaking his head. 'No, I don't have it.'

'I can sense it. I can smell your blood burning and hear your bones splitting. I followed it last night. That's how I found it. Surely, you can sense it. Surely, you know.'

'It's nothing,' Dreadaeleon said.

'Concomitant, if I can track you across an ocean through it, it is certainly not nothing. In fact, to even sense it at all, symptoms must be forming by now. Fluctuating temperatures? Loss of consciousness? Instantaneous mutation?'

'Flaming urine,' Dreadaeleon said, looking down.

'The Decay,' Bralston confirmed.

It was unthinkable, Dreadaeleon told himself. Or perhaps, he simply hadn't wanted to think about it. He still didn't want to. He didn't even want to hear the word, yet it was burned into his brain.

Decay.

The indefinable disease that ravaged wizards, that unknown alteration inside their body that broke down the unseen wall that separated Venarie from body, turning a humble vessel into a twisted, tainted amalgamation of errant magic and bodily function.

It was that which turned men and women into living infernos, turned flesh to snowflakes, caused brains to cook in their own electric currents. It was the killer of wizards, the vice of heretics, the consequence for disregarding the Laws.

And he had it.

He didn't question Bralston's diagnosis, didn't so much as feel the need to deny it anymore. It all made too much sense now: his sudden weakness, his use of the red stones, his altered bodily state.

But then ... how did you recover last night?

A fluke, perhaps. Such things would not be unheard-of. In fact, Decay's fluctuating effects on magic often resulted in sudden, sporadic enhancements. It all made too much sense, followed too cold a logic, too perfect an irony for him to deny it anymore.

'What ... ?' he said with a weak voice. 'What now? What happens?'

'Your master told you, I am sure.'

Dreadaeleon nodded weakly. 'The Decayed report back to the Venarium for ...' He swallowed. 'Harvesting.'

'We are wizards. Nothing can be wasted.'

'I understand.'

Bralston frowned, shaking his head.

'My duties require a survey of the ocean,' Bralston said, 'to scan for any signs of the heretic. After that, I shall return to Cier'Djaal. You will return with me.'

Dreadaeleon nodded weakly. A pained grimace flashed across Bralston's face.

'It's ... it's not so bad, really,' Bralston said. 'At the academy in Cier'Djaal, you'll still be useful to the Venarium. You'll be able to provide services in research, even after you're gone. And until then, you'll be cared for by people who understand you for however long you last.'

Dreadaeleon nodded again.

'Until then ...' Bralston sought for words and, finding nothing, sighed. 'Try to rest. It will be a difficult journey back.'

He left, disappearing into the village, and Dreadaeleon allowed himself to fall to his knees. Funny, he thought, how the very indication of a disease, the knowledge that life must end, made one suddenly feel as though it were already over.

Ridiculous, he told himself. *As though you didn't already know you'll have to die sometime. Hell, you've been with adventurers. You knew death was inevitable, right? Right. At least this way, you'll do your duty. You'll serve the cause. You'll enforce the Laws. You'll further knowledge. Harvesting ... well, that's just what happens. You can't begrudge them that. You use* merroskrit. *Someday, your bones and skin will be used by another wizard. Everything is balanced. Everything is a circle.*

He stared down at his hands: hands that had hurled,

hands that had held, hands that had touched. He estimated each one would yield about half a page, one full length of *merroskrit* when stitched together. He studied his hands, confirmed this guess.

And then he wept.

Lenk's first memory of this forest had been one of silver.

That night, long ago, even as his body had been racked with pain and his mind seared with fever, the forest had been something living, something full of light and life alike. The leaves were ablaze with moonlight, as though each one had been dipped in silver. The song of birds and the chatter of beasts had rung off the trees, each branch a chime that amplified the noise and sent it echoing in his ears.

That night, a week ago, he himself had barely had a drop of life left in him, the rest of his body filled with pain and desperation. That night, every time he fell, he could barely pull himself up again. That night, he had struggled to hold on: to life, to light, to anything.

This day, he stood tall. Despite the fresh stitches in his shoulder, he felt scarcely any pain. Despite the night before, he found his body light, easily carried by legs that should have been weaker. Despite everything, he found himself with nothing to hold on to.

And in the unrelenting brightness of midmorning, the forest was a tomb.

Mournful trees gathered together to drop a funeral shroud over the forest floor, each branch and leaf trying its hardest to block any trace of light from desecrating the perfect darkness. Life was gone, the forest so silent as to suggest it had never even been there, and the only sound that Lenk could hear was the wind singing wordless dirges through the leaves.

Had life been a hallucination?

It was not a hostile darkness that consumed the forest, but a hallowed one. It did not threaten him with its shadows, but invited him in. It whispered through the branches, commented on how tired he looked, how awful it was that his friends had abandoned him and let him wander out here all alone, mused aloud just how nice it would be to sit down and rest for a while, rest forever.

And he found himself inclined to agree with the procession of trees. A week ago, when it had been brimming with life, he had fought so hard to draw into himself, to survive for a bit longer. Now, as he stood, relatively healthy and free of disease, he felt like collapsing and letting the dark shroud fall upon him.

What had changed? he wondered.

'*Reasons, mostly.*'

He nodded. The voice rang clearer here. Perhaps because of the silence, perhaps because he wasn't fighting it anymore. Perhaps because he recognised the worthiness of its freezing words.

'Go on.'

'*Consider your motives between then and now. You clung to belief, then; a strong force, admittedly, but ultimately insubstantial. You desperately wished to believe that your companions were alive.*'

'They were, though. That kept me alive.'

'We *kept you alive,*' the voice corrected, without reproach. 'Our *determination,* our *will,* our *knowledge that duty must be upheld. That did not come from anyone else.*'

'It was the thought of them, though ...'

'*It was the thought of her.*'

'And she ...'

'*Lied to us, as did the forest.*'

Perhaps it had, Lenk thought. Perhaps there had never been any life here. Perhaps it was always dead and dusky. The other voice, Ulbecetonth's voice, had been with him, even back then, he realised. She was the fever in his mind, the hallucination in his eye, the will to surrender that pervaded him.

And she had bid him to seek the truth, to follow the ice.

The brook that coursed through the forest floor remained largely unchanged, its babble reduced to a quiet murmur, respectful of the darkness. He knelt and stared into it, saw empty eyes staring back at him.

'She might have been lying.'

'*Possibly.*'

'She *did* infect my thoughts.'

'*She did.*'

'But then, she also said she was trying to protect me. It's probably safe to say that I'm no longer considered worthy of protection by her anymore.'

'*We* did *kill a few of her children.*'

'Right. So … do I believe her?'

The voice said nothing. He merely sighed. It was a response customary enough not to warrant any greater reaction.

He stared into the water, uncertain as to what he would find. It flowed, clear and straight, as if to tell him that were answer enough. He frowned in disagreement. The last time he had stared into this river, it had frozen over, spoken in words that he heard in harsh, jagged cracks inside his head, a voice altogether different than the one that usually dwelt there.

Or had he even heard it, then? Ulbecetonth's feverish talons were inside his skull at that point, telling him terrible things, making him see wicked things. Perhaps the voice in the ice was just one more hallucination, one more reason to give up.

But it had spoken so clearly, telling him things in a language he knew by heart and had never heard before. It had whispered to him, told him of fate, of betrayal, of duty, of … of what? He bit his teeth, furrowed his brow, forcing the memory up through his mind like a spike. And when it rose, it drained the haze from his mind, left his sight clear.

Hope.

It had bidden him to survive.

And, at that thought, the forest's funeral ended and became death. The wind stopped. The last remnants of light vanished from above. The air became freezing cold. And with a cracking sound, the brook froze.

He looked down in it. Eyes that were not his own, nor had ever been in his head, looked back at him. They shifted, glancing farther down the river, and he followed their gaze. The ice crept up on spindly legs, gliding down the water, vanishing into the depths of the dead forest.

'It wants me to follow,' he said.

'*It does*,' the voice said. '*You won't like what you find.*'

'I know.'

But he rose and he followed, regardless, going deeper into the forest where nothing lived.

Because in the forest where nothing lived, something called to him.

Thirty-Seven

REMORSE

The bottle was without label, without an identity: an amber-coloured stranger standing in an alley made of murky glass, plying stale, sickly poison that bore no guarantee of quality or survival.

And Denaos threw it back along with his head, quaffing down the nameless liquor as though it were water. His stomach no longer protested, long since having grown used to the sudden assaults. His mind barely registered the introduction of a new intoxication, having grown too used to them.

His eyes were bleary from sleeplessness and drink as he stared across the small clearing from the log he sat on. He squinted, trying to see the trees, the leaves, the forest and only the forest.

No good.

The dead woman was still there.

Still staring.

Still smiling.

And to think, he told himself, *I had gotten so good at this.*

After so many years, so much meditation, so much prayer, so much liquor, he had stopped seeing her. Perhaps, in the periphery of his eye, he might have seen her peering around a corner; in a blinking moment of fitful half-sleep he might have seen the flutter of her white skirt; at the back of his head he could sometimes feel her looking at him. But those had been needle visions, fleeting pricks of a pin against his flesh that existed only in the moment he felt them.

This vision …

This was more like a knife.

A knife sunk deep into his skin.

Twisting.

He had given up trying to ignore her; by this point, it just seemed rude. She clearly wasn't going to go away. She wasn't going to stop staring at him, no matter how much he drank or wept or screamed.

So he stared at the gaping wound in her opened neck, the blood that wept without end down her white throat, and tried to understand.

A hallucination, probably, he thought. *I've been eating nothing but roaches for the past week, roaches known for spraying substances out of their anuses and probably undercooked, at that. Yeah, there's just enough weirdness about that for hallucinations to be all but certain.*

Of course, he reminded himself, he had seen her long before he had even sampled the bitter flavour of roach. It had all started back on the shore, amidst the corpse-strewn ruins. It had begun as soon as he heard the whispering, felt the slimy coils of the two-mouthed, angler-laden creature wrapping about his mind.

A poison of the mind, then, he reasoned. *It would make sense for a demon to be able to sink her … or its claws into my brain and leave them there. It makes as much sense as anything else we know about demons, anyway. I should probably ask someone … not Lenk, though.*

A wasted opportunity, he knew; Lenk had more experience than anyone else with demons. Denaos had reasoned as much when he looked over his shoulder after emerging from the surf the previous night, when he had seen the frogmen swarm over the sinking ship. When he had seen Lenk standing at the railing, staring out.

He hadn't been sure if the young man was even looking at him, but he had turned away all the same. It would have been madness to go back, he reasoned then; it would have been callous to abandon Asper as she pulled away from him, shivering and nude and huddling on the beach, not so much as blinking as he scavenged a blanket to wrap around her.

And it was better to leave Lenk to die, he told himself. *Yes, it was better to stay behind and watch him sink below the sea. You did the right thing ... you asshole.*

How Lenk had survived, he didn't know. Why he had gone to Lenk after Lenk emerged from Asper silently stitching him up, he didn't know. What led to him telling Lenk everything, about his deeper knowledge of demons on Teji, why he had never bothered to tell Lenk, why it wasn't his fault and why he was glad Lenk was alive and why he knew he should have gone back but didn't ... he did not know.

And when Lenk looked at him, unblinking, expressionless, with absolutely no scorn, no hate, no surprise for what the rogue had done and said: '*Uh-huh ...*'

Denaos wasn't sure why he felt like vomiting afterwards.

'That's it,' he whispered, his voice a hoarse croak. 'Not hallucination, not madness, not demons. This is all just a manifestation of a guilty conscience, a plague born of shame. How do these things work again? You acknowledge them and they go away.'

He looked up. He blinked once. He sighed.

'You're not going away.'

The woman looked back at him and grinned. She didn't say anything. She never said anything, except when he didn't want her to, and then always the same thing.

'*Good morning, tall man.*'

'Good morning,' he replied. 'How are you today?'

She didn't answer. She didn't stop grinning.

'Me, I'm fine,' he continued. 'I'm okay, anyway. Still alive … still healthy, mostly. My tastes are a lot more diverse lately. Not as much curry, but more roaches. Rich in fibre, probably. Good for the bowel movements.'

He cracked a grin. She grinned back.

'Last night was a little hectic. Sorry I wasn't there to say hello.' He smacked his lips. 'A friend was in trouble. Asper. You'd like her. She's a priestess. A good one. Went to temple every day before she set out with us, you know. Still prays a lot … or she did, anyway. She's a little bitter these days, losing faith in … pretty much everything. I can see it in her eyes.'

He glanced up, frowning.

'I saw it in your eyes a lot. In the beginning, at least, you weren't sure how to keep going. Not so much towards the end there … and …' His lips trailed from words to the bottle, sucking out another gulp of whisky. 'Yeah, it's cheap. I'm going to have to piss a lot later.' He chuckled. 'I think Togu thought it was quality. It was in his cabinet. Maybe he was saving it for something special.'

His nostrils quivered at the scent of smoke.

'Yeah … that was kind of special, wasn't it?' he laughed bitterly. 'I know you didn't like fire, but it's sort of what we do now. He betrayed us, and betrayal …' He stared at the bottle, wincing. 'I had to take it. I wasn't going to, but then I saw this.'

He held up his hand, the thick glove swaddling his skin.

'I remembered it. I couldn't leave it. I'm … I'm so sorry.'

His wrist tensed. There was a faint click. Before he could even blink, a thin spike of a blade leapt from the bottom of the wrist, dull and lightless. He stared at it through trembling eyes.

'A Long, Slow Kiss,' he whispered. 'You hated it. You thought it was what was wrong with everything about the city. I … it reminded me of you. Silf help me …' He winced. 'No, you hated Silf, too. You loved Talanas. Asper, she's a Talanite. She does …'

He drew back the tiny latch hidden in the glove, the spike retracting into the leather until it stuck with another clicking sound.

'I don't want her to see it. I don't want her to know anything about it.' He looked up, stared at her as she grinned at him. 'And that's why you've got to go.'

She grinned. Her neck continued to weep.

'Please.'

She wasn't answering.

'Go.'

She wasn't listening.

'If I keep seeing you, I won't be able to keep it hidden. If it's not hidden, if they *know*, they'll … they'll leave me. I'll never be able to make things right.' He looked at her pleadingly. 'But I'm trying. I'm *trying*. We're after this tome – it opens gates. It can communicate with heaven. If I keep it out of the hands of demons, gates stay closed and I can talk to Silf, I can talk to Talanas, I can talk to *any* of them. Everyone can! They'll be happy! Everything will be fine again and I … I'll …' He swallowed back tears. 'It'll work. I know it'll work. Everything will be fine after that happens. They'll forgive me. You'll forgive me … won't you?'

She did not answer.

'Say yes.'

She grinned.

'Please.'

The wound in her neck grinned broader.

'Say something.'

'*Good morning, tall man.*'

His wrist snapped, sent the bottle flying at her. She was gone when it reached her. It shattered against a tree trunk, a rain of murky glass falling upon the sand. Tears of whisky wept silently down the mossy bark.

The man was, Bralston thought, exactly as he remembered him.

Perhaps a little paler, with no more deceitful tan to mask his lack of a Djaalman's deeper bronze, but beyond that, completely the same. He still stood tall and lanky, long arms and long fingers. His face was still the kind of smooth, scarless angle that made one inherently suspicious of anyone who could maintain such a look for so long.

Bralston winced as he heard the bottle shatter against the tree.

The lunacy, though … that was new.

His eyes had a sunken desperation to them, as though they were trying to burrow deeper into his skull. The reek of liquor and fear was apparent even from the twenty feet Bralston stood, staring from the bushes.

He looked the same, but this was not the same man Bralston remembered from Cier'Djaal.

This was not the man Bralston had seen standing beside

her, the Houndmistress, with a smug chin raised high and eyes looking down upon the common man. This was not the parasite who had clung to her elbow at social functions, the insect that cowered behind her while she led the raids against the Jackals. This was not the liar's martyr that had been mourned with her death when he had disappeared from the palace on the night she was found dead, his blood covering the halls as she soaked in her own.

This man seemed far too broken, far too weary to bear the responsibility for over fourteen hundred dead by fire, stone and knife in the riots.

But there was no doubt. Bralston had seen him before. Bralston had heard the news of his disappearance. Bralston knew this man was supposed to be dead.

But he wasn't. This man stood here, while his mistress had bled to death. This man stood here, wearing a glove with a hidden blade, the favoured weapon of the Jackals. This man stood here, pleading the air for forgiveness, muttering familiar words, describing familiar crimes.

There was nothing to explain this beyond cold, ugly logic ... or a miracle.

Miracles were created by gods.

Gods did not exist.

Bralston narrowed his eyes, levelled his finger at the man from the underbrush. At a word, the electric blue leapt to his fingertip. At another, the man would be ash; a short death, a clean death. It would be over far sooner than this man deserved. But it would be over. Fourteen hundred bodies would be accounted for.

Fourteen hundred and one, he corrected himself as he called the word to mind.

The leaves parted from across the clearing, just noisy enough to keep the word from his lips. He turned and saw her, the priestess, approaching from the underbrush. The word instantly slipped from his mind as a frown found its way to his lips.

She looked exactly the same ... as someone else.

There was an emptiness in her eyes, not as consuming as the woman he had seen back in Cier'Djaal, the woman who had desperately tried to fold in on herself, but it was there. In her hazel eyes, he could see dead questions, dead dreams, dead hopes. It had all been replaced with a vague, gloomy wonder.

'What is the point?'

A question that he knew he could not answer, despite how much he wanted to. A question he knew this man could not answer, despite the way the priestess looked at him as she approached.

And yet ... approach she did, with a barely alive question in her eyes.

To the man he was so close to incinerating.

Right before her eyes.

He knew what would happen. He knew that the emptiness in her eyes would consume her wholly, that question snuffed out and leaving nothing but a wonder without an answer. No matter whom she had chosen to place her faith in, faith was all she had left.

And he decided, lowering his finger, that fourteen hundred and two lives was too many to give this man credit for.

Bralston would wait, then. Wait until she found herself with a cause. Wait until he found himself alone. It would be a monumental task, to keep himself from killing this man, this traitor, this murderer, this liar.

But he was a Librarian.

He could wait.

Denaos was a man of many fragments, Asper decided as he whirled on her. The masks he had worn, delicate porcelain facades that guarded him, had begun to crumble in different areas. The visage of the cynic, the sarcastic, the indifferent was gone from his face.

Caught without his masks, his face quickly tried to find a new one to don.

At the jaw, there was a clench of animal fury. Around the eyes, weariness and desperation. In the furrow of his brow, worry that bordered on panic. Which of these was the face that lay beneath them all, she was not sure. Nor did she care.

This wasn't about him.

She knew exactly why she stepped forward, however, under his wide and wary stare, before his tense and trembling form. She knew exactly why there could be no stepping back, no retreat back to contemplation and prayer.

That sort of thing never got anyone anywhere. This she knew now.

'You don't look well,' she said.

'Thanks, I haven't been sleeping well,' Denaos replied.

'You didn't sleep at all last night.'

'How would you know?'

'I didn't, either.'

Not for lack of trying, she knew. Exhaustion had come to claim her several times. Her eyes had fallen shut only as long as it took to see grins in the darkness, hear her own shrieks and hear no one reply back.

I asked ... I begged ... it was my moment of uttermost need. I always believed that—

No, no, NO! She gritted her teeth, forced the thoughts down her throat and into her stomach. *No more dwelling on it. No more fear. If you fear, you start wondering. If you wonder, you ask why.* Her frown broadened into a bitter gash. *If you ask, no one ever answers.*

She was keenly aware of the absence of a heavy weight that had once been upon her chest. To leave her pendant, her symbol, was blasphemous, at least as much as the suggestion she made by unlacing the front of her robes. The Gods, she was aware, would not approve.

This wasn't about them, either.

Bitterly, she hoped they were watching right now.

Though what was happening, she wasn't so certain of anymore. Nor was Denaos, it seemed, as he backed away from her like a hound beaten, glancing about nervously, hoping for a reward and fearing a lash, too scared to sit still, too curious to run outright. That was fine, she thought; his input was not needed.

This was her decision.

His back struck the tree and his eyes stopped their fervent flutter, focusing on her as she approached him. Her legs did not tremble as she feared they might have. Resolve flooded her body, turned to iron in her blood, so heavy that, with one more step, she tripped and was sent falling into him, her arms flying out to seize him.

His body was cold, she thought as her hands slithered under his vest, his flesh clammy and sweaty beneath as she pressed against him. She had expected him to be warm. His breathing was quick, erratic and hare-like. As she leaned up, thrusting her lips at him like weapons, she hadn't expected him to pull back, his eyes fighting against the urge to close and give in.

'You don't know what you're—' he began to whisper, silencing as she pressed a finger to his lips.

'I do,' she replied. 'I know exactly.'

697

He pulled back again, but she was swifter. She forced her lips upon his, pried his apart with her tongue. They came loose willingly enough after a time, as she had known they would. The man was, after all, a felon. He wanted this as much as she did. His reluctance was only due to her forwardness.

She confirmed this as his tongue came out to touch hers, hers wrapping about his, searching his mouth with a purpose she wasn't aware of. His body trembled; she pulled him all the closer. He made a soft moan; she drowned it with a chest-borne growl. She could feel him staring at her; she shut her eyes tighter. She didn't want to look at him. She just wanted to—

She was spared thinking of an answer as she felt his arms deftly slither up between them, breaking her hold. His hands lashed out with a fury normally reserved for combat, slamming against her and knocking her back. The iron resolve left her, a rush of leaden weakness flooding her and sending her crashing to the ground.

And when she met his gaze, it was not a look normally reserved for companions that he struck her with.

'I don't know what happened to you on the ship before I got there,' he whispered. 'I don't even exactly know what happened after. But no matter what it was, you don't want this.'

'I do,' she said, drawing herself up to her knees. 'It's my choice. *Mine*.'

'Not if you keep doing this, it isn't.'

'You're a brigand,' she whispered spitefully. 'What do you care where you get it? You think I couldn't do better? *I'm* the one settling here.'

'And you chose to do that?'

'It … it doesn't matter,' she said, wincing. 'I need this. I need to know that I can still … that it's still my …'

'Not this way.' He turned. 'Not with me.'

She watched him stalk away, his shoulders heavy, weighing down his stride. She whispered to him on a breathless, stagnant voice.

'I have been through …' She shook her head violently. 'I've given so much. And every time I ask for a blessing, try to take a favour, I am denied.' She stared fire into his spine. 'At the very least, I thought I could count on *you* to do what you always do. I should have remembered that what you always do is fail me in every way conceivable. You're pathetic.'

'I can live with that, at least,' he replied, continuing to stalk away.

'I hate you.'

'That, too.'

He disappeared into the forest. And she was left alone. She did not weep.

Who would hear it?

The stream continued through the forest, Lenk discovered, and its whispering voice went with it. It murmured between trees, whimpered under rocky brooks, roared through hard ground, grew softer as it thinned into shallows, grew louder as it deepened. Lenk followed it all, listening to it.

It was probably a bad sign that he was beginning to understand it.

Never long enough to get a complete sentence, sometimes not even a full word; the stream was always freezing as he walked past, its flows and ebbs becoming hissing, crackling ice every time he laid eyes on it. But when his own breath grew soft and the water was thin enough to freeze with barely a sound, he could hear it.

The words were ancient, or alien, or simply incomprehensible. He could not understand them, anyway, but he could grasp the message behind them. They were not happy words spoken from a pleasant voice. They uttered, decreed, spewed messages of hate, vengeance, duty.

And betrayal.

Always betrayal.

Every other word seemed to carry that frustrated, seething hatred born of treachery. It rose from the stream, hammering at the ice with its voice, its words mercifully muffled behind the frigid sheets.

It was probably a worse sign that the voice was familiar.

'I remember it,' he whispered, 'in the forest on my first night here. It spoke of betrayal then, too.'

'*This island is a tomb,*' the voice answered. '*The dead have seeped into it with all their hate and their sorrow. Most have had centuries to let the earth consume them and their emotions with them. For some hatreds, that's not nearly long enough.*'

'They sound so familiar, like I've heard them before.'

'*One of us has.*'

He frowned, but did not ask the voice anything more. He pressed on through the forest, following the winding stream and its angry voice. He couldn't tell if it was speaking to him. He didn't want to know. If he did, and if it was, he would want to turn back.

And turning back, returning to *them*, was not an option.

It never was.

Before long, he found the stream's end. Like an icy tongue from a great, black maw, it slithered into the shadows of a great cave set in the hillside. Here, the forest was at its deepest stage of decay. The leaves hung black off trees that had been brimming with greenery only a few paces back. The air was stale, stagnant and frigid.

It was most certainly a bad sign that he wasn't bothered by any of this.

He watched as the ice continued without him, continuing down its freezing, murmuring path into the darkness. His ears pricked up, however, as for a few fleeting moments, he could hear them: words, clear and coherent, echoing in the gloom.

'*Don't like it,*' a voice whispered. '*Don't like it and don't want to go in there. Not with him …*'

'*We have our orders,*' another replied. '*They've got to die, all of them.*'

'*They helped us at the battle, though, killed more demons than any—*'

'*Don't act like you haven't been thinking of it. They're unnatural. Abominations. Make it swift. In the back. Just don't look in his eyes.*'

'*Follow me,*' a third voice, cold as the air outside. '*This cave is supposed to lead to a way around the enemy. We will cleanse this earth of their taint. Our duty is upheld.*'

His eyes widened at the sound of it, the feel of it. It rang inside his ears as he had felt it ring inside his head before. Its rasping chill was all too familiar, the force behind it all too close to him. He heard it as it echoed inside the cavern.

He heard it as it spoke to him.

'*Go inside.*'

'What will I find there?' he asked.

'*Nothing good.*'

'Then why should I?'

'*We will only find truth in the dark places.*'

'I've gone this far living a lie. It's not been all bad.'

The voice didn't need to respond to that. Immediately, the memories of the previous night, of the screaming, of the backs of his companions, came flooding into his mind. He sighed, lowering his head.

'I'm afraid.'

'*Wise.*'

'I don't understand what's happening.'

'*You will.*'

An urge, not his own, rose within him and bid him to turn around. He beheld the figure instantly, standing upon a nearby ridge. A man, it appeared, cloaked in shadow with white hair. Lenk took in his harsh, angular features immediately, ignoring them as soon as he spied the hilt of a sword peeking over the man's shoulder.

But before Lenk could even recall he didn't have a weapon of his own, he found himself arrested by the man's stare. His eyes were a vast blue that seemed to take in Lenk as a shark swallows fish. They stared at him: intense, narrow ...

Bereft of pupils.

The man approached. Lenk found it hard to keep track of him as he walked down the ridge. His form was there, and not there, vanishing each time he stepped into a shadow, appearing when the wind blew dust that became his body. He took a step and was somewhere else, moving with an erratic fluidity Lenk had only seen in dreams.

He did not move as the man approached, held by his great stare. He did not move as the man walked right through him, unflinching. He turned and watched him disappear into the shadows of the cavern, vanishing completely the moment his foot touched gloom.

'This ... this isn't real,' he told himself. 'But it feels so ...' His head began to ache. 'Have I seen this before?'

'*One of us has.*'

He turned and saw more figures approaching over the ridge: more men, though softer of body and eye than the one that had just come. They approached in the same winking step, and each time they appeared in his vision, their faces were harder set. There was fear there, hate there, intent there.

They were clad in old armour, carried old blades, old spears. Their cloaks trailed behind them, stained and battered and torn. Clasping them together upon their breasts, Lenk saw a sigil.

An iron gauntlet clenching thirteen obsidian arrows.

'The House,' he whispered. He hadn't seen it since he had first accepted the task of pursuing the tome, but at a glimpse, he recalled it instantly. 'The House of the Vanquishing Trinity, the mortals who marched against the demons.'

'*Mortals have the capacity to march against many things. Enemies and allies alike.*'

'They're going to … ?' Lenk began to ask.

'*You know the answer to that.*'

'They're going into the cave.'

'*Answers lie in there.*'

'Should I … ?'

The voice said nothing. He was left standing, watching as the men vanished, one by one, into the cavern. He was left standing as the river fell silent. He was left standing, watching, wondering. Wiser, he thought, *not* to follow ghostly hallucinations into lightless caverns born of dead forests.

But he did. Going back, after all, was not an option.

It never was.

Thirty-Eight

THE DEAD, HONOURED AND IMPOTENT

Gariath did not fear silence. Gariath feared nothing.

Still, he found himself deeply uncomfortable with it. Ordinarily, discomfort wasn't such a problem; the source of it, after a few stiff beatings, would eventually become a source of much more manageable anger, which would warrant further beatings until only tranquillity remained.

But those sources of anger and discomfort were frequently made of flesh, meat. Silence was not. And he could not strangle the intangible.

He had tried.

And he had failed, so he remained in uncomfortable, awkward, intangible, fleshless silence as he stalked through the forest.

Occasionally he paused, fanning out his ear-frills to listen for an errant whisper, a trace of muttered curse, even a roach's fart. He heard nothing. He knew he would continue to hear nothing.

Grandfather had left him.

He wasn't sure what had happened to cause it, but he was certain of it now. Not merely because he hadn't seen, heard or smelled the ancestor since he had dragged himself out of the surf last night. It was a deeper absence, the perpetual, phantom agony of a limb long lost.

Or a relative ...

He continued on through the forest. The silence continued to close in around him, seething on his flesh as though it were new, raw. Not so unreasonable, he thought; he had lived his life without silence thus far. As near as he remembered, the *Rhega* were a people of perpetual noise, living in a world that thundered against them: the barking of pups met with the roar of rivers, the mutter of elders accompanied by the rumble of thunder.

Since then, he had experienced any number of howls, groans, shrieks, screams, grunts, cackles, chuckles and countless, *countless* bodily noises. That, too, seemed long ago, though.

For the first time, he heard silence.

He didn't like it.

And yet, he pressed ahead, instead of returning to the cheerful, stupid noises and their fleshy, meaty sources. Theirs was silence of another loud and useless kind, though today it had become a melancholy, self-loathing silence.

He had smelled them in a musky cocktail of guilt, hatred, despair and abject self-pity. All of them carried it, some daubed with scant traces of it, others wearing it like a mane about their heads.

Well, he corrected himself. *Almost all of them.*

It was unusual enough to find Lenk without a smell that it had given Gariath pause when they briefly crossed paths that morning. Usually, the young man bore the most varied odours, usually varying scents of exasperation. Today, when they brushed past each other without a word and exchanged a fleeting glance, he knew the young man was different. Today, the dragonman had inhaled deeply and scented nothing. Today, he had felt a chill when he met Lenk's eyes.

Just a fleeting sensation, there and gone in less than an instant; the human was the same human who had cried out like a coward last night, the same human who had fallen into useless babble, the same human whom Gariath had graced with one and only one glance before he leapt overboard to pursue the Shen.

But it had been clear in Lenk's eyes, in a silence that struck the whistle of the breeze dead, that Gariath was not the same dragonman from that night.

And that dragonman had told him nothing, about the pointy-eared one's plot to kill him, about the demons on the island, about the longfaces, about anything. Because the man he had seen was not the man from that night, and the man he had seen would brook nothing but silence.

He snorted to himself; too much silence, too little meaning in it all. It was starting to aggravate him. Absently, he began glancing around for things that would make the most noise when struck. Trees, rocks, leaves: all defiantly, annoyingly mute.

He pressed forward, stomping his feet on the earth as he did, crunching leaves under his soles. He needed to break the silence, he thought as he pushed through the underbrush and stepped into a great clearing amidst the forest. He needed something to speak to.

And, in the instant he felt the sun upon his skin, he knew he had found it.

He craned his neck up to take it all in: its massive, unblemished grey face; its weathered, rounded crown; its tremendous earthen roots extending into the lapping waters of a great pond.

An Elder, the familial rock from which all *Rhega* began

and ended, loomed over him. He surveyed it, unmarked
and unadorned as it was, and felt a smile creep across his
lips. The Elders were the basis, the focus, the stability
behind any *Rhega* family. And, judging by this one, it had
borne many burdens of many of his people.

His people.

They had been here in numbers great enough to raise
this rock and call it their earth, once.

Once ... He felt his smile fade at the words echoing in
his head. *And a long time ago.*

The scent here was faint; that couldn't be right, he
thought. The Elder was titanic. The scent of the *Rhega*,
of their memories, their families, their children, their
wounds, their feasts, their births, their elders ... he should
have been overwhelmed, brought low to his knees by the
sheer weight of the ancestral aroma.

But the smell was one of stagnant rivers, moss-covered
rocks. Not alive, not dead, like the rot between a dying
winter and a bloody newborn spring, barely faint enough
for a single memory, a single statement to make itself
known.

But it did make itself known.

Over and over.

Ahgaras succumbed to his wounds and died here, the scent
said.

Raha bled into the earth and died here.

Shuraga fell and, his arms ripped from his body, died here.

Ishath held his dead pup in his arms and ate no more ...

Garasha screamed until his breath left him ...

Urah walked into the night and never returned ...

Pups fell, elders fell, all fell ...

He drew in their scent, though he did so with ever-
diminishing breath, his heart conspiring with his lungs,

begging him to stop smelling the memories, to stop wrenching them both. But he continued to breathe them in, searching the scent for anything, any birth, any mating, any defecation, *anything* but this endless reeking list of death.

But he found nothing.

He felt them, each one of them, in his nostrils.

And in each expulsion of breath, he felt them, each one of them, die.

'Five hundred.'

At the sound of the voice, he turned without a start. His body was drained, a shell of red flesh and brittle bones in which there dwelt no will to start, to snarl, to curse. All he could do was turn and face the grandfather with eyes that sank back into his skull.

'Exactly,' the grandfather said.

'What?'

'There were five hundred *Rhega* that fell here,' the ancestor said as he walked wearily to the water's edge. 'I spent over a year taking in their scents to find their names, Wisest. I doubt you have that long.'

'I don't have anywhere to be.'

'You do ... You just don't know where yet.'

They stood, side by side, and stared. The waters of the pond lapped soundlessly against the shore. The wind in the trees had nothing to contribute. The Elder was the grave into which all sound was buried and lost, so inundated with death that even the great sigh of the earth was nothing.

'How did you find this place, Wisest?'

Grandfather's voice brought Gariath back to his senses, his attentions to the heavy object dangling from his belt. He reached down, plucked it from the leather straps that held it there, and held it up.

Grandfather looked up into empty eye sockets beneath a bone brow.

'I asked the skull,' Gariath replied.

'You went back to find it.'

'I needed to know what you wouldn't tell me. The skull knew.'

'The dead know.' Grandfather stared out over the pond. 'I had hoped you wouldn't have ears for their voices.'

'It didn't say much,' Gariath said. 'I could only hear fragments of words, like it was talking in its sleep. It knew where the Elder was.'

'All dead things know where the Elder is.' Grandfather sighed and made a gesture to the pond. 'It speaks because it can't remember that it should be asleep. Do what is right, Wisest.'

Gariath nodded, kneeling beside the pond to let the skull fall from his hands into the water. In its empty eyes, he saw a kind of relief, the same kind that followed an important thing remembered after having been forgotten for so long.

Or maybe I'm just seeing things.

It did not simply vanish into the water. Instead, it remained stark white against the blue as it fell, still vivid in his eyes no matter how much it shrank. The sunlight caught the water's surface, turned the blue into a pristine crystal through which he could see the muddy bottom and the stark white that painted it.

He stared into the water.

Five hundred skulls stared back.

'This was a pit when I brought them here,' Grandfather said. 'When it was all over, when I was the last one alive … I dug the earth open and lay them within. It rained – a long time it rained – and this pond formed.' He nodded. 'Rivers and rocks. The *Rhega* should lie in water.'

The sunlight was chased away by clouds. The water masked itself with blue again. Gariath continued to stare.

'How?' he asked.

'Same way everything died on this island,' Grandfather replied. 'In the great war.'

'Between Aeons and mortals? I thought the humans fought that.'

'They did. Would it surprise you, Wisest, that we fought alongside them? In those days, we fought along many creatures that you would call weak.'

'It does not surprise me. The *Rhega* should have been there to lead, to inspire, to show them what courage is.'

'And you know courage, Wisest?'

'I know what the *Rhega* are.'

'So did I, back then. So did we all. We thought ourselves full of courage ... That was reason enough to fight.'

'To hear the humans tell it, the Aeons threatened all mortals.'

'They did,' Grandfather said. 'But the *Rhega* were made of stronger things than crude flesh and bone. No matter what the humans tried to tell us, we were apart from their little wars. If we died, we returned to the earth and came back. Let the humans be concerned with heaven.'

'Then why did we fight?'

'We had our reasons. Perhaps life was too good for too long. Perhaps we needed to remember what pain and death were. I don't know. I've thought of a thousand reasons and none of them matter. In the end, we are still dead.

'But we fought, all the same, and in that day, we became a people obsessed with death. When the first *Rhega* died and did not come back, we turned our thoughts to killing.

710

If we did not kill, we died. If we did not die, we killed. Over and over until we were the red peak upon a mountain of corpses.'

'And you died in battle with the rest?'

'No,' Grandfather said. 'I should have, though. When the children of Ulbecetonth marched against the humans and the earth rattled under their feet, I marched alongside everyone. I climbed their great legs. I shamed the humans and their stupid metal toys by splitting their thoughts open.' His eyes narrowed, jaw clenched. 'I leapt into their minds. I tore them apart until I could taste their thoughts on my tongue.'

Gariath recalled the great ravine, the greater skeleton that lay within it, and the massive hole split open in its skull. He recalled how Grandfather had crawled into that hole and vanished, as he seemed to vanish now, growing fainter with every breath.

Suddenly, he sprang into full, bitter view with a deep, unpleasant laugh.

'And still, I am obsessed with death.'

'How did you die, Grandfather?'

The ancestor's body quivered and grew hazy with the force of his sigh.

'When I crawled out of that skull, when I stopped hearing the screaming, I looked and saw I was the only one left,' he said. 'The dead were everywhere: the demons, the humans, but I was the only one concerned for the *Rhega*, the only one concerned for the dead. The mortals had moved on, pushing Ulbecetonth back to her gate. I was left alone.

'So, I cut the earth open around the Elder and I dragged their bodies back, finding every piece.' He paused, glancing into the water. 'Almost every piece, at least. But the *Rhega* came back ... not born again, as they should have been, but as I am now. They still wanted to fight, they wondered where their families were, they had so many reasons and they were all so tired …

'And so, one by one, I bade them to sleep. Then I watched them sleep. I watched for so long I forgot the need for food, for water … and when I came back, there was no one left to bid me to sleep.'

He turned and stared hard into Gariath's eyes.

'When you are gone, who will bid you, Wisest?'

Gariath met his concern with a scowl.

'You think I'll die?'

'We all die.'

'I haven't yet.'

'You haven't tried hard enough.'

The dragonman offered the ancestor nothing more than a snort in reply, his hot breath causing the spectral form to ripple like the water at their feet. Gariath returned his stare to the water. Through the obscuring azure, he could feel their gazes. In the earth, he could smell their final moments.

But in the air, he couldn't hear their voices, not even the whispering sleep-talk of the skull. They all rested soundly now; staring, dead, utterly silent.

'What is it you feel, Wisest?' Grandfather asked. 'Hatred for the humans for drawing us into this war? A need for vengeance against the demons?'

'You can't read my thoughts, Grandfather?'

'I have been inside your heart,' the spirit replied coldly. 'It's not a place I want to go back to in the best of times.'

'Take your best guess, then.'

After a long, careful stare, the ancestor obliged him. His prediction was manifested in his great, heaving sigh. The accuracy of it was reflected in Gariath's unapologetic grunt of confirmation.

'What is it you plan to do, then?'

'The skulls are silent. Their scent is nothing but death,' Gariath said, folding his arms over his chest. 'This earth is dead. It has nothing to tell me.'

'The earth is dead, yes, but those that walk upon it still live.'

'I agree,' Gariath replied.

Grandfather's eye ridges furrowed, a contemplative look rippling upon his face.

'That is why I am going to find the Shen.'

And when the ripples settled, there was fury plain upon the spirit's face.

'The *Shen?*' Grandfather snarled. 'The Shen are a people just as obsessed as we were ... as *you* are.'

'Good company to keep, then.'

'No, you moron! The Shen are what dragged us into the war!'

'But you said—'

'I said we had a thousand reasons, and *none* of them mattered. The Shen were the original one, and they matter least of all.' Upon Gariath's confused look, he sighed and raised a hand. 'Shen, Owauku, Gonwa ... all descend from a single ancestor, born to serve Ulbecetonth. In them, we saw people who could not hear the rivers or smell the rocks. We were moved to sympathy. We gave our lives for them.'

'And they pay it back. I have seen them. They are brave; they are strong.'

'They are *dead*. They just don't know it yet.' Grandfather's lips peeled back, his teeth stark and prominent despite the haziness of his form. 'We killed for them. We died for them. And what have they done? They continue to kill! They continue to die!'

713

'For what they believe in.'

'What *do* they believe in, Wisest?'

'They are Shen.'

'That is not a reason to live—'

'And I am *Rhega*!' Gariath roared over the ancestor, baring teeth larger, sharper and far more substantial. 'I remember what that means. No *Rhega* was meant to live alone.'

'Then don't!' Grandfather said. 'There may still be more out there, somewhere. Go with the humans. Even if you never find another *Rhega*, you will never be alone!'

Gariath's expression went cold, the rage settling behind his eyes in a cold, seething poison, a poison he all but spat upon the ancestor.

'This is what it's been about, isn't it?' he hissed. 'This is why you told me to find Lenk. This is why you did not lead me here, why you tried to keep me from coming here. You would have me run into the arms of *humans*, like a fat, weeping lamb.'

'I would have you live, Wisest,' Grandfather snapped back. 'I would have you find more *Rhega* if you could. If you couldn't, I would have you die and have no need to come back. Amongst the Shen, you cannot do that.'

'Amongst the Shen, I can learn more. Do you know what it was like to hear the word *Rhega* instead of "dragonman"? Do you know what it is to smell things besides greed and hate and fear?'

'I know their scent, pup. Do you?'

'That's not important.'

'It is. You know what's important; you just won't admit to it. You know that the humans are important. You know that without them, you would have died long ago. After your sons—'

'*Never*, Grandfather.' Gariath's voice was cold, his claw trembling as he levelled it at the spirit. 'Not even you.' Waiting a moment, challenging the ancestor to speak and hearing nothing, he snorted. 'I kept myself alive. The fire inside me burned too bright to be contained by death.'

'Fires burn themselves out. The humans gave you purpose, gave you direction.'

'Stupidity.'

'Then why did you try to kill the shict when you knew she was going to kill the silver-haired one? Why did you go to save the two females you claimed to hate?'

'To kill, to fight'

'To what end? Because you *knew* that if they died, you would, too. In some ugly part of you, Wisest, you know it. Follow the humans. Live, Wisest. The Shen can give you nothing.'

He paused for a moment before turning and stalking away.

'They can give me answers.'

'They cannot,' Grandfather called after him.

'We'll find out. I am going to find the Shen, Grandfather. If I return, I will tell you what I've learned.'

'You won't return, Wisest,' the spirit shrieked. 'Wisest!'

He did not turn around.

'Gariath!'

He did not stop.

'*LOOK AT ME, PUP!*'

He paused.

He turned.

A fist met him.

Grandfather's roar was as strong as his blow. Gariath felt his jaw rattle against the knuckles, felt it course through his entire body. The silence was gone now. In the wake of Grandfather's enraged howl, the wind blew and shook the trees, the water churned and hissed in approval. Four hundred and ninety-nine voices found a brief, soundless voice.

Gariath could hear them, but only barely. Grandfather's roar drowned out all sound. Grandfather's fists knocked loose his senses as they hammered blow after blow into his skull, as if the spirit hoped some great truth was slathered upon his knuckles and would drive itself into Gariath's brain.

But Gariath's skull was hard. His horns were harder.

Grandfather learned this.

Through the rain of fists, Gariath burst through, a cloud of red mist bursting from his mouth to herald his howl as he drove his head forward and against the spirit's. It connected solidly, sending the ancestor reeling. He followed swiftly, going low to tackle the spirit about the middle.

Claws raked his flesh; he ignored them. Fists hammered his skull; he disregarded them. More than one foot found itself lodged in a deeply uncomfortable place; he tried his best to ignore that, too, as he hoisted Grandfather into the air and brought him down low.

And hard.

Gariath was panting. Grandfather didn't need to breathe. The spirit continued to lash with a vigour and hatred better suited to someone young. Or to a *Rhega*, Gariath thought, feeling a faint urge to grin. But his admiration lived only as long as it took for him to recognise the disparities between them. Gariath was bleeding flesh and rattled bones. Grandfather was rivers and rocks. The ending of this fight was clear to Gariath.

And his heart ached to finish it.

'You're tired, Grandfather,' he said.

And the spirit's eyes went wide. He did not stop fighting; the ferocity behind his blows only increased, his roar took on a new savage desperation.

'No, Gariath,' he snarled. 'I am not tired. I will fight you so long as I have to. I can't let you throw everything away. I can't let you end up like—'

'Go to sleep, Grandfather.'

Blood leaked from a split in his brow, weeping into his eyes. He shut them tight.

When he opened them, nothing remained on the earth beneath him but spatters of his own blood.

He clambered to his feet. His body did not cry out in agony. Rather, his muscles sighed and his flesh complained. Cries were for proud battles, wounds that had earned the right to scream out. This was not such a battle.

He carried his bleeding and battered body away to recover. He wasn't sure where the Shen came from, but he was certain he would have to be strong to reach it. The Shen were strong, after all. They were Shen.

And he was *Rhega*.

So were those who lay in the lake behind him. Their cries were quiet now, though. That brief spark of life that had surged through them had died, and the world had died with it. The wind was still. The earth was quiet. The waters were calm.

Silence settled over the clearing once again, as though it had never left. Gariath tried to listen to it, his distaste for it gone. It was preferable, he thought, for if he stopped long enough, if he let his ear-frills adjust to the silence, he could hear a single, solitary voice, not yet dead, far from alive.

It drew in a quiet breath. There was no breeze for its quiet sigh to be lost on.

He tried to ignore it.

There was ice.

Everywhere in the cavern, Lenk stared back at himself, his face distorted by the crystalline rime that coated the cavern walls, the dim light seeping through holes in the ceiling reflected upon its surface. At the mouth, it was mirrorlike, and he met his own worried gaze a dozen times over a dozen glances. With each step deeper, the rime solidified, became cloudy and thick.

His face became distorted in it: elongated, flattened, crushed, reduced to a pink blob, shattered into a dozen jagged creases. And through each mutation, each abomination, his eyes remained unbroken, unaltered, unblinking as they stared back at him.

As he continued down into the cavern, the ice became thicker, cloudier. He shivered. It was not the callous, emotionless cold that chilled him. Rather, the ice was heavier with more than just water, cloudier with more than just white.

Hatred.

It radiated off the cavern walls, a cold heavy with anger, crueller than any chill had a right to be, seeping through his flesh, into his bones and clawing at him with hoary fingernails from the marrow out. He felt it now, but while it was painful, it was not new. He had known this cold before. He had felt this hatred before.

'This can't be right,' he whispered, fearful of raising his voice that the ice might hear him. It was why he kept himself from screaming. 'There can't be ice in this part of the world.'

'*There is.*'

'It can't be natural.'

'*You forsook the ability to deny the unnatural long, long ago.*'

He said nothing, staring deeper into the cavern's rimed gullet. The light did not diminish, but it changed, shifting from the dying light of a golden sun to the dim azure glow of … something else entirely. He stared down it. He did not want to do more than that.

'*Go,*' the voice responded to his hesitation.

'I don't think I want to.'

'*Going back is not an option.*'

'It could be,' Lenk said.

'*They betrayed you.*'

'It's hardly the first time. I remember once, Kataria was eating something she said was rabbit meat and offered me some. It turned out to be skunk meat. She laughed, of course, but it's hard to feel bad when someone eats a skunk for the sole purpose of trying to trick you into eating it, too.'

'*Stop it.*'

'What?'

'*Stop trying to justify it. Stop trying to excuse it. Stop denying what is apparent.*'

'What's that?'

'*And stop pretending you don't know. I speak from inside you. We both know that they have always thought less of you.*'

'That's not entirely true.'

'*You brought them together. You gave them purpose, gave them meaning. You never asked for any of them. They came to you.*'

'Yes, but—'

'*They used you. You brought them salvation. You brought them hope. You brought them reason. The moment they had those, the moment you required aid, they abandoned you. They betrayed you. They betrayed us. That cannot happen. Not again.*'

'Not again? What do you mean?'

'*Go into the cave.*'

'I don't know if—'

'*GO.*'

The command came from mind and body alike, a surge of blood coursing into his legs of a volition beyond his own. In resisting it, he was sent to his knees, then to his hands as his body rebelled against him, torn between his will and another.

'*Resist now. I know you must, because I know you. You will always resist, at first. This is your strength. When you come to accept it, when you embrace us, we will be that much stronger for it.*'

He had no response, for he had no voice. His throat swelled up, was sealed as if by a hand of ice that gripped his neck and squeezed tightly. He gasped in breath, the cold cutting his lungs like knives. He felt his body go numb, so numb that he didn't even feel it when his face crashed against the cavern's floor.

It was not a darkness that overtook him, so much as a different kind of light. He did not fall, but he could feel himself struggling to hold on. He shut his eyes tight. He went deaf to the world.

Senses returned to him, after some time.

Not his senses, though.

Through ears not his own, he heard them: a dozen voices, rasping with frost, cold with hatred. They came drifting across his ears on icy breezes, whispering in words that he had heard before, in the stream and outside the cavern.

' ... *unnatural. The whole lot of them. Look at their eyes. They look at you and all they see is an obstacle. They'd kill you, given half a chance. Who cares if we're on the same side? Which god do they fight for? Not ours, I can tell you ...*'

'... this tome they're writing. What of it? The blasphemies in it, the sacrilege. They would aid and abet the Aeons even as they march with us against the Traitors of Heaven. Whose side are they on? Can't trust them, can't trust them at all ...'

'... see what they did to the priest? All he was did was dedicate the battle to the Gods. And they killed him. They didn't just kill him. They did to him what they did to the demons back on the beach. There's nothing right about dying that way ...'

'... not my fault. We have our orders. They had their orders. They chose to forsake them. They were going to turn on us, sooner or later. They look down on us. They hate us. They hate the Gods! They had to die. Not my fault I had to do it ...'

He rose, groggily. His legs were beneath him, he was certain, but he could not feel them. He was breathing, he was certain, but he couldn't taste the air on his tongue. He lurched forward, uncertain of where he was going, but certain he had to get there. His stride was weak, clumsy. He staggered, reached out for balance and laid a palm upon the ice.

Hatred coursed through him.

A voice spoke inside his heart.

'They're going to betray you.'

He reeled from the sheer anger that coursed into him like a venom. The ice clung to his palm greedily, unwilling to let him go. He pulled away, leaving traces of skin on it. He was in pain, but he could not feel it.

He continued, swaying down the hall. He brushed against the wall.

'It is in their nature. They are weak. Cattle.'

Agony; he was sure he should feel that. There was no time to dwell on it, no time to feel pain. Pain was fear, fear was doubt, doubt made strong wills falter and turn back. There was no turning back.

Another staggering step. Another brush against the ice.

'Man's destiny is his own to weave, not the dominion of Gods. They would seek to enslave mortals all over again, through churches instead of chains.'

More pain. More ice.

'The tome was written in case the House was wrong, in case we needed to destroy the Gods as well as the demons. It was written to help mankind. They cower before it, call it blasphemy.'

A light at the end of the cavern appeared: no welcoming, guiding gold, but something harsh, something seething, something terrifyingly blue. He continued towards it and the voice did not stop, whispering to him as the cavern grew narrower, as the ice closed in around him.

'We'll show them. We'll teach them. We can live on our own, without gods or demons. They will all burn. Mortalkind will remain.'

A wall of ice rose up before him, clear and pristine. A figure dwelled within it, a man cloaked in shadow.

'We have our duty. We have our commands. Darior gave us this gift that we may free mortals. We were made for greater things than heaven.'

His features were sharp and angular and harsh. His hair was white and flowing. His eyes were shut. His lips were shut.

'They are going to kill you. They are going to betray you. It is their nature. To let you live is to deny their comforting shackles. To let the tome survive is to acknowledge that they might be wrong.'

A dozen arrows were embedded in his flesh. A dozen knife hilts jutted from his body. A dozen bodies wearing battered armour and stained cloaks were frozen in the ice with him.

'Darior made us that we might serve a greater purpose. It is

our nature to cleanse, to purify, to kill. Demons, gods, heretics, liars, murderers ... any that would seek to enslave mankind. But it is their nature to doubt, to fear, to hate. They will hate you. They will betray you.'

Lenk felt his arm rise of its own volition.

'You cannot let them deny you this purpose. You cannot let them destroy you. You cannot fail. You cannot disobey Darior. You cannot abandon your duty.'

Lenk felt his hand fall upon the ice.

'You cannot let them stop you.'

Lenk felt the man's eyes open. Lenk stared into a vast, pupilless blue void.

'Kill them or they will kill you.'

And then, Lenk felt himself scream.

Thirty-Nine

THE KINDEST OF POISONS

In a blackening row, the frogs smouldered on a thin wooden skewer.

Kataria stared as their colours, the myriad greens and blues and reds and yellows, vanished under a coat of black as the fire licked at their bodies, made their bellies swell and glisten with escaping moisture. The frogs stared back at her, through eyes growing larger in their tiny sockets, the fear they could not express in life coming out in death.

Finally, with nearly inaudible popping sounds, their eyes burst. Naxiaw plucked the skewer from the fire, glanced it over, and handed it to Kataria. She took it from his hands, looking it over with a frown.

'You put them on six breaths ago,' she said, slightly worried.

'They are cooked in six breaths,' he said, his shictish deep and sure where hers was soft and hesitant.

'They're still toxic,' she replied, glancing at their glistening bellies. 'The poison hasn't evaporated from them yet.'

'That's why you use only six breaths.'

'So, they're still poisonous.'

'They are.'

'Why even cook them, then?' She managed a weak grin in the face of their charred countenances. 'Or do they just taste terrible raw?'

She looked up and found no grin on Naxiaw's face. He was staring at her.

Still, she noted.

And with an intensity too severe for the situation, as though whether or not she were about to chew up some roasted amphibians would answer a dire question she had been privately pondering for ages now, and whether or not she licked her lips afterwards would dictate what he did next.

Not for the first time, she found herself glancing to the thick Spokesman Stick resting against the rock he sat upon.

Saying nothing, she bit one of the toasted creatures from the skewer. They were bitter and foul on her tongue, the aroma of cooked venom filling her nostrils. They were quite toxic, quite terrible to taste; she found herself wondering again what the point of cooking them was.

Texture, perhaps?

She bit down. A pungent flower bloomed in her mouth, and her lips threatened to rip themselves from her face, so fiercely did they pucker.

Apparently not.

Yet, under his stare, she continued to pop them into her mouth, chewing them up as much as she could tolerate before they slid as greasy lumps into her belly. She met his gaze as she did so, watching him as he watched her, as he continued staring.

No, she realised as she saw the careful steadiness of his eyes, *not staring*. Her own quivered a bit. *Searching*.

She did not ask for what. She didn't want to know. She tried not to even think about it, for she didn't want him to find it. Yet with eyes and instinct alike, he searched her.

She had sensed him reaching out again, as she had all that

morning since rejoining him in the forest after reclaiming her clothes from the Owauku. She had sensed him peering through the veil of the Howling, whispering over its roar to her, trying to reach her through their communal instinct. Of him, she could sense nothing. Of her, it was clear by the faint twitch at the edges of his mouth that he sensed only frustration.

It was discouraging, she admitted to herself, that the connection they had shared on Sheraptus' ship had been lost so completely. There was a comfort in his instinct melding with hers, a soothing earth to bury her fear beneath, and she dearly wished to feel it again. How had it been lost? she wondered. What had changed since last night?

She fought to keep the despair off her face.

Oh, right.

Meeting Naxiaw should have been the first thing to do that morning, she knew. Going to Lenk should have been something that never happened. She had already made her choice between them, between a human she should hate and a people she should adore, three times. She had made it when she looked into his eyes. She had made it when she heard him scream her name and plea for help.

She had made it when she turned away.

She was shict, she told herself. Her loyalty was to her people. She owed him no excuses, would give him no reasons, would offer no apologies. And she had remained faithful to that vow when she came to him that morning, found him shrugging his shirt over a freshly stitched wound.

She had met his eyes, then, and was unable to say anything at all.

Perhaps that was why she unconsciously evaded Naxiaw's probing instinct: a fear he might see what happened that morning, a dread he might know why they couldn't connect, a gripping terror he might have a solution.

She looked to the Spokesman again.

She found herself surprised to see it there still and not, say, embedded in the skulls of one or more of the humans. Naxiaw had seen them, after all, when the two shicts had pulled themselves from the reaching ocean. He had paused, a mere fifty paces from them, and stared. The implications that had seized her with a cold dread then had surely dawned on him as well.

Despite his captivity, he was still fresh and energetic. Coming from a fight, the humans were not. He was still strong, limber and swift. The humans were weak, exhausted and burdened with each other. His Spokesman leapt to his hands like an eager puppy. The humans' weapons hung from their hands like leaden weights.

He was shict.

They were not.

She had braced herself, then. For what, she wasn't sure. The uncertainty paralysed her, rendered her incapable of doing more than staring dimly, unsure what more to do. A shict, she knew, would have rushed down with him against them. A companion, she told herself, would have stood between him and them.

But a companion would not have stared into her friend's eyes and turned away when he screamed her name.

And a shict would not have felt wounded when he stared back into hers the following morning and turned away when she said nothing.

Kataria had done nothing that night. Kataria continued to do nothing. As much as she cursed herself for it, that did not surprise her.

What did, however, was the fact that Naxiaw had

followed her example and let the humans be. Of all the qualities the *s'na shict s'ha* were legendary for, tolerance and patience were not among them.

Why he had vanished into the forest, continued to wait here, she did not know. Why he had met her with nothing more than an offer of cooked amphibians, she could not say. What he hoped to find in her as he stared at her so intently, she had no idea.

But she wished, desperately, that he would stop.

He might have picked up on that desire through the Howling. Or he might have seen her squirming upon her log seat with an intensity usually reserved for dogs inflicted with parasites. He looked away, regardless.

'Cook the poison from the frog and there is no point to consuming them,' he said, producing a pouch from his hip. 'Venom, you see, has a number of advantages.'

'My father said it's how the greenshicts keep their blood toxic,' she replied.

'Your father knew more about the *s'na shict s'ha*,' he paused, letting the word hang in the air, 'than he knew about his own people.'

'You knew him?'

'Many of us did. He was a knowledgeable leader. He knew what he was. He knew what he had to do. He knew he was a good shict, and so did we. He also knew the value of consuming venom.'

He reached into his pouch and produced a frog, still alive, its red and blue body glistening as it croaked contentedly in his palm, unafraid.

'It is a temporary pain and so snaps one from stupor,' he said. 'It sharpens the senses, makes one more aware of the weakness of lesser pains ... improves the function of the bowels.'

He said this pointedly, looking at her. She furrowed her brow in retaliation.

'*And?*' she pressed.

'And,' he continued, 'it is what cures disease.'

She stiffened at the word, gooseflesh rising on her back.

'One would assume,' she whispered hesitantly, 'that poison would make one as ill as disease.'

'Poison does not make one ill; it merely poisons. It is a temporary element introduced to a person's body. It enters and, assuming the host is strong enough, it leaves. If the host survives, she is more tolerant to the pain.'

He watched the frog as it tentatively waddled across his palm, testing this newfound footing.

'Illness is born of something deeper,' he said. 'It infects, festers within the host, not as a foreign element, but as a part of her body. And because of this, it does not leave on its own. Even if symptoms disappear, the disease lingers and births itself anew. Because of this, the host cannot wait for it leave. It must be treated.'

His fingers clenched into a fist. There was a faint snapping sound.

'Cured.'

She fought to hide the shudder that coursed through her, more for the sudden ruthlessness of the action than for the fact that he subsequently popped the raw amphibian into his mouth and swallowed.

'A cured illness is a purified body. It leaves the host stronger. But this is all assuming she recognises the illness to begin with.'

He fixed his penetrating stare upon her, sliding past her tender, exposed flesh, past her trembling bones, through sinew turning to jelly. He saw, then, what he had been searching for. She felt the knowledge of it in her heart.

'To infect without being noticed,' he whispered, 'is the nature of disease.'

She could not bear his searching stare any longer. She turned away. His sigh was something harsh and alien, unused to his lips.

'How long?'

She said nothing.

'What am I to tell your father, Little Sister?'

She shook her head.

'How am I to tell any of our kinsmen that you have been with humans?'

'Tell them nothing,' she said, biting her lip. 'Tell them anything; tell them everything. Tell them you don't know why and tell them that Kataria doesn't know, either. Or tell them I'm dead. Either way, we can all stop wondering about it and talking about it and thinking about it and get on with whatever the hell else we were doing before everyone started asking if Riffid even gave a crap if a shict hung around round-ears.'

Her hands trembled, clenched the skewer so hard it snapped. She looked down at it through blurred vision; she couldn't remember when she had started crying.

His stare was all the more unbearable for the sympathy flooding it. Sympathy, she noted, blended with a distinct lack of understanding that made his gaze a painful thing, two ocular knives twisting in her flesh with tears seeping into the wounds. And so she stared into the fire, biting back the agony.

'It's not what it seems,' she whispered.

'There are scant few ways for it to seem, Little Sister,' Naxiaw replied. 'They are not dead. You are not dead. Why, then, are you with them?'

She had been avoiding the question since the day she had walked out of the Silesrian alongside a silver-haired monkey. It had been easy to avoid, at first: just an idle wonder thrown from a clumsy and distracted mind. But Naxiaw's mind was sharp, practised. The question struck her like a brick to the face, and she found that all the answers she had used to excuse away the question before felt weightless.

For the adventure? In the beginning, she had told herself it was for that – the thrill of exploration and the lust for treasure. But shicts had no use for treasure, and the use for exploration went only so far as scouting for the tribe. There was no word for 'adventure'.

Friendship, then? As much as she knew she should loathe to admit it, she had become ... attached to the humans. There was no denying it after a year, anymore. But there was no word for 'friendship' in the shictish tongue; there was 'tribe'; there was 'shict'. That was all a shict needed.

Perhaps, then, because she found she had needed more than tribe ... more than a shict needed. But how could she tell him that? How could she tell herself that?

As the tears began to flow again, she realised she just had.

And she felt him: his gaze, his thoughts, his instincts. Naxiaw reached for her, with eyes, with frown, with thought, with ears, with everything but his long, green fingers. The scrutinising had not dissipated, but was mingled with an animal desire, an utter yearning to understand that made his gaze all the more painful, the wounds all the deeper.

He stared at her, trying to understand.

And he never would. There was no word for it.

If he didn't know what she was feeling, he must have seen something in her tears, felt something in her heart, heard something in her head that made him know all the same that she was feeling something no true shict should. His face twitched, trembled, sorrow battling confusion battling fury. In the end, all that came of it was a shaking of his head and a long, tired sigh.

'Little Sister,' he said.

'I'm sorry,' she whispered. 'I'm *sorry*.'

'They're *kou'ru*. Monkeys. *Diseases*.'

'But I've been with them so long,' she said. 'My skin hasn't flaked off; my heart hasn't stopped beating; my blood hasn't turned to mud. The stories aren't true. They aren't disease.'

'*They are*,' he snapped back, baring his canines. 'A disease does not merely infect and kill, it *weakens*. It makes us vulnerable to other sicknesses, deeper illnesses, ones that *cannot* be burned out.'

'Like what?' She was absently surprised to find the growl in her voice, to feel her ears flattening against her head as she flashed her own teeth at him. 'I've seen more in a *year* than most shicts will see in their lifetime. I've tasted alcohol, I've seen cities made of stone, I know what it means when a cock crows and what it means to drain the dragon.'

'Symptoms of a weak and ignorant breed, and you're infected with them.'

'It *can't* be ignorance to *learn*,' she snarled. 'A lot of what they know is useless, dangerous and stupid. But I've learned about farming, agriculture, digging wells. There *must* be a reason they became the dominant race. If shicts are to survive, then we have to—'

'*Reasons?*' He leapt to his full height, towering over her. 'There is a reason, yes. They are dominant because when we first met them, *we* had a disease. Understanding,

732

forgiveness, *mercy*,' he spat. 'These were the symptoms of an illness that claimed *thousands* of shicts.'

She found herself falling from her log in an attempt scramble away from him as he advanced, his long strides easily overtaking her. He leaned down, extended his fingers to her.

'The disease rises now and again. I was there the last time it infected us. I was there when I saw the *reason* humans were dominant.'

Quick as asps, his hands shot out and seized her by the face. His eyes were massive, intense and brimming with tears as he drew his face towards her own wide-eyed and trembling visage. Then, he uttered the last words she remembered before he pressed his brow to hers.

'*You see, too.*'

And then, there was fire.

It was everywhere, razing the forests in great orange sheets, writhing claws pulling down branches and leaves and blackening the sky. It roared, it laughed, it shrieked with delight: loud, too loud, deafening.

Not loud enough to drown out the screaming.

Children, men, women, elders, mothers, daughters, hunters, weavers, sitting, standing, drinking, breathing, screaming, screaming, *screaming*. She knew them all – their lives, their histories, their loves, their families – as each scream filled her ears, mingled within the Howling and became knowledge to her and all shicts. And she heard them all made silent: some instantly, some in groans that bubbled into nothingness, some in high-pitched wails that drifted into the sky.

She saw them: green faces, mouths open, ears flattened, weapons falling from long green hands. She saw the spears embedded in their chests, the boots crushing their bones, the thick pink hands that unbuckled belts, that dashed skulls against rocks, that thrust sword, stabbed spear, swung axe. She saw their eyes, wide with desire, vast with conviction. They looked upon the faces; they heard the screams. There was no language to let them understand what they did, and they did not try to understand.

The screams mingled as one wailing torrent, shrieking through her mind, bursting through her skull, flowing out of her ears on bright red brooks. She heard her own voice in there, her own sorrow, her own agony, her own tragedy.

Eventually, their voices stopped. Hers continued for a while.

She looked up, at last, and saw Naxiaw. His hands hung weakly at his side. He stared at her firmly. He did nothing more as she scrambled to her feet, staring at him with eyes bereft of anything but pure animal terror, and fled into the forest.

He stared, long after she had disappeared into the brush.

Then, he sat down, and sighed.

'I should not have done that,' he whispered.

'*She had to know,*' a voice deep inside his consciousness spoke: Inqalle, harsh and unforgiving.

'*You did as you must,*' another added: Avaij, strong and unyielding. '*Anything to make her aware of the disease. So long as she knows, she can fight it.*'

He said nothing in reply. Through the Howling, though, they heard everything.

'*You fear her weak,*' Inqalle said. '*I thought her weak, too. She lacks the conviction to kill the humans. She has had days, opportunities beyond counting, and she has done nothing.*'

'*If our plight, the suffering of our people, her people cannot move her,*' Avaij said, '*then perhaps she is too infected. Perhaps she must be put down.*'

'I have seen too many shicts die at human hands,' Naxiaw whispered harshly. 'Too many families severed, children lost … I will not let it happen again, not to another shict, not to her.'

He sent these words through the Howling on thoughts of anger, of frustration. The words of his companions came back on sensations of possibility, anticipation.

'*Many Red Harvests approaches,*' Avaij said. '*The idea here was to test it.*'

'*There are ways to save a host beyond putting it down,*' Inqalle said. '*Poison can be used to cleanse, to shrivel tumours and drive out diseases.*'

'I have seen enough of her heart to know that it will hurt her,' Naxiaw replied.

'*The nature of poison is to harm. The nature of disease to kill. It is your choice, Naxiaw.*'

He sat silently for a moment. His decision was made known to them in an instant, the Howling full of his cold anger and hardened resolve.

'The humans die,' he whispered. 'I will cure them.'

'*I am with you,*' Inqalle said.

'*As am I,*' Avaij agreed.

'*And we,*' their thoughts became synonymous, '*will not let another shict suffer.*'

The vigour that coursed through Lenk's body as he strode out of the cavern was one that he had not experienced in a lifetime. Maybe even his whole lifetime, he thought. His muscles were taut and tense; his body felt lighter than it had ever felt; his breath came in deep gulps of air too fresh to have ever existed on this stagnant island of death.

Life surged through him, a vibrant and untested energy that was nearly painful to feel racing through his veins. His mind was aware of his wounds and his scars, but his body remained oblivious. Still, that did not stop his brain from trying to make his body aware of its limitations.

This doesn't make sense, he thought. *Moments ago, I was unconscious. Hours ago, I was in agony. Days ago, I was …*

'*Look back far enough,*' the voice replied to his thoughts. '*You will find only pain, a dark and agonising nightmare, until this moment. You're awake now.*'

How?

'*Don't believe what the priests tell you. Life is not sacred. Life is simply a tool. Purpose is sacred. Without purpose, life is nothing but a long, pointless, empty sleep.*'

And our sleep has been long.

'*Too long.*'

And our purpose …

'*We know what it is.*'

To find the tome.

'*To slaughter the demons.*'

And from there?

'*You'll know by then. But for now …*'

He glanced up and saw Kataria's back. The shict sat upon a rock, staring into the forest. Lenk felt his hand tighten into a fist.

'*Remember your purpose. Remembers theirs.*'

'I will,' he whispered.

Her ears twitched. She glanced over her shoulder and frowned at him as he approached.

'You snuck up on me,' she said, slightly offended.

He said nothing. They stared for a moment. Her gaze was softer than he remembered. She shifted to the side, leaving a bare space of granite beside her.

'*Walk past,*' the voice urged his legs. '*Do not look. Do not think of her. Go forward.*'

She had abandoned him. She had looked into his eyes. His mind remembered this. His mind did not object as this vigour carried him forth and past her. Her hand shot out and caught his. He stopped. Her fingers wrapped around his.

His body remembered this. It did not object as she pulled him down to sit beside her.

Silence persisted between, but not within. A voice raged at him, hissed angrily inside him, told him to go up. He wasn't sure why he stayed sitting. He wasn't sure why her hand was wrapped around his.

'Through the neck,' she said, suddenly.

'Huh?'

'I've got your sword arm right now. If I had pulled just a little harder, I could have brought my knife up into your neck.' She sniffed, scratched her rear end. 'It wouldn't have to be instant, either. I don't think you could stop me if I ran away and waited for you to bleed to death.'

'*See?*' the voice roared. '*Do you see? Do you see her purpose? Do you see why she is a threat? Kill her. Strike her down! Strangle her now before she can kill us!*'

She hasn't killed us.

'*Yet.*'

Yet.

'I don't have my sword,' he said.

She reached down and plucked up a length of steel from beside the rock, handing it to him. The moment he clenched the weapon, the vigour inside him boiled instead of surged, his muscles clenched to the point of cramping.

'It washed up on shore just an hour ago. The Owauku wanted to throw it back before you could use it on them. I stopped them.'

737

'*It has purpose,*' the voice whispered. '*It knows what it is used for. That's why it comes back to us. It knows what it craves.*'

'I could,' he whispered, 'kill you right now.'

'You won't,' she said, not even bothering to look up. 'And I haven't killed you yet.' She smacked her lips. 'I've had so many opportunities. I've thought of a hundred ways to do it: poison, arrows, shove you overboard when you're doing your business ...'

'*Kill her now!*'

Right now?

'If I was a true shict, I would have killed you when I first set eyes on you.' She sighed. 'But I didn't. I followed you out of the forest. I followed you for a year. I tracked you to a dark cave that you went into and I waited on this rock because I knew you'd be all right.' She bit her lip. 'You're always all right.'

She bowed her head for a moment, then rubbed the back of her neck.

'And that's all I'm ever sure of these days. I go to sleep not knowing if I'll dream shict dreams or what shict dreams are, but I know you're going to be there when I wake up.' She blinked rapidly for a moment. 'And back on the ship, when I wasn't sure, it ... I ...'

The silence did not so much cloak them as smother them this time, seeping into Lenk so deeply that even his mind was still for the moment. He glanced at her, but she was pointedly looking into the forest, staring deeply into the trees as though she would die if she looked anywhere else.

Perhaps she would.

'How's the shoulder?' she asked.

'It's fine,' he replied. 'I've had worse.'

'You do seem to have a talent for getting beaten up.'

738

'Everyone's good at something.' He shrugged, then winced. The pain in his shoulder had returned; it hadn't been there when he had emerged from the cave.

'You should let me take a look at it,' she said. 'I don't trust Asper to do a good job anymore. She ...' She shook her head. 'She's distracted these days.'

'I'd rather you didn't.'

'I understand.' A bitter chuckle escaped her. 'I understand *that*. I understand *you*.' She sighed. 'And that doesn't feel as bad as I thought it would.'

He glanced down. Her hand had found his again, squeezing it tightly.

'What now?' she asked.

'With what?'

'Everything.'

'We go after the tome.'

'I thought you wanted to go back to the mainland, forget the tome and the gold.'

'Things change.'

'They do.' She rose to her feet, knuckled the small of her back, and loosed the kind of sigh that typically preceded an arrow in the neck and a shallow grave. 'And that's not fair.' Slowly, she began to walk away, slinking towards the forest. She hesitated at the edge of the brush. 'I'm not going to apologise, Lenk, for anything.'

'I don't blame you,' he replied.

For the first time, she looked at him. It was a fleeting flash of emerald, nothing more than a breath during which their eyes met. It took less than that for her to frown and look away again.

'Yes,' she said, 'you do.'

He didn't protest. Not as she said the words. Not as she walked away.

Forty

BROKEN PROMISES

A warm droplet of water struck his brow, dripped down a narrow cheekbone and fell to his chin. He caught it on a purple finger before it could fall and be lost on the red and black cobblestones.

The word for it, Yldus recalled, was rain. He knew only a little about it. He knew it fell from the sky; he knew it made things grow. There was meaning behind it, too. It was a symbol of renewal, its washing of taint and sin considered something sacred. This he had been told by those prisoners who had begged for water from the sky, from the earth, from him.

He had given none. He didn't see the point. Where he came from, things did not grow. The sky never changed. And as he looked up at the sky now, the rain falling in impotent orange dots against the burning roofs of the city's buildings, he wondered what reverence could possibly be justified for it.

The fires continued, unhindered, belching smoke in defiant rudeness to the meek greyness. There were faint rumbles of what was called thunder, but they did nothing to silence the war cries of the females or the distant cries of the weak and hapless overscum they descended upon.

He picked his way over the bodies, lifting the hem of his robes as he walked through the undistilled red smears upon the cobblestones. He glanced down an alley, frowning at the flashing jaws and errant cackles of the sikkhuns as they feasted upon the dead and the slow with relish. Their female riders, long since bored with the meagre defences that had been offered to them and subsequently shattered, goaded their mounts to gnash and consume with unabated glee.

Wasteful, he thought. Pointless. Disgusting.

Female.

He left them to the dead. His concerns were for the living.

Or the barely living, at least.

The road was slick with blood, clotted with ash, littered with the dead and the broken. Yldus searched the carnage with a careful eye. He had seen much more and much worse, enough to recognise the subtle differences in the splashes of bright red life. He saw where it had been squandered in spatters of cowardice, where it had leaked out on pleas to deaf ears, where it had simply pooled with resignation and despair.

His eyebrows rose appreciatively as he saw one that began a bright crimson and turned to a dark red as it was smeared across the road, leaving a trail thick with desperation.

He followed it carefully, winding past the stacks of shattered crates and sundered barrels, the spilled blood and split spears that had been the last defence the overscum had offered the females. Some had fled. Many had stayed. Only one lived.

And as the road turned to sand beneath Yldus' feet, he heard that solitary life drawing his last breaths.

The overscum lay upon the sand. Unworthy of note: small, soft, dark-haired, dark-skinned, maybe a little fatter than most. Yldus watched with passive indifference as the human continued to deny the reality of his soft flesh and leaking fluids, pulling himself farther along the sand, ignoring Yldus and the great black shapes that surrounded him.

Yldus glanced up at the warriors of the First: tall, powerful, their black armour obscuring all traces of purple flesh and bristling with polished spikes. The spears and razor-lined shields they clenched were bloodied, but stilled in their hands.

Yldus offered an approving smile; the First, as the sole females proven to be able to overcome their lust for blood enough to follow orders, held a special place in his heart. They could slaughter and skewer with the best of them, but it was their ability to recognise, strategise and, most importantly, obey that made him request their presence in the city.

He was after answers, not corpses. And this was delicate work.

At his approach, they turned, as one, their black-visored gazes towards him: expecting, anticipating. He indulged them with a nod. One of them replied, stepping forward, flipping her spear about in her grip and driving it down into the human's meaty thigh.

Delicate, as far as the netherling definition of the word went, at least.

He folded his hands behind him, closing his ears to the human's wailing as he approached, being careful not to tread in the blood-soaked sand. He stood beside the over-scum, staring, waiting for the screaming to stop.

It took some time, but Yldus was a patient male.

It never truly stopped, merely subsided to gasping sobs. That would serve, however. Yldus knelt beside the overscum, surveying him carefully, waiting for the inevitable outburst. The human looked back at him through a dark-skinned face drawn tight with pain and anguish.

'Monsters,' he spat out in his tongue, 'demons. Filthy child-killers!'

Defiance, Yldus recognised, saying nothing as the man launched into a litany of curses, only a few of which he recognised.

'Whatever it is you came here for,' the human gasped out, the edges of his mouth tinged with blood. 'Gold, steel, food … we have barely any. Take it and go. Leave the rest of us in peace.'

Rejection. Yldus still said nothing, merely watching as the man continued to leak out onto the earth, merely waiting until he drew in a ragged breath.

'Spare me,' he finally gasped.

Bargaining.

'Spare my life,' he croaked again, 'help me and—'

'No.'

'What?' The man appeared shocked that such was even a possible answer.

'You ask the unnatural,' Yldus replied. 'You are here, beneath our feet. We are netherling. Because of this, you are going to die. It will not be swift. It will not be merciful. But it will happen. Ours is the right to take. Yours … the right to die.'

'Then do it,' the human spat back.

'To demand is not your right. We require something in this city. You will offer it to us.'

'Why should I? Why *would* I? You've killed …' He paused to gasp, hacking viciously.

'We have. We do.' Yldus turned his gaze to the burning skyline. 'To kill, to bleed, to die. This is simply what

743

it means to be netherling.' He glanced back at the man. 'What does it mean to be human, overscum?'

'It means ... it ...'

'Hard to say, I realise. Females may only be concerned with your breed as to how much you glut their sikkhuns, but I have taken great pains to learn about your breed. It's been difficult, but I have learned something.

'To be human,' he said, 'is to deny. It is to fight, to flee, to beg or to pray, despite that each action leads to only one outcome. Your people can run, but we can run faster. Your people can fight, but we can kill them. Your people can pray ...' He glanced down at the man, taking note of the chain hanging from his neck. 'Hasn't worked so well for you, has it?

'You are faced with inevitabilities: you will die. We will have what we need. Your people will die. How many of them, though, is undetermined. To kill is female. I cannot stop them from doing this. To direct is male. I can point them away from your people, let your people hide, flee, think that their gods are listening to them while we collect what we require and leave.'

He regarded the man evenly.

'This is the choice you are offered. Deny it if you wish.'

The man's face was too agonised to allow for any lengthy contemplation. His answer was swift and tinged with red.

'What do you want?'

Yldus reached down, plucking the chain from the man's neck. It ended in a symbol: a crude iron gauntlet clutching thirteen arrows. He studied it briefly, then held it before the man.

'I know what this is,' he said.

'So?'

'So you already know what I want.'

'No,' he said, shaking a trembling head. 'No, I cannot do that. I swore an oath.'

'Oaths are broken.'

'Before the Gods.'

'Gods are false.'

'To perform a duty.'

'You have failed,' Yldus said. 'Whatever you might have done for those you looked to is no longer a concern. Whatever you might do for those who look to you can still be effected.'

The man's neck trembled under the weight of acknowledgement, forced him to nod weakly after a moment.

'The temple,' he said. He thrust a trembling finger to the distant cliffs and the humble building upon them. 'What you seek is in the temple, beyond the pool. Do as you swore.'

'It would be pointless,' Yldus replied, rising to his feet. 'I will do as netherlings do.'

'Then whatever you do,' the man said, grimacing, 'whatever makes you need that cursed thing … you will die.' He spoke without joy, without hate, without emotion. 'And whatever you are, you will remember this day. You will know what it is you're trying to kill. And you will know why we pray.'

He met Yldus' eyes. He did not flinch in pain.

'And I wonder who will answer yours?'

The man's eyes were still, rigid with insulting certainty. Yldus felt his own narrow despite himself. He raised his hand and levelled it at the man, his vision bathed in crimson. The man did not flinch.

The man did not breathe.

Yldus lowered his arm, letting the power slip from his hand and eyes alike. The rain fell a little harder now, its droplets cold on his skin. The sky was grey now, the orange of the fire-painted clouds going runny as the blazes fell to impotent smoke.

He spared only another moment for the sight of the sky-line, for the man, for this city before he trudged towards the distant cliffs, the metal solidarity of the First's footsteps following him.

'*UYE!*' one of the longfaces howled.

'*TOH!*' six replied in grating harmony.

And then there was the sound of thunder.

Hidden behind the largest of the pillars marching the circle of the temple's pool, the Mouth could not see the doors give way, but he heard them splinter open. He heard the sound of longfaces cursing as they made their way in; the defenders of Yonder had come here to the temple first, barricading the doors with crates and sandbags.

Not enough to stand against the invaders' ram, of course, but the people of Yonder knew nothing of the creatures that had come in great black boats to their city. They could not have been prepared for the merciless heathen assault that came to their streets on howling war cries and clanging iron. They were people of fear and memory. Those people protected their churches, as much out of instinct as out of principle.

Their dedication to defending the doors, and later the streets, had made it easy enough for him to slip in un-noticed. The longfaces were complicating things, though.

'*This* is why I hate coming in unannounced.' A voice echoed: harsh, iron, female. 'Look at what they put out to stop us. Wood. Sand. Barely more of an obstacle than the overscum. You know not a single female netherling died today?'

'As I planned.' Another voice replied: deep, arrogant, male. 'These were not creatures worth bleeding over.'

'If we had let them know we were coming, they might have been. They had weapons. They were clearly preparing for *something*.'

'They had spears. For fishing,' the male said. 'Like Those Green Things back on the island. *They* are chattel. *These* were obstacles. Neither are worth losing females over.'

'We've got plenty of females. What we don't have is things worth fighting.' The female muttered over the sound of more bodies entering. 'I heard the Master's ship sank. Everyone but him died in it. *That* must have been a fight.'

A chorus of female voices grunted their agreement.

'And now we have sixteen fewer females for the final attack,' the male replied wearily. 'I suppose I shouldn't be surprised that, yet again, no one but me seems to be taking account of the long term. We have more important foes than pink things.'

'Right, the underscum,' she said. 'But the Grey One That Grins says this thing will kill them, right? What's the point, then?'

'The point is to kill the underscum.'

'We've done it before. With the poison.'

'The poison is limited, and it's far too weak to destroy what we're meant to kill. This … relic, I believe it's called, will give us the edge we need.'

'We're netherling. We have enough edges.'

'And yet, here we are,' the male sighed. 'I don't ask that you understand, Qaine, merely that you do.' He hummed. 'The overscum said it was beyond the pool … but where?'

The female echoed his thoughtful hum. The Mouth heard her shuffle around the pool's perimeter. He slid lower against the pillar, shrouding himself further in the shadow of the temple. His hands slipped down to the satchel at his side, producing a short knife and the vial.

He stared at the latter intently. If he was discovered, there would be no time to use it, no time to deliver it to the pool, no time to free Daga-Mer, to complete his mission.

He had a mission, he reminded himself. He had a deal. He would deliver the vial, pour Mother's Milk into the water and free Daga-Mer. In exchange, he would remember nothing. He would be free of sinful memory, at long last. He would not remember the pain, the tragedies, his name ...

He had a name.

He grimaced.

The sound of stone shattering pulled him from his brief reverie. A cry of alarm was bitten back in his throat. He hadn't been discovered, he recognised. Rather, something had been shattered. The statue of Zamanthras that stood at the head of the pool, he recalled. Zamanthras was uncaring. Zamanthras did not save his family.

He had a family.

'*Hah!*' the female barked. 'See? Found it! It's like they say: Smash the biggest thing in the room and you'll find your answer.'

'No one says that,' the male replied.

'I say it. I'm a Carnassial. So *they* will say it now. Won't they?'

The females grunted their agreement, chuckling. There was the sound of stone sifting, rocks sliding.

'What ... *this* is it? It's just a heap of bones!'

'That's what we came for,' the male replied. 'Take it back to the ships. We're done here.'

'Done? The sikkhuns are still hungry.'

748

'They are always hungry.'

'The females haven't killed enough.'

'They will never kill enough.'

'There's still overscum here!'

The male paused.

'Find the ones with heads bowed, talking to invisible things. Kill them. Don't waste time on anything else. Ships need rebuilding, and Sheraptus is not pleased because of it.'

'Right, right,' the female muttered. The sounds of iron-clad feet shuffling rang out, then stopped. 'Well, well … what's *this* thing do?'

'We don't have time to—'

'It's *huge*,' another female interrupted. 'Look at it! It's got this big … big …'

'*Spiky* thing,' a third gasped. 'It's *spiky*! But how does it work?'

'No idea,' the first female grunted. 'It can't be that hard, though.' There was the sound of shuffling, knuckles rapping wood. 'There's some kind of … stick thing. What's it—?'

A snap. Wood rattled. Air shattered.

The Mouth froze as a purple blur fled past his pillar. He stared as it came to a halt against the stone. The netherling gasped, laying wide eyes upon him. She tried to say something through a mouth quickly filling with blood.

Possibly due to the massive spear jutting through her belly and pinning her to the wall. She squirmed once, spat once, then died upon the wall.

And a grating, wailing roar of joy swept through the temple.

'Did you see that? Did you *see it*? It was all—'

'*TWANG!* Yeah, and then it was all *fwoom* and she just went flying!'

'Look at that! Killed her right there! Look at her just hang there!'

'Could you make it *twang* faster? Could it be *fwoomier*?'

'Yeah, you could! Just put more spikes on it!'

'Right! More spikes and you could just kill *anything*.'

The low, morbid chuckle that swept the temple was the first female, Qaine.

'Yeah,' she said. 'We're *taking* this.'

'Quite done?' the male asked. 'Want to collect the one on the wall?'

The Mouth tensed.

'Who gets shot with a giant spike and deserves to get pulled down?' Qaine grunted. 'That's not a bad spike, though …' She hummed as the Mouth gripped his knife tighter. 'But we can make it spikier.'

'Shootier,' another female agreed.

'Stabbier,' a third said.

'*Twangier.*'

'Yeah,' Qaine said. 'Take it to the ships. Round up the sikkhuns. They've eaten enough.'

There was the sound of crates crunching under rolling wheels, grunts of effort as something massive was escorted out of the temple. A solitary breathing told the Mouth that he was not yet alone. He guessed by the lack of snarling accompanying it that the male still remained.

'You could have stopped this,' the male whispered.

The Mouth's eyes widened. He tensed, preparing himself. The knife was tight in his hand, though he wasn't sure how much difference it would make. The males used magic, he recalled. A flimsy little spike made of bone would be useless against such power.

Throw it, then, he told himself. Distract the male, then escape. There would be time enough to return later, to return to his home, to find what he had left behind, to say good-bye to ...

What about the mission? he asked himself. *What about the deal?*

'But you didn't ...'

The male hadn't struck yet. Who would he be talking to, then?

'Your people paint the stones red with their blood. Your shrines burn. You lay shattered on the floor ... and I walk away.' The Mouth could hear the sneer in the male's voice. 'If you were real, you'd do something.'

There was a long silence. The male waited.

And then turned and strode out.

It was some time later before the sound of dying and the war cries of the invaders faded outside. The Mouth waited quietly before he even thought to move.

And by then, he realised he was still not alone.

Soft feet on stone floors. Frantic breathing. Terror in every sound. Not a longface, then. Then there was the sound of slurping, the desperate gulping of water that belonged to the scared, the sick, the dying. He remembered that sound.

And as he turned, he remembered the girl. She stared up from the pool, wide-eyed beneath a mop of wild black hair. Her face was dirtier than before, covered in soot. Her hand was deep in the sacred pool, her cracked lips glistening with holy water.

No, he reminded himself, *waters of a prison, that which holds back Daga-Mer. You're to free him, remember? Remember?*

Of course he did. But he also remembered her, her fear, her desperation, her name. He opened his mouth to speak it.

'I don't care,' Kasla said before he could. 'It's not holy. If it was, She would have done something.' The girl pointed to the shattered statue of Zamanthras. 'And now nearly everyone's dead! Stabbed, bled out or eaten by those … *things*. And She did *nothing*.'

The Mouth followed her finger. Zamanthras' stone eyes stared at him blankly: no pity, no excuse, no plea for him not to do what he knew he must. He stared down at the vial in his hand.

Thick, viscous ooze swirled within. Mother's Milk. The last mortal essence of Ulbecetonth, all that was needed to free Daga-Mer from a prison unjust. He looked to the pool, and as if in response, a faint heartbeat arose from some unseen depth within the massive circle of water.

A distant pulse, reminding him with its steady, drumlike beat.

He leaned closer, as if to peer within, to see what it was he was freeing. He saw only his reflection, his weak mortality distorted and dissipated as ripples coursed across the surface. Kasla, the girl, was drinking again, noisily slurping down the sacred waters of her city's goddess.

The Mouth found himself taken aback slightly. It was just water, of course, but he had expected her to show more regard for that which her people revered.

But her people lay dying outside. No goddess answered their prayers, just as no goddess had answered hers. She drank as though every drop would be the last to touch her lips, as though she need not fear for anyone else. She was alone, without a people, without a holy man, without a goddess.

The humane thing to do would be to free them all, he told himself, to lift their sins of memory and ease the anguished burdens heaped upon them by a silent deity. To free them, he would free Daga-Mer, and be free himself. His own pain would be gone, his own memories lost, as would hers. And without anything to remember, they would be free, there would be nothing left, they would be ...

Alone ...

She looked up, panicked as he approached her. She backed away from the pool.

'Get back!' she hissed. 'I've done nothing wrong! I was thirsty! The wells, they're ... the things were drinking from them. I needed water. I needed to survive.'

The Mouth paused before her. He extended a hand, palm bare of knife hilt.

'Many people do.'

She stared at his hand suspiciously. He resisted the urge to pull it back, lest she see the faint webbing that had begun to grow between his fingers. He resisted the urge to turn to the pool and throw Mother's Milk into it. They were there, the urges, the need to do them.

But he could not remember why he should leave her.

Kasla took his hand tentatively and he pulled her to her feet. She smiled at him. He did not smile back.

'We both got here unseen,' he said, turning towards the sundered doors of the temple. 'We can help others get here, too, until the longfaces leave. There will be enough to drink.'

'The waters are sacred. They would fear the wrath of Zamanthras.'

'Zamanthras will do nothing.'

She followed him as he walked out the door into sheets of pouring rain and the impotent, smoking rage of fires extinguished.

'What's your name?' she asked at last.

He paused before answering.

'Hanth,' he said. 'My daughter's name was Hanta.'

753

She grunted. Together, they continued into the city, searching the fallen for signs of life. Hanth stared at their chests, felt for their breath, for want of listening for groans and pleas. He could not hear anything anymore.

The heartbeat was thunder in his ears.

Forty-One

COMPULSORY TREASON

Togu stared from the shore. When he was smaller, at his father's side, he recalled days of splendid sunsets, the sea transformed into a vast lake of glittering gold by the sun's slow and steady descent. He had always been encouraged by such a view, seeing it as a glimpse into the future, *his* future as chief.

Those had been fine days.

But he had learned many things since the day his father died. Gold lost its lustre. Treasure could not be eaten. And the sun, he swore, had been progressively dimming its light just to spite him, so that he could never again look at the ocean without seeing the world in flames.

Fire, too, had once held a different meaning.

He glanced to the massive pyre burning only a few feet away and licked his eyes to keep them from drying out. Just last night, this fire was a beacon for revelry. His people had gathered about it, danced and sang and ate the gohmns that had come from it. Last night, he had stared into the fire and dared to smile a little.

Today, he could not bear to look at it any longer than a few deep, tired breaths.

He had lit it over two hours ago. Only now did he hear the steps of heavy feet upon the sand. By the time he had turned to face the sound, Yaike was already standing over him, arms crossed, his single eye fixed upon the diminutive lizardman.

'You came,' Togu muttered.

'You lit the fire,' Yaike replied, making a point to reply in their rasping, hissing tongue.

'I did,' Togu replied in kind, wincing. The language always felt so unnatural in his mouth since he had learned the human tongue. Perhaps that was the reason Yaike looked down on him with disdain now.

Or one of them, at least.

'I was expecting Mahalar to come,' Togu muttered, turning away.

'Mahalar has concerns on Jaga.'

'Shalake, then. Shalake used to come often.'

'Shalake leads the defence of Jaga. Speak with me or speak to no one.'

'I have spoken to no one for many years,' Togu snapped back. 'I have lit *many* fires.'

'The nights are long and dangerous,' Yaike said. 'The longfaces prowl above the waves; the demons stalk below. The numbers of the Shen are limited, our time even more so. We do not need to make excuses to anyone.' He narrowed his eye. 'Let alone those who harbour outsiders.'

Togu turned toward the sea again, away from his scowl.

'The outsiders are dead.'

He felt Yaike's stare upon him like an arrow in his shoulder. He always had. That the Shen had only one eye did not diminish the ferocity of his scowl; it merely sharpened it to a fine, wounding edge.

'All of them,' Togu added.

'How did they die?'

'Most of them drowned,' Togu replied. 'But you already knew that. You sank the ship they were on.'

'You said "most".'

'One of them crawled back to shore. She was exhausted.' He turned back to face the Shen, his expression severe. 'I cut her throat.'

'She ...' Yaike whispered.

'Yes. She.'

He was not used to seeing Yaike grin. It was unnerving. Even more so when the Shen scratched the corner of his missing eye.

'Died swiftly?' Yaike asked.

'Messily.'

'Is that all, then?' the Shen asked.

'No,' Togu replied. 'The tome ...'

Instantly, Yaike's expression soured, grin slipping into a frown, frown vanishing into his tattooed green flesh.

'You don't need to know about it.'

'It came to *my* island. It drew the longfaces here. The demons were close enough to Teji's shores they could have broken wind and I'd see the bubbles. I deserve to know. The Owauku deserve to know.'

'There are no Owauku. There are no Gonwa. There are no Shen. There is only us and our oaths. Remember that, Togu, the next time you think such questions.'

'Oaths? *Oaths?*' He snarled at the taller creature, his size temporarily forgotten. 'For who do we swear these oaths, Yaike?'

'Our oath has always been to watch the gate, to wait for Ulbecetonth to—'

'I said *for who do we swear these oaths, Yaike?* I am well aware of what the Shen says our oaths are. I am well aware that we Owauku and Gonwa have no choice in swearing them. What I want to know is who? For who do we kill outsiders and spill blood?'

Yaike's eyelid twitched slightly.

'Everyone.'

'Including Owauku?'

'Including Owauku.'

'Including Gonwa?'

'Including Gonwa. We protect everyone.'

'Then tell me,' Togu said, 'why these oaths do not protect us. Tell me why the Gonwa are here on Teji and not on Komga? Tell me why their fathers and brothers die under the longfaces' boots while the Shen do *nothing*?'

Yaike said nothing. Togu snarled, stepping forward.

'Where were your oaths when the Owauku starved? Why did the Shen only come to Teji and kill the humans who would help us? Why did the Shen say nothing when I said my people could not eat oaths?'

Yaike said nothing. Togu stormed towards him, tiny hands clenched into tiny fists.

'Why did *I* have to kill the outsiders, Yaike? Why did I have to barter them to the longfaces? Why didn't *you* step in and protect us from the purple devils in the first place? Where were your oaths, then?'

Yaike said nothing. Togu searched his face and found nothing; no shame, no sorrow, no sympathy. And he sighed, turning away.

'If you can give me nothing else, Yaike,' he said, 'tell me what will happen to the tome.' At his silence, the Owauku trembled. 'Please.'

The Shen spoke. It was the monotone, the deliberate, the pitiless speech born of duty. Togu hadn't expected any great sympathy. But Togu hadn't expected to shudder at the sheer chill of the Shen's voice.

'The tome will be ours,' Yaike said. 'It will return to

Jaga. Mahalar will decide what to do with it. The oaths shall be fulfilled, with your cooperation or without.'

'It is in Jaga now, then? In Shen hands?'

'It is safe.'

Togu sighed, bowing his head as he heard Yaike turn and stride down the shore. He wasn't certain how far the Shen had gone, if he would even hear him, when he muttered.

'Is Teji safe, then?'

'Honour your oaths, Togu,' Yaike said. 'We will do the same.'

The footsteps faded into nothingness, leaving behind a cold silence that even the roaring pyre could not diminish. Togu stared into the fire, sympathising. He had stared at it, once, thinking it the greatest force of nature in the world. The power of destruction, of creation, feeding off the earth and encouraging growth in its ashes. In its lapping tongues, he had seen himself.

He still did.

For now, he stared at something gaudy, easily controlled and impotent against the forces around it. He stared at a tool.

'Did you hear all that you needed, then?' he asked in the human tongue.

Lenk stared at him from the forest's edge, nodding solemnly. He stepped out onto the shore, Kataria creeping out of the brush after him. She scowled down the beach, ears twitching.

'He thought you slit *my* throat, didn't he?' she growled. 'Did you see that smug grin on his face? Like he had done it himself ...'

'You took his eye,' Lenk pointed out.

'I would have taken the other one, too,' she muttered, adjusting the bow on her back. 'But *no*. *Someone* said we had to wait and listen.' She gestured down the beach. 'And for what?'

'The Shen have the tome.'

'And?'

'We're going after it.'

At that, both the shict and Owauku cast him the combined expressions of suspicion and resignation usually reserved for men who slather their unmentionables in goose grease and wander towards starving dogs with a gleam in their eye.

'To Jaga?' Togu said. 'The home of the Shen has never been seen by anyone *not* Shen. Only they and the Akaneeds know how to get to it.'

'That's fine,' Lenk said.

'You will probably die.'

'Also fine.'

'But why?' Kataria asked. 'What about returning to the mainland?'

'I have not seen any sign of Sebast or any rescue,' Lenk said. 'Have you?'

His gaze was expressionless, rid of any emotion, let alone accusation, yet Kataria squirmed all the same, rubbing her neck and glancing at the earth.

'No,' she said. 'But the plan was to get a boat and return that way, wasn't it?'

'Demons in the water,' Lenk replied.

'But—'

'Shen, Akaneed, longfaces, Deepshrieks …' He shook his head. 'Every time we seek comfort, every time we flee danger, it finds us.' His hand brushed the hilt of his sword, lingered there for a moment too long to be considered casual. 'This time, we go find it. We finish what we came to do.' He narrowed his eyes. 'We kill those who try to stop us.'

She stared at him searchingly.

'We?'

He turned to her, eyes hard.

'We.'

He stared out over the sea, then glanced to Togu.

'We'll need a boat,' he said. 'Supplies, too, and as much information as you can give us about Jaga and the Shen.'

'Asking a lot,' Togu mused, 'considering what I've already done for you.'

'Considering what we could have done *to* you, it's not unreasonable,' Lenk replied, his stare harsh. 'You betrayed us. We could have done worse.'

Togu nodded glumly, waving a hand as he turned and stalked towards the forest, towards his village.

'Take what you want, then,' he said. 'We were born in death. We will survive.' He paused, glancing over his shoulder at Lenk. 'If you don't, though, I won't mourn.'

'No one has yet,' Lenk replied.

Togu's eye ridges furrowed briefly as he glanced past the two companions. An errant ripple blossomed across the waves.

For a moment, he thought he had seen a flash of hair, green as the sea, pale flesh and long, frilled ears that had heard everything. For a moment, he thought he had heard a lyrical voice whispering on the wind. For a moment, he thought of telling the companions this.

But only for a moment.

Togu nodded again before disappearing into the brush. Lenk turned and stared out over the sea, either not noticing or ignoring Kataria as she turned an intent gaze upon him.

'Are you all right?'

'I'm always all right,' he said.

'I mean, are you well?' she asked. 'You've said barely a word since we got off the ship.'

'I'm trying not to waste my breath so much.'

'Look, about what happened …'

'Stop,' he said. 'Can you really think of any way to end that sentence that will change anything?'

She stared at him, frowned and shook her head.

'Then maybe you can save some breath, too.'

He turned to go, felt a hand on his shoulder. Something within him urged him to break away. The thought occurred to him to turn and strike her. Something within him did not disagree with that. He did neither, but nor did he turn to face her.

Not until she seized him by the shoulders and forced him around, anyway.

Her stare was intense, far too much for searching, for prying, for anything but conveying a raw, animal need that was reflected in her grip, her fingers digging into his shoulders. Her mouth quivered, wanting desperately to say something but finding nothing. Her teeth were bared, her ears flat against her head, her body tensed and rigid with trembling muscle.

He stared back at her, wary, his own body tightening up, blood freezing as something within him told him what was happening. This was it, it told him, the betrayal he was waiting for. She had done it before; she would do it again. The aggression was plain on her face. She was going to finish the job now. He should strike before she did so. Strike now, it told him, seize the sword and hack off her head. Strike.

Strike.

Kill—

And then, there was no more thought, no more action.

He had neither the mind nor the will for either as she pulled him close. There was only his body, feeling every ridge and contour of muscle on her naked midsection, each one brimming with nervous energy. There were only her eyes, shut tight as though she feared to open them and see anything in his.

There were only their lips pressed together, their tongues tasting each other, their hands, off weapons, on each other.

And the unending sigh of the ocean.

She pulled back, just as swiftly as she had embraced him. Her body still shook, her fingers still dug into his skin, her ears were still flat against her head. But her eyes were steady, fixed on his, unblinking.

'I can't change,' she whispered, 'anything.'

And she turned.

And she walked away.

And he stared after her, long into the night.

Forty-Two

THE ICE SPEAKS TRUE

Island of Teji
The Aeons' Gate
Time is irrelevant

*I lived on a farm before I became an adventurer. I had a mother,
a father, a grandfather and a cow. None of those are important. What is important is that I don't remember much about
them.*

Not much ... but a little.

*I remember that time seemed to stand still on a farm. We
lived, we ate, we planted, we harvested, we watched births, we
watched deaths. The same thing happened the next year ... for
as long as I was there.*

*This I remember. I remember it too well. Granted, the ad-
venturing life was not too different: we lived, mostly; we ate
things that we probably shouldn't have; we stabbed; we burned;
we once force-fed a man his own foot ...*

*Some part of me, I think, still suspected life was that way, still
thought that the world would never change.*

But I'm learning all kinds of things lately.

Things change.

*Weeks ago ... gold seemed everything. Gold was everything.
It would lead me back to the farm, back to living, planting,
harvesting, birthing, dying. That part of me that thought the*

world would continue as it always had wanted me to go back, to prove it right.

That part of me is gone, though. It was cast out. It was a blanket, something thick and warm that kept me sleeping. I'm awake now.

The cave ... I remember it. I remember it too well. I don't know his name. I don't know if he had family, if he ever planted anything or saw a child born. I don't know how he lived.

But I know who he was. And I know how he died.

He fought the demons, back during the war with the Aeons in which the mortals triumphed against Ulbecetonth. He inspired fear in his enemies and the House of the Vanquishing Trinity that he marched with, even as they called him ally. He killed many. His purpose was to kill.

His companions feared him: what he said, what he knew, what he was. They went into that cave. They killed him. They died with him. I stared into his eyes. I knew this. Some part of me remembered it, some part that I've been trying to ignore. I knew him.

And he knew me. And he spoke to me. And I listened.

And it all began to make sense. I've seen the way they look at me, the way they look away when I stare at them. When they need order, when they need direction, they turn to me. When I needed them, they abandoned me, betrayed me.

Maybe it was stupidity on the surface. Maybe it was their self-ishness, as I had suspected. Those might have been the shallows, but not the purpose. They had been waiting for that moment, the moment in which they could watch me die without retaliation.

They wanted me to die. They wanted to kill me. To kill us, but they couldn't.

The voice told me this. It's speaking so clearly now. It doesn't command me. I talk to it; it talks back. We discuss. We learn.

We reason. It told me everything about them, about their purpose. It made sense.

Things change.

They don't.

I learned this too well tonight.

The voice was speaking clearly, but I was still doubting it. I didn't see how they could hate me ... well, no, I could see how they could hate me, sure. They're assholes. But her ... I didn't believe it, not after that day.

So I watched her, as the voice told me to. I watched her go away. I followed her. I couldn't, too closely, of course; she would hear me. She would know. So I followed her as far as I could. I heard her. I heard her talk with other voices.

I glanced out from my hiding spot and saw him.

Greenshict.

My grandfather told me stories of them. Manhunters. Skinners. Seven feet and six toes of hatred for humans. I learned more about shicts than I ever thought I would; I learned that they weren't all bad; I learned about Kataria ...

But Kataria is a puppy. Greenshicts are wolves. They kill humans. This is their sole purpose. I know this. Everyone does. She knows it, too. And she told me nothing of them.

I couldn't tell what they were talking about. I didn't need to know. The voice did. It told me they were plotting my murder, that she would never be able to change her purpose, her desire to kill me for what I am, for what she was. She was speaking with a creature born to kill humans.

I believed it.

I left.

And everything became clear after that.

The tome is the key. The man in the cave told me that. There's more written on it than Miron would have me believe. His purpose was to lie and to obscure. Maybe there's something worse written in it than I would imagine. But maybe ... maybe there's something in it I need to see, no matter the danger.

And there is plenty.

The Shen are numerous, Togu has told me. They relentlessly patrol their island home of Jaga. They tattoo themselves with a black line for each kill they make, a red line for each head they've crushed. I've never seen one without at least three red lines upon it, the rest of them in black. They are violent; they are watchful; they live on an island that no one knows the location of.

And they have the tome.

I will go after it. I will find it. I will learn the truth inside it. I will take them, the betrayers, with me.

I won't give them another chance to kill me.

I will follow my purpose.

I will kill them all.

Epilogue

THE STIRRING IN THE SEA

Mesri had been a holy man, once: a revered speaker of the will of the Zamanthras. He had guided his people through many trials and many hardships. He was the chain that had held Port Yonder together. He was a leader. He was a man of the Gods. He was good.

And now, he was a fast-fading memory, his eyes shut tight and drifting beneath a cloak of shimmering blue as his body was commended to the depths. The last body to go under, the other victims of the longfaces' attack having since been offered to the ocean. It had begun reverently enough, with the ritual candles burned and the holy words spoken.

But the candles had been extinguished by a stray wave. The people did not know all the words. Mesri did. Mesri was dead. So was half of Port Yonder. And once that reality became too apparent, the funerals lasted as long as it took to identify the bodies and drop them into the harbour.

By the time they sent Mesri to Zamanthras, only two remained to watch him sink beneath the blue. Only Kasla. Only Hanth.

The girl peered out over the edge of the dock. 'Do we say something?'

'To who?' he asked.

She glanced around the empty harbour. 'To Zaman-thras?'

'Feel free,' he said.

Kasla inhaled deeply and looked for inspiration. She looked to the sky, grey and thundering. She looked to the sea, glutted with corpses. She looked to the city, its blackened ruin and blood-spattered sands. And so, she looked out over the ocean and spat.

'Thanks for nothing.'

They continued to stare at the sea, saying nothing. Neither of them felt an obligation to stay, to remain silent. Neither of them knew where they would go, what they would say.

'Are you going to stay?' Kasla asked.

'I am returning home,' he replied.

'You say that, but you don't look like you're from around here. Your skin is too white and your eyes are too dark to be Tohanan. And you very clearly don't follow Zamanthras.'

'Zamanthras doesn't tell me who I am. Neither do your people.'

She shrugged. 'I guess not. Still, you kept everyone safe while we rescued them from the longfaces. They'll welcome you for that.'

'That's fine,' he replied. 'I'm glad they're safe for now.'

'They are. We all are.' She reached out, slid a hand into his robe and smiled. 'Heartbeat.'

He turned on her. 'What?'

'I can feel it through your skin,' she said, running her fingers over his chest. 'You must be stressed.'

'I ... am ...' he said, nodding weakly.

'You need food. Fortunately, the cooks survived.' She patted him on the back and began walking to the wreckage of Port Yonder. 'Come on.'

He turned and began to follow. The water lapped at the docks. The sky rumbled. And between the voices of the storm and the sea, Hanth heard a whisper reach his ears from the waves.

'*Ulbecetonth honours her promises, Mouth.*'

He forced himself to keep going, to keep his eyes forward. He didn't dare look behind him for fear of seeing four golden eyes peering at him from the depths, a grey dorsal fin splitting the waters.

On the sands below, the females were joyous. The air was rife with the shrieking of Those Green Things as they were driven under lash and blade to chop more wood and haul it to the shore to be built into ships. The slightest excuse – a pause to take a drink, a load moving too slow – was used to justify an immediate execution.

'Shouldn't you stop them?' a rasping voice asked from behind him.

Sheraptus scowled; between the shriek of Those Green Things, the laughter of the females and the cackle of the sikkhuns as more and more corpses were hurled into their pits, the sound of the Grey One That Grins was just somehow even more grating.

'It's quite wasteful, you know,' his companion said. 'If you have no slaves, you will have no ships and you will have no way to find the tome.'

'No,' Sheraptus said, pointedly.

'No?'

'I'm bored with that. I found your stupid tome and it cost me dearly.'

'You've never given a concern for cost before.'

'That was before I lost my best warriors, my First Carnassial and my *ship* for the sake of a few pieces of pressed wood. This is no longer interesting.'

'There is still more to learn.'

'Of what? Overscum? They show up where you don't want them to and ruin everything. That's as much as I need to know and as much as I care to know. I've decided … we're returning to the Nether. There are plenty more wars to be fought there.'

'But so little power to be gained,' the Grey One That Grins urged. 'Consider all that you have found here; consider all that we have given you to fight Ulbecetonth's children on our behalf. The martyr stones, the poison …'

'The power I've found here is weak and fleeting. I've not yet met anyone who can best me.'

'No. Only those who can best your ship.'

'You are aggravating me,' Sheraptus growled. 'Consider my gratitude for the stones to be my aversion to killing you.'

'Most appreciated. However, I feel you may be a little shortsighted.'

'I also feel that way. I was apparently too hasty in offering such gratitude.'

'I simply mean to imply that you are letting your mood sour the potential for one of the greatest powers you've yet to see.'

'Power … is that all you think me concerned with?'

'No. *This* power, however, you might be … considering it comes in a form you will find most pleasing.'

Sheraptus paused, a smile growing across his lips as the Grey One That Grins drew the words out between his long teeth.

'The priestess.'

'What of her?' Sheraptus asked.

'Did you not sense something awry last night on your ship? A strength you have not tasted before?'

'I did … on the beach, as well. Her?'

771

'She possesses something not yet seen in *nethra*. Perhaps you are interested?'

'Passingly. In her, though ...'

'She attracts your ire?'

'We were interrupted. She did not scream for me.'

'I see. I can show you how to find her. I can show you how to harness her power for your own ends.'

'And in return?'

'The tome.'

'As you wish. The Screamer is out seeking its whereabouts right now. I suspect Those Other Green Things that sank my ship will be involved.'

'The Shen are powerful. It may take many females to wrench it from their grasp.'

'I have many females.'

'And the artifact,' the Grey One That Grins said, 'you returned it from Port Yonder?'

'Yldus arrived not long ago. I hardly see what you want with a pile of bones, though.'

'It will become clear, in time.'

'You say that often, I note.'

'I have little time to explain. My presence is needed elsewhere.'

'Of course. Vashnear will tend to your needs.'

He heard the Grey One That Grins turn on his heels and begin to walk away. Without turning around, Sheraptus called after him.

'This power she has ... and how to harness it ...'

'It will be a long process,' his companion said. 'Long ... and slow.'

And without a word, Sheraptus smiled, returning his gaze to the island below. The sikkhuns fed. The ships bobbed in the surf as supplies were loaded onto them. And the females were joyous.

So many steps, Mahalar thought as he climbed down. *Were there always this many?*

Not for the first time, he thought about turning around, returning to the top and sleeping for a few more hours. But his people were waiting for him below. They had requested his guidance.

He found the Shen gathered in a throng at the bottom of the massive stone staircase; he felt their yellow eyes upon him, heard the quiet hiss of their breath. At the fore of them, he recognised Shalake, heard the towering Shen's breath louder and angrier than the rest.

He bowed his scaly head to them as he was about to ask what they had summoned him for. That reason became clear as he recognised another presence amongst them: small, kneeling, quivering with fear.

Human, he recognised. *Humans here ... with Shalake.*

His heart sank. He knew what usually came next.

'Mahalar,' Shalake said. 'We found this one outside the reef. We await your wisdom.'

Of course, Mahalar thought with a sigh. *'Wisdom' is not often needed to sentence terrified humans to death. All the same ...*

He came before the human, smelled his frightened breath, the salt on his skin, heard the quaver in his voice.

'Your name?' he asked.

'S-Sebast,' the human replied. 'Of the *Riptide*, under the captaincy of one Argaol—'

'Sebast,' Mahalar repeated. 'What is it you've come seeking?'

'Our m-men,' the human stammered. 'Three men, two

women, one … thing. They disembarked weeks ago. We were supposed to pick them up weeks ago. But our crew … dead … slaughtered. And now, me …'

He let that thought hang, unfinished, in the air, clearly hoping for a denial, a shake of Mahalar's scaly, wrinkled head, anything that might suggest he would walk away from this.

Mahalar simply pulled a pipe from his robe and lit it, taking a few deep, long puffs.

'Where were you to meet them?' Mahalar asked.

'T-Teji, sir. It's supposed to be a trading post not far from—'

'We know what Teji is, human,' Shalake hissed. 'But apparently *you* do not. These waters are forbidden to humans.'

'We didn't know!' Sebast squealed. 'We didn't know, I swear! Let me go and I'll take my men away from here and never return.'

Mahalar looked to Shalake. 'His men?'

'Dead,' Shalake answered.

'W-what?' Sebast stammered.

'It is our way, unfortunately,' Mahalar said. 'We stand atop sacred ground, Sebast. Our charge sleeps deeply, and we take care that no one disturbs her.'

'Your charge?'

'It takes a long time to explain,' Mahalar said. 'A longer time to convince you. But we have been convinced for a long, long time. This is our charge. These are our oaths.' He shook his head. 'We break them for no one, Sebast.'

He glanced to Shalake, nodded. He felt the wind break as the great Shen's club rose into the air. He felt the air stand silent as the great Shen's voice followed.

'*SHENKO-SA!*'

'No! *PLEASE!*'

He heard the sound of a melon splitting, a sack of fruits hitting the earth. He smelled blood on the air and sighed.

'I am sorry, Sebast.'

'We do as we have to,' Shalake said. 'If he found those humans he sought ...'

'I know,' Mahalar said. 'But I was told you sent warriors to deal with them.'

'Yaike says that they are dead.'

'And who told Yaike?'

'Togu.'

'Then be on your guard. Togu has forgotten much in his time away.'

'We have not,' Shalake said. 'If they still live, we will kill them. The longfaces have been sunk, continue to sink as we find them. The demons ...'

'Are coming,' Mahalar said.

'You can sense them?'

'As easily as I can sense you.'

'How long?'

'Not very.'

'Why now?'

'They are called.'

Mahalar turned to stare up the great stone staircase. He could feel the mountain towering above him, smell the rain clouds that hung about its peak. And deep within its stone heart, he could hear a sound, fainter, but growing louder.

A heart, beating.

'She,' he whispered softly, 'is stirring.'

Acknowledgements

I poured a lot of stuff into this book. Mostly anger. But there was joy, love, humour and a bunch of other nice things, too. I would like to thank the people who pointed out just when I put too much love onto a page, because it was pretty gross, and those who thought there could have stood to be more anger from time to time.

Naturally, I'd like to thank my editors, Lou Anders and Simon Spanton, for their relentless work on it, and my agent, Danny Baror, for getting it into their hands. These are the men I respect so much I can't give them silly nicknames.

Not so for my gurus. I'd also like to thank Matthew 'Wouldn't You Just Kill Her' Hayduke, John 'Needs More Sex' Henes and Carl 'Okay, I Know That Sounds Cool, but Picture It in Your Head and Tell Me It Doesn't Sound Stupid' Cohen for providing their unique insights.

It was a collaborative effort. But I did most of the work. That's why I get more pages than they do.